I0780470

THE TAKING

THE SAVIORS OF PERSAL

BOOK ONE

MARGARET LOTT

ISBN: 978-1-969865-01-5 (sc)
ISBN: 978-1-969865-02-2 (e)

Rev. date: 09/22/2025

Dedicated to my beloved husband;
Booker T Lott, who's faith in me
and unfailing support has made the
publication of my book possible.

CONTENTS

PROLOGUE

571 years ago

Misha was weary. So very weary as she followed the others through the tall cedars and pines. Her fur brushed through ferns up to her waist before they crossed yet another stream. Right now, she would give anything to curl up under the fragrant cedar tree up ahead and rest. They had been traveling, searching, for almost two turns of the moon. Ever since the ground shaking had collapsed their home cave.

Misha still cried inside when she thought of her baby sister who had been buried by the cave along with two others of their clan, but she no longer wept tears. They only seemed to frighten Jacur and Myelou, causing them to cry as well, without quite knowing why. Unless it was the fear, they all seemed to feel, now that they didn't have a secure home. The biggest fear was that the shaking would come again and take more of them. There were only eleven of her family left now as it was.

Misha knew she was still considered a youngling. Until the next gathering, she was too young to mate. Too young to be listened to. But it seemed to her that Oyrane had passed three suitable caves in their quest, even though the ground shaking that had continued for several sun times had stopped over a turn of the moon ago. The sky water should be returning soon, and then the white cold would come. They needed a new home now.

On the other side of the stream was a large patch of ripe blackberries near a massive dead log, long ago hollowed out by insects and a respectable place to spend the night. Here Oyrane called a halt, and everyone flocked to eat the favorite treat. Next to the patch was a clearing and after Myelou and Jacur finished eating their fill, they took off chasing each other about the cleared ground, their hands and faces stained purple. Misha was watching them with a smile on her face when she noticed a shimmering in the air. What?

Surely that hadn't been there when they arrived. Really, what was that?

"No!" she cried, starting to rise just as Myelou ran unseeing toward this strange thing, followed closely by Jacur. As she got to her feet, they were swallowed by the shimmering. Just like a thrown stone is swallowed in a pool of water.

With a high-pitched wail, her mother, Creathe, chased after them without hesitation. Gifric reached to stop his mate, but he was too late, and as his hand followed her, it too disappeared. His eyes were wide as he snatched it back and glanced at it to make sure it was still whole.

Nervously, Oyrane stepped up next to Gifric while the rest of the tribe circled around behind, looking at each other in fear. None of them were interested in getting too close to this strange thing. Misha found herself watching her father, who kept looking at his hand, looking for an injury that wasn't there and then back up to the strange shimmering. It looked like they could see right through this thing, but Creathe and her children had not come out the other side.

Finally, Gifric broke the silence. "We must go after them. We have already lost too many. We must go after them."

Oyrane started, as one awakening from a nightmare. "Go in there? What kind of leader would I be to lead my people off a cliff just because some fell off accidentally? No, we will mourn them, but we must go on," he insisted.

"Yes, we must go on," agreed Jetmis, holding Masjoh close, as though Gifric had tried to take the child.

"Wait, what's that noise?" whispered Staoat, glancing around cautiously.

Then they could all hear it, the ever so soft tread of small feet on the forest carpet of dry needles and soft grasses. Then a pungent breeze confirmed it as a fragrant smell reached them; the small ones were here. Must be their younglings. Young enough to feel daring, perhaps to try to capture one of them. Usually, they avoided each other, but when there were many, and young, and foolish, sometimes they took captives.

Oyrane's hands flashed a signal for them to leave, quickly. Then they flashed again as he indicated the shimmer that had swallowed Misha's family was evil and to be avoided.

Which way to go? Misha looked to Gifric as their hunter to lead, but the sound of steps was coming from everywhere. Dispensing with the hand signals, Gifric spoke up, "Where would you have us go, Oyrane? They have surrounded us. There is only one place to go, isn't there? We must follow Creathe and the children. When you are surrounded, over the cliff may be the safest place to be," he said calmly, grabbing Misha's hand and walking into the shimmering that seemed to be waiting for them.

Misha tried to pull back, but her fear of the small ones was strong. Hopefully, she looked over her shoulder as her father disappeared to see if the others were following. She could see their frantic eyes darting about as they realized how few their options were. Her people were not fighters, as the small ones sometimes were. Her kind sought peace above all else. Capture, even for a short time would kill them. Reluctantly, they were following. Then she felt the strangeness washing over her as she walked through the curtain of light behind her father, and there on the other side, they were. In a strange cave made of piled stones with a hole looking outside to mountains with old trees, her father and mother and brother and sister and a small one like she'd never seen before.

Turning back to the 'something,' she watched Oyrane, the last of the family, reluctantly joined them. Together they stood and watched as the small ones in animal skins and feathers came together to stare at the ground and search the clearing to see where they had gone. All that remained of their passing were some of their footprints in the softer soil. Such big prints compared to those of the small ones.

The small ones outside, those who would take them if they could, couldn't seem to find them. The one small one, on this side, looked startled. They could handle him gently if they needed to. Perhaps they had found a place of safety.

CHAPTER 1

The Other Side of the Fountain

Outside it was raining. As always when it rained in Seattle, it was a chilly rain. A cold, wet greeting for the first day of summer.

Inside, Cheri stood sullenly, with her untamed long red curls falling across her face as she tried to eavesdrop on the public defender discussing her case and the conditions the judge had put on her release to Faye Chessman, her social worker. The small room they were in was overheated and beginning to feel stuffy even in her black leather mini skirt and white lace halter top.

"Miss Chessman, can I go get a drink of water?" she asked impatiently. She couldn't hear from where she was anyway.

Faye Chessman turned to look at her thoughtfully. "Well, Cheri, I've never known you to break your word. Will you promise me that you'll wait in the lobby?"

"Yeah, sure. You wanted me, you got me. For the duration. I ain't gonna run out in that rain anyway, no place to go so early." Hastily she gathered her fake fur coat and oversized purse and fled the room.

The heels of Cheri's boots rang hollowly on the green marble floor as she crossed the foyer to the water fountain.

As she turned, her eye was caught by the waterfall in the middle of the floor. It was a sheet of glass with water running down it framed on either side by fantastic statues. On one side was a unicorn and the other a dragon. Most fanciful for a serious courthouse. In a moment, the hordes would be let loose for lunch, but for now, the hall was almost empty. Thirst slaked, Cheri turned to watch the few people in the room. Watching people was part of her profession, one of the parts she liked. At fifteen, she had watched many people and enjoyed guessing who and what they were.

A very tall, striking black woman in a white raincoat over worn blue jeans blew in from outside and strode across the lobby, with tennis shoes squeaking, to the directory next to the waterfall. Just then, the elevator doors opened and let loose the civil servants and jurors going to lunch. The black woman, with long braids flying, backed against the edge of the waterfall to stand out of the way just as a short ball of a man stumbled and bumped against her. Cheri couldn't quite see what happened after that. Did the waterfall ripple? No, that wasn't possible. When the throng cleared, the black woman was gone, and the elevator doors were closing.

Surely, she must have gotten on an elevator. Where else could she have gone?

Cheri shoved her mass of red curls out of her eyes as the diminutive Ms. Chessman came down the hall from the public defender's office carrying a large briefcase and several loose folders held precariously in one hand. Ms. Chessman's blond hair was pulled back into a tight bun, and her large black-rimmed glasses effectively hid her eyes. As she had before, Cheri wondered what Ms. Chessman was hiding under her bulky, oversized clothes. Small to begin with, everything about her seemed designed to overpower any attractiveness lurking in there, somewhere.

The lobby was almost deserted again, and Cheri had

pushed herself away from the green marble wall to meet her temporary guardian when it happened, Ms. Chessman dropped several of the folders in her hands, and they went sliding across the floor in all directions.

"Oh dear! Not now!" she exclaimed in exasperation.

Shaking her head, Cheri bent to retrieve those coming her way, and Ms. Chessman went after the two heading for the waterfall. She rescued the first folder without further incident, but when she tried to pick up the one resting against the lip of the water catch for the waterfall, she tripped and put her hand out to the glass behind the water for support.

Cheri looked up from the last file to see Ms. Chessman fall slowly into the water as though there were no glass there at all with a silent rippling of the surface. Cheri barely noticed the small splash as her guardian dropped something into the water.

Astounded, Cheri ran across the room, picking up Ms. Chessman's last file almost absently as she studied the waterfall in front of her. Okay. There was a sheet of wavy blue glass with water falling on either side. Carefully, Cheri extended her palm against the water. Wet, it was definitely wet. Well, that's as it should be, but where had Ms. Chessman gone? Looking around to see if anyone were watching, Cheri straightened her hand and slid it through the water, expecting to reach the glass at any moment. Oh! That's not what happened. Her hand didn't encounter any glass, it just kept going, and it was disappearing. Startled, Cheri snatched back her hand to examine it. Well, it was still all there but wait! It wasn't wet. Even the dampness left from before was gone. Cheri continued to stare at the waterfall thoughtfully while she checked the ceramic knives Blue Dave had given her. Well, she had promised to stay with Ms. Chessman, and she had no doubt where she had gone. What was the worst that could happen? She'd get soaking wet, maybe?

Taking a deep breath and clutching the files, Cheri stepped on the edge of the basin and through the waterfall to wherever Ms. Chessman had gone. Ripple.

*****

On the other side of the waterfall was a round stone room filled with golden summer sunlight and cool mountain breezes flowing in through the open windows and three motionless people staring at her. The tall black woman had stopped in midyell, mouth still open, to watch the glass. Ms. Chessman was sitting on the floor where she had fallen and was staring past her with a dazed look. The third person, an incredibly frail husk of a man, wore a bemused smile as he watched from his chair in front of a crowded bookcase and a table jumbled with an astonishing array of books, papers, and strange paraphernalia. Cheri swung around quickly to look behind her, just in time to see a stone archway framing a strangely shimmering waterfall in the courthouse lobby. Tentatively she put out her hand to touch the water and realized she was touching brick instead. As she was pulling her hand back, the shimmering solidified and the waterfall was gone. Behind her, Cheri heard a loud gasp from the black woman while a very small sigh escaped Ms. Chessman.

Through the window, with open shutters, came the lush smell of a meadow and evergreen trees like cedars and pines. When Cheri looked out, there was a large meadow covered in yellow flowers, over a strange grass with purple tips.

"Well, evidently that is everyone. My name is Gaban, the wizard.

"May I inquire as to your names?"

The tall black woman seemed to be sulking, and Ms. Chessman appeared to be in a haze, so Cheri responded. "I'm Cheri Gaines, and this is Faye Chessman." Once again, Cheri looked at the third woman for a response.

"I'm Ebony Evans. Now, please explain what is going on so I can get back. I'm already very late for an appointment," she almost growled.

"We might as well go downstairs where we can all be more comfortable, and then I will be able to answer all your questions. You won't be going back any time soon," said the dry old...did he say wizard? Slowly he unfolded his incredibly thin form from his chair and led the way to the stairs. He was much taller standing than he had seemed possible at first, but he still wasn't much more than a walking skeleton about five foot, eleven inches. The frayed hem of his deep-blue robe swept the floor as he led the way.

Cheri bent to help Ms. Chessman up and handed her the folders she was holding before they followed Ebony and the old man. With a grimace, Faye took the time to stuff the folders into her briefcase. Well, whatever she'd gotten herself into now, it couldn't be worse than her life on the streets of Seattle.

The narrow spiral staircase that wrapped itself around the outside of the circular building was only wide enough for one at a time. Cheri let the still unsteady Faye go ahead and followed warily.

Gaban had gained level flooring at the first landing and was only a couple of steps beyond when Faye's feet slid out from under her. Dismayed, Cheri grabbed for a flying hand frantically and found herself tumbling helplessly just before Faye's collision with Ebony knocked her off-balance as well. A second later, all three were in a heap at the bottom of the steps.

"Oh dear, dear, dear," moaned Gaban, aghast. "Is anyone hurt?"

Somehow Ebony had landed on top. With difficulty and a hand from Gaban, she managed to regain her feet and turned to pull Cheri off Faye as she answered, "I'm not hurt, how about you two?"

Cheri shook her head in negation as she helped Ebony with the crumpled Faye. "Ms. Chessman, is everything all right? Are you hurt?"

"No. No. I'm fine. Not to worry, this sort of thing happens to me all the time. I've never really hurt anyone, not even myself," she said distractedly as she straightened her glasses and gazed about her. That distant look returned quickly as she took in her surroundings.

Continuing without further incident down another flight of stairs, they soon found themselves in a small sitting room, in comfortable, if mismatched chairs sipping herbal tea. A roaring fire was doing its best to take away the chill of the mountain air. There were two doors off the semicircular room and a view of nearby mountains through the window on the third.

"If everyone is settled, let me explain what has happened, and then I will answer any questions that you still have, if I can," said the old man in his dry voice. There was a raspy catch in it as if he didn't use it very often.

Taking another sip or two of his tea, he began, "I don't know where that place is that you have come from, but to me, it seems to be full of very strange people and wonderful things. Of course, you know where you have come from, you need to know where you are and how you got here. Please, excuse me, I have not had any company for some time. Let me start again.

"Two thousand years ago, the portal you have just come through was built to fulfill a prophecy, and now you are here. The prophecy tells us that when the end of ages and the beginning of the new age is near, a guide will come to show the way to salvation. Well, we read it as a guide, but evidently, we read it wrong. Anyway, it appears we have three guides.

That means that you are as much of a surprise to us as well. Anyway, when the portal was completed, eight of the twelve wizards were still alive, and three remained here to wait for the coming. In the years since, one by one the others have died, and I am the only one remaining to greet you. Uhm, where are you? You are in Persal, more exactly in the Hidden Valley, more or less in the center of Persal, high in the Forbidden Mountains.

"Why are you here? Like I was saying, as guides to our salvation. For according to prophecy, if you fail to help us, our world is doomed. As for returning to your world, I am afraid that won't be possible for at least a year. The portal only opens once a year, at the summer solstice, and it does not remain open any longer than it needs to. Do you have any other inquiries?"

"Why couldn't I return while the portal was still open?" asked Ebony angrily, waving the cell phone in her hand around wildly. Turning to Cheri, she asked, "Do you know I can't even get any bars here?"

In answer, Cheri pulled out her own phone, "Nope. No reception here either," she said as she put it back into her pocket.

"Please, you must realize, this is the first time the portal has ever been used or at least used as it was intended. We still haven't figured the other visitation out, but not to worry," explained Gaban slowly. "Anyway, there is so much even those of us who made it do not understand. I would theorize that it is a one-way door. At least until its purpose has been fulfilled. Once it had been used to come this way, it can't be used to return. At least during the same opening, we think."

"What do you mean you think? It was a while before I decided to follow Ms. Chessman. Why was it still open?" queried Cheri.

"That is easy. The portal only works for those it was meant

for. That evidently means the three of you. As for the other, as I said, this is the first time the portal has been used as it was intended. We've never had an occasion for anyone to try to return."

"Now for the hard questions," said Ebony, taking a deep breath. "You said you were a wizard and you built this tower two thousand years ago? How are we supposed to believe that? What kind of world are we in?"

"Yes, yes, of course. Well, every year, for two millennia, I have watched your world. In the last couple of hundred years or so I've seen many wondrous things. What I haven't seen there is magic as we know it. While magic has been dying on our world, or the good magic anyway, there are many magical things here yet."

"I'm in a fantasy, for goodness' sake!" said Ebony sarcastically. "What else can we expect? Elves? Unicorns? Dragons?"

"I do not know anymore. The dragons are yet alive, we think. Rumor has it Barakus has turned many of them against men and dwarves. Whether unicorns or elves have survived the last two thousand years, maybe you can discover," replied Gaban, sadly shaking his head.

Sitting next to Cheri, Faye began to shake uncontrollably. "Is there somewhere I can lay her down with warm blankets?" she asked in alarm. "I think she's going into shock. I've seen this before with people new to the streets."

"Oh, my dear, I am so sorry. Please, there are rooms here for you. Of course, we must take care of her immediately. I really did not think. This must be so traumatic for you all," fussed Gaban apologetically, showing them to comfortable rooms off the sitting room they were in.

In a flurry of activity, Ebony helped Cheri get Faye into a bed and under warm blankets. Ebony even followed Cheri's instructions, as the young girl took command. Gaban stayed out of the way, going down another flight of steps to the kitchen, leaving the three women alone.

Faye fell immediately into a deep sleep. Cheri sat on the edge of the bed, watching her while Ebony tried to pace the small room but soon discovered there was only space for three steps with her long legs. Frustrated, she sank into the only chair in the room.

"I don't think she believes any of this is real," commented Cheri, her eyes never leaving Faye's face.

"Do you? I'm certainly not sure I do. I just refuse to accept the alternative," Ebony replied in wonder.

Amazed, Cheri turned to meet Ebony's eyes as she answered. "I'm only fifteen, what do I know? I'd say that it's a fair guess to say we aren't in Kansas though, and it's a darn sight better than the streets of Seattle. For now, I intend to take things as they come. What alternative do we have? I do have one question though? Don't I know you from somewhere? You seem so familiar. Weren't you in a magazine or something?"

Ebony slowly exhaled a long sigh. "Yes. I've been a contestant more than once on *American Ninja*. Someone thought it was interesting."

"I remember, it was about coming back from a tour in Afghanistan and then choosing to go back as a medic," said Cheri. "I remember thinking how strong you were."

"Others might say I was insane. I would rather not relive that here, Cheri. Besides, I think that's all irrelevant now. You know, for only fifteen you really seemed to know what to do with Faye here."

Cheri looked up and grinned. "It's amazing what you learn when living on the streets. I want to thank you for treating me as if I just might know what I was doing. Most people dismiss young people as if they're idiots. It's shocking really, they go to all the trouble to educate us and then seem astonished if we know anything."

"I'm good with strains and breaks but nothing like this. Actually, you seem to be pretty bright. Why did you follow your friend into the waterfall?"

"I promised her I would stay with her and it isn't like I had a lot of good alternatives," said Cheri with a shake of her head and another glance to Faye.

Ebony tugged thoughtfully on a handful of braids as she continued, "As far as our situation goes, I think either you're right or we admit we've gone crazy, and even then, we'd have to live in the reality we've created so we're back to square one, aren't we? It sure pisses me off, though. To think these people can just bring us here like this. What right do they have?"

"People? Seems to me it was the wizards? Not only that, I got the impression they didn't make any choice, the portal or the prophecy or something did. I don't even think they were expecting anything like us. I don't know what they were expecting, but it's a fair guess that it wasn't us," said Cheri thoughtfully as she tucked the covers more securely around Faye.

"Well, I might have to give you that, even if I really want someone to blame right now. But...they didn't choose us, we just sort of happened, apparently. What could they possibly expect of three sisters of obviously different backgrounds to do? I mean, he, what's his name? Gaban? Anyway, he says he's been sitting here waiting for us for two thousand years, and now we're supposed to come in here and save their world when they couldn't or wouldn't save it themselves? Give me a break!" said Ebony derisively, throwing her hands in the air.

Cheri checked on Faye one more time before she rose and crossed to the window to watch the early sunset over the snowcapped mountains. "Listen, I have no more idea what's going on than you do. I just followed Ms. Chessman because I promised and because I guess I figured I didn't have anything to lose. What I left behind has got to be worse than anything I'm going to find here. Besides, I watched you and Ms. Chessman go through the waterfall, and I was curious. You know, curiosity killed the cat and all that?"

"Huh! Curiosity? Girl, you're just plain crazy. Personally, I was mad as hell. Especially when I tried to walk right back and bounced off that thing," said Ebony with a shake of her head.

With sudden energy, Ebony jumped out of the chair and opened the door. "Look, we can talk in circles all night and not get anywhere. I suggest we see if Gaban out there has any food. I'm getting hungry. Maybe we can get some more answers as well as food?" Then she looked back at Faye. "She seems to be only a little thing, but we women are stronger than most people give us credit for. We'll leave the door open, so you'll hear her if she wakes up, okay?"

Cheri turned from the window and nodded reluctantly before a shape outside the window caught her eye. It was a moon, a very large moon in a golden color she had never seen on the moon at home. With a shake of her head, she followed Ebony back to the sitting room where they found Gaban returning from the kitchen below with a large bowl of hot stew. The table was already set for four. Explaining that Faye wouldn't be joining them, she assured him she would be fine by morning. As they sat down to their stew and fresh bread, she only hoped she was right.

"You're a good cook. Or is this something you pulled out of your hat?" asked Ebony around a mouthful of stew.

"Pulled out of my hat? I do not understand?" queried Gaban, obviously puzzled.

"She's referring to your magic," explained Cheri. "Did you cook this wonderful stew, or did you just wave a magic wand or something?"

"Magic wand? What a strange way you have of speaking.

But to answer your question, no, I did not use magic. Using magic is dangerous these days, and I have had a great deal of time to become a very good cook."

"Dangerous? Why would using magic in an age of magic be dangerous? Especially now?" asked Ebony, suddenly alert.

"Barakus can sense magic being used, and we couldn't take a chance on the portal being found before you arrived," replied Gaban, calmly breaking off another piece of bread and buttering it.

"Barakus? This is the second time you've mentioned that name. Maybe you should tell us about him?" insisted Ebony sharply, putting her spoon down in her empty bowl and leaning forward aggressively.

"Oh dear. I really should not, you know. Gabriene can do this so much better than I can. He was there at the beginning, so he knows more than I do, you see. Barakus is the reason you are all here, of course, but what can I tell you that you are ready to understand?" flustered Gaban.

"Try us. Exactly what is it we are supposed to do? Why are we here? And who is Barakus? While we're at it, who is Gabriene?" pressed Ebony relentlessly.

"Gabriene?" responded Gaban, seizing the easiest answer first. "He's the only other good wizard yet alive. Actually, he's the master wizard who taught us all. Really, ladies, he has many more answers, but since you insist, I'll tell you what I can." Gaban sighed as he caved into Ebony's hard stare.

"Well, we don't know exactly what you are going to do, of course. If we knew that we could have done it ourselves, you see. Oh, dear, Gabriene really could do this so much better. I guess the one thing I can tell you is that Barakus is an evil sorcerer. A very long time ago, as Gabriene's most able pupil, he began to practice the forbidden magic. By the time Gabriene discovered what he had done, he had fled to Doome in the northeast and begun to learn black magic in earnest. He even learned to tap the power of the imprisoned demon Komarr. Gabriene tried to stop him, but Barakus's power was growing too fast. Then Gabriene gathered the twelve wizards together, and we all tried to attack him in his citadel at Mount Doome. His power was even greater there at the source. We were repelled, losing four of our brothers. After that is when we came here and built the portal, before Barakus grew strong enough to stop us, even here," explained Gaban quietly, drawing on memories from long, long ago. "As to why you are here? I only know the prophecy refers to you as guides. Gabriene has been studying the prophecy ever since the completion of the portal for answers to your questions. I am afraid you will need to wait until you can ask him."

"Well, fine. Let's go see this Gabriene. When Faye is ready to travel in the morning, we'll get on a plane or helicopter or something and go see him," said Ebony, satisfied.

"Plane? Helicopter? I do not understand? The horses should arrive in a day or two, and then you can begin your journey," said Gaban complacently.

"Horses?" yelped Ebony and Cheri in unison.

"Yes, of course, it is that or walk to get out of these mountains," said Gaban, clearly perplexed by their reaction.

"No car? How about a motorcycle?" Ebony asked desperately, her hopes sinking at the obviously uncomprehending look on Gaban's face with each new word.

"Ebony, I think we know why there's no cell phone reception," commented Cheri dryly.

"I am so sorry. Horses are all we have. Do you not have horses anymore in your world? I know you had some a century or so ago before the building was placed about the portal." Gaban asked in concern.

"Well, yes, we have horses, but that doesn't mean I've ever ridden one. I mean, they're only ridden for sport or for fun. If you really want to get somewhere, you use some form of motorized transportation like a car or one of those other things I asked about," explained Ebony despondently.

"We do not have these strange wonders you speak of. We have horses. Well, sometimes we have carts or carriages, but neither of those can get into these mountains. Do not worry, you will find it easy to learn to ride. Even our children ride safely. There is nothing to worry about," said Gaban, rising and beginning to collect the dirty dishes.

"Here, let me help you," volunteered Ebony while a pale Cheri returned to Faye's room to watch over the familiar face.

That night Cheri slept in the chair in Faye's room, and Ebony took the other bedroom on the same floor. Gaban's room was one floor above with two other empty bedrooms. Cheri's last thought as she pulled the quilt closer about her shoulders and drifted off to sleep was, *What have I gotten myself into this time? Wizards, dragons, and horses. Maybe this is just a nightmare after all. Maybe I won't have to get on a horse if I wake up at Faye's in the morning.*

*****

Debora could feel the cool night breezes blowing gently across her skin as she slept in her father's tent. She could feel the breezes, and she tried desperately to hold on to their caresses. She dreamed of things she had never seen. Things her father and mother had never seen. Water poured from the sky and drenched the land. A land that was not sand but grass and strange trees. Now, now she no longer felt the cool desert breezes but the water as it ran down her soft dark cheeks and drenched her long dark-auburn hair, plastering her sleeping Aht'chka against her skin. "No! This cannot be!" she screamed as she woke, staring blindly at the familiar stars over the Hamil Oasis.

"My dear, what is the matter? Debora, how did you get so wet? Why, you're sitting in a pool of water. What has happened here? Has some fool wasted water by throwing it on you? Debora, answer me!" came her mother's voice dimly as Debora began to shake uncontrollably, and tears added their water to her already wet face.

The children of Mojar were taught very early not to waste their water on tears, but Debora knew. She knew that tomorrow she would have to face the women of the Green Lizard tribe. Tonight would be her last in the life she'd always known.

Still sobbing, Debora licked her lips, "Salty, th-th-the water is salty."

"Of course, you're crying child," soothed her mother as she held her daughter.

"Nnn...no. Ddd...different. Saltier, sort of...odd?"

"What?" asked Terina as she raised her own arm and licked the water. Seawater, she'd tasted it once as a child. The tribe had visited Jahl, and she'd thought all that water would be clean and clear as it was at the oasis. Instead, it had been salty—and wrong. The water on her daughter was seawater, and they were hundreds of miles from the sea.

CHAPTER 2

What to Wear

In the morning, Ebony was awakened by Faye's piercing scream, denied even the luxury of believing for a moment that it was all a dream. Running into the next room, she found Cheri trying to calm the hysterical woman.

"It's all right, Ms. Chessman. We're all right. Don't worry, please. Please don't cry. Ms. Chessman, do you hear me? Do you know who I am?"

Closing her eyes very tight, Faye forced herself to take several deep, ragged breaths to calm herself before she nodded. "Ye...yes. I can hear you, Cheri. I don't know why you're in my dream, but I know you and I hear you. There's no reason for me to panic. In a little while I'll wake up, and everything will be normal again. This is just a dream. A very, very vivid dream but just a dream."

"Look, girl, the sooner..." Cheri stopped Ebony in midsentence with a hasty wave of her hand.

"Ms. Chessman, there's some fresh water in the pitcher over there, why don't you wash your face. We'll wait for you in the sitting room."

Rising to her feet, Cheri left the room, pushing Ebony out in front of her and closing the door. "Please, Ebony, maybe it will be easier for her to take later. Can't we let her get used to it slowly? Later is time enough for her to find out the truth.

Please?" begged Cheri, staring up into Ebony's warm brown eyes.

"I don't think I agree with you but sure, why not. I guess I wouldn't mind thinking I was only dreaming if I could. I just hope she snaps out of it before we need her for something. I mean, we have three options. One, we accept it's all real. Two, we've gone flat out crazy, and I sure don't want to believe that one. Or three, we're dreaming and to me that makes less sense than the first option at this point."

"I really don't think it can last too long, I mean, sooner or later, she'll have to realize that dreams don't go on forever," replied Cheri hopefully.

"Ah! Good morning. I see everyone is up. Wonderful! I will go down to the kitchen and finish up breakfast and bring it right up. I do hope you will forgive me, but I ate earlier. Old habits are hard to break," said Gaban cheerfully as he came up the stairs and saw them.

"Earlier? What time is it? Surely we didn't sleep that late," asked a confused Ebony.

"It must be two hours after sunrise. Please do not concern yourselves, I always eat very early in the morning. Even at this time of year, it is barely dawn when I sit down of a morning. Well, let me get your breakfast, I will be back directly." And Gaban was gone in a swirl of blue robes.

"Well, I'm going to take a minute to change, can I use your room?" said Cheri in a disgustingly cheerful voice.

"Girl, what are you so happy about so early in the morning? Nothing has changed since last night. Besides, what do you intend to change into? I didn't see you arrive with any luggage."

Grinning, Cheri held up her oversized purse. "I always carry at least two changes of clothes in here. The way I've been living, you learn to be prepared for anything. I also have a few new toothbrushes. I know you're taller than I am, but

I bet my underwear will fit and I have a smashing red mini dress that would look marvelous on you."

Ebony shook her head and laughed, "You are full of surprises, Cheri. I'll take you up on the clean undies, and a toothbrush sounds wonderful, but I think I'll stay in my jeans and sweater for now. You wouldn't have a clean pair of socks in there, would you?"

A few minutes later, feeling more refreshed, the three women sat down to breakfast, and Gaban removed the linen towel from a platter loaded with scrambled eggs, bacon, and biscuits.

Cheri and Ebony immediately helped themselves, but Faye held back, "What can I be thinking of? Do you realize how much cholesterol there is in that meal? I must miss these foods more than I imagined."

"Sure, but if you're just dreaming, what can it hurt to eat it?" asked Ebony innocently as Cheri glared at her across the table.

"You're right, of course. It's just a dream, and in dreams, nothing is real." Faye set about heaping her plate even higher than the other two. Of course, she had missed dinner the night before.

Ebony was watching Faye finish her third helping of bacon and eggs in awe when a cry came floating through the window from outside.

"Halloo, Gaban! Come on out, old man. I know you are there, and I know you have company, but that is no reason not to greet an old friend."

The three women rose as one, crossing to the window to throw it open, scattering several small bright purple birds who had been singing a cheerful good morning from the window sill. Below the window was an older woman with her gray hair sticking out of her bun messily. She was riding a brown horse with a golden mane, up the trail to the tower. She wore a slim riding skirt and a long-sleeved blouse and a fleece vest with a dagger at her belt. Behind her was a packhorse carrying what appeared to be bolts of colorful cloth, among many smaller bundles. She appeared to be very comfortable on the horse, and as she dismounted to greet Gaban, who had emerged from the tower, she was quite familiar with him as well.

Gaban laughed as he bent his tall thinness to embrace the short round woman. "Tasmin! How wonderful to see you. Don't tell me you're on the run again? I thought I told you it was time to go home and make babies."

Her smooth face creased in a broad smile, as Tasmin shook her head. "I did, Gaban, I did. I had seven, in fact. Now most of them have made me a grandmother. It's been thirty-five years! You, my old friend, never change. You look exactly the same, like you'll blow away in the next good wind."

"Never, Tasmin. There's more to me than meets the eye. The body can only grow so old before it stops to wait to die, my daughter, and I'm not going to die today. Now what are you doing here, when you should be taking care of grandchildren?"

"My grandchildren have parents who can take care of them better than I can. No, the portal called me, Gaban, and I brought enough material for three women. The time has finally come, hasn't it, old man? I bet you were surprised though. What I wouldn't have given to be there to see your face when they arrived." And with that Tasmin broke out laughing again.

"Humph! Well, we should not stand out here all day. Let me help you with all of this, whatever it is. It looks as if you intend be sewing for a month. There really isn't time, you know. In about a week, at most, Barakus will know that something is disturbing the fabric of Persal, and he will guess what it means for him. He will soon begin searching for my guests, and they must not be here when he does," said Gaban as he began unloading Tasmin's packhorse while she unsaddled her brown mare and set it free to roam the meadow.

"No, no, Gaban. I will not be doing all the sewing. Six women from the village will be arriving this afternoon. We will be ready to leave in two or three days, at most. I made the arrangements on my way up here. Now, why don't you take me in to meet your guests? There is so much we will have to say to each other," stated Tasmin blithely.

Hurriedly, the three eavesdropping women settled into various positions about the sitting room, trying to appear as if they hadn't heard a word. In only a moment they could hear footsteps as Gaban and Tasmin climbed the stairs from the first floor.

"Well, well." Tasmin beamed as she looked each of them over closely. "We do have an assortment here, don't we? Come, come, Gaban, introduce us so we may get down to work."

"Of course, my dear, you move so fast, you hardly give one a chance to think, you know," complained Gaban in good humor, "Now, let me see. This tall young woman is Ebony Evans, quite lovely, don't you think?"

"Please, stand up dear, oh my, yes. You would stand out in any crowd, I'm sure. We'll have to see if we can tone that down a bit when we're traveling, though. I believe we are to try to be inconspicuous. Don't worry dear, we'll work something out. Next, Gaban?"

"This appealing child is Cheri Gaines."

Cheri stood without being asked. "My, what striking hair. Perhaps we can pass her off as a Samalian, the coloring is right," Tasmin said musingly.

"And lastly, but certainly not least, is Faye Chessman," said Gaban with a final wave of his hand.

Hesitantly Faye stood as Tasmin crossed the room

for a closer look. "Well, I can't tell... Are you hiding from something, dear? It's really hard to see you behind those things on your face and under those bulky clothes. Well, we can sort that out later, I suppose. I, my dears, am Tasmin. I am to be your teacher here in this world. I will also make sure you have the proper clothes for our journey. Maybe we can adjourn to one of the bedrooms to take measurements? We haven't a lot of time to make you an adequate wardrobe. We can talk about people and social customs of the five kingdoms while we work."

Leaving no room for protest, Tasmin bustled the three women into Faye's bedroom and closed the door on Gaban. Looking lost, he stood alone in the center of the room, his eyes blinking rapidly for a moment before raising his shoulders in a resigned shrug and bending to clear the breakfast table.

"You know. You remind me a great deal of my grandmother," said Faye faintly as she watched Tasmin stand Ebony in the center of the room and begin to take measurements. "But then, I suppose you would. After all, it is my dream."

"What? What was that, dear? Now, Cheri, could you slide that chair over here, dear. I can't quite reach...there that's better. Ebony, honey, what's your favorite color? I'm afraid we'll have to go with dark colors for traveling, but I see no reason why we can't do better than that for more formal wear. It would be ideal if we knew how Mojar women dressed for travel or for formal settings, but we'll just have to make do," rambled Tasmin as she measured. She obviously wasn't paying any attention to what Faye had to say as she worked.

"Uh? Oh, well, wine or dark green, I guess. My costume is red. What's a Mojar?" asked Ebony, a bit overwhelmed by Tasmin's take- charge attitude.

"Costume, dear? Were you a player in your world? Your body is very well muscled. Perhaps you were an acrobat? Mojars are tall black people who live in the desert wastes in the western reaches of Persal. Unfortunately, I've only ever seen the men. Apparently, they keep their women close to home," murmured Tasmin absently as she checked her figures.

"Cheri, honey, come here, you're next."

"No, I mean, not exactly. I was a professional athlete. I was a regular on *American Ninja*, on television." Ebony paused as she registered the dumbfounded look on Tasmin's face. This was the first time she had even paused in her purpose since she burst in on their lives. "Uh, I guess you don't have television here, do you? I mean, I haven't seen a telephone, and no electric lights, and not even a microwave in the kitchen... Uhm, an athlete is someone who gets paid to swim or run or play a demanding game while others watch. Cheri, can you help me!" she cried as Tasmin, looking more and more confused, sat down on the chair with her mouth hanging open.

Cheri's eyes darted from one to the other while she stifled her urge to laugh. Hectically, her mind searched her memories of history for an apt reference. "Well, she was sort of like an acrobat and a knight, you know, when they joust. Lots of people used to watch her in her contests," she improvised.

"A woman? My, my, what a wonderful world you must live in. Are men also ath...letes?" Tasmin asked with a bemused smile.

"Oh, yes. In fact, women are just coming into their own in the last few decades. Before that, men thought a woman's place was in the home. More specifically, the kitchen or the bedroom," answered Ebony wryly, deciding Cheri's explanation was sufficient.

Rising again from the chair and resuming her measuring of Cheri, Tasmin said thoughtfully, "In some of the five kingdoms, men still like to think that way. Not in Jamben, at least not much. Women fight in the underground with the men, and all women are trained to fight when they are in their teens. It is their choice to marry or remain in the resistance for a while longer after that. Once the babies start to come, they have a need to stay home. Children come first in all our families, of course. Well, Cheri, I think that's enough for now," she said as she wrote down the measurements she had taken.

Cheri joined Ebony on the bed and leaned close. "I notice you didn't mention Afghanistan," she whispered to the black woman.

Ebony just shook her head. "It's not something I talk about," she whispered.

"From what I read, your convoy got hit, and some men died during your first tour. Then you requested a change to become a medic. You got the training and went back," murmured Cheri as they watched Tasmin motion Faye to stand and looked her over critically.

"I'd rather no one else know about all that, here," Ebony requested, never taking her eyes off Faye. Cheri nodded assent.

"What are those things on your face, dear?" asked Tasmin curiously.

Faye had been watching the proceedings with a giddy feeling as though watching a play she had stumbled into the middle of and paused a moment before raising her hands to her face. "These, they're my glasses. They help me see. My eyesight gets really blurry without them."

"Really? Well, ain't that something? What are you trying to see, dear? I mean, if you take them off, can you see me and Ebony and Cheri? Can you see our faces? Can you see the mountains? You won't stumble over your own feet, will you?"

"Well, yes, I can see all your faces, and no, my eyesight won't cause me to stumble," began Faye with a wry look to Ebony and Cheri. She was hoping they wouldn't mention the fall from last night. "I can see the mountains but not in any great detail. Mostly my glasses are for reading and computers. Uh...let's leave it at reading. It's just easier to wear them all the time than be putting them on and taking them off all day," admitted Faye as she corrected for her mention of technology.

"Computers? Never mind. I doubt I'd understand. You won't have much time or opportunity to read in the next few months, dear. Why don't we start by taking them off and putting them away, until you need them?" Tasmin insisted, removing the offending and unflattering black-rimmed glasses. "My, what beautiful deep-blue eyes. Oh, yes, that's much better. Now, I'm afraid dear that your clothes are much too bulky to measure through. Could you take off your skirt and sweater? You're so tiny, even shorter than I am. I'd be willing to bet there's a lovely figure under there as well."

"It's only a dream. It's only a dream..." Faye kept muttering to herself as she stripped to her camisole and underwear, all the while trying not to blush. She had always hated girls' gym in school for the lack of privacy. In fact, it was the only class she'd gotten a poor grade in, for not showering with the other girls.

"There, you see girls, I was right. I have no idea what you were hiding from under all of those clothes, but we'll bring out your best attributes, never fear. You have an absolutely lovely figure, not so skinny like these other two but not heavy either," continued Tasmin as she busily began measuring Faye and chattered about the best styles for the women to travel in. She never looked up to see Faye's red face as she was reminded of what she saw as her flaws. "Ebony, I think an outfit like mine would be best for you. Of course, it will look much better on your tall form. It's a shame you're so thin, but with your muscle, I have a feeling you would look good in almost anything. Of course, it would be much easier if we had a Mojar man for you to travel with."

"From what you just said, I doubt I would agree with that sentiment," muttered Ebony under her breath.

Tasmin heard her and looked up, "Well, I suppose we should leave such details to the portal. For Cheri and Faye now, I think fuller, divided skirts would be better. Not many Samalian women ride, of course, but enough do to make you not too noticeable, but they wouldn't dream of wearing Jamben fighter wear. Faye, dear, you're actually too tall to be a Jessamine, and even their children are plumper. Let me see, of course, Camir. I think you have the bearing to pass as a noble from Rim. No one would ever question you as a Camirian.

"What's your favorite color, Faye dear?"

"Brown, gray, tan," said Faye in a small voice as she started getting dressed again, but Tasmin just shook her head.

"You really have no idea how to set off your lovely pale coloring and deep-blue eyes, do you? Well, for traveling, we'll use dark blue. It's imminently practical. For your gowns, we'll use a blue to match your eyes with white trim to bring out the lovely roses in your cheeks," insisted Tasmin.

"Oh, by the way, Cheri, that pink dress you're wearing is pretty but totally unsuitable for your coloring, not to mention much too short. What other colors do you like?"

"Well, I wear red a lot. It gets me a lot of attention. I also wear a lot of black," Cheri answered defensively. There was no doubt in her mind that Tasmin wasn't going to like her answers.

"Red? Is that really your favorite color?"

"Well, no. Growing up in Seattle, I've always liked light green. Like the new growth in the spring." Admitted Cheri reluctantly, half expecting a comment from Ebony.

Fortunately, Ebony remained silent as Tasmin continued.

"Well, that's something we can work with. Red may get you attention, Miss Cheri, but I'd be willing to wager next year's crop of yamins that you'd be more fetching in the light green of your eyes or even in pale yellow. You can travel in dark green and black, but your gowns will be in a lovely teal silk I brought with me and a soft lemon- yellow brocade. Please, understand, I'm not just being bossy, your lives could depend on blending in as much as possible."

Tasmin looked at each woman closely, catching their eyes before moving on to make sure they had heard her before picking up her pad with its notes and headed for the door. "I hear my seamstresses arriving, I'd better get this information down to them so they can start right away."

Cheri crossed the room to close the door as Tasmin left, glancing into the sitting room to be sure it was empty. Leaning against the door, she looked from Ebony to Faye before the three of them burst out laughing.

"Did you see her face when I mentioned television?" asked Ebony when she could catch her breath.

"Not to mention telephones, electric lights, and microwaves. I'm sure she thought you were speaking a foreign language," gasped out Faye. "That was rather quick of you to define athlete for her that way, Cheri. What made you think of it?"

"I haven't had a lot of schooling, but I go to the library to read a lot. It's warm there. Anyway, it struck me that what I've seen here is somewhat medieval, I could only hope she knew of knights and jousting. Evidently, she did," revealed Cheri, almost reluctantly.

"Well, I for one am grateful you're so quick on your feet with things like that," enthused Ebony.

"Do you think she was serious, about our lives being in danger?" asked Cheri, suddenly serious.

"Don't be absurd! After all, this is my dream. We'll be just fine," answered Faye, dismissing Cheri's concerns categorically. "Let's go outside and look around. It's too beautiful of a day to stay cooped up."

The three women spent the day roaming the small valley meadow where Gaban's tower was. Cheri noticed many of the purple birds singing in the trees. They reminded her of canaries, except for their color. Occasionally the women were dragged into the tent that had been set up by the seamstresses for fittings where they shared the food the women had brought for lunch.

In the hour before dinner, Tasmin led them back into the tower to choose underwear from the supply she'd brought with her. The cobbler from the village had come to take measurements for new boots. Cheri suggested that she wear her own, but one look at the spiked heels and Tasmin shook her head. "Totally impractical! They wouldn't last an hour in the saddle. We must be prepared for almost anything, and I can't see you running across a plowed field or climbing mountains in those either."

At dinner Tasmin regaled them with tales of the peoples and customs of Persal, not incidentally imparting a great deal of information that might come in handy on their journey.

That night Cheri took one of the bedrooms upstairs with Tasmin and Gaban. The seamstresses went back to their village for the night. Taking their sewing and supplies with them.

*****

Meland had stood on the wharves of Lohi since shortly after midday, watching. Watching the gleaming white tower that dominated the harbor. It stood tall and straight on the largest and closest island in Mermaid Bay. It wasn't the only tower in the harbor, nor was it on the only island. She had heard it said; once there were twelve towers, one for each island, but the white tower has always been the most dominant. Of the others, two islands had sunk below the sea, and only the tops of broken towers were visible. The only other one still standing whole was a small blue tower to the east. The others had all fallen into ruin, and only some of their jagged outlines were visible from shore. She had even heard stories told in hushed whispers that once there was a thirteenth tower and a thirteenth island, destroyed by Gabriene when Barakus betrayed him.

Three miles, that was how far it was to the island. Everyone in Lohi knew how far it was, but no one ever went there. At least not that she had ever heard. Three miles that she knew she must travel, but it was three miles she couldn't bear to think about. Once she arrived at that tower, how could she be sure she would ever return? Even if she did, she would never be the same. And she must go alone, so she waited. She waited for the bustling activity of a thriving seaport to at least abate somewhat. She tossed her head, and her long black ponytail swayed as she waited impatiently for the sailors and dock workers to head for the taverns.

She slowly blew out a long breath to relax her tension. It would be dark soon, and they would all head for their ale. Then she could borrow a rowboat and begin her journey. She only hoped that Gerad, her brother, would wait until dark to give her father the note. She knew her father would never understand, but he would not come after her. Not to the tower.

CHAPTER 3

Shouts in the Night

It was still dark when Ebony woke with a start. Sitting up straight, she was trying to identify what woke her when the whiff of something acrid came again. Was that vinegar? It was very strong. She was already getting out of bed when the creak of a board outside the bedroom door caused her to grab the pitcher of water next to the bed as she scampered behind the door. Tasmin's warnings about danger were circling in her head as she took up her defensive stance.

The doorknob turned slowly, stretching Ebony's nerves to the limit before it opened and she found herself swinging the pitcher down sharply, smacking a small man in the head and knocking him out cold. Past him, in the sitting room, she saw several other men, two behind the man she'd knocked out, two opening Faye's door and several climbing up the stairs toward Cheri, Gaban, and Tasmin.

"Intruders!" she called loudly. "Intruders! Intruders!" she continued as she went on the offensive, barreling into the two still staring in confusion at their comrade on the floor. With a quick left jab, she took out the closest one on the right. Then she went into judo mode and turned quickly to chop down on the back of the neck of the other assailant. Three men were down, and the others in the room only knew about her attacks because she was busy warning her new friends. After that, she headed for the two men opening Faye's door. She was in full *American Ninja* mode now, and she was almost a blur as she spun about, disarming men with knives and swords before knocking them out. This was what had made her so popular on the show. When she started fighting, no one could stand in front of her.

As she turned back to the sitting room, she saw three very tall beings by the window, knocking out the smaller shadows. With a glance toward the stairs, she saw several of these tall, hairy people headed up the tower. Carefully she took a defensive stance. Just because the new entries into the fray had taken out some of her adversaries, it didn't necessarily follow they were friendly.

Now that it was quiet on their floor, Ebony could hear scuffling followed by a loud scream, which was followed quickly by a blinding flash of light coming from upstairs.

Suddenly Faye slammed into Ebony's back as she grabbed on for dear life. Trembling uncontrollably, Faye was obviously terrified. Ebony wasn't feeling very safe herself.

"Is everyone all right down there?" called Gaban's voice from upstairs.

"That depends. Are the newcomers friends or foes?" called back Ebony, still watching the three tall shadows across the room.

"Oh! Friends! Friends, my dear. Ochwatt! If you're down there, we need you, now! Tasmin, take Cheri downstairs and assess the situation there," said Gaban, taking command.

The tallest of the forms in the dim room separated himself from the rest to bound up the stairs four at a time. Boy, his legs were long! Then Tasmin and Cheri hustled down the stairs to check on Faye and Ebony. The other two friends by the window appeared to be watching for more attackers.

Cheri made a beeline for Faye, peeling her off Ebony's

back while Tasmin roamed the room, quickly dispatching any of the downed men who were still breathing.

"Tasmin! What are you doing? Couldn't we just have put them in jail or something?" gasped Ebony in horror.

"Three things you need to know, ladies. The first is about law enforcement in Persal. Barakus's priests and their soldiers are in charge of almost all law, if you want to call it that."

Suddenly she was interrupted by a loud howl from upstairs. It almost sounded like a wolf howl, but there was a human quality to it that made it heartbreaking to listen to. All four of the women gazed up at the ceiling, but when Ebony would have gone up, Tasmin put out her hand to stop her. "No, Ebony. This is a private matter," she said quietly as several more howls joined the first.

"Do you know what those...things are?" asked Cheri in a small voice.

Ebony and Faye looked at her blankly before mutely shaking their heads in denial.

"They're sasquatch! You know, the mythical giants from home? I saw them clearly when Gaban killed Barakus's men. Now, I think I might have been dreaming."

"What? You have accepted everything else that's happened as completely possible, but you balk at sasquatch? Cheri, I think you're insane!" cried Ebony in exasperation.

"This is real, isn't it?" said Faye in a small voice, looking around her at the dead men scattered among the shambles of the sitting room. Mutely she crossed to the nearest overturned chair to right it before sitting down.

"Oh, great! Faye wakes up and Cheri goes crazy!" muttered Ebony as she pulled her own chair up and sat down, shaking her head.

"Yes, our friends are, what did you call them, ah... sasquatch. They call themselves the People. They came through the portal over five hundred years ago when they were being hunted. Now they live in the mountains between this valley and Barakus's desert. Don't just sit there, help me dispose of our uninvited guests," said Tasmin, grabbing the dead body nearest the stairs to the kitchen. "Cheri, grab his feet."

Before Cheri could help Tasmin, one of the sasquatch by the window stepped up and grabbed two of the bodies. As he followed Tasmin out of the room, the other giant grabbed up two more as if they weighed nothing.

Over the next half hour, the eight men from the sitting room floor were removed and piled away from the tower. By the time they were through, the rest of the People and Gaban had joined them. Each of the People carried a body or two from the third floor and added them to the pile. The one Ochwatt carried was one of the People. The count of the enemy was fifteen. Fifteen men had been sent to kill them, and they might have succeeded if the acrid smell from the fur of their new friends hadn't woken Ebony.

"Tasmin, take the ladies inside and start straightening the tower, please. I'll take it from here," said Gaban solemnly.

None of the young women balked as Tasmin led the way. They didn't want to be here for this any more than Gaban wanted them to stay.

"Tasmin, you were telling us why it was necessary to kill those men?" prompted Ebony, a stony look on her face.

"Yes, where was I? Ah, I remember, the second thing you need to know is, those were Barakus's men. That means, sending them to the 'law' wouldn't have done any good. Then there's the third, most important thing. Barakus must not know, beyond a doubt, where the portal is. He made a good, probably educated, guess, but if no one returns, he'll still be guessing," said Tasmin as she crossed to the overturned table, just as a bright blue flash came from outside. It only took them a few minutes to straighten the sitting room, and there was only Ebony's broken pitcher in her bedroom to be cleaned up.

By the time they were through, Gaban and Ochwatt had rejoined them. The four humans sat in the chairs. Gaban was snacking on dried fruit to regain his strength, sapped when he cast the two spells. Ochwatt had made himself comfortable on the floor where they had cleared a space for him.

"Faye, why did you snap out of it? I mean, just like that you accept what's going on? What happened to your dream?"

"It wasn't a dream, Cheri. Oh, okay, I get your question. It wasn't the dream I questioned, but the nightmare that woke me up," answered Faye wryly. "Now, I want to know what's next? It doesn't look like a good idea to stay here."

"No, you're right. Pack what you need. We'll be leaving in fifteen minutes," said Gaban as he rose. The four women rose as well, heading to their rooms to pack.

Turning to his old friend, he continued, "Ochwatt, I want to thank you and your people. I am so sorry for Misha. If the people keep guarding the mountains, we can take it from here."

"No. Misha was mine. Barakus kill her. Killing bad. I go with. Stop the killing," replied Ochwatt stoically before crossing to the window and calling to his people outside in their guttural language. When he was through, his small troop trotted off silently, going home and taking Misha with them.

"Ochwatt! We need to travel quietly and unobserved. How are we going to hide you among our people? It's not just your height, it's your hair and maybe most of all your, uh, odor," protested Gaban.

Ochwatt's face broke into a big grin, "I do what I must. Tell me, I do." And he planted his legs. He wasn't going anywhere he didn't want to, that was evident.

As the women returned, Gaban muttered, "Remember, you asked for this. I'll be ready in a few minutes, ladies. Apparently, Ochwatt is coming with us," he said in exasperation as he took off up the stairs. He needed to secure the portal before he left and there were a few things he was taking with him.

The women and Ochwatt were downstairs saddling Tasmin and Gaban's horses as well as loading the packhorse with their few possessions. Ochwatt stood off to one side holding a lantern uncertainly as the horses shied away when he got near. That acrid vinegar smell was going to be a problem if Gaban didn't come up with a solution.

After filling his saddlebags, Gaban picked up the reins in one hand and his staff with a glowing blue stone in the other and led the way to about a hundred yards from the tower. Once there, he stopped. "Here, take my horse and keep going. Keep going," he insisted when Tasmin hesitated as well. "I'm just placing a protective spell over the tower. I'll catch up with you."

Nodding, Tasmin, who had reclaimed her lantern from Ochwatt, continued with Ebony, Faye and Cheri following. Ochwatt hesitated for a moment, but Gaban waved for him to continue as well.

Cheri turned to look back just as there was a bright flash and saw a blue dome appear to grow from where Gaban stood, circling around and growing higher until the tower was completely enclosed. Once it was complete, he sagged against his now quiet staff, and Ochwatt merged from the shadows to swoop him up and carry him to his horse where Tasmin and the women had stopped.

"Food...get me some fruit. I need the sugar," murmured Gaban as he lay against his horse's neck.

Tasmin, as usual, took charge and rummaged in his saddlebags, finding several apples on top. Below that was a large bag of dried fruit for another time.

Gaban devoured half an apple before he had the energy to sit up. "Okay, we need to keep moving. Ochwatt, Buttercup here is pretty mellow. She'll probably allow you to lead her while I replenish my energy."

Unfortunately, Buttercup didn't agree with the old wizard's assessment and shied away when the giant tried to approach the second time. It was one thing when he was with Gaban, but now that her master was on her back, it was a different matter.

"Here, let me do it," said Faye, stepping up to take the reins.

Again, Tasmin led the way while Gaban merrily munched on his apples. He was on the third one when Ochwatt stopped and turned his head back toward the mountains.

Suddenly alert, Gaban looked behind them. "What is it? What do you hear?"

"Fight! My people meet the enemy," he stated, suddenly showing signs of indecision.

"Tasmin, quick. We'll have to ride. Cheri, here, get up behind me," called Gaban, putting down his hand to help her mount.

With a deep breath, she followed his instructions, but she wasn't happy about it, not at all.

"Can either of you ride?" asked Tasmin, looking at Ebony and Faye.

Quickly, Faye handed the reins to the restored Gaban and headed for the packhorse. "I can."

"Ebony, come on. We need to get going. Now!" called Tasmin urgently as the tall black woman hesitated for a moment. But how could she refuse when Cheri was already mounted? With a sigh, she allowed Tasmin to leverage her as she jumped behind the saddle.

Tasmin, followed closely by Faye took off, but Gaban held

back for a moment, "Ochwatt, you don't have to come with us if your people need you."

Ochwatt's head jerked and then he turned back to Gaban. "The fighting stop. It be over. I come for Misha, friend Gaban. I will mourn later," he said, turning to run after the women. Buttercup caught up a short time later, and Gaban took the lead.

Cheri was flagging in exhaustion when she detected a general lightening in the sky ahead. What was that? A gigantic wall rose up in front of them. How were they supposed to get past that? Then the answer was revealed as a short time later, a very narrow bright beam of light found its way through a slender, defile directly ahead. It only lasted a couple of seconds, but she'd definitely seen it. Ah good, the wall was an escarpment and the defile passed through a rough split. Much better than a tunnel which was what she had been beginning to fear.

When Gaban reached the pass, everyone dismounted while Gaban and Tasmin put leather booties on the horses' hooves. When Ebony started to ask why Tasmin shushed her and motioned for everyone to remain quiet. Tasmin helped Cheri to mount up behind Faye on the poor packhorse before they continued.

Then Gaban turned Buttercup back toward the valley, "Ochwatt, if you'll go along for a little way, I just need to do another casting. This one might take a while."

Without a word, Ochwatt did as instructed.

Quietly, the women continued down the eerie canyon. Then, Tasmin's horse, Anabelle, loosened a stone that rattled a few feet before it came to a stop, but the noise it made continued on and on and on as its echoes repeated over and over. It kept getting louder as if it were building on itself and they had to cover their ears before it finally ended. No breeze invaded this strange place, and while there were evergreen trees in the heights above them, no sound of birds, purple canaries or otherwise, could be heard here.

Back at the beginning of the pass Gaban began casting another spell. Slowly, surely, the blue light started glowing from the tip of Gaban's staff. Even slower, it started to spread over the ground behind them, giving light to the trail and spreading to either side to cover the entire valley. There was a brief flash as this casting met the casting already protecting the tower and climbed right over it. Two hours later, Gaban was finally finished, and the entire valley floor glowed blue for a minute. Then the glow went out, and Gaban swayed in the saddle. A moment after that, Ochwatt was there beside him to keep him from falling and rummaging in the saddlebag for any remaining apples and the dried fruit. This time Gaban downed four apples before he was ready to continue. He kept munching on dried fruit as they rode carefully through the canyon.

It was an hour and a half of careful walking by the horses before the women emerged from the canyon of echoes and could see the broad Jamben plain far below them to the south. It was like standing at the top of the world. Again, the women stopped so Tasmin, with Faye's help, could remove the booties before they resumed their descent on the almost vertical trail at a cautious pace. In no time at all, the South Jamben Plain was lost behind a wall of strange trees with waxy leaves.

The smell of chimney smoke from the village wafted up to greet them through an evergreen forest that only faintly resembled the cedars and pines of western Washington. Cheri was trying to put her finger on what exactly wasn't right about them when Ebony's whisper distracted her.

"What was that all about?" she said with a jerk of her head over her right shoulder.

"That," said Tasmin, in her normal voice, "was Echo

Pass. It magnifies all sounds in it and repeats them almost endlessly. No one but the villagers and a very few others know of Gaban's Hidden Valley. For obvious reasons, we're trying to keep it that way. The pass can also act as an early warning for intruders that don't know it's properties."

"Oh, well, why didn't you tell us ahead of time? We could have really screwed things up," grumbled Ebony.

"You're absolutely right. I should have warned you, or Gaban should have, even though we were in a hurry. We'll simply have to keep reminding ourselves and each other that you know nothing about Persal. It would also be advisable to obey orders and gestures, when given, without question. Questions can always be answered later if we live long enough."

"Now there's a cheerful thought," said Cheri in an aside to Faye.

Faye simply patted the poor packhorse's neck affectionately and smiled. There was nothing she loved more than riding horses. Even a packhorse.

Soon after they lost sight of the plain, Gaban and Ochwatt caught up, and they caught sight of the village of Breymin, halfway down the steep slope. Just beyond the place where the forest seemed to end abruptly, and a wide chasm took over, the way was spanned by a narrow wooden bridge with a sturdy gate on the far side. Two well- armed men were patiently guarding the gate and watching the trail through the village for possible trouble. The kind of trouble they watched for was not expected to come from the bridge.

Gaban called for everyone to dismount before signaling Tasmin to take the lead. Then he stood in the way, effectively blocking the others from following immediately. "We need to cross one at a time. Breymin Village is scrupulous of its duties, including the care of this bridge, but there is no need to put undue strain on it," he said simply. Everyone else had dismounted by now, and all three of the strangers nervously edged toward the precipice to look down. Ebony made it close enough to see the sheer drop well. "There's no bottom! I can't see anything.

But the sheer walls going on and on."

Cheri's eyes snapped up to watch Tasmin with trepidation as she led Anabelle across the bridge. A moment ago, the bridge had appeared perfectly sound. Now Cheri thought it looked a little flimsy. The chasm seemed to act like a wind tunnel, causing Tasmin's skirt and cloak to whip about like a drab banner and the bridge itself complain in mournful creaks and groans as it took on their combined weight.

"I'll tell you what, I'll go around. I really wouldn't want to put any unnecessary stress on that old bridge," she volunteered.

"What!" began Gaban in amazement as he turned toward her.

"Don't be silly, Cheri. You'll be perfectly fine. If we're here for a purpose, it won't be a bridge that takes us out. I'll guarantee nothing bad will happen," insisted Faye sweetly as she stood near the edge stroking the packhorse's soft nose.

"Besides, there is no other way across. There, Tasmin's through the gate. Perhaps you had better go next. Ochwatt can go with you," decided Gaban.

"What? No! I'll go alone. I don't think any extra weight is a good idea." Taking a deep breath, she started across. "Don't look down. Don't look down," she kept repeating to herself as she stared steadfastly at the gate and tried not to think about how fragile the whole thing felt. She was nearly across when she stumbled and looked down at her feet. Crazily her eyes skittered off the edge of the bridge and tried to find the bottom of a bottomless abyss. Trembling uncontrollably, she stopped dead.

"Cheri! What's wrong? Look up, look at me! Come on,

you're almost here," came Tasmin's voice faintly, as if through a dense fog. Fainter still were the voices of the others behind her.

"I can't! I...just can't," she croaked hoarsely, her eyes never leaving the emptiness below.

The slight sway of the bridge increased dramatically as heavy footsteps vibrated from behind her. In alarm, Cheri turned her head just enough to see Ochwatt coming for her. When he reached her, he swept her up in one smooth movement, carrying her the last few feet to the gate where he deposited her gently.

She had regained her composure by the time everyone else was across, and mercifully no one mentioned the incident as they made their way into town.

CHAPTER 4

To Ride a White Horse

As they arrived, the people from town came out to greet them. The women from the day before instantly took note of their exhaustion and guided Ebony, Faye, and Cheri into a nearby house. Hustling them off to their rooms to get cleaned up and put to bed for some much-needed sleep.

Tasmin took the horses, including Buttercup, to the stables before making her way to the tavern and a bed of her own, but Gaban and Ochwatt stayed at the gate while the men charged with guarding the bridge dismantled the abutment and superstructure at the near end. It wasn't all that long before the bridge weakened and with the help of the winds from the chasm, the rest of the bridge cracked and broke, the ragged pieces spiraling down into nothingness.

Gaban was the only one not watching the bridge fall. Instead, he was watching the pass beyond. Now he was truly cut off from the valley he had called home for nearly two thousand years.

With a shake of his head, he turned to make his way to the Cock Crows Tavern where he would find food and a welcome bed. He had expended a great deal of magic in the last twelve hours and desperately needed to eat and sleep. Ochwatt stayed at his side, and Gaban glanced over at him with a questioning look. "Are you going to follow me around?"

"Yes," was the terse reply.

It was still early morning when the sound of several horses riding into the village followed by shouting from the direction of the bridge awoke the women from a sound sleep.

Instantly awake, Ebony rose and started getting dressed in the purple traveling clothes Tasmin had given her the day before. It was loose enough to be comfortable and close enough to not get in the way. The dark purple shirt was buttoned up the front with a wide collar, and the divided skirt was not so full as to hamper her movements nor too long since it stopped at midcalf. If anything, it was more comfortable than her jeans. Overall, she was pleased with her reflection in the tall pier glass that had been brought to her room. When she emerged, Cheri was already at breakfast, chowing down on the fragrant hot bread, eggs, and bacon. Her outfit was much more concealing than the girl was accustomed to with a high neck and long sleeves. She had left the top four buttons undone. The full skirt, divided for riding, came almost to her ankles. If they hit hot weather in their journeys, she was going to roast in all this heavy black tweed. The only redeeming feature was the vest which laced up the front and showed her figure to its best.

Faye came out of a third bedroom and seemed quite pleased with the demureness of her new clothes. The high neckline and concealing divided skirt suited her modesty just fine, but she wasn't so sure about the form-fitting bodice. She was also amazed at how flattering the dark blue was on her. Glancing over at Cheri, she shook her head. "In this world, I think a little more modesty is called for, please button up your shirt, Cheri."

Cheri frowned as she looked down at her blouse. "I thought this was more modest. Well, I'm not going to choke so how about we compromise," she suggested as she did up two of the offending buttons.

"Fine, but please remember, we're in a strange place, and we need to try to fit in, if we can," Faye instructed as she sat down to breakfast.

As they were finishing eating, Tasmin knocked on the door and opened it before they could answer.

"I hope you slept well. We have a great deal to do today. There will be final fittings for your gowns before you start taking horseback riding lessons. After yesterday there's no doubt Ebony and Cheri need those, anyway. Your horses arrived a few minutes ago."

"Is that wha...wuk uh?" asked Cheri around a mouthful of fresh bread.

"Cheri! Don't speak with your mouth full. To answer your mumbling, probably, if you were awakened by hoofbeats and yelling."

"Well, I'm ready to go," said Ebony, grabbing another thick slice of warm bread as she rose.

"I just got here," complained Faye. Let me grab a couple of peaches and some bread and butter, and I'll be right behind you.

Cheri rose without another word, but she did grab one last piece of the fresh, hot bread as the three of them followed Tasmin into the street.

Once there they caught sight of a man riding one horse and leading five other animals toward an open field just north of town. The field reminded Cheri of the meadow in Gaban's valley with its yellow flowers and purple-tipped grass waving in the fresh breeze. Three of the mounts were horses, and the other two were pack mules. Leaving on their bridles, he let the horses loose in the pasture while he removed the gear tied to the mules.

Before any of them could get a good look under his wide-brimmed hat, Tasmin hustled them into the community center where the seamstresses had set up. Amazingly, Ochwatt was already there being measured for pants, shirts, and a hooded cloak. He didn't even say hello when they arrived and ducked out the door as soon as he could. This was not comfortable for him.

For the next hour, the young ladies tried on their dresses and dodged straight pins. When Faye and Ebony were finally set free, they failed to notice that Cheri wasn't right behind them. Just as Ebony was turning to ask her a question, she ran up to join them.

"Where were you?" asked Faye, looking back at the center where the door was just closing.

"Uh, I just asked my lady for a quick favor. No big deal," she answered dismissively.

Faye glanced at Ebony, who arched a brow in reply. Neither thought they'd get an answer now, but both hoped it didn't mean trouble later.

"Come on, girls, time to meet your horses," called Tasmin gaily as she led the way to the field.

As they approached the horses, Faye's eyes lit up while Ebony and Cheri watched the horses with some trepidation. Gaban had told them they'd be traveling by horseback and these must be their rides. A piercing cry from above caught their attention, and they saw an enormous blue hawk spiral down from the sky to alight on the shoulder of the man who had brought the horses. He removed his hat in greeting when they stopped in front of him, introducing himself.

"My name is Falcon."

Cheri was staring nervously at the horses. Her heart sank, the moment she'd been trying not to think about was finally here. Maybe it wouldn't be so bad if she got the small one.

Ebony, on the other hand, was watching the wrangler carefully. Not for riding tips as she should have been, but for a sense of this man who would probably be teaching her to ride and most likely be accompanying them on their adventure. What she saw was a man dressed in greenish-gray buckskins and of medium height. Well, at least medium in their world. Maybe here he was really tall? Anyway, he was about an inch or so, shorter than her own five foot eleven. He was probably about a five foot nine or five foot ten. He sort of resembled an American Indian with his straight black hair tied back in a ponytail at his neck, black eyes and a beak of a nose. On the other hand, his olive complexion seemed more reminiscent of a Greek. 'Stupid, trying to compare nationalities here to those at home is like comparing apples and oranges," she berated herself silently when she realized what she was doing.

A startled gasp escaped from Faye drawing everyone's attention. Almost as if she were in a trance, Faye crossed the intervening space between herself and a pure white stallion that had evidently been giving the wrangler quite a problem. He even started to step between the two before Tasmin put her hand on his arm and shook her head.

At her approach, the stallion calmed instantly and arched his head to accept her outstretched hand on his nose. Sighing blissfully, Faye leaned her cheek against the horse's neck for a second before turning to the startled rider. "May I ride him, please?"

"Faye, do you think you should? I mean, if you're accident-prone," objected Ebony.

"Oh, I'm never clumsy on horseback. Sometimes I think it's the only place I really belong," replied Faye dreamily, her eyes never leaving the white stallion. "May I ride him?"

"Well, I'm not sure that's a good idea. No one else can even get close to him, but then, no one else can calm him down either. For the life of me, I have no idea why I brought him along. He's already been more trouble than he's worth. If you think you can handle him, let's saddle him up, and you can go ahead. Someone's going to have to ride him, and evidently it's going to be you," murmured the startled man, mostly to himself as Faye walked over to the saddles and Falcon pointed out the correct one. She quickly hauled the saddle and a horse blanket over to her horse and started saddling him with practiced moves.

Falcon shrugged slightly, and the hawk gave another harsh cry and hurtled into the air again with broad strokes of his bright blue wings.

"Astounding!" said Tasmin as she stared after the hawk as it flew off. "Absolutely amazing! Well, you must be the scout. My name is Tasmin. The young woman mounting the white is Faye. This is Ebony and Cheri. We will be your traveling companions. What did you say your name was again?"

"I'm Falcon, and the hawk is Amalee. Nice to meet all of you, I suppose. Maybe you can tell me why I'm here? I mean, a couple of weeks ago I got this urge, and every time I've tried to do something else, like choose a horse other than the white, everything would go wrong," said a very puzzled young man as he tried to saddle the spirited chocolate palomino gelding, which pranced as though showing off for the women. Cheri drew back in alarm, and Ebony shrugged before stepping forward. "How hard can it be?" she muttered.

"You've never been on a horse?" asked an astonished Falcon. When Ebony shook her head, he continued. "Let him smell your hand. Then start by talking to him. Give him a name. Tell him yours. He needs to get to know your voice and your smell," he instructed patiently, patting the large horse on his neck to calm him as Ebony came close. It seemed obvious to Ebony that all of Falcon's sympathies were with the horse, not her.

Ebony took a deep breath to calm her irritation with Falcon as well as her nerves. She started to speak but found her voice had taken a leave of absence. With another deep breath, she cleared her throat and tried again. Approaching the horse with her hand stretched out, she said, "Hi there. Aren't you beautiful? My name's Ebony, and I think you're a

George. The other George I knew was a blond too. Just don't run out on me like he did, okay? Do you like that?" she asked as she hesitantly stroked his soft nose. As she talked, she relaxed, and her smile was no longer forced. Watching the horse nuzzle her hand, Falcon handed Ebony a carrot to give to George and Tasmin drew Cheri over to the small pinto she had just finished saddling.

Cheri had been watching Ebony with interest, but now that she was in front of one of these beasts, she had stiffened up. She kept reminding herself she'd survived on the streets of Seattle for three years. Surely this couldn't be any worse than the first month when she had only been twelve.

"Mr. Falcon, is your bird a falcon? Is that why that's your name?" she asked the scout, trying to postpone the inevitable.

"She's a hawk, Lady Cheri, and please, just call me, Falcon. She did have something to do with my name, though. That's a long story, maybe another time. Let's worry about teaching you and Lady Ebony to ride."

"Quit stalling and relax, Cheri. Come on over to this pony, he's just a person, like you. Here are some carrots, take his reins, walk with him, and talk to him. Get to know him and let him get to know you," instructed Tasmin gently. "You don't have to ride him right away."

"A person? Huh! A really big person, I guess," said Cheri as she held the reins uncomfortably for a few minutes, watching Ebony get acquainted with George. Suddenly she was pushed gently by her pinto's inquiring nose against her shoulder. Giggling quietly, she reached up to pet the soft muzzle, "Hi there, Baby. I'm Cheri. Oh, you want a carrot, do you? Well, here then. Why don't we walk about a bit, okay?" Suddenly she found herself talking as if to an old friend.

Just then Faye cantered up on the white stallion, his long mane flying. Her eyes were sparkling, and her face was glowing as she tried to stop grinning. Pulling the horse to a stop, she let the grin slip free as she bent to pat his neck. "Isn't he marvelous? I never thought I'd see one, much less get to ride him. This is just like the most amazing dream."

"Um, Faye, surely you've ridden a horse before. I mean you ride quite well," stammered Ebony with an odd look.

Well, of course, I've ridden a horse, but he isn't a..." Faye's voice trailed away as the stallion shook his head vigorously, and she realized that no one else saw what she did. "Oh, I've been so stupid. You can't see it, can you? Uh, well, he certainly isn't an ordinary horse. He is just the most magnificent mount I've ever seen, much less been able to ride," she finished weakly, stifling a giggle.

Funny, she thought as she pulled up next to Falcon who continued the lessons for Ebony and Cheri. *I finally found a reason to be grateful for being twenty-six and a virgin, and I'm the only one who can see it. I wonder if anyone would even believe me if I told them?*

Once Ebony and Cheri were mounted, Falcon led the way with Amalee soaring high over his head. Tasmin headed back to town, certain they were in good hands.

Reluctantly, the two novices turned their horses to follow Falcon and Faye as the sun traveled across the sky and the purple canaries began their joyous song of greeting in earnest. For the next two hours, they cantered and walked around the open field. Getting used to their mounts and trying to learn what they would need to know over the next few weeks or months.

Faye was riding at a leisurely canter ahead of Cheri, and she watched her closely to see if there was a secret to riding a horse. One that could possibly make it more comfortable. Faye's hips rolled with the movement of the horse, and she appeared completely relaxed. How could Faye be so relaxed? How could Cheri learn to trust herself to such a large beast? With a shake of her head, she decided to make an effort to relax like Faye did but found herself tensing up again every few minutes.

Ebony's athletic background helped her master the basics of horseback riding by the end of the day.

Cheri, contrarily, had taken most of the day just learning to mount and stay on her pony. She did get in an hour of walking and trotting with Baby by the day's end, but her edginess had only softened slightly by sundown when they called a halt.

After dinner, the three women gathered in Faye's room to talk. Cheri lay gingerly on her stomach across the bed while Ebony leaned against the footboard. Faye rested easily in the chair.

"Ms. Chessman, where did you learn to ride like that?" asked Cheri curiously.

Faye laughed. "My father sent me to camp every summer between the ages of eight and sixteen. I don't think he knew what else to do with me. I found I had a knack for horses and riding the first year. When my father found out I'd been riding horses, he was upset, at first, until he talked to my instructor and found out I was good. He always considered me something of a klutz you see," she answered, bowing her head in embarrassment and allowing her loose hair to hide her face.

"I doubt I'll ever get the hang of it, but, Ebony, you were great. You had George galloping across the meadow before Baby and I were even walking."

"Well, I've always refused to let anything get the best of me. Falcon hardly spoke to me, and I had to prove to myself I could do it," said Ebony simply. Only her eyes betrayed a strange defiance. "Don't worry, Cheri. If we're going to be on horseback for some time, I'm sure you'll get the hang of it, eventually."

That comment caused all three of them to burst out laughing. At least until Cheri rolled over in the bed and let out a wail of pain. That only caused Faye and Ebony to laugh louder, right up to when Ebony tried to sit on the arm of the chair and let out a wail of her own, jumping back onto her feet.

Cheri and Faye burst into fresh laughter followed shortly by Ebony.

When she finally caught her breath, Cheri grumbled, "As sore as I am now, I don't think I can get on a horse again for a week, much less tomorrow."

There was a light tap on the door, followed closely by Tasmin carrying three jars. "Well, ladies, it's been quite a day. As of tomorrow, the easy life is over. In the morning we start for Lohi."

"Tasmin, I couldn't possibly!" cried Cheri in alarm, rubbing her sore backside. "I'm covered in bruises, and it's going to be a while before I can sit down. Not only that, my riding isn't even riding yet."

"I know, dear, but we really have no choice. Barakus already knows you're here. Put this ointment on your bruises tonight, and in the morning, you'll feel much better," she replied blithely, handing out a jar to each of them. "I'll teach you how to pack your saddlebags before we leave and we won't forget to pack it. It has many uses. I suggest you all get a good night's sleep."

Cheri rose stiffly and followed Ebony to the door, but as Ebony started to open it, she reached across and pushed it closed, again. "One more thing, Ms. Chessman. The horse, what did you name your horse?"

"Believer, Cheri, why?" responded Faye, looking at Cheri searchingly.

"There's something different about him, but I can't say what. You know, though, don't you? Why did you call him, Believer?"

"I have a bumper sticker on my car that says, 'Now I Believe in Unicorns.' That's why," answered Faye in a low voice.

"A little beard! I just realized that stallion has a little beard," gasped Ebony, leaning weakly against the door. "Is he really a unicorn?"

"Yes, he is. I was apparently the only one out there today who was a virgin, so I'm the only one who can see his horn. Oh, and it's absolutely gorgeous, like an iridescent pearl," answered Faye, full of excitement now that she could share her secret.

As Ebony and Cheri left, Ebony stopped outside the door. With a look at each of them, she commented, "I don't know what's in store for us, but I'm glad to have met you."

"Thank you, and good night, Ebony. Good night, Cheri," said Faye with a smile as she closed her door behind them.

"Good night, Ebony. Good night, Ms. Chessman," said Cheri with a smile of her own.

*****

Tasmin roused them from their slumber long before the first purple canaries began their trilling welcome to the sun.

She had them gather all their belongings in their hostess's sitting room. Since the villager had given up her home for a couple of days, they had complete privacy. Then began the process of deciding what could go and what had to stay.

First Tasmin had them go through whatever personal belongings they had brought with them and leave anything that was useless or unnecessary. She began with Cheri, who she caught before her makeup was on and stopped her from using any at all. She did agree to let Cheri bring it, once she promised to only use it under extreme circumstances. Then she went through the contents of Cheri's oversized purse. With determination, she put aside Cheri's hair straightener and hair dryer once she found out they needed a power source not available in Persal. Then she to put aside the inappropriate clothes Cheri always carried with her. Once she was through, she showed Cheri how to pack her saddlebags and a bedroll before moving on to Ebony's belongings. As soon as her back was turned, Cheri slipped a small bundle and her red mini dress into the bottom of her saddlebag.

The karate clothes in Ebony's gym bag proved perplexing to Tasmin, "What are these clothes for? They don't resemble what you were wearing when you arrived."

"They're clothes for, uh, some of my athletic exercises," Ebony explained warily.

"Well, bring them along, I suppose. I don't know what harm it can do. Perhaps we'll just say they're some type of clothing worn in Mojar," said Tasmin with a shake of her head. "What's this?" she asked, holding up Ebony's cell phone.

"Uh, it's a way to communicate over very long distances with anyone else who has one... Uhm, it's called a cell phone," stumbled Ebony. "They don't work here. We'll leave them."

"Good."

Faye had already left her briefcase and files behind in the tower. When they went through her purse, Tasmin insisted they leave the books behind. "If seen, they would be regarded suspiciously by the local population, and you can never tell who works for Barakus."

"Where's my cell phone? I had it in my hand when...," asked Faye, trailing off when she remembered.

"I think you dropped it in the pool at the waterfall," said Cheri, looking at Faye apologetically.

"Figures! I guess it doesn't matter now." Coming back to Tasmin's request, she reluctantly agreed. "Fine, but I won't leave my Bible!" she insisted.

"What is this book that makes it so important to you?" asked Tasmin, curious.

"It's the story of God and his son. I don't go anywhere without it."

"God? Not gods? Which god?"

"There is only one God, and he has one son. I'm not going to try to convert anyone to my faith, but I will take it with me," said Faye, holding the Bible tight, as if Tasmin were trying to take it.

"Well, I can't see the harm. Just be careful where you take it out, please," agreed Tasmin. Once that was settled, Faye packed her Bible and glasses in her saddlebag along with her new clothes.

After fighting to get the tangles left from yesterday's riding out of her hair, Cheri reluctantly pulled her curls into a smooth French braid down her back. If they were going to be traveling, something sensible was called for. Especially if they were going on horseback.

When Faye saw the braid, she exclaimed in delight, "Oh, Cheri, I really like your hair that way. It really frames your face instead of hiding it. That's quite a talent. I've never really known what to do with my hair."

"Thank you, Ms. Chessman. It's really not so hard. It just takes a little practice. Would you like me to do yours?" offered Cheri generously.

"Oh, yes, please. Maybe you can start teaching me how to do my own. I also think it's time you started calling me Faye, under the circumstances."

Before breakfast, Tasmin supplied three new pairs of custom- made boots that were amazingly comfortable. After a quick breakfast, they emerged into the town square where Falcon, Gaban, and a transformed Ochwatt were waiting.

"Wow, Ochwatt! You look, uh, almost normal, except for your height, of course," said Cheri, looking him up and down in wonder.

The sasquatch had been bathed, and his hair combed. He also had on a pair of extra-long pants that covered his feet. There hadn't been time to make him anything more than sandals. His enveloping cloak with its concealing hood finished the look. If you didn't get a good look under that hood, he mostly looked like an extra tall human with a full beard. He didn't smell half bad either, anymore.

"Humph!" said Gaban with a look over his shoulder at Falcon. "He'll do."

The horses were saddled and waiting, but Falcon was standing beside an odd assortment of weapons. "Take your choice," he said shortly. At their expressions of surprise and bewilderment, he continued, "We didn't take the time yesterday, but besides your personal daggers, each of you should carry other weapons for self- defense, at least. Take whichever weapons you're comfortable with."

"I realize this is going to come as a shock to you, but where we come from, normal people don't usually carry weapons," exclaimed Faye indignantly.

"Well, I guess that means I'll be training you in weapons while we're on the road. I wouldn't gamble on us having much time before they'll come in handy," replied Falcon brusquely.

"That won't be totally necessary!" exclaimed Ebony sharply, picking up a wide belt and a matched pair of short swords in their scabbards. She buckled them on before pulling them out to check their balance. "I learned something of how to use these in my martial arts training."

Stepping forward, Cheri picked up a set of throwing knives and started hiding them about her person. "I learned more than most people would believe on the streets."

Faye stood there a moment, looking into Ebony's and Cheri's defiant faces, before she stooped to pick up a quiver of arrows and a bow nearly as tall as she was. "Well, it so happens I do know a little about how to use these."

"Faye, are you sure?" asked Cheri nervously.

"Don't worry, Cheri, I know what I'm doing," said Faye as she strung the bow and pulled out an arrow in one smooth motion. Before anyone knew what she was doing, she had drawn and shot at a tree in the middle of the square, a hundred yards away, hitting a knothole neatly in the center. While they were still gaping, another arrow followed, splitting the first.

Roughly, Falcon reached out and grabbed her bow. "Don't let vanity make you foolish. Arrows aren't so easy to find that they should be destroyed needlessly. Your first shot proved your point," he growled, handing her a rawhide buckler for her arm.

Blushing furiously, Faye turned away and busied herself with unstringing the bow and hanging it on the high pommel of her saddle. The quiver of arrows she tied with her other belongings behind her. "Whatever this is, it's gone out of control," she muttered to herself.

"Fine, now that it's settled, let's be off," said Tasmin with a shake of her head. She had been watching from the sidelines with amusement teasing her lips.

Falcon mounted his own gray stallion, Wolf, and gathered the two mules behind him to wait. The other horses were already saddled, and the pack animals were laden with tents and supplies for several weeks. Tasmin's pack-horse had also been pressed into use and was tied behind Anabelle.

Cheri eyed Baby warily, but she had to admit, her backside had benefited greatly from Tasmin's ointment, and she might survive horseback riding after all, if she could stay on the beast.

Bedrolls and saddlebags secured, the women hugged Gaban with more fondness than their short acquaintance would normally warrant, but his was a familiar face in a strange world. Each of them shook hands with Ochwatt, even as he reacted to the gesture with some confusion.

"I'll explain the significance later, dear friend," promised Gaban from atop Buttercup with a smile. He and Ochwatt would be heading in a different direction and planned to meet up with the women and Falcon in Lohi. They all had a long way to go before they would meet again.

CHAPTER 5

Down the Mountain

Now that they were mounted, Falcon led the way with Amalee soaring high over his head. Ebony, Faye, and Cheri reluctantly turned their horses to follow as the sun found its way above the trees and the purple canaries began their joyous song to greet the day in earnest.

Once again Faye was riding ahead of Cheri and moving at a leisurely canter. Cheri watched to see if there were any secrets to riding that could possibly make it more comfortable. Faye was completely relaxed in the saddle, allowing her hips to roll with the gait of Believer. Cheri tried concentrating on relaxing, but just concentrating made her tense up again.

As they rode through the village, the six women who had helped sew their new clothes came out, and somberly waved to them before returning to their morning chores. Only the children acknowledged their passing, and they all seemed enthralled with Faye's white stallion. They knew what he really was.

Just as they were passing the last house, a girl not much younger than Cheri, came running out and grabbed her stirrup, looking up at her with eyes wide. "Don't be too hard on him, he's my brother!" she said as she trotted beside her.

"What? What do you mean? Who are you?" asked Cheri in confusion, looking to her companions for help.

"My name is Cantrice," was all she heard before the girl released the stirrup and was gone. Running back down the street to her home. Then the road turned steep as it headed down the mountain, demanding all her attention. Reluctantly she pushed the incident to the back of her mind.

Within moments, they had left even the most determined of the children behind, and the three women felt even more adrift than they had on leaving the valley.

Once they were away from the village, Amalee rejoined them, although she was still gliding on the thermals high overhead.

As their trek continued, Cheri detected the smell of cinnamon in the air. She was too busy concentrating on remaining on Baby's back and trying to relax in the process to search for the source. It became even harder to loosen up when she felt she was going to fly over the pony's head at any moment. Looking around her at the strange trees was a luxury she couldn't afford.

Faye was looking about at the tall, tightly packed trees with purple trunks and wide canopies in bemusement and Ebony was beginning to really worry about her. Was she drifting back into her delusion it was all a dream? Ebony edged nearer to Cheri when they reached a place that was wide and relatively level. "Cheri, have you noticed? Faye seems to be drifting. I'm worried she's going back to dreaming, so to speak. Any suggestions on how we can really wake her up?"

Cheri cast a quick glance Faye's way before returning her attention to Baby. "You're probably right, but how? Exactly? The only danger we appear to be in right now is in falling off these beasts. Sorry, Baby. Let's give it a couple of days, or until we reach the first town, okay?" And she let Baby pull ahead as the trail narrowed and continued winding its way through the thick forest. Abruptly, it made a steep hairpin turn, opening up a small space to catch a breathtaking glimpse of the downs far below for a moment. Then the trees closed in again, and all they could see was a wall of smooth, straight purple poles that smelled strongly of cinnamon and topped with wide-spreading branches like overlapping umbrellas.

Ebony stared after Cheri in frustration as George followed Baby automatically. She was staring after her two new friends and their mounts when she noticed how unbelievably white and clean Believer was. Even in all the dust from the trail. Well, if he really was a unicorn, maybe she should just leave Faye in his care.

They stopped briefly at noon in a small clearing near a babbling brook to stretch while eating cheese and bread. They washed it all down with cold clear water from the stream.

Amalee flew down to perch briefly on Falcon's shoulder and make small little sounds in his ear before she was off again.

"At least we probably don't need to worry about water pollution here," commented Cheri dryly, watching the blue-tailed hawk climb into the sky and soar out of sight, down the mountain.

"Maybe not here, but I wouldn't bet on it when we get closer to civilization. On our world, people at this stage used the rivers for sewers and the streets for garbage dumps. Any chance we'll find things better here, Tasmin?" asked Ebony.

"Just like home," mumbled Cheri under her breath.

"What you speak of was unheard of before Barakus gained control of most of Persal. Since then, many people act as if tomorrow, much less their surroundings, don't matter anymore. Too many people have given up, especially in the larger cities where Barakus's governors reside, and their lives are dictated at the whim of the priests with the help of the church soldiers," agreed Tasmin with a sad shake of her head.

"On the bright side, there are still good, decent people, even in the cities, and they try. Often whole neighborhoods have banded together to retain their dignity, but it is difficult. Many of the youth flee the cities and look for better lives in the country. When they are turned away they sometimes join highwaymen to survive. If they persist, they can usually find honest work. Many also go to sea," offered Falcon, darkly, keeping a sharp eye on the trail, both in front of them and behind.

Tasmin continued, "It's the older ones, who act as if nothing has changed that I find most deplorable. Those without hope can be roused. Those who are still trying will be ready. But those who are ignoring the problem won't welcome change. At least, not easily."

"I think it's time we moved on. We'll have to make camp before we reach the foothills as it is, but the sooner we reach the Haunted Forest, the better. Too many people have disappeared in these mountains," continued Falcon, mounting Wolf in one smooth movement. Without another word, the others also mounted and followed Falcon. Even Cheri, but nowhere near as gracefully. As they continued, each considered their own disturbing thoughts.

Ebony noticed a frown on Faye's face and uncertainty in her eyes as she looked around them. Perhaps she was beginning to realize just how dangerous their situation really was. One could only hope.

Just before dusk engulfed them, they found a small meadow near a clear stream and stopped to make camp for the night. Tasmin busily made supper from the fresh chicken they had brought with them while Falcon drafted Faye and Ebony to take care of the horses. Then he began teaching Cheri how to set up the tents.

After a hearty supper of bread and chicken, Falcon checked Ebony and Cheri out on their chosen weapons. Cheri had quite a good aim with the knives, but he told her to practice improving her speed. To Ebony, he gave a wooden practice sword and took up one himself.

Amalee was perched in a tree, watching, but now Falcon sent her away. "She gets upset when she thinks I might be hurt," he explained with a smile before they began.

Ebony's methods of spinning the swords in complicated defensive patterns before bringing them down for a striking blow was quite different from the graceful, almost dancelike motions Falcon employed, although they did have their effectiveness. Especially when she insisted on using two, one in each hand.

"You're quick, and you have good control, but in this world, it would be best if you also knew what to expect from your opponents," said Falcon dryly as he parried and got under her guard, pushing her off her feet and into the grass. "It would also help if you attacked more instead of just defending yourself. Your opponents won't be affording you the same courtesy."

Angrily, Ebony jumped to her feet in one fluid motion, and the practice session began again. This time Ebony did not neglect to attack, and Cheri had trouble telling who was getting in more touches than the other. As Ebony's blows became stronger, Faye and Tasmin joined her, and it became obvious Ebony was fighting in earnest.

The session ended abruptly when Falcon started advancing mercilessly, knocking first one sword, and then the other out of Ebony's hands and backing her against a tree. "Yes, Ebony, you have proved you can fight. But can you learn? Tomorrow, I will begin to teach you the forms for fighting with one sword, and we will practice every night between here and Lohi. Knowing what to expect from your enemies

be ready for the coming war. One more thing, when we meet people, do as I do."

"Yes, friend Gaban. Until we fight."

*****

With another dawn, the women were awakened by the purple canaries and another bright and sunny morning. A quick breakfast of cold chicken and hot tea and everyone pitching in to break camp and pack up, putting them on the road within an hour and a half. Speedy, considering they had three novices stumbling over themselves as they tried to learn the routine. Not to mention the time it took for Cheri to show Faye how she braided her hair before helping Faye braid her own.

The trees changed gradually as they continued to descend. First the trees with purple trunks gave way for an evergreen forest of pines with smooth white trunks, cedars with a bark the color of bright cranberries, and firs whose trunks were a strange blue-gray. They too grew fewer as aspen with dark-blue leaves and lavender bark, red leaf maples with a scarlet trunk to match, and unbelievably tall elms with leaves such a pale green that they appeared white at first glance infiltrated above the foothills to meet them. The glimpses they were able to catch of the birds and small animals scurrying out of the way left an impression of vague familiarity mixed with an oddness that only served to remind them they were truly in another world.

The Haunted Forest, when they finally reached it, wasn't at all what the name had led them to expect. The trees were the same red maples and ethereal elms scattered between new species, and it became harder and harder to find an analogy from their own world. Except for the gigantic oaks with trunks so dark, they looked black until a determined ray of sunlight hit them. This was hardly the bare dead trees with gnarled limbs surrounded by a gloomy atmosphere the name implied, instead they were surrounded by multiple shades of green, blue, and purple, the colors of thriving plants bathed in bright sunshine. The ground was now gently rolling hills interspersed with flat meadows.

The second night they made camp at the edge of a small clearing near a brook, and Falcon asked Cheri to help Ebony with the horses while he taught Faye how to set up the tents. Everything went fine until Falcon went inside the tent to raise the roof pole, and Faye tripped over the guy ropes tangling her feet while poles bounced off Falcon's head and canvas engulfed them both.

Falcon's cursing and Faye's yelp brought the other three running. The sight of the two of them tied up in canvas and rope with poles sticking out at odd angles was so ludicrous that Cheri found herself stifling her giggles behind her hand, and Ebony had a grin on her face from ear to ear. Meanwhile, Tasmin stared with eyes blinking before she allowed a loud guffaw to escape. That one sound was the breaking point for Cheri and Ebony as well, and all three were soon laughing uncontrollably.

Falcon had to shout to get their attention. "When you ladies find it convenient, Lady Faye and I would appreciate some help!" he said sarcastically.

Still giggling, the three women released the captives, and Falcon suggested it might be best if Faye returned to caring for the horses. He would train Ebony on tents, instead.

"This forest doesn't strike me as being particularly spooky," commented Ebony as they worked. "Why is it called the Haunted Forest?"

"It's not actually the forest, or at least not the trees themselves that are haunted, my lady. It's the stories of spirits seen out of the corner of the eye and a feeling of being watched, told by almost everyone who dares enter here.

People don't like things they can't explain so they call the forest 'Haunted,'" Falcon replied with a dismissing shrug. "There is no record of these spirits ever hurting anyone, so I wouldn't worry too much if I were you."

"Since I've never believed in ghosts, I'll try not to, thank you," said Ebony sarcastically, glancing over her shoulder to see if she could catch a spirit when she didn't think Falcon was looking. She didn't believe in ghosts, but her grandmother in New Orleans did, and she still remembered her ghost stories.

After Falcon and Ebony finished their practice with the swords, he took Faye aside. "Knowing how to shoot as you do is going to come in handy, but you really should know how to fight at close quarters as well. Let me teach you some basic techniques with your belt knife. Actually, I should teach all three of you these techniques.

He spent the next half hour taking turns showing Faye, Ebony, and Cheri different ways to use their knives to get the best effect.

Once, when he had his arms around the black woman, who was about two inches taller than he was, trying to show a particularly difficult move, Cheri thought she could hear grinding teeth. When she glanced at Ebony, she couldn't detect any clenching of the jaw. Maybe she was mistaken.

"You know, Faye, what you really need to learn is how to defend yourself against someone with a sword," he said when they were through.

"I've been watching you with Ebony. I really don't think I'm suited to the sword. Is there something else?" asked Faye uneasily.

"Why don't you let me teach them the quarterstaff. It wouldn't hurt for all three of them to learn. Would you find me four poles? We'll trim them up tomorrow while we ride. I can begin their training when we stop tomorrow night," volunteered Tasmin from her seat by the fire. "Now, why don't we eat?"

Dinner's main course was a brace of an animal that resembled a rabbit, almost. Falcon called it a habity. They were brought down neatly by Falcon's sling as they rode through the woods. When they were through cleaning up, the women retired early, worn out from the long ride and fresh air. Cheri only took the time to apply Tasmin's ointment to her bruises before she dropped off into a deep sleep, serenaded by what sounded like a nightingale above the tent.

*****

The birds never missed a note and the gentle breeze seemed to be rustling the leaves of the trees overhead as Ferney quietly made his way through the canopy, trying to get a closer look at the strangers. It was so seldom that strangers came to the Haunted Forest.

The breeze picked up as Istre rushed to catch up. "What are you doing? You know we aren't supposed to be so near to strangers. Our job is to watch them and make sure they leave the forest without discovering us," she trilled, sounding like one of the birds of the forest, but Ferney understood her.

"There's something different about these round ears though. Can't you feel it? I don't mean the old woman or the man and his hawk who went up the mountain a few days ago, I mean the others. There's something about them," he said, rubbing his thin, pointed chin earnestly. His long light-brown hair hung loosely to his shoulders, tied with a leather strap across his forehead.

"Yeah! They're young, and they're pretty if you like round faces and ears," she answered, her own pointed ears twitching indignantly as she tucked her loose hair behind them.

"Don't be a fool, Istre. Can't you feel it? It's like they're pushing the air around them, only that's not it. It's more than that, but it's less than that too. Follow me. I want to get a little closer."

"More than that, less than that! Just like a male, can't make up his mind. More like he doesn't know what he's talking about!" grumbled Istre as she followed.

Now they were over the picket line of horses, and Ferney let out a long low breath. "Well, will you look at that!" he said in awe.

Istre came up next to him, where he was pointing at a large white stallion, but no, it wasn't a stallion. It was a unicorn. "So? We've seen unicorns before. There are many living here in our forest," she queried in bewilderment.

"When was the last time you saw one with someone? Anyone? Much less the round ears?" asked Ferney in exasperation. "I told you there was something different about these strangers. Wasn't the small one with golden hair riding it when they got here?"

"You know, I think you're right. Isn't that the oddest thing? Doesn't one of Mexley's stories tell of a time when unicorns will let themselves be caught to fight the last battles or something?" asked Istre thoughtfully.

"I'm not sure, but I do remember something in a story. Let's go, I think we need to tell the elders," said Ferney with one last thoughtful look at the unicorn, tethered with the horses as if it were his idea. Ferney and Istre turned to leave just a moment before Believer opened his eyes and watched the departing elves.

"Well, we better hurry then. I heard Barakus has started the Taking and his priests are on their way. The elders want us to go to Forest City tonight before the soldiers can come."

*****

Ebony and the others spent the next two days traveling at

a leisurely canter interspersed with a restful walk, following a nearly invisible pack trail through the often-dense forest. Falcon frequently provided their dinners of soft, short-eared habities, squirrel-like greibals, or fat ground birds called whybras all brought down by a sling and small smooth creek stones he always kept handy as they rode. Cheri started keeping the wing feathers of the birds which were in vibrant hues of teal and purple.

Soon, whenever they caught sight of Amalee flying above or coming back to Falcon, Ebony felt reassured. It was like having a guardian angel watching over them. She didn't join them often during the day, but she seemed to be scouting for them all the same.

As they traveled, they fell into a routine for setting up and packing up that soon had their time in the morning down to just over half an hour. Faye soon became adept at braiding her own hair, and that alone cut twenty minutes from their time.

Each night their weapons training continued and all three women became proficient with the quarterstaff, practicing with Tasmin and each other every night. Ebony also spent time with Falcon, learning the forms of swordsmanship. Forms that had never been necessary before. In practice, she drove herself harder than anyone, and she learned quickly. It became harder and harder for Falcon to best her, but he allowed a small smile of satisfaction when he put away the wooden swords their last night in the Haunted Forest.

Shortly after they set out on their third morning in the Haunted Forest, the trees changed, bending in upon themselves as if in pain and their branches reached for those who dared pass as if to snare them in their clutches. The limbs were as white as bleached bone, and the leaves were small and red, like drops of blood. This was the edge of the haunted forest, and soon they broke through to a track between long rows of grapevines carefully tied and tended. Once clear of the forest, Cheri turned to glance back and understood why most would refuse to chance such a place. Haunted forest indeed.

For the first time since, leaving the mountain, brick farmhouses with thatched roofs could be seen in the distance. There was an orchard planted on the far side of the house, and a goat grazed in the yard in front. The women began feeling more at ease, knowing there were people close by again. It wasn't long before they came out onto a country lane angling from the northwest along the outskirts of the forest and continuing to the southeast. Falcon led them southeast for a short way until the lane met a well-traveled road heading east. The road sign pointed to the east, informing them Nelas was in that direction. A second sign, weathered clean, pointed to the west. Without a pause, they continued to canter down the deeply rutted road headed for what passed for civilization in this world.

That night, they stopped at a one-street village with the improbable name of Forest City, lined with red brick houses and establishments all roofed with thatch. They stayed at the only inn, whose wooden sign swinging over the door depicted a man with a wooden leg leaning on a wooden crutch, proclaiming it to be the One-Legged Man. Inside was a smoky common room filled with dusty farmers and other locals who all seemed to be talking to each other at the top of their lungs, but there were notes of frustration, anger, and sorrow in the voices as well. The serving maids, dressed similarly to Tasmin in loose blouses and slim split skirts, wove their way expertly through the crowd, trays of ale steins held high above their heads. Then, someone noticed the strangers standing at the door, and all eyes turned toward them as a hush fell over the room.

Falcon stepped forward. "If you have rooms, we'd be

obliged. We also need someone to tend to our horses," he said as the proprietor in his clean white apron pushed his way through the throng to help them.

"Certainly! Certainly! Ralf, go with this fine gentleman and see to his horses. Then help him bring up their luggage. Hop to it, boy!" said the portly man, motioning to a thin boy with unruly brown hair. Then he continued. "It isn't often we get strangers in these parts. Please excuse us if'n we've forgotten our manners. I be Mulk, owner of the One-Legged Man, named after my great ancestor who only had the one leg and said there was no better occupation for a man with one leg than selling drinks to men until they couldn't stand on two. Yes, yes, you ladies are tired and need your rest, and I be too busy running me mouth. Please follow me. How many rooms will ye be needin'? We have four fresh, clean rooms that my missus insists on changing every other day, even if they haven't been used. This way, this way now." And the very short, stout innkeeper led the way upstairs, his bald head gleaming in the lamplight.

"What do you think, Falcon? Three?" asked Tasmin as they followed their host up the stairs to the front of the building where their small rooms with low beamed ceilings were waiting.

"Two." He answered shortly, checking the hall for exits. "These two," he expanded, pointing to the two closest to the stairs.

Mulk turned to go back downstairs while they checked out the rooms. The mattresses appeared to be slightly lumpy, but the bedding was clean, and after almost a week of sleeping on the ground, the women were more than willing to be forgiving.

When Mulk was still at the top of the stairs, Tasmin stopped him. "That's quite a crowd down there for a weeknight. Isn't it unusual?"

"Yes, but it's the Taking, you see. The men come here as they can to lose themselves in drink and talk about what should be done. Not that anyone ever does anything. After all, what can be done? The poor women, I don't know how they get through it," said Mulk, shaking his head sadly. "No, I really don't know how they manage. Women are stronger than men like to admit, and that's a fact. Ye'll be wanting baths, I'm sure. Ladies always want baths. I'll send the tubs right up." And Mulk waddled swiftly back down the stairs.

"Baths!" exclaimed Faye and Cheri together.

"The Taking?" asked Ebony curiously at the same time.

"Yes, dear, I'm afraid so. But there's nothing for you to worry about, not yet anyway. Right now, we need only concern ourselves with a hot bath and a good night's sleep."

Faye followed Cheri into one of the rooms, leaving Ebony to share with Tasmin. "Where are you going to sleep, Falcon?" asked Tasmin, a frown wrinkling her brow.

"I'm not. I'll be in the hall, keeping watch."

"Not all night. Wake me when the moon is high. There are two beds in this room, and we can take it in turns," said Tasmin shaking her head as she returned to her room.

In the other room, Cheri sank onto the bed with a deep sigh as Faye joined her. I don't think any of this makes any sense, except for you."

"Ms. Chessman, maybe it would help if you tried to stop making sense of what's happening and just let it happen. We don't seem to have much choice or control over anything at this point anyway. I figure it's just best to take things as they come, one day at a time," said Cheri, watching her friend closely as she stood by the window.

"This is ridiculous. I told you, don't call me Ms. Chessman anymore. I've always hated that anyway. It makes me feel old. I mean really old. I'm only twenty-six. It also makes me feel like someone else is running my life. Then, what you just said doesn't help either. Call me Faye."

"Okay...Faye, you're rambling. Take a deep breath and sit down. What I meant is, we can't do much until we find out more. We still have free choice. Personally, I don't care much for the alternatives that have been presented yet. Maybe we can change our minds later if this turns out to be a poor choice," Cheri explained, trying to calm Faye down.

"That's what I mean, Cheri. You seem to have such a down to earth attitude about things. You don't analyze, you just take things as they come. Right now, you're my anchor. The only connection to the world we left behind," said Faye, turning her head as tears started to leak out of her eyes.

"Please, Ms. Chessman...Faye," cried Cheri in alarm as she rose to put an arm around the small woman. "Please, it will be all right, I promise you. You, and Ebony and I shall all get out of this just fine. We'll find a way to get home."

"You're sure? You're really sure?" sobbed Faye.

"Of course. I may have done a lot of questionable things, but have you ever known me to lie?" soothed Cheri, praying desperately that she was telling the truth and eventually they would be able to go home.

Faye smiled at the girl's optimism. "You're right, a bath and a good night's sleep in a bed will help me see things clearly in the morning. Thank you, Cheri. I don't know what I'd do without you."

While Faye undressed and slipped blissfully into the tub, Cheri pulled out clean clothes for both of them and wondered if they could get the dirty ones cleaned.

Faye emerged from the bath with a new sense of determination and a cheerier mood. She was also hungry, so she hurried Cheri through her own bath so they could join the others at a supper of roast chicken with light-green kine-on-the-cob and biscuits.

*****

As Gaban and Ochwatt crested the last hill and looked down on the red tile roofs of Jabar, Gaban shifted in his saddle. It had been much too long since he had traveled this far from his valley and his bones were telling him as much.

Ochwatt, with his long legs, was barely winded and seemed fascinated by all the new plants and animals he had seen since leaving his secluded mountains. He was especially interested in what plants were edible, and their evening meals had been interesting as he experimented with their stews.

Now, Ochwatt became especially intrigued as they approached the white buildings perched between the hills and an expanse of sand beyond that seemed to go on and on. Next to the town were two encampments of tents, one to the north and the other to the south. Between these was a huge tent with the sides rolled up housing market stalls. A few were still doing a brisk business, but many were starting to close up for the heat of the day, and the sides were being lowered as they entered the town. Gaban led the way to the largest building, the Inn of the Seventh Well. Already they could feel the heat of the sun beating on the town and the sands. The coolness of the inn was a welcome respite, even as they pushed their way through the crowd of merchants returning from the market for a tall mead.

Gaban began shouting in Ochwatt's ear until a hush fell over the crowd as their attention was drawn to Ochwatt. The Mojar were a tall people, but Ochwatt towered over everyone in the room. He even had to bow his head to keep from hitting the rafters. As his eyes darted around the room, he reached up a hairy hand to pull his hood tighter. "As I was about to say, I'll get us a room. Wait here," said Gaban, leaving Ochwatt at the foot of the stairs. After a couple of minutes, conversations around the room resumed.

Once they were in their room, Ochwatt posed a question. "Why we stop friend Gaban? The day not half-gone."

"You saw the market being closed out there? No one works in the heat of the day. From now on, we travel at night. The desert heat will kill us both if we try to travel when the sun is up. Besides, I must first find a guide. With any luck, we'll set out tonight. I know a man, if he's here, who should be able to tell me where I can find the Shik's tribe. Then there's one more thing. I, at least, need a bath and a rest in a bed. Even a bed like that one. From the smell of you, you could use a bath as well. We don't want to offend these people, do we?"

"This Shik? He not here? In city?"

"The Mojar are of the desert. They're nomads, Ochwatt. Only a few families will stay in the city for long and those no more than a year or two. Mojar are born of the sand, and from what I've been told, Mojar women go out into the desert to give birth. To be born of a city is a great shame and no woman would do that to her child.

"While the Shik is head of the council, he is not a king. He cannot order any but his own tribe. Still, I must appeal to Behnam for help. Then the best he can do is promise to call a conclave and ask. His word carries great weight, but he may not be able to sway all the tribes. They feel too secure in their desert. Now, I must find him, and I know just who to talk to. If you would please wait here? I have asked for water to be sent up so you can bathe."

With a sigh, Ochwatt nodded his assent as Gaban left.

It was over two hours later when Gaban returned to find Ochwatt combing through his thick fur, trying to get it dry. Now it was soft and silky, and he was stroking it absently, enjoying the sensation, as he listens to Gaban tell him of his failure and success. Perhaps bathing regularly had its benefits.

"The man I was looking for died about twelve years ago.

Apparently, I lost track of time in the valley. Here, let me get your back. What was I saying? Oh, well, I found another who knows where the Shik's tribe should be, and he'll travel with us. Not only that, both the Green Lizard Tribe and the Red Horse Tribe will be leaving tonight. The Red Horse Tribe is traveling in the right direction for a few days, and we can travel with them. They're the group of tents to the north of town. Now, I suggest you take a nap if you can. You've never traveled in the desert, and with your fur, the heat will be harder for you. They're bringing up fresh water for my bath now." He finished, pulling the screen across the corner for the bath.

Ochwatt eyed the too-short bed dubiously. The seven-foot-five- inch giant tried sprawling across it diagonally, but his arms and legs fell off the edges. With a "Humph!" he grabbed a blanket and stretched out on the floor where Gaban found him sleeping peacefully when he emerged from the bath.

CHAPTER 6

So This Is Civilization

Either the mattresses weren't as lumpy as they appeared or the baths had soothed their weariness, so they didn't notice, all three of the women slept peacefully that night. They awakened in the morning to the crowing of a cock in someone's backyard, but by now they were used to waking early.

Outside, it was raining. It was what the Irish call a soft rain, but it was still wet. After a good breakfast, Falcon handed them leather coats and large-brimmed hats to help keep them dry. Cheri couldn't help but remember what she'd said the night before about 'morning sunshine.' Faye just laughed at her. "Even you can't predict the weather, Cheri. Some things are out of our hands."

As they rode out, the women found the people of the village were in their doorways and windows, watching them ride by. In turn, they watched the people. While the people were mildly curious about them, showing special interest in Ebony, the anger and sorrow of the night before still lay over the town like a heavy blanket. Ebony found herself wondering where the children were. It was usually the children who showed the most interest in her dark skin.

Faye put all her attention on her 'horse' and, even through the rain, found things of interest in the passing countryside.

Cheri and Ebony tried to ignore the rain as they passed more vineyards interspersed with fields of grain. Occasionally they could smell a farmer's pigs or when a farmer was raising cows. It was the variety of vegetables being raised on small farms that really got their attention. Most of them were strange, but some appeared to resemble wheat, cabbages, or even melons and strawberries. The orchards had fruits similar to apples, peaches, and even cherries. Around noon, the clouds started to clear, and they stopped at a farm to purchase fresh fruit and vegetables while putting away their leathers. Now that the sun was out, the women opted to keep the hats. They weren't riding in a shady forest anymore.

Falcon led them at a leisurely pace for the next two days. Each evening they stayed at a village a little larger than the one before as they got closer to Nelas. The farmhouses, bordered by rock walls, were closer together as well, and they only saw Amalee briefly each day, flying high above. The only disturbing thing they noticed was the same sadness and anger they had seen in Forest City lay like a low cloud over each village they passed through. It even seemed to shadow the people they passed on the road.

As they neared the city, Amalee descended to alight briefly on Falcon's shoulder where she seemed to be whispering in his ear. Then she took flight, to soar aloft again, quickly disappearing from sight among the scattered clouds.

"She will rejoin us when we leave the city. She doesn't care much for the smell of civilization," Falcon explained tersely.

The women nodded in acknowledgment, but they were far more interested in the city.

Nelas at last! It was early afternoon when they passed through the gates of the thriving city. The wall around the city had once been quite high but was now broken in many places and the high weeds growing about the gates rusted open gave mute evidence that neither had been used for centuries. Just the same, guards in worn and dirty red uniforms with faded gold symbols on the tunics, lounged indifferently by the small guardhouse. As in the country, most of the shops and houses were of local red brick, but many of the roofs here were of wood shingles or dark-gray slate, instead of the cheaper and more-flammable thatch common in the countryside. As expected, the alleys were littered with trash and refuse; the clean country air had been left on the far side of the wall.

Looming over all, the spires of a black stone temple dominated the rest of the city, diminishing even the impressive government buildings made of imported granite that they could glimpse toward the city center. Ebony urged George up alongside Tasmin. "That seems to be a forbidding place. Tell us about it," she requested, nodding to the spires bristling with spikes.

"It's Barakus's attempt to form a religion with himself as some sort of god. He had those monstrosities built in many cities throughout Persal and sent his Komas priests with their soldiers to man them. Once a civilian goes inside there, they are never seen again. It's said terrible things happen in there. That's why people avoid it. Except for the priests themselves, of course," she replied in a disdainful tone with just a hint of sadness. "It's said the temple here in Nelas is the greatest built by that Doomed wizard."

Ebony backed off and took another long look at the threatening facade of the building and shuddered.

The building's shadow fell behind and Tasmin's despair dissipated as they followed Falcon through the bustling city streets. Frequently they had to push their way through congested intersections, before reaching a prosperous-looking inn not far from the east gate, and quite a distance from the temple whose Komas priests answered to no one except Barakus.

The sign above the inn pictured a man in the typical Jamben costume of a loose white shirt tucked into baggy brown trousers and knee-high black boots. This man's vest was red and embroidered with bright yellow flowers. He was carrying a clutch of bright green birds in his left hand with his bow, and a quiver slung over his right shoulder. The Huntsman.

Falcon left them soon after they had been shown to their rooms and headed for a nearby blacksmith. One of the pack-mules had a shoe coming loose that needed attending.

After Tasmin had their luggage sent up to their rooms, she suggested, "Why don't we visit the bazaar? I think it will give you an insight into the people and the way they live. It will also give us an idea as to how well you can blend in with the locals. Well, all except Ebony, of course. It's time we learned these things. It won't take Barakus much longer to catch up to our trail. I'm sure he's already following your eddies in the tides of Persal."

All three women were curious about this strange world and, with a quick glance at each other, turned eagerly to follow Tasmin out of the inn, smiling like children let out of school. The people in the street were intent on their daily business and paid the strangers little heed.

The anger and sorrow that had been so evident in the smaller towns appeared to have been swallowed up in the furious activity of the city. Hidden unless you noticed the people seldom smiled or that there was a tightness about the eyes that betrayed their troubled hearts. Most revealing of all was the absence of small children playing on the doorsteps or running through the streets. Something was definitely amiss in Jamben.

"Tasmin, what is wrong?" started Cheri, to be cut short by an abrupt hand motion from Tasmin.

"Not here," she whispered. "I'll answer your questions

later, in private. Now, here is the market square. Let's browse." She insisted.

Restraining their curiosity, for now, the women found themselves fascinated by the baskets, pottery and especially the jewelry of the area. Each of them had been given a small bag of local coins by Gaban, and they now splurged a little to buy a trinket or two. Tasmin wandered on ahead, leaving her charges to barter on their own.

Finished with their purchases, and well aware that they'd more than likely paid too much, the women were walking on across a narrow alley to catch up to Tasmin, a few stalls down. Suddenly, several rough-looking men who had been lounging against the walls surrounded them, blocking their way, leaving the alley as the only exit.

"Get behind me," hissed Ebony, motioning with her hand for Faye and Cheri to proceed her into the narrow passage. Reluctantly, they complied.

While they had left most of their weapons at the inn, Faye was suddenly grateful local custom decreed she wear a dagger at her waist. She wasn't sure that it would do much good against six burly men.

Meanwhile, Cheri was berating herself for leaving the extra knives she'd been wearing in her saddlebags for the last three days. Somehow, she hadn't felt as threatened as they neared civilization. Fool! She of all people should know better.

Faye and Cheri moved quickly toward the far end of the alley, hoping to reach safety until Faye stumbled on a loose brick. As Cheri bent to help her up, two more men appeared and began to advance on them from the far end. When they turned to see how Ebony was doing, they saw she had stopped halfway between their pursuers and themselves instead of following. Unsure what to do now, and reluctant to leave Ebony, they paused to watch their friend as she turned and with a powerful kick knocked the nearest grinning thug against the wall. Startled, Cheri turned her attention back to the two newcomers. She had her belt knife, but she would need another.

"Faye, quick, give me your knife. I don't have my throwing knives with me," she said, putting out her hand as she watched the men advance.

Confused, Faye pulled her gaze from Ebony, who was using her martial arts skills to keep the first three men in the lead at bay in the tight quarters and looked at Cheri. "Quickly, Faye. Your knife!"

"Yes," she answered as she fumbled at her waist.

Impatiently, Cheri reached out and took it from her hand before she could drop it. Now, the question was, where could she inflict an injury that would stop them without killing? She wasn't ready for killing. Seeing her knives, ready for throwing, the two men paused to assess this development.

Meanwhile, Ebony's karate and tae kwon do was quickly taking its toll on all six of the original attackers whose blood seemed to be everywhere. They had no idea how to react to this type of fighting, and there was no room to spread out and surround her. Even their daggers and short swords went flying when they got close to Ebony's hands or feet.

Help finally arrived in the form of a very tall black man with red- brown hair worn in long curls to his broad shoulders. His oddly golden eyes seemed to shine in the dim light as he dispatched the two men at the far end of the tunnel-like alley with two well-placed knife throws before he passed Cheri and Faye to reach with one long arm past Ebony. With one quick motion, he turned the last attacker to face him, bringing his sword up under his chin. Falcon came up behind him just in time to prevent more bloodshed. "We might need some answers from this one, first," he said, glancing sardonically at the seven men littering the ground and Cheri still standing poised to throw her knives.

Faye stood against the stained wall staring in disbelief at the bodies of the fallen men in horror. Cheri reached out and grabbed her hand in reassurance, "It's all right. We're safe, now."

"Are we? How can we be safe when people keep trying to kill us?"

"Having fun, ladies?" came Tasmin's dry inquiry. "I thought the idea of this excursion was seeing if we could avoid being noticed. Oh, well, too late now. I suggest we return to the inn immediately and leave the questioning to Falcon and our tall friend here. Come, ladies, straighten your clothes and try to act as though nothing untoward has happened. Maybe somebody will actually believe it," she muttered this last to herself as she herded them in front of her.

Everyone was subdued when they returned to the inn. Tasmin asked for a private dining room and two flasks of wine. They waited for the wine in silence, each lost in their own thoughts. When the wine arrived, Ebony and Cheri each helped themselves and drank their first glass quickly. No one bothered to remind Cheri she was too young. Faye was still shaking from their encounter, and Tasmin made the reluctant woman drink the first glass of the sweet red wine to help calm her nerves. Faye reached out her glass to Cheri as she refilled her own for seconds.

After finishing the second glass, a newfound strength filled Faye's eyes as she sat up straighter. "I think it's time I started participating in this new world instead of just being an observer," she said with determination.

"Good for you, dear. I'm sure we'll need your help," said Tasmin.

Ebony opened her mouth to explain to Tasmin what had happened in the alley and why she had no choice but to fight.

She quickly changed her mind when she saw the worried frown on Tasmin's habitually cheerful face. Tasmin did not ask any questions; she merely stared thoughtfully into the empty fireplace.

It wasn't long before Falcon and their erstwhile rescuer joined them. "The men were waiting for them. They were hired to bring them to the temple, dead or alive. He couldn't tell me how he knew he had the right women. I suspect Barakus had something to do with that, although I haven't the faintest idea what."

"Can he tell that we're women? Does he know there are three of us? Does he know already what we look like?" asked Ebony.

"I don't know if he knows you are women, nor do I know if he knows what you look like, but I doubt it. It's probable he can tell by the disturbance in the tides of the life of Persal that there are three. Maybe not. I'm only guessing, but perhaps he had a way to implant the knowledge of the tides in those men. Gabriene will know more. We need to be aware that he will soon know you are women, if not what you look like," explained Tasmin wearily. "And what of our tall friend, here?"

"Well, whatever Barakus knows, or doesn't know, those thugs won't be adding to his information. May I introduce, Behnam, Shik of the Kodul, chief among the seven tribes. He heard the ruckus and came to help. He already knows a great deal."

"I do not think that is a problem. Barakus doesn't own the Mojar nomads. They are probably the only really free people left in Persal."

"Thank you, madam. You are most gracious and also most correct. A Mojar would rather die than aid Barakus or his scum from the temples. Is it permitted for me to know the names of the ladies I saved?" inquired the tall man, giving them all a flourishing deep bow from the hips, although his golden eyes hadn't left Ebony but briefly since he entered the room.

"Yes, of course. May I introduce Ebony, Faye, and Cheri. I am their teacher, Tasmin."

"Saved? *You* saved us?" sputtered Ebony in outrage. "I had most of those men out before you got there. If you hadn't interfered, I would have finished them. I do believe the last one was ready to run when you showed up."

"Yes, and if he had run, we wouldn't know what we now do. Worse, Barakus would know more than he needs to. None of those you put down was in any condition to answer questions yet, and we couldn't give the church soldiers time to arrive," put in Falcon casually.

"Ebony, that is no way to thank a man who would certainly have saved you if you'd needed it!" admonished Tasmin acerbically. "Well, bickering isn't going to help us any. What are we going to do now?"

"They'll keep coming, won't they?" asked Cheri, penetrating right to the problem.

"Yes, of course. There are a great many inns in the city, and several closer to the market than this one but we obviously aren't safe remaining in Nelas. We'll have to leave as quickly as possible," said Tasmin, rising to take charge, as usual.

"Madam Tasmin. Since I am merely wandering anyway, and even with the obvious capabilities of your companions," Behnam made a deep bow, nearly touching the floor, in Ebony's direction before he continued, "Surely another sword could prove useful. As I have said, Mojar are all enemies of Barakus. If he is your enemy, then I am your friend."

"The enemy of my enemy is my friend?" asked Ebony archly.

Behnam raised his left eyebrow slightly, and a smile played at his full lips as he repeated the deep bow in assent.

"Thank you. I believe you are right, things are going to be

much more dangerous from here on out, and we can certainly use all the help we can get," agreed Tasmin. "Besides, no use trying to deny a gift of the portal."

"I think we need to split up and meet somewhere outside the city," suggested Falcon.

"Marvelous idea," agreed Tasmin. "Behnam, if you would escort Ebony, the two of you should pass for a Mojar couple, even as rare as it is to see a woman of your people away from their desert."

"What! Why?" yelped Ebony in objection, rising from her chair. Looking about for support her eyes came to rest on Cheri. The last thing she wanted at this point was to be alone with this arrogant man.

"Ebony. It's the only thing that makes sense, and you know it," put in Cheri firmly, acting as if she were the adult. "I think there's more to consider than our personal feelings at this point. What happened in the alley should have convinced you of that as well."

Ebony snapped her mouth closed in exasperation.

"Fine. Now I think Falcon and Faye should leave together and Cheri will stay with me. If we leave by separate gates and keep the three of you apart, perhaps the disturbance in the tides will be too small to detect long enough for us to get a good head start, anyway," said Tasmin, finishing their plans. "I think we'd best take time for a quick meal. I believe the innkeeper has a hot mutton stew on the stove. There's no telling when we'll have time for more than cheese and bread in the next few days.

"Falcon, if you would see that our horses are ready to leave, I'll order dinner. Master Behnam, perhaps you should go to your inn and make your own preparations."

"As you desire, madam. But may I suggest that if Lady Ebony were to go with me to my lodging, we could eat there and we would be splitting these lovely ladies up even sooner," recommended Behnam smoothly.

"That's a good idea. Before you leave, we need to decide where to meet," said Tasmin.

"If Lady Ebony would get her things, I will help Falcon with her horse, and we can pick a spot we're both familiar with. After all, speed appears to be essential."

"Yes. Ebony, please go fetch your things. The innkeeper said ours would be the first two rooms at the front of the inn."

Ebony rose and bowed gracefully to Behnam. "Since it appears to be inevitable, sir. I shall see you in the courtyard," and she left the room with her head held high, followed quickly by Falcon and Behnam. Cheri rose as well as she took it upon herself to find the innkeeper and order their dinner.

"If you're feeling up to it, Faye, I believe we have a few minutes to fetch our things from our rooms. Every minute could make a difference at this point," Tasmin said gently, patting her shoulder.

"Thank you, Tasmin. You've all been most patient with me. Well, you don't have to coddle me any longer. I've known how to take care of myself for some time, and I'm sure I can be a help as well," Faye asserted, standing to follow Tasmin from the room.

Dinner was eaten quickly while Tasmin and Falcon discussed the details of their cover stories for leaving the city. Falcon also took the opportunity to explain to Tasmin where he and Behnam had decided to rendezvous, at a high rock outcropping just off the main road that followed the Green River from the east side of town. Behnam and Ebony would be using the west gate, as though they were headed back to Mojar. They were taking Tasmin and Cheri's horses with them. It was decided that Falcon and Faye would take all the pack- animals back out the way they had come to the north. That left Tasmin and Cheri to travel on foot, through the east gate, and over the bridge. Luckily, they had the shortest distance to go. For them all, it was going to be a long night.

*****

Carlise awoke with a start and sat up, pulling her long brown braid over her shoulder and twisting it nervously. Despite her best intentions, she had dozed off and the dreams were there again! The dreams of a tall white tower in the middle of an expanse of water larger than Carlise had ever known. It was the ocean. The ocean that uncle Joban had told them about so many times. Why should she dream about the ocean? And the tower? She had never heard of this tower. It was beckoning to her. Calling her. The tower had been calling her every night for eleven nights. Each morning she found it harder not to pack up and go. Go where? How? And she was afraid! So very afraid! Where would she be going? How would she get there safely? And most of all, she was afraid of what would happen to her once she arrived.

Well, she had prepared all her life to be a resistance fighter of Jamben. She was supposed to leave next first day with Merind. That was over now, but surely, she could face whatever fate had in store for her instead. One thing was sure—she had to stop fighting it. She no longer had the strength to fight it. In the morning she would talk to old uncle Joban to see if he could tell her where she would be going. Perhaps he might even travel part of the way with her? She knew, somehow, that he could not go to the tower. That she had to do alone.

*****

Ebony picked at her supper sullenly. No matter how much sense it made, it galled her that everyone seemed to be making decisions for her. She wasn't in the military, anymore. Behnam watched her with obvious amusement. Well, he could afford to be amused. He'd gotten what he wanted, obviously.

"What was that Shik of whatever all about anyway?" she asked, breaking the uncomfortable silence.

"What?" Behnam asked, startled. "Ah, that. Nothing. Nothing of importance."

Raising her right eyebrow in disbelief over a spoonful of thick soup, Ebony decided not to press further. If he wanted to act mysterious, she didn't need to let him know she was curious. Suddenly amused by his attitude, she smiled as she tore off a hunk of warm bread and buttered it liberally.

When the last of the soup was gone, Ebony followed Behnam out to the stables where George, Baby and Tasmin's Anabelle were waiting for them with Behnam's magnificent black stallion. "Wrap your cloak tightly about you and pull up the hood. It will make you less noticeable. They may even take you for a thin man," he instructed as he mounted in one smooth movement. He pulled his own cloak close but left the hood down.

Irritated at being given orders, Ebony bit her tongue and pulled herself into George's saddle before complying with Behnam's reasonable recommendation. At this point, the last thing she was going to do was let him know how angry she really was.

Behnam caught the reins to Baby and handed them to Ebony before he took Anabelle's reins in his own hands. "Keep close and follow my lead," was Behnam's last terse advice before leading the way from the inn courtyard. As they passed under the inn's sign, the breeze caused it to squeak loudly, and Ebony looked up involuntarily. A woman falling into a bucket of splashing water, The Fallen Woman.

Very funny, Ebony thought. *Very, very funny.* And she couldn't resist a deep chuckle as their horses made their way through the dark and almost deserted streets.

*****

Faye and Falcon rode out of the courtyard of the Huntsman with the three pack-animals in tow. Falcon had spread a large brown blanket over Believer to make his white coat stand out less, and they both were dressed in dark clothes with cloaks pulled close. Faye had her hood pulled up over her golden hair. Falcon left his own hood thrown back and his hat pulled low as he watched those they passed in the streets carefully. At each intersection, he paused to check the cross street and to listen before continuing across. The only real noise they heard came from the occasional tavern they passed. They had the entire width of the city to traverse before they would be safely outside the walls.

The reins of the pack-animals were tied behind Believer, leaving Falcon as free as possible. Each time they stopped, Faye found herself holding her breath and her heart was beating so loudly she was sure it could be heard above the clatter of the horses' hooves.

They were skirting the center of the city, keeping at least two streets between themselves and the temple when the measured beat of marching boots could be heard. Falcon motioned for Faye to stop, but she had already pulled Believer up, and her eyes were wide when Falcon glanced at her.

"Church soldiers," he whispered. "Follow me." And he turned his gray stallion into the next alley, stopping halfway down. He dismounted and talked quietly to Wolf for a moment before walking back to the street, stopping just inside the alley. The sound of the soldiers grew nearer and nearer as Faye's nerves stretched in agony at the waiting. What she really wanted to do was run, but the noise in the nearly abandoned streets would only give them away. *I will not act stupid, again!* she told herself sternly as she huddled in the saddle wishing the soldiers would just go away.

An eternity later, about eight minutes in real time, the

small squad of soldiers passed them by and continued up the street to stop at an inn in the next block. Falcon came to Faye's side. "They didn't see us. Let's try to walk quietly out the other end of this alley."

Without waiting for a reply, he walked up to Wolf and picked up the reins. Faye resisted the urge to tempt fate and look over her shoulder as Believer and the pack-animals emerged from the narrow lane. When Falcon stopped a block later to remount, Faye let her breath out in a rush. Just realizing that she'd been holding it.

Falcon turned to smile at her. "Hopefully, that's as close as we'll come until we reached the gate. We're more than halfway there, now."

Nervously, Faye tried to smile back. "Don't worry, I've been praying ever since we left the inn. I'm sure we'll be fine. I just have to remind myself sometimes."

Falcon nodded once before he resumed their careful trek across the quiet city.

*****

Having less to carry, Cheri and Tasmin had left the inn twenty minutes before Falcon and Faye. They walked quickly, keeping to the shadows as much as possible and trying to look like farm women kept late at the market. They were carrying their saddlebags in baskets bought from the innkeeper for this purpose.

Cheri followed Tasmin with strangely mixed emotions. She almost felt at home, wandering the streets of a city at night. Even a city as different as this. The garbage in the streets was basically the same, if a little more foul, and the closeness of buildings was somehow reassuring in this new world. She was also afraid. Almost as afraid as when she'd first begun to live on the streets when she was twelve, but not quite. After all, she'd managed then, surely she could manage now. But most of all, she was excited. There was no doubt that this could be considered an adventure, and her life in Seattle was never that.

The wall loomed ahead, and the open gates showed evidence that an attempt had been made very recently to close them. There were twice as many guards as they'd seen at the north gate coming in and they were more alert, as if they were waiting for something or someone.

Tasmin and Cheri had stopped in the shadows across the street from the gate, and they were reasonably sure they hadn't been seen yet.

"Well, let's see if they believe our story," said Tasmin, adjusting her basket on her hip. Just before she stepped into the torchlight illuminating the gate, she pulled back again. "Drat! A priest! He can probably sense you."

A glance across the street confirmed that a very short, bald priest had just emerged from the guardhouse. "Maybe not, not if he thinks what he's feeling is something else."

"Cheri...what have you got in mind? If he can sense you, how do you propose to confuse him?" demanded Tasmin apprehensively.

"Just answer one question, is there any prohibition against sex in this priesthood? Just what kind of priests are we talking about?"

"Well, they're priests. They take bribes, frequently, under the assumption that what Barakus doesn't know won't hurt him. They do fear him, so they won't purposely cross him. They seem to be susceptible to most vices, as are all men."

"Great! I haven't got a lot of time to explain, but my experience has taught me, when you get more than one sense stimulated in a man, lust takes precedence. Besides, who in their right mind would walk right up to the enemy?" answered Cheri cryptically. "Here, hold this while I change. If this works, you can go through while I'm talking to that clergyman. Believe me, no one will even give you a second look."

Reluctantly, Tasmin held Cheri's cape to hide her from view as she rummaged through her saddlebag and pulled out her red mini dress and a package she had gotten from one of the seamstresses in the mountain village. She changed quickly, the package proving to be a long red skirt and a pair of low shoes that gave a semblance of decency to the outfit, but not much. Rapidly, Cheri unbraided her hair and shook out her curls, with a quick swipe of bright-red lipstick she was ready. She pulled the neck of the dress down to reveal her shoulders before packing her clothes and putting her saddlebag in Tasmin's basket, under the loose sacking. Finally, she trotted back up the street to toss her basket into the last alley they had passed.

Standing very straight and still for a moment, Cheri took a few deep breaths and fluffed her hair one more time before placing her hands boldly on her hips and sauntering up the middle of the street in plain sight toward the amazed priest and leering soldiers. Brazenly she sashayed up to the priest, carefully smiling suggestively at each of the soldiers as well. "Hello, there. I'm kind of lonely, do you know anyone who might have the time to keep me company?" she asked in a sultry voice Tasmin had never heard before.

The priest puffed himself up importantly. "These soldiers are on duty. They have better things to do than entertain you, miss."

"Well, what about you? Surely, they can spare you for a little while? I mean, if anything important happens we won't be far away," invited Cheri, running her hand over his bald pate and trying not to faint from the odors of sweat and sour wine.

Seeing Cheri's success in distracting the guard, who were snickering as they tried to get Cheri's attention, a bent Tasmin shambled through the gate like a tired farm woman who still had a long way to go.

"Your invitation is tempting, very tempting," he said, leering lasciviously. "Unfortunately, I'm going to have to refuse you tonight. Perhaps we can enjoy one another some other night. Tonight, I'm on temple business."

Cheri pouted prettily and batted her eyelashes at him. "Oh, what a shame. I promise, you would have remembered me for a long, long time. Perhaps another night I can show you what I mean," she promised with a suggestive smile as she turned and swayed out the gate and across the wide stone bridge over the river. Turning often to smile at the bemused priest until she was sure she could no longer be seen. Stopping her masquerade, she stifled her giggles as Tasmin dragged her off the road and into the bushes to quickly change her clothes again.

"That was quite a performance, I must say," said Tasmin with a shake of her head. "Cheri, child, why do I have a sinking feeling that you're going to continue to surprise us all?" She laughed softly. "The man didn't even notice when you walked out of the city."

"Amazing how men's glands can make them lose all sense, isn't it?" giggled Cheri.

Once she was changed, Cheri threw her saddlebags over her shoulder as Tasmin followed suit and threw the last basket behind a bush before starting their long hike to the rendezvous.

*****

Ebony and Behnam rode quietly through the streets, occasionally hearing marching feet a few streets over, but not actually encountering any soldiers until they reached the gate. As with the east gate, the west gate was well guarded and a portly priest of medium height with dirty, unkempt hair was waiting as well.

Behnam stopped their horses well down the street to appraise the situation. "It seems we are expected," he commented. "I see no alternative except to continue with our charade. Do not speak for any reason. Mojar women do not speak to strange men. Ever!" And he spurred his black stallion ahead, leaving Ebony fuming once more.

They approached the gate at a sedate walk, pulling to a halt when two guards stepped in front of them. "Halt! What is your business, leaving the city at this hour?" demanded the taller of the two.

Behnam drew himself up in his saddle, emphasizing his height, "I am Behnam of Mojar. My concubine and I are returning to our home. We travel at night, as is our custom. Only a fool travels during the day in the desert sun."

The priest stepped forward and started to put his hand on Ebony's horse, the hiss of steel as Behnam began drawing his sword stopped him. "Do you insult me! No one may come near what is mine. Surely you know enough of my people to know the consequences of such an act!"

"I beg your indulgence, sire. We are searching for strange women from a strange land. Something I...felt made me think your lady might be one of them," explained the priest as he backed away hurriedly.

Behnam burst out laughing. "I was warned when I decided to give in to Myla's whim to see strange lands with me. Have you never wondered why you have never before seen a Mojar woman in your lands? Even as covered as she is? Even at a distance? A Mojar woman casts her spell and draws men to her. Even in our camps, our women are guarded closely. What you feel is nothing more than that, I assure you."

"Perhaps you are right, sire. As you say, I have never before seen a woman of Mojar, and I was led to expect a stronger pull from the one we seek. Be on your way then," said the priest, smiling suggestively at Ebony as he stepped aside and motioned the soldiers to let them pass.

In distaste, Ebony pulled her cloak closer as she passed the smarmy man. All too glad to leave him behind.

*****

Falcon and Faye reached the north gate without further incident. They noticed immediately the increase in guards from that afternoon and Faye pointed to the tall thin priest standing in the doorway to the guardhouse, smoking a pipe.

"Well, they're definitely expecting us. Let's hope they can't detect a single disturbance," said Falcon, urging Wolf ahead with Faye close beside him.

When the guards noticed them, two moved to block their way and four more fanned out to either side. The priest strode forward to stand pompously in front, vainly stroking his carefully groomed beard. "Halt!" he commanded, raising his left hand.

Falcon reined in, and Faye followed suit, trying to assess their options as she did so.

"What is the meaning of this?" demanded Falcon impatiently. "Since when are honest traders detained in Nelas? Does the priesthood demand new bribes on top of the exorbitant taxes we are already charged?"

"Sir! You demean my profession. We seek no fees. The temple has entrusted us to find a woman for our arch prelate, Barakus. The delay will only take a moment. If you have just cause for traveling at such an hour, you will be permitted to continue," explained the priest indignantly.

"If Barakus wants a woman, I believe you are looking in the wrong part of town. I have heard that a certain type of woman is found in the northern quarter in abundance and to suit almost any taste." Falcon laughed.

"Please, sir! To speak of Barakus in such a manner could be considered blasphemy! Unfortunately, there isn't time to deal with this now. I will let it pass. So you know, Barakus is looking for a specific woman, not a whore!"

Falcon doffed his wide-brimmed hat and bowed from the saddle. "My apologies to Barakus, sir priest. I meant no offense. Obviously, I have only my darling wife with me. Surely Barakus hasn't taken to stealing another man's wife?" said Falcon in apology.

"Would you mind if she lowered her hood, sir?" asked the priest, stepping closer to Believer, who suddenly lowered his head and turned it toward the priest, his horn glowing threateningly to Faye's eyes.

"Do you mind, dear? The sooner we satisfy his curiosity, the sooner we may be on our way." Falcon shrugged indifferently, as his right hand moved slowly toward the hilt of his sword.

Faye boldly put her own hand on the dagger at her belt as she threw back her hood arrogantly. "There, sir, are you satisfied? I'm quite sure I do not resemble the woman you seek."

Suddenly the priest was confused, "For a moment I thought... But no. No, it wasn't as strong as it should have been anyway. You may go."

The guards stood aside insolently as Falcon led them out the gate. "By the way, dear, may I inquire as to how you are familiar with the northern section of the city? On one of those boring trips you have taken without me, perhaps?" asked Faye loudly. Since her back was to the gate, she felt safe in smiling broadly at Falcon when he turned to look at her.

"Why, not at all, darling. I have merely heard of it from fellow traders. You know how men will talk of such things," he said with a sly grin as he urged Wolf into a canter down the road.

CHAPTER 7

A Ride through the Country

Falcon and Faye rode east down the highway for about two miles before turning south to circle through the fields, heading for the river. Falcon was hoping to find a ford for crossing. He really didn't look forward to waiting for daylight and swimming the horses across.

Two hours later they arrived at the banks of the Greene River, and he dismounted to break off a long branch, using it to test the depth of the fast running water. The pole came back from as far as he could reach with about three feet of it wet, but in the dark of the moonless night, it was hardly evidence of a safe crossing point.

Reluctantly, Falcon returned to Faye. "There's no way to tell if it's possible to cross here, or even if it's safe to attempt to swim. We'll have to wait until first light."

Smiling, Faye dismounted. "Well, at least we're out of any immediate danger. Waiting doesn't seem to be such a terrible thing to have to do. I don't suppose we can have a fire?"

"No, if they begin to search the countryside it would give us away," agreed Falcon and added with a smile, "That was a nice touch back at the gate, questioning my knowledge of the northern quarter of the city."

Faye smiled impishly. "Well, since you assigned me the

role of your wife, I thought it only appropriate that I stay in character."

*****

"Slow down, Cheri. We're not in a footrace. In all probability, we'll reach the rendezvous long before anyone else. We had a bridge for crossing the river. They must find alternative ways across. I'm sure it will be tomorrow morning before we see them again. And my old legs tire easier than yours," admonished Tasmin with a forgiving smile.

"I'm sorry," said Cheri contritely. "It's just that I'm having such fun. I know it sounds crazy, but this is a real-life adventure. We're fairly safe at the moment, aren't we?"

"At least until they discover we've left the city. Hopefully, only good honest people saw us together or saw us leave. Unfortunately, some people make a little extra money selling information to the priests," explained Tasmin wearily. "Enjoying herself? Humph, it must be youth!" she muttered to herself.

"Oh, come now, Tasmin. You can't tell me the little deception at the gate wasn't fun. The danger of getting caught just adds a little spice."

"I can tell, I'm going to have more gray hair before this is all over."

Cheri laughed gaily. "Pooh! All your hair is already gray. Don't go blaming that on me."

"That's the only reason you won't be giving me any more gray hair." Tasmin sighed in exasperation. "Cheri, my dear, you know more about men than a girl your age should."

Cheri sobered for a moment. "You're right about the men though... You know, I was brought here for a reason and perhaps using whatever knowledge or skills I possess is part of that reason."

"Well, there's one skill I have no intention of letting you

use, my dear. So don't even think about it. Keep an eye out, we should be reaching that pile of rocks soon, and then we'll be able to make camp and get some rest. We'll need all the rest we can get. We're going to have to move much faster from here on. Until we reach Lohi, anyway."

*****

Once their horses had rounded a curve and they were out of sight of the gate, Ebony brought George even with Desert Wind. "Consort? You couldn't have given me the dignity of a wife?"

"A Majoran woman has never been seen outside of Mojar. I might explain indulging a favored consort, but a wife would never be allowed the liberty of leaving the protection of the tribe," explained Behnam equably, golden eyes intent on the road.

"And I suppose you have both, so you're quite familiar with all of this," she said acidly.

"No... Actually, I have neither yet. This is something every Mojar child knows. Our women are protected and held precious."

"Well, if no Mojar woman has ever been seen outside Mojar, I hardly think these people would know the difference."

"Perhaps they wouldn't know, but I would," insisted Behnam as he spurred Desert Wind into a canter, leaving Ebony to catch up.

They continued south silently beside the river at a ground-eating canter. It was several miles before they reached a small house and Behnam reined in his black stallion and dismounted.

"Wait here. I will only be a moment," he called softly as he strode to the door and knocked loudly.

"The ferry doesn't cross before morning. Go away!" yelled a gruff man's voice from inside.

"Surely if one is willing to pay extra, an exception can be made," coaxed Behnam loudly.

In a surprisingly short time, a light was seen at the window, and the door opened a crack to reveal the unshaved face and greasy brown hair of the ferry master. He looked up at Behnam slowly before he peered into the dark at Ebony for a moment. "Well, Master, a Mojar, isn't it? I don't get many Mojar wanting to cross here. Most go into Nelas and use the bridge," commented the burly man sourly, slowly stretching himself to his full five-foot eight inches as he pulled his suspenders over his broad shoulders, getting ready to barter.

"Cheap lot, yer kind, as a rule," he grumbled, eyeing Behnam doubtfully. "How much extra was ye talkin' about?" he asked suspiciously.

"Yes. Well, usually we prefer to travel through the cities. Some of us are a little uneasy with so much water. Unfortunately, my consort here has never seen a river and I promised her a ride on a ferry," then Behnam lowered his voice to a conspiratorial whisper. "There's always the romantic aspects of a crossing with a woman afraid of so much rushing water," he winked.

The ferryman glanced toward Ebony again as greed filled his eyes, "There's that, I suppose. I cain't figure it meself. Cain't see much of 'er from here. Hope she be worth it. It'll cost ye."

"Sir, you have no idea of the worth of this woman. She is rarer than the great blue pearl of Comari and more priceless than the lost Baraga rose. I'll pay three dragos now and five more when we're across," offered Behnam in a voice of command that betrayed a certain impatience.

"Five now and five when you're across. In gold," demanded the ferryman quickly, hurrying down to the ferry to lower the ramp for the horses and loosen the ropes.

Behnam followed, allowing his eyes to flash gold for a

moment before he counted out five coins with a nod. "But be quick about it. My consort is weary of waiting."

Behnam returned to Ebony and helped her dismount, taking the opportunity to murmur in her ear, "Don't ask why. Just act afraid of the water. Stay close to me and jump into my arms when the ferry leaves the shore."

Ebony tossed her braids in irritation but bit her tongue despite what she considered a rather obvious ploy by Behnam and deferentially followed him as he led the four horses onto the ferry. The ferryman now seemed quite eager as he pulled up the horse ramp behind them. Slowly, they moved away from the bank, and the swift current of the river tugged at the raft. Dutifully, Ebony obeyed Behnam and jumped into his arms, just slightly unsure of the consequences if she didn't. Unexpectedly, there was a comfort in being held there that Ebony refused to acknowledge.

The small man soon showed how he had earned his broad shoulders and large arms as he pulled mightily on the ropes, and their progress became steady. The hard work didn't keep the greasy man from leering at Ebony when he thought Behnam wasn't looking. Ebony's stomach just had time to become uncomfortably queasy from the rocking of the raft when they bumped into the far bank, and the other ramp was dropped, allowing them to disembark.

Ebony remounted George while Behnam counted out five more coins. The ferryman stood and watched them ride out of sight before reboarding the ferry and starting his return trip.

The long night of riding was beginning to tell on Ebony, and she found herself dozing off almost immediately only to have Behnam suddenly turn Desert Wind off into a newly plowed field. George followed automatically, a docile Baby and Anabelle trailing behind. "Whoa, Desert Wind. Hold it here," he said, looking over his shoulder with a thoughtful frown. "You know, he had every reason to be suspicious of us. I really don't see why we should make things easy for our pursuers, do you?"

"What?" asked a groggy Ebony, shaking her head to clear it. "Where are we? What do you have in mind?"

"Just take these," he said, dismounting and throwing her the reins for his horse. "Keep the horses milling about in circles for a while and make false trails out of the field in a couple of directions. Then take the grass verge east for half a mile before returning to the road. I'll meet you there. I have an errand to run."

"Behnam, what do you have in mind?"

"Don't you think it might slow anyone who might try to follow us if the ferry rope happened to snap?" he mused with a wicked smile on his full lips.

"It might be helpful, but the ropes looked almost new to me," objected Ebony obtusely.

"Even new ropes have their weak spots at times, especially if they have a little help." Behnam smiled with a gleam in his eyes as he turned away to start jogging back up the road. Keeping to the grassy sides.

"Surely you're not going to cut the rope while that poor man is in the middle of the river?" Ebony called after him in outrage.

"Of course not. What do you think I am? A barbarian? I think if I continue back at this rate, by the time I get there, he should be docked and back in his bed. Besides, I'm not going to cut the rope at all. I have something else in mind. I wouldn't think it will break until sometime tomorrow," he said glibly as he disappeared into the night.

"Well, it may be you're not a barbarian, but you certainly resemble one at times," muttered Ebony knowing he could no longer hear her as she encouraged George to trot around the field with Desert Wind, Baby and Anabelle trailing behind.

An hour later, her mission accomplished, Ebony was

waiting impatiently for Behnam and beginning to worry about him when he appeared out of the darkness and remounted his horse. "What did you do to your hand?" asked Ebony in alarm.

"This? I happened to cut it, and a little fell onto the ropes. It's such a shame, really. You'd be surprised how much rats enjoy the taste of blood. They'll eat anything with blood on it until all traces are gone," he said with a smile.

Ebony gasped in surprise as she realized what he had done. Before she could say anything more, Behnam spurred his horse, and they were once again cantering east along the river highway. Ebony found herself giggling as she pictured the look on that nasty man's face when the rope broke, hoping Behnam the arrogant couldn't hear her.

*****

Patrice woke with a start as the door to the cottage burst open. Then her mother screamed, and she broke into action. "Missy, Hender, wake up! We have to get into the hidey-hole! Now! Keep quiet and move! Hurry!"

"Mama, I want Mama!" whispered Missy. At least trying to keep quiet.

"Not now, Missy. Mama will be all right. They're looking for us, not grown-ups. Hurry! Into the hidey-hole!"

Her parents were yelling downstairs, but boots were climbing the ladder. Quickly, Patrice closed the door to the hidey-hole in the wall. Silently she prayed to the old gods to keep them hidden.

In the loft, she could hear two men rummaging around in the room, tearing it up, looking for them. Then one of the men started going around the room, tapping on the walls with his staff. They were going to find them. They were going to find them, and there was nothing they could do. Please, someone, help us!

A few minutes later, the three of them were being dragged out the door while other soldiers held her mother. Father was lying still on the floor, and she couldn't tell if he were still breathing.

Roughly, they were piled into a wagon with bars on the high windows, and all the other children from town between five and twelve were in the wagon with them. They hadn't missed one. Not one had gotten away.

*****

Falcon woke Faye before dawn began to think about a new day. She stretched to get the kinks out that come with sleeping against a tree and tried to peer at the river in the pale light. A sharp cry that she recognized brought a smile to her lips.

Looking up, she saw the hawk perched on a branch overhead. "I see Amalee has found us. I still can't see much more of the river than last night. Are you trying to tell me you can tell if the river is crossable here?"

"By the time we're packed up, Amalee will be able to see enough, even if I can't. We don't want too much light. That would make us too visible, and there's no cover out in the water," said Falcon as he checked the loads on the pack animals. "By the way, you can swim, can't you?"

Faye rose and crossed to the bank to feel the water before she answered, "As a matter of fact, I can. But even if this is summer, that water's very cold."

"Don't worry, the sun will dry us out, once we're on the other side. I suggest you wrap your cloak up in this and tie it on the back of Believer though," he said as he tossed her a large square of rough cloth coated with wax.

Faye glanced again at the increasingly visible river before complying.

As usual, Falcon was right, when they had everything

checked and stowed there was indeed enough light to see the far side of the river. As for the river itself, it flowed steadily at this point. Apparently in no particular hurry but too deep to ford. They were going to have to swim for it.

They both mounted, and Faye followed Falcon down the gentle slope and into the water. Falcon had tied the other horse and two mules in a line behind Wolf. "Try to stay upstream from me, if you can," he called. "That way, if an animal breaks free, the two of you won't tangle."

"Right," answered Faye as she urged Believer to try the water. For the first time, he balked at one of Faye's commands. "Come on, Believer, we can do this. We're special, you and I, we can do anything, together," she coaxed. Finally, the reluctant unicorn stepped into the chilly water and proudly swam out into the current. Very soon Believer was soaked and Faye was wet above her thighs. Water had already filled her boots, and she was thoroughly uncomfortable.

Amalee watched them from a tree on the bank of the river for a moment before flying low with her strong wings to the other side. Landing on a stump to wait. Evidently, she thought they were somewhat handicapped in having to cross the river so clumsily.

Their trip had barely begun before the pack-horse started to panic, pulling at Wolf and the two mules, trying desperately to break free. Wolf tried to ignore the antics of the other animals and strained valiantly toward the far bank. Faye looked at the commotion and bent forward to talk to Believer. "Help them, please."

Believer's eyes rolled toward her in reproof before his horn started to glow. A glow that spread, reaching out to touch first the thrashing horse, then the mules, calming them and encouraging them to follow Wolf. When the glow touched Wolf, he rolled his eyes and shook his mane in protest. With a nod to the stallion, Believer withdrew his help, concentrating on the other animals instead.

Halfway across, true daybreak greeted them, and the rising sun brought with it a rising mist off the river. They never quite lost sight of the far bank, but by the time Believer emerged from the water, the fog was dense enough to obscure the road.

"Now what?" asked Faye belligerently as she dismounted to drain her boots. "How do we find your rendezvous now? In this stuff, we're more likely to get lost or lose each other."

"You certainly woke up on the wrong side of the tree this morning, didn't you?" commented Falcon tersely, emptying his own boots before Amalee hopped from her stump to perch on his shoulder.

"Actually, I have no intention of getting lost. Once we gain the road, which, by the way, is only fifty feet to the east, I'll know where we are, and in a very short time, you can rejoin your friends. As for losing you, didn't you just tell Believer that the two of you could do anything? Give him his head, he'll keep us together."

"I'm sorry, Falcon. I am in a foul mood, aren't I? I apologize for taking it out on you. I don't know if it's the lack of sleep or the tension last night or that very cold bath we just had, but it's not really your fault. Well, except maybe the bath."

Falcon laughed. "I accept your apology, and I apologize for the necessity of the bath. We should be grateful for this fog, though. It's going to make it very hard to follow us. Even if Amalee does dislike it as much as you do. Let's go. The sooner we get there, the sooner we can get in dry clothes. Everyone else should be waiting for us." And Falcon led Wolf the rest of the way up the bank to the road. In a short time, they were headed east and away from Nelas.

*****

Ebony watched Tasmin making tea at the small fire built in a sheltered area against the tall rock, while Cheri combed and braided her long black hair for her. Behnam was busy with the horses, although his eyes seemed to stray their way more than was necessary. Why did the man irritate her so? He really wasn't bad- looking. He just had this attitude, like he was a king or something and used to getting his own way.

"Tasmin, do you think Faye and Falcon are all right?" asked Cheri for the fifth time.

"Of course, I do, child. Falcon is a very capable man, and I have a feeling you aren't the only one who is going to surprise us on this trip. Faye had strengths that haven't been tested yet."

Then, through the mist came the eerie sound of hoofbeats and jingling harness echoing off the rock outcropping and everyone froze. The sound came closer and grew louder as Behnam's hand went for his scimitar. Then it suddenly stopped. Cheri let out a yelp of surprise as a whiff of a breeze revealed Falcon's big gray stallion looming out of the fog, followed closely by Faye on Believer and the pack animals. All of them, except Beleiver, still damp.

"I see you had to swim across," commented Behnam dryly.

"And I'm sure you convinced the ferryman. Won't that leave a trail?" asked Falcon as he dismounted.

"Perhaps, but one they'll have a hard time following. It seems some rats have been chewing on the anchor ropes on this side, for some reason. I would guess the ferry is going to break free and head downstream in the very near future."

"Faye, you're shivering. Ebony, Cheri, hold this blanket. Faye, dear, bring your saddlebags and change clothes. Then I want you to wrap up while I get some hot tea into both of you. Falcon, are you also going to change or are you going to be a hardheaded fool?" broke in Tasmin, taking charge, as usual.

"I have been taking care of myself for years, and I am still here. I fully intend to change, madam," said Falcon formally, rolling his eyes at Tasmin's back, busy over her tea kettle.

Once Faye was settled at the fire, and Falcon was sipping his own tea, Ebony crossed to him. "Falcon, may I speak to you, alone, for a moment?" she asked.

"Certainly, my lady. Perhaps over by the horses?" he agreed, allowing her to lead the way.

Behnam was returning from caring for the animals that had arrived with Falcon and Faye and stood aside to allow them to pass. Ebony graced him with a nod which he returned with a slight wave of his left hand, drawing Tasmin's attention to the crude bandage he had wrapped around it.

"What happened to you? You didn't mention a fight last night," she asked, rising and taking his hand in hers.

"This? It's nothing, dear lady. Certainly not a fight. You might say a sacrifice was called for, that's all," answered Behnam, futilely trying to retrieve his hand.

"Sacrifice! Well, let me at least treat and bandage it properly," insisted Tasmin.

Finally, alone with Falcon, Ebony revealed what was on her mind, "Falcon, I need to know...I mean, there really hasn't been an opportunity to ask before, did I...in the alley, did I... uhm...," she stammered to a stop, dropping her eyes and turning away in embarrassment.

Gently, Falcon took Ebony's shoulders in his hands and turned her to face him. "Look at me! Ebony, look at me!" he commanded sternly, waiting until she raised her eyes. "You knocked those five men out. Behnam and I dispatched them to save all our lives, but you...did...not...kill...anyone. Make no mistake, they would have killed all of you, if we had given them a chance, but you haven't killed anyone," he averred, staring steadily into her eyes.

"What we're into, it's really that dangerous, isn't it? I mean, I...we—Faye, Cheri, and I—might have to kill people to survive. For all of us to survive, I mean," she said slowly, the harsh realities of this world finally coming home to her.

"Ebony, I won't lie to you. I don't know what kind of world you come from, whether it's better or worse than ours, but I know that our world is not gentle, and these are dangerous times. Even more so for the three of you. What you and your friends are being forced into is going to be the worst it has to offer. Before this is all over, I would be very surprised if each of you didn't have to kill, at one time or another. Remember, it won't be just your survival or the survival of those in our party. Our entire world depends on what happens to the three of you. On the other hand, those of us who travel with you will be doing our best to ensure your survival."

"You paint a rather gloomy picture."

"Well, it's not going to be a court ball, but I doubt if you'll be bored and there will be times when everything seems very far away, and life is almost normal. Don't worry, I have no doubt at all that all of you are strong enough to get through whatever happens," Falcon reassured her awkwardly. "I think we had better be returning to the others. We should be leaving soon."

"Thank you, Falcon," said Ebony sincerely. "You've been very comforting. No, that's not quite the word. Helpful, anyway."

Falcon laughed and bowed gallantly to Ebony, motioning for her to lead the way.

Back at the fire, Faye was nursing her third cup of herb tea and staring into the mist nervously.

Cheri was watching her and shuddered, "I know what you mean, Faye. I wish this dreary fog would burn off. While we wait, Tasmin, would you please tell us about this... Taking we keep hearing about?" she asked to change the subject.

Tasmin shook her head despairingly. "A few centuries ago, Barakus began sending special troops throughout most of Persal, kidnapping our children, ages about six to twelve. The first time, the people banded together and took them back. When Barakus's men returned, they killed the fathers and any small children they had left behind. Only the women were left to grieve and bury their dead. The original children were still taken to Doome. Sixty-two years later, Barakus sent men again. This time, the women refused to allow any interference. Since then, every sixty-some years, Barakus takes more children. The event has become known as the Taking."

"That's awful. So they just show up and take the children. There must be thousands of them. What does Barakus do with them?" asked Faye with a perplexed frown.

"No one knows for sure, but we don't think they're mistreated. When they arrive at the seaports to board the black longships, they appear well fed and in good condition. Well, that's enough of that. Drink up your tea," insisted Tasmin, pouring out the remains of tea from the pot.

"Well, this fog won't remain indefinitely, and right now it's our best friend. I suggest we get ourselves together and head out as soon as possible. I'd like to be as far from this highway as we can should anyone come looking. I think it's best we head due east into Samal. We can catch the White River at Dink," suggested Falcon.

Behnam had been watching Ebony and Falcon closely since they returned, but now, he nodded agreement and turned to bring the horses up without a word.

"I'll help with the horses," said Cheri, surprising everyone except Behnam, who didn't know her yet.

Tasmin, Faye, and Ebony gathered together the few things they had out while Falcon scattered and buried all trace of their campfire.

"What's Mojar like?" asked Cheri impishly.

"Desert, sand, and beautiful star-studded skies. The

green of our oasis is appreciated since it is so rare. Here the abundance is taken for granted and wasted. In Mojar, nothing is wasted," answered Behnam with a smile, suddenly liking this forward child.

"It sounds harsh but beautiful, too. Where we come from, at least the part of our world we come from, it was always very green and wet. I think I wouldn't mind being somewhere hot and dry for a while," she commented thoughtfully. Suddenly feeling like a child, she ran the last few yards to give her pinto pony a hug. "Oh, Baby, I know you don't believe this, but I actually missed you."

Behnam smiled and shook his head as he checked the horses that had remained saddled and tied the pack-animals to the saddles of Desert Wind, Wolf, and Annabelle. Cheri took the reins of Baby, George, and Believer and led the way back to the others. "By the way, may I call you Ben, for short?" she asked impulsively.

"I beg your pardon? You wish to call me what?"

"Ben. You know, like a nickname. Where I come from, people give nicknames to people they like."

"In my land, names are sacred. Do you not confuse the spirits with too many names?"

"No, I don't think so. I really haven't thought too much about it. Maybe, sometimes, we're trying to confuse other people anyway. I'll call you Behnam, if you want, but Ben would just be a term of affection. I don't know why, but I like you," she explained shyly.

"You're an amazing child, Cheri, and I find myself inexplicably liking you as well. I tell you what, just between you and me, you may call me Ben," he acceded with a gracious bow.

Cheri was giggling softly with delight as they entered the campground and Ebony looked up, startled. Amazingly, she found herself wondering what could have made Cheri laugh, nothing Behnam had ever said to her had ever struck her as particularly humorous.

The morning was still young as they mounted and rode out, across the fields, avoiding farmhouses and roads. They were all still exhausted from the previous night, but none of them were under the delusion that it would end soon. Their times to sleep would be short, and they would be riding hard for the next few weeks. After that, it would depend on signs of pursuit. Even without anyone behind them, they had no way of knowing what Barakus might have waiting ahead of them.

Amalee took off again, soaring out of sight above the fog until they left it behind with the river.

CHAPTER 8

Flight of the Unicorn

Falcon took the lead as they headed across the country at a ground- eating canter, slowing to a walk occasionally to give the horses a breather before picking up the pace again. Most of them had no more than a nap in the last thirty-six hours, and Faye could see the punishing pace was taking its toll on everyone except Falcon, Behnam, and herself. Falcon and Behnam were probably used to this sort of thing, but she wasn't quite sure why she wasn't tired. She did have a hunch, and when she looked at Believer's glowing horn, she was almost certain.

They managed to ride for about three hours before Ebony called out, her voice breaking with fatigue, "Plea...," she began and then paused to cough before trying again. "Please, we need to get some rest. Cheri's almost asleep on her pony, and she doesn't ride that well as it is." Her shoulders were set stubbornly, refusing to give in to her own weariness.

"We haven't gotten far enough. They know where we have to be headed. It won't take them that long to pick up our trail." Falcon called back in objection, although Faye thought she detected a tired note in his voice as well.

"The ladies are weary, Falcon. Perhaps we can at least slow to a walk again," suggested Behnam reasonably.

Reluctantly, Falcon slowed his horse, and the others

followed suit. At this pace, Ebony found herself napping in the saddle, a feat she would never have believed a couple of weeks ago. Tasmin seemed to be napping too when Behnam called a halt. Cheri had fallen asleep on Baby's back, and when the pony halted, she slowly toppled out of the saddle.

"Falcon, we have to let the ladies rest. Let's find a place to sleep while it's daylight. Even the horses can't continue at this pace.

Besides, if we don't get our rest, we won't be able to run or fight if we see signs of real pursuit," called Tasmin wearily as she pulled Anabelle up and dismounted to check on Cheri. "Please, find us some cover."

"The woods ahead ought to provide a good place. I'll go scout it out. Be right back," he called back, pulling on Wolf's reins as he turned a tight circle before galloping into the stand of trees.

"Cheri dear, are you alright?" inquired Tasmin gently as she put her arm beneath Cheri's head.

"No, Mom, it's not time to get up yet. I just want to sleep. Please, let me sleep another five minutes. Then I'll get up. I promise," mumbled Cheri groggily.

"Well, I don't think she's going to be able to ride the rest of the way," commented Ebony with a wry smile. "If we weren't so exposed, I could easily lay down right here and join her."

"Put her up with me," commanded Behnam. "She can ride with me and Ebony can bring her horse. We shouldn't remain out here where someone may see us. There are still too many farms about."

Once Cheri was nestled in front of Behnam, they were able to follow Falcon into the trees. They rode for another ten minutes before Falcon stepped out from behind a tree. "This way," he said, motioning. "There's a large thicket over here that should shelter us well enough today. I'll have Amalee warn us if anyone comes near. We'll need to be on our way again shortly after nightfall though. We have a long way to go, and I don't want to try second-guessing Barakus's next move. Whatever else he does, he's sure to have his soldiers and priests looking for us in every city between here and Lohi."

Except for Cheri, who never woke up, they ate a quick meal of bread and cheese before rolling up in blankets on the hard ground. Behnam was taking the first watch since he had rested most of the day before their hasty departure from Nelas. Faye lay in her blankets until even Falcon was snoring before she got up again and walked over to Behnam.

"I'm too tense to sleep just yet, and I think Believer may have picked up a stone. I want to check on him and then I'll try to sleep again," she said casually.

Behnam looked at her oddly, but all he did was nod. Trying to be inconspicuous about it, Faye pulled one of Believer's forelegs up and pretended to check it while she loosened his halter, tied to the picket rope. "I know you've been helping me, Believer, but I need you to help everyone and the horses too. The next couple of weeks are going to be very tiring for those of us who aren't magic. We'll need all the help we can get. I'll trust you to take care of Behnam so you can get to everyone else," she whispered as she stroked his horn before she returned to her blanket.

Behnam had watched Faye closely although he couldn't hear what she said. After she was settled in her bedroll, he found himself staring thoughtfully at her white stallion. There did seem to be something different about the steed. For one thing, neither of the other stallions seemed to mind when he was around, and that wasn't normal. Stallions always wanted to fight for domination, always. That's why they had made a point of keeping Desert Wind and Wolf apart. Finally, with a troubled shrug, Behnam resumed his watch, ignoring the restless stomping and occasional whinny coming from the horses behind him.

Despite the harsh training of life as a Mojar, Behnam soon found it hard to keep his eyes open and leaned wearily against a tree for just a moment. Was that the white stallion moving through the trees? When he went to check the picket line, the stallion was where it had been before and appeared to be asleep. It must all have been his imagination. His mind must have wandered for a moment. A couple of hours later, he woke Falcon so he, too, could rest, even though he didn't feel particularly tired anymore.

When dusk came, Falcon woke the women to a small fire well hidden behind a log. He had steaming tea and four fat habities roasting over the fire. "I felt we could chance a hot meal tonight. It might be the last chance we get for some time," he said.

"A wonderful idea, Falcon. Where did you find the habities? They smell marvelous," complimented Tasmin, absently sipping at her cup of tea.

Falcon gave his ponytail a distracted tug, "I'm not sure. They just ran into the clearing and sat there, staring at me until I reached out and grabbed them. It was almost as if that was why they came. As though they'd been bewitched or something. I've never seen anything like it before, and I'd rather not see it again," he said quietly, his gaze never leaving the fire.

Faye allowed her gaze to travel to Believer who arched his neck in a nod. Trying not to smile, she sat at the fire and filled her mouth with meat instead.

Ebony looked at Falcon oddly before she squatted by the fire and took the piece of meat he offered her. "Well, I feel like a new woman, anyway! It's amazing what a little nap can do, isn't it? Why worry about one more strange thing in this strange world?"

"Well, I don't feel tired anymore, but I'm certainly hungry enough. Do we still have some of that bread to go with this?"

asked Cheri, taking a large bite from the habity leg she'd been given.

"Sounds like everyone is going to be able to ride all night. If the horses can stand the pace, we should cover a lot of ground tonight," commented Behnam thoughtfully as he turned from where he was standing to look at the horses. In the dim light, the only one who really stood out at this distance was Believer, who seemed to glow. There might come a time when that white coat was a liability.

Faye saw his look and followed his gaze with a small smile. She'd been right. Believer was able to take away their fatigue. She'd have to find a way to leave him free each time they stopped to rest.

Within twenty minutes they were mounted and on their way again. Since this was Tasmin's homeland, well known from her days in the Jamben resistance, she took over the lead and Falcon dropped back to cover the rear. She set the pace at a ground-eating canter, making conversation impractical as they traveled through the darkness.

After an hour, Tasmin slowed them to a walk and began alternating an hour at speed with an hour walking. While they walked, they were able to eat cheese and bread while in their saddles. As the dawn blushed the eastern horizon, Tasmin led them to a well-hidden cave that was obviously used frequently. There was a creek running through it for fresh water and a fire already laid. There was even ample room for the horses in the back.

"Quite a hideout you have here, Tasmin. If we can find places like this all the way to Dink, things will be easier than I thought," said Falcon appreciatively.

"Unfortunately, in two more days, we cross over into Samal. Once we cross the border, there are fewer places like this, and I only know where one of those are. We should be fairly safe for the next three days though. After that, we'll have to rely on luck."

"Maybe not. I've ranged over quite a bit of this part of the world in my life. When we leave your last haven, I'll take the lead again. It will help if we make sure our path goes through at least some of the Singing Forest. The trees there are, well, different," explained Falcon as he stared at the horizon from the mouth of the cave.

Faye and Behnam had volunteered to put the horses up while the others made camp and started dinner. "That stallion of yours, he isn't like any horse I've seen before. I can't quite put my finger on what makes him stand out, but stand out he does," complimented Behnam as they unsaddled the mounts and tied them to the picket line with the pack animals freed of their burdens.

"Why, thank you, Behnam. Of course, I think he's special, but coming from you, that really is a compliment," answered Faye, being deliberately obtuse. She knew Behnam was fishing.

"That isn't exactly what I meant. I think you know that, Lady Faye. You don't have to tell me what it is unless you want to, but do you think we should be keeping secrets from each other? It might be important at some point in our travels."

"Well, I can't tell you why. It's not my secret. Will you promise not to tell the others yet?" she asked, waiting for his nod before she let out her breath. "Believer can renew us so we don't tire so easily. I don't know how, but he can. I realized it yesterday when everyone was so exhausted. Everyone but me," admitted Faye reluctantly.

"And the habities?"

Faye shrugged. "I'm not sure. Maybe?" she admitted.

"That's what I thought. Well, if that's all you can tell me, why don't we put him here on the end and drape his reins over the picket line?

I'm taking the first watch again, this morning."

"We aren't that tired today. Let's give him the day off. Right now, we have no idea how long he can renew us without draining himself. From what I've heard, we may really need his help before we're through. And, Behnam, thanks for keeping our secret," said Faye gratefully.

"For now, thy secret is safe with me. But please, ask your beast to not put me to sleep while I'm on watch. As a Mojar, to sleep on watch is death. I'd hate to have to commit ritual suicide," he requested formally, although Faye thought she detected a gleam of humor in his eyes.

The next few days followed the same pattern. Tasmin led the way, Falcon and Behnam took turns watching the rear. Every other night, Believer was set free to revive the travelers and their mounts. Faye was beginning to worry though. The only one who appeared to be tiring after a week was Believer. A glance she shared with Behnam when Believer stumbled told her he, too, was concerned.

In the early evening of the first night they were in Samal, they passed within a half mile of a village. Tasmin and Falcon decided it was a good time to buy more bread and cheese while finding out what kind of information they could gather. They left the others concealed in an old, overgrown orchard while they were gone.

Behnam helped himself to a treat of fresh, ripe fruit from the orchard while he guarded the perimeter and waited. Cheri soon followed suit and chomped on one of the strange produce hungrily while Faye and Ebony hesitated for a moment. The odd fruit was bright green with a pebbly surface, similar to an avocado, but when bitten into, it was soft and slightly tart. The meat was a deep purple and juicy sweet. Whatever it was, it was delicious.

Once she had tried them, Faye eagerly pulled out a piece of waxed cloth and picked several of the fruit for their next meal.

Then she offered one to Believer who snorted disdainfully and tossed his head. Obviously, he wasn't impressed.

*****

Falcon and Tasmin entered the village separately. The better to gather information as well as food. It was late for Tasmin to arrive at the market place, but she found most of the stalls still open. An unusually large crowd was standing about talking. No one seemed to be shopping, the merchants themselves were too involved in the gossip to pack up and go home. There was certainly something unusual going on. Slowing her pace, she paused at several stalls near different gatherings to see what she could learn.

"Priest? Here? Now? That's never been heard of before," a woman said to her companion.

"Well, they were here today. Asking strange questions too, they was. My Bolt was at the Talking Cock when they come in. They had their dirty soldiers with them too."

This was not good news, but she needed to be certain they were looking for them. Tasmin moved on to the next stall and paused again.

"Asked about a woman and her companions, they did, but when Geff asked them what the woman looked like, it seemed they couldn't agree. One said she was short and blond and rode a white horse. Then another said that when he saw her, she was young and sassy and had bright-red hair. The third one insisted she was tall and a black Mojar woman. As if anyone's ever seen one of them outside of Mojar. Said a big Mojar was traveling with her as well. If you ask me, they was all drunk," said one of the men, laughing at his own joke as the others joined in.

Falcon opened the door to let himself into the Talking Cock tavern, and the clamor he could hear out in the street died instantly. Every eye in the room turned to look at him curiously before they resumed their idle chatter. Saucily, the barmaid came over to him. "There's a table over there in the corner where a body might be able to think. Can I get you a pint of ale? A nice strong man like you must get awfully thirsty."

Smiling down at her pale-red hair done in elaborate braids wrapped about her head, Falcon nodded his agreement. The volume of the discussion was rising again. With no one person to listen to, he couldn't make out enough of what was being said to make senseof it. When the maid brought back his sour ale, he grabbed her plump hand and motioned her to bend down so he could talk into her ear. "What's going on here? Something unusual happen?"

After a quick glance about the room to be sure the innkeeper was still busy talking, the pretty redhead pushed in close to him on the bench. "These fools are talkin' as if the world done come to an end. All that really happened was some priests, and their soldiers, come to town from the west. Some say Nelas. Anyway, they said they was lookin' for someone. Funny thing was, they didn't seem able to agree on who they was lookin' for. Now don' ye think that was odd? Lookin' fer someone but not knowin' who? They only seemed to ken it were a woman. Anyway, there's some who would tell ye they was drunk, but I ken drunks and they wasn't. What they seemed like was scared, although they tried to act tough to hide it. You ken, like little boys do? You ken what's really odd. My great aunt Jebel told me the only time the priests ever come to this town in two thousand years was for the Taking. The Taking was a week and a half ago, there warn't no need to come back fer that, now was there?" she told him, as though she couldn't stop talking once she started. Finally, she seemed to remember her job. "Well, they've gone now, it's done and over. You be wantin' a room fer the night? Ye be a well set up man, I'd deem it a real pleasure to warm yer bed up fer ye right cozy."

"No, thank you. Another time perhaps? I really hate to disappoint a lady, but I have appointments in Nelas," Falcon declined gracefully, flashing his most charming smile. "I could use some bread and cheese for the road though."

The redhead gave a pout as she rose. "I bet ye ain't never disappointed a woman in yer life. I'll be lookin' fer ye when ye come back this way then." She laughed over her shoulder as she swayed her way through the crowd to get his order.

As Falcon was making his way to the door, he overheard one of the men. "They said she must be a witch who kin turn into almost any shape. How are we supposed to recognize her if'n she kin do that? I ask ye?"

"All I'll say is, if'n she's got the filthy priests worried then more power to her. She can't be bad if'n she's against that lot," his companion answered. A chorus of "Ayes!" rose in agreement around him.

Falcon met Tasmin just outside the village, and they knew by the look on both their faces, they had heard the same disturbing news. Without a word, they made for the orchard.

Reining in, Tasmin whispered quietly, "The tidings aren't good. There have been priests here looking for you. Right now, the people are laughing at them. They seem to be looking for one woman with three descriptions. But it's still not good for us. Let's get to a safe place before we discuss it. We're too exposed here," said Tasmin, turning Anabelle southeast, away from the orchard and the village. Soon they were surrounded by heavy woods.

Behnam was bringing up the rear, just downwind of Faye. "What is that smell, Mistress Tasmin? It seems to be getting worse the deeper we go into these woods."

"Yes, I can smell it too. We aren't going to have to sleep with that, are we?" asked Faye.

Bringing her horse back to Behnam and Desert Wind, Tasmin stopped and grabbed Believer's reins. "Faye! You didn't by any chance bring any fruit from that orchard back there with you, did you?"

"Why, yes, I did. I thought they would go lovely with breakfast. Why?"

"Get them out! Now! Quickly, girl, there's no time to lose."

"All right! They're right here on top. What's the big deal?" asked Faye as she pulled the bundle of fruit from her saddlebag.

"Another case of me not telling you enough, that's all," said Tasmin as she grabbed the package and threw it to the ground. The now thoroughly rotted fruit fell out and revealed itself to be filled with horrible large green bugs.

"Yuck! What happened? They weren't even ripe when I picked them," said Faye in disgust as the others gathered around.

"Those are Princess Pears. Barakus put a spell on them two thousand years ago. On the morning Jamben's new queen was to be crowned, she ran from all the pomp and circumstance and found her way into the garden to have one of her favorite fruits before being caged by the affairs of state. When she took her first bite, she turned into crystal. They found her there a few moments later, but it was too late. Gabriene was summoned. Princess Areola's heart was still beating. Therefore, no one else could take her throne. She still lives, after a fashion, in the throne room in Elans, but Barakus's governor rules the land.

"Gabriene was furious! The princess was the first of the royal families attacked, you see. He couldn't do anything to Barakus, so he took it out on the Princess Pear instead. It would be good to eat, if eaten immediately, but within a few minutes of being picked, it would start to rot and crawl with bugs. That's why the orchard has been abandoned. There is no profit in those pears anymore. Come, we're almost there."

When they were settled in an abandoned mill by a dry stream five miles farther on, Tasmin and Falcon relayed the news over a cup of hot tea.

"Mostly the people think the priests may be a little crazy. They're sure anyone who is tying knots in the tail of the priests can't be all bad," finished Tasmin. "But if anyone should see the three of you together, they'd quit laughing. Especially you, Behnam, with Ebony. The two of you stand out like a sore thumb. I hate to say this, but I think we need to split up again. The way we did in Nelas. This time we'll regroup in Dink."

"Shouldn't we change partners? Surely, if they have descriptions of us, they also have descriptions of our companions. Falcon said they described Behnam. From what I've heard, the only one they might not know about is Tasmin."

"Ebony's right. We should change, but I can't get over one thing. Ebony herself would only be more noticeable if she were with Falcon or me. I think Faye should go with me if we're being forced to separate and Cheri can go with Falcon, but I just see no alternative. Behnam will have to stay with Ebony. If there were only some way to disguise you, Ebony."

"I think I'll check the horses," said Ebony, unable to refute their arguments. She had forgotten Behnam was on watch outside, and as she was petting George, he walked up behind her.

"Something has upset you, lady. Is there anything I can do?" he asked.

"Do? It's all your fault in the first place. Because your people treat women like cattle and keep them hidden, it's evidently not safe for me to travel without your company," she answered acerbically. Turning her head away from him.

"I'm sorry, my lady. Our traditions are very old. We are only trying to protect our women, not cage them. You do not understand our customs, that's all," said Behnam consolingly. "Is the thought of having to spend time alone with me so abhorrent to you?"

Ebony whirled to look at him. "It's not that, Behnam. If your women weren't so 'protected,' I could go anywhere and not cause comment. I could travel with anyone, and no one would think it was strange. There are cultures like yours on my world where they refuse to let their women learn, all in the name of protection. Did it ever occur to you that when you protect women too much, you're taking the decisions from their hands and actually caging them? Did it occur to you you're treating them like possessions? Maybe you're just keeping them for yourselves. What real harm is done if someone else sees them? Are you so afraid you can't keep them if they are seen by a white man? Would it be so bad if one wanted to marry someone who wasn't a Mojar? Don't Mojar men ever take white women as wives?"

"As wives? Not and remain with the tribes. Some have been known to take white women as consorts, but that has nothing to do with it. Perhaps you should learn to accept things the way they are instead of fighting them all the time, Lady Ebony. Instead of questioning the ways of our people," retorted Behnam stiffly.

"Apparently, that's what I'm going to have to do, for a while. But I'm going to serve notice here and now, Behnam, I wasn't raised to accept the unacceptable without a fight. If the opportunity arrives for me to change things, believe me. I will!" retorted Ebony in a harsh whisper before she turned on her heel and stalked away.

A bemused Behnam stood there, watching her leave. Why did he desire this strong-minded woman who seemed to be all fire and ice?

That evening, as they prepared to leave, Cheri produced a solution to their dilemma. "Why doesn't she dress like a man? When I first went on the streets, I dressed like a boy, thinking it would make me safer. They're looking for a Mojar woman with a Mojar man. If she dresses like a man, they'll be seeing two Mojar men. No woman."

"That would work! I could dress like Behnam. Wrap my braids in a turban and dress as a man. Then I could travel with Falcon when we split up. My dressing like a man would make me less noticeable anyway," agreed Ebony, eager for a way out of being a meek Mojar woman.

The others stared at her thoughtfully for a moment before Tasmin nodded in agreement. "I don't know why none of us thought of this before. It's the perfect solution. Although traveling with Behnam would still be for the best. Behnam, loan her some of your clothes."

"Allow a woman to dress as a man! That is unthinkable, mistress!" cried Behnam in outrage.

"Allow? Allow? This is what I was talking about. You don't allow me to do anything!" screamed Ebony. "In my world, I not only dressed as a man, I led men in battle, so don't tell me what a woman shouldn't do!"

"In battle, really? Amazing. Now, calm down, Ebony. Behnam, besides the fact she's right, why?" asked Tasmin reasonably.

"It simply isn't done. Women aren't... They can't... I mean, it isn't done," he finished, lamely looking at the glare in Ebony's deep- brown eyes helplessly.

"Well, if you've exhausted your brilliant arguments, I think you should give her a spare set of clothes. Even you must be able to see it's the most logical solution," prompted Tasmin one more time.

Without another word, Behnam stalked across the mill floor to his pack and produced the needed clothes. The women retired to another part of the mill to help Ebony get into them amid a chorus of giggles. When they reemerged,

Behnam looked her over with a critical eye and adjusted some of the ties and belts here and there before wrapping a turban around the braids that had been pulled up. When he was through, he nodded curtly and strode off to check Desert Wind.

Tasmin looked after him with a frown for a moment before turning her attention back to the problems at hand. "Cheri, you'll be traveling with Falcon. It's not common, but occasionally a Samali woman will marry a man from another place and move from her family. Your story will be that you are newlywed and traveling to southern Swaloh, where Falcon has retired from the sea to farm. Believable enough, but you'll have to share a room while you travel. Remember, Falcon, we're trusting you in more ways than one."

"Me! Madam, I have never found it necessary to rob the cradle, and I will not begin now. Cheri is as safe with me as with a palace eunuch from Rim," objected Falcon hotly.

"Cheri, I'm also relying on you to behave yourself. You promised on the road from Nelas, and I will hold you to it," insisted Tasmin with a narrow look.

"I'll second that notion, Cheri. Stay out of trouble," said Faye helplessly.

"Faye, my lady Tasmin, I am but a young bride, innocent and shy. So very shy that I may insist that my husband wait until we are in our own home before I can allow him to touch me," protested Cheri with wide green eyes.

"Now that's an excellent suggestion, Cheri dear. Try to keep it up for the next week and a half, will you? And, Falcon, don't underestimate this young lady. She's not everything she appears to be.

"Faye, can you act haughty, overbearing, arrogant? I think we should pass you as a spoiled aristocrat from Rim, and I will be your duenna. You got bored in the great city with its constant games and politics and set off for adventure. Now you are just weary and dirty and tired of lumpy beds. You can't wait to return to your dear father in Rim, even if it does mean you'll have to marry Delphord Waydon. We'll make him a young philanderer who wants to marry you for political positioning. You'll need to whine and complain of everything all the time," asked Tasmin, embroidering on the story as she went.

"Well, I'll do my best to act like a spoiled child, but what if someone asks me about Rim? I don't even know where it is from here or what country it's in. Is it a country?" asked Faye, considering the part.

"I'll fill you in on its politics as we ride. For now, Rim is the capital city of Camir, far to the east of here. Falcon, will you ask Behnam to join us? We need to know what routes we'll each be taking and where to meet again in Dink."

Tasmin and Falcon spent the next few minutes mapping the different ways they could each get to Dink. None of them would take the most direct route, and they should all arrive within a week and a half to two weeks. Falcon was familiar with Dink and suggested they meet at the Golden Stag Inn, positioned in the middle of the city.

It was agreed Faye and Tasmin would take two pack animals, and Cheri and Falcon would take the other. Behnam informed them Mojar relied only on what they could carry on their own mounts. It was decided to leave in half-hour intervals.

When Cheri and Falcon rode away from the others with the pack- horse in tow, she couldn't help but feel she was leaving her family, again, and found herself looking back frequently until long after the trees completely blocked the view. Amalee's presence high overhead was a strange sort of comfort.

CHAPTER 9

Our Separate Ways

Ebony watched Faye and Tasmin disappear among the trees. She was alone with Behnam and would be for a week or more. How was she going to get through this? His arrogance made her hackles rise, and now he would be upset she had gotten her way. That could only make things worse. There was no denying his present mood was all her fault. Even if she was right.

"Do you really believe you can act like a Mojar warrior?" he asked with deadly quiet from the fire behind her.

"I can fight if I need to. You've seen that," she responded without turning around.

"Yes. You are a formidable opponent. But the way you fought is not the way of a Mojar warrior. A Mojar warrior fights with a sword, like this," he said, drawing his long, curved blade.

"I can use a sword if I must. I'm also quite sure you can teach me to use one more effectively. If I remember correctly, you also fight with knives," she challenged as she turned to look carefully at the blade and the way he held it.

"We only use knives to protect the helpless. When we cannot get in close enough to fight with honor."

"Helpless? I was hardly helpless, but that doesn't matter now. What does is, one of the reasons we've split up is to avoid attracting undue notice and having to fight. If we do need to fight, I doubt if most will question how we do it."

He stared at her thoughtfully for a moment. "Perhaps you are right. I hope you are. How do you intend to pass as a Mojar male in town? You are a formidable woman, Lady Ebony, but you are still a woman. Even dressed as a man."

Ebony laughed. "Don't worry, Behnam. I have known you long enough now to imitate your ways. It isn't hard to swagger and be arrogant, you know."

"Ah, lady, is that how you see me? How little you know of me yet. Well, show me! Convince me you are a young Mojar male."

Ebony squared her shoulders defiantly and strode across the room in a fair parody of Behnam's style. She stopped, with arms crossed, waiting for his response.

Behnam burst into laughter. "Yes, yes, I think you can pull this off after all. Just remember, even among Mojar warriors, there are distinctions. I think perhaps we should say you are my younger brother, Cadir. No one will question it when you defer to me."

"Defer! But I thought we'd be traveling as equals!" objected Ebony.

"There are no equals, Ebony. This is my world now, and I know the way of it. Besides, do you think anyone would believe you were my superior?" explained Behnam patiently.

"Perhaps not, but in my world, all men are created equal."

"Created equal, maybe. Can you honestly tell me that they stay that way? No, Ebony. On any world, some men have done more with what they have been given than others. There are no equal men, or women. Only equal opportunities. I'm sure it's been a half hour by now. We should be on our way, Cadir."

*****

They had ridden south for over an hour, and real darkness

had just overtaken them when Cheri and Falcon saw the lights of a farm ahead. Under the guise of their new identities, they had no reason to believe they wouldn't be well received and proceeded accordingly.

Falcon was leading the packhorse, and Cheri kept Baby close to Wolf as they rode into the farmyard and the dogs began barking. There was a loud bang, and when they looked up toward the stone house with its slate roof, a short round woman with a large ax was outlined in the doorway. "Who be ye? Don' move jus' state yer business from where ye stand! One wrong move and I'll call the dogs on ye!" she called out.

"We didn't mean to disturb you, mistress. We saw your lights and hoped to find a warm room and perhaps a soft bed. My bride and I are journeying to my homeland. I'm afraid we kept going at the last town when we should have stopped," called Falcon, removing his hat as he moved Wolf into the light and motioned Cheri to move closer. Cheri pulled down the hood on her cloak so she could be seen clearly.

"Yer bride, ye say? She seems to me to be a might young. How old be ye, missus?"

"Sixteen, mistress. My pa has six girls and only one son to help about the place. He said it was high time I had a place of me own and quit moochin' off'n him," improvised Cheri.

"Aye! Men do be like that at times. Ye said ye was journeying to yer homeland, sir? Well, ye certainly don' look to be from these parts. And where be that? This farm ain' on the way to anywhere," inquired the woman suspiciously, still holding the ax aloft.

"I'm from southern Swaloh, mistress. My wife's people are from up near the border of Jamben. We're traveling this way because I promised my mother I would look up a distant cousin. Last we heard, he was living somewhere about the north side of the Singing Forest. Perhaps you know of him?" answered Falcon guilelessly.

Abruptly, the woman started to laugh as the ax head dropped to the floor with a thump. "Aye, I've heard of him. The tall, dark woodcutter who lives on the edge of the Singing Forest is almost a legend in these parts. His folks 'ave been here for a good long time. Since the time of the shadow, some say. They always marry girls from afar. No one's quite sure where. That alone makes for a legend 'round here. Dog! Get yer brood away now, ye hear!" she finished. Calling off her dogs.

"Well, I guess ye be all right. Come on in, don't keep yer bride out there in the damp night air. 'Tis already beginnin' ter feel a bit like fall, ain' it. Don' ken what an early winter will do ter the crops. Come in, come in. There be hot stew on the settle and a clean bed in Matew's room. What be yer names, now?" she rambled as she ushered them into the house and set them down at the table. "Cato! Where ye be, lad? We've got company, and their horses need tendin' to. Cato!"

"Please, mistress. Don't bother. I'll take care of the horses. Is there room in the barn?" volunteered Falcon, jumping up again and heading out the door as though trying to escape the woman's chatter.

"Ah! Where be me manners? Me name be Mistress Bye. Me husban' be back afore two dawns have brightened the sky. Tha's why Matew's room be empty the nigh'. Here, eat some hot stew, girl. If'n yer husban' be like mos' ye'll need yer strength, dear," she rambled as she prepared a second bowl of stew and set it to cool for Falcon.

"I didn' ketch yer name, dear? An' yer husban's?" she asked as she settled down across from Cheri.

Cheri quit blowing on her hot stew, surprised at being given an opening to speak. "Me name be Cheri, Mistress. Me husban's name be Falcon. I'd like ter thank ye fer yer hospitality. Yer most kind," she said shyly, imitating the local patois.

"Falcon? Seems like an odd name, don' it? Well, I guess it's the way in Swaloh. What's yer last name, Cheri dear?"

"Uhm... That's not the custom in Swaloh. To have last names, I mean. At least not with the sailors, or so Falcon done told me. Just more baggage ter carry, Falcon says. Only the landlubbers keep their surnames. 'Course, we be goin' ter be landlubbers now, I guess. Falcon says he's got a nice little farm waitin' fer us," she said, wishing fervently for Falcon's return.

"That's right, mistress. I suppose I should take back my surname, now. But it'll have to wait until we get to Lohi, so's it can be recorded proper like," said Falcon as he came back into the room with their saddlebags. "Cato found me and insisted on finishing the job so's I could eat. That's a fine boy you've got there, ma'am."

"I see," said Mistress Bye, eyeing them both closely as she shoved the still steaming bowl of stew across to Falcon. "How'd it happen tha' ye came so far ter marry, Falcon? Surely ye could 'ave foun' someone closer?"

Falcon smiled broadly before he took another large mouthful of stew. As soon as there was room in his mouth for words, he began, "It began in Lohi, Mistress Bye. Three years gone. Cheri's father, Damet, was visiting Lohi. Seems he had a nephew who wanted to become a knight and his brother was too sick to take him for the trials. Anyway, we met up in a tavern when he saved my life from an irate lady. When I asked him what I could do to repay him, he said when I was quit of the sea, I could come to his farm in Samal and marry one of his daughters. Since I always did like redheads, it seemed like a reasonable deal to me.

"I made me fortune and quit the sea three months ago and bought my farm. Then I came to claim my wife. Personally, I think I got the best of the deal from all sides," he finished, leaning back from a now- empty bowl.

"And did he get it? The nephew, I mean? Did he get to become a knight?" came a deep voice from the door, startling Cheri, who turned in her seat to find herself staring up and up, past unbelievably broad shoulders to a wide, open face with a nice smile topped by an unruly mop of light red curls. Mistress Bye's son was about six-foot four inches tall, and very large for a Samali.

"Well, he got in as a squire. It takes years to become a knight proper, you know. Another five years or so and he'll be allowed to compete in the great joust," said Falcon with a broad smile.

"Tha's enough, young man. Off to bed with ye now. Don' be pesterin' Falcon about that nonsense," interrupted Mistress Bye, shooing her oversized son up the stairs as though he were still a wee bairn instead of a young giant.

"Ah, Ma! Ye ken I wan' ter be a knight proper. Pa says I may try, when I'm of age," complained Cato as he stomped up the stairs.

"Be that as it may, young'un, these be newlywed folk. They don' wan' ter be spending their ev'in jawin' wit ye. Good nigh' Cato," insisted Mistress Bye with a scowl and a shake of her head.

Falcon stood and stretched with a mighty yawn, "Aye, mistress. You're right. We should be getting up to bed. We've a long way to go tomorrow. Come, Cheri, it's time we settled down to rest," he finished, reaching a hand down to help Cheri rise.

Cheri was amazed to find herself blushing furiously as she kept her head lowered. She didn't need to pretend to be shy. A few weeks ago, she would never have believed she would be able to blush again. The shy smile she gave her hostess as she followed the good woman up the stairs wasn't faked. Their room was a low space under the eaves, and Falcon brought up the rear with their saddlebags.

"There be fresh water in the pitcher, missus. Let me get ye a clean dryin', and I'll let ye be. Good nigh', sir. Good nigh', Cheri dear," said the good woman as she left the soft sacking towel. Just before she closed the door behind her, she stepped close to Cheri and whispered, "Don' worry, lass. It ain' so bad an' ye get used ter it."

Finally, alone in the room with Falcon, Cheri looked up at Falcon as she covered her mouth with her hand to stifle a giggle. Falcon was standing, with hands on hips, grinning down at his charge. "Well, missus. I think we've passed our first test quite well. All we need do now is remember our story for the next time," he said roguishly, his voice low.

Cheri found herself blushing again as her gaze slid past the bed that looked much too small, even though it took up most of the room. "You need to rest, Falcon. I'll take the floor tonight," she volunteered, keeping her voice low as well.

"Don't be silly, Cheri. Just throw me that extra quilt. I'm so used to sleeping anywhere. I'll probably sleep better on the floor," he insisted. "Don't worry, Cheri. As I told Tasmin, your virtue is safe with me."

Abruptly, Cheri turned away to strip to her chemise before she crawled between the cold sheets. A lump had formed in her throat. Her virtue was safe? What virtue? Turning her face to the wall, she was amazed to find tears on her cheeks. For some reason, she couldn't stop crying.

Cheri's natural ebullience had returned by morning, and she was up early, although her slightest movement brought Falcon instantly alert. Quickly he pulled on his boots. "I'll go get the horses ready while you clean up and get dressed. We should be on our way as soon as we've eaten."

"I'll be right down, Falcon," she assured him. She could hear him as he met up with Cato in the hall. It appeared Cato was going to get his chance to ask about the knights of Lohi before they left after all.

*****

Aliand emerged from the rented carriage that had brought her to the wharves of Lohi and looked around as though not quite sure how she had gotten here. Absently, in a gesture that was mostly habit, she patted her pale-gold hair that had been woven in the elaborate braid so popular in Rim now. She had left Leha sleeping at the inn, and it was very late. As the carriage clattered away on the cobblestones, she absently smoothed the skirt of her green silk gown and took a deep breath before allowing herself to gaze across the water at the white tower. The one she had been trying so hard not to look at.

It gathered all the starlight and all the moonlight, reflecting it back until it glowed as if with a light of its own in the dark night. Even when the clouds covered the stars, the tower could still be plainly seen. There was no doubt; it was the same one. The one that had been haunting her dreams for what seemed like forever. The one that had been calling her, beckoning to her. The tower she couldn't resist.

She wondered briefly what her father would do or had done when he found her gone. The Baron of Phym was not an easy man. How long would it take for him to notice his fourth daughter was gone? He had twelve daughters and sons, but his pride would never allow a precious daughter to leave. Whatever her reasons had been. They were too valuable for the power they could buy with the right marriage. It was entirely possible he could start a war if he thought a rival had stolen her away. Well, there was nothing to be done now. Whatever he did, she would go to the tower.

Drawing another deep breath, she untied the closest rowboat and climbed awkwardly into it. Primly she spread her skirts on the crude wooden bench and gingerly grabbed the oars in her silk-gloved hands. Once she started her clumsy rowing, she continued doggedly, gaining some mastery as she went. She seemed not to feel the blisters that rose and burst to bleed on her ripped gloves. No matter what, she had to do this.

*****

Tasmin and Faye rode east for two hours before they made camp for the night. From now on they would be traveling in the daytime, like respectable people, and they needed their sleep.

"What can you tell me about Rim and Camir? Tasmin?" asked Faye over her cup of herb tea.

"Let me start by telling you its history. When Barakus was gaining control of the lands in the east, he didn't do it with war. He was much more devious than that. One by one he destroyed the ruling families and replaced them with his regents and governors, backed up by the priests and church soldiers. He also cast a spell on the regular armies, causing them to lose heart when their rulers were gone. Those who escaped his influence were few, and they formed small pockets of resistance which are still out there. He used a different method with each country. For each one, he chose the most effective.

"In Rim, the capital city of Camir, the royal family was very large. King Absonth and Queen Maydene had sixteen children, and the king's brothers also had large families. To kill the entire royal family required something ingenious. Barakus came up with a very insidious plan. Somehow, he developed a disease that only affected the members of the royal family. It is said, even the bastard offspring of the family succumbed. He released it in the city during the winter festival when almost all members of the family should have been in the city. A few distant cousins had been snowed in at their country estate in the far north, but when word reached them and they came into the city during the spring thaw, they too contracted the disease. There have been rumors for centuries that one of the royal children, the third son Patrit, had been hunting and survived. The retainer who was with him on the hunt had spirited him away to another land, and his descendants would return when the city was once more safe.

"That's why there is no royal family in Rim, although there is much vying for the position of regent. They deceive themselves they hold the throne for the heir and Barakus allows them to delude themselves. Each time a regent dies, a new one must be elected by the noble houses and the buying and selling of favors for power is common. It is said that loyalties change with the weather in Camir. Aristocratic ladies spend their time trying to outdo themselves in dress and power as well. The more beautiful the girl, the greater the gain for her father. It's quite simple, really, nothing is done in Rim without great thought given to the advantages that can be gained. The current regent has been ill for some months now, and the 'game' always gets more frantic at these times. Our story is quite plausible.

"One more thing, these 'nobles' have become so caught up in political intrigue that they have neglected, even abused, their people and value them only for the service and power they give their master. They're treated as property, not people. Mostly it is an unpleasant place unless you're of noble birth," added Tasmin, wrinkling her nose in distaste.

"You want me to pretend to be one of these people? You may have to remind me, but I'll do my best," commented Faye as she rolled over in her blanket and fell instantly asleep.

Tasmin sat very still, watching her charge sleep and listening intently for any change in the rhythm of the woods, as she sipped another cup of tea. What kind of place did these strange young women come from? Each of them was so very different from the others, yet they all came from the same city.

Tasmin woke Faye as dawn was blushing the horizon, "Faye, dear. Give me two hours to sleep before we set out for the road. You might want to start getting ready. Wear the deep-blue riding outfit with silver embroidery. When I wake, I'll dress your hair in an elaborate style. Oh, and one more thing, keep your bow and arrows handy. If you listen to the songs of the birds, they'll warn you if anyone is coming. Good night, dear."

Faye spent the first forty-five minutes of her watch cleaning up and changing. She knew she could trust Believer to be on watch as she donned her new riding habit. Smoothing the fine blue material over her hips she found she actually wished she had a mirror to see how she looked in the dark blue with silver trim. It fit her better than anything she had ever worn before coming here. If she even had Cheri's hand mirror, she might get an idea of how she looked. Funny thing, that, she'd never cared much what she looked like before she came to this world. Well, it was just curiosity, anyway, she told herself as she loosened the French braid she had gotten used to wearing and began to brush her hair

Leaving her hair loose, she fished her Bible and glasses out of her saddlebag and settled on a rock to read. Her hair fell forward about her face as she lost herself in the story of Ruth. She was so absorbed in the timeless story, it was a moment before she realized a sudden hush had fallen over the woods. Believer's whinny and sudden restless stomping brought her back to her job.

She jerked her head up to look at the unicorn before she followed his gaze, her hand moving slowly to pick up the strung bow and waiting arrows by her side. She notched an arrow and pulled back the bow as she stood, turning around, checking the entire perimeter carefully. There was a rustling in the brush a little off to her left, and she brought the arrow up to her chin, ready to fire. "Who's there? Whoever you are, come on out where I can see you."

There was more rustling in the bushes before a shriveled man in ill-kempt clothes poked his small face, surrounded by dirty red hair and a scrawny red beard, into the open. "Don' shoo', miss. I don' mean no 'arm. You ask in de village. Doph don' do no harm ter no one," he cried in a high, whiny voice as he stepped around a tree and into the small clearing. His small eyes darted restlessly about as he talked.

Faye heard Tasmin's step behind her as the small man dropped the bag he'd been carrying and started to reach a hand inside. Faye let fly her arrow deliberately, tearing through the man's sleeve but missing his arm and pinning him to the tree behind him, leaving the bag on the ground.

The strange man's eyes flew wide and he let out a yelp of surprise, "Please, madam, Tell the lady I only wanna giver 'er a gif'. There's a brace of nice plummy whirrers in de bag. I ken ter give us'n a good dine. There ain' no 'arm in tha'," he beseeched Tasmin.

Tasmin glanced once at Faye, who was holding another arrow pointed at the helpless man. Silently she nodded before Tasmin crossed to the bag. Carefully staying out of the line of fire, and as far from the stranger as possible, she picked up the bag and dumped its contents on the ground. Two fat birds that resembled quail came tumbling out, and Faye relaxed her stand although she did not put down the bow.

"Cook the whirrers, Mistress Tasmin. It will break the monotony of travel fare. Ah, how I miss the meals at my father's table! While it's cooking, you can do my hair. I certainly can't continue this way. I don't know which is worse, sleeping among the animals in the open or in the lumpy, bug-infested mattresses provided by the inns," she complained arrogantly, ignoring the man who was still pinned to the tree.

"Miss, sure ye ain' goin' ter leave me stuck here!" called Doph plaintively.

Faye refused to answer him. Instead, she looked at Tasmin, with one raised eyebrow.

"My lady does not speak to the likes of you, cur. She has decided to be generous and leave you where you are, for now. If we were back in Camir, she would have you shot for daring to talk to her. But she understands the customs are not as civilized here. Now, just behave yourself, and she may set you free when we depart. And don't underestimate her aim with that bow. If she'd wanted to hit you somewhere else, she would have," said Tasmin with a glance lower on his body before she busied herself with the whirrers. Once they were cleaned and cut and sizzling in the pan, she braided and looped Faye's long blond hair into a style that was extremely elaborate and highly impractical. Perfect for their charade.

Doph glowered at them from his tree as they ate heartily of his whirrers, and Tasmin repacked the horses. He could easily reach up and pull out the arrow, but Faye's bow was kept close, and Tasmin had drawn her dagger. The remains of the whirrers, as well as a hunk of bread, Tasmin lay on a stone next to the now-dead fire. The rest of his belongings lay as if forgotten on the ground in front of him. Mounted and ready to leave, Tasmin glanced at Faye questioningly and waited for her nod before she rode over and retrieved Faye's arrow. "Thank you for your gift. It was enjoyable," she said as she followed Faye from the clearing.

Doph scurried across the clearing to get his food before some other vermin did. Chewing thoughtfully, he watched the ladies depart with narrowed eyes. "Ye'd best watch behin' ye, lady. I don' take kindly ter yer ways. I ain' good enough fer ter eat wi' ye? Perhaps we meet again, and I have the upper hand? Perhaps, there even be a profit here some way?" he muttered to himself around a mouthful of whirrer and bread.

*****

Behnam and Ebony rode through the night, coming at last to a wide deserted highway. That changed rapidly as night gave way to morning and more and more travelers joined them. Many of the people they passed looked like tramps and vagabonds who wandered from village to village in search of work and food. Some of the men, who traveled in small groups, were singing lustily of knights and brave deeds as they headed for Dink. Occasionally they passed a farmer and his cart headed to the market in the next town.

As they rode, traffic bound away from Dink also made its presence felt. Peddler wagons and merchant trains raised clouds of dust that followed them on their way to the many villages of Samal for the late summer trade. They found it prudent to keep their mouths and noses covered during much of the day.

The two of them, with their dark skin in a fair-skinned land, caused a lot of heads to turn. No one seemed to stare at them overlong; however, they had their own concerns. While Behnam's steady gaze, which Ebony tried to emulate, may have had some effect, it was evident other Mojar had been seen in these parts in days past.

When able, Behnam trotted down the center of the road, arrogantly ignoring those around him, making others move aside as Desert Wind stepped proudly and George followed suit. Ebony copied the way he sat his horse and tried not to think of the poor men who were scrambling out of their way. Even Behnam was forced to give way for the wagons. Especially the large boxy wagons with high windows that passed in groups of two or three. These were always surrounded by rough men in dark-brown shirts and suede vests and jackets. As the wagons passed, the chatter of the people on the road would calm, and they would stare at the wagons in a strange mix of sorrow and anger. Once they were gone, the people would begin talking again but now in angrier voices. When one such group of wagons passed, Ebony thought she heard muffled crying over the sound of creaking leather, jangling harness and the metal wheels on the road.

Instead of scrambling into the ditches on either side to avoid the wagons, Behnam merely pulled aside and waited. Giving them no more space than absolutely necessary. Once, while waiting for a merchant's wagon, a drover started as though to whip them out of the way, but Behnam simply watched him with an impassive stare. The merchant stood up quickly and grabbed the drover's arm. "Are ye daft, man? Don' ye know, if ye strike a Mojar, it'll be yer life! He's no harmin' us. Let 'im be," he called frantically.

Unconvinced, the drover stared at Behnam a moment longer as the wagon pulled on past.

When the last wagon was gone, Behnam returned to his rightful place, in the middle of the highway. "Is that absolutely necessary?" asked Ebony from behind her scarf as she pulled George up almost even with Desert Wind.

"Don't question me, Cadir. These people know the place of the Mojar warriors. It's time you did as well," he replied tersely before cantering ahead, again.

They rode on until midday when Behnam finally stopped in a small clearing for lunch. He left Desert Wind untied as he sat on an exposed root and leaned against the tree, munching peacefully on bread and cheese, washed down with cool water from a nearby stream. Ebony glowered at him as she followed suit. This trip was going about as she'd feared, and this was only the first day.

Finished with his meal, Behnam leaned his head back and shortly began to snore. Amazed that they weren't continuing, Ebony decided to take a nap of her own as she leaned against a warm rock.

It seemed to be only a moment later when a loud whinny from Desert Wind awoke both of them. From where Ebony now lay, beside the rock, she looked up to see Desert Wind rise up on his hind legs as he tried to protect Behnam and herself from intruders.

Three uniformed men on horseback were advancing with drawn sabers. Springing to her feet gracefully, Ebony drew her sword and prepared for battle. Looking around, she saw Behnam was already on his feet, scimitar in hand.

Suddenly a fourth rider appeared. "Ho, men. What goes on here? We're supposed to be protecting travelers on this highway, not accosting them. Lower your weapons!" the newcomer commanded.

"But, sir! The priests are looking for two Mojar. There's a handsome reward, and these may be the two," protested one.

"Since when do we work for the priests, Sergeant Pitt? Besides, if you would listen to reports more closely, you would know that they are looking for a Mojar and his woman. Not two Mojar men. My apologies, gentlemen. Rewards can make fools of the best of men. I see I will have to teach them that if they go up against the Mojar, they must outnumber him ten to one."

Behnam bowed deeply and saluted the man with his scimitar before returning it to its scabbard. Ebony followed suit, not quite sure what had just happened.

"No harm done, Lieutenant. But it takes more than ten men from the wetlands to take down a Mojar warrior." He laughed while his deep voice implied there would have been bloodshed in another moment. "What's this about a reward for Mojar? I like not the sound of that."

"Yes, it's those fool priests. One thousand decars for a Mojar and his woman. They claim they're somewhere in Samal. They claim she is a witch and the church needs to question her. It has even been reported Barakus himself is interested in this woman."

Behnam's deep laugh echoed through the glen. "Lieutenant, how many years have you been protecting the highways of Samal? In all of those years, how many Mojar women have you seen? If a Mojar is indeed traveling with his woman, I too would like to see him. At least long enough to remove his head for breaking our customs.

"That's what I thought when I heard the report, sir. Personally, I think some of the priesthood have lost their minds. Their stories are very confused. To be honest, I don't think they know who they're looking for. Again, my apologies, sir. Once you arrive in Dink, if you need any assistance, ask for Lieutenant Vedar," he finished with a salute before following his men back onto the road.

Ebony stared speechlessly at Behnam for a moment, but as she was about to ask a question, he shook his head sharply and crossed to check on Desert Wind. "This has nothing to do with us, Cadir. It is time to be moving on. I would like a hot meal this evening. Let's not waste time getting to the next village."

They arrived at Bakir as the sun was setting. The Baker's Daughter was the only inn, and many heavily guarded wagons were lined up outside. Apparently, a merchant train had gotten there first.

Behnam rode into the stable yard and called for a hostler to care for their horses. "Take good care of our mounts, man. Desert Wind has been known to get even when he's mistreated, nor would I take kindly to ill treatment for his friend," he instructed seriously as he grabbed his gear from behind the saddle. Ebony hastened to follow suit.

The common room was crowded, and Ebony managed to stay fairly close to Behnam as he made a path to the center of the room where they were also the center of attention.

"Innkeeper! Have you a room for two tired travelers for the night? And hot food? My brother and I are weary as well as famished!" he bellowed to the room at large. Causing an instant lull in all conversations.

A man of average height and extraordinary girth waddled out from behind the bar. His short hair and long beard of flaming red framed a smiling face covered with freckles. "I be here, gentlemen. Good man Davir at your service. You have come in good time. I have two beds in a room with four yet. Another half hour and there would not be even that."

"Ah, my good man. We're willing to pay extra, in gold, for a room to ourselves. We have been traveling for days with only our horses for company, and we would not want to offend anyone unfortunate enough to room with us. Are you sure arrangements cannot be made?" Behnam asked as he jingled a small purse of coins that suddenly appeared in his hand. Several customers close by laughed at Behnam's little joke before returning to their own concerns.

The innkeeper's eyes gleamed at the sound. "Ah, well, sir. Perhaps arrangements can be made, after all. Please, there is room for you to eat in peace in the private dining room while I see what might be done. My wife and daughter are wonderful cooks and bakers. You'll find the food well worth it, I assure you."

"I'm quite sure you will be able to accommodate us, good sir. I have faith in you," acceded Behnam graciously as he pocketed the purse and followed their host to the dining room.

Once they were alone, Ebony finally had a chance to speak up. "We're going to have to share a room? I was hoping for a long bath and a room to myself tonight."

Behnam arched a brow at her. "What a strange idea. Only very wealthy and foolish merchants pay to have separate rooms. And of course, ladies. Since we are merely brothers and tight-fisted Mojar at that, I will be doing well if we avoid sharing a room with others, as we came close to doing tonight. As for a bath, I wouldn't count on that before we reach Dink, at least. That is not how men travel. I will order a pitcher of hot water which you may use first, but that is the best I can do without calling undue attention to us. Cadir, you must accustom yourself to these things if you are going to learn the ways of all Persal."

Ebony stared at the table in front of her in dismay. This trip was going to be much, much worse than she had ever imagined. Suddenly the hectic life she had led in Seattle seemed like a distant dream. This reality was becoming a nightmare.

*****

In the caravan of the Mojar, Ochwatt would have been impossible to hide so Gaban didn't even try. On their first day out, young boys followed the hairy giant cautiously. Ochwatt, in return, allowed his lips to curve into a smile, but for the most part, he ignored them. At first, they just followed, but when he did not respond, they started running up to touch his cloak, laughing as they ran back. Suddenly, Ochwatt grabbed one small boy with a curly mop of hair as he approached, swinging him high in the air before tucking him securely under his arm while he kicked and screamed. Laughing, the other boys began running in circles, about the giant, snatching at their friend. Dismissively he continued to stride next to Buttercup, Gaban's horse, as if they were merely a swarm of pesky flies.

Gaban was chuckling atop his horse when the children noticed the small smile on Ochwatt's face, and their leader called them into a huddle. Their friend had ceased to struggle, looking up at his captor, wondering what was next. The women and warriors traveling nearby were watching the exchange as well. All were curious about Gaban's strange friend.

Then came the attack. Two of the boys started running around Ochwatt and his burden, trying to distract him as three more came running up behind. The first one stooped low and allowed his friends to run up his back so they could jump on the giant and try to wrestle him to the ground. Now Gaban and the other adults burst into laughter in fact as Ochwatt tried to dislodge the boys on his back without giving up his first prize. He was twisting and turning in the effort. The boy under his arm began struggling again, making it even harder on the poor sasquatch, who suddenly turned in a complete circle before seeming to lose his balance and fall to the ground. Setting all the boys free in the process. By now everyone was roaring with laughter, and Ochwatt added his bellow to the merriment. Until, that is, he raised his bowed head, revealing his wide grin and the mouthful of fangs behind it. Then the women gasped and drew back, the boys went screaming to hide among the camel's legs, and two of the warriors began to draw their scimitars.

"Now, now! No need to be alarmed. Ochwatt is a peaceful man. 'Tis only his smile. No man can control his smile," Gaban reassured them quickly.

Ochwatt's smile faltered as he stood, looking about him in confusion. Seeing everyone staring at him, he bowed his head shyly. "Well done, Sir Ochwatt! Well done!" exclaimed the Shakir as he rode up to join them. "I can see a great advantage to that grin of yours, but well done in playing with my son Bashnir. He hasn't had such fun in quite some time."

The young boy Ochwatt had held captive jumped off the front of his father's stallion to run up to the sasquatch and bow almost double. "Thank you so much, sir Ochwatt," he said solemnly.

"Good fun," agreed Ochwatt, smiling with closed lips

at the boy. Gaban watched him thoughtfully. *Perhaps... hmmm... Yes,* perhaps.

"I insist, you, Master Ochwatt? Is that how it's said? And of course, Gaban must join us for dinner. You can tell us of your home." That night over the brazier in the Shakir's tent, Ochwatt was a great favorite, answering as best as possible the many questions about his people and their lives.

CHAPTER 10

The Song of the Woodsman

It was mid-afternoon when Tasmin and Faye came to the sleepy village of Dacora and Tasmin urged Annabelle up next to Believer. "My lady, I believe this might be a good place to stop for the night. We cannot be sure of reaching another town before nightfall. There's an inn just up ahead," she said in a voice that managed to sound cultured and carry well at the same time as she pointed to a sign so weathered the girl with once-bright-red hair could barely be seen running down a hill. The Running Maid.

"What a lovely idea," agreed Faye, covering her surprise by pulling ahead again and leading the way into the stable yard of the inn. The stench of the stable wafted out to meet them. "Perhaps the innkeeper can even find a tub so I can bathe properly before dinner. It's amazing how quickly dirt and grime lose their attractiveness.

"You there! Come help me down from my horse. Have someone bring our things to our room," she said airily to the men lounging in the door to the stable as a suddenly restive Believer shied away from the men's approach. "One more thing, your stable is a bit...ripe. Perhaps you can put our horses in the paddock? And...take very good care of our animals. My stallion here can be very ill-tempered when he feels any of his friends are being mistreated. Now, Believer, will you behave if they do?" she crooned sweetly with heavy emphasis on *they*. Believer gave a vigorous nod, sending his mane flying as he eyed the man approaching him with a dubious eye.

Reassured, Faye grabbed her bow and quiver before she turned to stride across the courtyard and up the steps to the common room. She walked into the dim room with its smoke-blackened windows and beams and was crossing the rough and dirty floor when she tripped and started to fall, only to catch herself on a grimy table.

"Oh, my lady! Are you all right? You must be tired after the last weeks on the road. Innkeeper! Quickly, a glass of your best wine! And rooms, we require two rooms for the night!" cried Tasmin as she came up behind Faye and helped her into a chair that hadn't seen a cleaning rag in some time.

"Ye do, do ye? Let me see the color of yer coin first. Then ye can have me best room. But only one fer the two of ye. I'll 'ave other payin' customers afore the night falls," said the thin, surly man in a dirty apron as he emerged from behind the bar to greet them.

Tasmin looked upon their would-be host with narrowed eyes for a brief moment before returning her attention to Faye. "Perhaps we should travel on, my lady. We might be able to make it to the next village yet tonight," she suggested quietly.

"Now, Jem. Be that a way ter greet yer guests?" came a booming voice from the dim recesses of the room, followed shortly by a large man with faded red hair. A younger man, even larger, and with redder hair, was right behind him.

"These be poor days ter be too quick to trust to strangers, Geo. I don' take any without seeing the color o' dere coin," answered Jem defiantly.

"I do believe yer eyesight be as bad as yer manners, an' we all ken ye never learnt those. These be ladies. Women of quality. Can ye not see that the Miss needs a reviving drink of wine, Jem? So bring out yer best and mind ye, I'll ken if'n it be lesser! If need be, ye kin put it on me tab an' I'll settle in the morn. Oh, and be sure it be a clean flagon ye be usin'!"

Jem paused before telling Geo what he could do with his wine and took another long look at his new guests. Faye looked up and found herself staring deep into pain-filled eyes.

Pulling his glance away, Jem finally responded, "Aye, Geo. Ye be right. Ye heard Master Bye, Besi! Beg pardon, ladies. Yer refreshment will be right out," he said, motioning to the slovenly barmaid behind him to hurry up as his eyes kept returning to Faye's.

"It be about time ye came ter yer senses, Jem. Allow me to introduce myself, Geo Bye, and this be me son, Matew. Our reluctant host here be Jem Derf," said the large man with a gallant bow. "Do ye have a room fit fer these ladies, Jem?"

"Thank you for your aid, Master Bye. Master Derf. You've been most kind. Do you have soap and hot water available? It's obvious they seldom use it," answered Tasmin with a deep curtsy for Master Bye.

"If'n they dinna have any, I'll see they get some, dear lady."

Faye raised her head as her wine was brought. She didn't bother to acknowledge the maid who brought it, but she turned instead to Geo. "Perhaps they can be persuaded to use some on our room and bedding? If this room's any indication, it could surely use it," she asked quietly.

"I'll see ter the cleanin' of me best room meself," insisted their host eagerly.

"Ah, no need ter take time from yer busy schedule, Jem. Me boy Matew here don' have nothin' to do right now. Make sure they work as they would fer yer mater, son. While yer at it, I'm thinkin' it would be comfortin' ter sleep in a clean bed oursel's the night," said Geo, sending his oversized son off as if he were a small boy.

"Aye, Father. I'll roust the help from their gamin' and teach them ter work," agreed Matew with a grin as he left with Jem for the back of the inn, calling loudly for the maids and the pot boys.

"Please, Master Bye, be assured we can pay our bill. Is there a special reason for our host's unfriendly reception?" asked Faye curiously.

"He's been summat grumpy and slovenly since his wife died a year gone, but a few days ago, three priests arrived with a small group of church soldiers. They all stayed here. They and their horses ate heartily and left in the morning without payin'. They told him it was in the service of the church, and Barakus remembered those who served his church. Nearly broke him, they did. Made 'im even grumpier an' he ain' quite recovered yet. He never was too fond of the church, any more'n the rest of us, but he's got a real grudge agin 'em anon. As ye kin guess, he don' do too well here in the best of times. There's many who'd rather sleep in the woods than share a lumpy bed with bed bugs and vermin. 'Course, there won' be no vermin in yer bed when Matew gets done. No one's more of a stickler fer cleanin' than his mam, my Mata. Don' worry, she's trained our boys well."

"Thank you again, Master Bye. Will the food be edible? If the kitchen is as ill-kempt as this room, I have little hope for it," said Tasmin with a rueful shake of her head and a little smile.

Geo returned her smile with a grin of his own. "The baker down the road sells wonderful meat pies. If'n I hurry, I should be able to catch 'im afore he closes. Why don' I just nip down an' pick up a few? Matew and I could do wit' a good hot meal. It not be as good as my Mata but then few kin cook like her."

"Master Bye, our debt to you just keeps growing. Perhaps there is some way we can repay you?" asked Faye generously.

"No need. No need. Mata'd box my ears if'n I did else an' she heard. There's shame enough for the entire district in the greetin' ye received. I'll be back soon."

The wait for Geo was beginning to wear on Faye's nerves, and the common room had begun to fill up when Matew returned. "My ladies, even Ma wouldna be shamed to offer ye that room now. I've even taken the liberty to order up a 'clean' tub and hot water. After sittin' in this grimy place, I thought ye'd appreciate it."

"We do indeed, Matew. I wonder what could have happened to your father. He left shortly after you did to fetch us all some meat pies," commented Tasmin.

"So sorry ter 'ave kept ye waitin', dear ladies. There was a ruckus out in the stable, and I had to send for Jem. It seems to be all settled now though," came Geo's booming voice as he returned.

Faye straightened up with a look of alarm. "In the stable? Are Believer and Anabelle and the mules all right?"

"Oh, aye lady. They be in much better shape than the stablemen. Seems they couldn't get that stallion of yer'n to go into the stable. Nor would he let them take any of yer other animals in. The stablemen were coming out on the worse end of the argument when I arrived. I took one look at the stable and told Jem they might 'ave better luck if'n they'd take the time to clean out the stalls good and lay fresh straw. When I returned just now, Jem had things well inhand. All the animals 'ave been stabled and brushed good, and they do be quite content. I'll say this, yer visit is certainly shakin' this place up and not aforetime, neither," explained Geo as he handed a pie of generous portion to each of the women and sat down to begin eating the three he'd brought for himself, and Matew did justice to a like amount.

"I think ye'll be all right in yer room tonight, ladies, but to be safe, Matew and I will be in the next room should ye be needin' us," said Geo when dinner was done, and they all rose to go upstairs.

"We're most fortunate to have found two gallant gentlemen

as you and your son, Master Bye. Most fortunate indeed," murmured Faye as she mounted the stairs to the long-awaited bath and a clean bed.

*****

Behnam checked on the horses, giving Ebony a moment's privacy and a chance to clean up before he returned. When he did get back, he pushed his bed against the door before he lay down fully clothed. "You'd better sleep light tonight, brother Cadir. Some of those fools in the common room were eyeing my purse and are thinking they might surprise us," he said as he rolled over and closed his eyes.

Ebony paused before blowing out their candle to stare at him. Evidently, there would be no real rest tonight. With a heavy sigh, she pulled her boots back on before getting into bed and pulling the thin blanket over her head.

The exhaustion of constant travel the last few weeks overcame her, and she was sleeping soundly when a sudden banging disturbed her. Without thinking twice, she rolled off the bed and hugged the floor, looking for her rifle and finding a sword instead. "Incoming!" she called out before remembering where she was.

"Cadir! On your feet!" barked Behnam, his commanding voice penetrating the fog of memories that threatened to take her over the edge.

Instantly, Ebony sprang to her feet and adopted a defensive posture as she peered around in the gloom. There was a thin shaft of moonlight piercing through the shutters on the window, giving just enough light to reveal three or four shapes wrestling to push open the door as Behnam could no longer hold it and let it go. Their attackers tumbled through in a jumble of arms and legs. Behnam stood over them with an upraised saber. "Cadir! It appears we are no longer welcome here. Grab our things and open the shutter. Perhaps if we leave by the window, we can avoid their friends downstairs."

Wordlessly, Ebony obeyed. When she opened the window, she was relieved to see the roof of a shed was just off to the left and easily reached from their room. She hadn't looked forward to jumping two stories to the hard-packed earth of the stable yard. With a last glance at Behnam, who was engaged in battling the would-be thieves, she grabbed both the saddlebags and swung herself out the window and onto the roof below. She reached the ground safely and hurried into the stable to saddle the horses, praying all the time Behnam would be right behind her.

George was saddled, and she was trying to get close enough to Desert Wind to saddle him as well when the sound of battle died for a moment, and a large shadow blocked the door. Instantly, she dropped the saddle and assumed a defensive posture. Slowly she started circling for a better vantage point. "Cadir! It's me, Behnam. They won't be delayed long. Watch my back while I saddle Desert Wind," he whispered loudly as he strode to his restive horse who calmed immediately at the sound of his voice.

Ebony nodded once and went to watch the door, George's reins in her hand. Peering outside, she noted five furtive shapes darting from shadow to shadow across the courtyard. "They're coming."

"Another moment and we'll be away," panted Behnam as he cinched tight the girth and reached for his saddlebag.

But they didn't have another moment as three of the shadowy men burst through the door. Ebony was waiting for them and took the first one down with a sharp blow to the back of his head as he passed. The next one went down right on top of his friend when he encountered her foot with his chin. The third one skidded to a stop in midstride as he tried to comprehend what had happened. Ebony didn't give him much time as she advanced from the side and grabbed his sword arm, flipping him onto the hard ground and wrenching his sword lose at the same time.

"Mount up! We'll ride over any who are still intent on attacking us," called Behnam as he swung into the saddle and walked his horse over to cover her as she mounted.

Ebony didn't have to be told twice. She vaulted into the saddle and followed Behnam at a gallop out of the stable and through the yard. Someone was closing the five-foot-tall yard gate, but without even pausing, Behnam and Desert Wind sailed over it. Ebony had never jumped a horse before, but she didn't allow herself time to think about it. She put her heels to an eager George and followed suit.

Two miles out of town, Behnam led the way into the woods, and they slowed their horses. Then Behnam startled Ebony with his deep laugh. "We make a good team, Cadir! They never had a chance. If you were not a woman, you would be a mighty Mojar warrior."

"Ah! But I am a woman, and I am also a warrior, Behnam. I am simply not Mojar," corrected Ebony. "Where I come from, we do not limit people as you do."

"I am beginning to see this may indeed be a good thing. One day you must tell me of this strange land you come from, but for now, we must find a place to rest. Those were not merely thieves, I'm afraid. There were too many, and they were too persistent. My guess is, they did not believe us about the Mojar woman. Either they saw through your disguise, which I doubt, or they thought we knew where she was. Either way, we cannot travel as openly as we'd hoped," said Behnam seriously.

"My guess is, all Mojar, traveling in any part of Persal, outside of Mojar itself, is going to come under suspicion. If you all traveled more among these people, with your women, things would be much easier for us right now and harder for Barakus."

"Perhaps, my dear brother, perhaps. But there's no use wishing for things we cannot have. We cannot change the past. Only the future is ours to shape as we will and as fate allows. I suggest we travel deeper into these woods before our recent past catches up with us," said Behnam, leading the way deeper into the trees and away from the road, leaving Ebony to follow as she would.

*****

Cheri was content to let Falcon lead the way through the countryside as they left the Bye farm. The morning air was still a bit chilly, but the sunrise promised it would soon burn off and she wanted to indulge herself in taking in all the strange and wonderful things to be seen in this magical land.

Except for the colors of their wool, which seemed to be in all shades of the rainbow, the sheep grazing in the fields looked about the way sheep had looked in books at home. Cato was already in the field with a hoe, weeding between the rows of high stalks that most resembled blue corn. Turning to look behind her one more time, she saw Mistress Bye bent over a washtub, scrubbing clothes and she waved.

As they left the farmhouse behind, she noticed bright-red birds similar to finches that sang out a glorious greeting as they neared until they scattered in alarm as Amalee swooped down to rejoin Falcon. Falcon had told her it would be another day and a half of hard riding before they would near the forest itself. There they would be safe, for a while.

"You promised once to tell me Amalee's story and how you got your name. Seems like this might be a good time," said Cheri, deliberately casual.

Falcon glanced at her out of the corner of his eye. "I suppose you might be right. I would rather tell you alone anyway. The truth is, I do not know who I am or where I come from. The traveling people found me one day in the far south of Jamben.

Very near the Arid Mountains that border Mojar. They guessed my age to be about one year at the time. I was alone, except for Amalee. They are great ones for omens, and they first thought she was a falcon, so they named me Falcon. I was grateful for their care and love, but although Wachee raised me as her own, I never felt as if I belonged. Not really, anyway. Amalee never left me for long, and she is the one I belong with. Anyway, when I got old enough, I started traveling on my own. I know more now than I did then. I know I am not of any of the races of eastern Persal, and I'm obviously not of the Mojar in the west. One day I will sail to the south and travel to the north to see if the myths and stories are true. Perhaps I will find my people in one of those lands. If not, I may finally even travel to Doome, in the northeast."

"For your sake, Falcon, I hope you do find them one day. And when that day comes, I hope it is all you hope it will be," said Cheri sympathetically before asking, "Can you understand Amalee? I mean, when she nibbles at your ear, does she talk to you?"

"We are family. Cannot everyone understand their families?" asked Falcon in reply.

"I suppose they should, but I never found that in my family." She said as she pulled Baby back to follow Falcon again.

Now that they were out of sight of the farm, Falcon urged Wolf into a ground-eating canter, not slowing to a walk until just before they stopped for lunch.

"The woodsman you talked about last night? Do you know him or had you merely heard of him?" asked Cheri over her fresh bread and cold chicken sent by Mistress Bye.

"We've met. More than once. I'm a traveler, Cheri, with no home. There are things I have in common with Bass that no one else can understand," answered Falcon, a distant look in his eyes.

"Does he travel too?"

"What? No, no. I mean, he has a home. He has never to my knowledge traveled farther than Dink where he sometimes takes logs to sell for lumber. Mostly he only goes as far as the village of Danfer where fine furniture is made. He and his fathers before him supply most of their wood."

"Oh, I understand," said Cheri as she rose to walk to the creek for some cold water.

Stunned, all Falcon could do was stare after his young charge in confusion. Somehow, he believed she really did understand.

Even though Falcon continued to push them hard on the road and they slept quickly that night, it was early the next afternoon before they could see the forest clearly.

The pace was tiring Cheri, and she had been daydreaming when she looked toward the trees again. Ahead she could finally see the tall, straight trees, their stark white trunks soaring twenty, forty, maybe as much as eighty feet above the ground before the masses of green leaves that topped them began. Above the trees soared large birds that could be hawks, falcons, or eagles. Trying to take in everything at once, Cheri noticed an old, dead snag of a tree in a fallow field nearby with four or five crows perched on it. Oddly, they seemed to have nothing better to do than watch them ride by. At least until Amalee stooped for the kill, scattering them all while picking one out for dinner.

As they drew nearer to the forest, first she caught a whiff of carnation in the air. Then she began to hear an odd sound. It appeared to be someone singing, but there was no sign of anyone around, and she couldn't make out the words. Urging Baby past the packhorse and closer to Wolf, she asked, "Falcon, what is that noise? It sounds like singing. I thought Mistress Bye said there wasn't another farm between her place and the forest?"

"She did. There is no farm in this area. Listen awhile longer and see if you can tell me where the singing is coming from, little one. If you haven't figured it out by the time we reach the trees, I will tell you then," promised Falcon with a secretive smile.

"All right, I will. Can I assume it isn't those birds?" she asked, pointing above the trees. When Falcon nodded, she continued excitedly. "I've always loved mysteries."

"And a challenge as well, I'll wager," responded Falcon in a low voice that Cheri could still hear, even under the flutter of wings as Amalee took flight again, heading back for the crows behind them who took flight and headed north with a purpose, unlike any birds scattering in fright she'd ever seen.

Shrugging, she merely grinned broadly as her eyes scanned their surroundings, hunting for the source of the song.

By the time they were only a couple of hundred yards from the trees the smell of carnations was everywhere and Cheri pulled Baby to a halt, realizing in disbelief where the song had to be coming from.

It had been getting easier to hear the song as they traveled, although there were still no words. Amazingly, the volume was not really louder, and this had been puzzling her. "It's the trees!" she exclaimed in wonder. "The whole forest is singing."

"A great deal of it, yes. Isn't it wonderful? This is the only part of the world where the singing trees will grow. Before Barakus's time, all the great courts tried to grow their own singing trees. None of them succeeded. The trees sing here, for the occasional traveler or those willing to live close, like my friend the woodsman. In fact, in recent times, the last thousand years or so, their singing has become known as the Song of the Woodsman. That's why there are no farms closer than Bye's. Many people have superstitions about this forest and don't want to be too near. There are many who say spending too much time in the Singing Forest can drive a man mad. Many men avoid it for that very reason," explained Falcon, smiling broadly.

"Obviously you don't believe that or we wouldn't be going there. Oh, and the song is so lovely. I can't imagine ever getting tired of it." Cheri sighed dreamily.

"The trees like you, little one. They sing a different song for everyone and for you they've chosen a song especially sweet. There is no evil in the Singing Forest for the noise it makes for those with a deceptive heart is raucous indeed. For Barakus's priests the trees are said to reserve the most terrible of sounds. That is why, although few wish to visit the trees themselves, they are considered sacred, and no one cuts down the singing trees."

"Not even your friend, the woodsman? If he's a woodsman, surely he cuts down something?" protested Cheri.

"If you look closely, there are many other trees in this forest as well. He cuts down quick-growing trees like ash for firewood in the winter and hardy old trees like oak and wild cherry for furniture. He sometimes even cuts down the cedars and pines that grow close to the base of the Arid Mountains to take to Dink for building. He cuts judiciously, and the entire forest is better for it. No, Bass would be the very last to cut down the singing trees. He's the only man I know who lives among the trees. His family has lived there for generations, and the Samali still consider him an outsider because his hair is black and not red."

"Will we be stopping to meet this friend of yours? How long will it take to get to his cabin?" asked Cheri, suddenly very curious.

"Three or four days, depending on how fast we can travel. Amalee will spend the time with her kind, high in the trees. She will only rejoin us after we have left. She knows nothing can harm us here since the trees seem to like you and I've always gotten along with them. We should make good time indeed," said Falcon over his shoulder as he entered the narrow trail that seemed to head straight into the woods.

"That long? Oh well, so much longer to enjoy this enchanting singing. Right now, it reminds me of a lovely church choir I heard once. It was raining out, and I hid in the back of the church to stay dry. Of course, it smells better than incense. I was never a fan of incense," reminisced Cheri.

"Church choir?" asked Falcon, perplexed. "The only church we have around here is Barakus's church and the only singing you're likely to hear there would be produced at the prompting of the torturer. I can't even imagine going into a church for any reason, much less to stay out of the rain."

"Oh! Our churches are nothing like that! Most of them, especially where I come from, are churches dedicated to Jesus Christ. A man most believe was our savior. They are meant to be places of worship and sanctuary. The singing is for worship and joy. They sing joyful praises to the Lord," explained Cheri.

"A savior? Isn't that what you and your friends are supposed to be for us? Our saviors? When this is over, should we erect churches for you?"

"What? Oh no. No, no, no! What I didn't tell you was that Jesus was more than a man. He was also the son of God. The churches are built to his father as well as him," protested Cheri hastily.

"The son of God? Which god? Some people here believe in many gods. Barakus is said to worship the seven deities of the underworld. Each land had many gods before Barakus's shadow fell upon Persal," inquired Falcon curiously.

"We've...well, most of us have been taught there is only one god. There was a time many gods were worshiped, but we only acknowledge one God now. Is there maybe one god, perhaps with no statues, who is common to all the lands of Persal? Maybe one that Barakus took particular pains to try to eradicate? The underworld has always taken the greatest pains to destroy the faith of those whose beliefs were on the right track."

"There have been rumors of one such as that, but I don't know much about it. Well, aren't we being serious for such a beautiful summer day? Why don't we take advantage of the weather and the straight path the trees have provided and let the horses run for a while?" said Falcon as he heeled Wolf into a gallop, forcing a laughing Cheri to try to keep up with the packhorse trailing Wolf.

*****

Tasmin woke Faye as the cock crowed. "Come, dear, we've a long way to go before we sleep tonight. Especially if you want to sleep in a bed."

"Sometimes I think beds are highly overrated. Particularly when they're this lumpy," moaned Faye as she rolled off the mattress to sit on the edge. "There are many reasons I won't be sorry to leave this particular inn, though. I know Matew saw to the cleaning of this room, but all night long I felt as though bugs of some sort were crawling all over me."

"Be that as it may, get up and get dressed. I'm going to go see if Geo or Matew is about. I'll wager our horses will be saddled faster if one of them requests it. Apparently, they command quite a bit of respect in this village. When I come back, you can let me do your hair before we go down for a quick breakfast," said Tasmin as she bustled about the room, packing items they wouldn't be needing before they left.

As Tasmin opened the door, Faye shook out her blond curls and made her way to the tin pitcher of water to wash her face. Tasmin's yelp of surprise startled her just as she was lifting the pitcher to pour some water out in the basin, causing her to spill water everywhere.

"What?" she asked, looking at the door as Tasmin closed it hastily behind her.

"Matew! What are you doing out here? Have you been sleeping in front of our door?" came Tasmin's shocked voice.

"Sleepin'? No, ma'am. I been standin' watch since about midnigh'. Ever since pa woke me ter take me turn," said Matew honestly. "Pa woulda kilt me if'n I had fallen asleep."

"That really wasn't necessary, you know. Oh well, no help for it now. As long as you're here, would you be so kind as to go have our horses prepared to leave? We won't be staying much longer than is necessary to settle our bill."

"Yes, ma'am," acceded Matew, already halfway down the stairs.

When Tasmin stepped back into the room, Faye was reluctantly putting the clothes she'd worn the day before over her clean underwear. Somehow, airing them out just wasn't a good substitute for a clean change of clothes.

Downstairs they found the most bizarre activity going on in the common room. There were young men running everywhere as they helped the maids wash the windows, scrub the floors, and scour the tables. Jem the innkeeper was dashing between the common room and the kitchen, supervising everything. This morning, even his apron was clean.

"My goodness, Master Derf. Whatever has prompted this sudden leaning to cleanliness?" inquired Tasmin sweetly, deftly repressing a smile.

Jem glanced once at Faye's face before answering. "Yer horses, madam! Or at least that blasted stallion of yer'n, my lady," he cried with a slight bow in their direction. "When my guests came in last night, after stabling their horses, they wouldn't let me hear the end of it. How I treat animals better than paying customers. Many actually offered to pay more to sleep in the stable loft, with the horses. Yer stallion has forced this on me, my lady."

"Ah. Well, good sir, I'm quite sure it's all for the best. I think you'll find a little work and a lot of soap will soon see you more than recovering whatever losses you may have suffered recently. I can guarantee custom will be picking up immediately. Now, if you'll take this, I'm quite sure it will cover our bill," finished Tasmin, smiling broadly as she handed him five pieces of silver.

"Thank ye, ma'am. This is more than generous, I'm sure. Ye probably be right about custom pickin' up. When ye come agin, there'll be a room awaitin'," he called after them following them out the door and standing on the step, broom in hand, his somber eyes never leaving Faye.

Outside, Geo was waiting with fresh, hot meat pies and a packet of fresh bread for their trip.

"Master Bye, you must let us reimburse you for the expense you've incurred on our behalf, at least," insisted Faye as Tasmin accepted the gifts.

"Nay, nay. I'm right pleased I could help ye. Ye can pay me back by takin' Matew wit' ye."

"What? Isn't Matew returning with you to your farm?" asked Tasmin as Faye looked at her in confusion.

"Aye, my lady. The boy be tellin' me he has an urge ter travel wit ye a way, and when I tried to tell him nay, I could nay speak. I've giv'n him what I could, but that's no much. I'd appreciate it if'n ye'd help feed him in the towns. In the country, he be real good with his sling and likely ter provide ye with succulent meats. Ah, here he comes now," explained Geo, looking over their shoulders at the sound of approaching horses.

Turning, the ladies found themselves looking up and up as Matew approached on a very large draft horse that matched the large frame of Matew perfectly. The young man was leading their mounts and staring at Believer with a bemused expression on his face.

"Well, my lady Faye. It appears we're to have company for part of our journey. I have no doubt that his companionship will prove beneficial in many respects. Thank you again, Master Bye. We'll eat our pies on the road. We really must be going," said Tasmin as she mounted Anabelle.

"Yes, Master Bye. Thank you for everything. Perhaps we'll meet again and when we are able to thank you more properly," called Faye as she mounted. She kept glancing at Matew with a worried look on her face. She had no doubt he could see Believer as he really was, and the unicorn wasn't even trying to disguise himself as he had done so frequently in other villages. She was going to have to talk to him as soon as possible about keeping Believer's true nature a secret.

"How far do you plan to travel with us, Matew?" asked Faye as they rode out of the courtyard, and she noticed even the inn's faded sign was being painted. Evidently, Master Jem wasn't a man to do things halfway.

"I'm right sorry, my lady. I don't rightly know. I mean, I guess I'll stay until I don' feel needed any more, and I won' know that until it happens, will I? I'd guess at least as far as Dobe, maybe farther. Where do ye be headin', anyway?" asked Matew apologetically.

"Matew, I don't mean to be secretive, but I think it's best if we don't tell you any more than you need to know, for your own safety once we part company. Right now, all you need to know is we're going to pass through Dobe," answered Tasmin before Faye could speak up.

"Pa tol' me ye was on a chancy journey. Don' worry none. I no be afeared of danger. Ma has tol' me off'n enough I wouldna fear the evil one hissel' if'n he walked up ter me. I don' think I be that stupid but most thin's I don' worry about too much."

"Yes, I'm sure," said Tasmin with a shake of her head as she urged Anabelle into a ground-eating canter and Believer took the cue as well as the lead, effectively limiting any chance for conversation for the time being.

CHAPTER 11

It's a Long, Long Road

Behnam had insisted they ride until daybreak although Ebony was sure their pursuers had given up long before. When he finally called a halt near a stream babbling its way through the woods, all she could think of was sleep. It was funny, she'd been traveling like this for weeks, but this was the first time since the first day out of Nelas she could remember being really tired. Stubbornly, she insisted on taking care of George herself before she lay on the ground with her saddlebags for a pillow and fell asleep. She was going to pull her own weight if it killed her.

For two days, they slept under logs and bushes while Behnam continued to push them at night. On the third morning, she rebelled. "Behnam! There is no longer anyone chasing us. With the way things are, if we arrive in Dink too early, we will be in more danger there than we could possibly be on the road getting there. You may not have noticed it, but I am dirty. I am sweaty. I smell. And so, by the way, do you. There's a waterfall over there with a nice deep pool under it, and I intend to take a bath and wash my clothes. What I would appreciate from you would be a guarantee of some privacy. Unless you can give me one believable reason why we should continue to punish ourselves and the horses."

Shocked at her defiance, Behnam could only stare at her

mutely, which Ebony took as an affirmative answer. "Thank you. Please don't come too close. I wouldn't want to have to hurt you," she snapped as she grabbed her saddlebags and strode across the clearing, stepping behind a bush before she began to disrobe.

Behnam found himself smiling as he turned away, and his years of living in the unforgiving desert took over, his senses automatically scanning their surroundings for possible danger. He could hear Ebony singing softly as the waterfall splashed down on her, cleansing her skin. When her singing cut off abruptly, he instinctively whirled to see what the problem was only to watch her rise, with her back toward him, from where she had been swimming underwater. On her lower back, he spied a tattoo of something strange with wings and two heads. In the beauty of the scene, he had momentarily forgotten he was to give her privacy until she called out. "Behnam! If you've satisfied your curiosity, do you think you could turn around again? Now? I'm beginning to get chilly, and I'd like to get out."

Behnam laughed and started to turn away as she reached for the piece of cloth she planned to use as a towel when he realized what he had seen out of the corner of his eye. Spinning back, he sprinted across the clearing and dove for Ebony, landing them both in the deeper part of the pool. Pushing her away from him, he regained his footing and drew his scimitar, slicing the air beneath the branch of an overhanging tree.

Ebony saw something go flying to land on the narrow beach. As Behnam bent over to catch his breath, she could see the body of an oversized snake still dangling from the branch. Its head was missing. Clutching the sopping wet cloth she still held against her body, she pulled herself against Behnam and shuddered, scanning the other trees near the pool for more. "It's a snake! Where did it come from? Is it poisonous?" she asked in a babble.

Still panting from his run across the clearing, Behnam looked down at her appreciatively before he answered. "Yes, I think it's poisonous, but don't worry. You should be all right now. Except for mating season in the spring, these snakes are solitary creatures. Preferring to hunt alone."

Following Behnam's gaze, Ebony looked down at herself as she pulled away from him again. Blushing furiously, she pushed Behnam hard, causing him to tumble back into the water before she made her way to the beach, pausing curiously to examine the snake's triangular head. As Behnam resurfaced, he called out, "Don't touch it! There's still venom on the horn at the top of his head."

Without bothering to answer, she grabbed her saddlebags and stalked behind a bush. "You might as well take a bath yourself since you're already wet," she called back. "I'll keep watch for you."

Looking down at himself, Behnam shrugged in acceptance and began stripping off his clothes, revealing a broad, well-defined back that Ebony could see as she peered through her bush. She watched him rinse his clothes well before laying them on the sun baked flat rocks beside her own nearly dry ones and grabbing her bar of soap. Forcing herself to turn away, she snatched her still damp Mojar clothes and, a moment later, reappeared to sit on a rock in the middle of the clearing as she dried her braids. With a show of indifference, she kept her back to the pool, only occasionally glancing in her mirror as she checked her hair. She tried not to give herself away by looking in the mirror too long.

When Behnam emerged from the pool and redressed, he finally agreed it was probably safe to return to the highway and try their luck again in the throng traveling to Dink. With any luck, there would be other Mojar traveling as well.

Curious, Behnam looked over at Ebony as they prepared to leave, "What did you mean back at the inn? When you called *incoming*?"

Looking up at the tall Mojar, something like pain flashed in her eyes before she answered. "It's nothing, and I don't want to talk about it. You wouldn't understand anyway."

Behnam frowned thoughtfully at her bent head before he mounted Desert Wind. "Let's go," he said tersely.

They spent the early part of the night heading toward the highway before making camp. Behnam and Ebony rode out onto the road early the next morning, before too many people, carts and wagons would slow their progress. Behnam cantered down the road with his usual arrogance. "Why don't we just wave a flag telling them where we are?" asked Ebony sarcastically, keeping her voice low.

"The people here expect the Mojar to behave in a certain way, Cadir. Acting like less than we are would only make us stand out more. We can hardly expect to pass for a local here. Our hair isn't red enough." Behnam laughed, his eyes never leaving the growing crowd of mostly red-haired men and women around them.

Ebony had to smile to herself as she was forced to agree. The pale, freckled faces that predominated in the crowd only seemed to emphasize their own dark complexions. Trying to be inconspicuous here would be like trying to hide a lion in a litter of kittens.

*****

Much to Falcon's amazement, fascination and eventual annoyance, Cheri had taken to singing with the trees. Apparently, if she would start singing a song, the trees would simply change their song to match hers. This would have been all right if she had sung any of the ballads he was used to, but while her repertoire was varied, it held nothing he recognized. Even the type of music she sang rang oddly in his ears. There was no way for him to join in. He had tried a couple of times to begin the singing himself, but the trees simply ignored his efforts. This was especially galling since he had been known in the past to earn his way as a troubadour and in his opinion, Cheri's voice was sweet but untrained and hardly spectacular.

For two days she had sung songs with such confusing words:

> I thought love was only true in fairy tales
> Meant for someone else but not for me
> Love was out to get me
> That's the way it seemed
> Disappointment haunted all my dreams
> Then I saw her face, now I'm a believer[*]

And:

> I come home in the morning light
> My mother says, when you gonna get your life right?
> Oh, mother dear, we're not the fortunate ones
> Girls they want to have fu...un
> Oh, girls just want to have fu...un[**]

And:

> Sugar, ah, honey, honey
> You are my candy girl
> And you got me wanting you
> Honey, ah, sugar, sugar[***]

----

[*] "I'm a Believer" by Neil Diamond
[**] "Girls Just Want to Have Fun" by Cyndi Lauper
[***] "Sugar, Sugar" by the Archies

Then there were the ballads that didn't even tell a story. When he'd mentioned this particular omission, Cheri had been silent for a few moments before she sang a song called "Demons,"* which told a story, of sorts, but one he couldn't quite understand. No doubt about it, he was grateful they would be reaching Bass's cabin any time now. It seemed the trees liked her singing so much they had opened a direct path to Bass for them.

Cheri and the forest were singing a song called "Amazing Grace." Cheri said it was a hymn and Falcon found it comforting even if he wasn't quite sure what it meant. She was still singing as they rode into the small clearing around Bass's cabin. Bass himself was standing on his porch, waiting as the setting sun bathed his tall, well- muscled physique in red and gold.

His eyes took in Falcon at a glance before his searching gaze swept past him and fastened on Cheri as if he'd been expecting her.

"Good day, friend Falcon. Who is this adorable child who has so bewitched my trees that they have been singing her praises for the past two days? A wood sprite, perhaps?" Bass asked in greeting, his vivid blue eyes never leaving Cheri's face as he ran his fingers thoughtfully through his unruly black hair.

Cheri had stopped singing as she returned his stare, smiling shyly at the compliment. "Bass, you appear to be fit, as usual. This is Cheri. Not a wood sprite, I believe, but you may find her story even more amazing."

"Will the two of you stop talking about me as if I weren't right here? I would also appreciate it if you would cease calling me a child and remember I'm a young woman," broke in Cheri in exasperation.

"My apologies, Lady Cheri. You're quite right, of course. In fact, there are several ways I've been remiss in my manners.

Lady Cheri, may I introduce myself, my name is Bass. Jarl, were he still with me, would never forgive me if he knew I'd left you sitting on your horses for so long. Won't the two of you come in and join me in a hot meal?" amended Bass with a low bow.

"Who's Jarl? What did you mean when you said I'd bewitched your trees? I have no real magical powers, you know. We just enjoy singing together," babbled Cheri defensively as she dismounted.

"Jarl was my manservant and guardian. His family has served mine for generations. He died several months ago. As for the trees, perhaps yes, perhaps no. I have lived here all my life and my family for many generations before me. Never has it been known for the trees to sing with anyone. Until now, they have always persistently sung their own songs. Whether it is magic or not, I cannot say, but there is no doubt there is something special about you," explained Bass as he helped Falcon unsaddle the horses and take their bundles from the packhorse.

When they were through, Bass ushered her into his cabin while Falcon put the horses in the paddock next to the small stable. There was a succulent roast, summer green beans, and baked purple potatoes waiting for them at a table set for three. "You were expecting us!" she exclaimed in surprise as she mulled over what he'd said. It seemed a bit strange to her that a woodsman would have a manservant.

"Yes, of course. The trees always tell me when company is coming. They also tell me what kind of company to expect. That is why I did not greet you with ax in hand," said Bass calmly as he motioned for her to sit and sat at the head of the table himself. Falcon was quick to join them.

"Are you coming with us, old friend?" asked Falcon as he chewed on a generous piece of roast meat.

"My wagon has been loaded for a week, yet every time I

think it's time to leave, something keeps me here. Lady Cheri, you must be the one I've been waiting for?"

Cheri spluttered around a mouthful of food for a moment before she could choke down enough to get the words out. "What do you mean you've been waiting for me? Falcon, why are you assuming Bass will be joining us? Would someone please tell me what's going on?"

"Remember that compulsion I had that brought me to, uh, meet you? Well, I had that same compulsion to come here. I even mentioned coming through the Singing Forest before we split up with the others. Until that happened, I thought we would all be coming here. When we separated, I realized it would only be the two of us. I simply assumed Bass was having a similar experience. Why else would we be here?" explained Falcon.

"Ah! Yes, I see," said Bass. "Not only have I been waiting here, but I usually take oak and cherry wood to the village to be made into furniture at this time of year. Today my wagon is loaded with the best ash in the forest for firewood, which seemed most strange. 'Tis the wrong time of the year to make much profit on firewood. I have also packed for traveling in the winter although summer is not half-gone. Why don't the two of you tell me why?"

Falcon looked to Cheri in confusion for a moment, "Uh, perhaps you can do this better than I?"

"Well, I guess. Apparently, my friends and I have been brought here from our world because of some prophecy. Something about saving Persal from Barakus. On our travels to Lohi to talk to Gabriene, we've been picking up companions, whether we want them or not. It looks like you're going to be next. As for the firewood and the winter clothes, well, it looks like you know more than we do. Although Mistress Bye did say something about unseasonably cool nights, didn't she?" elaborated Cheri obligingly.

"Yes, she did. Perhaps winter will be very early this year?" ventured Falcon.

"Then that would be very early indeed. Does Barakus know that you are here and why?" asked Bass.

"I was afraid you were going to ask that. I'll tell you what, if I can have a nice hot bath somewhere private, I'll let Falcon tell you what's happened to us so far and you can judge for yourself. As for the future, I'll tell you what Tasmin keeps telling us, we have to wait until we see Gabriene in Lohi," offered Cheri as she finished the last of her potatoes and rose from the table.

"There's a tub in the next room and water boiling on the hob. Just let me fill your tub and get you a towel, and we'll leave you alone while Falcon and I talk," offered Bass genially.

Cheri settled back into the welcome hot water to soak and stared at the beamed ceiling thoughtfully. Things were becoming stranger and stranger as they traveled. "I wonder what's happening to Faye and Tasmin? I hope they're not having any difficulties. On the other hand, Ebony and Behnam are probably fighting more with each other than anyone else. I just hope they all make it in one piece to Dink," she murmured aloud.

*****

The pouring rain had long ago plastered Beloria's red hair to her head, and her serviceable brown cloak was no protection at all, but she continued to row. Her muscles ached, and her work-hardened hands had started to bleed from blisters raised by the unfamiliar task, but she was almost there. Suddenly a loud thump from the boat hitting the jetty knocked her from the wooden seat. Righting herself and turning around, she saw she was against the stone dock, and the white tower was looming above her. She had arrived.

Hurrying, now, she tied the boat to a docking cleat as she

had seen at the wharf in Lohi and scrambled up. Holding up her skirts, she tried to run, but the rain and wind made it difficult. She had to slow anyway when she reached the end of the pier and started climbing the rough-cut steps that zigzagged up the stone estuary.

Breathless, she paused for just a moment and looked again at the white tower that had haunted her dreams and driven her here. Dreams that had been a relief from the other ones. The strange dreams that had been haunting her since she was seven, where she was always running. Running from an unseen hunter. Every time, when she had finally lost the hunter and paused at a pool to cool her thirst, she looked down to see her reflection. Only it was never her reflection. Once she had been a red-stripped badger. Another time a red stag. Always a different animal but always red. When she woke in the morning, her nightgown was ruined, full of snags and small holes and covered in mud. Her hands and feet were muddy and bruised as well.

Now she was here, and maybe this tower would protect her from the other dreams or maybe it would help her understand them. Once again, she looked up at the towering white edifice and smiled. Now that she had arrived, why did she feel as though she had come home? The storm seemed to slow, and she ran eagerly to the door at the tower's base to knock. There was no doubt in her mind she would be welcome.

*****

Faye, Tasmin, and Matew had traveled for two days, stopping at another dusty town and staying at another dingy inn each night. Faye actually welcomed returning to the saddle each morning since sleeping on a lumpy mattress did little to relieve her fatigue. On the other hand, Believer did wonders for her well-being.

The first day out, she had drawn Matew aside when they

stopped late in the morning to eat their still warm meat pies. "Matew, what do you see when you look at Believer?" she asked.

"Why, Lady Faye!" he began in an excited voice.

"Hush! Keep your voice low!" commanded Faye, clamping her hand over his mouth. Once he had nodded in agreement, she removed it again.

Matew's eyes were large with suppressed excitement as he forced himself to whisper, "I see a unicorn, of course, my lady."

"That's what I thought. Matew, has it occurred to you most people can't see him that way? Most people, including Lady Tasmin, only see a fine white stallion."

"Really? How very odd. I wonder why that be, my lady?"

"It's quite simple, really. Only virgins can see a unicorn, Matew," explained Faye gently.

Matew blushed furiously, "Well, I be savin' meself fer marriage, my lady. It ain' like I haven' had offers," he mumbled defensively.

"Of course! I knew that, Matew. After all, what woman wouldn't be honored to give herself to a fine young man like yourself? In fact, I'd guess when you go into town with your father there are some women brazen enough to throw themselves your way. Aren't there?"

Matew had been puffing himself up at Faye's words, "Ye don' ken how for'ard some of those town girls be, my lady."

"No, I suppose I don't. What I really wanted to talk about is how important it is not to let anyone know Believer is anything more than an ordinary horse. Do you know what some people would do if they found out?" urged Faye gently.

"Not even Lady Tasmin?" he asked in amazement.

"Not even Lady Tasmin. You see, it's not our secret, is it? It's Believer's secret. Of course, Lady Tasmin would never betray him, but the more people who know, the greater the danger he is in. You do understand, don't you, Matew?" pleaded Faye, her blue eyes meeting his pale-green ones.

With another shy smile, Matew nodded. "Aye, Lady Faye. I understand. Don' worry, I ain' never betrayed a confidence in me life an' I won' start now. I 'ave only one more question, my lady. Are we the only two who ken? I mean, can't anyone else see him in the villages or on the road?"

"Well, being a unicorn means he has powers. Among them is the power to masquerade as a horse, when necessary. Although he doesn't seem to bother with children for some reason, when there are any around. Now, I want to thank you, my friend. Believer knew he could trust you. Now I do too," she assured him with a smile as she returned to the fire where Tasmin was brewing her tea.

Faye had put the whole thing out of her mind, and now it was the morning of the third day, and it showed all the signs of being as uneventful as the last two. Tasmin was pleased things were going so well, but Faye, who had led a rather mundane life before finding herself in this strange land, was about ready for something to happen. It seemed to her all the quaint little villages and picturesque inns were becoming one in her mind. The absence of young children was also depressing, and she was beginning to think she didn't want to know where they were. They would be arriving in Dobe tonight. Perhaps a Samalian city would at least offer some variety.

They had been riding near the center of the road, as usual. It was the best place for people on horseback unless a wagon demanded precedence. Those on foot or with push barrows usually converged to one side or the other, the easier to move out of the way when necessary. Behind them could be heard a commotion and Faye turned in her saddle to investigate. A troop of soldiers escorting a coach was riding at a fast trot down the middle of the road, sending everyone running for the ditch on either side. Tasmin and Matew were hastily urging their horses and the mules into the field just beyond the ditch. "Faye! Quit daydreaming and get out of the way!" commanded Tasmin frantically.

With a shrug, Faye did as she was told, albeit a bit slower than Tasmin would have liked. She was quite sure she'd never been in danger. After all, Believer would protect them both.

She had just joined Tasmin and Matew, who were off their horses and bowing, when the entourage came alongside and a voice from within the carriage called a halt. Despite Tasmin's urgent motions, Faye remained seated and watched calmly as the soldiers, who appeared to belong to the church, judging by their ragtag appearance, came to an undisciplined halt and their leader rode back to check on his passengers.

None of the people huddling in the ditches moved as three priests emerged from the carriage in deep discussion. Tasmin and Matew stood up behind Faye. Matew had his staff in his hand, like a walking stick. "Captain! Have that young woman come here! Immediately!" shouted the tall thin one as he stroked his well-combed beard, pointing in the general direction of Faye.

Without waiting for the ill-kempt soldiers to approach her, Faye sat very straight as she urged Believer forward. Ignoring the captain as he tried to get her to dismount, she addressed this priest she remembered all too well and who appeared to be in charge. The same one she has last seen with Falcon at the gates of Nelas. "You wished to speak to me, sir priest?" she inquired in the haughty voice she had perfected in the last few days.

"Yes, young woman. You appear to be familiar. There is also something else, something I sense. Have we met before? In Nelas, perhaps?" he asked, searching her face carefully.

"I, sir? I think not. I usually don't associate with, ah... those of the priesthood," she answered disdainfully.

"Perhaps I was at the gate when you left the city, in the evening, about ten days ago?" he pressed. His associates were carefully watching her and keeping an eye on the crowd at the same time.

"In the evening? Ten days ago? No, no…I left the city at least two weeks ago, early in the morning. Too early for me, I must admit. In Rim, I seldom rise before midday. Besides which, I would not press my stallion by traveling the distance in only ten days," returned Faye, improvising.

"Wat! What about her companions? Neither of them matches the descriptions we have. Didn't you say that the fair woman you saw was with a lean, swarthy man with long, brown, straight hair? Look at that boy! Does he appear to fit the description you gave? Then there's the other woman, nowhere was there mention of another woman. Surely this, this sense that Barakus has given us has been confused with something else. It doesn't feel as it should. Perhaps it is the sight of an attractive woman, again," hissed the portly priest with unkempt hair as he glanced derisively at their companion.

"We all know you are quite the ladies' man, Wat, but we haven't time for this now. We must be on our way," hissed the short bald one, blushing as he returned to the carriage followed by the portly one who had to be pushed up the steps by two of the soldiers.

"One more question! Your name, please, and those of your companions. Also where you hail from?" asked Wat persistently.

"I am Lady Faye Goran of Rim, sir. My father is the Duc D'Orleans of Camir. In all probability he will be the next regent," answered Faye, drawing herself up proudly. "The Lady Tasmin is my duenna, and we have hired this young man from Samal for protection on the road."

"I will remember that, my lady. I will remember," he said

as he rejoined his friends and motioned to the captain to continue the journey.

When their dust had cleared, Faye found Tasmin and Matew had returned to her side while their fellow travelers were climbing out of the ditches, staring at her and murmuring among themselves. Matew looked around for a moment before twirling his staff expertly, in a subtle threat and the crowd sorted itself out as they resumed their journey to Dobe.

"Faye! What were you thinking?" hissed Tasmin furiously as she pulled Anabelle against Believer, forcing him back to the side of the road. Pulling close, she looked Faye in the eye.

Faye responded casually. "Why, I was just behaving the way the nobility of Camir would be expected to behave, Tasmin."

Matew pulled up against the other side of Believer. "What did you expect me to do, Lady Faye? Fight that whole troop of soldiers?" asked a perplexed Matew towering over the two women from his red-and-white draft horse, Dobbin.

"Don't be silly, Matew. Of course not. I knew it would never come to actual combat," said Faye confidently.

"What do you mean you knew? How could you know? When will you get it through your head, the priesthood has the full weight of Barakus behind them? Especially now? To defy them could bring the wrath of Barakus down on you, and sadly there would be few who would dare to help if it came to that," insisted Tasmin vehemently.

"Tasmin, have you ever actually met a Camir noble? How would they deal with such a situation? I was quite civil. I answered all their questions. I simply didn't bow to them. From what you told me, the Camir nobility doesn't bow to anyone. Although they might make an exception if their lost king were found."

"You took a terrible chance, Faye. It was reckless and inconsiderate, no matter how well you may have been staying in character."

"My lady, I know I be a brawny man and can beat any ten normal men if things had gone wrong. The church soldiers are known to be a sad lot, so I may be able to beat fifteen of them, but there were twenty-five of those scrawny rats today, and I be not so sure I could have held me own," objected Matew.

"Matew, please! We would not have expected you to fight alone if it had come to that. Lady Faye and I are quite capable of puncturing some of those dirty rags they call uniforms. Be that as it may, it wasn't necessary. This time. Well, I suggest we get on our way. The day is getting longer, and we've a ways to go before we reach Dobe," said Tasmin, deftly ignoring Faye's logic.

"Tasmin, Matew, whatever you may think, please be assured we were never in any danger. You'll just have to take my word on it," insisted Faye as she urged Believer into the lead, winking at Matew as they passed each other.

As they rode out, Faye bent over Believer's mane to pat his neck. "We know something they don't, don't we, Believer? You and I together are a team that can't be beaten," she whispered.

Matew urged Dobbin up next to Believer. "It be the unicorn, don' it, Lady Faye?" he whispered so Tasmin, at the rear with the mules, couldn't overhear.

"Yes. But please, remember your promise."

"Aye, my lady. Aye," he answered thoughtfully as he dropped back to the rear again.

*****

It had been raining for two steady hours by the time Behnam and Ebony arrived at the muddy town of Palade that evening. Palade was large enough to be a town. Larger than the villages Ebony had seen so far and except for the main road, the streets seemed to be a little better than narrow alleys. Perhaps it would look better in bright sunshine, but it was late, and Ebony was cold, wet, and hungry. She was in no mood to give the town the benefit of any doubts she had.

Behnam inquired at all four of the inns the town boasted about a private room, but none could be found. In fact, most of the inns had no room at all. Just as Ebony was about to suggest they settle for a hot meal and a spot on the common room floor, Behnam returned with news. "This is the last inn in town, and we have our choice. We can sleep in a bed with four other men or in the stable with the horses."

"Thank goodness! I hope you told them we'd take the hayloft." Ebony sighed wearily.

"I did, but you should know the roof leaks over the hayloft. They were in the process of repairing it when the storm hit. We may not be able to stay much dryer than we are now. Also, there's a chance others looking for shelter from this storm will be joining us," warned Behnam as he led Desert Wind toward the ancient stone stable that was apparently under repair.

"Right now, I don't much care. As long as I have time to get into dry clothes first, I can put up with anything. As the first, we can at least find the driest spot to sleep," she answered as they passed beneath the swaying sign depicting a bright blue ox. *The Blue Ox? Did that mean Paul Bunyan had slept here?* she wondered through a fog as George stepped into the warm stable. Well, if nothing else, the body heat from all the horses should keep them warm tonight.

"In that case, Cadir, I suggest you allow me to take care of our horses while you hurry about your change. I'll try to stall anyone who comes in," offered Behnam graciously.

"Thank you, Behnam. You can be sweet when you want to," said Ebony contritely before she climbed into the loft, smelling of sweet, fresh hay, and found a corner that wasn't currently leaking in which to hurriedly change.

She had just gotten out of her wet clothes when it occurred to her—she didn't have any dry Mojar clothes to change into. All she had were the clothes Tasmin had provided and her karate outfit. That was it! It wasn't exactly what she needed, but it was the closest she could come to on such short notice. As she was pulling everything out of her saddlebags to get to the garments packed at the bottom more than a month ago, she heard voices below. Oh no! Someone was here. Maybe they were just bringing in a horse, but she couldn't take the chance. Frantic now, she dumped everything into the hay and pulled her white suit and black belt out of the pile.

Suddenly Behnam's voice raised so she could hear what he was saying. "Ah, brother! It is lucky indeed that you will be joining us. It is so rare to find another Mojar so far from our own sacred sands. There are few who care to venture out among the barbarians."

"Even among these people, one can find men of honor, Behnam. It is just a shame they seem to be so rare," came the strange voice as it moved closer. Hastily Ebony pulled on her dry clothes. "Come, let us get settled. I can't wait to get out of my wet tabanak."

"I quite agree. I have bribed one of the stable boys to go to the inn for hot stew. I do not care to go out in that downpour again myself," agreed Behnam as he took the lead. His head cleared the loft floor just as Ebony was tying her belt, remembering to leave it loose enough to not be revealing. Hastily she grabbed a length of cloth and wrapped her long braids out of sight.

"Ah, Cadir! I see you have changed. That's good. I know our mother coddles you and she would never forgive me should you fall ill on foreign soil. He is our mother's youngest, and our father allowed her to spoil him. While she could not keep him at home any longer, she made me promise nothing would happen while we were traveling among the pale skins," he explained to the man below him on the ladder. "Cadir, this is Kali, eldest son of Shemar of the Maudi tribe."

"Well, I know how mothers can be," came the strange voice in reply as Behnam finally allowed him to finish the climb into the loft. As he appeared, Ebony saw a Mojar of incredibly good looks. His curly hair was long and wet about his face, which had a strong nose and straight lips curled into a smile. His hazel-green eyes were dancing with mirth, despite his wet attire. As he settled down near herself and Behnam, he began to peel off the loose wet clothes to reveal a well-muscled torso. Ebony busied herself with repacking her saddlebags. Keeping herself turned away as she tried to keep him from seeing what she had in her hands and forced herself not to stare. Behnam also stripped out of his wet clothing, and soon the two of them were in nothing but their loincloths. Trying to hide her shyness with busy work, she found a rail to hang her clothes on to dry, and when Behnam tossed his wet clothes to her, she hung those up as well.

Kali stepped over to hang his own clothes and plucked at her sleeve. "What strange clothes are these? I have never seen their like before," he asked with a raised eyebrow.

"We found those in a bazaar in Jahl last year. A trader had a few he had bought from a distant land. Even he wasn't sure where they were from. Cadir has taken a fancy to wearing them when his clothes require cleaning," answered Behnam lazily as he lay back on his bedroll.

Mercifully the stable boy arrived with hot stew, fresh bread, and three bowls before Kali could ask any more questions. They were all soon busily engaged in eating. Once the meal was completed, Ebony wrapped herself in her own bedroll and turned toward the wall to sleep. It would be best to allow Behnam to deal with Kali tonight.

CHAPTER 12

Flight of a Thousand Hawks

The storm that hit Ebony to the northwest missed Dobe entirely, and Faye was delighted! Dobe appeared to be the closest thing to real civilization she had seen yet. While the design and buildings of the city were ancient beyond imagining, it was a city well cared for. The broad stone walls were still high and in good repair. The massive wooden gates with their shiny brass fittings looked relatively new, as if they had been replaced not more than five or six years ago. The people who lived here were still putting value on their lives.

The three of them passed through the gates and onto the uneven cobblestones with barely a glance from the smartly dressed city guards, although they did stop a man who looked rough around the edges and was carrying a pair of axes on his back, for questioning. These were not the slovenly church soldiers she had seen before. These were men who had some pride. Barakus may hold most of this land in a death grip, but obviously, not everyone had given up the fight.

Faye was so enchanted by the clean, wide avenues with their parklike rows of trees down the center she failed to notice the two church soldiers who broke away to follow them once they were away from the gate. Matew, temporarily separated by the crowd and following a short distance behind, saw them clearly. They were two of the soldiers from the road, which was suspicious. Discreetly he rode up next to Tasmin and nodded in their direction.

"Thank you, Matew. I am aware. Do not worry about it. I will take care of it shortly," she replied quietly, not changing her pace or appearing to be concerned. "Follow me."

Obediently, Matew dropped back into the crowd, making way for a gaily colored vendor's cart crossing the road.

They traveled for some distance before Tasmin turned into the bustling courtyard of a large and prosperous inn. The sign with its three red bells proclaimed it to be the Inn of the Red Bells. As soon as they arrived, the innkeeper in his starched white apron stretched about his amazingly round belly was bustling down the steps and shouting orders to his stable men. "Shut those gates! Do ye intend to allow all the beggars and stray dogs in Dobe into my courtyard? Quickly now! Quickly."

Tasmin had dismounted and was standing next to Anabelle as their host sent anyone who appeared to be too idle about their work. Faye and Matew dismounted next to her.

"Tasmin, my dear! That is you, isn't it?" he asked in a much lower voice, once the gates were closed and the soldiers were on the outside.

"Yes, it is, Master Griggs. After all of these years, it appears I am working again," said Tasmin, smiling up at him.

"It also appears you be havin' similar problems, again. Follow me and we'll send ye on yer way. It will be some time afore they know ye have eluded them, I promise ye," he said, leading the way into his suddenly deserted stable. At the far end, he pressed on a panel and a tall, thin door appeared. Large enough for the horses to pass, one at a time. Rising on tiptoe, Tasmin kissed Master Griggs on the cheek before she led the way into a passage too narrow to be called an alley.

"Tasmin, what is this corridor? Where are we going?

What's going on?" whispered Faye frantically once the hidden door had disappeared behind them.

"Hush, child. I'll tell you later. There are many things going on here that I don't have time to explain now," shushed Tasmin in a low voice.

"Tell me about it," muttered a bewildered Faye. She was about to open her mouth as though to speak again when a stern look from Tasmin convinced her to hold her peace, for now.

As they wound their way through the twists and turns of the passage, Matew let out a whistle of appreciation while Faye looked at the high walls towering overhead and shutting out most of the light, totally lost. They had gone some distance before Tasmin pushed at a section of the wall in front of them that looked like all the other walls they had passed, and another door opened. This one led to a small area behind the stable in another inn's courtyard. "Wait here and be quiet," said Tasmin commandingly as she handed Anabelle's reins to Faye.

Faye was filling up with questions and beginning to fidget when Tasmin finally returned with a man who could be the twin of Master Griggs, only rounder, if that were possible.

"Welcome! Welcome to the Red Crown! Please, follow me and I will see you are properly settled in your rooms. Tasmin, my dear, I presume you'll be eating in the private dining room? I have an excellent roast pig available tonight, or perhaps the roast beef? Chicken? I know, I'll send in a selection of meats with fresh bread, potatoes, cheese, fruit, and jibbers. The jibbers just came in this morning, very succulent, very fresh. Come, come children. Jepper, see to our guests' horses and bring up their saddlebags," babbled their host as he led them around to the busy courtyard.

"Butter, you haven't changed a bit! You still don't allow a

body to get a word in edgewise." Tasmin laughed with a wry shake of her head.

"Nor have you dear friend, nor have you," rejoined Butter with a hearty laugh of his own as he led the way through the airy common room with its many windows and down a short hall to the private dining room.

This room had a large, well-scrubbed wooden table, surrounded by twelve high-backed armchairs with leather seats. The walls were lined with bookshelves crammed with books. Matew's mouth opened in awe as he crossed to the nearest shelf and started to read the titles in a low voice. "*The Champions Ride Forth.* Oh, wouldn't Cato love that one. And look! *The Travels of Chiad.* I never thought to get a chance to read that. What a wondrous place. Never have I seen so many books. Master Butter, you must be wealthy indeed. Cato will never believe it!"

Tasmin was glancing around as though she had come home after a long time and was looking to see what might have changed. "It hasn't changed a bit, Butter. You know, I think I actually missed you and this place," she said with a wistful smile.

Faye also studied the rest of the room for the first time as she waited impatiently for Butter to leave. There were several windows, placed high to allow in the light but ensure privacy at the same time. There was also a fireplace at one end of the room, but this was July and no fire was laid today. Except for a little dust on the books, the room was spotlessly clean.

"I'll leave you and your friends here while I make all the necessary arrangements for your stay, dear lady. I can promise you won't be disturbed."

"Thank you, Butter. As usual, you and your brother have served well," congratulated Tasmin as the door was closing behind their host.

Once the door was closed, Faye turned to Tasmin and let

the questions loose. "What was that all about? Where are we? I got completely lost in that labyrinth back there. Why did you suddenly feel all of this need to secrecy again? Tasmin, what's going on?"

"Why don't you sit down and make yourself comfortable, dear? I'll explain as best I can," urged Tasmin as she crossed to Faye and gently pushed her into one of the plush chairs. "You were too busy looking at Dobe to notice the church soldiers following us from the gate, but Matew and I did. It seems your friends back there on the road haven't given up on us yet. The little escape route we took back there is part of the underground. Any time there are church soldiers after you, you are aided, without question. If the church soldiers are after you, you must be on the right side. Also, I know the Griggs brothers from when I was still active in the resistance. Right now, we are very near the east gate. We'll leave shortly after the gates open in the morning. Our biggest problem is, after your little conversation on the road today, you and Believer have become very conspicuous. After dinner, I think Matew should hit a tavern or two to see what gossip he can pick up while we discuss what we can do in the way of damage control. One thing is sure—changes have got to be made. Right now, I think I'll clean up before we eat," she finished rolling up her sleeves and crossing to a low table with a washbasin in one corner.

Contritely, Faye followed suit while Matew waited for them to finish before washing his own hands.

They had barely settled at the table when there was a light tap on the door followed by Butter himself as he held the door for his kitchen boys carrying enough food for twenty. First, there was a large pork roast as well as a good-sized hunk of roast beef and a roast chicken. The meats were followed by a huge bowl of potatoes, another of a vegetable that resembled broccoli except it appeared to be a little blue and leafy. Then came a serving maid with three baskets of freshly baked rolls and another maid with a wheel of cheese on a tray. Finally, a younger boy appeared with a large basket of fruit and a bowl of freshly churned butter. Faye's hunger took over as the three of them sat down to eat, so she put her misgivings regarding Tasmin's changes aside, for now anyway.

They'd been eating for a good fifteen minutes before Matew looked up from his third heaping platter of food. "Lady Tasmin, ye be more knowin' about this town than I be. Mayhap ye ken which taverns I be most likely to hear what we need?" he asked around a mouthful of pork and potatoes.

"I probably could, but I think it would be best to have Butter give you the directions you need, Matew. I haven't been here in years, and while things change slowly in Dobe, they do change. As soon as you've finished with that platter, I'll ring for Butter and explain things to him," she answered, smiling as Matew looked at the still full table and then his crowded plate. Apparently, he had planned to eat quite a bit more before calling it quits. "Don't worry. I'll be sure we keep the food warm for your return. You won't go to bed hungry tonight, Matew. Oh, and I'll ask Butter if you can have one of his prize books. For me, he might let one go," she promised.

"Yes, my lady. Thank you," he said as he returned to the task of eating the food on his plate.

Faye had filled up rather quickly. She'd found the blue jibbers especially good although she'd rather enjoyed the roast beef as well. Now she decided it was time to open the conversation with Tasmin while she munched on a delicious green fruit that tasted somewhat like a nectarine only somehow more succulent. "Isn't Butter an unusual name for an old man, even here?" she asked.

"Actually, it's a nickname. As I heard it, when he was a child, he was always called Butterball, and as he grew up it was shortened to Butter. He takes it in good humor, and only his friends call him that. Everyone else calls him Master Griggs, like his brother," Tasmin explained with a fond smile.

Matew was about finished with his meal, so Tasmin rang the bell sitting in front of her on the table. Butter appeared almost immediately. "What more can I do for you, Tasmin? Would the ladies care for a hot bath now?" he asked hospitably.

"That sounds like heaven but not yet, Butter dear. Right now, our friend Matew here needs some directions to a tavern or two where he might find information on the activities of the priests in these parts without arousing suspicion. Perhaps you can help him?" she asked sweetly.

"Do ye gamble, boy? Throw the dice? Play crowns and swords? Tiles and sticks? Perhaps a little stones?" asked Butter curiously, waiting for Matew's head to shake after each inquiry before he finally asked about stones and got a nod. "Well, not the best, but it will do. Are you any good at it?"

"I always beat me brother Cato and lately I been beatin' pa more than not. I only played in the village a few times, but I won more than I lost. Why?"

"Well, the best way to learn what you want to know is to get a man to talking while his mind is on gambling. Tasmin, if you can give the boy some money he can afford to lose I have just the place in mind. Remember, boy, you're not going out there to win, you're trying to get information. It shouldn't take more than a game or two in each tavern to learn what you need," finished the innkeeper as Tasmin fished several silver and brass coins from her purse to hand to Matew before he was ushered from the room.

Finally, Faye and Tasmin were alone and could discuss the matter of her disguise and what to do about Believer. "Tasmin, earlier you mentioned my stallion had become as conspicuous as I had. You also said something about changes to be made. What did you mean by that?" she asked hesitantly.

"Well, obviously those three priests, at least, have their

suspicions about your identity, dear. After your encounter on the road a very good description as well. It wouldn't do us much good to disguise your looks and then put you back on that horse who stands out as much or more than you do, does it?" answered Tasmin as she took a sip of her wine.

"You're saying we should get rid of Believer, aren't you?" said Faye, her voice rising.

"Yes, dear, I'm afraid so."

"But you can't, you just can't! I mean, Believer is special. Remember what Falcon said about bringing him up to the valley? He's part of everything, just like I am or you. We simply can't leave him behind," objected Faye vehemently.

"You may be right, Faye, but I don't see what else we can do. He won't let anyone else ride him, and even if he did, he'd still stand out. I simply don't see any other way than to trade him for a less conspicuous mount."

"Okay. Tasmin, come with me. It's time you learned Believer's secret," said Faye standing and heading for the door.

Without a word, Tasmin rose and followed. She'd been suspicious of something going on she hadn't been told. It was past time she knew what it was.

Faye led the way to the stable and Believer's stall. After checking that they were alone, she turned to Tasmin. "Come closer. Yes, that's it. Now, close your eyes. Let me take your hand. There, do you feel it? It's Believer's horn. He's a unicorn," she explained, whispering the last part as she watched for intruders.

Tasmin's mouth had fallen open as she stroked the horn for a moment. When she opened her eyes, it wasn't there although her fingers could still feel it. "A unicorn?" she breathed. "Rumors said they were all gone. It's amazing."

"Let's go back in before someone wonders what we're doing," said Faye, pulling the awed Tasmin with her.

Tasmin was thoughtful as they returned to the dining room where only the fruit remained.

Once the door was closed, Faye continued, "Remember how exhausted we were the first two days out of Nelas? Afterward, we all seemed to catch our breath, and it wasn't nearly as bad? That was Believer, sharing his power. He can also disguise himself. He's been keeping virgins from noticing him in the towns and villages since we left Gaban's mountain, except Matew, of course. I think he can make himself look like another horse entirely. I know he can if I explain it to him."

"Why didn't you tell me this earlier? It could have made things so much easier if you had."

"I couldn't. It wasn't my secret. It was Believer's. I'm sorry," answered Faye contritely.

"Who else knows?" demanded Tasmin firmly.

"Well, Ebony and Cheri have known almost from the beginning, and Behnam found out the first day on the run from Nelas, and of course, Matew. Oh, and the children in the village guarding the valley. They could see him as he really is," admitted Faye.

"Matew! You told Matew and you didn't trust me with this secret?"

"No! No, I didn't tell Matew. He's a virgin. He has always been able to see Believer's horn. Believer trusted him. I asked him not to mention it when we left Dacora, that's all."

"Faye, dear, do you have any more surprises for me? Anything else you've been keeping from me that I really should know?"

"No. That's the only secret I've been keeping, I promise."

"All right, I guess that takes care of your...mount. Do you think he can appear to be a plain brown gelding? I know that may be asking a bit much, but it would certainly help," asked Tasmin in defeat.

"I'm not sure about that, but I'm fairly certain he can make people just not notice him at all, like he wasn't even there, sort of. Maybe it's more like they can't remember what he looks like, just an ordinary, nondescript horse. I think. Why don't I ask him to try it on you before we leave in the morning?" asked Faye hopefully.

"Fine, whatever works. Now that I know he's a unicorn, I won't worry about him anymore. What about you? We aren't going to be able to continue with our present story, not after what you told those priests. Do you have any ideas on how we can make you less conspicuous? Or can Believer make people forget they saw you as well?" inquired Tasmin dryly.

"Well, maybe while I'm on his back, but actually I was thinking more of taking my cue from Ebony. They are looking for women, or a woman. I thought perhaps I could dress as a male. With my shortness and slim figure, I could pass for a boy of about, uhm, fifteen or so?" submitted Faye helpfully.

"A boy? Hmm, a boy. Yes, I think it might even work. You know, the more I think about it, the more it's actually quite a good idea. It would be even better if you had red hair and looked more like a local. We could say you're Matew's little brother. We'll have to claim you're fifteen or there will be questions as to why you were missed in the taking. I've seen you hide in loose clothes and I think this could really work," exclaimed Tasmin as she warmed up to the idea and stepped to the table to ring the bell again.

It was only a moment or two before Butter appeared again. "Butter dear, we're ready for our baths now, and I need you to get a few things for me. We're going to need some henna. At least enough to turn our blond friend here into a strawberry blond or a little darker. Then we're going to need about three boys' shirts and three pairs of pants to fit her. You know, the kind that a boy of about fifteen would wear. Finally, a few pair of hose, a pair of shoes and a cap. Once you've sent for that you can tell your people we'll be ready for our baths in about twenty minutes. Oh, and, Butter, I'll need a pair of scissors in our rooms. By the way, I promised Matew there would ample food available for him when he returned, please see to it. We wouldn't want him to fade away, would we? One other thing, do you think I can persuade you to part with one of your books? Matew looked like he could get lost in here and I told him I would ask," said Tasmin, spewing out directions so fast Faye couldn't keep up but evidently the efficient Butter could.

"Right away, Lady Tasmin. Your rooms are the two in the back by the outside stairs, and you'll have everything you need shortly. Lady Faye, could you stand up for a moment so I can get the size right?

Thank you," said Butter looking her over critically before once more slipping out the door.

Tasmin was striding purposefully through the door behind when Faye realized what had been said. "Scissors? Did you mention scissors? I thought I could just tuck my hair under a hat or something. I've never cut my hair before, Tasmin."

Three hours later, Matew tapped on the door to their room, and Tasmin let him in. He was grinning broadly as he handed her a full pouch of coins. "Yer won' believe wot 'appened! I won! I tried ter lose, just to make it look like I was the country boy they was takin' me fer, but they was so easy, I couldn't seem ter hep meself. I think I just about tripled yer money, Lady Tasmin."

"I do hope you didn't draw any attention to yourself in the process? The last thing we need now is more unnecessary attention," said Tasmin as she eyed the pouch doubtfully.

"I tried ter be discreet, my lady. I never won too much from any one man, and I traveled to four different taverns. By the way, where is Lady Faye? I have tidings fer ye both," he insisted.

The young boy with bright-red hair that had been moping on the bed with an open book and something strange on his face raised his head, "Here I am, Matew. I guess if you didn't recognize me, at least the disguise will work. Just call me Fred from now on," she said glumly.

Matew's jaw dropped in disbelief as he sank into the only chair. "Be that really you, Lady Faye? I just thought ye was some boy as worked fer Master Griggs," he said in awe. "What's that on yer face?" Tasmin broke in before Faye could explain, "It's not important. I do believe our ruse will actually work. Just quit pouting, Faye. Your hair is still below your shoulders, and it will grow again. The red should fade after a few washings. Just tie it back before we leave in the morning. Now, Matew, what is your news?"

"Huh? Oh, yeah. I almost forgot. Seems about an hour after those priests arrived today, they lit out again. Headed almost direct south. The word is they was really travelin' too. They warn't usin' no carriage this time an' they was ridin' across country. Looks like they ain' too interested in Lady Faye anymore," said Matew triumphantly.

"What! You mean I didn't have to go through all of this? Are you telling me I cut my hair and allowed it to be dyed this awful red for nothing?" wailed Faye in despair as she ran her fingers through the offending locks. Her hair had been such a pale blond that the henna had taken easily and turned it to flame.

"Faye, dear. It's not for nothing. They did leave soldiers who would recognize you at the gates after all. Regardless, by the time we reach Dink, it will be necessary. It might also help if you can't be traced leaving Dobe. Please, quit acting like a child. My real concern now is for Ebony and Cheri. It's possible they may have learned the location of one or both of them. I hope this doesn't mean they are in more trouble than they can handle," mused Tasmin with a worried frown.

"Oh, dear. Of course! Well, I'll just have to pray for them a little harder tonight," said Faye contritely.

"Prayer, dear? I assume it's to your gods where you come from. Do you really think they can hear you here?"

"I believe there is only one god and I believe he's everywhere. Since he can do anything, I don't see why he can't watch out for us while we're here," insisted Faye, turning her back and bowing over her clasped hands.

"Ah, yes. Perhaps we should all be getting some sleep? We'll be leaving early tomorrow. Your room's next door, Matew, and I'm sure Butter has seen to your snack," said Tasmin with an odd look at Faye's back. "Oh, and this book is for you."

"A book of my own? Oh, and it's the *Travels of Chiad*! Thank you, my lady and good night. I must tell Master Griggs thank you as well in the morning. I sure don' see what's wrong with red hair though," said Matew under his breath as he closed the door behind him.

*****

A multitude of stars blanketed the desert sky like dew on a mountain meadow in the early morning, and the Amnon moon turned the sands to silver as Gaban, Ochwatt, and Denahr, their guide, topped the last dune before the Third Well. The last oasis before the sea and this was where Shik Behnam's tribe was said to be. There, spread across the sands, under the tall palm trees, they could see the tents. The Wild Horse Tribe was still here. Hopefully, so was Behnam.

The wolfhounds barked, raising a ruckus as they rode into camp. A few minutes later, the three of them were ushered into the largest tent where they were greeted by a tall, well-muscled man with mahogany skin and pale-yellow eyes. "Greetings, travelers. Welcome to the Wild Horse Tribe. Come in and be welcome."

As they settle on the bright cushions and rugs lining the floor of the tent, the man introduced himself, "I'm the A'sah Shakir, Fahbha. Please, refresh yourselves from your journey, then we will talk," he invited as draped and veiled women provided water and clean rags for washing the grime from their hands, cooling fruit juices and a pale-green and wrinkled fruit that grew on the palms surrounding them.

After washing, Gaban took some of the tada and encouraged Ochwatt to enjoy them as well. "Is Shik Behnam here? I have come a long way to talk to him," asked Gaban respectfully.

"The Shik was called away, quite suddenly. To the wetlands. He left me in charge," answered Fahbha, smiling broadly while his eyes kept returning to Ochwatt.

"I needed to warn him, war is coming. He needs to get the tribes ready," said a distraught Gaban. "Can you call the conclave?"

"No. Only a tribe leader can do that. You are Gaban the wizard, yes?"

"Yes. How do you...?"

"Behnam told me to expect you. He had a dream a few weeks ago. The next morning, he called Yamama. After speaking with her, he put me in charge and told me to expect you. Then he left for the wetlands. He said he'd been called. He also left me a message if a conclave were called," explained Fahbha. "That is all I know."

"What's in the message? Does it support a call to war?" asked Gaban urgently.

"I do not know, Gaban. He did not say, and the message is sealed. Only to be opened at a conclave."

"May I talk to this, Yamama? Perhaps he can tell me more."

"Yamama is not a man, master wizard. She is our wise one and very old. She has not been able to speak since she was a child and received the gift. What she heard from Behnam, she cannot tell us."

"Then how does she communicate with Behnam? Why call her if she cannot tell him about his dream?"

"She has other ways of communicating. With touch and the mind.

Only the Shik can hear her."

"Fahbha, I thank you for your hospitality, but I am tired. Is there somewhere we can sleep? We must leave for the coast tonight. I hope to find a ship to Lohi. I have done what I could."

"Of course. Behnida, please escort our guests to their tent. I will see you all tonight for dinner before you leave."

*****

The morning sunshine was streaming through the window, illuminating Cheri as she sang cheerfully while she washed the breakfast dishes. Falcon and Bass were harnessing the draft horses for the trip to Dink, and she could safely pretend this sweet little cottage in the wonderful Singing Forest was hers. At least for as long as it took her to finish the dishes and repack her saddlebags. It was nice to have someplace she could pretend was home again. She couldn't remember the last time she had felt this way.

"Cheri! As soon as you're through there, we're ready to go. We'll be traveling much slower now, what with the wagon and all," called Falcon from the door.

Cheri turned her back as she answered. "I just wanted to leave things straightened up. I'll be right there."

Falcon paused a moment before he went back outside, but he knew what he had seen. He had seen the sunlight from the window glinting off a tear on Cheri's face. Tough, smart little Cheri had a soft spot in her somewhere.

A short time later, Cheri emerged from the cottage and tied her saddlebags onto Baby's saddle before mounting. Bass had offered her a seat on the wagon, but one look at that hard, board plank had convinced her she'd rather ride her pony. Besides, she was getting used to Baby's company.

Bass clucked to the horses, and they were on their way. Falcon had tied their pack-horse to the back of the wagon to make it easier for him to scout ahead. Cheri moved up beside the wagon so she could talk to Bass over the jingling of the harness. "How long does it usually take you to reach Dink with a full load?" she asked.

"Usually, if there aren't any problems, three days. Why?" he answered.

"Nothing, really, it's just we were making such good time before. I'd hate to have our friends waiting too long for us. It could be dangerous for them, that's all," she answered, suddenly feeling a little shy.

"Don't worry, little one. We'll be there in good time. I'm sure your friends are fine. Barakus may be trying to force it early, but I'm sure it isn't time yet for either side to triumph. This quest you're on has just begun. Why, you haven't even got all the companions together yet. I've studied the prophecies myself, and a great deal has to happen before anything will be decided. I'll admit I don't understand all of it. In fact, I don't even have a complete copy, but what I have tells me we've barely begun," Bass reassured her.

"Really? You know something about the prophecies? Can you tell me about them? No one seems to want to tell us anything. They keep saying we should let Gabriene tell us. Seems he's the expert or something," prattled Cheri eagerly.

"Whoa! Hold on there, Cheri. I said I know a little about the prophecies, but believe me, what everyone's been telling you is correct. You need to wait for Gabriene to tell you about them. He's the only one who can answer all your questions. I promise," protested Bass holding up his hands to stop her.

Pouting slightly and admitting momentary defeat, she

rode ahead a short distance so she could say goodbye to her friends, the trees. She could already see the edge of the forest approaching. For some reason, she couldn't explain she chose the lonesome ballad "Five Hundred Miles" for the last song they would sing together.

Amazingly, when the trees sang it, it didn't sound so lonesome. Instead, it almost sounded like a promise that she would be back.

When they left the last of the tall trees behind, the song seemed to follow them down the road, calling Cheri back. To take her mind off them, she dropped back next to Bass and the wagon again. "Aren't you concerned about your cottage? I mean, someone might come by and take your things?" she asked.

"No. Not at all. You see, the forest will protect it for me. No one will even be able to find it unless the trees know they will do no harm," he assured her with a shrug.

"What do you mean no one can find it? The road leads straight…" began Cheri as she turned to point to the road behind them. Only, the road through the trees was gone! The road they were on led to the edge of the trees and turned south, never entering the forest at all. "What? What happened to the road? It was right there a moment ago. It just disappeared! That can't be! It's impossible!"

"Little one, do not question how a thing can be. Just accept it, on faith. Here, everyone knows the singing trees have a magic that is more than merely their songs. Surely where you come from some things have to be accepted on faith alone?"

"I've been told so, yes. I never believed it before. Not really," muttered Cheri, as much to herself as to answer Bass's question.

"Then perhaps you should think again. There are a great many things logic can't explain, and I do not think it can be so very different where you come from. After all, can you explain how you got here?" teased Bass with a straight face.

"No. I mean, it had something to do with the magic of Persal, but since we don't have any magic like that, I don't know why it worked in Seattle," admitted Cheri.

"Yet you do accept you are here? By magic? This isn't a hallucination or a dream?" prodded Bass relentlessly.

"I may not have learned to accept too many things on faith, Bass, but I have had to learn to live in the here and now. Even if the here and now resembles a fantasy," acknowledged Cheri with a little smile. "I guess I'll have to accept roads that are there one moment and gone the next."

"Well, don't worry too much about it. The road will always be there, should you need it. I can also guarantee the road ahead won't change at all. Around that bend up there is the village of Danfer, my closest neighbors. Beyond them the road winds between hills and fields to Dink. There aren't any more towns or villages, but there is an inn we will be stopping at tomorrow night. Tonight, I'm afraid we'll be sleeping in the woods. The road between Danfer and Dink isn't well-traveled so there are few amenities," said Bass expansively as he slapped the reins to keep the draft horses moving.

Falcon had ridden ahead when they left the Singing Forest behind, and they could see him returning now. "The village seems normal. Looks like things should be peaceful enough, at least until we're a couple of miles out of town," he said as he turned Wolf around next to them.

"Trouble? Why would we be expecting trouble?" asked Cheri, glancing around her in alarm.

"Cheri! I thought you realized by now even if there is no reason to expect trouble, we should always be prepared for it. Don't worry, Amalee is keeping watch. We won't be caught unprepared," reassured Falcon.

When he mentioned Amalee, Cheri craned her neck to spot the hawk who had left her friends in the forest and was gliding far above them. Reassured, she laughed at herself.

"You're right, Falcon. I guess our time in the forest made me forget for a moment. Don't worry, I won't forget again."

It only took them a few minutes to travel through the sleepy village on its one street. There were a few waves and smiles for Bass as they rode through and stares at the strangers, but no one stopped them to ask questions. Out here, on the edge of nowhere, people had learned knowing too much about what other people are up to can be dangerous.

A few miles out of Danfer, Falcon rode ahead, leaving Bass and Cheri alone, again. "Tell me about your world. Is it so very different from this one?" asked Bass curiously.

"Different? Yes, very different. If I were to tell you what it's like you would really think it was full of magic, but it isn't. Things may seem magical are quite simple, really. They just haven't been thought of here yet, that's all," said Cheri, a little afraid of saying too much.

"I suppose I could take your word for it, but why don't you convince me?"

"Well, we have carriages that move without being pulled by an animal. They're called cars, and they run on an engine, uh, machine, that does the work. We also have similar machines to carry people through the sky. We have another machine that allows us to talk to people across many miles as though they were in the same room. I wouldn't even know how to begin explaining computers and the internet."

"Do you really want me to believe there is no magic involved with these wonders?" he asked incredulously.

"We call it science. Even the wizard Gaban said our world was filled with many wonderful things, but there seemed to be very little magic left. I guess you'll just have to take my word for it. On faith," Cheri teased with a coquettish smile.

Bass allowed himself a hearty laugh, "I guess you're right. I will have to take it on faith."

They were about ten miles out of Danfer when they stopped

for lunch. Cheri and Falcon had just dismounted to join Bass where he was getting out their meal when Amalee came hurtling down to a hard landing on Falcon's shoulder. After she'd been there a moment, she took off again and headed back toward the forest.

Nonchalantly, Falcon grabbed a piece of bread with one hand while the other pulled up the string on his bow. In a low voice, he filled them in. "Amalee has informed me a small force of church soldiers are trying to surround us, and they appear to be ready for battle. She's gone for help, but in the meantime, we're on our own."

With a small nod, Bass sauntered over to lean against the wagon while he munched on his bread and cheese. Cheri tried to imitate their style while she walked across to Baby and started rummaging in her saddlebags while checking on the placement of her knives. She certainly hoped it was indeed a small force. There was no guarantee they could even hold their own against an equal number much less two or three to one. One thing for sure, she was going to make them pay dearly to get anywhere near her.

Suddenly the horses started to get restless, and Cheri glanced over at Wolf and noticed Falcon had set him free so he could easily maneuver. Briefly, she wondered if she should do the same with Baby, but just then there was a rustling in the bushed not thirty feet away from her. She spun to see three men rise up and come running at her. All her instincts from living on the streets came back as she remembered how she had fought off four toughs intent on gang rape shortly after Cap Howe had taught her to defend herself with knives. There was no time to check on what Bass and Falcon were up to but from the sounds of the commotion they were busy anyway.

Those running for her hadn't bothered to pull their weapons. "Well, you're about to learn what a mistake you just made," she muttered under her breath as she let fly with the first two knives. The man on the right fell as a knife buried itself in his thigh. The man right behind him grabbed at his shoulder and snarled a curse but kept on coming. The third man drew his sword without slowing down. This was getting serious! These men weren't going to scare away like the toughs had. The only way to slow them down would be with mortal wounds.

"Okay, if that's the way you want it." She gritted her teeth and let fly with two more of her knives. The first knife struck to the heart of the man with the sword, and blood was spurting everywhere. The other sliced deep into the neck of the man with the wounded shoulder, he went down, blood flowing freely. Cheri didn't have time to worry about the downed men. She had other priorities. Was there anyone else attacking or could she help her comrades?

Looking around, she saw Bass fighting off two scurvy looking men with precise swings of his ax. He looked as though he were chopping down trees. The three men at his feet attested to his prowess. Falcon had downed four of his attackers with his arrows before the remaining men could get close. He was presently engaged in fighting off a fifth with his sword. While she watched, Bass downed each of his remaining attackers with two more powerful swings of the bloody ax while a lunge put an end to Falcon's last opponent.

A groan from behind Cheri drew the attention of all three of them and they turned in that direction to find the man she had wounded in the thigh attempting to drag himself away. Falcon and Bass caught the man for questioning while the carnage in front of Cheri suddenly made her feel very queasy. "Excuse, me," she whimpered as she fled behind the nearest tree and was heartily sick. Afterward, she couldn't make herself return to all that blood. This wasn't just another horror movie. This was all too real.

As she was busy being sick, she suddenly heard horses galloping down the road as a greater force of slovenly soldiers came barreling around the curve. There were at least thirty of them along with three priests. Falcon grabbed his bow, and Bass had an ax in each hand as they drew near. "Attack! They have killed soldiers of Barakus's church! Blasphemy!" called the skinny priest as he took in the carnage around them.

From behind the tree, Cheri could hear the distant cry of hawks, eagles, and falcons approaching from the west as Amalee brought her friends to help. Before anyone could engage in battle, they swooped from the sky. Their attack surprised and disoriented the soldiers, most of whom screamed in terror and tried to flee. The few soldiers not terrified tried to fight back, but they were fighting their horses as much as the birds. The three priests were calling out conflicting orders.

"Fight them! They are but birds. Kill the men! We must have the woman!"

"Flee! Barakus has abandoned us!"

"Barakus is with us. We will overcome the birds. Find the woman!" The battle, such as it was, was over quickly, and thirty-seven—no, thirty-eight men were dead. Two soldiers and a priest had fled with several birds giving chase. Most of the dead were killed by the birds, but it was the two she, Cheri, had killed that she kept seeing. The thought of it made her retch again on a now empty stomach. The hawks swooped over the sight one last time before returning to the forest, leaving Amalee and the three birds that had died behind.

Falcon and Bass left her alone while they learned what they needed to learn from their captive before Falcon dispatched him.

Then they buried the birds but left the men piled away from the road. There wasn't time to bury them properly. Cheri wove through the trees parallel to the road, unable to return to the wagon even after the bodies were gone. The sun was dropping low on the horizon when Falcon brought Baby and Wolf to her, and she could hear the harness of the wagon as it started to roll again.

Wordlessly Cheri climbed on Baby's back and allowed him to follow Falcon and Wolf where he would. Right now, she just didn't care.

Several miles down the road, they pulled over to make camp for the night. When Falcon pulled Cheri from the saddle, she had started to shake. "Bass! Quickly! Get a blanket for Cheri. She's going into shock!"

Soon she found herself enveloped in warmth and a cup of hot tea was pressed to her mouth. She drank without thinking. Right now, she didn't want to think about anything, but she couldn't help it. She kept seeing her knives enter those men and their blood spurting out. She was so ready to just wake up in Seattle and find this had all been a bad dream. Only she knew she wouldn't be waking up in Seattle. Not in the morning and maybe not ever again.

"Cheri? Cheri, can you hear me? Cheri, you're going to be all right. Do you hear me? You're going to be just fine," came Bass's soothing rumble, intruding on the wall she was trying to build around herself.

"Am I? Am I really going to be all right? Thirty-nine men died today, and they're never going to be all right again. I killed two of those, or was it three? What makes you think I'm going to be all right?" she hissed as she threw the dregs of her tea at the fire.

Then she found herself enfolded in Falcon's strong arms as his soothing voice come to her. "I know, Cheri. I know. It's a hard thing to do. Kill a man. If we hadn't, more if the birds hadn't come, they would have killed us all, if you were lucky. More likely they would just have killed Bass and I. Who knows what would have happened to you before you reached Barakus, much less afterward? Our world can be a harsh one, Cheri. Just remember, it's also a beautiful one. Try to put this in the back of your mind and in a few days the memory will start to fade. In time, it will seem like no more than a distant dream."

"No! That's just it, you don't understand. I have what is called a photographic memory. Once I see something, it's there, all of it. It will come back in full force and without warning for the rest of my life. Whether I want it or not. I never forget anything. Ever," she sobbed on his shoulder bitterly.

"Photographic?" asked Bass, looking at Falcon who merely shrugged his ignorance.

"Technically it's called eidetic, but let's just call it a perfect memory, if you want. Me, sometimes, like now, I call it a nightmare memory. It's a curse!" she choked out before burrowing closer to Falcon and letting the tears wash over her. Gently he continued to hold her until she fell asleep, but when he tried to lay her on the bedroll, she clung to him desperately, unwilling to let him go, even in her sleep.

With a small smile of resignation, Falcon settled beside her and managed to fall asleep himself.

CHAPTER 13

The Protectors?

Behnam and Kali woke early the next morning and redressed in their loose clothes. Ebony pretended to be asleep until Behnam suggested they see about breakfast and leave his lazy brother to sleep a little more. Laughing, Kali agreed.

As soon as they were gone, Ebony hurriedly got into her own dry clothes and packed both her and Behnam's saddlebags. She had managed to get all their gear down to the horses in only two trips when the two men returned, munching on hot fresh bread and pieces of chicken.

"Cadir! I see you're up. Good, good. We must be getting on the road. Here, I brought you breakfast. Eat up while I saddle the horses. Oh, and I have great news! Kali is also bound for Dink, and we have decided we should travel together. Isn't that an incredible coincidence? We'll have the company of our countryman for a while longer," said Behnam a little overzealously.

Ebony tried to make herself smile warmly at Kali and Behnam, but her heart was sinking. For the next two days, she would have no privacy at all. Things had been bad enough when it was just her and Behnam. At least Behnam knew who she really was and allowed her some leeway when they were alone. With this Kali around, she wouldn't even be able to talk without running the risk of rousing his suspicions. Well, one thing, nothing else could possibly happen to make this trip any worse!

As they were leading their horses from the stable, they could see seven large men with more muscles than brain lounging by the gates. Ebony didn't pay too much attention to them as she mounted George. She was trying to be inconspicuous as she watched Kali and his off-white mare prance vainly about the courtyard. She didn't want to give him the satisfaction of knowing she'd noticed his horsemanship.

Behnam appeared to be taking a long time double-checking Desert Wind's girth before mounting, but in reality, he was checking the men out carefully. Kali had finally settled his mare and was smiling, as usual, apparently without a care. Wondering why Behnam was taking so long, Ebony finally followed one of his glances and noticed the toughs at the gates. Oh, dear, they seemed very interested in the three of them.

Finally, Behnam was through, and they were headed out of the courtyard. "Doesn't it seem to you like there be too many Mojar about this year, Derb?" asked the smallest of the group. He was only about five-foot eight inches, but his muscles were as large as those of any of his friends. None of them appeared to be underfed or strangers to hard work.

"Yeah! Especial since the priests seem awful interested in 'em. It would seem to me our damp air might not be too 'ealthy. Not this year, say wot?" commented a second thug.

"Ye'd thin' they would be afeared of drownin' in all our water, would'n ye?" piped up a third.

"I heard a rumor once aboot a Mojar bein' able ter outfight any five of us wet landers. They don' look so tough ter me. Maybe they just been gettin' by on their reps?" commented the first one, his upper lip curling into a sneer.

"One thin's fer sure, they ain' never had ter deal wit us afore," agreed the second as the entire group joined in the laughter.

Once through the gate and in the street, Behnam gave Desert Wind his head and the Blue Ox and the town it was in were soon far behind them.

As they slowed to a canter a mile down the road, Kali urged his mare alongside Behnam. "I don't think we've seen the last of those fools, friend."

"Neither do I, Kali, but they do not worry me overmuch. I know the fighting skills of myself and my brother and I have no qualms as to your skills as well. When they decide to attack, no doubt they will come out of the fight worse than we do," answered Behnam with assurance.

Ebony was dying to ask about this fight they were expecting, but she didn't want to have to rely too much on keeping her voice deep enough to pass for a young man's. Frustrated, she followed behind, hoping Behnam would find an opportunity to talk to her before anything happened.

One thing, Kali seemed to have decided to ignore her. As Behnam's younger brother, she evidently wasn't worth talking to. She found herself torn. She didn't know whether to be angry or relieved at being so easily dismissed.

When they paused for lunch, Behnam called to Ebony. "Help me take the horses to the creek for a drink, Cadir! They are thirsty too."

Ebony jumped almost eagerly to obey. This would be their chance to talk. "What's going on? Why are you letting Kali tag along with us?" she asked in a fierce whisper.

"I could see no way around it, but do not be too concerned. There is no reason for us to tell him anything. I certainly don't want him to realize who and what you really are, I promise you," he replied calmly in a low voice.

"What about this fight the two of you seem to be expecting? What do you intend to do about it? Take your afternoon siesta as usual?"

"No. I think staying on the move might be the wisest

choice, but if a fight finds us, we will not run away. There are always a few who think our reputations are not earned. They persist in testing us. We cannot stop them if they initiate a confrontation. Besides, with the rumors of a Mojar woman about, especially one Barakus is interested in...well, let's just say they may have more than one motive. It is not beyond the realm of possibility they are seeking a reward. Do not concern yourself too much, Kali and I can take them if necessary, and I meant what I said when I assured Kali, I had no doubts as to your abilities. Come, Cadir, we had best return to the road. We have a long way to go yet today," said Behnam, turning away and leaving a worried Ebony little choice but to meekly follow.

Ebony spent the rest of the day watching for an ambush that never came. Behnam and Kali spent the same time laughing and joking as they cantered along, telling tales of Mojar heroes and pale villains or stories of great trials suffered by this tribe or that. Every time Ebony would take the time to watch as they rode ahead of her, it seemed she would hear Behnam asking Kali another question beginning with "Do you remember...?" or "Did you hear...?" or "Do you know...?" If he missed Mojar so much, why had he come here at all? Just to make her life miserable?

At dusk, they stopped near a small stream in the woods, shortly after Kali had brought down two whybras with a sling.

Being the youngest, Cadir was expected to clean the birds before dinner as well as cook. Meanwhile, Behnam and Kali took care of the horses before sinking to the ground and diving into the roasted birds. While she did dishes, they laid out their bedrolls by the dying fire then Behnam announced he would take the first watch and marched off to patrol through the woods.

Against her will, Ebony found herself drowsing off almost at once as she curled up in her own bedroll and turned her back to Kali on the other side of the glowing embers. She wasn't sure why, but she didn't want to fall asleep while they were alone. Irritated, she shook herself and lay back to see how many of the constellations she could name. She had no idea whether any of them were the same as she knew from home, so she made up her own names. The only one she knew from her world was the big dipper, nothing she could see looked like that. That one over there looked like a Falcon, the bird, so she called it that. Another appeared to be a short round woman with untamed hair, like Tasmin. Oh, and the one over there was a group of proud, arrogant stars, something like the arrogant Mojar, Behnam.

A half an hour later, as Ebony was nodding off, again, Behnam returned, stopping by her bedroll. "Sleep now. Don't worry while I'm on watch. Keep your sword handy. You may need to be alert when Kali takes the watch," he whispered, his eyes never ceasing their scan of the dense woods around them. Before she could reply, he was gone.

Right! Like she was going to be able to get to sleep now, she thought while she turned restlessly onto her side.

It seemed only a heartbeat later when Behnam was shaking her awake. "Do you think you can pretend to sleep yet stay awake for awhile? I'm going to wake Kali for his watch now. It is only a couple of hours before dawn. I need you to watch Kali."

"Sure, I can keep an eye on him, but I thought all Mojar could be trusted," she answered in a low voice.

"At one time, so did I, but I find I don't feel I can trust this man, and that worries me greatly. Perhaps I am wrong, but I will not bet our lives on it," said Behnam, his eyes watching the still sleeping Kali closely. "Pretend to sleep, Cadir. I must wake him now."

Frowning, Ebony closed her eyes and concentrated on breathing easy while Behnam woke him. Once Behnam was settled in his bedroll, she allowed her eyes to slit slightly as she watched Kali from under her long lashes. He was leaning against a tree, his eyes sweeping around and through the trees. It seemed to Ebony they were also watching Behnam closely. Waiting for him to fall completely asleep perhaps? As usual, he appeared to be ignoring her entirely. As if he didn't think of her as a threat.

As dawn approached, Ebony's eyes kept trying to close so she could drift off to sleep. Kali wasn't doing anything. He barely even moved for the next forty-five minutes, almost as if he wasn't worried anymore about the toughs at the Blue Ox. Suddenly, he straightened up and walked around their camp and into the forest. Nervously Ebony kept him in sight as her heart started to race. She could almost feel the adrenalin surging through her body as he disappeared behind some trees. A few minutes later, he was back and watching Behnam carefully. Restlessly, his eyes darted about the campsite as he resumed leaning against the tree.

He probably just went to the bathroom, Ebony thought in disgust as her heartbeat began to slow again. A soft rustle alerted her, and she found herself shouting for Behnam as she sprang to her feet, her short sword in one hand. Behnam was on his feet, and Kali was rushing to their side as the men from the Blue Ox burst into their clearing. Forming a triangle where they could protect each other's backs, the three found themselves in a battle. Ebony's sword was a blur as she countered the first assailant's clumsy attempts with his rusty sword. To her trained eye, it appeared he hadn't had more than a few lessons with it, if that. It only took her a few short minutes to parry a final thrust and get under his guard with a killing blow. Before she could do more than ascertain Behnam and Kali were still on their feet and two more of the attackers were down, another came at her. She thought this was the one they had called Derb the day before. In his hand was a stout pole about as long as he was tall. Ebony wasn't about to make the mistake of thinking he was no match for her sword. She knew better. From the way he carried it, she would be willing to bet he was better with his staff than the first had been with the sword.

Briefly, she debated with herself about tossing the short sword aside and relying on her other skills but saw no reason to reveal too much too soon. Warily they circled each other as the battle pulled the three companions apart. As they circled, she could see Behnam and Kali each battled one remaining attacker. That meant four were down. Without warning, she started to attack, fighting his spinning staff and trying to guess where it would be next. With the staff in his hands, he was amazingly graceful and, as she had feared, very good. She knew her chances against him as long as she used the sword alone were small, so as she leapt over a sweep designed to knock her off her feet, she decided it was time to do the unexpected and pushed herself into a spin over his head to land on her feet behind him. Before he could figure out where she was, she had stepped up behind him and pressed the sword point firmly against his kidney.

"Don't move. Drop the quarterstaff, or you'll join your friends," she said quietly. Firmly controlling her anger as her eyes took in the aftermath of the fight. There were six bodies on the ground, but Behnam was still standing, even if he was holding his upper arm to staunch the flow of blood. Kali was also on his feet and appeared to be unharmed.

"Well, well. What do we have here?" he asked as he started to cross to Ebony and her prisoner. His words seemed to be for the man at sword point, but his eyes were on her, taking inventory from head to foot. They also seemed to be judging what they found.

She couldn't decide what judgment he'd come to when she heard Behnam's shout as he tried to lunge across the dead fire and tripped on the stones. "No! Cadir, stop him!"

It was too late. While she had been watching Kali's eyes, a knife had flown from his hands and blood was spurting from her prisoner's neck. He sank to his knees in slow motion and hung there as if in prayer for a long time before finally falling on his face in the dust.

Ebony stood there stunned, staring at the dead man at her feet in disbelief before she raised her eyes to Kali, "Why? He had surrendered. There was no reason—" she asked in a low growl, trying desperately to control her anger.

"Reason? Of course, there was a reason. He is a barbarian, and he dared to attack us. What is more, he knew who you are. We could not merely let him go once he knew that, could we?" answered Kali calmly, his easy smile returning to her face once more.

By now Behnam had reached Kali's side and spun him about. "He could have answered questions first! He may have had valuable information. Who trained you that you should forget the first rule of taking prisoners?" he demanded harshly.

"In the tribe of Maudi, we are taught not to take prisoners. Water is too scarce for enemies," replied Kali as he shook Behnam's hand from his arm. "You may rule in Mojar, but you do not rule here, Behnam," he spat as he walked over to Ebony and picked up a handful of braids. "Perhaps you should replace your turban, Cadir. I would hate to have to kill an innocent man if he were to see a Mojar woman," he said with a slow smile before walking away.

Ebony's mouth opened in shock as she grabbed her braids and began frantically searching for the missing turban. "Oh, my lord! Oh, Behnam, I'm sorry," she apologized as she found the folds of cloth lying in the dust.

"Do not be disturbed, Cadir. I will take care of this. How depends on what Kali intends to do with this information. Why don't you clean up while we...talk," said Behnam, his eyes never leaving Kali, who had packed up his bedroll and was saddling his horse.

"Clean up? I'll thank you to sit down, and I'll clean you up first! I refuse to budge until you allow me to wash and bandage your wound," insisted Ebony defiantly.

With a sigh of resignation, Behnam sat on a log and allowed Ebony to tend him, but his eyes never left Kali as he waited for his reply.

"I do not intend to *do* anything, Behnam. Just because I do not acknowledge your status here does not mean I am no longer a Mojar. I do not serve Barakus or his priests. In fact, I had my suspicions about your 'brother' at the Blue Ox. If you will let me, I would like to help," he said smoothly, his charming smile never slipping as he finished with his horse.

Behnam's eyes continued to bore into him hard for a long minute before turning to the carnage on the ground as Ebony tied off his makeshift bandage. "For now, I will accept that, Kali. But be aware if you defy me again, I will take whatever steps I deem necessary to protect Cadir. I suggest we hide these bodies before we move on. No reason to put anyone else on alert here."

"Cadir? Surely such a lovely woman has a name more fitting than that?" asked Kali as he bent to help Behnam carry the bodies deeper into the woods. His eyes and his smile were for Ebony as she bent over the stream to splash cool water on her face before hiding her braids once more in the hot and itchy turban.

"There is no need to know more, Kali. Cadir will do as well as any other name. It will help us all remember she is my brother. At least for our purposes. Cadir! When you can, pack our horses. We should be ready to ride from here as soon as possible. We'll eat in the saddle," commanded Behnam, giving no one the opportunity to argue as he carried another body into the thicket he had chosen to hide them in.

As they disappeared, Ebony sat back on her heels to watch after them. Kali said all the right things, but there was something about him. He radiated danger, not to mention that trip into the woods just before the thugs attacked. Maybe it was just the way he smiled all the time or perhaps it was the way he looked at her. Or maybe, just maybe, it was the way he made her feel when his eyes were on her. Suddenly she was very glad she had Behnam watching out for her. She had a feeling he was the only thing standing between herself and that man. She wasn't sure what she thought would happen if he wasn't there.

*****

Warm sunlight, singing birds, and the smell of a roasting habity finally roused Cheri from her sleep in the morning. For a minute or two, as she sat up and stretched, she was able to push the events of the previous day into a deep corner of her mind, and she smiled.

As the memories came back, she refused to let her smile fade; instead, she thought of all the lovely songs she had sung with the trees of the Singing Forest. For a brief moment, her smile turned wistful as she thought of returning to Bass's cottage and living with the trees. They would keep her safe. She knew they would. But no, not yet. She had a job to do.

"What happened yesterday? They seemed to be lying in ambush. Did they know we were coming?" she asked, looking fully into Bass's eyes as he handed her a cup of tea.

Both men heaved a sigh of relief as Falcon added another piece of wood to the fire. "Yes. We're not sure how, but the Komas priests knew you would be coming out of the Singing Forest and about where. Right now, it doesn't matter how they knew where you would be. What really matters is there will be more, and they will be searching for you all the way between here and Dink," he commented calmly, deciding to follow her lead and let sleeping wolves lie.

"Okay, what do we do now?" she asked, watching both men carefully.

"Well, uhm…we've come up with a plan," muttered Falcon as he exchanged a guilty look with Bass.

"Little one, we've come up with three options. Why don't we tell them to you, with the good and bad sides and see what you think?" suggested Bass returning her gaze honestly. "First of all, it seems to me to be important I deliver this load of wood to Dink. All the options are built around that. The first idea was to have you and Falcon ride in the woods, at night, trying to keep out of sight during the day. Of course, I'll be restricted to the road and traveling by night with the wagon would be suspicious. Since the Komas are looking in this area, they probably won't restrict their search to just the road. Especially if those men are found."

"Secondly, we discussed you and me taking off across country directly for Dhwittle while Bass continued to Dink alone. The main problem is, the Komas are probably looking in that area as well, and since they don't know who you're traveling with, one less fighting man could make things worse, not better," submitted Falcon as he took the cooked habity off the spit, tearing off a leg and handing it to Cheri.

Shaking his head, Bass continued, "Finally, we came up with a third option. The Komas are looking for a woman, or three. With or without companions. They are not looking for two men traveling along this road. One with a load of firewood to sell in Dink. The other is a horse trader who has a special-order pony for a wealthy merchant's young son in Dink. These two travelers have met by chance and have decided to travel together. These men will not be questioned too closely and should have no trouble getting past the patrols."

"Well, that sounds just fine and dandy for the two of you.

What do you plan on doing with me? Am I to suddenly become invisible? Or am I to ride in a sack on the packhorse?" Cheri demanded, accepting another piece of habity and a hunk of bread. She was famished, but she refused to think of the reasons why.

"Oh, no! No, Cheri, we would never do that to you," objected Falcon fiercely.

"Well, not exactly, anyway. What we've done is make a small space for you, in...the...woodpile...," Bass finally admitted, munching on his own piece of habity innocently.

"I'm what! To ride curled up in a hole in the woodpile? All the way to Dink? How often do you intend to let me out? Will I have to sleep there as well? How big is this, small space, anyway?" Cheri asked in rapid-fire.

"If you're through eating, why don't we take a look at it? Then, if you really don't like the idea, perhaps you can come up with a better one?" suggested Bass, getting to his feet and walking toward the wagon.

Cheri followed him and took a better look at the load. It appeared a bit higher than the day before. Bass walked around the back and pulled five pieces of wood out of the way to reveal her new home.

Doubtfully she peered inside. They had used her saddle to help hold up the wood and give her space, and it looked roomier than she had imagined. Carefully she climbed onto the wagon and crawled into the space and turned around. Then she started to laugh. The longer she sat there, looking at the light and airy "room" and at the two bewildered faces peering in at her, the harder she laughed. Finally, she crawled out again and reached up to kiss first Bass and then Falcon on the cheek, her grin never fading.

"It's lovely! I lived in a dilapidated cardboard box for three months. It was smaller than that. In Seattle, it rains most of the time, so the cardboard was usually soggy. I can stay in there for what, two, maybe three days? There's even room for my bedroll and saddlebags. Don't worry, guys. I'll do what I have to, to reach Dink. I promise you. Another thing, about what happened yesterday? Well, uhm…"

"It's all right, Cheri. We understand. You don't have to say anything," said Bass reassuringly.

"Yes, yes, I do. I have to say it. I don't like what happened yesterday, but I have accepted it was them or us. I've also accepted it will probably happen again. As long as no one expects me to like it," she insisted doggedly.

"None of us like it, Cheri. If any of us ever do, we might as well be on Barakus's side," assured Falcon grimly, handing Cheri her knives without a word.

"Cheri, why don't you wash up? There's a stream right over there, and Falcon and I will pack up," offered Bass, his relief obvious as he headed back to put out the fire.

*****

When Tasmin woke Faye the next morning, it was still dark out, and the single candle did little to brighten their room. Sleepily, she sat up and pulled her brush out of her bags to run through her hair. Her eyes were still closed as the brush slid down and…fell…off…the end of her hair. Her eyes flew open in astonishment as she automatically tried again. Again, the brush ran out of hair long before it should have. A memory of the previous evening returned in force as she looked down at her cropped, red hair. Alarmingly, she wanted to cry again. Her hair had been her pride and joy. It had never been cut before. Hastily she brushed what remained back and tied it at the nape of her neck and slammed a wide-brimmed cloth hat over it. Out of sight, out of mind. It wouldn't do any of them any good if she started crying about it, again.

They ate a hasty meal of fresh bread and cold roast before going down to their horses, saddled and ready in the inn's courtyard. After a brief conversation with the unicorn, Faye was able to convince Tasmin Believer could go unnoticed when he chose. With a sigh, Tasmin reluctantly left first, riding through the nearby city gates as they opened, alone. Matew and Faye waited an interminable five minutes before they rode out of the Red Crown to mingle with the crowd, following at a maddeningly casual pace. Believer had changed as they left the inn behind to a plain brown mare with a dark mane. Gone was the white stallion that gleamed in the sunlight.

As they neared the gate, Faye spotted a Komas priest she hadn't seen before watching the early morning throng intently. Even going so far as to check under the hoods of the women leaving the city. Then his head snapped up suddenly and began turning in her direction as though he could sense her. Remembering she was just a young Samalian lad, she turned her attention to the people around her and deliberately kept her eyes away from the black-robed cleric.

Quickly the man began to shout orders at the local guard. "Close the gates! Surround this crowd. I want to talk to each one of them!"

The crowd made room around the excited man as it increased its pace, and Faye and Matew were able to urge their horses a few steps closer to the gate.

"Belay that order! I do be the one to give orders here. You may be the servant of Barakus, but the city council do be the ones who decide if the gate do be closed. Has word come from them that I haven't heard?" objected a burly man in shining armor, his hand resting comfortably on the hilt of his sword.

The gate was only twenty paces away now. In just a few minutes they would be through.

"There's no time for that, man! The one Barakus seeks is here! Somewhere in this crowd! At least restrict their movement to allow only one through at a time so I may find her!" insisted the frantic Komas, his eyes still sweeping the crowd as if to find the source of some disturbance.

Ten more paces and they would be through the gates. Then they could ride like the wind, if necessary.

"What! You want me to stop people from leaving? Don't be daft! These gates and walls are to keep people from coming in, not leaving," stated the captain of the guard, crossing his arms on his chest and planting his feet as though he were rooted to the spot where he stood.

They were finally passing through the gate where the throng had to skirt around five sly-looking men on horseback just watching the crowd as it passed. No matter, they were going to make it. Faye wanted desperately to urge Believer into a run the minute they were through, but Matew was grabbing her reins. "Now, Fred, don' go runnin' off half-cocked. No need to tire old Brownie early on. We've a long way ter go afore we get back ter the farm, and pa'll tan yer hide if'n Brownie comes up lame," he said in a low voice.

Faye hung her head as she listened to the last word from the guardsman. "You bring me an order from the council, and I'll do whatever they command, but I don't be no lackey to the likes of you. Now get out of the way of these honest people so they can be about their business."

Finally! They were outside the walls, and Matew picked up the pace to an easy canter without looking suspicious. The wild-eyed priest had looked directly at them more than once, but each time had shaken his head in denial. The two Samalian youths couldn't possibly have any connection with the woman Barakus was seeking. They certainly had nothing to do with the lady of Camir on a white stallion that old fool Wat had told him to watch for.

The woods were allowed to grow no nearer than half a mile from the walls of Dobe and Tasmin waited to join them shortly after the first red pines and blue maples were behind them. "Well, I see you made it all right. I was beginning to get worried, what with the Komas watching the gate."

"For a few moments there, so were we. Thank goodness the city guard has no love for Barakus's priests." Faye smiled in reassurance, not realizing she was revealing her dimples.

"Oh, dear. Faye, do you think you can try not to smile for the next few days? Try to scowl like a naughty boy who's being forced to do something he doesn't want. Those dimples of yours completely destroy your disguise," fussed Tasmin as she vainly tried to tuck in a stray wisp of gray hair.

"My dimples? Really. You know, I'm not really an actress. First, you ask me to pretend I'm snobbish nobility. Now you want me to be a sulky boy. You'd think I was brought here to learn to act instead of using my own talents. Whatever they are," muttered Faye.

"Yes, dear. That's just the look I had in mind. Now, we really must ride. We're days behind the others and all of those church soldiers and Komas priests riding south have me worried about them. I don't think they're going to be too safe if they have to wait for us very long in Dink," said Tasmin with a worried frown just before she urged Anabelle into a gallop, trusting the other two to keep up and the farmers and pilgrims traveling the road to get out of the way.

It was late afternoon, and they had left almost all the foot traffic behind when the highway curved south to follow the banks of the White River roaring far below them toward Dink. Even here, three hundred feet above the water, the foaming river sent an endless mist around them, and the woods and hillsides were a palette of multihued vegetation.

They hadn't been traveling by the river for long when the dense woods on their right began climbing steep hillsides, crowding them closer to the edge overlooking the angry river below and Believer pulled up, refusing to go further. Tasmin and Matew had pulled ahead about a quarter of a mile and disappeared around the next bend when Faye quit fighting the unicorn and bent to touch his horn. "What's the matter, boy? We've pushed you harder than this before. What's wrong?"

Abruptly she sat straight again and pulled her bow from beneath the saddle girth as she reached into her pocket for a dry wrapped cord to string it with. There was something dangerous, waiting for them just ahead. She had no idea what but the sense of danger coming from Believer was too strong to ignore. She belted her quiver to her hip and slipped on the rawhide buckler. Once Faye was armed, Believer proceeded at a somewhat slower pace.

As they neared the turn Tasmin and Matew had just ridden around, Believer slowed to a walk and Faye began to realize the only sound was the distant roar of the river, now five hundred feet below them. The woods on the steep hillside were completely and unnaturally still. Every nerve jangled as she notched an arrow and held it ready.

Believer moved soundlessly as they started around the steep angle of the road and heard voices ahead. "Come on, big boy. We ken ye won last nigh' an' we ken ye won big! Why don' ye just toss over yer winnin's an' we might e'en be lettin' ye and the ol' woman go."

Swinging one leg over Believer's neck, Faye slid to the ground, never losing her grip on the bow and proceeded on foot. Believer was right behind her as she edged into the woods and peered around a smooth red trunk. Matew and Tasmin were stopped about a hundred yards up the road by four of the five unkempt men she had seen that morning at the city gates, without their horses. "Okay, where's your friend?" she murmured to herself in a low voice as she scanned the woods for movement, hoping it might give away the fifth man. He must be watching the horses somewhere safe. She could only hope he didn't show up unexpectedly.

When she saw nothing unusual, she returned her attention

to the scene on the road. Tasmin and Matew had been forced to dismount and walk to the edge of the river gorge. "Well, there's no time to worry about it anymore. Believer, watch my back," she whispered as she flitted from tree to tree, closing the distance between herself and the men holding her friends.

By the time she reached the spot she'd chosen, she was shaking, and she took a deep breath before closing her eyes and saying a silent prayer. When she opened her eyes, her hands were steady, and the bow was already more than halfway drawn to her ear. Quietly her arrow flew and found the thigh of the man standing beside Matew, the momentum propelling him over the edge of the gorge to the river below.

Her second arrow found its mark in the arm of the man who was holding a sword to Tasmin's back, and he toppled, his sword arm flinging out and the sword went flying in a long arc through the mist before disappearing from sight.

By the time the third arrow was on its way, Believer had charged past her going for the man on her left. Before the two remaining men could react the arrow's target, the man on her right turned in time to take the point meant for his shoulder in his arm instead, causing him to drop his sword with an oath. The fourth man was scrambling to get out of Believer's way when another arrow whistled past him to hit the first man in the shoulder, making him drop his weapon. Matew darted to retrieve the third man's sword while Tasmin held another at knifepoint. He held his bleeding arm and watched Tasmin's grim countenance before craning his neck to eye the sheer drop to the river only a step behind him.

The third attacker sprang to his feet as Matew whirled to face him with the sword, effectively blocking Faye's aim. Without lowering her bow, Faye emerged from the wood, keeping an eye out for the fifth man she knew was still out there. Before anyone could say anything, the attacker next to Matew lunged at him clumsily, obviously unaccustomed to wielding a blade. Matew barely deflected the blow as he stepped aside. He seemed reluctant to injure his opponent which made him hesitate. The two circled each other with clashing blades but no telling blows. All the while, the assailant backed himself toward the woods and Faye. When he backed into her belt knife, he dropped the sword quickly and stopped.

"I'm sorry, Matew. I really hate to break up your little game, but I believe we're in something of a hurry. Also, there's a fifth man out there, somewhere," she said sweetly, barely remembering not to smile. In the woods, she thought she could hear the sound of several horses running away. Well, that took care of the fifth man.

Tasmin prodded her captive over to meet them. "I thought you said you hadn't attracted any attention with your winnings last night? Even street thieves can jeopardize what we do."

Matew's head was going back and forth between the two women. He seemed to be at a loss as to whether he should be angry at Faye or shamefaced in front of Tasmin. In disgust, he finally picked up the other fallen sword. "Do we want to keep these?"

"They're not worth it. Throw them into the river. These pathetic excuses for men would only cut themselves if they were allowed to keep them. Oh, and, Matew, would you be so kind as to bring me some rope from the gray mule? We will show more charity than they deserve and tie them to a tree. The patrol from Dobe should be coming by in the next few hours or by morning at least. We'll let them explain how they got there. They should be properly grateful since I'm sure they intended to encourage us to go swimming," answered Tasmin, beaming on them with her sweetest grandmother smile.

Faye turned her head to hide her own smile behind her hand. Believer snorted and stepped back from his hostage, tossing his head proudly. "Well, I don't think the man who was watching their horses will be around to set them free. At least not very soon. I have a hunch he and the horses have been taken care of," she commented, keeping a guard on what she said as she watched Matew tie the three men to a tree. Anyone who walked by would be sure to see them, but it wasn't likely anyone, but the patrol, would approach such rough-looking men.

Once they were well tied, Tasmin approached the wounded men with her knife, her stride filled with purpose. As they flinched back, she reached out and cut the torn sleeve off one of their shirts to turn it into a crude bandage to tie over his wound after putting tree moss on it. "That should not only keep you from bleeding to death, but it should also keep infection away. That's saying a lot since it appears to have been years since you bothered to bathe last," she commented caustically. Without another word, she bandaged the wounds on the other man as well.

Watching her, Faye suddenly realized she had wounded this man. Even if he was a scoundrel, he was a man. Worse, she had killed another. She hadn't meant to, but her arrow had knocked him into the river. Her eyes stretched in horror, and she started to tremble as Believer came up behind her and put his head-on her shoulder. A few tears managed to fall even though she suddenly felt much better, resigned that she had done what needed to be done. After all, these men would have killed them all, given a chance. She still felt remorse it had been necessary, but nothing more. With a small sigh, she swung onto believer's saddle and waited for Tasmin.

Tasmin turned from the thieves to join Faye and Matew as they waited on their mounts. Wearily she hoisted herself onto Anabelle. "Let's ride, children. We have a long way to go yet today."

CHAPTER 14

Swim to Dink

The rays of the setting sun splashed shades of amber, scarlet, and violet through the low-lying clouds to strike the high yellow walls of the large city sprawled in the valley below as the three riders pulled their weary horses up at the edge of a small stand of red pines.

The chocolate palomino tossed his head impatiently as Ebony took it all in. The White River dropped four hundred feet from its narrow canyon to Lake Djara in the majestic Kanada Waterfall and quickly spread out behind Dink. The lake itself was dotted with colorful sails atop small fishing boats, some of which were headed for the beach and a fishing village outside the walls at the southern edge of the city. The city itself was in better repair than Nelas had been. The walls were intact, and the gates looked strong. From here, it appeared to be a thriving, busy community with throngs of people at each of the three gates. On the bustling waterfront were larger river ships loading and unloading cargo. More could be seen beyond the fishing village as they headed downriver toward Dhwittle.

Ebony could almost believe this place was as peaceful as it appeared if it hadn't been for the massive, dark-gray, almost black temple towering over the center of the city.

"I still say that three Mojar arriving separately on the same evening will be just as noticeable as three Mojar arriving together. With the climate of the countryside, all Mojar are bound to stand out more than ever anyway. We'll just have to take our chances on getting through the gates together," insisted Kali, again.

"Why don't we swim around the walls? They don't go very far into the water, and they don't appear to be well guarded either," asked Ebony thoughtfully.

Kali's mouth dropped open in a gape, and Behnam scowled at her. "I would have thought it obvious from our departure from Nelas that Mojar do not swim, Cadir. No, the gates are the only way," he said grimly.

"Well, maybe you can't swim, but Desert Wind can. All horses can. Surely you can hold onto the saddle and let him do the work? Unless the two of you are afraid?" she taunted mercilessly.

"It doesn't sound like a very good idea to me. If we're caught it'll be obvious, we have something to hide. There's no reason to assume we can't get through the gates safely," blustered Kali, apparently upset about something.

"There's also no reason to assume we can. If we wait until after midnight, even the activity on the wharves should be minimal. We can cover the head of your mare, Kali. They won't even see us. The way I see it, it depends on how afraid of water you are."

"Kali, didn't you say there was a Mojar merchant living here? His place wouldn't be very secure if we were seen going there. I think Cadir is right, we'll swim around the north wall tonight," decided Behnam, capitulating in what amounted to a low growl.

Kali snapped his mouth shut on any more objections while Ebony tried unsuccessfully to hide her satisfied smile as they turned their horses back into the stand of trees to wait.

The moon was a thin sliver playing tag with the clouds

when midnight finally arrived, and Behnam reluctantly led the way down into the valley. Cautiously they made their way to the base of the waterfall before heading the short distance along the lakeshore to the wall where it continued two hundred feet into the lake before stopping. Now Ebony was going over the instructions again in a low whisper. "Tie your clothes to the top of the saddle. We don't want to be seen in the streets soaking wet. Just remember to hold on tight to the saddle horn. The horses should automatically follow me, once you get them into the water but hold your reins, so you don't lose control. They might also decide to swing back to land before we clear the wall. It wouldn't hurt to kick your feet, as long as it's underwater. Try not to splash. Are we ready?"

Kali jerked his head once, and she wasn't sure whether it was a nod or a shake, but his teeth shone in the darkness as though he were smiling, as usual. Okay, nothing to worry about. Behnam merely grunted. Since he hadn't done much else since she'd challenged them to do this, she took that as a yes.

She was wearing no more than her black camisole and the wide pants from her karate outfit as she led George into the water, she could only hope the white of the pants would be too deep in the water to be noticed. Kali and Behnam had stripped to loincloths. She grabbed for the saddle horn when the water covered her shoulders, so far, so good. She could only hope the muted sounds in the water behind her weren't loud enough for anyone to notice. Curious, she craned her neck to see how they were doing. Behnam and Desert Wind were so dark she couldn't so much see them as see the absence of starlight glittered in the water. She could just make out Kali against his mare, bringing up the rear. Except for the mare swinging a little wide of the wall, he seemed to be fine.

Returning her attention to the wall, she saw she was almost to the end. This was going to be the trickiest part. They knew no one was on the wall overhead, but until she rounded the end, they couldn't be sure no one was watching on the other side. Taking a deep breath, Ebony let go of the saddle horn and slipped the rest of the way into the cold water to swim ahead of George. This is why she had convinced them she should go first. She could swim around the end of the wall, effectively leaving her horse behind while she checked quickly for a guard. Once she had determined it was safe or not, she could either keep going or urge George to turn around and head for the shore. The worst part was, she would only have a couple of seconds to decide.

Peering around the corner in the dark, her eyes scanned quickly for anything that moved. There! By the wharf ahead! What was that? Oh, just a skiff bobbing in the water. No one seemed to be in it, and the dock itself was empty. With a gasp, Ebony allowed to let herself breathe again as she tugged on George's reins and regained her hold on the saddle horn. Unless someone came in the next ten minutes, they were going to make it.

Just then she heard a noise behind her. Turning to look, she saw Kali was clinging tightly to his saddle horn with both arms, holding himself too far out of the water, causing his horse to panic. Gritting her teeth, Ebony turned about, handing the reins of George to Behnam as she swam past. "Kali, stop it!" she hissed, putting a hand on his arm to calm him. "Trust your horse. Do you want us caught? Now, calm down!"

Gently she continued to talk to him until he relaxed his hold on the saddle and slid back into the water. "Are we all right now?" she finally asked. When Kali nodded in return, she turned back to Behnam and George, swimming gracefully.

"It never happened," ground out Kali as she took back the reins of George.

"Behnam, do you have any idea what he's talking about?" whispered Ebony, just loud enough to be heard as her teeth flashed in a smile.

"I thought there was simply a problem with his horse, Cadir. Was I mistaken?" responded the Shik blandly.

The smell of tar was prevalent as this end of the long waterfront of Dink consisted of dry docks for repairing the larger ships after they had hit a snag on the trip upriver. At this late hour, the workmen had gone home, and a night watchman dozed in a dimly lit gatehouse on the city side. Cautiously, Ebony was leading the way toward a vacant ramp when she heard a crash followed by a loud oath, then all was silent once more. Alarmed, she swam instead under a nearby dock and motioned frantically for Behnam and Kali to follow, hoping they could still see her. Thankfully the horses could touch bottom here, and it was possible to get them to hold still.

Almost as soon as they were all out of sight, they could hear the faint scrapes, grunts, and groans of several men carrying something heavy. The clouds cleared for a moment to reveal six or seven men loading boxes into the skiff tied to the next pier. The same one Ebony had seen earlier. Then four of the men got into the boat and started rowing out into the lake while the others ran quietly back the way they had come. Ebony noted with interest they were not headed for the gatehouse with its single lantern before she turned to see where the skiff was going. Out in the lake, she could just make out the silhouette of a small ship with no running lights. But there, a single lamp flashed twice toward shore and then was hidden again. Smugglers!

Well, now their company was gone, they had best be going themselves. Leading the way again, Ebony urged George up the ramp, hoping his hooves on the bricks weren't loud enough to rouse the guard. Once off the ramp, the ground turned to mud, a blessing in disguise. At least in mud horses wouldn't make a great deal of noise.

Instead of heading for the gatehouse, Ebony headed the direction the smugglers had gone. Apparently, they had another way into the boatyard that wasn't watched.

When they emerged on the city streets through a breach in the fence, Behnam grabbed her arm. "Wait here a moment. I'll go cover our tracks," he whispered, once more taking command as he disappeared.

Ebony scowled after him in exasperation.

"Perhaps now would be a good time to get dressed, Cadir? We might draw some attention if we are seen in the city streets like this," suggested Kali calmly, the dim light flashing off his teeth, revealing he was smiling, as usual.

By the time Behnam returned, both Ebony and Kali had donned their clothes and Kali calmly set about cleaning the mud from the horses' hooves while Behnam dressed. In a very short time, they were following Kali through back streets and alleys to his friend's house on the south side of the city.

*****

"Uhmmmm," moaned Ebony drowsily as she burrowed deeper into the soft feather bed and tugged the blue and white quilt over her head. The sunlight streaming through the window had been trying to wake her for some time now, and she had a suspicion it was winning. "Oh, I give up!" she exclaimed, tossing back the comforter and staring in disbelief at the tiny blue flowers painted on the walls above the wainscoting. She thought they were close to bluebells. Apparently, she had climbed out of that lake and landed in heaven.

"Oh, marvelous, dear. You're finally awake. Now, don't

budge an inch, I'll be right back with your breakfast, or perhaps you'd rather have lunch now. It's one span past high sun, you know. No, I guess you don't know. Oh, there I go again, nattering on about nothing and you must be starving. My husband says it's my one fault, bless him," said a slightly plump woman with carrot red hair and deep-blue eyes as she poked her head around the door before bustling in to straighten a picture hanging perfectly straight here or move a delicate knickknack there. Before Ebony could get a word in, she had bustled out again.

Strange, she thought Kali had brought them to the home of a Mojar merchant. Whoever the woman was, she acted like the mistress of the house, not one of the servants. Ebony was sure Behnam had told her Mojar men didn't marry any but Mojar women. White women were only good enough to be concubines, even if often favorite concubines. Perhaps this merchant who chose to live in the wetlands of the whites didn't agree with that policy? Something to think about anyway. If Behnam could be wrong about this, what else could he not know about his people?

In a very short time, the bustling woman in her deep-blue silk dress and a dainty white apron trimmed in lace that was certainly never intended for serious work returned. She was followed by a young girl who bore a striking resemblance although her skin was a lovely mocha color, and her hair was a deep auburn. The girl carried a large tray covered with a white linen cloth. When she set the tray down on the table by the window, the girl lifted her own voluminous apron that effectively covered her green calico dress and bobbed a curtsy before leaving, her wide green eyes never leaving Ebony's face until the door closed behind her.

"Please excuse Melind, my lady. We've never had the privilege of meeting a woman of my husband's people before. We have often been honored to host men from Mojar, but this is the first time for a woman. My husband says this is because you are the first Mojar woman to ever leave the land of her people. Oh, there I go, babbling again. Please, eat. I have fresh honey rolls, the kind my husband taught me to make as they do in the tribe of Lumni. I also have tada, those strange fruits only grown in the desert. My husband says they grow on tall, straight trees with no limbs and incredibly wide leaves. I would like to see those trees someday. There is also sliced ham and goose, and look, fresh strawberries. We usually don't have any this late in the season, but the plants began to bear again a couple of weeks ago. It was the strangest thing, really. I don't understand it, but my husband tells me not to question the hand of fate. Let's see, now that you've gotten something in you, I'm sure there are a lot of things you'd like to know?" said the mistress of the house, finally winding down.

"Well, yes, there is. To begin with, I'm afraid I can't remember your name, and you've been such a gracious hostess," said Ebony, smiling an apology as she raised a plump strawberry the color of golden honey to her mouth and took a bite. Oh! What marvelous flavor. Ebony doubted she'd ever tasted anything more refreshing or sweeter.

"Oh, my dear, it's not your manners that are out of place, it's mine. You came so late last night we were never properly introduced. My name is Nattie D'Orean, mistress of this household and wife to Omis D'Orean, Mojar merchant and councilman of Dink. Please, call me Nattie. Master Behnam said your name was Cadir, but that doesn't sound like a proper name for a lady to me."

"Well, it's not, really. As you have noted, it is usually not allowed for a Mojar woman to travel in the outside world. For my safety, I've been traveling as Behnam's brother. Even though I am not in disguise in your home, it is for the best if I keep the name, at least for now. Please, call me Cadir. I'd like us to be friends. Where is Behnam? I can't imagine him sleeping this late," she asked curiously as she buttered her third honey roll and piled it with slices of roast goose.

"Oh, no. He left this morning, right after breakfast. He said something about finding out the news, but I had a feeling there was something more he was going to look for as well.

Ebony sat up and put the strawberry she was about to devour back on her almost empty plate, "And Kali? Did he go with him?"

"No. I heard Master Behnam ask him to stay here to protect you. For some reason, this caused Kali a great deal of laughter, and before he could recover, Master Behnam shook his head and was gone. He's been brooding in the drawing room ever since. In itself that is most strange. I have never seen Kali brood about anything, and he has been a guest here often.

Nodding thoughtfully, Ebony rose from the table almost reluctantly. "Thank you, Nattie. Thank you very much. Do you know what I'd like now? A nice, hot bath. Bathing in cold streams and swimming in your even colder lake just aren't the same."

"Of course, Cadir. In fact, I've had a bath readied for you in the dressing room, there. Is it true? Did you really get Behnam and Kali to swim in the lake? I haven't even been able to get Omis out in a fishing boat or on one of the riverboats. Before you get in the tub, would you allow me to take your measurements? I'll see that a decent gown is made for you to use during your stay. It won't take my women but an hour or so, and we have lovely red silk that will compliment your coloring. Now, I won't take no for an answer. We've had the silk gathering dust for some time now. Omis bought it without consulting me and the color's all wrong for all but the rarest of Samalian women. He'll never be able to sell it here anyway," insisted Nattie as she whipped out a cloth measuring ribbon and proceeded to turn Ebony this way and that, making notes of her findings.

"You know, Nattie, I do have other clothes to wear," Ebony said helplessly, looking about the room for her saddlebags.

"Yes. I know. I saw them. They are either that awful Jamben style which is well suited for traveling but not for a drawing room or gowns so rich as to grace a palace. None of them are suitable for Dink, I'm afraid. I've had them all cleaned, by the way. Now, don't worry about it. I've said the dress will be finished before dinner, and it will be. There! Your bath is waiting on the other side of that door. Would you like me to send in one of my daughters to help you? Be assured none but a member of our family will actually see you while you are here," she assured Ebony innocently, still intent on writing down the measurements of the dress.

"No! No, that's quite all right. I'm quite capable of taking a bath by myself. Thank you, Nattie. Thank you for everything," answered Ebony hastily, flushing as she slipped through the door into the dressing room and her waiting bath.

It was another hour before Ebony emerged from her room wearing her wine-colored riding outfit. Even though she disapproved, Nattie had seen there was no choice until the new dress was finished. Feeling like a new woman, she made her way downstairs and found Kali pacing restlessly in the drawing room with a scowl on his face. Nattie had been right—he was brooding.

"My, my. Has someone put a bee in your bonnet?" said Ebony coolly as she sank gracefully into an empty pale-green armchair.

"Ah, Cadir! Don't you look absolutely lovely? Do you realize this is the first real opportunity I've had to see you dressed as a woman? Of course, I would be even happier if you were wearing and Aht'chka. I doubt there is another woman in Dink who would be more exquisite," complimented Kali gallantly, his ever-present smile firmly back in place.

"Why, thank you, kind sir. Surely you managed to see more of my charms last night, even in the dark? Be that as it may, it does not explain why you were scowling so when I came in," she persisted.

"Scowling? Me? I wasn't scowling, dear Cadir. I was simply lonely and pining away for your company. It was no scowl you saw, only devastation. As for the other, as a gentleman, I would never speak of such things," he insisted as his eyes strayed to the window and the busy street beyond.

"Well, have it your way, Kali. My personal guess is it's not my presence you miss but Behnam's. I get the distinct feeling his whereabouts interest you far more than how I am dressed," she said calmly with an amused smile as she rose from the chair and began wandering around the cool green room, examining books and knickknacks at random. There was no doubt Nattie had good taste, even if her rooms did tend to have a slightly cluttered look.

"Of course, you are right again, dear Cadir. I do not mean to neglect you, but I am by nature a curious man. Perhaps you know where Behnam has gone? With the unrest in Samal, I worry about our friend. If I knew where he was headed when he left, perhaps I could find him to be sure he is safe and well?'

Ebony couldn't help allowing a small laugh to escape. "I'm quite sure Behnam can take care of himself, Kali. He isn't a small boy, after all. Unfortunately, I'm afraid I can be no help in any case, Behnam left long before I woke and he left me no message. Since I have never been to Dink before I'm also sure your guess would be better than mine on how to locate him."

"I do have an idea or two, but he has effectively tied me to this house," Kali muttered in a low voice, probably not intending to be overheard.

"I heard. I also heard you laughed when assigned to 'protect me. So why are you still here?"

"I reconsidered and felt I could augment your skills if it came to it."

"Ah, well, since we both appear to be prisoners in this house, can you teach me how to play this game?" she inquired, stopping at a small square table with a game board and small pieces of ivory and jade laid out in what appeared to be a random pattern.

"Yes, It's Marjaduk. An ancient game said to date before the time of Barakus. Before the time of Gabriene himself, even. The figures are of mythical creatures some say once shared Persal with men but have not been seen since Barakus called upon the dark powers," he said, giving in gracefully as he seated himself across from her and began to explain how to play the game.

Ebony smiled to herself as she looked closer at the intricately carved pieces. The one in her hand was a unicorn, and she knew unicorns were neither mythical nor extinct. Paying scant attention to Kali's directions, she examined each piece carefully. The short, squat one appeared to be a dwarf, and the tall thin one with pointed ears must be an elf. On Kali's side of the board, there was no mistaking the dragon with his outspread wings. Gaban had told them the dragons still raided over the Forbidden Mountains. There were others on Kali's side of the board resembling trolls or ogres, and both sides held figures she didn't recognize. The front rank of her men would have resembled pygmies, if they had been carved in obsidian. The front line on Kali's side looked more like toads than men at all. If two of these "myths" still existed, how many more of them did?

Kali had finally gotten her attention again and was patiently teaching her the basic rules of the game when boots could be heard coming down the hall from the kitchen. A moment later, Behnam appeared.

"Ah, I see you have found a way to pass the time. Good, we may be here for a few days before I can arrange passage on a suitable ship," he announced as he strode in and dropped into one of Nattie's sturdier armchairs.

Kali placed one of his trolls, making ready to capture Ebony's last elf before raising a questioning eyebrow. "Is that where you've been all day? Looking for 'suitable' ships? You should have told Omis before you left. He knows all the ships arriving and leaving Dink. It is his business."

"Yes, but the less known about our business, even by our friends, the safer for everyone. Omis and his family cannot tell what they do not know once we are gone. I have had a long and tiring day with little food. I believe Omis himself is due home at any time. Our gracious hostess informed me this morning dinner would be about half an hour after his return. It surely must be time to clean up. Ah, and here is the good lady now," he exclaimed, rising graciously to his feet and bending low as Nattie entered.

"Oh, Master Behnam, please do not rise on my account. You are an honored guest in our home. I hate to interrupt your game of Marjaduk, Lady Cadir, but Behnam is right. It is time to change for dinner," she insisted, practically pulling Ebony from her chair and pushing her ahead of her out the door and up the stairs.

Ebony looked back once at the confused expressions on Behnam and Kali's faces before allowing herself to be hustled off to her room. As she suspected, the dress was almost ready, but three young girls were waiting for her to try it on, so they could mark the hem. The deep red was indeed attractive on her, but she wasn't so sure about the tightly laced, low-cut bodice even with the sheer lace blouse under it. She had often worn less clothing in public in her life in Seattle, but somehow this was more...more feminine and alluring.

She couldn't put her finger on it, but somehow it almost seemed indecent. Thankfully, Nattie had kept the rest of the styling simple, unlike the majority of ruffled and ribboned dresses she had seen on the women passing by in the street that day.

Nattie took her long braids and pulled them to the top of her head before pinning them under to create luxurious loops, giving her a regal air before she would allow Ebony to leave the room. When she finally descended the stairs for dinner, following Nattie by a couple of minutes as instructed, she had to hold herself stiffly erect to steady her nerves. The overall effect was a grand entrance. As she swept across the hall, and into the drawing room, Behnam was facing the door and the first to see her. She could have sworn his golden eyes grew wide, and his mouth parted slightly for just a second or two, but then it was gone. Kali and Omis turned from their game of Marjaduk to follow his gaze. They exhibited much less control in their responses. Omis smiled broadly and bowed almost to the floor, something she would have thought impossible for a man of his girth, before crossing to take her hand in his. "Ah, how absolutely enchanting. This is a much better way to greet a guest than in the middle of the night, Lady Cadir. My home, my heart and my valor are yours to command."

"Master D'Orean, you are much too kind. You and your lovely wife have done too much for me already," she protested with a dazzling smile.

Kali stepped in front of Omis and nudged him aside, none too subtly. "My dear Lady Cadir, you are absolutely ravishing. That color is positively perfect for you. Now, I must remedy a terrible oversight. In our short acquaintance, I have neglected to tell you what glorious eyes you have. I have never seen such a warm, dark brown in anyone's eyes before. I have certainly seen nothing even close in Mojar."

Flushing slightly, Ebony lowered her eyes to the carpet, delicately worked in shades of green to resemble the leaves of a thousand different trees. Before she could think of what to say, Behnam stepped up. "Madam D'Orean, I do believe one of your lovely daughters is coming to tell us dinner is ready. Cadir, would you do me the honor?" he asked, taking her left hand and placing it on his right arm before she could refuse.

Nattie had been standing by the door, enjoying the effect she had created, and was hardly expecting this turn of events. Flustered, she looked toward the kitchen where indeed her youngest daughter Agail was coming down the hall. "My, my, Master Behnam, it appears you are quite right. It is time to go to dinner."

During dinner, Behnam regaled everyone with spirited stories of Mojar men who became enamored of chieftain's daughters. Of course, the chieftains didn't want their daughters to marry this particular Mojar warrior, for one reason or another. Nattie's three daughters listened, entranced, as Jadar defied Shakir Amir and ignoring the fact their two tribes had a blood feud, fought his way past all guards to take Armialady from her father's tent. Tragically, he accidentally killed Amir at the doorway before they made their escape, killing her love for him at the same time. By the time a dessert of delicate pastry covered with a sweet fruit sauce was served, the three girls all but ignored it as Behnam finished the tale of Valir and Jennai who's love was doomed when Jennai's father claimed Valir wasn't good enough for his daughter and had been promised to Mara, a man old enough to be her father. In desperation, Valir gathered his ten brothers, and they attacked Jennai's father's camp, but during the ensuing battle, Jennai is struck with a knife from one of her father's men and was killed. When Valir found

Jennai, she was dying, and he was able to give her one last kiss. When her father took her body to be prepared for burial, Valir wandered away into the desert and was never heard from again.

"Ah! Behnam, you have captivated the imaginations of my daughters. I'm afraid it will be some time before they will be willing to settle for the husbands, I might find for them here," lamented Omis as he rose from the table.

"Don't be absurd, Omis. It is you who does not want them to leave." Nattie laughed as she roused her daughters to clear the table.

"My dear wife exaggerates. I have no objection at all to my dear song pipers flying from the nest."

"Then why have you found fault with anyone who has been bold enough to dare to court them?" asked Nattie with asperity as she followed her guests down the hall.

"That is quite simple to answer, my dear. There just aren't any men suitable for them here. I have been considering returning to Mojar to find husbands, but I fear I have spoiled them. In Mojar they would find their lives quite changed, and I am not sure they could adapt." Omis sighed as he returned to his seat at the Marjaduk table where his game with Kali was as yet unfinished.

Reluctantly Kali joined him as Behnam and Ebony laughed with their hosts at the problems of finding the right husbands for their daughters. Nattie picked up her embroidery and settled into an armchair near the cold fireplace, leaving Ebony and Behnam to the settee.

Almost as soon as they were seated, Behnam began shifting his position, trying to get his large frame comfortable in the dainty piece of furniture. "The D'Oreans have a lovely garden behind the house. Now that it is dark, I thought perhaps you would enjoy seeing it," he finally suggested with an encouraging smile.

"I would love some fresh air," admitted Ebony, somewhat surprised at the offer but willing enough to get out of the house if only for a few minutes.

What she could see of the garden by the light of the stars and sliver of moon was indeed lovely, and the odor of many flowers in bloom was intoxicating. At first, she thought she could detect something very much like lilacs, but as they walked, it gave way to a smell similar to roses but with a touch of cinnamon. How unique and intriguing. Then Behnam led her to a quiet arbor covered in a vine similar to wisteria. Here, when she closed her eyes, she felt as if she had walked right into the flower. "Is this what it's like to be a bee?" she whispered.

"What? Cadir! We may not have long to talk alone. I need to tell you what I learned or perhaps didn't learn today," whispered Behnam as he pulled her down on a bench beside him.

"Oh! Yes, yes, of course. Tell me what you found out," said Ebony, sternly rousing herself from the romantic spell the night and the garden had cast on her.

"No one else has arrived yet. As near as I can tell, we are the first. I made some discreet inquiries at the Golden Stag about Falcon and Tasmin and only mentioned in passing they would have traveling companions. Then I spent the rest of the day at the tavern across the street, watching for them. It may be several days before we can leave and this is the safest place for you," Behnam said, apparently unaware of having disturbed her mood.

"What of the church soldiers and the Komas priests? Do they know we are in the city? Are they even acting suspicious?"

"No. Not yet, anyway, but if you were seen on the street, I'm sure they would soon begin looking. I can see your point about how a black woman would stand out less if more Mojar women were allowed to travel," he admitted reluctantly.

"Can't we at least tell these lovely people the truth?" she implored. "I really hate to lie to people who have been so kind to me."

"It's for their own safety. You know that. The less they know, the less the danger for them. They are well aware you are sought by the church of Barakus. They have heard the descriptions and the rumors. Even if they hadn't, they would know by the lateness of the hour when we arrived, not to mention Kali's slip when he mentioned swimming around the wall," insisted Behnam.

"You're right, but I...," began Ebony, only to be cut off sharply as Behnam took her in his arms and began kissing her thoroughly.

Startled, Ebony pushed against his chest as she struggled for a moment until she unexpectedly found herself responding and her arms found their way around his neck to pull him closer with no conscious thought from her.

Just as she found herself melting into his embrace, he raised his head and looked up the garden path toward the house. "He's gone. I don't think he overheard anything."

"What? Who?" breathed Ebony huskily, her heart still pounding like a skittish colt.

"Kali. He was here. Probably looking for you. I thought it best to let him think we were lovers," he explained, obviously pleased with himself.

Ebony's hand had drawn back and let loose to slap him before either of them knew what she intended. "How dare you! I don't care what else is happening, you had no right to do that!" she growled, jumping to her feet and running back up the walk before she tried to tear him apart.

Behnam sat very still on the bench watching her go, a smile growing into a grin across his face.

*****

Huge waded a few feet into the pounding surf, putting the front of the outrigger canoe into the water in one smooth motion. "We're here," he said simply, grabbing a sack from the canoe and walking back up the beach to dry land.

Ciral tried to hide the mischievous smile, spreading across her mahogany face, behind her hand as the three equally dark men holding up the back of their craft struggled to maintain their balance and put their end down on the beach gently.

"Yes, I know, Huge. We have reached the eastern water the wise ones said would be here," replied Cirroc, refusing to let himself get angry at Huge. Huge wasn't really being sarcastic, he was just slow, and sometimes he forgot other men were not as strong. Huge had never done harm to a woman, and he was unbelievably gentle with small children and animals, he reminded himself as he strode to the water's edge to gaze out over the surf. He refused to rise up on his toes to get a better look. Experience had taught him the difference of two inches never gave him much more to see. He would see it all anyway since Ciral was determined to have her way and continue this madness.

Resolutely, he turned to look at the dainty black girl in her long white robe whose long golden braids and pale-gray eyes were more familiar to him than his own short blond curls and stormy-gray eyes. She was the reason they were here. When she drew herself up to her full height of three-foot two inches, she somehow managed to command them all, now, but he was at a loss to explain how or why. It was hard to believe she was the same girl he had grown up expecting to marry. Since she started dreaming, she seemed to have forgotten they had been betrothed since birth. At one time he had just accepted, the whole village had accepted that they would marry when she came of age. Now the wise ones have told them she must go to this strange white tower somewhere in the eastern sea. When he had asked if they would still marry, they wouldn't or couldn't tell him.

With a sigh, Cirroc stretched to his full three feet and six inches, easing his tired muscles. Then he rejoined the rest of their party as they finished making camp for the night. Saith and Saird stood together, as always, near the fire. Their three-foot seven inches frames cast such slight shadows here where the expanses of land and sky made him feel small for the first time in his adult life. He had been surprised when they had volunteered to come, but as children from the only double birth the people of Hawart had ever recorded, this was not the first time they had surprised people over the years. He still didn't know why they were here, but neither one had suggested turning back, even once. Not even when the giant cats had surrounded them, and he had been sure their trip was about to end rather drastically. Nor when their would-be attackers had inexplicably turned and disappeared into the rocks and grass they called home. Quietly they watched Huge, at a full four feet tall, the tallest man of Hawart, as he skinned the habity he had brought down with his sling when they had stopped at high sun in this strange and unfamiliar landscape binding the two Great Lands together.

Again, Cirroc glanced about nervously. So far, they had been lucky; they hadn't met any of the people who lived in these lands. He really wasn't looking forward to meeting the giants they had been told lived in the Great Lands, although he knew they would meet them soon enough. Once again, he gazed almost in awe at Ciral as she walked to the shore and stood staring at the sea they would be taking to go even farther from their home come daylight. How could she be so calm when she had been told she must go to live with giants? Possibly for the rest of her life? Women! He never would understand them.

*****

Gaban, Ochwatt, and Denahr had been traveling across the endless desert dunes for two days and had three days to go before reaching the port city Jahl. Suddenly a wall of sand arose in the west. There was no outrunning a haboob. Hurriedly, Denahr slid off his camel before it could kneel. "Sandstorm! Quickly! Off your horse. Get it to lay down. Ochwatt! Take this and create a tent over yourselves and the horse. I'll be right there."

Without question, both Gaban and Ochwatt obeyed. This was Denahr's land. Only he could keep them alive. Gaban took his staff and set it up as a tent pole while Ochwatt wrapped the long piece of silk around the top and spread it over them. Silk had an unusually tight weave making it especially effective for keeping out the sand. A moment later, Denahr joined them with the camel's saddle. "We'll have to wait it out here."

"What of camel?" asked Ochwatt.

"They're made for this. They have two eyelids for keeping out the sand, and his hide is very tough. He's sleeping with his back to the storm. He'll be fine."

"How long can this last?" asked Gaban dejectedly. Not only was this trip wasted, it now looked like he would never reach the port of Jahl.

CHAPTER 15

Out of the Woodpile

Cheri knew when they passed through the gate into Dink because the impossible happened. The cobblestones caused the wagon to bump along even worse than it had for the past eternity. Well, one consolation, it was hardly likely she could possibly get any more bruises when her bruises already had bruises of their own. Things had been made even worse by the incessant patrols of church soldiers forcing her to remain in her cubbyhole almost the entire three days. Except for necessary trips into the woods, this woodpile had become her prison and torture chamber. "Oof!" she whispered as Bass managed to find another pothole. Well, at least this time the wood overhead hadn't fallen in on her as it had twice during the trek. If it weren't for the saddle, she would have been crushed. After the second time, she had almost refused to ride this way anymore, but with the Komas patrols, it was much too dangerous not to.

She was beginning to think they were going to have to travel all the way across the city before stopping when Bass turned the horses abruptly and came to a halt. "Hie there, Tahat! I have a shipment for you."

"So early? 'Tis still midsummer, Bass old friend. What will I do with firewood at this time of year? Do you know something I don't?" came the voice of a young man followed by approaching steps.

The useless springs of the wagon squealed in protest as Bass jumped to the ground. "Let's just call it intuition. Besides, this will be my only delivery this year. I'm going on a trip to visit relatives in Lohi. Do you know anyone who would like to buy my wagon and horses? I may be gone for some time."

"Ah! Well, that be another matter. I may have use for them if the price is right," said the high voice, fading as he moved away to inspect the horses.

A few minutes later, Tahat had gone to count out Bass's coins for the wagon, horses, and firewood. Bass was able to come to the back of the wagon unobserved. Gingerly he removed the concealing pieces of wood and helped Cheri to the ground. "Falcon is waiting halfway down the street, to the left of the gate. Follow him, and he will lead you to the Golden Stag. I'll meet you both there later."

With a silent nod, Cheri resisted the urge to stretch out the kinks and rub some of the more bruised parts of her anatomy as she crossed to the gate and looked quickly about. Before proceeding, she took a moment to brush wood chips out of her hair and resolutely straightened her shoulders. Finally, ready, she sauntered through the gate as though she belonged exactly where she was. She had donned her red dress with the red overskirt she'd had made in the valley. She knew there was some risk in wearing it again, but unless she was seen by that particular priest, it was the best disguise she had.

Falcon had been inspecting one of Wolf's shoes and shook his head once as Cheri emerged. He put it down gently and led his three horses away. Nonchalantly, Cheri headed in the same direction, carefully smiling at the men she passed, usually if they were with another woman. No use inviting trouble.

They had passed four or five cross streets and as many alleys before Falcon turned onto a boulevard divided by large strips of landscaped parks filled with a myriad of flower beds, artfully designed bushes and shaded by ancient trees. On either side of the parkways were shops of all sorts with an occasional house sandwiched between. They had gone about three and a half blocks when Cheri paused to look into the window of one shop cluttered with a wide variety of things to tempt one's fancy. Oh, but it was the bolts of silk in marvelous hues of green, blue, and yellow that really caught her attention. There was one bolt of an iridescent sea green that almost appeared to flow like water. She found it absolutely captivating. As she was turning to leave, she noticed the tall brick house next door was set back a few feet from the street, and Cheri thought she glimpsed a swirl of red and a familiar face. Her mouth was partly opened when she looked ahead and realized Falcon would soon be disappearing in the growing crowd. If she didn't stop daydreaming, she would end up lost for sure.

Without appearing to hurry too much, Cheri managed to close the gap until she was only half a street away from Falcon and the horses again. Then two things happened at once. The garish red door of the house on the corner ahead opened up, allowing five fluttery women with overdone makeup and frilly dresses in bright colors to emerge amid calls of "Don't forget my lace!" and "Get me some blue ribbon, Katharyn."

Laughing and chatting, the women didn't notice Cheri behind them at all, and they almost didn't notice the squad of church soldiers escorting a Komas priest crossing the wide street and partially hidden by a high hedge. When they did, they began to call to soldiers they knew. Some of the soldiers began to call back and wave when their sergeant cracked an order, bringing them all to attention.

That was when Cheri got a good look at the priest riding

in an open carriage. The round face running high up his forehead to meet a short fringe of hair atop his pate was all too familiar. Well, she could only hope prostitutes were the same everywhere as she quickened her pace and managed to insert herself into the middle of the women. Still babbling of nothing behind their busy lace fans, they crossed the street. Taking one last look at the priest, she could see him looking around at the other pedestrians as he called a halt in the middle of the intersection. Grumbling under their breaths, pedestrian traffic went around while teamsters reined in restless horses and mules and cursed the Komas more audibly while impatiently waiting for him to move. Doing her best to make herself inconspicuous, Cheri bent her knees and stayed behind the wide skirts the other women wore. None of her new companions even looked at her as they continued to chatter about the men they would conquer with their new dresses and if they seemed to close ranks a little. Well, who would notice that with a group of pretty young women?

They had traveled the length of the next block before the sergeant could be heard ordering the troop to continue. Daring to stand to look, Cheri saw the short Komas was standing in his carriage now, still looking for something when the carriage jerked forward, causing him to topple into the seat as they moved out of sight. Once they were gone, Cheri frantically looked ahead to see Falcon had once more stopped, this time to inspect one of Baby's hooves.

"Well, dearie, what'd you do? Roll the priest when he began snoring?" asked one of the ladies protecting her.

"No. Not exactly. But thank you. I really mean that. If he had found me, I'd really be in trouble now," enthused Cheri as she tried to worm her way between their wide skirts.

"New in town, aren't you, dearie? You know, you look like you've got potential, with the right clothes and some more makeup. Why don't you come back to Carrie's house with us?

It's a good sight safer than working the streets," said another in a sky-blue dress.

"Thank you for the offer, but I can't, really. I'm going to Lohi as soon as I can arrange passage. I figure it's the one place that greasy Komas can't follow me," insisted Cheri, wondering why it was so much harder to get free of these women and their multiple petticoats than it had been to get in.

"Ah! I thought a few times about going to Lohi meself, lassie. All those strapping knights, not to mention the sailors. 'Course some say the knights be sworn to celibacy, but I've never believed that. Well, we'll wish ye luck then, lassie. Glad we could be of help," said a third woman in an unflattering dark yellow as she moved aside to release Cheri.

"Thank you. Thank you again," said Cheri as she made her way toward Falcon once again. She was so ready to get to the Golden Stag.

At the third cross street, Falcon led the horses around the corner to the right. Cheri was less than four buildings behind, but when she turned the corner, he was nowhere in sight. Had she lost him so quickly? Frantically she turned and looked the other way, even though she knew he had turned here. Looking again to the front, the creaking of a sign swaying in the breeze caught her attention, and she looked up. A magnificent stag, head held proudly, freshly painted in gold. Of course, they were here. Falcon had merely led the horses into the courtyard.

Now came the trickiest part of their plan. Cheri was to give him time to settle in the common room before wandering in and appearing to proposition him. Once she was settled in his room, she would effectively disappear. The entire scheme depended on the landlord. If he was a prude or if his wife were to find out, she could be out on her ear before reaching the safety of that room.

Taking a deep breath, she sashayed saucily toward the

open gate, trying to see if Falcon were still there. Yes, there he was, giving instructions to the hostler while a servant from the inn came running to collect his belongings. Finally satisfied, Falcon turned to walk into the inn by the side door. The glance he gave to his surroundings before closing the door behind him could have been casual, and he only allowed his eyes to rest on her as a prospective customer might for a moment. Finally, he was gone. Now came the most dangerous part. She needed to wait about ten minutes before going in by the street entrance.

Looking around, there didn't seem to be any dark corners for her to loiter unobtrusively in. It was still early in the day, which posed another problem. Most streetwalkers wouldn't even be out looking for business for several hours. Well, hanging around here could only get her in trouble. Perhaps a short walk in one of those parks on the boulevard? *An innocent enough pastime*, she thought.

Turning about the way she had come, Cheri returned to the beautiful tree-shaded boulevard and watched the well-dressed people strolling in the park for a moment before crossing the busy street and strolling down the flagstone walk, looking for an unoccupied bench. It felt so good to just sit still for a moment as the heady fragrance of flowers washed over her.

A moment was all she got. No sooner had she settled herself somewhat comfortably on the least bruised part of her bottom than a stern male voice came up from behind her. "Well, well, what have we here?"

Startled, Cheri jumped slightly as she turned around to see a rough-looking man in a sharp-looking guardsman uniform. Her first thought was, *At least he isn't a church soldier.* His next words made her heart jump in her throat. "I'm going to have to arrest you, miss."

"For what? I haven't done anything?"

"You're in the Grand Boulevard Park. That be enough."

"I'm really sorry. I'm not from around here. I didn't know it was against the law. I just wanted to sit for a minute. I'll leave right now," she answered uneasily as she rose to her feet.

"You should know that doesn't excuse you. Breaking the law is breaking the law. Come along with me, miss," he insisted, reaching for her wrist.

Just as she was getting ready to bolt, a handsome young man dressed in tight trousers of an expensive-looking gray material and a crisp-white linen shirt with a bold-blue scarf tied casually at his throat strode up. His pale-blue woolen jacket, with a deep-blue scroll elegantly embroidered about the hem and up the sleeves, was casually unbuttoned. "Is there a problem here Officer Easom? Surely this young woman hasn't bothered anyone?"

"Well, no, sir. She was just sitting on the bench. If she's your guest then accept my apologies, sir," said the guardsman, some of the gruffness bleeding out of his voice.

"Yes, I think she is, now. I'll take care of it from here, Corporal." "Yes, sir," said the corporal with a smart salute before resuming his patrol of the park.

"Don't you know the parks in the Grand Boulevard are reserved for the aristocracy? Or at least for those with enough money to buy their way in? Young woman, I do believe you were in danger of being arrested," he said, softening his words with a charming smile.

"I'd like to thank you properly, but I really must be going," said Cheri as she turned to leave.

She had gone no more than a step when she was firmly halted by the gentle but strong hand that was suddenly holding her wrist. "No need to rush off, my dear. Since 'guests' are also allowed. You are now officially my 'guest.' Perhaps we could take the opportunity to get to know each other better?"

"Look, I didn't mean anything when I sat here. Honest. I just got into town today. I didn't know! Now, I really need to be going. I have an appointment that's waiting for me," begged Cheri. She'd promised Tasmin not to get into any trouble of this sort. She had to get out of it somehow.

"My, you do work fast. You only got here today, but already you have an appointment? The least you can do is tell me your name as we walk to meet this appointment of yours. I'll start out. My name is Vera Joph. Now, it's your turn," he insisted as he firmly placed her hand on his arm and calmly started walking toward the street.

"Cheri. My name is Cheri. I met this fella on the road. He said if I met him at the Golden Stag, I could stay in his room tonight and he'd buy me a meal. He's also going to give me some silver in the morning," she said sullenly, improvising as they walked along.

"Ah, well then, the fellow does indeed sound like a gentleman. I'm sure he won't mind if I tag along to meet him. There's something about you I find truly intriguing, Miss Cheri."

"Vera? Ain't that a girl's name? It doesn't exactly suit you."

"Actually, it's short for my real name. I don't usually tell people my real name," he said, and she could feel the sudden tenseness in his arm.

"Really? Why not? I mean, it can't be much worse than Vera, can it?" she persisted.

"People in Dink have learned not to laugh at Vera, the full name is my business," he said formally, his handsome face turning grim as they crossed the street.

"Look, Cheri is not my real name either. If I tell you mine, will you tell me yours? I hate unsolved mysteries," she cajoled, blatantly using her most devastating smile.

"What kind of name could a little thing like you possibly be hiding?" he asked, suddenly intrigued.

"Well, you have to promise not to laugh. And don't forget, once I tell you my real name, you have to tell me yours."

"Agreed."

"My name's really Charity. Ain't that a lousy name for someone in my line of work?" she admitted ruefully.

Vera's smile had returned, although, true to his word, he wasn't laughing. "You're quite right. That does not suit a woman in your profession. Although I believe it does suit you as a person."

"Don't go sayin' that, now. You don't even know me. Anyway, it's time for you to tell me what Vera stands for," she insisted as they climbed the steps to the Golden Stag.

Vera paused with his hand on the latch. "Don't worry, I never renege on a deal," he assured her as he lowered his voice to a whisper. "My full name is Veracity Alagaro Joph."

"Oh! Are you?" she asked as he opened the door and allowed her to proceed him into the common room.

"Truthful? Yes. With a name like that, I've never dared not to be. You've no idea of the number of scrapes the name got me into as a child. I had to learn very early how to fight," he said drolly, a twinkle in his eyes.

Now, Cheri allowed herself to laugh as she glanced around for Falcon. There he was, sitting by the windows with an untouched ale and a scowl on his face that would peel the paint off walls. "Oh, there's my appointment now. He doesn't seem very happy with me, does he? Perhaps I should go explain things to him?"

"I wouldn't hear of it. It's my fault he's angry after all. I'm sure once he hears you were a damsel in distress, all will be well," insisted Vera calmly, leading the way to Falcon's table.

"My good sir, may I introduce myself? My name is Vera Joph, Second Prelate to the Council. I do hope you will accept my apology if the young lady is a bit late? She was in danger of being picked up by the city guard for sitting in the Grand

Boulevard Park. Unfortunately, a few hundred years ago, those with power or money decided the park should only be for themselves and their guests. Cheri's presence, while most delightful, violated that law. Until I made her my guest, anyway. Then I insisted on escorting her here, to keep her from accidentally getting into more trouble," he explained graciously.

Falcon had calmed down by the time Vera finished his apology. "Then I am indebted to you. Perhaps you would like to join me in an ale? I'll be right back, once I've settled Cheri in her room. I've made arrangements for a bath, and we wouldn't like it to grow cold."

"I'd be delighted. As I'd guessed from Cheri's description of you, you are indeed a gentleman." Vera smiled as he sank into a chair and propped his feet on another. "I do hope, little lady, I may have the opportunity to see you again, in the future?"

"You've been most kind, Sir Vera. Thank you," mumbled Cheri with a nod as Falcon firmly turned her about and walked her up the stairs to her room with a large feather bed, one chair, and a small table. True to Falcon's word, a nice hot bath was waiting behind a screen.

"What were you thinking of? I've been worried to death! Getting yourself arrested! Cheri, I have no idea how we would have been able to find you, much less get you out if you'd ended up in Dink's jail! I knew this whole idea was too risky," growled Falcon as he closed the door behind him.

"I didn't get arrested! Just almost. It may not have been a foolproof plan, but it was still the best one we could come up with. Besides, didn't Bass tell us to some extent I'm protected by the prophecies? At least in the beginning? I'm also ready to tell you it's just terrible the people who need beauty in their lives the most, the poor and needy, are kept out of the Grand Boulevard Park," said Cheri defiantly, eyeing the hot water longingly. "Now, shouldn't you rejoin your guest and let me get into that bath before it cools?"

While Cheri soaked her bruises in the hot water, she speculated on how Falcon intended to deal with Vera. She had a hunch Veracity Joph wasn't going to be a man easy to get rid of.

Finally, the water cooled too much, and she emerged to rub herself briskly with a soft towel. Oh, what heaven to be back in a semblance of civilization! After treating her bruises with Tasmin's slave, she slid into a loose shift and curled up in the bed and ran through selected memories of all she'd been through since stepping through the portal in an effort to remain awake until Falcon returned, hopefully with Bass. She had something important to tell him, didn't she?

The crowing of a cock on the roof of the stable awoke her early. In this day and age, chickens were kept even in the cities. Drowsily she roused herself to find the chamber pot behind the screen in the corner and nearly stepped on Falcon, asleep on the floor. "Umph!

Oh, what are you doing there?" she mumbled as she continued on her mission.

Groggily Falcon sat up and clutched his head. "Dying, if I'm lucky and quit yelling! You know, I've never met a man who could drink the way your friend Vera does. If it hadn't been for his help, I would never have made it up the stairs. Of course, I had to come in here, and I suppose I more or less passed out on the floor, waiting for him to leave."

Cheri giggled maliciously as she returned from the corner. "Well, that's what you get for spending your nights carousing, Falcon dear. Now you're up, any chance for breakfast? Apparently, I missed dinner last night, and I'm famished!"

"Ugh! How can you think of food at a time like this? Especially when this is all your fault! All right! Give me half an hour to drown myself in a horse trough, and I'll see what

I can do. I'll also see about bringing Bass back with me, slave driver," complained Falcon grumpily as he staggered to the door.

Falcon gathered himself together in an effort to at least appear under control and strode stiffly from the room, chased away by Cheri's cheerful laughter.

Twenty minutes later, an extremely damp Falcon returned with a large tray of food and followed by Bass, who was doing a poor job of not smiling at his friend's discomfort.

Cheri had dressed in her dark-green traveling dress and packed her red dress at the bottom of her saddlebags. After yesterday's incident, she hoped she would never have to wear it again.

"Well, what's going on? Is Faye here yet? She asked around a mouthful of food.

"Actually, no. No sign of her or Tasmin or Ebony although a Mojar who's description could fit Behnam was here day before yesterday. He described me rather closely. I find it disturbing he may be here without Ebony. I suppose it could have been someone else, most people in these parts have had few dealings with Mojar and one looks pretty much like another. If that's the case, why would he be looking for me?" admitted Falcon with a perplexed frown.

"Oh! Didn't I tell you? Ebony's here. No, I guess I didn't have time," said Cheri, returning their incredulous stares with wide-eyed innocence. She continued with a sweet smile, one she had often practiced before. "I saw her. In the window of a house somewhere down on Grand Boulevard. As I was walking by. She was wearing a lovely red dress. I told her she'd be smashing in red."

"Well, it's good to know it was Behnam asking for me and not someone else. I guess we'll just have to presume she's safe where she is until he gets in touch with us. Unless Cheri can remember exactly where this house was?" asked Falcon sarcastically.

"Now, I ask you, Bass, does that sound fair? I certainly would have told him sooner, if he hadn't spent the night carousing with the Second Prelate to the Council. I mean, really! Yes, I can tell you where it is. Three and a half blocks from where we turned onto the Grand Boulevard is a shop with the loveliest silks in the windows. The house next door is tall and made of brick and set back a little from the street. I remember that especially since it's the only house I passed with any sort of a front yard," Cheri informed them both haughtily.

"Actually, Falcon, why don't we go downstairs and see if Behnam shows up again. If it truly is him, I'm sure he's watching for your arrival. We won't try to seek them out right away. It's most likely safer for Ebony if we follow his lead," suggested Bass as he pushed Falcon out the door, turning to smile understandingly at Cheri.

"Bring me a book!" she called as the door closed.

Cheri was smiling to herself as she continued to gorge on fresh- baked bread and sample the juicy fruits on the tray. There was a lot to be said for freedom, and no one appreciated it more at the moment than Cheri, now that she was free of the horrid woodpile.

*****

A long black braid in each hand, Briar Rose's deep-brown eyes were troubled as she stood on the quay watching impatiently for the sails of her greatfather's small boat to disappear over the western horizon. He had looked at her most oddly just before he left, but the strange light in his dark-blue eyes had fled so fast she had thought perhaps it was merely the sunrise reflected there. If he had really known what she was going to do, surely he would have tried to stop her? Well, he was gone, and no one else would be able to block her plans now. With a little smile, she tossed her braids over her shoulder and casually walked back up the quay, refusing to break into a run now. She had waited so long already, surely another hour or two would make no difference.

As she followed the path inland, Petare with his rumpled dark brown hair appeared from around the bend, coming toward her with a determined look in his innocent mahogany eyes. When they drew even, he turned congenially and fell in beside her. "So your greatfather left this morning? It's been a long time since he's left Jessamine," he commented casually.

"Yes, yes, it has," she agreed in a noncommittal voice, stubbornly refusing to look at him.

"My father says the last time he left he waited for one of the horse boats," he continued.

"I wouldn't know. I wasn't even born yet." What did he want now?

"My father says Jakar hasn't gone to the mainland since he was a small boy."

"Petare! Why don't you just say what's on your mind and leave me alone?" she asked in exasperation, her look finally meeting his as she stopped on the path and placed her small hands firmly on her hips.

"I was just wondering where he was going and why he was going now, that's all," he answered petulantly, eyes downcast under her glare.

"Well, I don't know. Does that satisfy you? Just because he's my greatfather does not mean he tells me everything he is going to do. Now, will you please go find someone else to bother? I have things to do," she insisted as she turned to stride away.

"Wait, Briar Rose, please don't be angry with me! I was just curious, that's all. What things? Can I help?" he asked desperately as he ran to catch up.

"No! You can't. Sometimes a woman just wants to be alone. I'm going to take my new boat out for the day, just so I can think. Alone," she fumed, not even turning to look at him as she increased her speed.

Petare's face registered hurt and confusion as he finally stopped to stare after her. She was practically running, now that they were nearly at the base of the Oracle Tree. "I wonder what's gotten into her?" he said to himself.

A half hour later, Briar Rose returned, carrying a basket with her lunch in it, to find Petare seated on a rock, patiently waiting. Sometimes it seemed to her as if he had always been patiently waiting, for her.

"Petare! I told you I want to be alone, today," she said with a contrite smile.

Petare's familiar smile, the one smile that always kept her from really being angry with him lit up his face. Before she could respond, a blur swept past Briar Rose to tug on Petare's sleeve, "Petare! Petare! Guess what? Janlyn has asked us to take the horses to the hill today. Us! Come on, he's waiting," babbled Jerym excitedly, completely ignoring Briar Rose. Petare returned her look of relief with one of utter bewilderment before allowing Jerym to pull him away.

He knows. He knows something is going on, thought Briar Rose frantically as she hurried to the cove and her waiting sloop, the Bonnie Jean.

Within minutes her lunch was stored with the other things she had been packing away since the dreams began. Before she climbed into the boat, she stood to look back at the gigantic Oracle Tree that twisted its way into the sky. The tree that was their home, dominating and protecting Jessamine. One last look and she cast off. Finally, she was on her way! As she rounded the point and the wind caught her sails, she headed the boat to the northeast with all the instincts of a born sailor. She didn't know how she knew, but there was no doubt in her mind, the White Tower that haunted her dreams was there waiting for her. Just a ways over the horizon.

*****

It was high sun and Falcon's appetite and good humor had both returned with a vengeance. He and Bass were regaling each other with tales of adventures only slightly embroidered for the sake of the listener while they savored a hearty meal in the common room when Behnam finally put in an appearance. He gave their table only the merest of glances as he sat at another and ordered lunch. Sensing his caution, Falcon waited until after he was served before he crossed to his table. "Mind if I sit down? My name is Falcon, and I have a Mojar friend named Cadir, perhaps you know him?"

"Cadir? Cadir is my youngest brother. I am Behnam, Shik of the Kodul. Cadir has often spoken of you and your lovely bride. How pleased he will be when I tell him one of his friends is actually here," answered Behnam, somewhat cautiously, his eyes traveling to Bass, seated across the room.

"He is here then? How wonderful. Please, I am being rude, Behnam. Come, let me introduce you to a recent traveling companion of mine. It appears we are going the same way. Bass, this is Behnam, brother to my dear friend Cadir. My bride came to care a great deal for Cadir when we traveled together, Behnam. Perhaps you could be persuaded to come up to my room and tell her yourself he is well? She worries so."

"I would be honored to meet your bride, Falcon, and perhaps we can speak of your travels as well?" responded Behnam with a stormy look on his face as he allowed Falcon and Bass to lead the way.

*****

Cheri was lying on her stomach on the bed, feet waving

in the air, totally involved in the *Adventures of Alezand Bruit*. One of the books she had persuaded Bass to bring her from the Golden Stag's private dining room where their congenial proprietor, Alad Geoff, kept a small library. Abruptly the door swung open, and Falcon strode in followed closely by Bass and Behnam.

"Ben! You're really here! Where's Ebony? Is she all right?" she asked excitedly as she bounced off the bed and flew into the big man's arms.

"Good afternoon, little Cheri. I'm glad to see you as well. Ebony's doing quite well. I left her in a safe house, possibly the only place in Dink where she is safe. Actually, I left her playing Marjaduk with her latest suitor," he responded with a brief smile as he extricated himself from Cheri's embrace.

"Falcon, is it safe to be bringing another into our confidence?" he queried with a worried glance at the silent Bass.

"Behnam. You of all people should know we don't choose to be here but are chosen by the prophecies. I knew I had no choice but to travel to the Singing Forest and find the woodsman. When we arrived, he was waiting for us. We would not have confided in him otherwise," answered Falcon reasonably.

"Yeah, Ben, give us a break. I think we know what's at stake as well or better than you by now," put in Cheri defensively.

Behnam sat in the only chair with a sigh. "I do apologize, my friends. I have not been so lucky with the man who chose to travel with us. Ever since he joined us, I have felt nothing but an urgency to get Ebony away from him, despite the fact he has been most helpful and found us a most inconspicuous place to stay here in Dink. I cannot explain how I feel, but my concern is there all the same."

"It appears feelings are all we have to go on for most of our decisions in this situation, isn't it? After all, no one has ever had to deal with the portal or the prophecies before, have they?" asked Bass thoughtfully.

"No. I guess they haven't. You're right. Please accept my apologies and take my hand in friendship," insisted Behnam, extending his hand to the woodsman.

As they shook, Falcon asked, "Since we're calling the shots by feelings, is Ebony safe with him?"

"Yes, at least for now. He is quite enchanted with her, and there are others there as well."

"That may pose another problem. How does she feel about him? Will we be able to sneak her away when Tasmin and Faye arrive?" asked Falcon with a worried frown.

"I'm not sure how she feels about him. They're friendly, but sometimes I have seen her leave the room abruptly when he enters. I have a plan for when it comes time for the two of us to leave without being followed. It would be for the best if someone else were to make the arrangements for the boat. I'm rather conspicuous," he replied with a determined scowl.

A light knock at the door interrupted the conversation, and Behnam and Bass disappeared behind the screen as Falcon opened the door. "Yes?"

"Please excuse the intrusion, Master Falcon. Sir Vera is downstairs and would like to know if you would join him for a pint of ale. He said something about aiding you in your search for a ship to take transport to Dhwittle," explained Alad Geoff apologetically, trying not to look at Cheri, sitting on the bed.

"Thank you, Master Geoff. Please tell Sir Vera I'll be down shortly," answered Falcon with a brief smile as he closed the door.

"Behnam, I do believe our problem may be solved. I will accept whatever proposal Sir Vera may offer while Bass makes alternate arrangements. I must be going but let Bass know when and how to contact you when we are ready to leave or when the rest of our party arrive," said Falcon in hushed tones. Cheri thought she detected an evil gleam in his eye just before he slipped out the door.

"I wonder what he's got in mind?" she pondered aloud. "I do hope he doesn't anger Sir Vera, whatever it is."

"Sir Vera? Not Vera Joph, I hope?" queried Behnam with a worried frown.

"Yes, why?" said Bass, with a puzzled expression.

"I heard rumors in the tavern about how Vera Joph achieved his position and wealth so quickly due to some sort of alliance with Barakus or his church. Of course, rumors of this sort could get started due to someone's jealousy, but we're in no position to be taking chances," explained Behnam, still frowning at the closed door.

"Vera? I don't believe it!" exclaimed Cheri defensively. "He saved me from being arrested by the guard yesterday. If he were working for the church or Barakus, surely he would have turned me over to the Komas priests?"

"Perhaps, perhaps not. If he does intend to do so, he wouldn't want you in the custody of the city guardsmen though, would he? As I said, some rumors get started out of spite or jealousy and aren't based on truth at all. Now, I must be leaving. Bass, could you show me to the back stairs?"

A moment later, Cheri was alone with her book again, but it was some time before she even pretended to read it. Behnam's words about Sir Vera had disturbed her deeply. What were they going to do if they couldn't even tell the good guys from the bad ones?

CHAPTER 16

Horse of a Different Color

Sir Vera did indeed book passage for Falcon and Cheri. The *Gray Gull* was to set sail in three days.

For two days Behnam kept to his routine and drank sparingly at the Blue Moon Tavern across from the Golden Stag. Every afternoon, Bass joined him for an hour or two before dinner time.

For two days, Cheri's bruises healed while she fidgeted in her room and devoured the books Bass brought to her.

For two days, Bass prowled the waterfront, keeping tabs on which ships were about to sail for Dhwittle.

For two days, Ebony played endless games of Marjaduk with Kali and laughed as though he were joking whenever he tried to get romantic.

For two days, Falcon drank and gambled with Sir Vera who seemed to have taken an uncanny liking to him. He kept him dicing until Master Geoff pushed Falcon up to his room and politely ushered Sir Vera out the door in the wee hours of the morning.

For two eternities, they all fretted about the fate of Tasmin and Faye.

On the morning of the third day, Bass joined Behnam at the Blue Moon shortly after breakfast. "We're running out of time. The ship Sir Vera has booked is scheduled to leave at moonrise tonight. If Tasmin and Faye do not arrive in time, we see no alternative but for Falcon and Cheri to board. The rest of us will wait here for the ladies and catch up to them in Dhwittle."

"If they arrive today? In time?" asked Behnam.

"In that case, I have made friends with Captain Jefler of the Jayhawk, who has agreed to take us all and our horses. If they arrive in time, we must be aboard ship no later than sunset tonight. As long as we travel by river, there can only be one destination. If we can continue to stay a step ahead, we have a chance," explained Bass, running his fingers through his unruly curls. "They are cutting it a bit short though, aren't they?"

"They did take the longest route. Still, I would have expected them no later than yesterday afternoon. I must admit I have been tempted to ride out on the highway to Dobe and look for them," grumbled Behnam, pushing away his untouched ale.

"Perhaps, if there had been anyone else who could safely watch over Lady Ebony. As it is, there has been increased activity among the clergy and the thugs they call soldiers. Inquiries at the inns and such. Luckily, no one has yet admitted to the presence of Miss Cheri. Some sort of gentleman's code, I believe," muttered Bass in a low voice as he stared into his own tankard of ale.

"I've heard. Might be more a matter of dislike for the priests but I've also been concerned. It wouldn't surprise me if they began a house to house search within a day or two. Even though Omis is on the council we can't be sure how much longer Lady Ebony will remain safe. There's also the matter of Lady Faye's getting into the city without being discovered. The longer we remain here, the more dangerous it is for all of them. Maybe it's for the best if Falcon and Cheri leave on the *Gray Gull* tonight? It might also be a good idea if

Ebony and I sailed on the Jayhawk. You could remain here to wait for the other ladies."

"Not a bad idea. I'll need a password, so they'll trust me. Let me wander over and see if I can pry Falcon from Sir Vera for a moment or two. It might be for the best if you sailed separately anyway. Keep the disturbances from the ladies diluted for a while longer? I doubt I'll have any trouble recognizing your friends. You've all described them to me often enough. Have you figured out how to get Ebony out of the house without Kali knowing? From what you've told me, he's been very attentive, despite your claims to romantic attachment," agreed Bass with a sudden grin as he rose to go. It would feel good to be doing something constructive again. Almost anything.

"Actually, I have. I've even enlisted the aid of Mrs. D'Orean. In the name of romance, of course," said Behnam, returning the grin.

Bass laughed and gave Behnam a sly wink. "Of course. In that case, I'll try to meet you and Lady Ebony on the ship an hour before sunset tonight."

Sir Vera was in the midst of what appeared to be a rather long- winded story, so Bass went upstairs to tell Cheri of their latest plans. Falcon had seen him and was certain to find an excuse to see Cheri soon. When he left Cheri, Bass went to his own room and confirmed his gear was ready to go. He had already decided to wait until they reached Lohi to purchase a horse since the next two parts of the trip would be by ship. Satisfied he could leave at a moment's notice; he left by the back stairs and made his way to a small gate leading into the alley. If for any reason he was being watched, he didn't intend to make things easier for anyone.

It was noon when Bass entered the Rooftop Gardens and settled at a table overlooking the North Gate. The Rooftop Gardens was the most prestigious café in town and therefore the most expensive as well. Most of the politics of the city were conducted here, and usually the gossip heard here was based on fact. Being on a rooftop gave it the added advantage of allowing Bass to eat and drink while appearing to idly watch the traffic coming and going at the city gate without taking the chance of being asked to move on by the city guard. Keeping a watchful eye for the missing ladies, he ate slowly and drank sparingly while allowing stray conversations into his thoughts. You never knew what the politics of a city might reveal.

As the day wore on, he began to despair of Tasmin and Faye arriving in time to catch the ship. It was getting late. The gates would be closing soon. He had finished an extended lunch and was sipping a particularly fine Jamben wine when a slight disturbance at the gate caught his attention. The sleepy priest assigned to watch the gate had started awake and was yelling for the guard to have everyone stop! Quickly, Bass scanned the crowd but couldn't spot anyone who looked like the women he was searching for. The closest was an older Jamben woman on a small mare who could be Lady Tasmin, but she appeared to be with two youths with red hair sharing a large draft horse and leading an overladen mule. One of the youths had his arm in a sling. There was no sign of the blonde Lady Faye on her white stallion.

Bass leaned over the rail as he watched the Komas carefully. He seemed to be trying to get closer to the Jamben woman and her party, but he abruptly turned aside to question a group of several red-haired farm women who were right behind the small party, allowing them to proceed unchallenged through the gate.

"They must be there," Bass muttered to himself as he surveyed the growing crowd again. Intrigued, he took a closer look at the older woman and the young men on a dun gelding.

Dun gelding! he thought in amazement as he rose from his

seat and dropped a silver coin on the table. He was sure he had seen a draft horse the first time. Glancing again at the priest, he saw he was helplessly mired in the group of Samali women, indignant at being detained.

He wasn't sure why, but all his instincts told him to follow the strange trio as they headed down the Grand Boulevard. When he reached the street and managed to catch up to the trio, the boys were riding an appaloosa. Very strange indeed.

Even though he was on foot, the crowded street forced the pace of the horses to slow, making it easy to keep his quarry in sight. Cautiously, he moved closer as they neared the turn to the Golden Stag. The larger of the two sharing the changeable horse seemed to be scanning the crowd in all directions, as though expecting trouble.

Turning the corner behind them, he saw they were indeed going into the courtyard of the Golden Stag, but before he could follow, the front door of the inn opened for Sir Vera as he ushered Falcon and Cheri down the steps and into his waiting landau carriage. "Don't be absurd, dear Falcon. Of course, I intend to see my dear friend and his lady to the ship. I know it's early yet, but I thought Cheri might like to see something of the city before you leave. I've taken the liberty to have my man take your horses ahead and my carriage awaits. Who knows how long it will be before we meet again, after all?"

Cheri hid a smile behind her hand as Falcon tried to accept graciously since he had no choice. More than once, Falcon had told Bass how much Sir Vera's high-handed attitude irritated him. He must really be chafing at having the care of his horse taken from him.

Once they were gone, Bass made his way into the courtyard and managed to catch the Jamben woman as she was crossing to the inn, followed by the husky young man who was even larger than he'd appeared on horseback and the slight boy. The horses were being led into the stable now included a spirited black stallion that would be the envy of a Mojar. Curiously, the boy looked over his shoulder with a worried frown as they stopped.

"Excuse me, my lady? Please excuse me for being forward, but it's possible we have friends in common. Is your name Lady Tasmin by chance? A Lord Falcon asked me to watch for you."

"Perhaps...did he give you a token or a password, by chance?" she asked hesitantly.

"Believer. He seemed to think it would suffice," admitted Bass quietly.

The woman had been carefully memorizing every detail about him, but now she smiled brightly. "Why, yes, I am Lady Tasmin. If you don't mind, perhaps we could talk inside. It's been a tiring trip. Once I can sit still for a moment, we can talk of mutual friends."

Returning her smile, Bass bowed gracefully as he held the door for her and her companions, still wondering where Lady Faye might be.

When they had settled into their seats and wine was sitting in front of Tasmin and the boy while the youth and Bass hefted an ale, Tasmin took charge. "Sir, could you be so kind as to tell me your name? I would also be grateful if you could tell me where I might find Lord Falcon. When I last saw him, I had entrusted him with a valuable item to take care of for me."

"My name is Bass. Many people call me the woodsman. Falcon told me of your trust, dear lady. He asked me to assure you the item is quite safe and still in his possession. It is my understanding you also left another treasure with his dear friend, the Mojar Behnam? That item was still safe when last I saw that worthy gentleman only this morning. Unfortunately, Falcon has been forced by circumstances to board a ship bound for Dhwittle tonight. Benham has booked passage for all of us on another ship leaving in about an hour and a half. If the treasure you retained is also safe, and if we hurry, we can catch up with Behnam and sail with him at sunset," answered Bass, picking up on the oblique reference to the women.

"The woodsman? The hermit? I have heard tales of you. You are somewhat of a legend. It is even said you have been sheltered by the Singing Forest for centuries. As to your inquiry, let me assure you, I would never allow such a prize out of my sight. If speed is needed, we are prepared to leave immediately. Matew, are you still tied to traveling with us?" she asked, turning to the larger young man.

Bass allowed the conversation to fade to the background as he turned to take a closer look at the slight boy with shoulder-length red hair. The clear blue eyes that met his were framed by a face much too delicate for a boy, and when he smiled, there was a disturbing hint of mischief in those eyes.

"Aye, it do feel different now, but no less urgent. I do be traveling on a way with ye yet."

Tasmin nodded slightly, as though his answer were no more nor less than she expected. "Then run out and get our horses and gear ready to go. We won't be but a moment longer here."

"Lady Tasmin, may I inquire who our young friend might be?" asked Bass, his eyes never wavering from his inspection.

"I am sorry, Master Bass, I should have introduced you earlier. May I present Fred. Sometimes known as Faye," she finished, dropping her voice to nearly a whisper at the end belying the gleam in her eyes.

Bass raised an eyebrow and sat back, "As I suspected. Let me retrieve my pack, and I'll meet you in the courtyard. We really must hurry to make the ship," he said, turning his attention back to Tasmin as he rose and headed upstairs, two steps at a time.

"Pleased to meet you, I'm sure," grumbled Faye as she glared at his retreating back.

"Come, boy, we've no time for sulks. We'll have days of rest once we're safely on the river," admonished Tasmin as she wearily pushed herself back on her feet and headed for the door.

A few minutes later, Bass was leading the way through the back gate and into a narrow alley, shaded by buildings three and four stories high on either side. The smell of the garbage littering the way made Faye wish they were back in the clean country air, and the eternal gloom made her look around warily for the hidden eyes she was sure she could feel watching them.

For the next forty-five minutes, Bass led them through a maze of similar alleys and back streets not much larger or cleaner, until, just as Faye was certain they were going in circles, the flavor of the air changed. The unmistakable odor of fish and river weeds rushed to meet them on a freshening breeze. They had arrived at the docks.

Bass waved them to a stop and left them in an alley piled with trash and garbage while he led the mule to the wharf and the captain of the Jayhawk. "Ho! Captain Jefler! Have my friends arrived?" he called jovially as he wove between the stevedores still hauling crates of unripe seed fruits and bales of Cathira furs up the gangplank. Sailors aboard were stowing the cargo in the hold while others on the dock were trying to rig a black stallion in a hoist and having a great deal of difficulty. The chocolate palomino gelding was waiting on the dock. A scowling Behnam was watching the procedure with obvious dissatisfaction.

"Ah, yes, Master Bass," exclaimed the barrel-chested man with a bald head through his drooping blond mustache as he clapped Bass heartily on the shoulder. Bass managed to maintain his balance and he didn't wince, but Faye was sure the friendly gesture had smarted anyway. The two men of Mojar you arranged passage for are already here, but we are having trouble loading their horses into the hold. I hope you realize I'm leaving valuable cargo behind to make room for the horses? Livestock does take up more than its share of space, does it not? What of the ladies you were expecting? Will they be here soon? It is close to sunset now, and my men have almost finished loading. If they can get that Doomed stallion aboard, that is."

"My dear captain, you have been paid well for the transport of the horses. As for the ladies, alas, one has fallen ill and will not be able to join us, and the other has insisted upon bringing two serving lads along. They are waiting across the way there. As soon as your men can load her horses, we can be on our way. I'll escort the lady and her companions to their cabin myself," insisted Bass heartily as he nodded briefly to Behnam and clapped the captain vigorously on the back, motioning to Tasmin's small party to emerge from the alley.

Tasmin heeled Anabelle, and the mare's hooves echoed hollowly on the wooden pier. When she didn't hear Believer follow, she risked a glance over her shoulder. Believer, in the guise of a pinto mare was patently refusing to move as Faye and Matew tried to urge him forward. Sensing something was amiss, Tasmin turned her gaze steadfastly on the waiting Jayhawk and tried to listen over the bustle on the dock for any unusual disturbance. Believer had been right too often to ignore. If only Faye would remember that.

Now, as she listened, Tasmin could hear a faint sound, as of many boots, marching. It appeared to be getting louder, closer. Soldiers! Probably church soldiers. Coming in this direction. Hopefully, when Faye and Matew heard them, they would slide deeper into that foul alley. Reaching the bottom of the ramp, Tasmin dismounted calmly and led Anabelle up the ramp. "Master Bass, the boy's horse has a problem with a shoe. The boys will be along shortly. Captain, sir, my mare here is quite used to traveling. Would it be possible to tie her to a rail and spare her the indignity of being hoisted into the hold? In fact, perhaps it would be better all around if all the horses were kept topside. We wouldn't want you to miss any of your custom by leaving cargo behind. My servants will keep the area spotless for you," she babbled in her best imitation of a noblewoman used to getting her way. Completely ignoring the clamor of stomping boots and rattling armor as the approaching soldiers rounded a corner and their lieutenant, mounted on a bay gelding brought them to a halt at the end of the wharf.

There were two Komas priests in an open carriage following the soldiers, and they both jumped out, yelling and gesturing at the confused lieutenant.

"There is one on the ship. I can feel it strongly!" insisted the short, thin one who looked as if he hadn't seen a good meal in some time. His arms were waving frantically in the officer's face.

"No! Back there, by the warehouses! There's definitely one over there!" bellowed the priest of medium height and maximum girth. "Quickly! Send your men down that alley! Search the warehouses!" he insisted, trying to get the confused soldiers to follow his lead.

"In the alley?" came the querulous voice of the first. "There is something? Maybe?" he admitted in obvious confusion.

At the same time, the fat Komas glanced at the ship where Captain Jefler, Bass, Behnam, Cadir, Tasmin, and various sailors were staring at the tableau on the pier. "The ship? Perhaps you're right? There is a definite pull," he boomed, further confusing the soldiers and their leader.

Just then a palomino stallion with two women, the one in

front a tall Mojar and the one clinging to her a petite blond, came galloping from the alley in question and raced down the wharf to disappear up a side street back toward the city center. Both priests shouted, "There they are! Two of them! Don't just stand there, after them!"

The officer was instantly back on his horse and sped off to give chase, shouting "Follow me!" while the Komas priests scrambled back into their carriage to follow the awkwardly running soldiers.

As they disappeared from sight, a husky young man and a boy emerged from the alley and walked calmly down the dock to the waiting ship.

"Quit yer gawkin'!" yelled the quartermaster to the stevedores and sailors who were laughing loudly at the whole performance. "The pilot says we sail at sunset and by Doome, we'll sail at sunset. Any cargo left on the dock comes out of your share. Hop to it lads!"

Faye took the reluctant mule's reins from Bass and led him up the gangplank behind Desert Wind while Matew brought up the rear. As soon as the pack-mule was tied with the others, Fred ran to the rail, his frantic eyes watching the sun as it settled nearer to the western edge of the lake. "Oh, Lady Tasmin! Please, tell them they must wait for Believer to return. He won't be long, but they really must wait for him!" he cried, clutching the woman who put her arms around the youth.

"How much would it take you to wait another fifteen minutes, Captain?" inquired Tasmin archly, pulling out a pouch heavy with coin.

"I do be sorry, dear lady, but we canna wait for anyone or anything. If we delay by even fifteen minutes, it will be days afore the harbormaster will allow me to sail at all. These times are set most carefully. While the White River do appear to be wide south of here, there are places where it is not safe for two ships to meet. Besides, something tells me you would not like to wait for a week or two to leave yourselves?" said the man with a sympathetic shake of his head. "Whoever has not made it will have to find his own way," explained the captain as though he'd had this conversation before.

"Nooo! Wailed Faye as the sun began dipping behind the city and the last of the cargo was lowered below. Frantically she ran to the rail as the gangplank was raised and the hatch covers battened down. "Come on, Believer! You can make it!" she murmured to herself as ropes were cast off and the jib sail was unfurled.

"If it can be done, Faye, he can do it," whispered Tasmin at her side.

"Remember his name and believe in him," insisted Matew as he joined them.

"There! What was that? Was it hoofbeats! Yes, it must be! Look down the quay! Was that a white blur? It's Believer! Look there. Here he comes! Come on, boy, you can make it!" called Faye eagerly, trying to ignore the rapidly growing expanse of water between the ship and the pier.

By now everyone not actively engaged in getting the ship underway had gathered at the rail to watch the white stallion as it raced toward them. Several male voices joined Matew, and Faye in urging the horse on.

"Come on!"

"You can make it!"

"Look at that horse run, he's almost flying!"

"Keep coming!"

"You're almost here!"

Five feet from the end of the dock, the animal came to a screeching halt, and silence descended on the ship. His eyes were rolling as he stared at the stretch of water.

"Come on, Believer! You can do it! I know you can. You can

do anything! Believe in yourself!" called Faye, her soft voice carrying clearly across the water.

Tossing his head, Believer wheeled to canter a hundred feet down the quay. There he reared in a sharp turn and began galloping toward the ship once more. Picking up speed rapidly, his legs were a blur, but his eyes never left Faye's face as he sprang from the edge of the dock and seemed to fly across the water between them.

Hastily, everyone cleared the deck to give the valiant horse room as he touched down gracefully, almost in middeck, and trotted daintily across to Faye. Every voice rose in a cheer except Faye's who unaccountably found herself crying in the white stallion's mane.

"All right, ye lubbers! The show's over. Back to work. We've got a long way ter go this night," bellowed the captain, leaving his passengers alone.

Matew, why don't you supervise the unloading of the mule. Lady Tasmin, with your permission, I'll help Fred tie up Believer and remove his tack and then we can all go below," suggested Bass, his eyes never leaving Faye's bent head.

Jumping to comply, Matew did his best to watch the sailors swarming over the ship as they moved out into the lake.

While tying Believer loosely to the rail near Anabelle and unsaddling them both, Bass bent to whisper in Faye's ear. "That's a neat trick your stallion has, making people see him as something's he's not. One time he's a brown mare, another a roan gelding. But if we don't want to answer a lot of awkward questions, perhaps you can suggest, since he came aboard as a white stallion, he remain one until after we disembark at Dhwittle?" he proposed before he stood with the saddlebags from both horses slung over his shoulder.

She could only hope Believer would cooperate since she was only asking him to be himself. Faye had a suspicion he had been enjoying his new game entirely too much.

*****

The sandstorm had been particularly fierce and lasted two days. Gaban was wondering if the fates were conspiring against him for some reason. After two thousand years of patiently waiting for the savior...saviors, to arrive, it should have been easier to wait for two days now, but it wasn't. Now, things would begin moving quickly.

They could smell the salt of the sea before they crested the last dune before Jahl. When they did reach the top of the pile of sand, Ochwatt came to a sudden halt and stared at the expanse of the ocean beyond the port and the ships in the bay.

"Gaban pulled Buttercup up next to him. "It's quite a sight, isn't it? That's the Roonagon Sea. Stretched from Mojar past Hawart in the northeast and Sanaagal Peninsula to the south. On the other side of the peninsula, it becomes the Great Southern Sea. From now on, stay behind me on the left, you're going to be my bodyguard. I can't hide you, so I'll put you to use. How can anyone question who or what a wizard uses for protection? If you see danger, feel free to smile."

At the last comment, Ochwatt grinned fiercely in reply.

Nodding, Gaban and Denahr led the way down the slope to the bustling port. Like Jabar, there were few buildings beyond the inns and taverns. Most residences were tents. Any shops to be found were run by men from the wetlands. In Mojar, even wetland women were discouraged from being out in public.

Once their guide had been paid, Gaban headed straight for the wharves. Examining the ships with a practiced eye, he stopped at each one he deemed seaworthy to discuss with the captain his destination and when the ship was due to leave.

After the fifth one, he turned back to look down the line. "Well! As I suspected, we missed our ship. The one we should have been on left yesterday. We'll go back to the *Flying*

Dolphin. They're leaving with the morning tide in two days. No one is leaving earlier, and the ship and captain appear honest enough," he commented absently to Ochwatt as he set off to the other end of the pier.

With a shrug of his massive shoulders, a gesture he had picked up from some of the Mojar, Ochwatt followed.

CHAPTER 17

Muddy Memories

Ebony lay despondently on the short, narrow bunk built against the bulkhead, wishing she were on stable, dry land facing the priests and their soldiers or maybe...dead. Anywhere but on this heaving, wallowing tub where her stomach betrayed her and all her strength had abandoned her. She was physically fit, for pity's sake! Not someone weak or fragile.

She had felt uncomfortable since coming aboard, but once the sails were set, and they set off across the lake toward the river, the rising wind had conspired with heaving waves to send her stomach lurching. Feeling queasy she opened a porthole for fresh air. Soon, even that was of no help and by the time Tasmin and Faye had arrived in the cabin, she was hanging her head out the porthole, retching miserably. As usual, Tasmin had taken over and soon had her drinking a vile potion before firmly pushing her back on the bed with cool cloths on her forehead.

Now everyone had crowded into the cramped cabin stealing all the air as they exchanged stories. She tried to listen to take her mind away from her problem as Bass and Behnam related their adventures. It seemed Tasmin was insisting on knowing why Falcon and Cheri were traveling on another ship before she consented to tell them why she and

Faye were almost two days late. What Ebony really wanted to know was why Faye's beautiful blond hair had been cut and dyed red. All in all, it seemed none of them had found the trip to Dink an easy one.

*****

Faye moved across the small cramped cabin, to stare out the portal in the stern. She didn't want to hear Tasmin's version of what had happened. They lost Matew's horse and a mule and almost lost Matew as well. She could still hear the screaming of the mule, stopped abruptly by Matew's knife. It was all her fault, no matter what Tasmin said to the contrary.

Closing her eyes, she could feel the rain coming down in the hills above the gorge. For three days they had been drenched, everything they owned was saturated, and sleep had been hard to come by. She was exhausted as Believer lagged behind Tasmin and Matew, each with a mule in tow.

Today Believer was a dapple-gray stallion. She had avoided asking him to relieve their fatigue or even to keep them dry the last two days. If she hadn't known it was impossible, she would have said the unicorn had pouted when she first asked him if he could disguise himself. After that, she was leery of asking another favor. Now there seemed to be no help for it. If they were to continue, they needed their strength.

As Faye leaned forward to make her request, Believer stopped abruptly. If he hadn't raised his head in alarm, she would have slid off right over his withers. Awkwardly managing to sit up, she leaned out, trying to see around the curve in the muddy road, above the raging White River, where her friends had disappeared. Someone was shouting up there. When she couldn't get Believer to move, she slid off his back and grabbed her bow. A nicker from the unicorn and the weapon was dry and ready to use.

"Thanks, Believer. Let's hope I don't need this," she

whispered as she hugged the hill and edged around the curve. Ahead she saw Tasmin and Matew as they dismounted while five bandits held rusty swords pointed at them. *Did one of them look vaguely familiar?* Oh no, not again. Gulping reflexively, she stepped back and took a deep breath before stepping into the open and letting her first arrow fly. That arrow hit the thug with his blade pointed at Tasmin in the shoulder with a "thunk." Her second arrow was already speeding toward the man facing Matew and hit him in the leg, felling him with a howl.

Now Matew and Tasmin sprang into action as the other three men reacted. Two turned to face Faye, and one started racing for her as she let another arrow fly, grazing his cheek and making him angrier as he kept coming with his dagger raised. The training Faye had been getting the last couple of months paid off as she dropped her bow and drew her sword with one fluid motion. Unfortunately, two things held Faye back from fighting effectively: even with the superior weapon and the man's ineptitude, she didn't want to kill another man, and two months did not a true swordswoman make. Unfortunately, he didn't seem to have the same reservations about killing her as he parried her first cut and tried to get closer to make his dagger more effective. Faye danced aside, trying to keep her distance while her friends battled their own assailants.

Matew had grabbed his staff from his horse as soon as Faye's arrow sent the man holding a sword on him to writhe in the mud. His quarterstaff was spun to counter every attempt another man was making to impale him.

Tasmin had punched the leader after the arrow hit his shoulder, putting him on the ground. Now she had Anabelle with one firm hoof on his chest while she faced the fifth man who actually seemed to know how to handle his sword, which was in slightly better shape than those of his companions.

As the battle continued, Faye kept dancing back, barely aware where she was when, finally, the man pushed her sword down with his blade and lunged forward. Faye didn't even try to respond as her training took over and her sword came back up to slice his groin while he managed to get in a shallow scratch across her stomach. Stumbling, she fell back as the man grabbed himself and lurched toward the gorge. That was when the rain caught up to them, and half the road started sliding. Sliding into the river sixty-five feet below. The man Faye had just dealt a mortal blow was still alive and the first one over the edge. Unaccountably, Believer appeared behind Faye at the last moment, grabbing her cloak in his teeth and pulling her back to land with an undignified "Oomph!" on her backside.

Abruptly, the ground began to tremble and shake as a larger section of the road settled, slipped, and finally slid down the gorge. Believer was still pulling Faye back as she felt the ground falling beneath her. Thankfully she slid easily while getting covered in a thick coat of muck.

The mudslide continued for what seemed to be an eternity. Finally, the ground stopped shaking although she was still trembling. Dazed, she struggled to a seated position and looked around. Behind her Tasmin was standing with legs spread wide over her second opponent while she tried to quiet Anabelle and the remaining mule. Matew's horse, the second mule, Matew, and his adversary were gone! North of them the new chasm had washed away the road and now extended right up to the bluff cut out of the mountain. It was going to be some time before this road could be repaired or a new one made over the top of the mountain towering above the cliff face.

Then Faye started making out the sounds coming from the muddy gully, and she fumbled as she tried to pull out of Believer's grasp. She was just getting up as Tasmin finished tying her captives to the mule before walking them down the road to a tree growing out the side of the cliff several feet south of the catastrophe. The two women hesitantly approached the edge of the slide at the same time. Believer stood just behind Faye as he stretched his neck to get a better view.

Her gaze found Matew's horse first. He was only using his right foreleg. The left, the left foreleg was dangling, broken. Both animals were lost to them, even if they could have found a way to haul them back onto the road. "Oh please, please, Lord, make Matew all right," she prayed fervently, closing her eyes for a moment.

"There, there he is. Just the other side of the mule. Can you see him, Faye?" called Tasmin, yanking on Faye's sleeve. "He appears unconscious."

"Yes, I see him. I can't see any of the bandits that went over with him. There were three of them, weren't there?" Faye asked as they took in the desolation. "Is Matew dead or just out cold?"

"Unconscious! We're going to assume the best until proven wrong! As for the other men, good riddance to bad rubbish."

"Okay... How are we going to get him out of there if he's unconscious? Oh no! Look, look at his horse! It's...it's..." Faye gulped back a screech and covered her face as the flailing horse slid over the edge and into the river below with one final, terrible scream. "Well, he's out of his misery, now. Our problem is Matew. One of us is going to have to go down there and tie a rope to him so we can drag him out. I'm afraid that I'm a little out of shape for acrobatics these days," said Tasmin, rising from her knees and heading for a pile of rope when she stopped. "You're bleeding, let me bind that first."

"Me?" whispered Faye to herself as she surveyed the muddy slope. She was going to have to travel to reach Matew.

Obviously there really was no other choice. She wished the poor mule would quit screaming.

A short time later, Faye was ready. One rope tied firmly around her waist, and a small shovel was tied to her belt in case she needed to dig Matew out. Just before she was ready to leave Tasmin handed her a belt knife. "Here you'll need this as well."

"What for?" she asked, staring at it in confusion.

"For the mule, of course. Did you intend to let it die slowly?"

I guess I was trying not to think about it," she admitted as she slipped the sheathe onto her belt and rebuckled it.

"All right, you're tied securely to Anabelle. I have another rope tied to Believer, and I'll throw it down once you reach Matew. Watch out for the mule. He's dangerous. It's best to come up to him head-on and talk soothingly to him," she instructed, repeating their plan.

Faye took one last look at the mudslide. It appeared to be changing moment by moment in the continuing rain. Well, getting down wouldn't really be the problem. Any way she went, she was sure to end up sliding most of the way. The best she could hope for would be to maintain control and land as close to Matew as possible without getting too close to the hooves of the desperate mule between them. Taking a deep breath, she closed her eyes for a brief prayer for all of them before she sat down and slid over the edge into the new and unstable gully. If she didn't do it quickly, she might chicken out, and she didn't have that luxury, for Matew's sake.

The rope went taut almost immediately as Tasmin tried to help guide her, walking Anabelle slowly toward the edge. Warily, Faye put her hands out to either side, trying to steer in the right direction. If she started skidding too close to the mule, Tasmin would stop Anabelle and try to guide her from another direction.

Slowly, so slowly, she approached the upstream side of

the mule. The closer she got, the more apparent it became the only way to reach Matew would be to put the poor animal out of his misery first. What was the matter with her? Wanting to put it off was only selfishness on her part. At least it looked like she would be coming up on it head-on. In reluctant preparation, she eased the knife from its scabbard into her slippery, muddy hand. She would have wiped off the mud, but by now she was covered with it. As she slid into the rock pinning the mule, she carefully tried to stand, speaking softly to the terrified animal. Here the slide had uncovered a flat rock, making the ground slightly more stable. Leaning on the boulder she gingerly edged around to the mule and lost her footing, sliding into the animal, causing his pain to increase as his head whipped frantically about. "I'm sorry, boy. I didn't mean to hurt you. I...I've come to help you. Easy boy. Easy," she crooned, hoping the sound of her voice would help calm him down some. She hated lying to him, but soon enough he would be out of pain, so it wasn't really a lie.

"There, boy. Easy, boy," she continued, trying not to think about what she had to do as she edged nearer and nearer to his vulnerable throat. Then two things happened at once: her foot found a baseball-size rock, rolling her ankle out from under her, causing her to lose her balance, and the mud started moving again.

With a startled shriek, Faye landed on her bottom and found herself sliding right under those deadly front hooves. In a totally reflexive move brought on by sheer terror, she found herself lying flat in the mud as her momentum increased and she slid to safety. Once she was clear of immediate danger, she flung out her arms in a futile attempt to find something, anything stable to hold on to and the knife went flying out of her slippery grip and over the edge of the crevasse. She was brought up short of the gorge itself by a sudden yank on the rope at her waist. Then steadily, Anabelle pulled her back from disaster and away from the weakening but still dangerous mule as well.

Inching carefully, she worked her way back up the steep slope. Thankfully, Tasmin was keeping the tension on the rope steady so even when she slipped; she didn't lose much ground, or mud. Whatever. Finally, she reached a stretch not quite so treacherous and gained her feet, waving to Tasmin above. "I lost my knife!" she called, only hoping Tasmin could hear over the drumming rain. "I'll have to get to Matew before I dare approach that animal again!"

"I can't see Matew anymore! That last slide changed his position! Tell me what you need!" came Tasmin's voice, a thin sound in the fury of the storm.

Faye wondered if the downpour had really gotten worse of if it were just that she felt wetter and colder. Eew! There was mud in her drawers as well as everywhere else.

"Give me some slack! This stretch is fairly level, and I think I can work around to Matew without getting too close to the mule! Oh, and a hot bath waiting for me would be marvelous!" she called back as she lowered herself to her hands and knees for maximum stability. Cautiously, she started to crawl up the slope at an angle that should clear the mule and bring her close to where Matew was the last time she saw him.

Every few feet, she seemed to slide backward, but Faye was fairly certain, in the limited visibility, she was very near her destination. Then her hand came down on something soft that wasn't pure mud. Stifling a yelp, she yanked back. When she couldn't see what she'd found, she tentatively reached down again and dug in the mud. A hand! Matew's hand! Where was the rest of him?

"Please, oh please, God, let him still be alive," she whispered over and over in fervent prayer as she frantically dug his arm out of the mud. It appeared to be just under the surface so perhaps it wasn't as bad as it seemed. Finally, she reached his shoulder and found his face barely clear of the muck. Bending close, she tried to determine if he were still breathing. No, she couldn't quite tell. There was too much interference from the rain and wind. If he were breathing, it was much too shallow.

"Matew! Matew, can you hear me?" she yelled as she freed his neck to check for a heartbeat. There was no response but wait, was that a pulse? It seemed dangerously weak, but what did she really know of such things? At least he was still alive

"He's alive!" she called up to Tasmin before returning to the job at hand.

What she needed to do next was finish digging him out. As she started tugging on his left arm she elicited a weak moan from him. Carefully she continued her excavation until she found where his arm was bent in the wrong direction. Momentarily, she paused. It was broken, what now? Looking down she realized there was only one way. Determinedly, she removed her shirt and used it as a makeshift sling and tied the arm to Matew's body before clearing the mud from his torso. Gritting her teeth, she ignored the moans and whimpers of pain coming from the young man. She still had to free his legs but she thought it best to tie the rope to him first, in case the mud decided to slide again.

Well, once she found Matew's knife she could release the poor animal whose screaming had diminished to a feeble echo of its former volume. Finally, she would be able to catch and tie a rope around Matew so he could be pulled out. That's all she had left. After what she'd already gone through, it should be a snap.

"What am I doing here, anyway? I'm a nice, quiet social worker. In archaic terms I'm an 'old maid.' I go to work. I read. I mind my own business. I play the piano. This is not my life!" she muttered as she finished excavating the arm as gently as she could with her hands.

"Tasmin! Throw me the rope! I want to secure Matew before I go any farther," she called, standing as best she could in the slippery muck and waving at the blurry cliff.

A moment later a call came back. "Heads up! Here it comes!"

Faye thought she could see something coming at her, but it fell short, striking the back of the dying mule, causing him to scream in fresh terror. Well, it must be about time to take care of that little detail while she was at it. She really shouldn't put it off any longer. "Wait here, Matew. I'll be right back," she said to the unconscious young man as she bent over to retrieve his belt knife.

Matew's knife was too big for Tasmin's sheath, so she settled it firmly behind her belt. She didn't want to take a chance on losing another knife. No matter how much her mind or stomach rebelled, she couldn't allow the miserable mule to suffer any longer.

"Poor boy. I know you're hurt. Let me help you, boy. Let me take all the pain away," she crooned as she crossed the few feet between them, hating herself for what she had to do.

Amazingly, the mule seemed to calm down this time at the sound of her voice, or perhaps he was merely too weak to fight any longer. Whatever the cause, he didn't protest when she started patting his neck. Her vision was blurred by more than rain as she buried her face against his mane to wipe her tears. She remained there for only a brief moment before pulling the sharp dagger and raising it to stab where she thought his artery was. She did it so fast his last scream died as it was born and she was the only one who could hear it. "I'm sorry. So very sorry," she whispered, replacing the knife in her belt even though every instinct told her to throw it away. She knew too well Matew would need it again.

With a heavy sigh, she pushed away from the mule and pulled on her rope so she could lie across his back. She could feel Anabelle helping her from her end, so Tasmin was still watching. Once her own rope was in position, she reached for Matew's rope and retraced her knee marks to her still unconscious friend. As fast as she could with her slippery hands, she tied the rope around his chest just below his arms. Making sure to be especially gentle with the broken left arm. Once he was secure, she resumed digging to free his legs.

She had cleared the mud to just below Matew's knees when there was a rumbling and shaking. The mud was on the move again. This time the dead mule and the boulder he was crushed under were sliding away faster than the area where she and Matew were. The bad news was, the boulder was going to snag their ropes and take them with it. It took Faye only a moment to assess the situation. Dropping the shovel, she took Matew into her arms and held on tight. A second later, the ropes caught, and Matew was pulled free from the suction of the mud as they started to slide. Depending on how far they went, the least she would need to do would be to keep them both from being buried, again. In horror, she watched the boulder as it got closer and closer to the edge of the chasm. If it went over, the chances of either of them surviving was slim. Frantically, she pulled the knife and started slicing at the ropes. She didn't dare count on Tasmin letting them go from her end, although she found herself praying, "Please, Lord, please save us. I know you sent us here for a reason. Save us, and I won't question you ever again."

She looked up briefly, in time to see the dead mule disappear over the edge. Just then, her rope snapped, but she was only halfway through Matew's. Wildly, she sawed at his rope, refusing to give up. Oh, no! There went the boulder. Their speed was accelerating drastically when *snap* went Matew's rope and the two of them slid to a stop against a rock outcrop, less than three feet from the edge.

She was breathing raggedly, and her heart was pounding

as she stared at the river below. "You're beautiful," came a whisper in her ear and she looked over to see Matew, looking at her with a silly smile. She knew what she must look like right now, covered from head to toe in mud and muck. She couldn't help it; she burst out laughing.

Abruptly, there was another shift as the earth settled again, and they started sliding around the outcrop and nearer the drop. She stopped laughing abruptly.

"Uh, I think we'd better see what we can do to get out of here," she suggested, cautiously getting to her knees.

"Where are we? How did we get here? Ow! What's wrong with my arm?"

"Explanations come later! How are your legs? Not broken? Good! Let me help you get to your knees, and then we crawl, uphill and to the left. You go first, I'll follow," she instructed as she dug in the toes of her boots, trying to get traction.

Matew made slow progress, but with Faye's help it was progress. There were several times they slid backward and had to start over before Faye felt they were close enough to the southern edge of the slide to get help from above.

"Tasmin! Tasmin, can you hear me!" she called hopefully, noticing the rain finally appeared to be slackening. Weakly, she raised up on her knees and waved. She was much too tired to even try to stand up. It just wasn't worth the effort. When there was no immediate answer, she was ready to panic. "Tasmin! Believer! Anyone up there?"

"We're right here, dear!" Tasmin's voice was music to her ears and couldn't she see Believer's horn, shining through the rain? "One of the ropes snagged, and I had to cut it free before the horses were dragged over the edge with you. I've been making a harness so Believer and Lady can work together to haul both you and Matew up together on our last rope. Heads up! Here it comes!"

This time the rope landed only two feet in front of Matew,

who reached over and grabbed it. "Here, let me tie it around you," he offered.

"With one hand? I think you'd better relax. You're along for the ride, this time, Matew," she insisted, taking the rope from him and pulling a good length down so she could tie herself on and have plenty of rope to tie around Matew's considerable chest just below her. With slippery, muddy hands, it seemed to take forever, but finally they were both tied securely. She had tied them close enough for her to cradle his broken arm, trying to keep it from being injured any more.

"Take up the slack!" she called. A short time later, she felt a tug as they began to slide up the slope. Was it her imagination, or was it steeper and higher than when she went down?

Four feet from the top, Faye felt a small jerk. When she looked up, she could see a spot on the rope, two feet above her head. The rope had begun to fray. "Tasmin! The rope's breaking! Pull us out of here, fast!" she screamed, closing her eyes in prayer.

While she was imagining the rope breaking, sending the two of them over the edge of the gorge and into oblivion, she missed the miracle. Believer's horn lit up the gloom of the slackening rain, and the rope started mending itself.

In the meantime, there was a sharp slapping sound, and they were jerked unceremoniously up the last few feet and onto what was left of the road. A few seconds later, there was a loud *snap*, and the rope took off after the horses, leaving them gasping and sore in the mud.

Faye lay there for a very long time, catching her breath and trying to assimilate to still being alive and the ordeal was over. Tasmin cut them free and began expertly setting Matew's arm while she pretty much ignored Faye, lying in a filthy, exhausted heap on the ground.

*****

Reluctantly, Faye brought her attention back to the ship's cramped cabin and the end of Tasmin's version of the story. Unfortunately, as she had when telling Matew what happened, she made it sound as if Faye were some kind of hero instead of someone who caused so much death and destruction. They had left the two surviving highwaymen tied to a tree for someone else to find.

"You know, the more I think about it, the more I'm certain the whole thing was Barakus's work," Tasmin concluded thoughtfully.

"Why?" asked Behnam curiously.

"Several reasons. The first being the unseasonable storm. Normal storms, this time of year, never last more than a few hours. The one that found us lasted for days, more like an autumn storm. Secondly, the road. Part of a highway that's stood all kinds of weather for centuries collapsing right where we were when we were most vulnerable? We already know Barakus can sense the 'saviors.' Thirdly, we could only be headed to one place, and he set a trap," she said reasonably.

"It could have just been a freak storm. The road washing out right there, right then. Just a coincidence, right?" argued Faye weakly, wanting so much to believe Tasmin but needing to be convinced.

"Think about it, Faye. An hour after we got on the road again, the rain just stopped. It didn't really taper off, it just stopped, and the sun started coming out of the clouds almost immediately," insisted Tasmin gently.

"She be right, Faye. Don't forget, when we reached the other side of the mountains, we all noticed how it looked like it hadna rained for several tendays on tha' side. We all thought it be odd. Seems ter be Barakus ter me," confirmed Matew excitedly. He knew only too well Faye blamed herself for it all, even though she had saved his life as well.

Faye was ashamed to realize there were tears of relief in her eyes. It hadn't been her fault after all.

Just then, Ebony woke and leaned over the side of the bed to vomit ignominiously into the basin Tasmin had set on the floor. In seconds, the men made their excuses and were gone. They left the small cabin considerably less crowded as Tasmin bent to tend the sick woman.

Faye stood by the window, taking in the night air from the lake. "Men!" she said in disgust, trying to think of a good reason to follow them. Ebony wasn't going to be the best traveling companion on this leg of the journey. Well, she was supposed to be a boy, sufficient excuse to remain topside most of the time. With that thought, she slipped out the door.

CHAPTER 18

Rolling on the River

Tasmin's concoctions seemed to have no more effect toward calming Ebony's poor stomach than they did on stabilizing the incessant rolling of the ship. She nibbled in disinterest on the hard crackers, hardtack?, and sipped weakly on a clear broth whenever Tasmin insisted. In between, she swallowed the water and bitter wine being pressed on her. She simply didn't have the strength to protest. She refused to admit to anyone else, but having something on her stomach when she decided to heave a few minutes later was better than the dry heaves. It would be so much easier if she would just die and get it over with.

In her more lucid moments, Ebony got the impression Faye was always gone. Usually when she woke, it was to find Tasmin in attendance. Not that she was up to being good company, but still, she thought this should bother her. If she could only bring herself to care about such things.

On one such rare occasion, when Faye was there, she asked for her version of the disaster on the road and was hardly satisfied when told that there had been a washout on the road, taking two animals with it and almost taking Matew, Faye's new friend, as well. Since he was unconscious, she had been required to go after him so the remaining horses could pull him back up to Tasmin. Somehow, Ebony was sure there was much more to the story, but then Tasmin returned with more broth or wine, and Faye beat a hasty retreat. Every time she asked Tasmin to tell the story, she had just finished a sip or two of wine or tea and found herself unable to stay awake past the beginning. The only thing she was fairly sure of was little, unassuming Faye was somehow a hero. Now there was an unlikely thought.

Topside, Faye was having the time of her life exploring the ship with Matew. Since she was posing as a boy, no one, including her friends, dared suggest climbing the rigging or taking a watch in the crow's nest was inappropriate. At the same time, since she was a paying passenger, she wasn't expected to work for anyone except Tasmin.

As Tasmin's servant, she did have to help Matew clean up after the animals several times a day and occasionally help below decks with Ebony. Matew tried to do as much of the dirty work above decks as his arm would allow. His gratitude seemed to fall short of taking turns in the sick room. Faye just gave him a disgusted look and kept working. There was no need to arouse any suspicions, or at least any more than Believer already had.

Her main concern was that in the hot summer sun, the sailors and Matew shed their shirts and worked bare-chested or at best in skimpy vests. She took a great deal of teasing about being overdressed and shy for two or three days. Stoically, she decided ignoring them would be the best choice.

Early in the voyage, there had been some comments about Lady Tasmin sharing her cabin with the Mojar, Cadir. At least until Behnam took out his long, curved knife to clean his fingernails while commenting casually to Bass, "You know, my brother has never been on a ship before. It really isn't surprising he should be susceptible to the landlubber's sickness common among many who don't make the water their home. I'm sure in due time he will overcome this temporary weakness. We are grateful to Lady Tasmin for nursing him." The look in his eyes when he looked up made it clear any further comments by the crew would be taken badly on his part. The Mojar reputation for a quick temper and a ruthless nature took care of the rest. The official story was, the good Lady Tasmin had volunteered to tend the sick man. Perfectly natural, since they apparently already knew each other. No one mentioned it was just a bit odd for a Jamben Lady to be traveling in such diverse company. Jambens were known to have odd friends everywhere.

Matew was enthralled by the life aboard ship and adapted quickly, even with his broken arm in a sling. He quickly learned the names of all the sails and which side was port and which starboard. After the first two days, Faye was having more fun irritating Behnam and Bass, who thought her behavior inappropriate. The first time Behnam could get her alone in the men's cabin, he chastised her soundly. "Lady Faye," he began.

"Fred, Behnam. Fred. What if someone hears you?"

"All right, Fred. You really shouldn't be taking such chances. This is no way for...you...to...act. It isn't proper," he lectured.

"On this ship, I'm an ordinary fifteen-year-old boy. Don't you think it would cause more comment if I didn't want to explore the ship from top to bottom?" she teased.

"Possibly, but we could have claimed you were ill as well."

"And confine me in the cabin with, uh, Cadir, barfing everywhere? I don't think so. Besides, it's much too late for that now. Look, I'll be truthful with you, Behnam. I'm enjoying my chance at a second childhood. I didn't have much of a childhood the first time around. My father's ideas of having fun were things like going to concerts, plays, or the opera. Mostly we just read books. The only time I actually got to be a kid was at camp. I'm quite sure once we reach Lohi, if not at Dhwittle, I'll have to grow up and act like a lady again. For now, just let me be a kid, okay?" she implored.

"Oh, all right...Fred. Just please, please be careful. We can't afford any accidents," he said, giving in with a rare smile.

"One other thing, please don't tell the others what I just told you. There's no reason for them to know, is there?" she asked with a saucy grin.

"What? Did you just tell me something? I can't seem to recall."

"Thank you, Behnam. Thank you," she said, giving him a quick peck on the cheek before rushing out the door and back up on deck.

Behnam stared after her with a bemused expression. What a strange woman she was. On the other hand, none of the three women from the other side of the portal were like any ever seen in Persal before.

*****

Much to Cheri and Falcon's dismay, Sir Vera had taken a cabin for himself on the *Gray Gull* as well.

"I had business in Dhwittle that needed tending, and when you said you needed to go there, well...it seemed ideal we travel together. How could I pass up the opportunity to travel in company with such a lovely young lady as well as my new friend, Falcon?" he explained glibly as he stared deeply into Cheri's eyes.

Stubbornly, Cheri decided to ignore Falcon's warnings. She had been cooped up entirely too much of late. First traveling in that bug- infested woodpile and then in her room at the inn. She simply wasn't going to put up with it any longer. Besides, she rather liked Sir Vera's company. She hadn't had much opportunity to meet a real gentleman before. They didn't need to worry too much about it until they tried to lose him in Dhwittle anyway. They had at least a week and a half of traveling to go before his presence could become an issue. In the meantime, Cheri intended to enjoy herself.

The first full day out, Cheri donned the iridescent green/blue dress Ebony had sent to her while they were waiting to leave Dink. The fit was perfect, and she'd had plenty of time to hem it. Now, looking at herself in the pier glass in her cabin, she felt a bit like she was playing dress-up. The skirt was still long, filled out wide by many lace petticoats it swept the floor gracefully. She'd seen the same on the ladies of Dink when she'd arrived. The square-cut bodice was high enough to be considered demur, even by Tasmin, and the long tight sleeves came to a point on the backs of her hands. All in all, she was quite pleased with the effect, even if she wasn't quite sure she knew the person in the mirror who returned her stare. She hardly looked like a veteran street urchin now.

Putting the final touches on her hair, piled in loose curls on top of her head, she left her spacious cabin and swept up the wide steps of the ladder to the deck. In daylight, it was easy to see the *Gray Gull* was a luxury passenger ship, catering to the wealthy who wished to travel. "Cheri, girl, you're traveling in style now," she murmured to herself as she looked around at the neatly uniformed crew in their bare feet and the highly polished woodwork and brass. This was definitely a classy way to travel.

Sir Vera was at her side almost immediately. "My dear Lady Cheri. So good to see you up and about. I missed your company greatly in Dink," he said as he gallantly bent to kiss her hand.

"Not too much, I think. From what I heard, you were almost completely occupied with Falcon. I barely even got to see him, you kept him up so late. I'm sure between the mead, the dice, and Marjaduk, you hardly had time to spare me a second thought," she rejoined, smiling brightly.

"You wound me, Lady Cheri. Actually, you were never far from my thoughts, which is probably why Falcon won so much more than he lost." He sighed, dramatically clutching his chest in mock pain.

Cheri laughed. Yes, this was going to be a most enjoyable trip. Talking with Sir Vera was a form of verbal fencing. It would be nice to play innocent games with a man for once.

"That is the loveliest dress you are wearing. It appears new. Was it one of your many admirers who gave it to you?" he inquired smoothly.

Cheri smiled wistfully, and her eyes grew distant. "It was indeed a gift, a very special one, but not from an admirer. Merely a gift from a friend," she murmured more to herself than Sir Vera as an odd thought occurred to her. *A friend, I don't think I've ever had a woman friend before. Certainly never one who thought of me and what I would like. Especially without concern for themselves. Wow!*

"My dear Lady Cheri, I would be such a friend, if you would let me. Perhaps an emerald necklace to go with your lovely gown?" suggested Sir Vera, a hint of something menacing in his voice startling Cheri back to the here and now.

Cheri giggled, trying to make light of it all. "No, I don't think so, Sir Vera. I don't think emeralds would be an appropriate gift. We hardly know each other, after all. Thank you for the lovely thought, though."

"I don't think you believe I just want to be your friend. You wound me to the heart, Lady Cheri," he protested.

"I am indeed sorry, but the answer is still no. To really be a friend, don't you think we should first get to know each other? This is really only the third time we've met. Why don't you tell me about the politics of Samal?" she inquired, fending him off nicely.

"Such a dry subject for one so young? Surely I could

entertain you better with tales of the hunt or fables of quests from long ago?"

There was a sharp cry above them, and Cheri looked up to see Amalee circling above, now they were away from the city. Sir Vera followed her gaze. "There, see? Let me fetch my bow, and I will show you my prowess as an archer. I've been told I'm the best shot in Dink if not in Samal," he bragged, turning to return to his cabin.

Hastily, Cheri grabbed his arm, "I would really like to know more about the way Samal interacts with the rest of Persal, but if you prefer, tell me tales of your childhood. All I ask is you leave out anything bloody, like hunting poor defenseless birds and animals. I do hate violence so."

This time it was Sir Vera who laughingly capitulated. The rest of the morning was spent in talk of the Samalian Council. In Sir Vera's opinion, they were mostly puppets for Barakus and his priests. They certainly never dared oppose his church openly. The only ones who resisted the priests at all were the city guard and the patrols. They were led by Major Talkurt, and he kept his men well trained. He also kept a superior force in each of the cities of Samal. The church priests were not a match, and they knew it. In many other ways, Barakus and his church ruled in Samal. Most of the people just tried to go on with their lives. They lived by the theory if you ignored it, it might go away. At the very least, if it didn't go away, maybe it wouldn't bother you personally. In the meantime, the council tried to find ways to gain privileges for themselves and their friends, like keeping "undesirables" out of the Grand Avenue Parks.

Cheri smiled and nodded. She was listening intently while she watched the prow of the ship cut through the crystal-clear water. Occasionally she even asked a pertinent question. "Why don't you start to change things? At least things like the restrictions in the park? Surely you have some influence?" she asked, slightly alarmed by what he said. She thought

Tasmin would be proud of her; she was doing her best to learn more about this strange world called Persal.

*****

Six days on the ship and Faye had not only enjoyed the heights of the crow's nest, but true to her taunt, she had learned about the rats and foul-smelling bilge water infesting the depths. Now she truly had explored the ship from top to bottom, and the novelty of behaving like a fifteen-year-old boy was beginning to wear a little thin. The only liberty she still savored was the view from the crow's nest. It was dawn, and she was dreamily watching the sun returning from its nightly voyage to other lands when she heard a shout from the watch behind her to the captain below.

"Vortex three mals ahead, Captain! Off the port bow! Wide waters to the starboard side!"

Her curiosity aroused, Faye peered around his broad shoulders at the river ahead. Controlled pandemonium broke out on the deck below.

"Pilot! Head for the starboard bank! Reef the sails, we don't want too much speed. Mate, send a man to watch the bow and have half the crew ready to shove off if we get too close to the bank. There was a sandspit building near here the last time we passed on that side. We don't want to be stranded if it's still there when the vortex shifts again!" came the captain's orders in rapid succession.

The man on watch glanced down at her as she peered up the river and pointed to a spot off to the left side of the river. There. There was something causing a great deal of disturbance in the water. No, the water itself was the disturbance. A whirlpool! Oh my! Barely to the left of the middle of the river was a whirlpool! How were they going to manage navigating around it?

Excited, Faye scrambled down the ratlines to the deck so

she could get a closer look. Until now, she had begun to get used to everything looking sort of fuzzy, but now she wished it were safe to wear her glasses. She could only hope she would get close enough for a good view as she headed for the bow where Matew had already posted himself.

Captain Jefler and his mate joined the pilot at the tiller where all three were needed as the outer current caught the ship and tried to pull it toward the Vortex. Slowly, steadily, the Jayhawk edged closer to the calmer waters on the right bank of the river. Then, just before the bow drew abreast of the disturbance, they broke free and were once again in the river current. Faye breathed a premature sigh of relief before she noticed the tension on the ship was continuing to rise as they tried to edge past the danger. The man on watch in the bow never let his eyes stray from the water ahead as he looked for the possible sandspit.

Faye and Matew had been watching the whirlpool, and as it passed, they made their way down the port side of the ship. They were amidships where Tasmin had already joined Bass and Behnam when they heard a cry from the bow. "Sandspit! Dead ahead half a mal. Turn two legs to port!"

Faye took one look at the men at the helm as they took two steps to the left, heading them back toward the hazardous current before she started running after the captain, back to the bow, Matew right behind her. When she arrived, even she could see the ripple in the water caused by the hidden threat. "I don' like the looks of this at all, at all," muttered the Captain with a worried frown. "This sandbar should na be so large so soon."

As the ship turned, she divided her attention between the two hazards. Surely it would be better to be grounded than swept into the Vortex? Again, she could feel the slight tug of the current as the ship came near the edge of those whirling waters and the sandspit began to slip behind them. Finally, just when she was sure they wouldn't make it, they were clear. The Vortex was behind them, and it was safe to head for the middle of the river again. Faye found herself meeting Matew's eyes and returning his grin. There was something invigorating about coming close to disaster and winning. She had certainly never encountered anything like this at home. This strange new world seemed to make her come alive.

Below decks, Ebony awoke with a start. Something had changed! Something was wrong. The ship was turning. Were they there, finally? "Tasmin?" she called weakly as she struggled to sit up slowly and look around the dim cabin. When there was no answer, she started to panic as she realized for the first time since the voyage began, she was alone.

Carefully, not daring to move too fast, Ebony swung her legs out of bed and rose unsteadily to her feet. That was another thing, the sounds of running feet coming from above implied a lot of activity. What could be happening? Then there was a sharp tug in the motion of the ship as the current suddenly changed, and her stomach lurched uncomfortably. She took one shaky step toward the door before she realized she would never make it up the ladder. Perhaps she could see enough from the porthole? Grimly, she hung onto the upper bunk and took one shaky step at a time until she could sink on to the trunk under the porthole and look out.

It took a few minutes for what she was seeing to register with her brain. There, outside her window and a little bit toward the front of the boat was a whirlpool! They were all going to drown! Just then, the current lost its hold on the ship, and they appeared to be merely sailing calmly past the danger. Uneasily, she watched as the maelstrom seemed to come closer and then past her window. Just when she thought they might make it, the heading of the ship changed slightly, and they seemed once again to be pulled into the outer reaches of disaster. What could the captain be thinking? Abruptly they were past the whirlpool, and the ship was once again in safe water.

Ebony leaned in exhaustion against the bulkhead, far too tired to even think about returning to the bed. Nothing she had ever faced at home had affected her like this. She was too sick to take the strain; that must be it. "I don't think I like this world very much," she muttered to herself.

*****

It hadn't taken Cheri long to realize her traveling clothes were more comfortable as well as practical during the long, hot days aboard ship, and she had returned to them gratefully although it was customary to dress formally for dinner.

After six days on the *Gray Gull*, it would have been impossible for Cheri not to have met her fellow passengers.

Mr. and Mrs. Cubbitt were a very sweet older couple, enjoying an early retirement from the bindery business he had recently turned over to their only daughter and her husband. They were a matched pair, both being a little short and more than a little stout with graying hair beginning to fade the orange-red of their younger years. Mrs. Cubbitt had early on decided Cheri needed a woman to protect her and had accordingly taken her under her wing.

Mrs. Highho stood taller than she was, her hair piled high and a shade redder than anyone else in Samal and her up-tilted nose always in the air. Cheri was half afraid if it rained the lady might drown. She was traveling with her thoroughly dominated maid who was only seen on deck twice a day and took her meals alone in their cabin. She had been scandalized when she learned Cheri was traveling with two men but no duenna. Since then, she had done her best to ignore Cheri completely.

Mr. Hapton was an exceptionally tidy man of average height, and in Samal, average coloring. Unspectacular thinning red hair and a smattering of faded freckles. He was in the glass business in Dobe and this was the first time his dominating wife had let him leave home without her. Unfortunately, she was home with a sick mother. On more than one occasion when Cheri had found herself alone with the good gentleman, he had tried to get a little too familiar. It was a shame his wife had missed the trip after all. The man definitely needed a keeper.

Mr. Herron and Mr. Craane were sharing a cabin, partners in a soliciting firm. They were both tall and very thin with sharp beaks for noses. Cheri thought their names were very apt. They stayed holed up in their cabin working on something mysterious, only emerging for meals which they ate hurriedly and in silence before returning below decks.

The last cabin was occupied by a well-dressed character with shifty eyes and a sinister look about him. He refused to give his name, so Cheri dubbed him Bugsy. He always seemed to be everywhere, watching everything. He never answered direct questions, but he seemed to listen intently to every word everyone else said. He made Cheri more than a little uncomfortable. She made up her mind early on to ignore him.

She saw little of Falcon on the trip since he left her to Sir Vera and seemed to prefer the company of sailors, much to her irritation.

After two days of lectures on the politics of not only Samal but of Jamben, Swaloh, and Camir as well, Cheri encouraged the Cubbitts to regale her with tales of their travels. They were returning to Dhwittle from Elans in Jamben where they had seen Princess Areola, the Crystal Princess. They had been awed to see the heir of Jamben who had been turned to crystal nearly two thousand years ago, but they could still see her beating heart. Legend had it that while Barakus could cage the body of the princess in crystal, he couldn't still the goodness of her heart.

They were all seated at the lunch table set up on deck. It was sumptuously laid with succulent roast beef and tasty, if purple, potatoes and a large bowl of exotic fresh fruits. Cheri had let it slip this would be her first visit to the fair city of Dhwittle, and the Cubbitts were interrupting each other to tell her of the Dhwittle Menagerie. In all their travels there was no other city with one half as complete.

"In the ancient days the menagerie was said to have held such things as unicorns and dragons." Mr. Cubbitt bragged with a cherubic smile.

"Yes, yes. Many things are said of the old days, dear. But Lady Cheri isn't interested in myths. She wants to hear about the white lanther. A gorgeous cat from the southern continent where it is said to be under snow most of the year, my lady. He is pure white and taller than most men when standing on all fours, the cat this is, not the man. His mane is as of silver. He is said to be the only one in captivity," interrupted Mrs. Cubbitt, patting her husband's hand affectionately.

"Oh, how sad. In captivity and alone. She, or is it a he? must be so lonely," said Cheri with a frown.

Just then the mate approached to whisper in Captain Brogre's ear. Rising, the good captain bowed graciously to each of the ladies. "If you will excuse me, we are coming up on the Vortex, and I must see to our safe passage beyond it. Lady Cheri, if you have never seen our Vortex before, perhaps you would like to come to the bow where the view is better?" he invited before walking hurriedly away.

Instantly the ship erupted into a flurry of activity as the mate relayed a series of rapid orders and the pilot turned the wheel sharply to port. The sails were being furled as Cheri grabbed another fruit resembling a cross between a strawberry and a pear and rose to comply with his suggestion. *Vortex? What did that mean?* The man had aroused her curiosity.

As they neared the left bank, several sailors who had doffed their shirts and put on long leather vests grabbed long ropes and mounted the bulwarks. Cheri forgot she was posing as a lady, and stooping low, she grabbed an armful of skirt and set off at a run to the bow of the ship.

Once her vantage point was reached, she looked at the swirling waters ahead and gasped in alarm. The currents of that deadly whirlpool must be too strong for the boat! Then the men in leather vests stepped onto the bulwarks, and all swung over the water to the bank of the river. Why were they leaving? Surely, they had seen this before? Then she heaved a sigh of relief as the men still aboard ship began throwing heavy ropes, as thick as her arm and with a loop at one end, to each man onshore. The men ashore pulled it over their heads and arms to settle it around their waist before taking off running at an easy lope to keep abreast of the ship while pulling slightly toward the bank. Well, the men were built like wrestlers, they might be sturdy enough to hold the boat out of, what did the captain call it? Vortex? Involuntarily, Cheri's eyes returned to the Vortex, and there was Falcon, standing beside her.

"Can we make it? It seems so, I don't know, determined somehow," she whispered in awe.

"Ships have been getting by the Vortex for centuries, Cheri. I wouldn't worry too much. This skipper seems to be taking more precautions than most," he assured her with a smile.

Mrs. Cubbitt had come up on her right side, much to the vexation of Sir Vera. "Quite a sight, isn't it, Miss Cheri? It is said the Creator put it there to relieve the monotony of the voyage down the river. It moves from one side of the river to the other on a predictable timetable which is why the time the ships leave port going either way is so rigidly controlled," he lectured behind her.

"Well," fluttered Mrs. Cubbitt, seemingly out of breath, "Speaking for myself, I think I would rather have joined the young men on the shore. I'm quite sure their view is every bit as good as ours."

The men all chuckled with good nature, "There, there, dear. I'm quite sure we're safe or the captain would have said something. Isn't it strange, we've traveled through four countries in the last two years, and the most amazing sights are practically in our own backyard?" soothed Mr. Cubbitt, a tinge of excitement in his voice.

"Mara, dear! Whatever are you doing on deck?" exclaimed Lady Highho, apparently more astounded at finding her maid topside than at the awesome force of nature off the starboard bow.

Just then, the captain came up to the cluster of passengers at the rail. "I invited her to see this, my lady. No one should miss such a sight when the opportunity presents itself. It isn't often most of us come so close to destruction and still pass it by. I want all of you to rest assured we are in no danger. The channel is very deep on this side of the river."

Overhead, Amalee wheeled and screamed, trying to warn Falcon of the oncoming danger. Throwing back his head, Falcon uttered a harsh cry in response, and the hawk flew off to perch atop a high tree downriver where she could watch.

Cheri watched the current in morbid fascination as they drew abreast of the Vortex. The passengers moved together, as though mesmerized, down the rail to the middle of the ship, following the whirlpool.

With a start, Cheri grabbed Falcon's arm, "It's getting closer!" she breathed.

Behind her, Sir Vera laughed, "Of course it seems that way as we move along the side. It's really nothing to worry about. I've taken this trip many times, trust me."

"No. No, she's right! Look there! The Vortex is starting to move back toward this side of the river!" confirmed Falcon.

Hearing this, Mrs. Cubbitt promptly screamed and fainted into her husband's arms.

A moment or two later they could all feel a definite tug as the current started to grab at the ship. Followed almost immediately by the sound of a loud *snap!*

Whirling around, Cheri was just in time to see one of the sailors onshore, close to the bow, go flying out of control into the bushes near the river as the frayed end of his rope whipped back toward the ship. The muscles on the rest of the men bulged as they tried to keep the ship close to shore. The two men left holding the bow seemed to be sliding toward the water as more men from the ship rushed to join those on land.

Looking about, she noticed the captain had left them to join the pilot and the mate as they struggled with the tiller against the current of the insistent Vortex. There was no doubt now the whirlpool was returning to the right side of the river.

Mrs. Highho was crying and clinging to her maid, Mara, while Falcon rushed to see if he could help the sailors still onboard. After a minute or two, Sir Vera joined him. The other male passengers tried to comfort the women, not knowing what else to do.

Mr. Hapton tried to put his arms around Cheri to comfort her. Adroitly, she stepped away. "I think I'd rather see if I can help," she said acerbically and headed for the other side of the ship, taking up a position next to Falcon to watch the ropes for signs of wear so a new rope could be set out before another snapped.

"Raise the sails! We'll need to make a run for it! She's turning!" bellowed Captain Brogre from his place at the tiller and seven of the crew nearest to Cheri and Falcon hastened to obey.

One high scream could be heard from above as Amalee

returned to her circling. There would be no way for Falcon to convince the bird to leave them now.

Cheri and Falcon spread out as they each tried to watch several ropes at once. The men onshore strained harder, and Cheri wasn't sure what would break first, the men or the ropes. Were they being pulled closer to the river or was it just her imagination? Then she saw several of the straining men on shore slide sideways, toward the water as the boat lurched away from the bank. The sails had caught the wind, and their speed was increasing. The men ashore began to trot to keep up as they continued their struggle, but was it all too late to beat the advancing Vortex?

"No!" screamed Cheri. The Vortex couldn't win! The prophecy was supposed to protect her!

Impulsively, Cheri grabbed two of the ropes leading to the men onshore, her eyes meeting theirs, as they battled to keep from being pulled into the river. It was as though an electric shock ran through the hemp while moments later the two men pulled with extraordinary strength. Strength they hadn't known they had. Encouraged, Cheri moved over to two more ropes, and the same thing happened. After two dozen men began to pull with superhuman strength, the ship slowly, then with increasing ease began to edge ahead of the Vortex. Abruptly, Cheri fell as the Vortex reluctantly let them go. They were clear! They had made it. Cheri slumped on the deck in relief and inexplicable exhaustion, ignoring the continuing bustle around her as the ship prepared to slow, allowing the drained men on shore to reboard.

Falcon and Sir Vera reached her at the same time.

"Lady Cheri! What happened! What did you do?" gasped Sir Vera, a speculative gleam in his eyes.

"Cheri! Are you all right? You really shouldn't scare me like that. I think you'd better rest now," insisted Falcon with a worried frown. Ignoring Sir Vera and the other passengers and crew, he lifted her in his arms and carried her to the safety of her cabin.

Just before they made their way into the gangway, Cheri heard a scream from Amalee and looked up to see her flying off. Evidently, she believed they were safe now too.

Alone int her cabin, Falcon gently lay her on the bed before standing and shaking his head sadly, "Whatever you did, I should be grateful. At least we're still alive, but whatever were you thinking? We're not supposed to draw attention to ourselves. What you just did must have been like the tolling of bells to Barakus. How do you propose to explain this to the other passengers?"

"I don't know right now. I guess I'll let the prophecy take care of it," she replied in a small weak voice as she suddenly started to shake uncontrollably. "Shhhock. I...I...I-I'm going into shhhock!" she managed to get out.

"Here, let me wrap you up, you're freezing," responded Falcon swiftly, pulling the quilt on the bed around her tightly. Now he was feeling guilty about scolding her. When the quilt wasn't enough, he opened the quilt, lay next to her, and pulled the quilt close again. He needed to add his body warmth to bring Cheri through this.

When Cheri finally stopped shaking, she was asleep. Checking her carefully, Falcon eased his arms from under her and tucked the quilt tightly about her again. He still had no idea what he was going to tell the passengers and crew about what had just happened.

*****

The merchant ship Profit entered the Jamben port of Moonraker Bay with the afternoon tide. Gaban and Ochwatt left the vessel as soon as the gangplank hit the dock, looking for a faster ship to take them on to Lohi. Captain Wender planned to stop at every port between the two, selling and buying cargo. Gaban was feeling a greater urgency and was desperate to get to Lohi where he could talk to Gabriene.

Striding purposefully, he scanned the docks to see what sort of ships might be available.

Then he saw the raker. A closed-hull ship with two rows of oarlocks on either side, two masts and painted black. "Doome! Barakus has started the Taking. Why now? He hasn't sent his ships in over seventy years," he muttered, more to himself than Ochwatt.

As always, Ochwatt listened carefully to everything Gaban said but saved his questions for later. The ship the wizard was looking at was long and sleek and looked like it might be faster than any others he could see. When Gaban headed to the next pier and a sleek schooner with three masts, he merely filed it away to be questioned later.

The *Flying Seahawk* was indeed a fast ship, but Captain Ta'Jar wasn't headed to Lohi. "I'm headed to the southern continent, Master Gaban. I have acquired a map, and there's great profit to be had from such a voyage. Why should I consider changing my plans?"

"This would only be a slight delay, and I can guarantee a great profit at the end. Gabriene himself will pay a large bonus for getting us there early."

"Ah! Tempting. The menagerie in Dhwittle is willing to pay five thousand dejars for a female white lanther to partner with the one they have. If you cannot do better than that, I must be heading south," said the captain regretfully.

"I can give you two thousand dejars now, and Gabriene will be giving you five thousand when we reach Lohi. It's only a slight delay, after all. You'll still get to the southern continent and your female lanther."

"You have a point. Twice the profit with only a little more of the work. All right, agreed! We can leave as soon as you have your things aboard."

CHAPTER 19

Off Again, On Again

Cheri woke to a light tapping at her door, followed by the fluttery, round form of Mrs. Cubbitt and an imperious Lady Highho. "Oh, my dear, you haven't even started to dress for dinner, and everyone's so excited! Surely, you've had enough rest by now. Mind you, I didn't see it myself since I was unfortunately indisposed. I do have such a delicate constitution, you know. Anyway, I hear you were just marvelous! All the sailors say you quite simply inspired them to do more than they thought they could," Mrs. Cubbitt twittered as she bustled about the small cabin, pulling out Cheri's lemon-yellow chiffon dress and several suitable slips.

"Yes, dear girl. They've actually declared you the heroine of the day, although I must say I still don't quite understand what you were supposed to have done. I mean, all I saw was you touching their ropes. I could have done that much. Well, no matter, come, come dearie. Do get up. Dinner is in only half an hour, and they all seem so set on seeing you," said Lady Highho, half graciously as she picked up Cheri's plastic brush and stared in bewilderment at the small pile of French clips, cloth-covered elastic scrunchies, and the banana comb Cheri had left on the vanity.

"Oh, dear," Cheri muttered under her breath as she jumped up and reclaimed her brush, incidentally positioning herself between the lady and the vanity before she could get a close look at her small collection of cosmetics. "Half an hour? No problem! I'll be right up. Tell you what, ladies, it's so crowded in here, I'll bet I can get ready faster on my own. Why don't you both go on up and tell everyone I'll be there in a jiffy?"

"Jiffy?" inquired Mrs. Cubbitt, screwing her face up in confusion.

"Shortly. Just tell them I'll be up soon," corrected Cheri hurriedly as she ushered them toward the door.

"I'm sure you are quite right about the space, but perhaps I can send Mara to help you with your hair?" conceded Lady Highho in a skeptical tone, clearly voicing her doubts as she stared in dismay at Cheri's unruly mop of red curls.

"Now, don't be silly. I'm used to taming my hair. You two just run along now so I can get started," insisted Cheri as she finally got them into the hall, retrieving her clothes from Mrs. Cubbitt just before closing the door firmly behind them and throwing the bolt.

With a sigh of relief, she leaned against the door and started to giggle at the odd looks the two women had exchanged. Obviously, they weren't sure what to make of her. She certainly didn't fit into any categories they knew of.

Turning from the door, she caught a glimpse of herself in the pier glass and sobered instantly. What a mess! She looked like she had just climbed out of bed and had slept in her clothes. Of course, she had, but she had less than half an hour to pull herself together!

Forty minutes later, the vision of loveliness emerging from the ladder barely resembled the tousled child of a few minutes earlier. Her gown floated about her like a lemon mist, and her long red curls were pulled back with the aid of the banana comb into long, fat ringlets she had pulled forward to fall over her left shoulder. A touch or two of cosmetics had sufficed to subtly smooth over any remaining signs of tiredness. She thought she was ready to greet the crew and her fellow passengers.

She was wrong. The rousing cheer the sailors greeted her with gave her pause. Even more so when it was joined by the passengers as she stepped on deck. Noticeably quiet were Lady Highho, who apparently considered herself above such things, and Bugsy, who was watching intently from the port rail.

Before Cheri could worry too much about either of them, the crew snapped to attention where they were lined up along the starboard rail and saluted smartly. Her fellow passengers fell quiet as Captain Brogre crossed the deck to stand at attention before her.

"Lady Cheri, your courage in the face of imminent disaster today was an inspiration to us all, but mostly to the gallant men of my crew. Never before have I witnessed them putting forth such heroic efforts and while I commend each and every one of them, they insist it was when you touched their ropes, they felt renewed energy and they had the strength to fight the Vortex. This day will be remembered forever in the histories of Samal," he said formally before taking her hand and kissing it. "We would be honored if you would be our guest at dinner this evening," he finished, barely waiting for her nod before placing her hand on his arm and leading the way to the head of an extra-long table.

The passengers were quick to find places at the top of the table, arranging themselves automatically according to their social standing. Hesitantly, the crew began filing across the deck toward the far end of the table.

Cheri smiled warmly, allowing her dimples to show charmingly. "Excuse me but wouldn't it really be more fitting to honor those brave men who really saved us all today? Please, gentlemen, won't you take your places here, at the head of the table? Lady Highho, I don't see Mara anywhere.

Surely on an occasion such as this, she should be included? Falcon, be a dear and fetch her, please," she requested reasonably, meeting Falcon's grin and sending him a wink in the resulting confusion of everyone changing places.

When everyone had once more settled into the seats, Sir Vera sat near the middle of the table looking confused. Lady Highho was clearly aghast to find herself seated between the cabin boy and one of the sailors. Mara was sitting between the first mate, who seemed especially taken with the mousy woman, and a sailor near the top.

The burly sailors, who usually kept aloof, quietly going about their duties, suddenly found themselves the center of attention and many ducked their heads in embarrassment.

As the first course of succulent pork roast and baked waleys were brought out, Cheri paused to wonder how Falcon had worked the miracle of making them think she had merely inspired them. She wasn't even sure what had really happened herself. Looking up, she met his gaze at the far end of the table, and they exchanged a secret smile.

"By the way, Captain, what happened back there?" asked Sir Vera as he helped himself to several generous slices of waleys.

"I have no idea, good sir. The Vortex wasn't due to turn for at least two hours. In all my days of sailing the White River, I've never seen it happen before."

"Don't the prophecies speak of common events happening out of time, or something? When the awaited one arrives, I mean," asked Mr. Herron timidly.

"Well, it does speak of upheaval and turmoil, but I'm not sure if what just happened qualifies," said Mr. Craane soothingly.

"I have another question," put in Cheri, changing the subject. "I didn't see any wreckage on the banks of the river. What happens to ships that get caught by the Vortex?"

The captain's dark eyes met her green ones for a long time before he answered, "It has only happened a few times over the centuries. Do you really want to know now? This is hardly a fit conversation in front of ladies."

"I hate to burst your bubble, Captain, but women are hardly as fragile as you seemed to think. Please, I really want to know," she implored, sending him her most winning smile.

With a heavy sigh and a look around the table where everyone was waiting, he explained, "When a ship dares get too close to the Vortex, it keeps it. It's never been known to return so much as a broken board or a scrap of sail."

"Thank you, Captain. I appreciate your honesty."

*****

It was early morning two days after passing the Vortex, and Faye leaned contentedly on the rail of the small crow's nest, watching Ebony as she slowly practiced the graceful movements of tai chi on the deck far below. She had no idea exactly what had caused it, but Ebony's seasickness seemed to have miraculously disappeared immediately after passing the Vortex. Since then she had spent most of her days on deck, disguised as Cadir and going through the graceful movements of her martial arts.

Behnam and Bass were also watching. Behnam from the base of the mainmast where he stood straight and tall, his arms crossed over his massive chest. Bass, from the top of a nearby hatch cover where he had taken a seat.

Then Faye spotted Matew, easing around by the horses to get behind Ebony. He was going to try to imitate her again. Awkwardly, one arm still in a sling, the large young man tried to copy Ebony's fluid movements as she flowed from one stance to another. Actually, Faye wouldn't have minded doing the same, but two things stopped her. She didn't want to appear too graceful in front of the crew who apparently thought it was some sort of Mojar ritual or something. She also didn't want to look a fool in front of Bass and Behnam if she lost her footing.

As Ebony finished her exercises, she caught a glimpse of motion behind her and turned with a grin. "Matew! Why didn't you say you were interested in learning tai chi? I'd be happy to teach you. If Lady Tasmin has no objections."

"The boy hasn't enough to do anyway. It will keep him out of trouble. As long as you take care with his arm, please go right ahead, Cadir. I'm quite sure the discipline would be good for him," said Tasmin, looking up from her sewing with a particularly devilish smile.

Bass rose from his seat and joined the others. "You know, Cadir, those moves of yours are all very interesting, but what good are they?"

From her crow's nest, Faye grinned and glanced at Behnam who also allowed himself a small smile as he settled casually against the mast. He obviously felt they were in for a good show.

Ebony, on the other hand, didn't allow a smile to reach her lips, but Faye was sure her brown eyes were sparkling as she turned to look Bass over appraisingly, pausing significantly at his well-muscled chest and arms. "I'll tell you what, Bass, why don't you try to attack me. I mean, seriously attack me. Any way you choose. From the front, from the back, anything you choose," she invited in a quiet voice.

Sensing something was up, the crew began to look for good vantage points, some even choosing the ratlines to better see the competition between the lightly built Mojar and the burly woodsman. Quietly they began making bets on the outcome.

As Ebony continued to just stand there, waiting, even turning away slightly to wink at Matew, Bass appeared to be confused. Almost desperately, he glanced at Behnam. He found no help there as the tall black man merely shrugged. He didn't want to fight a woman. It had seemed like a harmless question, but since the crew believed her to be a young man, there was no way to back down now. Worse, Ebony didn't even appear to be paying him any attention.

Abruptly, Bass turned and rushed at Ebony only to find himself greeted by laughter as he stumbled right through the spot where she'd just been. Startled, he turned to see she was still there, or nearly so. She'd only moved a step, and she appeared to be still waiting for him to try to attack. With a frown, he came at her more slowly, arms raised in a fighting pose. As he swung on her, her own hands raised to block his punches so quickly he couldn't even see them coming, and there was even more laughter from the watchers as the betting increased. *What was going on here, anyway?* he wondered as he danced back a step or two to reassess his strategy. When he did so, Ebony calmly turned her back on him and looked up at Faye in the crow's nest. Deciding this might be his only chance, Bass rushed up to grab Ebony around the throat only to find himself flying through the air, landing on his back on the hatch cover he'd so recently vacated. He let out an "Oof!" as the wind was knocked out of him.

By now the crew were bending over, holding their sides; they were laughing so hard, before collecting on their bets. Bass caught his breath and rolled over to stare in awe at Ebony. Behnam came up behind him to help him to his feet, whispering softly in his ear, "You never had a chance, dear friend. My brother went easy on you."

Still stunned, Bass looked in disbelief, first at Behnam then at Ebony. At least the crew didn't know she was a woman. Wouldn't that really make them howl?

Gracefully, Ebony put her hands together, fingers up, and gave him a deep bow. Then she glanced around at the other men, "Since you all find this so amusing, perhaps some of you would be interested in having a lesson of you own?" she invited.

Most of the crew glanced at each other nervously, reluctant to be the first volunteer and as a couple of men near the front hesitantly raised their hand, Goff stepped through their ranks to stand in the open space, with Ebony. "If that invite be open to all, I be the one," he rumbled from deep inside.

Ebony didn't even flinch as she looked him over. Of course, she'd noticed him before. You'd have to be blind to miss him. He was an inch or two taller than Behnam and half again as broad in the shoulders and chest as Bass. He had pale-red hair and skin so fair even living life outdoors as he did his arms and his nose were constantly red and peeling. With graceful courtesy, Ebony repeated the bow she had given Bass.

Alarmed, Behnam stood straight and clenched his jaw to keep from saying anything as the giant rushed her only to find she'd stepped aside as she'd done earlier.

"Be ye goin' ter fight or be ye goin' ter run?" he bellowed as he turned to come at her again. On the rails, the gambling had gained momentum.

With a slight shrug, Ebony set herself in a horse stance and waited. More slowly, Goff advanced again, only to find every move he made to strike out, or to grab at her, was brushed aside.

"Fight, ye landlubber! If'n ye canna knock me doon, it dinna count!" he shouted in frustration as he continued to try to reach Ebony.

Abruptly, as he advanced, Ebony moved a little closer to the giant and turned slightly aside as she brought her bare right foot up and hit Goff sharply on the left side of his head, causing him to stagger and fall on one knee. She danced back lightly as she assessed what damage had been done.

By now a hush had fallen over the onlookers. Goff was the

ship's champion, and there had never been a man who could beat him.

"I said doon an' I mean all the way doon, boy," Goff grumbled as he stumbled to his feet again.

Ebony shook her head slightly and went on the offensive. Hands and feet seemed to blur as she simultaneously countered his every move and managed to land several blows of her own. Finally, she was able to throw him off-balance as she whirled behind him and gave him a powerful chop to the neck, sending him sprawling onto the deck.

It only took a stunned moment for the crew to glance from their fallen comrade to Ebony and back again before they let loose with a rousing cheer as losers paid on their bets.

"Port, 'round the bend!" came the sudden call from the watch next to Faye in the crow's nest and instantly the crew scurried to prepare the ship for docking, leaving Goff where he lay.

Flush from the exertion of the fight and still breathing heavily, Ebony crossed to where Behnam and Bass were helping Goff rise to put out a hand. "You put up a good fight, Goff. It was quite a challenge," she said sincerely.

Goff scowled down at her for a moment before breaking into a grin, shaking her hand very firmly. "I'll say this, Cadir, ye be no boy but a man grow'd. I havena had as good a fight since last I was in Lohi. If ye ever need a fightin' partner, just send word," he said warmly before running aft to help ready the anchor.

Wryly, Ebony rubbed her hand. "That's the only thing he did that hurt me," she muttered.

"As I'm sure he intended, Cadir. As I'm sure he intended. Just don't dismiss his offer. He was most sincere, and he will honor it if you ever have the need. Come, we must gather our things to disembark at Dhwittle." Behnam laughed as he put his arm across her shoulder and guided her toward their cabins.

On her other side, Bass grumbled, "You'll have to show me how you threw me, sometime."

"I'd be happy to oblige, Bass, but for now I want nothing more than to get off this heaving ship." She laughed in reply.

Land! At last! The thought gave wings to Ebony's feet, and in only a moment, she was in her cabin pulling on her boots and watching Tasmin and Faye gather their carefully packed belongings.

Before the crew had finished tying up the ship or the gangplank had hit the pier, a small man with a neatly trimmed blue-white beard and long white hair flowing from under an oversized red hat with a large white plume hopped aboard, settling his short sword on the hip of his red suit and using a strangely twisted staff to clear a passage.

"Ah. The good Lady Tasmin. We meet at last. I have a carriage waiting to take you and your charges to a safe place, but we really must hurry," he chattered amiably in a deep voice as he greeted them all with a formal bow, sweeping the plume of his hat on the deck.

"Your traveling companions can bring the horses, but we really must be on our way," he insisted when the small group simply stared at him for a long moment. Finally, Behnam bent over, picked up the small man, and lifted him to eye level. "I suggest you tell us first who you are and how you knew we'd be on this ship," he snarled with a fierce grin.

"Don't be foolish, we're wasting time! Oh, all right. I can see you won't budge until you're satisfied. Just put me down, friend Behnam, and I'll tell you what you want to know," he capitulated in exasperation, waving his staff menacingly.

Slowly, very slowly, Behnam complied while Bass and Matew stepped closer to keep him from running off.

Indignantly, the small man straightened his red jerkin

before sweeping off his absurd hat again and giving Tasmin and the others another deep bow, "I, my dear ladies and gentlemen, am Jakar. A halfling of Jessamine. Perhaps you have heard of my people and their talents?" he asked graciously.

The quick look Tasmin and Bass exchanged spoke volumes. "Say no more, Sir Jakar. We're right behind you," said Tasmin firmly, ushering the confused Faye and Ebony before her down the gangplank toward the carriage as she called orders over her shoulder.

"Matew, run! Help Bass and Behnam fetch the animals. I suggest we all hurry as Jakar has so wisely suggested. Come along everyone, come along," she kept insisting, never lessening her own pace as Bass and Matew headed for the horses, followed shortly by Behnam, who looked after them for a moment, shaking his head in confusion.

There was indeed an enclosed carriage waiting, and the little man ushered the three women and their saddlebags inside with a low comment to Tasmin before closing the door and clambering up to take the reins.

Bass, Behnam, and Matew had barely reached the dock when he slapped the reins, and the carriage headed out at a quick pace, going west-southwest, toward the sea.

Behnam and Bass swung easily into their saddles, Bass riding Ebony's chocolate palomino, George, with Anabelle and the mule in tow, they took off at a canter to catch the disappearing coach.

Matew was left behind, trying to convince the restless Believer to hold still and let him mount.

Finally, just as the others were disappearing down a windy street, Believer got very still, his ears cocked forward, and Matew managed to hoist himself into the saddle. Unfortunately, once he was mounted, Matew couldn't seem to persuade Believer to move faster than a walk. To make matters worse, a troop of church soldiers came out of a side street, pushing and shoving anyone who didn't clear a path out of their way. They were led by a tall, husky priest riding alongside the captain.

With a twitch of his ears and a loud neigh, Believer reared up on his hind legs and broke into a gallop, going the wrong way! Ignoring Matew's frantic pull on the reins, the errant unicorn turned into the main thoroughfare going south, toward the center of the city.

Glancing over his shoulder, Matew saw the priest urge his horse after him, leaving the troop captain to give a hurried order to his men to hold and search the ship before he urged his horse into a gallop, following the priest and Matew.

Racing along, Matew tried in vain to bring the animal under control, cursing all the while, "You Doomed animal! What in Doome's gotten into you?" he yelled as he pulled sharply on the reins again. He just couldn't understand why Believer was doing this to him. He was never going to be able to find the others again.

Finally, the burly priest caught up and was able to grab the rein on the left while pulling his own barrel-chested gelding to a stop, forcing Believer to stop as well.

"Back there...for just a moment...I thought...I felt... something," panted the priest, his grip on Believer's reins tightening.

"This certainly don't look like no witch to me. Looks more like a stable boy on his master's stallion. Why'd you take off running like that, boy?" growled the captain who had arrived a few seconds after Believer was brought to a halt.

"I didn't do anything! It was this hardheaded horse! I guess he was restless after being on the ship for so long. Once we reached the dock, he just took off!" objected Matew, taking his cue from the captain's comments, giving Believer a hard glare. At least the delinquent unicorn hadn't resumed his trick of changing colors and breeds yet.

"He certainly appeared to be trying to stop the beast, but still I felt...something. Bring him with us back to the ship, perhaps we'll get more answers there," ordered the priest in bewilderment. Handing the reins over to the captain.

Unfortunately, Matew was well and truly caught as they led an unreasonably spirited Believer back to the ship.

*****

Bouncing over the cobblestone street in the carriage, Ebony was cursing mildly, and even Faye could be heard muttering as they tried to keep their balance and change their clothes at the same time.

"Mumf!" said Ebony as they hit a particularly large pothole. "Why is it so important we get wherever we're going looking like women again?" she asked as she was finally able to settle back and tuck her blouse into her maroon riding skirt.

"Jakar has assured me it would be for the best," answered Tasmin calmly, as though that explained anything.

"Oof!" gasped Faye as she was bounced off the other side of the carriage and into Tasmin, again. "That's another thing! Who is this Jakar that we should simply put ourselves into his hands like this? Is he some kind of Hobbit or something? How do we know he's not taking us straight to Barakus's priests?"

Tasmin smoothed her own split skirt as Faye returned to her side of the carriage and reached across to try to help Ebony arrange her braids, set free of the turban at last. "Hobbit, dear? Sometimes you say the strangest things. Jakar is from Jessamine. The fabled island in the Great Southern Sea. Only the truly lost and the Jessamines themselves can find that island. The island is famous for two things: their great Chardell horses—the best war horses in the world— and their seers. The great seer Jarok gave us a great portion of the prophecy. He was from Jessamine. If Jakar insists there are good reasons for doing things this way, he has seen the alternatives."

"A seer? You mean a psychic? Someone who can see into the future? I mean really see into the future? Don't you think you're pushing our gullibility a bit too far?" scoffed Ebony.

"Where did you think the prophecy came from? Think! He knew exactly where and when to meet us. He's never met any of us before, but he recognized us, even with your disguises. Of course, he's a seer," said Tasmin with an arched brow.

"Yes," breathed Faye in awe as she brushed her short red hair back in a long barrette to make it appear longer. "Don't you remember, Ebony? He knew Tasmin's and Behnam's names. Besides, in a land full of magic and unicorns, a seer shouldn't be that big of a stretch."

"Perhaps you're right. I guess it's because we have so many charlatans who make false prophecies back home. Being skeptical comes with the territory," mumbled Ebony, not convinced but grudgingly willing to concede the possibility.

Abruptly, the carriage pulled to a stop, throwing Tasmin and Faye back in their seats with Ebony in their lap.

"We're here. We're here. Is everyone decent?" called Jakar just before opening the door and popping his head in. "Good. Good. This is for you, Lady of Hope. Eat it up. We'll be boarding soon now," with a gamin grin he handed a small cake to Ebony and was gone again.

Ebony's mouth had dropped open, and she found herself holding the cake and staring at the closed door.

"What was that all about? What did he mean by Lady of Hope? Ebony, what did he give you?" asked a very curious Faye as she pushed the dazed Ebony off her lap.

"What? Oh, this? I have no idea. It looks like a cake," answered Ebony as she disentangled herself from the other two women.

"Well, eat it girl. I'm sure there's a reason for Jakar's giving it to you. Get away from the shade, Faye! Jakar told me to keep them pulled until he comes for us. We're not safe yet," said Tasmin, exasperated with both of them.

Ebony dutifully nibbled on her cake, but her mind was evidently a million miles away. Tasmin thought she heard her whisper, "Hope."

Reluctantly, Faye pulled back from the window, "It's so stifling hot in here. Is anyone else suffocating? Besides, it looks to me like we've been going in circles. We're still at the docks. The only difference I can see is the ships outside are quite a bit larger," she said petulantly as she sank back into the seat.

Ebony swallowed the last bite of her cake. "More ships? Please, please, don't tell me we're getting on another ship. I haven't fully recovered from the last one!" she wailed in dismay.

"What are you talking about? I thought you'd gotten over it. I mean, well, you've been acting normal ever since we passed the Vortex. I just assumed Tasmin's tea had finally started working, or something," said Faye in perplexity.

"No, it just took the Vortex trying to pull our ship to oblivion to make me realize something. I reminded myself we have been in constant danger since we got to Persal, and I decided if I were going to die, I wasn't going to do it while lying in bed feeling sorry for myself. It is absurd to cave in to seasickness.

"All right. So how did you get over feeling so sick? You certainly didn't look queasy when you sent Bass flying across the deck," inquired Tasmin, leaning forward to hear better.

"I never did conquer it completely. I simply decided to put the mental disciplines of my training to work, and I was able to control it. Practicing my forms helped as well," she explained with a shrug. "You know, the queasy feeling never quite went away until just a moment ago. About the time I finished that little cake Jakar gave me. Faye's right, it is unbearably hot in here."

"Ladies, gather your things, we're ready to board. Come, ladies. I apologize for the delivery, but you won't be safe until you're on the ship," came Jakar's deep voice as he rapped on the door.

Tasmin had already repacked their bags, so they handed them out to Behnam and Bass before emerging to all the bustle and smells of any waterfront, but this time the air was flavored with salt. They were close to the Great Southern Sea.

As she reached the ground, Ebony stood straight to stretch after the confines of the carriage and took a moment to look around in dejection. Their destination was obviously a very large ship with several towering masts. What was that? Across the wooden wharf from the waiting ship was a long, sleek, black ship with a black dragon on the prow. The men preparing her for sailing were burly and gruff, and several church soldiers were guarding it. Very ominous.

"Oh, look!" called Faye, pointing at the figurehead mounted on the bow of their ship. It was a white unicorn dancing in the waves and on the side of the ship was the name, *Unicorn's Magic.*

Tasmin leaned forward and put a hand in the middle of their backs, pushing them gently to get them moving. "A good omen, I would say, but let's get aboard. We're not safe yet!" she whispered as she propelled them up the gangplank.

Jakar scampered ahead while Behnam and Bass led the horses aboard.

Ebony picked up her pace and stalked up the ramp to the deck of the ship, reaching it well ahead of the others. Once there, she turned to wait impatiently for them to join her, obviously upset. "Look, just because we're dressed like women again doesn't give you the right to treat us like brainless, helpless females!" she growled in a low voice.

Bass had been looking at the newly feminine Faye as though at a stranger. It was hard to believe this lovely woman was the same tomboy, Fred, he had watched climbing through the riggings on the Jayhawk only that morning. Reluctantly, he turned to Ebony and grinned while rubbing his back. "Believe me, I'm well aware you're far from helpless. The fresh bruises on my back are testimony to that!"

"Whatever has gotten into you, Ebony? You know we respect your intelligence as well as your fighting skills," asked Tasmin acerbically, never letting her smile slip as she cocked her head curiously. "As your duenna, it's only proper for me to be right behind you and for your servants, Behnam and Bass to bring up the rear."

"Well, what's going on? Does anyone know why we're here instead of somewhere out of sight waiting for Cheri? You hustled us onto this ship fast enough, but we're still in plain sight to anyone who chances by. One other thing, if this ship tries to set sail before Cheri is onboard, I'm getting off! Even if that means I have to jump over the side and swim! I think the three of us have been separated too much as it is," she rambled recklessly. "Can anyone, please, just tell us what's going on?"

"Someone? Not just anyone? I guess that makes me a somebody," piped up Jakar as he climbed a stack of nearby crates waiting to be stowed in the hold and sat down with his strange staff across his knees. He was now at a height where even Behnam had to look up at him. "This ship is safe, 'tis safe indeed! Sent by Gabriene himself, in faith, hope, and charity. All can be seen upon this ship from land or sea, except the three. There's a spell, you see."

"What? What does that mean?" asked Faye in bewilderment.

"It's quite simple, dear. Gabriene put a spell on this ship making you, Ebony and Cheri, when she arrives, invisible to anyone not onboard," translated Tasmin with a smile.

"That's another thing. Where's Cheri? How do we even know if she's still safe?" insisted the still agitated Ebony.

"Fret not, fret not. She's safe for now, even though surrounded by those who may wish her ill. Soon enough I'll go fetch her, and they won't find her, look where they will. 'Tis all arranged, there'll be no harm. Have faith, keep hope, just trust my charm," chanted Jakar blithely.

"Where's Believer?" asked Faye abruptly, her alarmed gaze lighting on the horses and the mule picketed by the mast. "For that matter, where's Matew?"

"Uh, we're not quite sure, Faye. Believer seemed to be giving him some sort of problem when we left, but as you've so often told us, sometimes we need to trust his actions," replied Behnam, not meeting her blazing blue eyes.

"Actually, we were so intent on catching up with the carriage it was a few minutes before we realized he wasn't right behind us and after all, the two of you are our main concern," insisted Bass.

"Well, go find them! They're lost! They could be in trouble! How do you expect them to find us in this huge city when they don't know where to look?" cried Faye in panic.

"Don't fear for the unicorn nor the boy. They're busy playing decoy," soothed Jakar.

"That's another thing. What's with the doggerel? Why are you suddenly speaking in rhyme? Bad rhyme at that? Someone should teach you how to rap," insisted Ebony sarcastically.

"Rap? What's rap? Well, never mind. Sometimes it happens when I speak of visions. I have no control at all, you see. Oh, good. It's gone. It can be so embarrassing. In the meantime, you, young lady, can quit being so testy. You're not suddenly going to get sick again. The cake I gave you was a temporary cure for the landlubber's illness," replied a nearly normal Jakar. "Well, I have things to do before Cheri arrives, just remain on the ship," he finished, flashing them a grin and a bow before running down the gangplank to his coach.

As he left, Ebony's attention was again caught by the black galley with its single mast across the quay. "Tasmin, what is that? It looks malevolent."

"Ebony, we have other things to worry about. All will be explained when you're safe in Lohi. Let's get settled in our cabins."

CHAPTER 20

The Calm before the Storm

When Matew was returned to the Jayhawk, flanked by the priest and the captain of the troop, they were greeted by the tough old sergeant who had been left in charge. "The women told ter us warn't here, sir! They was a couple o' Mojar onboard, but they warn't no female. The smaller one beat one of da swabs pretty bad in a fair fight just dis morn. He showed me 'is bruises. The only woman onboard were an old Jamben wi' a couple young servin' boys. The youngest of them spent mos' o' 'is time aloft. Ain' none of de crew lef' de ship if'n ye wants ter talk to dem again. As for dis boy, dey say he be bringin' 'is master's new stallion from Dobe. Summat aboot a wager."

Matew sat a little straighter. Perhaps they would get out of this mess yet. No thanks to Believer. "As I said, sir. I would like ter thank ye fer comin' ter me rescue. Kin I tak' dis beast ter me master now? He'd get terrible angry if'n this horse weren't in top form when I get 'im dere.

"I didn't do it to save you, boy! I know I...felt...something. Something important. Well, whatever it was, it wasn't you and it's gone now," grumbled the priest as the captain threw Believer's reins back to Matew.

"Yes, sir, but thank you anyway," repeated Matew as he tugged on a lock of his hair that had fallen into his pale green eyes. Bowing from his saddle, he turned Believer away and urged him into a trot. Once again, when he tried to prompt Believer in the direction the carriage had taken, the animal balked and took his own path, two streets over. As they left, Matew could hear the captain barking at his subordinate.

"Sergeant! Ye say the crew's still aboard? Where are the other passengers? Why haven't they been detained!"

"They be gone when we got here, sir. Left as soon as the gangplank dropped."

Well, he may be free to go, but as far as Matew was concerned, they were still lost with no clue on where to go, "Well, this is a fine mess you've gotten us into, Believer," he muttered as he gave up trying to control the beast.

Once away from the wharves, Believer picked up his pace to a canter and the twisty street left the riverfront far behind. Abruptly, Believer took a left turn into a shadowy alley, heading in what Matew thought might be the right direction.

When they crossed the street at the other end, a shaft of sunlight caught them, and he looked down to find himself riding a stocky roan with a short, black mane. Dismayed, he covered his face with one hand. "Oh no! Not again!" he moaned as they entered another dim alley.

A few minutes later, they emerged from the second alley into a busy street and headed southwest. They had just rounded a sharp bend when they were crowded against a building on the left side of the street to let several coaches pass, headed toward the river docks.

"Wait! Isn't that Jakar on the lead carriage?" exclaimed Matew. After all, how many little men with blue-white beards and dressed in red could there be in Dhwittle? Tugging on the reins, again, he allowed himself to hope he wasn't lost after all.

Believer nodded in agreement with his question but mulishly continued on his chosen course.

"Well, let's follow him! He must know where the others are!" urged the frustrated young man, frantically trying to pull the unicorn around. As the last carriage disappeared around the curve behind them,

Believer gave a stubborn shake of his stubby black mane and broke into a canter once more. Matew had no choice but to hang on.

"Well, it's not as if there were any doubt as to who was in charge. I guess I'm only along for the ride," the burly redhead sighed in defeat.

With a gentle nicker, Believer bobbed his head in agreement.

*****

"Uhm," moaned Cheri as she rolled over and rubbed the sleep out of her eyes, vaguely wondering what woke her when it came again, a very light rapping at her door. Groggily, she rose. "Who's there?" she called sleepily.

"Falcon. Let me in!" came back a hoarse whisper at the crack in the door.

Suddenly alarmed, she pulled back the bolt, allowing her friend to slip in and close the door quickly behind him.

"What's wrong? Are we discovered?" she asked in a low voice.

"Nothing's wrong. I just needed to see you alone, that's all. We have to make plans for Dhwittle."

"You woke me up with the rising sun to make plans? Are you crazy?" she complained quietly as she flopped on the unmade bunk, sitting cross-legged, making the oversized shirt she had been sleeping in ride up her calves. Falcon turned his head away and coughed in embarrassment.

Cheri was amazed to feel herself blush and quickly pulled a quilt over her lap. "Well? I'm waiting. What couldn't wait until after breakfast?" she whispered.

"If you weren't so hard to get alone during the day, I would have let you get your beauty sleep. As it is, we arrive in Dhwittle today, and we haven't discussed how we intend to slip away from your 'ardent admirer,' Sir Vera!"

"Okay, fine. Tell me the plan and let me get back to sleep," she said, yawning hugely to emphasize her point.

"That's part of the problem. I haven't been able to come up with anything. Almost everything I can think of depends on what we find when we arrive. We're due to put into port in the early afternoon, so we won't have the cover of darkness to help us, but hopefully there will be crowds of sailors and stevedores on the dock, probably."

"So...getting lost in the crowd is one possibility but probably rather slim. What else might we expect?"

"If a passenger ship is making ready to head upriver, there will be passengers, their retainers and well-wishers milling around. The more people the better. If there are enough, we might manage to get separated from Sir Vera and lose ourselves in the shuffle. On the other hand, if it's relatively quiet, I suppose we'll have to make a diversion of our own. The main problem with all of this is the danger of getting split up."

"Well, one thing we can rely on is our fellow passengers right here. I'm sure Lady Highho will be insisting she get preferential treatment of some sort. That will be a diversion of its own. What about Amalee, can she help us out? Personally, I think we should keep an eye on Bugsy. I don't trust that man. Other than that, I suggest we rely on the fates and our own wits. We'll figure it out when the time comes." Cheri shrugged, lying back down and closing her eyes.

"Cheri! Sit up and pay attention! We may have to rely on the fates, or prophecy, for an opening but we have to be ready to seize whatever opportunity presents itself," hissed Falcon in disgruntlement as he turned a chair around to straddle it.

With a pout, Cheri rose to get her brush, taking impish delight in Falcon's discomfort as she brushed her hair and her long shirt hiked up even higher. "I really don't see any point in talking about it. We both know as soon as there's an opening, we need to ditch Sir Vera without losing each other. No sweat! If we can't do it on the docks, we're sure to find a chance once we're in the city proper. Until the chance presents itself, what other plans can we make?" she asked with her most innocent smile, dimpling at him sweetly.

"I can see talking to you is useless. You better get up and start packing. From the looks of this place, that's going to take a while. You need to be ready as soon as we've docked," growled Falcon, heading for the door. "I need to take care of Wolf and Baby before Sir Vera does it for me."

"Just a minute, let me check the hall. I have my reputation to think of, you know?"

Cheri gave a quick peek into the companionway before letting him out. While they had been talking, dawn had broken, and some of the passengers were beginning to stir. Before Falcon was well away from the door, Sir Vera emerged from his stateroom and could see Cheri's door closing over the taller man's shoulder. For just a second, he allowed his anger to blaze in his eyes.

Falcon glanced back over his shoulder before giving the other man a lazy smile and a wink. "Wonderful morning, isn't it, Sir Vera? I was just about to take a stroll around the deck before breakfast, care to join me?"

Gracefully, Sir Vera bowed in acceptance, but Falcon was sure he could hear teeth grinding behind the suave smile. If necessary, perhaps he could create a diversion with Sir Vera's unwilling help? Concentrating on Sir Vera, Falcon failed to see another door at the end of the companionway closing slowly.

Cheri was wearing her green traveling dress when she

emerged on deck for breakfast. Sir Vera immediately began crossing to her, but somehow, Falcon got there first, going out of his way to be charming as he escorted her to the table. Sir Vera was holding her chair when they got there. Then with deep bows and barely civil smiles, they took seats on either side of her. Without a doubt, Falcon was up to something, and she wasn't sure she was going to like it.

A few minutes later, Mrs. Highho surprised everyone by appearing for breakfast. Her usual habit had been to sleep in, emerging at noon. "I was so excited about arriving in Dhwittle today. I just couldn't bear another minute in my cabin! I do hope I don't suffer for lack of proper beauty sleep!" she gushed and was properly rewarded by compliments from Captain Brogre and Sir Vera.

Amazingly, even Falcon was ready with a gracious word. "I am sure, dear lady, your beauty transcends any need for mortal rest. For true beauty is merely the soul shining forth from your face," he said as he rose to bow gallantly while the captain held her chair across the table from Cheri.

"Why, thank you, Sir Falcon. You do flatter me," she responded with a blush as she sat down and beamed at them all.

Cheri suspected there was more to the smile the lady sent her way than mere goodwill, just as she was sure there had been a slight level of sarcasm to Falcon's compliment. She wished she knew what was going on.

Only moments later, Lady Highho's glass of black currant juice slipped from her hand and went running across the table to seek comfort in Cheri's lap.

While Cheri moved quickly, it wasn't quite fast enough, and when she stood, the entire front of her skirt was stained a deep purple against the forest green.

"Oh my! I'm so sorry, my dear. I've no idea why I'm so clumsy this morning. Please, let me have Mara get that stain out for you. If it's not done right away, it will set. She's a wonder with stains!"

"Thank you, Lady Highho. As soon as I change, I'll be sure she gets it. Can she have it clean before we reach Dhwittle?" asked Cheri, dabbing ineffectually at her split skirt with a white linen napkin before giving up and returning to her stateroom. This day had not started well, and it appeared everything was just getting worse.

*****

Jakar pulled his caravan of closed coaches to a halt outside a tall brick house with a slate roof in the middle of a narrow lane. When the door opened, a plain young woman with bright-red curls and wearing a dark-green traveling skirt and vest emerged.

"No, no, no, Jinjer! The plan has changed since I saw you last night! You must wear the black, not the green," jabbered Jakar in a frenzy as he descended from the coach box, waving his staff about wildly.

"Las' night ye were sure it be the green! Now it be the black? Would ye make up yer doomed mind? If'n I change, I won't do it again, mind ye," said the woman sourly as she flounced off, slamming the door in his face.

"Don't worry, I won't," he muttered as he began to pace on the sidewalk. "Just hurry! We're already cutting it close!" he yelled up at an open window. Thankfully, he couldn't quite make out her reply. He had a feeling he wouldn't like it.

Ten minutes later, with Jinjer properly clad in black and safely out of sight in the third carriage. Jakar took off so quickly, the pedestrians were jumping into doorways for safety and shouting curses after them.

"We're cutting this too close to Doome," Jakar grumbled to himself as he urged the poor horses to go even faster on a short, straight stretch.

Two blocks from the riverfront, Jakar finally slacked off the pace, slowing the horses to a more sedate trot. They would need a chance to cool before they arrived, and even the urgency of the situation wouldn't prompt Jakar to misuse the animals.

Finally, Jakar turned the corner onto Dock Street and led his train of coaches up alongside the docking *Gray Gull*.

Jakar was off his coach and up the gangplank, bowing low to Lady Highho, before anyone had a chance to disembark. "My lady, I have a fine coach waiting to take you wherever you wish to go in the style you deserve," he said, sweeping his large hat and its exotic plume on the deck. "My very best coach and most capable driver awaits your pleasure. Boggs! Help this lady with her luggage."

Before Jakar's arrival, Falcon had been about to pick a fight with Sir Vera, but the little man's appearance stopped him dead in his tracks. He stroked his chin thoughtfully as he watched the little man in the red suit charm the other passengers.

As the crew hoisted Wolf, Baby and Sir Vera's mount, Imp, as well as the packhorse from the hold and onto the dock, Jakar approached the Cubbitts and quickly persuaded them into his second coach. Before they left, Mrs. Cubbitt embraced Cheri in a tearful farewell.

Finally, he walked up to Cheri, Falcon, and Sir Vera, executing another of his flamboyant bows. "Dear lady, gentlemen, I have a grand coach waiting to take you where you would go with as much comfort as if seated in your own parlor," he said smoothly, meeting Falcon's look of recognition with a grin and a wink as he straightened to his full three feet six inches.

"My friend and I have our own horses, but I'm sure the lady would appreciate such a gentle ride," Falcon agreed quickly. Wouldn't you, Lady Cheri?" he insisted sternly as she opened her mouth to protest.

After a thoughtful gaze at Falcon's set expression, she reluctantly agreed, "Actually, I think I might at that."

"Marvelous, then I shall leave the lady in your capable care, sir coach master." Falcon smiled with a low bow, allowing the little man to lead Cheri to the third coach while he joined Sir Vera on the gangplank. "I do have this pony to deliver, perhaps you would be so kind as to escort Lady Cheri to the Shepherd King, where we will be staying for me?" he said, distracting the gentleman effectively while Jakar spoke to Cheri in a quick, low voice.

Startled, Sir Vera allowed a suspicious look to cross his face before he agreed and left to mount Imp and take up position near the third coach, which promptly took off.

Jakar was busy, back on the ship, settling the rest of the passengers into the remaining coaches. When he was through, only the last coach remained without a passenger, and the other five had gone their separate ways. Swaggering down the gangplank with a satisfied grin on his face, he clambered onto the box and took up the reins, slapping them down on the hindquarters of the horses.

Falcon had been fussing with the tack on Wolf and the baggage on the packhorse, stalling his departure. "It's been a long time, Jakar. I don't suppose I should be surprised to see you here, old friend. I must say I am relieved. I did not want to start a fight to get us safely away," he said as he pulled up alongside the coach. Baby and the packhorse were trailing behind docilely.

Jakar emitted a loud belly laugh. "It seems to be my destiny to pull you out of tight spots, friend Falcon. I find it telling that the only distraction you could think of was a fight, though. Now things will really get interesting," he said with a wide grin as he set his team off at a smart pace.

*****

It was a dispirited Matew, who arrived at the bay aboard his stocky roan. As far as he was concerned, there was no way they were ever going to find Lady Faye or Lady Tasmin again. Believer had really messed up this time.

"Matew! Matew, over here. We're over her, Matew!" came Lady Faye's voice clearly. Startled, he looked up and scanned the docks and the decks of the nearby ships while Believer whinnied a reply of his own. On the right was one of Barakus's famous black galleys, they wouldn't be there. Next to it was a shore hugging trade ship with only a small watch crew aboard. On his left was a galleon that had seen better days and was getting ready to cast off. Ah, just beyond that was a four-masted barque with Bass striding down the gangplank to meet him. Curiously though, he couldn't see Lady Faye anywhere and he was sure it was her voice he'd heard.

"Well, Matew! You're a sight for sore eyes. Lady Faye was sure we'd lost you and Believer, both. I must say though, you've hardly returned the animal in the same condition as he was when we last saw him." Bass laughed, with a critical gaze at the stocky roan.

"Hardly my fault, Bass. This animal has had me dancing to his tune all over Dhwittle. I guess I'm just lucky he knew how to find Lady Faye again, or I'd still be lost. Where is she? I thought I heard her voice," grumped Matew as he dismounted, still upset with the unicorn.

Grinning, Bass glanced over his shoulder at the ship. Lady Tasmin and Behnam could be plainly seen watching them from the gunwales, but of Faye and Ebony, there was no sign. "Come aboard, mate, and all will be made clear to ye," he grinned, tickled at his own pun.

*****

Cheri had climbed into the third carriage at Jakar's insistence and stifled a shocked scream. There on the carriage seat was a young woman, just a few years older than herself, with long red hair, almost the same shade as her own. The face was a little plainer, perhaps, but if you didn't get a clear, close look, the woman could be mistaken for her, she supposed. Strange, very strange. Shaking it off, she followed Jakar's instructions. With a grin and a saucy salute to the stranger, Cheri quietly slipped out the other side of the carriage and began to sidle along the row of coaches to the last one. Sir Vera was mounting his horse as she edged past the fourth team of horses, and as Imp turned restlessly, she took a step and froze behind the coach itself, hoping he hadn't noticed her. Of course, he thought she was in the third coach, so he really wasn't looking for her, either.

Two coaches later, she was brought up short as Bugsy stopped by his carriage to peer around suspiciously. Why did that man always appear to be snooping about in the wrong place at the wrong time? Finally, he climbed into his carriage, and his driver moved up a bit as Cheri scampered past, slipping into the last carriage to wait. At this point, it didn't look like she was going to get to see as much of Dhwittle as she had of Dink, little as that had been. All of this sneaking around was beginning to make her wonder if she really were better off here than back on the streets of Seattle? Well, here she did have plenty to eat, usually, and nice clothes and no one had tried to molest her yet. There were still plenty of people trying to tell her what to do. If so many people weren't trying to kill her, she'd almost be tempted to return to the streets where she was her own boss.

*****

Ebony was leaning thoughtfully on the gunwale, watching the stevedores loading the long black galley across the way with uncharacteristic haste and angry, hopeless looks. Except for the color it resembled a Viking ship, but even so, there was something odd going on there, she just couldn't seem to put her finger on what. For one thing, they didn't seem to be loading anything resembling cargo, only ship's stores and a lot of those. The ship wasn't built to be a passenger ship. It was too cramped and dirty to attract paying customers. Now that she thought of it, the wharf traffic seemed to eddy to their side of the dock as people swerved to avoid the sinister ship, averting their gaze and sometimes with tears in their eyes. Strangely, it seemed important for her to know what it was about the ship making it so different from the others lining the wharves. She turned to see if Tasmin or Bass could answer her questions when Faye came running across the deck, jubilant from her reunion with Believer.

"Oh, Ebony! Have you seen Jakar's horse? He's huge! He looks a lot like a Clydesdale except he's black with white markings. I just love their black feathering. Bass tells me he's called a Chardell, and Matew's all excited because they're so rare. Apparently, only the Lohi knights ride them.

"I don't know why, but I feel so free! I mean, here we are on a ship protected by Gabriene, so we're safe from those awful priests and their soldiers. As soon as Cheri arrives, everything will be perfect!" she gushed, still retaining the childish enthusiasm she'd let loose while masquerading as a boy.

"Faye, do me a favor, take a good look at that galley over there and tell me if you see anything..., I don't know, wrong about it," asked Ebony urgently. It seemed to her, the feeling of...evil was growing.

Startled by the sudden change in subject, Faye looked up at her dark friend for a moment before turning to study the ship in question. After a few minutes, she straightened up with a perplexed frown. "I'm not sure why, but it seems awfully spooky. What does it have to do with us?"

"I'm not sure, but I know it's important for me to know

more about it. Look, why don't you cover for me? I'm going to get a closer look," said Ebony impulsively.

"What? Wait, Ebony! You shouldn't leave the ship," objected Faye in a weak whisper. Ebony was already down the gangplank and mingling with the stevedores as she tried to slip across to the other ship. "You're not protected out there," whispered Faye to her retreating back, glancing around nervously to see if any of their friends had noticed the departure.

Spotting some barrels of fresh water yet to be loaded, Ebony made her way up the dock before crossing over and slipping between the bales and boxes to get a closer look. Finally, she was next to the strange black ship and wondering what her next move should be when an odd sound reached her from beyond the hull. What was that? It seemed like it could be crying. Moving closer still, Ebony put her ear to the bulwark, wishing the bustling crowd would be quiet. There! There it was again, only clearer. It was crying. It sounded like children crying and was that other childish voices trying to comfort them? This ship was full of children. How ridiculous! They hadn't seen any children in Persal since they left Breymin, the hidden mountain village just outside Gaban's stronghold.

Cautiously, she raised herself on tiptoe to peer over the low gunwales, through the railing. Of course, no children were visible. Only rough sailors with whips and an odd golden coloring, watching over underfed men chained to the oars and rougher-looking soldiers. Not the sloppy church soldiers they had encountered before. These were men of discipline, in clean uniforms. They reminded her of marines, except for their faces. Those looked deadly. Well, soldiers who served on ships were marines, weren't they? Abruptly, the door to the gangway opened and a tall, harsh-looking man, thin with a beak of a nose, stepped out, but before he could close the door, she caught a glimpse of several children sitting listless on the steps. They didn't even try to break for freedom, but Ebony still did not doubt they were prisoners of some kind. Slowly, grinding her teeth in anger, she lowered herself to a crouch and slipped away before she was seen. There was nothing she could do here alone. Perhaps her friends could help. There had to be something they could do.

*****

When the captain opened the door to the deck and the sunlight came in, Patrice was blinded for a moment, so she closed her eyes and tilted her head to the sun. It had been so long since she'd felt the sun on her face. The transports had only had small windows at the top of the walls. Very little light or air got in. Now, aboard this ship there only seemed to be darkness and the crying of the small ones. The older ones, like herself and Hender, had quit crying by now, at least when the little ones could hear.

After a minute or two, her eyes had adjusted, and as she opened them and lowered her head, she saw a dark face staring at her. She wasn't sure if it were a man or a woman, she'd never seen anyone with skin so dark before, but there was something there that made her wonder. There was a lot of anger, but not at her, and a determination. Just before the face dropped below the gunwale, she felt the stirrings of something inside her. She wasn't sure, but it almost felt like hope.

*****

A few minutes later, Ebony was making her way back up the gangplank to the *Unicorn's Magic*. Onboard, Tasmin's normally placid expression had been replaced by one of mixed fear and disapproval. Disapproval seemed to be winning. Bass and Behnam wore equally stern expressions as they stood on either side of Tasmin with arms crossed on their chests, like bookends. As she stepped a foot on deck, she thought she detected a hint of relief in Behnam's look as well. No, surely it was just her imagination.

"What do you think you were doing? Do you have any idea how much danger you were in out there? If you were seen returning to this ship, you wouldn't be safe, even here! Neither will the rest of us," snapped Tasmin angrily.

"I, uh...I'm sorry, Tasmin. But if I don't know how much danger we're in, it might be because you haven't told us everything. I had to know more about that ship. If you know anything about that, it would be a start," rejoined Ebony defiantly, returning Tasmin's glare with one of her own, ignoring this previously unseen aspect of Tasmin's personality.

"What? What are you talking about? When have I not told you something you needed to know? Exactly what is it you 'think' you needed to know that you couldn't have asked one of us? Apparently, your curiosity was so aroused you ignored everything you've been told. Do you have any idea what you risked just now?"

"I was very careful not to be seen. I had no intention on risking our lives. Really, I didn't. I had to know more about that ship. Something about it made me...feel...I sensed evil. I also felt an urgency. It was important for me to see for myself. Do you know it's apparently full of children? Do you know they are crying?"

"You risked much more than merely our lives. Before this is through, all our lives might be forfeit. I will not have them wasted on a whim before we begin. Now, come, you deserve better answers to your questions about the Black Ship," said Tasmin, wearily, leading both her and Faye across the deck to sit on a hatch cover.

"That ship is one of Barakus's black galleys. Those children are of the Taking. I told you of it before. It must be one of the last ships making ready to leave for Doome. To tell you the truth, I am surprised it is still here. Usually, they are long gone by now. No one does anything because we are all powerless before Barakus's wrath. It's not as if they haven't tried. When they did, the children were killed, mercilessly, in front of everyone. They had to stop and just hope for the best. No one knows why Barakus wants them, so they learned to let them go. Usually the Taking takes place every sixty to one hundred years. It's only been seventy-six since the last one.

"If you felt an urgency to know, I will not say there was not. You could have found out merely by asking," she finished.

"Maybe. Maybe not, but I don't think so. I think it is important for me to know here," said Ebony, lightly touching her heart. "Not here," she finished, touching her head. "Hearing the cries made it real to me, not just some far away story happening to someone else on the six-o'-clock news."

Faye nodded in understanding while Behnam, Bass, and Tasmin exchanged glances, relaying she'd lost them with the last phrase.

Before anyone could say more, there was a clatter of coach wheels and horse hooves followed by a hail from the dock, "Ahoy the *Unicorn*! Make ready to sail!" came the booming voice of Jakar.

"Cheri! She must finally be here!" yelped Faye as she rushed across the deck to peer over the rail. The sailors were making ready to cast off the lines holding them to the dock in response to commands the captain was barking quickly to his crew. Falcon was already leading Wolf, Baby, and the packhorse up the gangplank while Jakar helped Cheri alight from the coach.

"Cheri! Cheri, we're up here!" called Faye excitedly before bursting into giggles when Cheri looked right past them. She only had a moment to be confused as Jakar took her hand, rushing her up the gangplank. As soon as they were all aboard, the gangplank was hauled up, and they pushed away from the dock. Faye, Ebony, and Cheri squealed in excitement as they shared hugs. They had only known each other for a short time, but they were already family.

When Ebony looked up, again, she saw they weren't the only ones leaving Dhwittle. The Black Ship had also set out and was rapidly making for the harbor entrance under power of the galley's sweeps.

"Ebony? Ebony, what's the matter?" asked Faye, looking into those dark eyes and seeing them flash gold with anger and frustration. When she didn't get an answer, she followed the other woman's gaze and nodded in understanding.

Once clear of the harbor, the sleek build and the multitude of sails on the *Unicorn's Magic* allowed it to easily cut through the waves, passing then leaving the black galley, with its solitary sail and shelved sweeps, far behind. Amalee swooped out of the clouds to perch momentarily on Falcon's shoulder, causing Ebony to smile, before the hawk took off to find a perch on the crow's nest, startling the sailor on watch.

With one last look of regret and sorrow at the Black Ship, Ebony joined the others to catch up on what had happened while they were separated. Perhaps, now, she would find out what really happened to Faye in that mudslide. She'd slept through the last telling.

*****

The *Flying Seahawk* sailed past Dhwittle without a pause and far enough out to sea to avoid all traffic coming from the port.

Captain Ta'Jar preferred the deep sea, away from land. The great expanse of water didn't disorient him or his crew as it did so many who lived on the sea and preferred staying within sight of the coast.

All this water made Ochwatt uneasy, but the only indication was when he would begin pacing toward the end of day. He spent most of his time standing in the bow, watching the water break against the hull.

"How are you doing, Ochwatt?" asked Gaban, coming up to stand beside him.

"Doin' what, friend Gaban?"

"Uhm, oh, well, does all of this water bother you? Make you feel uneasy or queasy? After all, you've never seen the sea before or been away from land."

"I...fine," he answered tersely.

"Another week or so and we'll be in Lohi. Actually, sooner with the speed we've been making," Gaban elaborated. He'd long ago found out that Ochwatt wasn't much for conversation.

"Good, friend Gaban. What be those?" asked Ochwatt, pointing into the sea.

"What? Oh, I'm not quite...Captain Ta'Jar! Could you tell us about these amazing fish?" called Gaban across the ship.

"Not fish," said Ochwatt.

"What? Oh, here he is. Captain Ta'Jar, what are these?" asked Gaban as the captain joined them, and he pointed to the leaping animals chasing the ship.

"That's the narwhal. Some look at their horns and believe they're related to unicorns, but I don't know that they have any magic."

"Not a fish," Ochwatt repeated.

"Actually, he's right. They're mammals, like whaltes or sea cows. At least that's what I've been told. They give birth. Fish don't do that."

"They not just animal. They more," insisted Ochwatt, bending over the railing, which only came up to his thighs, to get closer.

When Captain Ta'Jar started to argue, Gaban held up his hand to stop him. "What do you mean more?"

By now Ochwatt was reaching his long arm down toward one of the narwhals who was moving closer to the ship. "They smart. Like you, Gaban. Really smart," came his voice as he leaned a little more. In alarm, both Gaban and Ta'Jar grabbed for the giant before he toppled off the ship. They tried to steady him but not pull him back. Finally, his hand touched the narwhal horn, and it started to glow, spreading up Ochwatt's arm until he was glowing as well. When it touched Gaban, he gasped in surprise and awe. Here was pure magic. Captain Ta'Jar cried out in alarm and snatched his hands away from Ochwatt, breaking the connection. When the giant started to tilt toward the sea, the man grabbed him again and shouted orders for a rope.

Before the rope reached them, Ochwatt leaned back and stood straight. "They say they stay with us. They my friends now," he said simply, still watching the animals frolicking in the waves.

"Having narwhals escort a ship is considered good luck. Now we know we'll have safe sailing," commented the captain before returning to the helm, head shaking.

CHAPTER 21

In the Eye of the Storm

Two days later they were well out to sea when the wind turned about and began blowing right at them, pushing before it a long gray wall of roiling clouds. As the sails began to luff, Captain Aberon started shouting orders to set the ship to tack slightly to starboard and make ready for a storm. Faye was nearby, and she could swear he was muttering about never seeing the weather change so abruptly before, not in twenty-three years on the seas, as he strode toward the bridge.

Within half an hour, the crew had secured the animals in a makeshift corral between the mainmast and the mizzenmast. Faye stopped to give Believer a reassuring hug, but maybe it was Believer who was doing the reassuring. Then the storm arrived, carrying a solid wall of rain with it, and Faye and the others ran for their cabins. Amalee had flown to Falcon's shoulder shortly after the wind picked up, and now, she stayed there as he went below. It was the first time any of them had seen the bird take refuge inside instead of flying to safety. They were in for quite a storm.

Within minutes, only the crew and the helpless animals remained on deck. The crew were still battening down the hatches and lashing down the reefed sails before the gale's force could shred the canvas. Sitting listlessly in the dim cabin she shared with Cheri, Faye wished she dared light a lamp to read by, but the danger of fire was too great. Then there was a blinding flash followed a few minutes later by deep, rolling thunder. Moments later she was fighting to stay in her bed as the waves continued to grow and tossed the ship from side to side. The hull of the ship groaned in protest. The next time the lightning came, the thunder came sooner. She was beginning to think Ebony wasn't the only one who would need Jakar's little magic cakes when there was a rap on the door, followed closely by Jakar himself with two of those cakes. Behind him, Ebony held on tight to the door jam while she waited impatiently for him to leave. Then she grabbed a corner of Faye's bunk and sat.

"You know, the more I think about that Black Ship of Barakus's, the more I believe we have to stop him, somehow. If we're here for any purpose at all, part of it has to be to save those children," she said urgently, speaking loudly to be heard over another roll of thunder.

"Didn't you hear what Tasmin told us? They tried, three times, hundreds of years ago. Why should it be any different now?" argued Faye, shrugging in resignation.

"We're here to change things, somehow. Well, I can't think of a better way to start. Didn't you say the priests came for them again? Maybe the problem isn't getting them back. It's having a safe place for them once they're free. If we free them, we won't send them home, at least not right away," interjected Cheri thoughtfully, barely managing to say it before more thunder could drown her out.

Right then the ship crested another wave and dived deep into the trough on the other side, throwing the three women together at one end of the bunk. The timbers of the ship creaked loudly in protest. "Maybe you're right, but it won't do us much good if we're at the bottom of the ocean," grumbled Faye as she pushed Cheri away and pulled herself off Ebony. This time the lightning and thunder came simultaneously.

"Don't be ridiculous. If there were really any danger, someone would tell us. I'm sure the captain and crew have weathered worse storms before," insisted Ebony, praying silently to herself it was true but not quite believing it as they were flung to the other side of the bunk.

Incongruously, Cheri began giggling, "Well, if we don't want to be covered with bruises, much less break any bones, I suggest we each find a good spot and hold on. It looks like it's going to be a bumpy ride."

Just as Faye settled herself on the floor, holding tight to the table bolted to the deck, the door slammed open, and Behnam stood there, bracing himself and bending slightly to avoid hitting the low ceiling with his head. "Are you all right?" he yelled, trying to be heard over the howling wind and the sound of waves pounding the sides of the ship.

Ebony waited for another peal of thunder to pass before raising her voice to answer. "We're fine, so far! How bad is it?"

There was barely a pause between flashes of lightning and rumbles of thunder now, but there was a momentary lull in the motion of the ship as it seemed to be climbing impossibly high to crest another wave and Behnam managed to cross the room in a strange angle and grab at the upper bunk before the ship began the long slide down the other side. His place at the door was taken by Falcon with Amalee still clinging tightly to his leather shoulder pad. "I've never seen a storm so bad, especially at this time of year. It's even worse than the one that sank the *Voyager* and washed me up on the shores of Jessamine, five years gone," he called, carefully making his way to a chair firmly anchored to the decking. Amalee glided across the room to clutch a rail across the top of a high cabinet of books above the desk, grabbing hold like she never intended to move again.

A short time later, Matew and Bass helped Tasmin into the

room and across to another secure chair, followed by Jakar who even managed to shut the door before a sudden descent down the crest of a wave changed everything, causing him to fall and roll across the floor where he came up against the bunk at Cheri's feet.

The two of them were laughing as she helped him get to his feet and gain a firm grip on the bedrail. "What are you laughing about? I see nothing funny here. If you can see the future, why didn't you see this coming? Surely, we could have waited a day or two before leaving Dhwittle?" asked Faye, yelling to be heard.

"Sometimes you either laugh or you cry, Lady of Faith, and no good ever comes from crying. If we'd waited another hour in Dhwittle, you would be enjoying the hospitality of Barakus's priests, now. As for this storm, even I can't see what shouldn't be. Perhaps you should rely on your faith now," he hollered above the thunder, tempering his words with a cheeky grin.

"This storm shouldn't be here. I foresaw calm, safe sailing all the way to Lohi. I don't know why it's here or where it came from, but it shouldn't be here," continued Jakar, scratching his head in puzzlement.

"Barakus! Of course! It's the only explanation. He must have called up this storm to stop us," said Tasmin with a look of disgust she hadn't thought of it before.

"But how? I thought he couldn't see or sense us on this ship," asked Faye, her voice so small it could barely be heard over the fury of the storm.

"He may not know exactly where you ladies are, but if he has eliminated all other possibilities for your departure from Dhwittle, and I'm quite sure he has by now, he has to know you're somewhere at sea. If this storm is his, he's using some very strong magic. Even dark magic takes a lot out of a wizard to conjure something this big. He can't keep it up forever."

"Oh, that's swell! Now what do we do? How do we fight someone we can't see out in the middle of the ocean?" asked Ebony sarcastically, glad her face couldn't get as pale as Faye's or Cheri's. Cheri's freckles were stark as another flash of lightning lit the room for a moment.

"We don't! We just hope the crew can keep us on course and afloat until we reach the Gate, five miles out of Lohi. It's the gap between the two long peninsulas guarding Mermaid Bay. Once there, Gabriene's magic will take over, and we should be out of danger," explained Falcon, swaying as the ship was hit broadside with a wave.

"Jakar! You said you couldn't see this storm coming because it shouldn't be here. What do you see now? Do we arrive safely in Lohi?" asked Bass, turning to the small man in red.

Jakar got a strange, faraway expression on his face for a few moments before he answered, "It's fuzzy, and it flickers back and forth. In one I see a great expanse of calm sea littered with debris, pieces of burned wood, rope, charred sails, trunks, that sort of thing," he began with a deep frown.

"Do you see anyone? Anyone alive?" interrupted Cheri, fascinated.

"Cheri! Please, don't be so morbid!" admonished Faye, clinging even tighter to the table.

"And the rest, Jakar, what do you see?" asked Bass, urging him to continue.

"I also see the *Unicorn's Magic* run aground on a wooded beach with many injured survivors. Lastly, I see the ship sailing into port at Lohi. It is still raining, but the winds have died down, and everyone onboard is safe," he finished, shaking his head as he came back to himself

"Well, which one is true? I've never wanted to know my future, I prefer to think I make my own destiny, but I'll make an exception this time," growled Behnam, irritated at all the water without any sight of land.

Jakar's eyes focused on the tall black man. "I don't know. At this time, it could be any of the three or something in between," he answered helplessly.

"Do you know what makes the difference? Why we get one outcome instead of another?" asked Tasmin, shouting to be heard as more thunder rolled overhead.

"I'm sorry, no, I don't. It doesn't work that way. I can see how things might be but not what makes it so," he answered, his eyes and mouth drooping in failure.

"No need to be sorry, friend Jakar! You've told us more than we knew a few minutes ago. Now we have to decide what we're going to do about it," said Falcon heartily.

"Of course! That's it!" shouted Cheri gleefully. "We simply need to do something about it!"

"What are you talking about, child? Barakus is too far away for us to fight now. What can we do?" asked Tasmin, shaking her head.

"That's the point, we don't have to fight Barakus, only his storm," argued Cheri, leaning forward intently.

"Fight the storm! Are you crazy?" screeched Faye, her blues eyes going wide.

"Wait, I think I almost see what she's getting at. Go on, Cheri," encouraged Ebony with a strange gleam in her eyes.

"Sure, we can do it. There's never been a precedence for the three of us before. When there was no obvious way into Dink for Behnam and Ebony, Ebony found a way. A way that neither Behnam nor Kali would ever have dreamed of, much less dared if it weren't for her," she explained, ignoring the scowl clouding Behnam's face. Eagerly, she continued, "When the mudslide took two of your animals and almost took Matew as well, Faye found the way and the courage to get him out of there alive. Finally, when the Vortex turned early and tried to take the *Gray Gull*, I somehow managed to give more strength to the crew, and we made it past. There is something in the three of us. I don't know what, but it makes us and those around us…I don't know…do more…or be more than they knew they could be."

"You know, she could be right," admitted Behnam grudgingly.

"I think she probably is. You should have seen her when it looked like the Vortex was going to win." Agreed Falcon with a nod."

"I did find the courage before, didn't I?" asked Faye wonderingly as she frantically grabbed at the table leg again to keep from sliding across the dangerously tilting floor. The flashes of light and the rumbles of thunder were almost continuous now.

"And of course, we have Believer. I would think he could help," said Tasmin thoughtfully as she looked at Faye.

This comment brought a startled look from Falcon, but before he could say anything, Tasmin continued. "Tell us what you have in mind, Cheri."

Cheri stood and swayed as she held tight to the bunk, "I don't know. I mean, it's not like I actually have a plan or something. Look, when I responded to the Vortex, it was just that, a response. I don't know how it was with Faye and Ebony, but well, for me it was just a reaction to an unacceptable alternative. What I do know is, whatever we do, we can't do from here. We have to go up on deck."

Faye pulled herself to her feet as Falcon put out a hand to steady her, "I was afraid you were going to say that," she growled loudly through clenched teeth, grabbing her cloak.

Just as Ebony was rising to her feet, the ship gave another lurch, flinging her into Behnam's lap. "That's assuming we can get there without breaking any bones," she snapped, pushing herself up roughly.

"Well, there's only one way to find out," said Bass, opening the door and letting in a rush of water and cold, wet air before heading to the gangway.

*****

Patrice held Missy's head as she leaned over to vomit once again. Hender and the little boy on her other side were both thrown about as the Black Ship *Barracuda* mounted another giant wave washing over the children. The vomiting continued throughout the hold, and Patrice was unsure if it was the pitching of the ship or the vomit- laden water swirling across the deck, causing it anymore. Whether or not they would survive this storm was the question she was really concerned about. She could hear the men above as they yelled at each other. It gave her the distinct impression they didn't know how to sail through a storm like this. She was fairly certain some of the children wouldn't survive as they were tossed about, and the water got deeper. At the very least, there would be broken bones.

Suddenly, the ship shuddered as it scraped against a rock and the yelling from topside increased. What were they doing so close to land?

A few minutes later, the hatch was lifted, and the children were hustled out of the hold and into the lifeboats. Patrice managed to keep Missy with her, but Hender was pulled away and put into another boat with the other boys. They had run aground on a reef a mile from shore. The water inside the reef didn't heave as much as the storm-lashed waves they'd been cresting a moment before, but the rain and wind didn't cease. The men's muscled arms strained as they rowed against the tide. Wet, bruised, and worried sick about her brother Patrice barely noticed the rain washing away the vomit and other sour smells from the ship. With any luck, the ship would be beaten to splinters by the waves crashing against the reef, and they wouldn't be going to Doome after all.

When they reached the beach, Patrice started looking for Hender. Where was her brother? But there were guards already on the shore, keeping the children in small groups and they wouldn't let her keep looking as she tried to walk down the beach. "My brother, please! I need to find my brother!" she pled as Missy started trembling and coughing. "Missy, she's sick. We're all sick. We need to get out of the rain."

The guard, as usual, ignored her, but a few minutes later another soldier ran up. "There is a village down the beach. We need to get the children there. You know Barakus insists they arrive in good shape. Move them, now! It's small but we'll all crowd in any way. Come on, get them moving. Carry any who can't make it on their own." And he was gone, on to the next group.

Patrice picked up Missy as their guard roused the exhausted children around her and started herding them toward the distant lights. Barakus wanted them well when they arrived. *Was that a good thing?* she wondered.

*****

Debora stood on the stone dock of Lohi watching the water pouring from the sky and drenching the land. This land of green grass and too many strange trees terrified her. Then she forced herself to peer out into the bay, looking at the tall White Tower, ignoring the water as it ran down her soft dark cheeks and drenched her long dark-auburn hair, plastering her white Aht'chka against her thin frame. It was just like her dream so many weeks ago, only this time it was no dream. This time it was real.

Behind her, her uncle Ranjua and her brother Jondor held the reins of their horses while they looked about them nervously. Until now, they had avoided towns and cities, not wanting to be seen. They still weren't sure they were safe, even here. No matter what she tried to tell them, this land was just too strange, too wet. Uncle Ranjua had been as far as Nelas before, which is why he had come along, but none of them had ever been this far into the wetlands. For two turns of the moon, they had traveled, across the strange landscape. Circling terrifying lakes and crossing horrible rivers, all with more water than any of them had seen in their lives. Now they were here.

Drawing herself up to her full five feet nine, Debora turned to the two men. "This is as far as you may go. From here I must go on alone. Go to the castle in the city, you will be welcome there," she said with more courage than she felt.

"Debora, I promised to see you to this place you must go. I will not leave you now!" objected Jondor, drawing himself up to his full six feet six-inch height as though he were already a warrior.

"No, Jondor. Chenauylt made us promise we would do as Debora says, once we reached the great salt sea. It is time to let her go," insisted Ranjua, putting his hand gently on his nephew's arm. Before he left, he turned to Debora. "We will wait at the castle until it is time for you to go home, my brother's daughter. I do not understand why you need to be here, but we will wait as long as necessary." And then they were gone, disappearing into the rain.

*****

Knowing there was nothing she could do on deck, Tasmin stayed in Cheri and Faye's cabin with Jakar and Amalee. She would have to trust the men to keep her charges from being washed overboard and hope Cheri was right, and they really could fight a storm Barakus had made.

As the small group approached the door at the top of the ladder, they realized it was the source of the water flooding the passage as it swung viciously back and forth, making a loud banging barely heard above the thunder and the howling wind. Falcon started up the steps when the door was suddenly slammed shut. As he struggled to open it, it wouldn't budge. "It's jammed!" he called, trying again. Then, just as unexpectedly, it was flung open by a malicious gust of wind full of rain and sea water, instantly drenching them all and throwing Falcon to the floor. "Are you sure this is such a good idea?" Faye yelled to Cheri, standing next to her.

"Not at all, but the way I see it, it's either this or we go down without a fight. I'd rather do it this way," Cheri yelled back as Falcon got to his feet with Bass's help and dashed up the ladder, grabbing ropes that were strung up for the crew to navigate the slippery deck.

Fighting the wind and water all the way, they made it to the mainmast. The ship groaned as if it were going to shatter at any moment. There, Falcon found a secured rope. While taking it firmly in hand, he was almost blown back into Behnam who steadied him, keeping them both on their feet. Regaining his balance, he tied the rope around Faye's waist. "With this on, at least you won't be washed over the side!" he hollered in her ear.

Nodding once, Faye pulled the sturdy wool cloak off and handed it to him. As wet as it was and with the wind whipping it about it was worse than useless. Then she let Bass take her back to the mast, where she could face the storm. Believer was tethered nearby, and he came close to nuzzle her neck reassuringly. With him there, she watched the lightning as it forked all around the ship. She wished she could be as brave about this as Cheri and Ebony. Wasn't lightning attracted to tall things? Like this mast? She was sure she'd heard of it hitting trees. She shuddered involuntarily. For heaven's sake, she didn't even know what she was supposed to do, but she calmed a little as Believer's horn started to glow, causing the crew to back away.

While Bass made sure Faye was safely tied to the mast, Falcon retrieved another length of rope from the mizzenmast, and now Matew and Cheri were bracing against the wind as they made their way, carefully, to the stern.

Before Cheri reached her post, Behnam and Falcon were

fighting their way into the wind on either side of Ebony, taking her to the foremast in the bow.

Once they were tied, they tried to see each other through the driving tempest. Now what were they supposed to do?

Captain Aberon and two of his crew were at the helm, struggling to keep the ship cresting the waves. He had seen them but only had time to shake his head as though they were crazy. He didn't have time to worry about his passengers. They were too busy fighting the worst storm ever recorded on the Great Southern Sea. Another thought briefly crossed his mind. Gabriene had made it clear there was something very special about these three women. Maybe, just maybe, they could help keep his ship from being torn apart by the wind and waves or set afire by the lightning.

Once the three women had exchanged the one look, they lifted their faces into the storm with eyes closed and Believer's horn started to glow. Dimly at first then bright enough for those amidships to see. Abruptly it leapt from Faye, through the dark of the storm to Cheri at the mizzenmast and finally to Ebony at the foremast. As it spread, it grew brighter and spread across the deck and up the masts to encompass the entire ship. There wasn't a soul above decks who didn't pause to stare. The rain still came, but the wind seemed to break on an unseen bow, six feet ahead of the ship's prow. Going around them to either side. They could still hear the wind's howl and the roll of thunder, but the lightning seemed to skitter away. To port or starboard, ahead or astern, no longer coming close enough to be dangerous. Slowly the wind on the ship slackened to a wind just brisk enough to power the ship. The waves calmed from forty- and fifty-foot crests to a mere five to fifteen feet. They hadn't stopped the storm; they had only made a little pocket in its center for the ship to ride in.

Falcon strode up to the captain, where he stood dumbfounded at the helm. "How many days to Lohi, Captain Aberon?"

"Days? I have no idea. We'll have to take a reading to determine our position, if we can," he answered, looking at the overcast sky. "If we're anywhere near to on course, and sailing into this wind, another six to nine days, maybe."

"That's not good enough! I don't know how long the unicorn and these women can keep this up, but I doubt they can last that long! Why don't you and your crew see if you can't cut a few days off that," insisted Falcon with a worried frown, turning to find Bass behind him.

"I think we're going to have to start giving them a breather right away. Faye's already exhausted. I'm going to take her below to get dry and rest," said the big man.

"Good idea, there's no way all three of them can maintain this for days. We're going to have to do this one at a time. I suggest you set your men to using everything they've got or we still may all drown," growled Falcon to the captain, stalking off to check on Ebony and Behnam while the captain sent his crew scrambling to raise the sails and begin the tack that would enable them to sail into the wind.

Since Ebony was the strongest of the three women, she volunteered to take the first watch, reassuring the men, "Maintaining this pocket is much easier than creating it was."

As they were discussing the best place for Ebony's watch, Cheri arrived and suggested, "The bow, it clears the path of the ship." When everyone nodded in agreement, Matew helped Cheri back to her cabin.

As soon as she was in Tasmin's capable hands, Matew returned to the deck and Believer. Making sure the unicorn had whatever he needed. He only wished he could give his strength as well.

A few minutes later, Jakar came topside, crossing to the horses. "Come, boy! Let's make sure all of these animals are well fed. Believer can draw on their strength as well as his own. Let me just explain things to Tiny, he'll make sure they all understand," said the little man as he climbed the nearby ratlines and swung himself onto his massive draft horse.

"You're going to talk him? And you expect him to understand and tell the other horses? I mean, I know Believer understands us, but after all, he's a unicorn!" objected Matew as he dipped out buckets of fresh water for each animal. Then he spread the hay that was only wet on the bottom, the top being covered in oiled cloth.

As he worked, Jakar continued the conversation, "Of course, boy. Of course. Even ordinary horses can understand their owners. They just usually pretend they don't because they're contrary beasts. The Chardells of Jessamine not only understand, but they're eager to please. As for Tiny here, he and I have been together since his birth, fifteen years ago. We communicate quite nicely, we do."

Matew stood staring in awe until Jakar finished talking and listened closely to a few whinnies and nickers before he slid back down to Tiny's broad back where he stood up and did a flip to the deck. "Do you understand him? What did he say?" he asked.

"Said he already had it under control and where are his oats?" said Jakar with a straight face, but when Matew jumped to comply, he burst out laughing. "Now, now, Matew, don't let Tiny get away with telling you what to do. Let them have their hay first, then we'll move Tiny next to Believer. He'll need his strength the most. When that's done, we can get the crew to help us rig a sail as a cover."

*****

Briar rose was still half a mile out from the Gate to Mermaid Bay and could see the low sand dunes on the twin peninsulas when the blue sky turned dark, and she found herself in the middle of a squall. Frantically, she reefed her sail and tied the rudder to head aslant the wind, toward the mainland as she took up the oars. She had listened often when her greatfather talked of the mainland. Lohi was protected by Gabriene's spell all the way to the Gate. No storm had ever penetrated Gabriene's safeguard, except for the needed rain. If she could keep her bearings on the Gate, she'd be fine. She had barely begun when needles of lightning began streaking from the sky. Well, no one had said this was going to be easy.

It took her two hours to cover half a mile, but abruptly, she realized the wind was no more than a brisk breeze and waves had died to rolling swells, the sound of thunder seemed to be coming from the other side of an invisible wall. She had made it! She was through the Gate!

Drenched and weary to the bone, she forced herself to row for another fifty strokes before collapsing on her oars and turning her head to watch the storm as it beat furiously on the other side of the breakwater. Gabriene's barrier still held. She only needed a moment or two to catch her breath before raising her sail. There had to be at least five miles to go before reaching Lohi, she thought, as she shipped her oars and lay down on the seat. "I'll just close my eyes for a couple of minutes," she mumbled as she fell asleep.

With a start, Briar Rose woke! How long had she slept? Oh no, the dim glow of the sun through the rain was far to the west, turning the clouds a pale pink topped with a deep purple. She must have slept at least two hours. Where had this storm come from? This was usually the dry season. Surely the sky had to run out of water soon! Well, no use crying over a torn sail, she might as well be on her way. She did feel better for a having slept as she raised her small triangular sail and set her rudder in the direction of the tall White Tower in the middle of the bay. Lohi, beyond, was barely a smudge on the skyline in the dusky light, but the tower seemed to shine. Taking one last look at the storm still raging a mile away, she was grateful she hadn't drifted back into it while she slept.

As she was about to turn away, her eyes caught sight of something odd. A strange longboat with two impossibly thin and shallow keels connected by curved poles fore and aft. It didn't even have a mast. Instead, it was rowed by several people with dark skins and light hair, all in the starboard keel. It was emerging from the storm as it made its way through the Gate.

Briar Rose only watched for a moment. She had never seen a craft like theirs before, and she had no idea who they might be, but some people liked to interfere where they weren't wanted. You never knew. She was too close to her destination to be stopped now. Setting her jaw stubbornly, she slipped the rope tied to the boom, allowing the sail to catch the wind, sending her small skiff skimming across the water. She doubted anyone with only oars could possibly keep up, much less catch her.

A few minutes later, sure they were far behind, Briar Rose looked over her shoulder to see the strange boat a little closer than it had been. Impossible! They couldn't be gaining on her.

Expertly using the wind to maximum advantage, Briar Rose concentrated on leaving the strangers behind. Half an hour later, she turned again, expecting to see them far behind her. No! They were about as far away as they had been the last time she looked. What was that? They were closer. They were still gaining on her! How was this possible? Another time and place, she would like to ask them about their strange boat and those oars. What was with those oars?

They were close enough to see them now, and they were longer and shaped like broad, flat paddles. She could see where they would be better for pushing the water than what she was used to. Maybe that was the secret.

Now she could see the people clearly as well. There were five of them, four men and one woman. They all had dark skin with fair hair, and unless her perspective was off at this distance, she didn't think they were much bigger than she was. Not from the mainland, then. Her greatfather had always told her the people on the mainland were very tall and, except for the Mojar, who knew little of water, light-skinned. Where could they be from?

When her sail started flapping, she was brought back to the task at hand. She hadn't been paying enough attention and lost the wind. Disgusted with herself, she set her mind on the job of getting safely to the White Tower. She was almost there! Besides, if she did her job right surely, they would soon tire and fall behind. Even if they didn't, perhaps these strange people weren't trying to stop her after all. They must be here on business of their own. What conceit, to think they might even care where she was going.

Unwilling to believe the two-hulled craft could possibly beat her sleek sloop, Briar Rose set all her skills to reaching the tower before they passed her on their way to Lohi. A persistent beam of sunlight found its way through the clouds skimming the horizon, briefly illuminating the tall white spire. One last beacon before the sun set altogether.

The pace of the other boat never seemed to diminish as she fought to get the most out of the fickle wind. At times, her sailboat almost skipped across the waves, at others, the boat was making headway much too slowly for the impatient girl. Bit by bit, the other craft continued to gain. It seemed to be going toward the tower as well, ignoring the lights of the city on the shore.

Luckily, a bright light shot out from the top of the tower before full dark, letting Briar rose keep her heading. Finally, it was time to slow or crash on the rocks at the base of the tower island, and the other boat shot past, drawing up quickly at the end of the short pier when all the paddles were abruptly put in the water for maximum drag. A moment later, Briar Rose brought her own craft around, settling against the other side of the dock and jumping out to tie it up, glowering at the others as the woman, no, girl, got out of the double- hulled boat and shook her head sternly when one of the young men tried to follow. Obstinately, she pointed toward Lohi itself, the city lights barely visible on the shore, three miles away.

The men radiated a great deal of reluctance as they left the girl behind. The youngest was a few years older than Briar Rose, and he seemed especially reluctant as they disappeared into the dark.

Well, no reason not to be a good sport, they had won, fair and square, she thought as she tossed her dark braids behind her and crossed the sturdy stone structure to the other girl, who happened to be exactly her height. Somehow that seemed strangely familiar. "Hello, my name's Briar Rose of Jessamine. That's quite a boat you and your friends have there."

"Thank you, yours seems to handle quite well too. I know Cirroc was impressed. My name's Ciral of Hawart," she answered, furtively brushing away a tear before taking Briar Rose's extended hand.

A shock ran through Briar Rose's body at the touch, like nothing she had ever felt before. Startled, she pulled her hand away, "What was that!" she yelped as she stared at Ciral with her mahogany skin, golden braids, and pale eyes. Why was she so familiar? Her face was like one of her childhood friends but not. Of course, all her friends had light skin and dark hair with dark eyes. This stranger had very dark skin, almost black, with pale-blond hair and gray eyes. The whole thing was just a bit spooky.

"I...I don't know. Perhaps we should go up to the tower, and get out of this rain," suggested Ciral hesitantly, her eyes looking strangely into Briar Rose's before she picked up her small bundle and turned to lead the way.

Hastily, Briar Rose followed, suddenly not wanting to look as though she didn't know when to come out of the rain. "Of course, that's it! The storm! Somehow the storm caused that shock. I've felt something like it before!" she exclaimed in relief.

Ciral looked over her shoulder doubtfully. "Well, maybe, but I thought it felt... Well...never mind. You're probably right."

*****

When the storm hit the *Flying Seahawk*, Captain Ta'Jar's first move was to head south, away from the oncoming tempest and land. The narwhals stayed with them. When they couldn't escape the storm entirely, and most of the sails were reefed, they sped ahead, taking point. As the storm followed them, increasing in intensity, their horns started to glow and the winds afore the ship slackened while the lightning was sent astray.

Ochwatt stood on deck, watching his new friends. When one of them dropped back next to the ship, and he bent over to touch its horn, the glow brightened. Gaban and the captain panicked, worried about how far Ochwatt's reach extended. When he slumped back onto the deck, his energy spent, Gaban ran over in alarm. The captain sent crewmen over to tie a line to the giant. If he decided to do that again, they didn't want him overboard.

Once he was covered in blankets and secured with a line, Gaban turned to the captain. "How long do you think this will delay us?" he asked with a worried look to the north.

"I've never seen a storm like this before. As long as it lasts, we don't dare head north. Not even with the narwhals to help us."

"I'm a bit rusty, but I'll see what I can do to help. I only hope the saviors are already safe in Lohi. Maybe I should have stayed with them?" muttered Gaban, turning to join Ochwatt and the narwhals.

CHAPTER 22

Safe Haven

Fatigue etched every line of Ebony's body through the oiled slicker the captain had provided as she leaned against the foremast. She had only been out here an hour, this time, but it felt more like twelve. The last four days were wearing them all down.

The first, long day, Ebony had lasted four hours before she fainted and woke to find Behnam carrying her below while Cheri rushed to take her place. Cheri pushed herself beyond her strength and also lasted four hours, only to be carried back to the cabin by Falcon. That was when Tasmin put her foot down, insisting they each take shifts of no more than three hours at a time. When she relieved Faye, the petite blonde, could still walk, although she was leaning heavily on Bass.

For the next two days, they were able to maintain the pace. Three hours on deck with Believer and the horses, five hours to sleep and a hearty meal or two to keep up their strength. Then it began all over again. On the third day, Faye fainted after less than two and a half hours. Tasmin refused to listen to Ebony and Cheri when they wanted to continue doing three hours. The shifts were shortened to two hours.

Now, at the beginning of the seventh day, Ebony wasn't

sure she could last another fifteen minutes, much less another hour. She had no idea what was keeping Believer going.

Abruptly, she found herself fighting harder. This was not the wild winds they had been fighting; even then, they were barely keeping the storm at bay. It felt more like it did at the beginning. When they had to force the storm off. Wide-eyed, with a sense of panic, she looked around. Believer's glow was dimming, and it felt as though someone were draining what little strength left to her. "Believer! What's wrong with Believer!" she shouted, as she watched the drained unicorn sinking slowly into the straw. Next to him was an exhausted Tiny, drooping but still standing. Sprawled on the deck were five sleeping horses, one sleeping pony and one stubborn mule, still on his feet. They were no longer able to maintain the shield. Jakar and Matew had never left the animals. In just those few seconds, Believer's glow winked out completely. The storm returned with a vengeance, as though determined to crush these puny beings with the temerity to dare fight it.

Before the sails could be hauled in, the howling wind had most of them in shreds. While the crew was lowering their remains, a bolt of lightning streaked down to the mizzenmast, shattering the spar and sending the topsails crashing into the ratlines of the foremast, fouling them beyond hope. Luckily, the torrential rain extinguished the fire almost immediately, leaving the crippled ship and its crew fighting the howling gale and towering waves for their survival as Bass and Falcon managed to extract Ebony and get her to safety below decks. The door had been tied open, and Faye was awake, trying to keep Cheri from rolling out of her bed where she still slept the sleep of the near dead. Ebony was helped into the other bunk, where Behnam reached across to hold her in. She was too spent to object,

"How...how much further?" she whispered groggily, fighting sleep.

"I must get up... Believer needs me," muttered Faye, trying to rise.

"No. No, he doesn't. It's over, Faye. Believer can't continue. It's up to the crew now," said Bass, pushing her back down.

"I'm not sure how close we are. Falcon's gone to talk to the captain, but I'm not even sure he knows. You get your rest, all of you. You've done all you can," said Tasmin.

"Who's taking care of Believer? Is he all right?" asked Faye.

"He's asheep, Faye. He's just asheep. He kept it up as long as he cou...," comforted Ebony, her voice slurring with sleep as she began to snore gently.

Faye giggled as Cheri tried to roll out of the bunk, again. "Well, I don't think I'll tell him she called him a sheep. He might take offense."

Behnam responded with a deep laugh. "No, but we might want to tell Ebony the next time she gets too serious."

"Why, Behnam, I don't think I've ever heard you tell a joke before!" said Tasmin in mock awe, smiling broader than usual as she got a better grip on her chair.

"You know, we all seem to be a bit jovial considering there's a storm outside desperately trying to sink the ship," interjected Bass from his position at the foot of the bed.

"We're just punch drunk or something. You know, lack of sleep?" explained Faye with a silly smile.

"I'm sure that's part of it, but I think it's also because we've done all we can, now we just need our faith, and trust the prophecies," said Tasmin, glad her padded form kept her from sliding around in the chair as the cabin tilted from side to side.

As the door at the top of the ladder flew open, the wind blew the rain before it down the passage and into the open door of the cabin before it could be caught and closed again. A moment or two later, the ship began climbing a towering swell, sending Matew sliding past in the passage, followed closely by Falcon, who managed to grab the doorjamb and make an entry so graceful he appeared to have planned it that way. "Quit lying about and get in here where you can get dry!" he hollered down the hall to Matew before making his way to the railed table and grabbing on tight, spreading his legs for stability.

"How far to Lohi?" asked Tasmin urgently.

"How's Believer? Will he be all right?" queried Faye at the same time.

"How's the ship holding up?" questioned Behnam, scowling fiercely to cover his worry as the ship let out a loud groan.

Matew was almost to the door as the ship crested the wave and headed down the other side, accompanied by blinding flashes of light and deafening thunder. Frantically, he grabbed the doorjamb as his feet went flying out from under him again. The muscles defined his shoulders, and his arms bulged as he pulled himself back to the door one handed and managed to wedge himself in the opening.

"One thing at a time, please," implored Falcon during a pause in the thunder. "Captain Aberon believes we're only a few miles from the Gate, four or five at most. Now that they're fighting the wind, it's going to be tough going to reach it. He says the *Unicorn's Magic* is a tough ship and well-made but what he didn't say was, no ship was made for a storm like this. Given enough time, it could still shatter. As for Believer, I'm just not sure. Jakar is staying with the animals, all of them. He has a way of calming them, but even he isn't sure about Believer. He told me if any other creature, even a Jessamine Chardell, had put as much of his heart into something as Believer did, it would have broken long before now. He isn't sure it hasn't. Jakar told me our best hope lies in knowing no one knows about unicorns anymore. They are obviously stronger than any could have expected. We just have to have faith he's strong enough."

Bracing herself against the upper bunk, Faye stood up. "I have to go to him. He needs me," she said.

"Are you crazy?" asked Behnam, reaching out to stop her but missing as she stumbled to the table.

"There's nothing you can do. Jakar is already doing what needs to be done," insisted Bass, beginning to reach for her but forced to hold where he was when the ship gave a sudden lurch.

"You don't understand! Believer calls me. He needs me. I must go to him," sobbed Faye trying to pull away from Tasmin's hold and make it to the wall where her slicker had been hung to dry.

"Don't worry, she won't get past me," volunteered Matew from the door.

"Wait! Let's hear her out," called Falcon. "All right, Faye, tell us why you think you can help Believer."

"I don't know exactly. He's calling me. I know my being with him will make the difference. Besides, what difference does it make if I'm on deck or down here when the ship breaks up? Please? I have to go to him," she implored, looking to each in turn.

Looking deep into Faye's distressed blue eyes across the table, Falcon nodded. "She's right. What difference does it make? Besides, we've been going on 'feelings' for days now, or we couldn't have survived this long. Let me help with your slicker."

"If she must go, I'll go with her," insisted Bass, suddenly pushing away from the bunks to stand next to Faye at the table.

"Don't be a fool, Bass. You've been doing quite well, but you've never been on a seagoing vessel before. I've sailed many times, and this isn't the first storm I've weathered. I'll take her and I don't need someone else to have to worry about when I do it," exclaimed Falcon, dismissing the bigger man's offer as he helped Faye into her slicker.

"Yes, isn't that how you met Jakar? Being shipwrecked and washing up on Jessamine's shore? I think the last few days on this ship has given me enough experience. Besides, there's no such thing as enough experience to cover this storm," insisted Bass, bracing his feet to tie his own slicker firmly.

"I survived, didn't I? I know how to do that much," growled Falcon with a stubborn glare over Faye's head.

Tasmin smacked the top of the table with the flat of her hand, instantly getting everyone's attention. "Boys! Quit squabbling! Bass is right. He has as much experience with this storm as you do. If Faye feels she needs to go to Believer, she needs to go now, not after you've fought for the privilege of accompanying her. There's no reason you both can't go," she said sternly.

Just then, everyone grabbed onto the closest handhold to keep from being thrown about as the ship trundled down yet another wave and Cheri groaned as she was tossed against the bulkhead, finally waking up. "Well, I suggest the three of you get going. Matew, come over and help hold Cheri so she doesn't break anything. I'm going to proceed on the assumption we're going to survive this. After which I'll be quite happy if I never again set foot on a ship. There's entirely too much water, if there's enough to float a ship," grumbled Behnam sourly. The man was not a comfortable sailor.

Tactfully deciding to ignore their earlier quarrel, as well as each other, Bass and Falcon made a chain from the table to the door, steadying Faye. Then they held her back as she tried to rush ahead to the ladder.

On deck, Falcon took the lead, keeping Faye close behind with Bass behind her, holding her waist, as they used the guide ropes to make their way to Believer and Jakar. As they got close, Faye took advantage of a brief moment when the storm wasn't trying to tear the ship apart and broke free to rush to the unicorn's side.

"Believer! Believer, are you all right? Jakar, is he...is he...?" she wailed above the howling wind and crashing thunder as they huddled over her still friend, her eyes never leaving the unicorn, lying on the deck.

"Faye! You shouldn't be out here!" objected Jakar, glowering at Falcon and Bass accusingly. "But since you are, he still breaths but that is all I can say. His breathing is very shallow, and his heartbeat worries me, but he is still alive," said the little man, putting out a hand to pat her gently on the back.

Trying in vain not to cry, Faye lowered her head onto Believer's neck, hugging him tightly. "Get better, my friend. You have to get better," she whispered.

Through the storm, she couldn't hear his heartbeat, and only the occasional rise and fall of his rib cage gave evidence of his breathing. Desperately, Faye rose to her knees and bowed her head, hands clasped tightly before her chest. Bass and Falcon, on either side, reached out to hold her steady, and she prayed. She didn't know anything about the beliefs or gods in this strange place, and even if she did, she couldn't pray to them. She had to pray to the only God she knew. "Dear Lord, please bring him safely through this. Please don't let him die. He's done so much for us. He doesn't deserve to die. Please give him back the strength he has given for us. And please, save this ship from the storm. In Jesus's name, amen."

"I don't know what god you prayed to, child, and I've never heard of this Jesus, but it seems you pray a very powerful prayer," commented Jakar in wonder, looking around in disbelief.

"Not a powerful prayer, Jakar. A powerful god, the only one there is."

Falcon and Bass were both staring at Faye in wonder before Falcon turned to the bridge, "Captain! Captain Aberon! How far to the Gate?"

"Land ho!" called the watch, halfway up to the crow's nest, where he'd headed as soon as the winds had let him.

"How far? Is it the Gate?" the captain called back.

"Almost to his perch, the call came back, "Aye, Cap'n. 'Tis indeed the Gate, near a league away," they could see the sailor turn as he looked behind them, pointing excitedly. "Sir, look there! The storm's afollowin'!"

Bass, Jakar, and Falcon rushed to the rail to look astern. Sure enough, the storm was a short way behind them, but it wasn't gaining. In fact, they appeared to be leaving it behind.

"Strange, it looks like Gabriene's shield has grown. Usually, it doesn't protect until you're safely in Mermaid Bay," murmured Jakar, his gaze returning to Faye where she was speaking softly to Believer as he clambered to his feet, splaying his legs for balance. Once he was on his feet, she grabbed some oats to give the unicorn.

Falcon looked over at her thoughtfully, "She said, she prayed to a powerful god. Do you think she is a priestess of this god of hers and simply hasn't seen fit to tell us?" he whispered to Bass.

"Perhaps, perhaps. I think, if she hasn't seen fit to tell us, I don't think we should ask. If she's a priestess, she'll tell us when the time is right," replied Jakar thoughtfully as he stood next to them, before walking away to check on the horses and see how they fared.

Bass stared at the small woman for a long moment. "A priestess?

Surely not," he mumbled to himself as he followed the others.

*****

Gabriene sighed as he settled back in the comfortable brown chair with the stuffing coming out and glanced about his sanctuary. Before *they* started coming, it had merely been his workshop. Now, it was the one place they were forbidden to come after he had caught Meland and Beloria cleaning up. They had barely started, but it had been days before he found everything again. He much preferred it the way it was, cluttered and dusty, with everything right where he could find it. There were books and scrolls and maps scattered everywhere. On the bookshelves, on the tables, on the other two chairs in the room, on the floor. Here and there were odd-shaped glass containers with blue, red, green, orange, and black liquids inside. Under the south window was a large table cluttered with gray and brown pots and jars of all sizes, a mortar and pestle, and a variety of arcane paraphernalia, including an assortment of bowls with strange berries, roots, and stones. Next to these was an exceptionally large book, open on a stand. By the west window was a tall bookcase with ancient scrolls tucked between several glass globes, each with its own scene inside. On a perch by the east window, was a fat barn owl who spread his wings and gave Gabriene a haughty look before returning to sleep.

"Sorry, Boswell. I didn't mean to disturb your sleep. It must be all this noise. I just can't seem to extend the spell of safety any further," said the very, very tired old man over the sounds of children playing drifting up the stairs from below.

Boswell opened one eye and stared at him skeptically.

"All right. Maybe it isn't the noise, but it's not what you're thinking, either. I'm not getting too old to cast a proper spell, nor am I getting rusty. I will admit I'm too old to be trying to train all of these young girls coming to my doorstep.

Silently, Boswell closed his eye again.

"Well, well. What am I supposed to do with them all? I

know there must be a reason why seven girls, each with innate magical talent, should show up after nearly two thousand years without a new sorcerer, but I haven't got time to train them. Not now. Just testing them to see where their talents lie has been a strain and I'm still not sure about those last two. The Jessamine and the Hawarti. I can sense ability in them, but I haven't been able to figure out what it is. All of this just when the prophecies are being fulfilled. Do you know the three who came through the portal should be here any time now? If they survived Barakus's storm, that is. Well, I've done all I can. I'll have to leave the rest to prophecy," rambled the old man, pushing himself out of the cushions of his chair. As he turned, he grabbed a gnarled staff and stumped to the door. "At least old Gaban should be here soon. I only wish we could have left a guard on the portal. Now, I must turn these girls over to him while I help the three saviors in their quest," he rambled to himself.

Wearily, Gabriene descended to the next level of the tower where his uninvited and unexpected charges were supposed to be practicing and exploring their talents. The lively chatter that only seven little girls in early adolescence can generate increased, causing the old man to smile momentarily. Ever since Meland of Lohi had first arrived, her innocence had begun making him feel younger as well, with each addition the effect multiplied. It was almost like finding a fountain of youth. At any other time, he would have been thrilled with the challenge of teaching adepts how to use and control the magic touching their lives. Now, there simply wasn't time. Just before making the last turn in the curving staircase, he wiped the smile from his face. It wouldn't do to let the girls know how much he enjoyed their company. They were almost impossible to control as it was.

*****

The crew of the *Unicorn's Magic* had salvaged enough sail to rig the foremast and the jib once they were in safe waters again, but the ship could hardly regain her earlier speed, and it took almost all day for the once-proud ship to limp into harbor with its valuable cargo. As they approached the dock, they could make out a short, round figure, hooded in a plain brown water-repelling robe alighting from a carriage. Leaning heavily on his staff, the unassuming figure approached the ship as it was tying up and threw back his hood to reveal a well-tanned bald head shining in the drizzling rain. He was the oldest man Cheri had ever seen. The creases and seams of his face made even Gaban seem young. Finally, she met his eyes, eyes that twinkled like a young boy about to play a prank or a man about to realize a dream. Trying to stay out of the way of the sailors lowering the gangplank, he leaned his staff in the crook of one arm and began rubbing his hands eagerly.

"Ahoy! Captain Aberon! I see you made it. I knew if anyone could, it would be you. Not that I expected Barakus to brew up that horrendous storm, but then perhaps I should have. One should never underestimate one's enemies, they say. After over two thousand years, you would think I would know better, wouldn't you? Well, well. Enough about that. All that matters is, you made it safely. You were able to pick up your passengers, weren't you? They are safely aboard, aren't they?" he chattered excitedly.

"Aye, Master Gabriene, sir! They're here all right. We'd never have made it without them. I do wish you'd warned me though. I didn't expect what I found, beggin' yer pardon, sir," came the captain's hearty reply.

"Warn you? Warn you about what? I do hope you had no trouble finding them. It was the one part I couldn't be sure of when I sent you out. Well, well. Never mind. Where are they? What are all those women doing onboard? I thought it was understood you were only to pick up the designated passengers and anyone traveling with them? Well, well. I suppose it's too late now to do anything about it. I've waited two thousand years to meet these men, and now I find I can't wait any longer! Permission to come aboard," rambled Gabriene as he trudged up the gangplank.

Onboard the ship, Cheri and Faye were no longer able to stifle their giggles while the others respectfully tried to hide their smiles. Gabriene was definitely in for the surprise of his life when he met the portal's chosen saviors.

Once aboard Gabriene stood beaming at Behnam, Bass, and Falcon with a damp and miserable Amalee on his shoulder. "Well, well. You're finally here. Not exactly what I expected but then I suppose Gaban briefed you well and helped you with your clothes. I expected him to give you more than an overgrown boy as a guide. Since you're here, I guess, no harm done. You know, I've had a look or two through the portal myself over the years, and I must say I didn't expect you to be anything like this."

"Well, to tell you the truth, sir, we're not anything like this ourselves. That is, we are, but those who came through the portal aren't. I mean, well, we aren't the ones you're expecting. We've just been helping them get here," stumbled Falcon nervously.

"Perhaps I can best explain things," volunteered Tasmin, stepping forward. "Master Gabriene, these three lovely young women you see before you are the ones who came through the portal. May I introduce Lady Ebony, Lady Faye, and Lady Cheri. I am Tasmin of Jamben, and when the portal called me, Gaban put me in charge of their well-being. This gentleman is Falcon. He was also called by the portal to be our guide and provide the horses. The hawk on his shoulder is his companion Amalee. The Mojar is Behnam, Shik of the Kodul, he came to our aid in Nelas and volunteered to join us. Young

Matew felt the call in a small village on the way to Dobe. Sir Bass is the woodsman of the Singing Forest and was waiting for Falcon and Cheri when they passed his way. He has been a great help. And last but certainly not least is Sir Jakar of Jessamine. He was able to get us safely through Dhwittle and onto your ship in record time and with very little notice. Now, it's been a rather harrowing trip for us all, but especially for these three lovely women without whom we would never have made it, so perhaps we can find somewhere dry that doesn't toss about so much? We've waited this long, surely another few hours while my charges recuperate won't matter that much?"

Abruptly, Gabriene realized his mouth had fallen open sometime ago, and he snapped it shut. "Yes, yes, of course. It's only I'm so surprised. I mean, I expected warriors, generals, leaders. That's not to say you can't lead us of course, but I never expected—that is to say, well, you are women," he said in obvious confusion.

"As though women can't be warriors," muttered Ebony under her breath, too tired to start a fight.

"Don't tell me we've outrun the rumors of Barakus looking for three women?" asked Behnam loudly, bowing respectfully to the venerable sorcerer, trying to draw attention away from Ebony's disgruntled mood.

"Well, well. Not exactly. I did hear something about that, but I dismissed it as pure nonsense. Another error on my part, obviously," grumbled the ancient one distractedly. "Let's get you up to the castle where you can rest and bathe then we must talk. Plan our next move."

Ebony yawned hugely. "Actually, once I've had a hot bath and a good night's sleep, the first thing we need to know about is the prophecy. It seems to be doing a good job of running our lives since we came to this crazy place. I think it's time we knew more about it."

"The prophecy? Oh, yes, of course, you wouldn't know much about it, would you? I do apologize, I appear to be getting a bit absentminded of late, but then I've had so much on my mind. What with those little girls and all. Well, well. If we're not going to meet until morning, I suppose I have time to return to my tower and retrieve the prophecy. So unlike me, to have forgotten to bring it," he grumbled as he headed back down the gangplank to the waiting carriage. "I'm afraid there's not enough room in the carriage for all of you, but the ladies are welcome to join me. At least it's out of the rain," he called back over his shoulder as the men started leading the horses to the dock.

Cheri gave baby's black and white coat a rueful pat before following the old man. "I think we can wait a while longer, Baby. I'm sure we'll be riding together soon."

Ebony took one look at the gray sky and gave George a quick hug on his neck. "I never thought I'd say this, but I'm sure I'd be more comfortable on your back, my love, but it is drier in the carriage. I'm so tired of being wet. Bass, will you take care of him for me?"

Faye gave Believer a long hug before turning away, "I'd rather be with you, regardless of the weather, but you still need to rest. I'll ride with the others."

Tasmin merely patted Anabelle as she passed, "Matew, would you take care of her for me? I'm afraid the storm was a bit much for her."

Once Gabriene and the women were settled comfortably in the well-sprung carriage, Gabriene rapped on the roof, and they were off at a sedate pace. The men filed in behind, making quite a caravan.

Inside the carriage, Gabriene was still staring at them with a stunned expression. Absently, he reached over to Faye and picked up a lock of her hair, "Is this your natural color, child?" he asked.

"This? No! Not at all. It's just part of a disguise. It just seems to be the one part taking its time going away," she answered in disgust.

"Well, well. I'll have Madlene give you some of the shampoo I made for her. It will fix you right up. Oh, my... women. Uhm, of course, that could be it. Yes, yes, it could," he muttered distractedly, his mind moving on to other things.

Faye doubted he would remember the shampoo, but she would.

She'd just have to find out who this Madlene person was, that's all.

Luckily, the castle wasn't far, although it was immense, on the scale of one of those fairy-tale castles in Germany. Nothing else Faye had seen, heard, or smelled brought home to her exactly what kind of place they were in as vividly. The carriage drove up the long drive to the portico erected above the door and stopped. As they emerged, there was an army of servants, waiting quietly. In front of them was a large woman with brown hair pulled back in a bun at the nape of her neck. She was wearing a clean, starched dress of gray satin and rustled as she stepped forward to curtsey gracefully. The domestics behind her followed suit and bowed or curtsied according to their sex. "Welcome to Castle Tinora, lords and ladies. My staff and I are yours to command. If you need anything, anything at all, we will do our best to provide it," she said, rising and smiling broadly at all of them, obviously a little unsure which ones they had been expecting.

"Well, well. Madlene! So good of you to be waiting. May I introduce Ladies Ebony, Faye, Cheri, and Tasmin. Please be sure they are given the very best rooms, and I believe hot baths were mentioned. We also need suitable guest quarters for Shik Behnam, Lord Falcon and his hawk, Amalee, Lord Bass, and Sir Matew. Master Jakar, I would be pleased to make you a guest of my tower. It has been many years since

I've has a Jessamine seer for a guest. You are a seer, aren't you?" said Gabriene in his usual garrulous way.

Madlene had already motioned for porters and maids to help guide their guests upstairs, and stablemen had been sent for to care for the animals. Scampering forward nimbly, Jakar grinned. "Yes, yes, I am a seer. Any other time, I would be honored to be joining you, but I believe you have among your guests, one Briar Rose from Jessamine. Right now, it would be very detrimental for her to know that I know she is there. She needs to believe she has broken free of the ties of home. No, I really must refuse. Don't worry, we will have ample time to talk in the near future," he said, bowing low with an elaborate flourish of his red hat, the white plume sweeping the ground. Straightening, he turned to follow the others into the grand hall with its carved pillars, crown molding, parquet wood floor, and elaborately painted ceiling. He had to skip spryly to catch them as they made their way up the wide staircase with its carved wooden banister and wrought iron balusters looking like grapevines climbing around in sweeping curves.

CHAPTER 23

The Face of Prophecy

Madlene caught up to her guests as they were stopping outside the first door in the empire wing. "I'm sorry to have been delayed. Master Gabriene had further instructions for me. This room, I think, would be for Lady Ebony. The colors suit you, my dear," she said graciously, opening the door to a large bedroom with a heavy four-poster bed. The spread and the drapes were a deep rich wine-colored velvet while the bed hangings were a soft, lustrous dove gray satin. The rug covering most of the polished wood floor was an intricate design in both colors. All the woodwork gleamed with years of care and beeswax in the light of a dozen or more candles about the room. On the stone walls were tapestries with glorified scenes of battles between knights and fanciful monsters. While the tapestries gave the room a masculine note, Ebony found the overall effect comforting. Exactly what a guest room in a castle should look like.

"Ah! This is lovely. Thank you," she said as two maids bustled in with pitchers of hot water and fluffy towels.

"Since it will take a while for the water to heat for your baths, I thought you might like to clean up enough for a light meal. Either here or downstairs, if you're hungry, that is?" said the efficient Madlene.

"Actually, a good hot meal would go down well. Where are Cheri and Faye staying?"

"Lady Faye will be next door, and Cheri is across the hall. Don't fear. You need not be separated from your friends. You're safe here, you know," she assured them all, leading the way to Faye's room.

Half an hour later, dressed in dry clothes and cleaned up some, Ebony crossed to Faye's room and knocked on the door.

"Come in," came Faye's voice.

The hangings, drapes, and carpet inside the room were done in shades of blue accented with white lace. The delicate spindle bed had a white-lace canopy. Here the tapestries were of unicorns. Sometimes in a group of two or three at a pool in a forest, sometimes alone with a maiden with long blond hair dressed in white.

Cheri was already there, lying across the bed. "Isn't it cool? Don't you think it fits Faye to a tee? I mean, it even has unicorns. I wonder how they knew?" she asked, bouncing up on her knees.

"What? I don't know. I'm beginning to think we shouldn't question anything we find here since none of it makes a lot of sense. Where's Faye?"

"Here I am. About as ready as I'm going to be," she said fretfully, stepping from behind a delicately painted blue silk changing screen and crossing to the dressing table with its smoky mirror. Absently she picked up a brush to run it through her red hair. "I only wish I could have washed this color out of my hair first."

"Come on, you've lived with it this long. Surely you can live with it a little longer. I don't imagine there'll be a lot of people there tonight. Just us and whoever owns this castle and maybe their family. Nothing at all to worry about," reassured Ebony gently.

"Besides, I've rather gotten used to seeing you in that color of hair. If only you had the freckles to go with it," chimed in Cheri with an impish grin and a saucy toss of her own red curls before she leapt off the bed and darted for the door, just ahead of Faye and Ebony.

When they reached the ground floor, they just followed the sound of male laughter to find the dining room. Falcon, Behnam, Matew, Bass, and Jakar were already there, standing around a gleaming table stretching for at least ten feet down the room. It was set with very thin, delicate, porcelain dishes and crystal goblets trimmed in gold, which were only outshone by the glitter of the golden flatware and silver candelabra. Amalee had found a perch on the back of a chair. For a change she seemed to have chosen to stay with Falcon this time. There was no sign of their host or hostess.

When Tasmin arrived a moment later, Madlene was right behind her, "Lords, ladies, dinner is served."

"Won't the owner of the castle be joining us?" asked Ebony curiously.

"Of course, but you're already here. Didn't you know? Gabriene! He has forgotten to tell you, hasn't he? I should have known. This castle was built and originally staffed in the first three hundred years after the prophecies became known. It belongs to the savior of Persal. I presume that is one or more of you?" she answered calmly.

"It's been staffed for almost two thousand years? You don't mean you're...," squeaked Cheri in disbelief.

"No, no, child. The posts we hold are hereditary. It is considered a great honor to be on the staff of the savior's castle. Now, I must ring for your dinner to be served before you starve. Please be seated," explained Madlene, crossing to pull the cord that would ring the bell in the kitchen.

The light meal she had promised was brought in by a long stream of servants. First, there was a maid carrying a tureen of steaming vegetable soup, followed by a footman with a large ham. Next were a series of maids with fresh bread and rolls in four varieties, five vegetables including those purple potatoes Cheri had become so fond of, and last but not least, the chef himself arrived with a succulent roast bird, the size of a goose. The wine steward topped it all off with a mellow white wine. Once they were served the main meal, the procession continued as the sideboard was loaded with a variety of pastries and two large bowls of fresh fruit.

When all the servants had finally left the room, Faye leaned across to Ebony. "If this is a 'light' supper, can you imagine what a feast consists of?"

Cheri giggled as she took small helpings of everything that looked appetizing. Unfortunately, when she looked at her plate, that appeared to be everything. Oh well, she was hungry after the waterlogged rations on the ship. Still, a little embarrassed, she looked around at the others and saw her plate was positively barren compared to what the men had piled on theirs. Amalee was picking disdainfully at the plate of cooked meats Falcon had given her.

Before Ebony began eating, she glanced around the room with its well-cared-for furnishings. "Don't you think it's just a bit spooky? A castle built almost two thousand years ago and just sitting here, empty? Waiting for us to come?" she asked.

"Aren't you the one who just told us not to question anything in Persal? What makes this any stranger than anything else we've seen here?" rejoined Faye as her head rose from saying grace.

"We were told to expect a savior. The least we could do would be to make ready for their arrival. Give them an honored place of their own," said Tasmin complacently.

"Yes, I suppose you're right, but I just can't shake this feeling there's something wrong about it all. Well, if it's important, it will come to me," capitulated Ebony, giving into her hunger with gusto.

As they were finishing their meal, Madlene appeared. The housekeeper seemed to have a way of knowing when she was needed. "Dear ladies, if you are through, the water for your baths is ready to be sent to your rooms.

"A hot bath? Madam Madlene, I will follow you anywhere. Lead on," said Cheri dramatically.

At the door to Faye's room, Madlene handed her a cut-glass bottle in the shape of a dolphin. "For your hair, Lady Faye. Gabriene mentioned you might need it. He says I'm being foolish, but I know it not only restores the color of your hair, but it will make it thicker and grow faster. Sometimes he underestimates himself," she said with a smile before turning to go.

"He remembered. I'm surprised, he actually remembered," murmured Faye as she closed the door and crossed to the large copper tub steaming behind the screen in the corner.

*****

The next morning, the rain was reduced to a fine mist as Cheri woke and stretched in her soft bed filled with down. Hers was a cheerful room done in green with delightful yellow flowers. The tapestries were woodland scenes which unfortunately also meant one or two included the hunt. Those she tried to ignore; instead, she concentrated on all the good things that were hers this day. After supper and a hot bath, she had slept like a baby, and she felt wonderful. For the first time in a long time, she could be reasonably sure she was safe. She hadn't felt this secure since before her father left them. Well, she knew better than most, security and comfort never last. She was going to enjoy it while she could.

Half an hour later, dressed and hungry, Cheri followed her nose back to the dining room where the others were already taking advantage of a buffet breakfast waiting in silver chafing dishes. Heaping eggs, bacon, fresh bread, and lush yellow strawberries on her delicate porcelain plate, she joined them, pausing briefly to lift a lock of Faye's blond hair. "You know, you're right. Stick with blond hair. You don't have the panache to get away with being a redhead." She smirked.

"Don't be impudent, Lady Cheri! Personally, I think Lady Faye is lovely regardless of the color of her hair, although I must say she has an almost ethereal beauty, as a blond," blustered Bass, beginning in outrage but finishing by blushing and staring at his plate as though he'd said too much.

"Why, thank you, Master Bass, but I would appreciate it if you didn't say such things, please. I was raised to believe beauty is not something to be proud of and all of this talk is making me very uncomfortable," objected Faye, her face flushing in embarrassment.

"Now, why would anyone want to do that to you, dear girl? I admit that beauty isn't the most important thing in life, but why try to deny what you've been given? It's not exactly a curse, either," admonished Tasmin, a frown on her genial face.

"Compliments make me uncomfortable, that's all."

"Okay, okay. I'm sorry I even mentioned your hair, Faye, but I'll bet you're glad it's back to normal. Well, have we heard yet from Gabriene? Personally, I'd like to know what it is we're supposed to do here," inquired Cheri, skillfully changing the subject.

"Don't be so impatient, Cheri. I'm quite sure Gabriene will be here soon. You've waited this long, another half hour or so won't make much difference," chided Tasmin with a shake of her gray head, stray wisps already escaping her bun.

Ebony sighed as she nibbled on a slice of...well, she hoped it was a peach. "She's right, girlfriend. At least we should all finish eating breakfast before having to worry about it."

"I'm sorry, but being the savior of a place and not having the faintest idea how to go about it is nerve-wracking. I mean, we never asked for this, and so far, we haven't the faintest idea what it's all about. Not really," said Cheri, around a mouthful of bread, not letting her impatience interfere with eating.

"Cheri, don't talk with your mouth full!" admonished Faye as she pushed away her own plate. "I know what you mean, though, until now we've been too busy to worry about it. Now, all we have to do is sit here and wait."

Behnam's deep laugh rumbled out, "Amazing! The three of you are so impatient to put your hands into the snake pit before you check and see if the vipers are sleeping. Considering what you've already been through, I'd think you'd realize by now that things are only going to get more dangerous from here on out."

"Since we've been told, repeatedly, we can't avoid our destiny, why wait? The sooner we get this over, the sooner we can go home," rejoined Ebony testily, as she rose to leave the table.

Having finished, the others followed with Amalee gliding smoothly to her favorite perch, Falcon's shoulder. Curious, they wandered down the great hall, looking into open doors as they went. Next to the dining room was a large sitting room, chairs, settees, and couches scattered about in small conversational groups. Across from the sitting room was a conservatory, filled with weak sunshine and an interesting variety of plants. The next door was closed, and Ebony stepped up to open it. Inside was the library. Walls covered in two stories of shelves filled with books and scrolls, except for the occasional window with its deep window seats. Comfortable-looking wingback chairs were scattered here and there to take advantage of the light given off by table lamps filled with oil. In one corner was an intricately carved desk with a matching, high-backed chair, while in the center of the room was a table only slightly smaller than the one in the dining room, with several chairs placed neatly around it.

Cheri found herself irresistibly drawn to the tall shelves of books. The others followed. Faye eyed the books almost hungrily as she pulled out her glasses to read the titles. Ebony crossed to a low table beside one of the wingback chairs and picked up the book someone had left there, while Tasmin settled herself into a chair and watched the others. Jakar had already climbed the ladder to check out the books on the top shelves while Bass held a book almost reverently.

Behnam stood in the middle of the room, just staring, as though uncertain where to start. Matew's eyes were large as he looked bout the room nervously, shifting on his feet by the door. When Gabriene arrived, he pushed the husky youth ahead of him so he could get through the double doors with his armload of scrolls. "Well, well, we're all here, I see. I hope you had a good night's sleep. We've got a long day ahead of us. Sorry if I'm late, those girls at my tower, well, I'm really not much good with children. This whole thing has been most unsettling. Now, where is the first scroll? It must be here, somewhere. I know I had it when I left this morning," he rambled as he scattered his scrolls on the table, startling Amalee, who flapped her wings in agitation before flying from Falcon's shoulder to perch on an empty bookstand near the window.

"And good morning to you, Master Gabriene," said Tasmin sweetly as she rose and crossed to the table to see if she could help him.

"What? Oh, yes, good morning, good morning to you all. I'm afraid I've been rather a recluse for many years now, and I tend to forget the social graces, now and then. Please excuse my lapses. Ah, here it is," he said, nodding absently to each of them as they gathered around the table. "Since you have never heard the prophecies, I felt it best we begin at the beginning. Please, please be seated. Make yourselves comfortable," he urged as he sat on a wingback chair in the middle of the table and unrolled the chosen scroll carefully before beginning to read.

> "Darkness has descended on the land, but we get by
> Through upheaval and turmoil,
> Afore the redemption doth arrive, there will be changes
> And there will be tears.
> To save Persal we will have to face ourselves and our fears
> As common events happen out of time
> From afar will come hope When hope is gone
> Faith when faith is forgotten
> Charity when we feel most alone
> In days to come, to save us from ourselves
> Shall appear from an unknown place
> A beguiling wake-up call
> Swiftness to learn, agility in practice
> Joy in providing for others as need is seen
> For a time, great jubilation shall spread across the land.

"Please bear in mind, Jarok came to me with these first prophecies two hundred years before Barakus showed up on my doorstep. I had forgotten them until it was too late. Of course, this part is talking about when Barakus appears on the scene. He was a strange child when we first met, only about thirteen or fourteen, I'd say. A very handsome boy, almost delicate features. While eager to learn, I had more difficulty with him than with any of my other students. It was like he looked at things differently, somehow. In fact, it was somewhat like the problems I'm having with my new students. Oh well, let me see, where was I?

> "Then this one who brings such joy shall step beyond the
> limits of our world
> Unwilling to be confined to what should be done That
> which is forbidden shall be done

When success is shown, and approbation is looked for
Shall it be said, "Am I not god?"
Then the favored one shall believe
Nothing should be denied
It is time I learn what is forbidden
When refusal comes, and refuse you must, it will be the beginning
Of the end of our world, as is known.

"It was shortly after Barakus's great sin that I remembered the prophecy, but by then, it was too late. He had fled to the land of Doome and was fast becoming stronger even than I, although a foolish old man's pride was slow to admit it."

"Gabriene, what was Barakus's 'great sin'? Just what did he do that made him think he was a god?" asked Cheri curiously.

"Rumors have said it's one thing, some have said another, but there are only a few left who know. I suppose if anyone has a right to know the truth, it would be the ones who'll have to correct what happened after. Let's see...," began Gabriene thoughtfully.

"Uh, excuse me, Master Gabriene? Lady Tasmin? I haven't quite known how to say this, but I...well, I won't be going on with you and the ladies. It's not that I'm a coward, you see, it's just, I feel my place is here, somehow. I thought I'd start over at the knights' academy, if they'll have me," stammered Matew, his voice fading on the last sentence. "I just thought you ought to know before you go telling any secrets I shouldn't know," he finished in a rush.

Tasmin rose and gave the nervous young man a hug. "Don't fret about it, Matew. I always suspected you wouldn't be satisfied just following us around. Look at you! You're built to be a knight yourself someday. Your destiny lies there, beyond the wall. Go with the good."

After this announcement, everyone rose to say goodbye to

their friend. Faye waited until last. "Make me proud, Matew. Don't ever make me regret hauling you out of the mud," she mumbled, giving him a fierce hug and brushing away the tears glistening in her eyes.

"Never fear, Lady Faye, as soon as my arm heals, I'll make you proud of me. Then I'll write me pa, askin' him to send me brother Cato. Looks like we're goin' to need all the strong backs we can get," he answered with a grin.

Falcon's head snapped up. "Cato? That wouldn't be Cato Bye, would it? I thought you reminded me of someone. We met him and your mother on our way to the Singing Forest."

"Yes, sir, that would be me family. I'll tell them I met you when I write. Well, I'd best be goin' on me way. I don't have any place stayin' here," he said, turning and leaving the room quickly, hoping no one saw his eyes shine.

"Well, I'll be switched. Seems we met his family on their farm about the same time you were meeting him and his father in the village," mused Falcon as he sat down again.

"Some say it's a small world, but I'd still say it was a strange coincidence," admitted Faye, shaking her head in wonder.

"Excuse me, Master Gabriene, ladies and gentlemen, I thought you might like some refreshment. I've brought some cool peach cordial," said Madlene as she bustled in from the hall, followed by a footman and a maid with silver trays topped by crystal goblets and decanters glistening wetly. They placed them quietly on the table and a moment later they were gone, Madlene closing the doors behind them.

"Harrumph! Well, yes, I am a bit parched. A cool drink would go down easy about now. Lady Tasmin, would you do the honors? Now, let me see, where were we? Ah, yes, coincidences...actually, I don't believe it was a coincidence at all. You see, your movements have been fairly easy to follow ever since you left the mountains. I can't tell you who was doing what all the time, but you were hardly quiet in the magical ambiance. Did any of you have a knack for magic in your world? No? well, it still seemed..., well, no matter.

"Anyway, the first big ripples you sent out after your initial arrival, happened in Nelas. Actually, there was one big splash then several smaller ripples. Shortly after that, you appeared to be on the run and smaller ripples could be felt but they weren't yours. At least I don't think so. I'm not sure where they came from, but I'll work on that too. Now, when Falcon and...," said Gabriene, pausing to take a sip of the cordial Tasmin handed him and gaze thoughtfully at the three women, noticing Cheri's eyes flick uneasily, "Yes, Cheri, I believe, reached the Singing Forest, well, that sent so many ripples I would have thought the rocks would vibrate from it. As for those who went through Dobe, I picked your currents up while you were still in the woods. I'd say you met someone there and from the vibrations of those currents, I think it was someone a little...unsavory. As for those traveling cross country, well, you were hardly quiet in the currents either. No, it strikes me there are no coincidences where the three of you are concerned. I believe the magical currents of Persal are bending themselves around you, somehow. The problem is, I haven't figured out how to teach you to be quiet about it, even so Barakus isn't as aware as I have been."

"Master Gabriene, that is interesting and possibly even useful, but that isn't where we were. You were about to tell us what Barakus's 'great sin' was," reminded Ebony, a bit impatiently.

"Ah, yes," sighed the old man, settling back in his chair, his eyes growing distant as he stared at an old memory. "Barakus had learned all I could teach him, yet he wanted to know even more. One day, when I was away from my tower, he started rummaging in my manuscripts and found an old scroll that I thought I'd burned long ago. It told of how you could take an ordinary beast of the woods or fields and give them the power of intelligence and speech. This is a forbidden thing, known only by a few and never before has anyone dared to tempt the Creator and try it. Barakus...well, he was always bold and reckless. There was nothing he would not dare. He took the scroll and fled Lohi, going to a far place, seldom visited by men, to raise the animals so they could worship him. The only fortunate thing was, he chose a small animal that was gentle and kind by nature. That's when he found that he could give them speech and thought but could not make them be other than what they were. As soon as the deed was done, we sorcerers knew, and we set out to search for the one who had turned to evil. Of course, Barakus knew we were coming, and he fled to Doome, where evil teachings were easy to come by. I went to the marshes of Zabir and found the poor creatures but not before much damage had been done. I set out to protect them as best I could, but I could not undo what had been done. By the time we found Barakus, he was firmly entrenched in Doome. That was when I discovered his powers were as great, or greater, than my own. The best we could do was try to keep our side of the Forbidden Mountains free, but one by one, Barakus found ten of the good sorcerers and killed them, leaving only Gaban and myself to defend it all.

"Gaban was needed to watch and guard the portal, so that left only me. Bit by bit, I was beaten back to this small corner while Barakus sent in his priests and armies across Persal. The people tried to fight back, at first, but what can an ordinary mortal do against forbidden magic? They never had a chance. Not a chance," finished Gabriene, nodding off in his chair.

"I do believe the sound of his own voice has put the old geezer to sleep," said Jakar, a bit less than respectful.

Just then there was a snort followed by a gentle snore

from the chair. "It sounds like you're right, but what do we do now? I don't much like the idea of sitting here watching him sleep until he decides to wake up again," said Bass with a small smile.

"I've a hunch he can sleep through anything. Why don't I continue reading the prophecy where the master left off? Here, Behnam, old fella, hand me that scroll," suggested Jakar helpfully as he hopped up on the seat of his chair and stretched for the scroll.

"Well, I suppose it really wouldn't do any harm, and he does look like he could use the sleep," agreed Tasmin, shaking her head reluctantly.

"Let's see, where were we? Ah, here it is," began Jakar, scanning down the scroll quickly.

> "An age shall pass, and Charity will become lost to survival Who shall hear us crying?"

At this Cheri's head snapped up in wide-eyed astonishment.

> "An age and an age shall pass, and Faith will become lost among the ashes
> Who shall we pray to then?"

Almost involuntarily, Faye's hand came up to her mouth, and she started chewing on her thumbnail.

> "An age, and an age, and an age shall pass, and Hope shall evaporate as smoke from the fires of our passion,
> Leaving us dry as empty husks with no tears for crying."

Ebony stiffened for a moment before making herself relax and glancing around to see if anyone had noticed.

Without raising his eyes, Jakar commented, "Sounds like

the early times of Barakus before people learned to live with what they couldn't change.

> "You will know the end has begun when the house of forever fails and appears to be gone.
> In this illusion shall you know the time to span worlds is near."

Gabriene snorted and sat up. "That would be when the ruling house of Camir, in Rim, all came down with some disease, and they all died. What was really strange, only members of the royal family died. Of course, there were a lot of them. Very prolific, they were. Thank you, Jakar. My voice isn't used to all that talking."

"Oh, Master Gabriene, I didn't mean to...I only thought, since you were sleeping and already knew all this...," stammered Jakar in embarrassment.

"Now, now. You are doing me a favor, and I did need the rest. Don't worry about it."

"Master Gabriene, what does the prophecy mean when it says it will 'appear to be gone'? And there was something about an 'illusion'?" asked Ebony curiously.

"Well, it's said that when they were through burying the royal family, one member, Patrit, the youngest son of King Abnoth and Queen Maydene, was missing. One of the servants remembered that the boy and his retainer had been hunting when it began. Since the boy was never found, it is thought his retainer took him somewhere safe. The people of Camir have been waiting for his descendant to return ever since. Even the most ambitious of the nobles has never dared declare himself king."

"Spanning worlds, that's the portal, isn't it?" asked Cheri, beginning to enjoy herself again.

"You're absolutely right, Lady Cheri. Of course, it's easy to figure out what the prophecy means when you have history to help you. It's what's yet to come that makes it hard," said Gabriene with a smile as Jakar continued.

> "Do not hesitate,
> Do not delay,
> When the princess under the mountain sleeps in crystal,
> Your time for finishing the gate will be short indeed."

"Princess Areola of Jamben and the princess pears," breathed Tasmin, interrupting Jakar yet again.

"Well, well. So sorry about that. Only goes to prove nothing good comes of losing your temper," mumbled the wizard.

"Ahem, yes. Well, if I may continue?

> "Do not despair
> While the end has begun
> It may yet be halted
> Build the gateway into a strange land
> Through it shall come guides to salvation."

"Guides to salvation? Not exactly the same thing as 'saviors,' is it?" pounced Ebony triumphantly.

"Maybe not, but the end result will be the same, won't it?" answered Behnam with a grin.

"Not necessarily," objected Ebony tersely.

Jakar glared at them both for a moment before continuing.

> "When all the ages are past, and the end seems certain
> Learn to live anew, and our crying will be heard.
> The gateway will open and promises kept
> Our tears will finally be dried
> When Hope, Faith, and Charity shall enter our world fully grown
> Having the eyes of a child

Seeing our world as a new creation
Our redemption is at hand.”

This time, Ebony, Faye, and Cheri all gasped aloud at the same time, drawing everyone's attention to them.

“What? What is it? Cheri? Faye? Ebony? Are you all right?” asked Tasmin, rising abruptly from her chair and beginning to move toward them in alarm.

“No! I mean, yes! I'm fine,” said Faye hastily, waving Tasmin back to her seat.

“Me...me too. I think,” seconded Cheri, her eyes wide as she stared at the scroll in Jakar's hands.

“Yes. It's just...just...,” mumbled Ebony, shaking her head as though to clear her thoughts.

Gabriene sat forward eagerly. “It's something in the prophecy, isn't it? You know something about what this passage means? That's more than I can say, and I've been studying this for near on to two thousand years. What did you read, Jakar?”

Jakar looked uncertainly from the three women to Gabriene before looking down at the scroll and finding his place.

“When all the ages are past, and the end seems certain
Learn to live anew, and our crying will be herd.
The gateway will open and promises kept
Our tears will finally be dried
When Hope, Faith, and Charity shall enter our world
fully grown
Having the eyes of a child
Seeing our world as a new creation
Our redemption is at hand.”

“Ebony, what does that mean to you?” asked Falcon, staring directly at the dark woman.

"Well, it's silly, really. I just wasn't expecting...Ebony isn't my first name. It's so old-fashioned. I never liked the name, so I use Ebony instead," stumbled Ebony, her voice dropping to a hoarse whisper as she continued. "My name is Hope. Hope Ebony Evans."

Faye's eyes widened in surprise, "Really? How odd. I mean... actually, my name's Faith, after my mother. When she left us, my father took to calling me Faye. When I heard Jakar just now...I was surprised. I hoped it was just a coincidence...," she said, her voice trailing off as she started chewing on her thumb again. Worried, she glanced around the table, remembering what Gabriene had said about coincidences.

It was deathly quiet as all eyes turned to Cheri. "Okay, okay. So my name's not Cheri! What was I supposed to do? What kind of name is Charity for someone in the profession? I mean, men tend to get the idea I was giving away my...wares," she said defensively, her face turning a bright red.

"Ah, of course. Well, now we know. Hope, Faith, and Charity have entered our world, fully grown. What about the part that says 'with the eyes of a child'?" asked Bass, trying to follow the line of clues emerging from the prophecy.

"Oh, I think that definitely fits," piped up Faye, nodding for emphasis.

"Sure, seeing some of the wonders of your world mas made me feel like the child I should have been," agreed Cheri.

"I'm sorry, I don't quite understand. Except for Cheri, you're grown women, how can you see 'through the eyes of a child'?" asked Behnam in confusion

Ebony pursed her lips for a moment in thought. "Well, let me see if I can explain. Okay, I've got it! Behnam, you grew up in the desert, right? I'm thinking there was very little in the way of flowing water or forests, am I right?"

Behnam nodded, his expression showing he wasn't sure where this was leading.

"All right, all right, just stay with me for a moment. Think about how you felt, I mean really felt, the first time you saw, say a forest, or better yet, a river, or the sea, all that water. All of those things must have been amazing to you. Think of the wonder of a small child when they first see something new, or amazing. It's not, of course, but it is to them. Well, that's the way we feel when we first encounter some of the amazing things you have here in Persal. Pink and blue sheep? Ours only come in white, black, and brown. They may be ordinary to you, but to us, they're what dreams and legends are made of."

"Exactly! Like the first time, I saw Believer! Who would have thought unicorns were real?" agreed Faye, her eyes shining.

"Or that marvelous Singing Forest! That just blew me away!" sighed Cheri dramatically.

"Yes, and the Vortex is rather impressive! To the best of my knowledge, we have nothing like that where we come from. That's not to mention things like magic and sorcerers, and we've even heard of a rumor of dragons. Where we come from, the scientists have explained the magic right out of almost everything," finished Ebony, with a slight shrug.

"Well, well. I'd say that was sufficiently explained. Please, Jakar, continue," urged Gabriene.

"Ahem!" said Jakar, clearing his throat.

> "The guardians will be few
> New ones to join in
> While the way to our deliverance
> Will come from another place and time
> Redemption has always been with us."

"The guardians? That must be you, Master Gabriene and Master Gaban, of course, you can't get much fewer than that," offered Falcon.

"Yes, I considered it a possibility myself. At least for the last few years. After the others were killed by Barakus, but who are the new ones?" asked Gabriene.

"Well, as guardians, what you and Gaban have in common is magic. Wouldn't that mean the new ones would also have something magical about them?" asked Jakar.

"Oh! Oh no! You can't mean those little girls coming to the tower? I mean, we haven't had any new apprentices for nearly two thousand years, and suddenly seven show up on my doorstep. Surely, we can't trust the guardianship of Persal to seven little girls. Can we?" objected Gabriene, his face going pale.

"Well, whatever you think, I'd say that's exactly what we've got," said Tasmin with a straight face while Cheri tried to stifle a giggle.

"Did anyone else notice we were called 'guides'? Sounds to me like we're only here to show the way. Since redemption has always been with you, I would say the people of Persal are expected to actually save themselves," commented Ebony acidly. "What's the next part, Jakar?"

> "The companions will come from far and near,
> Some will think they know why they are there.
> Others will only follow because they must.
> In the end, all will know they were destined
> To do their part."

"I'd say that was pretty clear. Lady Tasmin, Falcon, Bass, and I are the companions. I know it certainly fits me," offered Behnam smugly.

"What! What about me? I know I'm a new addition to this expedition, but don't count me out yet!" objected Jakar, hopping up on the table and crossing it to meet Behnam, eye to eye, almost.

"Settle down, Jakar. Behnam didn't mean anything by

it. Besides, I think there will be several others to travel the dangerous paths our 'guides' must lead us on. What we have here, today, is just the beginning," said Gabriene, pulling Jakar back to his seat while Tasmin patted Behnam's hand placatingly.

Smiling, Behnam bowed across the table. "I do beg your pardon, friend Jakar, I did not intend to forget our brave and true friend. Please believe me when I say it was an oversight."

"Harrumph! Oversight? Easy to overlook, eh? Yes, and you must forgive my temper, friend Behnam. My wife has often told me I am too hasty by half. An unfortunate trait in a seer," replied Jakar, retuning the bow.

"Please, continue, Jakar. We're coming to the part that will tell us what is next, I think," urged Gabriene, getting everyone's attention back to the prophecy.

> "In Hope is Spirit
> In Faith is Heart
> In Charity is Strength
> View the world through a strong spirit
> Behold the world with a virtuous heart
> Witness the world with the purity of strength
> See the world as a whole
> Not torn apart and divided
> Know yourselves as complete
> No differences as matters
> With unity, all things are possible."

Jakar glanced up to see if anyone knew what the prophecy was talking about. When no one volunteered any ideas, he continued.

> "Hope shall be found in hopelessness.
> When revealed to the world
> Hope shall be reborn.

So are the signs, you are on the right path
Stolen children, plucked from Evil's Claw.
Hidden well in the branches of a tree.
Spread the word, tell one and all
Let Hope be reborn once they're free.
Find joy in providing for others as need is seen
For a time, great jubilation shall spread across the
land."

"Stolen children! I knew it! At least we know where to begin," said Ebony triumphantly.

CHAPTER 24

The Tournament of Lilies

"What? What are you talking about, child? What children?" gasped Gabriene in astonishment.

"Why the children of the Taking, of course," insisted Ebony, sitting back in her chair with a smug look of satisfaction, obviously under the impression she had explained everything.

"Whoa! Hold it just a minute! Before you let Ebony get up on her soapbox, please, can we talk about this over lunch? I'm starving, and Ebony will argue forever," wailed Cheri as she rose from her chair, staggering expressively toward the door.

Behind her, Faye started laughing as Bass scratched his head, "Soapbox? What's a soapbox and why would Ebony wish to get up on one?" he asked.

Ebony was trying unsuccessfully to stifle her own laughter as she rose, following Cheri out the mahogany door. "An old joke from our world. Maybe, someday, I'll explain it to you," she managed as her laughter erupted.

The other men shrugged as Bass looked to see if any of them understood the reference. Still shaking his head, he followed the women to the dining room.

"Master Gabriene, should we take the scrolls of the prophecy with us? Will they be safe out in the open here?" asked Jakar with a worried frown as he hesitated at the library door.

"Well, well. Perhaps you're right. Let's put them in here," suggested the wizard, glancing around before crossing to the desk and opening the top drawer. "There, all safe and sound. After all, we are in the middle of Lohi and in the Castle Tinora. Where could they be more secure? Now, let's see what's for lunch. Since the child has mentioned it, I realize I am quite famished myself."

In the dining room, Madlene had a lunch of cold meats, with fresh, warm bread with butter, green salads, fresh fruit and a variety of cheese laid out on the buffet. This time there was only enough to feed a small army.

Ebony queued up behind Cheri and began filling her plate. Behind her, she could hear Faye muttering to herself, "Since this isn't a dream, I suppose I should begin watching what I eat, again. I don't want to return home with a cholesterol problem."

Ebony turned with a pile of roast goose poised on a fork over her plate. "Whatever are you talking about? These people have never heard of cholesterol," she said in disbelief.

"So what? Just because they've never heard of it doesn't mean it doesn't exist. Isn't it bad enough I drink wine and ale now? Do you know I had never tasted alcohol before I came here? What if I become an alcoholic?" objected Faye, making a point of putting only salad and fruit on her plate with a little bread.

"Well, who would have guessed? Seriously, I'd say the chance of you becoming alcoholic are pretty thin, even if someone in your family was. I mean, think about what we've been through. From what we've been told, that was only a warm-up. I think our chances of dying from, oh, say, an arrow or maybe a knife, are much more likely than cirrhosis of the liver or heart disease. From what I've seen, I would wager you've never been more active. Doesn't exercise have something to do with your cholesterol level?" insisted Ebony, letting the roast goose fall onto her plate and heading to the table.

Faye stood there gazing at the meat for a moment before taking generous helpings of both roast lamb and goose. "Eat, drink, and be merry and all that, I suppose," she said with a smile as her blue eyes met Ebony's brown ones.

Jakar, being only two hundred and eleven years old, easily managed to beat Gabriene to the buffet and had settled into devouring his generous helpings of just about everything before the ancient one finally joined them. After downing a generous draft of wine and refilling his goblet, Gabriene turned to Ebony. "All right, Lady of Hope, tell us what that last passage on the first scroll was referring to," he urged.

"I thought it was obvious. We must rescue as many of the children who are victims of the Taking as possible. I've talked to several of our 'companions' as well as Captain Aberon of the *Unicorn's Magic*. They have told me what happened when Barakus started taking the children. When did they stop trying? After the second time? The third? The fourth? Children and their parents died. If they made it home, they came for them again, and again. The captain also told me the Black Ships gather at Yves in northern Zabir before heading back to Doome. The last Black Ship left Dhwittle when we did, and we quickly outdistanced it. When I asked the captain about it, he said they were really poor sailors, staying close to shore. In all probability, they found a safe cove to ride out the storm, if they were lucky. We need to muster a large force of fighting men and transport them by sea. We can lie in wait somewhere and rescue the children. The biggest thing is finding a safe place for them to hide," explained Ebony emotionally.

"Well, well. That could explain the first part, I suppose. Did anyone tell you the name of the strait between the Raserei Ocean and the North Sea and Doome? No? I thought not. It is called the Strait of the Claw. Do you know why? Because of a terrible monster living there beneath the waves. It's not a creation of Barakus, but he has found a way to persuade or trick it into allowing his ships, and only his ships, to pass unharmed. If his ships break free to the open sea beyond, it will all be over. We cannot follow into the Claw," expounded Gabriene, forcefully.

"Right, well, it's not like I didn't expect obstacles. We'll rescue as many as we can before they get that far," insisted Ebony refusing to be swayed.

"We'll circle back to that. If we succeed, where are we supposed to hide, what? Thirteen, fourteen, fifteen thousand children? More? In trees?" asked Cheri practically.

"Not trees, young one. The prophecy said, 'Hide them well in the branches of a tree.' There's only one place fits that description, Jessamine. The great Oracle Tree protects us all, and we have room on our island for a few children. Barakus cannot follow us there," explained Jakar, chuckling gleefully.

"Must be one heck of a tree," muttered Cheri, shaking her head in disbelief.

"Well, well. Of course, Barakus foiled by his own spell! What a great jest!" chuckled Gabriene, howling in glee. "Before I met Barakus, he was saved from a shipwreck by the Jessamines, and when he gained the power, he protected them from all evil by making it impossible for anyone who wished to do Jessamine harm to even remember Jessamine existed much less find it. Now only the natives of Jessamine and those few in dire need, such as those shipwrecked, ever go there. It's perfect, but we'll have to send supplies."

"At least the last part is pretty straightforward, once people learn their children are safe, they will dare to hope again and maybe to fight," said Faye.

"Seems to me, the next step is to get an army together and get them to Yves as quickly as possible. There appear to be enough ships in the harbor to carry them," said Ebony, ready to settle down to business.

"Ah, dear lady, you will see our finest this afternoon, at the tournament," answered Gabriene with a secretive smile.

"Tournament? What tournament? We don't have time for games, Gabriene. Those children need us."

"Knights? Jousting? That sort of tournament?" asked Cheri, scooting up to the edge of her chair in excitement.

"Well, well. Of course. What other kind of tournament could there possibly be? Lady Ebony, this tournament is an annual affair, scheduled a year ago. Long before you arrived in Persal. As it is, we delayed it until you could get here. We're using it to announce your arrival and introduce you to the people. They've waited their entire lives for you, you know?"

A bloodcurdling scream, followed by a loud crash killed any further questions before they were born and everyone rushed into the grand hall. There they found a maid with her back pressed firmly against the wall opposite the library door, eyes wide in alarm. The tray she had been carrying was on the floor, a stain of peach cordial flowing from the shattered decanter.

Tasmin rushed to help the poor girl who fainted in her arms when she touched her. Tasmin was lowering her to the floor as the men dashed into the library.

In the hall, Faye wrinkled her nose in distaste. "Ugh! What is that smell?"

Cheri looked down the hall and gasped. "What was that? There, down the hall, where it turns. I thought I saw a...a shape. A strange, black...shape," she stammered uncertainly as Bass, Behnam, and Falcon, emerging from the library, took off running, turning into the narrow servant's hall. Amalee quickly outdistanced them in the pursuit.

Then the women heard Jakar exclaim in dismay. "Oh, no!

I only hope he didn't..." In a rush, he made his way across the room to the desk.

Looking inside, the women could see the disarray. Books were strewn everywhere. Jakar stumbled and almost fell twice before he reached his goal. By then, Gabriene and the women were watching his progress from the doorway.

Slowly, as though afraid of what he might find, Jakar looked into the open drawer. When he raised his dark eyes to meet Gabriene's blue ones, they knew before he said it, "They're gone. The scrolls are gone. I guess you'll have to go back to your tower and get another copy."

"Well, well, about that. You see, I can't exactly," admitted Gabriene reluctantly.

"Master Gabriene, what do you mean you can't? You can't go back to your tower right now? Or there isn't another copy?" asked Ebony suspiciously.

"Well, well. Neither of those, either, I'm afraid. Of course, I could go back to my tower, but, well, you see... I don't have another copy. Not here," he stammered, glancing at Jakar for support. "It's not as if there aren't other copies! Precautions were taken. There's a copy in Rim, at the Royal Library and another in Elans."

As the men returned, it was Bass's turn to get a stubborn look on his face, his jaw set.

Jakar glanced at him before speaking. "No, I don't think Rim is the wisest course. If you don't mind my saying so, Master Gabriene. Perhaps we should go to Elans after the children are safe? Gentlemen, did you find the intruder?"

"No, he disappeared," confessed Bass with a scowl.

"It. It was only vaguely manlike. It moved...oddly," interrupted Cheri with a shudder.

"All right, it. That actually, makes sense of some of the footprints we found. Gabriene, are there hidden passageways in the castle? We think, by virtue of the slimy, wet footprints left behind, it might have come through the sewers," answered Falcon thoughtfully. "I would have thought those were covered with grates?"

"Well, well, yes. There are escape passages for the safety of the saviors. If it comes to Barakus sending troops to attack us here, as unlikely as that might be," admitted the wizard with a worried scowl.

"If the enemy knows about those passages, they aren't very safe, are they? I think we'd better make sure that's not the case," suggested Bass.

"Well, well. One of the Imaldi at the tower had dreams of being different animals. I wonder if she might have a 'talent' we can use?" ruminated Gabriene thoughtfully. "Madlene, send someone to the tower to retrieve Beloria."

"If you have seven girls cooped up in that tower of yours, perhaps we should retrieve all of them?" suggested Tasmin, shaking her head at the folly of men.

"Well, well...that might be for the best. It is getting crowded. In the meantime, there is a map of the castle here somewhere. I'll have the passages searched and all the entries blocked or guarded. Now, Jakar, why shouldn't we go to Rim?"

"Isn't it apparent? We haven't much time if we're going to save those children. We've already agreed, it's what we have to do. Let's take care of them first, then we can worry about the rest of the prophecy," stated Ebony emphatically, her hands on her hips as though ready for a fight.

Behnam allowed a small smile to play about his lips as he agreed with her. "She's right. If we don't start out right, who knows what the ending might be? It may mean disaster."

"Well, well. I suppose you've got a point. Right now, we'd best start getting ready for the tournament. It will begin in about two hours," agreed Gabriene, sighing as he took another look at the mess in the library.

"Master Gabriene? How could this happen here? I thought we would be safe in Lohi. How do we know we won't be killed in our rooms?" asked Faye nervously.

"Even here, Barakus has spies, my dear. I'll have Madlene set guards at your doors. All shall be secured. The doors, the sewers, all will be barricaded or guarded. Once that thief reports to his...its... master, Barakus will know, for sure, you all survived his storm. I would imagine he won't be in a good mood when he finds out, or for some time thereafter," said Gabriene with a chuckle.

"You mean, until now, he thought we might be dead? He wasn't sure? If he only suspected, he'll soon know now?" So we're in danger, again?" asked Cheri incredulously.

"Well, well. The ship was protected, of course. It didn't allow your 'ripples' to escape, so to speak. I've been protecting Lohi for centuries, but unfortunately, my powers aren't great enough to do much more than that. If you travel, and I'm with you, I can contain them again, possibly confuse things. I would wager he had already guessed at least one of you were alive by the time you escaped the storm. In those few hours, between the end of the storm and when you crossed the Gate and entered Mermaid Bay, he couldn't quite be sure if you'd survived or not. I myself couldn't tell if the ship had sunk or not until you entered the bay. I will tell you there is no place in all Persal more secure than Lohi. With a few precautions, we can assure you will not be killed in your beds."

Tasmin turned to the three ladies, ushering them toward the stairs. "Since we can no longer review the prophecy, for now. It may take us some time to find the proper attire and do your hair. This is your first formal presentation to the knights of Lohi and the nobility of Swaloh, I'm sure you wish to be at your best."

As they mounted the stairs, Cheri glanced over the ornate banister. She saw the men retiring to the drawing room with a footman carrying wine and Madlene's forces were already descending on the mess in the library. When they returned, there would be no sign of the intrusion. She did wish she knew what it was she had seen scurrying down the hall. It certainly didn't look human as its slimy footprints attested to.

*****

Seeing no particular urgency, Ebony and Cheri followed Faye into her room, only to find Madlene had been keeping her women busy. A lovely new dress of old rose-pink satin with ivory lace on the low bodice was lying on the bed.

Faye picked it up and held it against herself as she stared at her reflection in dismay. "Oh dear, I really don't know if I can take being on public display. Especially in this."

"Don't be silly, girlfriend. It's a lovely dress, and you're going to be devastating in it. In fact, you'll probably outshine us all," scoffed Ebony.

"You don't understand. That's exactly what I'm afraid of. Not that I'll outshine you. With your coloring, you'll get most of the attention, but I was raised to believe humility and modesty are the two greatest virtues."

"So now we know why you were hiding yourself under those ugly, bulky clothes and behind those unattractive glasses as long as I've known you," said Cheri in disbelief.

"I felt my attire was appropriate for my position," replied Faye stiffly.

"Well, this attire is appropriate for your present position. What's wrong with being pretty? It isn't a sin, you know," insisted Ebony wryly.

"You just don't understand," wailed Faye, sinking despondently to the edge of her bed.

"So explain it to us," said Cheri, making herself comfortable in a well-cushioned chair.

Faye sat for a moment with a faraway look in her eyes.

"I've never mentioned my mother to you, have I?" she asked at last.

"No, I always got the impression she'd died when you were a little girl. You talk about your father all the time," answered Cheri, getting curious.

"Well, she did die, for me anyway. She was a very beautiful woman. Very vibrant and she laughed a lot. She was very, very different from my father. I remember him saying how lucky he was and sometimes he'd look at her as though he wasn't sure how this lovely creature had come into his life. That was when he still told me with pride how much like my mother I was.

"When I was about six, she just wasn't there anymore. My father had always been a studious, austere man but after she left, he withdrew into himself. It was as though whatever life was in him had come from my mother. Shortly after she left, he began telling me it was my mother's beauty that had ruined our lives and beauty was only an illusion. When I was fourteen, he let it slip, if mother hadn't been so very beautiful, no one could have stolen her from him. That's when I knew she had run off with another man. He told me I must guard against my beauty so it wouldn't ruin lives, like my mother's beauty had ruined ours. I felt I mustn't flaunt my looks or I would betray my father. You know, I never understood why she left us. Why did she leave me?" wailed Faye, tears streaming down her cheeks.

Faye tried to stop crying as Ebony held her close. "There, there, honey. I'm sure she had her reasons. Maybe she thought she was already taking too much from your father to take you, too."

"Didn't you ever hear from her again? What happened to her?" asked Cheri, intrigued.

"After my father died, I found a few letters, unopened. She'd run off because a man offered her a career, acting in television. I guess she had a part in a soap opera for a while. Father never let me watch them. He said they were trash. Usually, we watched public television. The letters only covered about four or five years, and then they stopped. I don't know where she is now. She could be dead." Faye sighed as she regained control.

"Look, I sympathize, but it was literally in another time and place, so get a grip, girl. Your father used his heartache and inability to admit he couldn't provide what your mother believed she needed to shame you. It wasn't your fault. Can beauty be a curse? Yes, but it needn't be. It's how you perceive your beauty that makes you who you are. Not the beauty itself, Faye. You can accept that you're a beautiful young woman without letting it rule your life. Wash your face and put on this lovely dress. I think Tasmin said the tournament would begin three hours after high sun and we need to be seated before it can begin. Cheri, we'd better be thinking of getting ready ourselves," counseled Ebony, standing and dragging Cheri from her chair.

*****

The nobility and wealthy merchants were already seated around the outdoor arena and commoners were crowded at the far rail when Ebony, Faye and Cheri were at last allowed to leave their carriage. They arranged themselves behind six young girls throwing delicate pale-green lilies of the valley in their path as they proceeded them into the arena where three high-backed chairs and Gabriene were waiting on a raised platform.

Suddenly, four trumpets rang forth with a fanfare, causing the waiting audience to fall silent and rise to their feet. Urgently, Tasmin got them walking as the trumpeters continued with a processional. Ebony in emerald green and Faye were side by side, followed by Cheri in dark blue silk and pale blue lace. Tasmin, in a sedate, shimmering gray, stayed a step or two behind. As they passed, the assembled dignitaries bowed or curtsied. The three women allowed themselves to exchange one amazed look before continuing.

Just before they reached their seats, they came to where Behnam, Bass, Falcon, without Amalee, and Jakar were standing. Ebony was startled when the first three bowed. Contrariwise, she wasn't surprised at all when Jakar swept his impossible red hat off his head and bowed to sweep the white feather on the ground, he was always doing that. Amazingly, his feather managed to remain a pristine white.

Finally, they reached the platform and succeeded in making passable curtsies before Gabriene motioned for them to sit down.

The fanfare of the trumpets rang forth once more, and the grand procession began. Leading the way were about two dozen small boys, spreading more of the fragile lilies of the valley. Then the knights, in full armor under colorful tabards, entered, five abreast mounted on magnificent Chardell horses, trained for battle and draped in the colors of their knights. Each horse was led by a squire carrying a bright banner. The horses pranced across the parade grounds with arched necks and precise, high steps, carrying their riders proudly. Each silk banner and tunic was decorated in the colors and symbols chosen for him when he gained knighthood. As they rode, silk shimmered in red and white, green and yellow, blue and silver, black and orange, and purple and deep pink. The combinations and designs seemed endless, as did the procession.

Gabriene, sitting between Cheri and Ebony beamed as if they were his children. "Well, well. Aren't they a marvelous sight? Of course, only the top two hundred are allowed to participate. We actually have over seven thousand five hundred active, trained knights in Swaloh. That doesn't count the ones living in other parts of Persal. Twenty-five hundred are here in Lohi. These, these are the best of the best fighting men Persal has ever seen!"

Ebony pursed her lips skeptically, "Well, perhaps, but I find it hard to believe anyone can fight effectively in all that armor."

"Well, well, do not be deceived. When they wear their armor, they are very hard to kill. Harder, anyway. Only the bolt from a crossbow can penetrate it easily, even their swords, battle-axes, and maces require a great deal of force and skill to succeed. Don't worry, the men beneath are as fit and well trained as is humanly possible," he assured her.

Once all two hundred knights, on their horses, accompanied by their squires, had finally assembled, they turned in ranks to face the dais where the women were sitting and the horses bent their knees in a bow as their riders bowed their bare heads, helmets held under their left arms. Beside them, the squires bowed low. For a moment there was dead silence, now the clanking of armor and jingling of harness had ceased. Then Cheri jumped to her feet and began clapping excitedly in appreciation. Hesitantly at first, growing as it spread around the arena, she was joined by everyone else.

When the horses rose, Gabriene stood and suddenly seemed much larger than life as his white robe began to glow. In a deep voice that filled the arena, he began, "Lords, ladies, citizens and assembled knights, welcome to the Tournament of Lilies. It is an especially proud day for all of Persal and I am gratified to introduce you to our special guests. Those we have awaited for so long, the ones destined to lead us out of fear and bondage..."

At this point, Gabriene was interrupted by a boisterous cheer from the gallery, gaining in volume as it was repeated around the arena.

Finally, the crowd settled down and let Gabriene continue. "Please, welcome to our world, Gentlewoman Ebony, our Lady of Hope…"

Ebony's eyes were wide with amazement as she stood, smiling tightly. "Gentlewoman? Me? You can tell he doesn't know me very well," she muttered under her breath.

"Gentlewoman Faye, our Lady of Faith…"

"He's making us sound like saints. A bit blasphemous, wouldn't you say?" said Faye, forcing herself to smile and nod gracefully to the cheering crowd.

"And, Gentlewoman Cheri, our Lady of Charity," he finished with a bow and a sweep of his arm as he returned to normal size. He stepped back, everyone' attention focused on the three of them as the six young girls threw more lilies in front of them.

Under cover of thunderous applause and a tight smile, Cheri grumbled, "I can't be a saint! I'm quite sure I destroyed all possibility of that long ago!"

Still smiling and nodding, Faye allowed herself to chuckle, "Not really, dear. Look at Mary Magdalene."

"Haven't you heard? Mary Magdalene wasn't a prostitute. It was propaganda by the men who decided what we should know and what we shouldn't, or something," objected Cheri, drawing on her prodigious memory.

"Humph!" snorted Ebony. "I suppose anything is possible, but the first one who kneels to me is going to regret it!"

As the knights filed out, the crowd was once again able to converse with each other before the games began. Cheri was surprised when no one approached them. Then Tasmin leaned over and explained, "Gabriene hasc made arrangements to keep everyone from approaching you now. He's informed them it's for the best they wait until the ball."

"Ball? What ball?" asked Faye in alarm.

"Why, the one tomorrow night. It will officially welcome

you to Lohi nobility. Didn't we tell you about it?" asked Tasmin.

"No, you didn't. I for one can't dance," whispered Faye furiously, trying to keep anyone from overhearing.

"Oh, dear!" was all Tasmin could gasp out before Cheri chimed in. "Neither can I. It wasn't exactly necessary in my prior life."

Tasmin turned to Ebony hopefully.

"Sure, I can dance, but I would be willing to bet the kind of dances I know won't be on the agenda."

With a heavy sigh, Tasmin shook her head. "Well, there's nothing to do but give you all dancing lessons, tomorrow morning."

The trumpeters gave another fanfare, and the tournament began. Eight at a time, the knights raced down the arena, collecting four- inch rings tied with bright ribbons on the points of their lances. In the second contest, the rings were not much bigger than would fit on a big man's thumb, Ebony noted those who had done poorly the first time weren't still in the lists the second time around. She also couldn't help but be impressed by the performance of two men, a well-muscled man with long blond hair flying behind him and wearing scarlet and white, and a wiry Mojar, his dark-reddish curls cut short, dressed in sapphire blue and silver. The two seemed to be crowd favorites. They were evenly matched as well as highly skilled. As the contests got harder and the riding skills more complex, she couldn't help cheering them on, along with the rest of the crowd.

It was dusk when the competitions were coming to an end, and eight men had earned the right to show their skills in the joust. Torches were lit around the arena, spreading pools of light across the field while the onlookers were served a supper of roast quail, seasoned potatoes and hearty burgundy wine or ale. This was supposed to be a light meal to be followed later by a real dinner. Ebony was still having trouble with the purple potatoes.

Gabriene stood as another flourish of trumpets sounded, and the first two contestants entered the field and took up positions at opposite ends of the arena. The knight on their left was wearing black and white in a checkerboard pattern while the other knight wore a yellow and green harlequin tunic. They turned their horses and saluted the ladies on the dais with upraised lances before facing each other and lowering visors. Gabriene raised a red scarf and dropped it, signaling the charge. The two men leaned forward as the horses started racing toward each other and the one in yellow broke his lance on the other knight's shield; a roar went through the crowd. Pulling up at the other end of the field, a squire rushed out with a fresh lance. Again, the crowd fell silent as the two men on their massive mounts rushed toward each other. This time, the black and white knight went flying from his horse as contact was made. Hastily he scrambled to his feet as the other knight dismounted and his squire handed him a sword and shield. The black-and-white knight's squire rushed to him with a battle-ax, and the two men approached each other warily.

Suddenly alarmed, Ebony leaned over to Gabriene. "This is just for show, isn't it?" she asked. "They don't really intend to harm each other, do they?"

"What? What was that, dear? Well, well, this isn't supposed to be a fight to the death, you know, but injuries have been known to happen. Don't worry, no one has died in years," he answered distractedly, rising to cheer as steel blade met steel armor.

"Gabriene! Listen to me! This is ridiculous! We don't want to watch men who are on our side breaking each other's bones!"

"Don't worry, dear. They're used to it. A little irritating, perhaps, but once they mend, they're back in the fray," he assured her, reaching over to pat her hand, his eyes never leaving the contest on the field.

Agilely stepping away from a thrust of the broadsword, the black and white knight countered with a mighty swing of his battle-ax, landing squarely on the yellow-and-green knight's back, sending him sprawling. As the crowd roared its approval, Ebony held her breath, watching carefully as two squires rushed out to help him up. He was half carried off the field. At least he didn't appear to be too badly injured, the armor taking the brunt of the blow.

Faye and Cheri were enjoying themselves immensely as the winner of the first bout fought with a challenger. The basic process was repeated, over and over again, in the third and fourth contest. Then, in the fifth bout, as a knight in aqua and gold faced off against a knight in orange with blue trim, they were both knocked to the ground on the first pass. The orange and blue knight chose a broadsword while the knight in aqua and gold picked a mace. Whirling the spiked ball menacingly, they circled each other in the middle of the arena. Then the man with the mace lunged forward, bringing his weapon down where the other man's head should have been. When he didn't connect, he was momentarily caught off- balance, and the orange-and-blue knight brought his two-handed sword down forcefully on the other man's arm. The stricken knight let out a bloodcurdling scream and dropped the mace as blood quickly soaked his tunic. Immediately, there were squires and men, Ebony hoped were doctors, rushing to his aid while the crowed rose to cheer the victor.

Ebony looked around in shocked horror and outrage. Cheri was bent over, holding her stomach with one hand and her mouth with the other. Faye's eyes were wide with disbelief, and all the blood had drained from her face. Ebony thought she might be in shock. Before she could move, Tasmin beckoned to nearby servants who brought towels and cool water.

Without allowing herself to think about it, Ebony came to a decision she'd been wrestling with since the jousting began and rose to her impressive five feet eleven inches of height, letting her ice- cold fury take over as she stepped regally to the front of the platform and waited.

Slowly, almost cautiously, an expectant hush, broken here and there by quiet whispers, cut off abruptly, as it spread through the crowd. The increased excitement level of the assembled throng made it evident they expected a special honor for the valor of the triumphant knight.

Eyes wide, the color slowly coming back into her face, Faye scanned the crowd as she rose to her feet, stepping forward to join her friend. One look up to Ebony's clenched jaw confirmed her fears. "Ebony! I'm as shocked as you are, but remember, these people are on our side. We need all the friends we can get," she hissed in a low voice.

Cheri gulped as she straightened up and stepped to Ebony's other side. "Don't forget, this is a far different world than ours, with different ways. Think, when in Rome, do as, etc. Try to be tactful," she mumbled, eyes darting around uneasily, looking for the quickest exit.

Ebony gave each of them a tight smile. "I'm always tactful. Besides, their ways aren't different, only outdated. We started changing this world the minute we walked, or fell, through that portal. It's about time we did it deliberately, don't you think?" she said so low no one else could possibly hear.

Finally, the arena was deathly still, waiting to see what the saviors of Persal were going to say.

Ebony stood there, apparently quite calm, and let the moment stretch until it seemed about ready to snap before she began, "Gabriene, noble guests, gallant knights, and dear friends. The skill, bravery, and honor shown by your knights are no less than to be expected from those who come to Lohi in dedication to the fight against Barakus. This knight..."

Sir Gurmail, came Gabriene's quiet voice, somewhere inside her head.

"Ahem, yes, this valiant knight, Sir Gurmail, has proven his skills and worthiness to join in the great battle to come," she broke off as a great roar of approval resounded from the crowd. This time, the silence came more quickly when they realized she was waiting to continue.

"We, my friends and I, come from a far land with different customs, so bear with me if I overstep my bounds," she added with a smile, pausing briefly for the polite ripple of laughter to subside.

"In that land, I too am a warrior," this time there was more laughter until the crowd noticed none of the three women were smiling this time. When it cut off abruptly, the assembled guests were looking at each other in confusion. Ebony took a deep breath. "In our land, I am a warrior. Because I am a warrior, I understand the need to prove yourself on the battlefield. The need to win. To tell you the truth, without this need, we'd have no hope of winning the war about to begin. Make no mistake, it will be a war, and in that war, we will need all our brave knights fit and ready to fight.

"Therefore, as much as I appreciate the skills and bravery you all have shown, as much and more I deplore the terrible injury suffered by..."

Sir Lakhvir, come Gabriene's voice, again only this time she was expecting it.

"Sir Lakhvir," she continued with barely a pause. "Ladies! Gentlemen! Knights! We can't afford the luxury of damaging our own warriors just before the battles begin. While I would love to see the outcome of this competition, I...we...can't remain and watch the blood of our friends spill on the sands of this arena," she finished, turning to leave the way they had come, Faye and Cheri right behind her.

"Wait! Please, dear ladies, wait!" called Sir Gurmail from the arena floor, rushing forward with his free arm outstretched, to intercept them. "You are right, of course. The battle is finally upon us, and we have grown careless with two millennia of waiting. Please accept our apologies, and remain to see the end. We will continue the matches with our wooden practice weapons, and I guarantee, the most damage we will inflict will be a few bruises and headaches quickly recovered from."

Ebony turned to the waiting knight and smiled brightly as she inclined her head regally. "In that case, we should be honored to remain," she said, leading the way as the three ladies returned to their seats.

Gabriene was staring at them with a strange expression on his face.

"I didn't know she could do that. Did you know she could do that?" whispered Cheri, taken by surprise by Ebony's speech.

Faye was staring at Ebony thoughtfully as she shook her head. Just when she thought she was getting to know these two women, they surprised her all over again. Huh! She was supposed to be an expert in social science! Shouldn't that give her some insight?

*****

The tournament continued with battles just as fierce and competitive but no more broken bones or bloodshed. Sir Gurmail won the next two competitions before he was finally beaten by a knight in gold with black rampant lions. Ebony wondered how much of the good knight's final defeat was the skill of the new champion and how much was Sir

Gurmail's own fatigue. All of that activity in heavy armor had to be exhausting.

Finally, the dashing Mojar knight Ebony had noticed earlier appeared in his brilliant sapphire blue and silver, his white warhorse prancing impatiently as they waited for the jousting to begin. His opponent was a young knight dressed in green and white who had just fought hard to beat a talented opponent in a close battle. The Mojar was fresh but probably six or seven years older than the victor, besides which the younger man had about twenty pounds of muscle on the slight black man. Maybe, just maybe, this would be an even fight.

It took three brutal passes with their lances before the Mojar managed to unhorse the knight in green and white. Once they were both on the ground, the Mojar's weapon was a heavy wooden practice sword while his opponent chose a cumbersome wooden mace. They fought hard and with great skill, both coming close to disabling the other several times, before the Mojar lost his footing after avoiding a particularly close pass with the mace and went down, into the packed sand. Swinging his mace confidently, almost cockily, the young knight closed in for the winning blow, only to find he'd taken too long as the Mojar managed to roll slightly to one side, avoiding the mace again and rolling back with a telling thrust of his sword. As the younger man went down, the Mojar rose to his feet, holding the sword on his opponent's neck so there could be no mistake.

The crowd broke into a mighty cheer as the loser was helped off the field while the winner, Sir Suvaat, remounted to take on the champion. It was the blond Ebony had taken note of earlier, Sir Galad. On the first pass, both contestants were unseated. The weapon of choice for both of them was the wooden sword, and the fighting was furious. Watching closely, Ebony noted they were fairly evenly matched. It might just come down to who had the most stamina or if one of them got in a lucky strike.

In the end, it appeared to be the latter when, after a particularly furious bout of swordplay, Galad found an opening and scored what would have been a killing blow under the left arm had they been fighting with steel. Gallantly, Sir Suvaat backed off and saluted his opponent with the sword while Sir Galad did the same. Then the triumphant knight mounted his horse and rode once around the arena to the deafening cheers of the crowd. He ended in front of the saviors where he and his horse gave them another bow. The three ladies stood as one and curtsied to the victor in return.

CHAPTER 25

Shall We Dance?

In the night, the *Flying Seahawk* limped into Mermaid Bay and made its way to the docks in Lohi. Nobody was waiting to greet Gaban and Ochwatt when they disembarked. Stoically, Gaban led the way to the castle while people in the streets moved aside, staring oddly at the giant striding beside him and his horse Buttercup.

*****

At the castle itself, breakfast had just ended, and while Tasmin gathered Faye, Ebony, Cheri, Falcon, Bass, and Behnam in the ballroom for dance lessons, Gabriene went to the west wing where the Imaldi had been housed the afternoon before. He was looking for Beloria. They needed to talk about her dreams of being an animal.

"Well, well, child. Please, tell me again of your 'other' dreams. The ones about the animals," cajoled Gabriene softly as he led the red- haired twelve-year-old to the servant's hallway where the intruder disappeared. Waiting for them was Jakar.

"Wahl, inna dreams I were al'ays runnin'. Runnin' from a hunter like smoke. Ever' time, when he was gone an' I could stop I'd be at a pool. When I bend ter slake me thirst, I'd look

438

inter me 'flexion. On'y de eye be mine own. Oncet I were a red-striped badger. Another time a red stag. Al'ays a differen' animal but al'ays red. In a morn, I be covert wit' mud and bruisers and me sleep gown be all torned," she related shyly, reluctant to share.

"Do you think you actually become an animal? Is that why you were muddy in the morning?" prodded Jakar softly.

"Uh, maybe... But I don' wanna do it! I on'y done it asleep. I don' ken I be achange," objected Beloria nervously.

Gabriene cocked his head as he looked into her eyes. "Have you ever changed while you were awake?"

"Wahl, I started oncet, when I be angered. It scairt me and I stopped. On'y me hands started ter be differ, I thin'."

"Well, well. Do you understand, now, the changes are from your magic? The magic that brought you to me?"

Reluctantly, Beloria nodded.

"We're here, in a castle, and if you lose control, we can help you. I promise," said the soft-spoken wizard, trying to reassure the nervous girl. "Let me tell you what happened. Yesterday, we had an intruder. Lady Cheri said it wasn't quite human, and it came and went leaving only some odd, slimy footprints. While we were at yesterday's tournament, the castle guard scoured the castle for possible entryways and found nothing beyond this point. What we need to know is, how did it get in? Where did it go? And if at all possible, what it was. Maybe as an animal, you could answer these questions?"

Beloria looked at the two men for a long moment before answering. "Mabet?" she acknowledged reluctantly. "Boots I dinna ken 'ow."

"When you started to change before, what was happening?" prodded Gabriene.

"Ever' time I be aboot ter turn, I be scairt or angered. I do na ken 'ow ter do it a purpose."

"Well, well. That's encouraging. Don't you see? If you can control it enough to stop it, you don't need to fear it. You can use this ability. You can turn into animals, and I have a hunch you can even pick which animal as well. Would you be willing to try to turn into a small animal?"

"Yes, but 'ow?" asked Beloria as she embarked on a frustrating morning.

*****

In the ballroom, four musicians waited to play while Tasmin taught them all to dance. Only Bass, for some reason, knew anything about the dances of Lohi society. That in itself seemed odd for a man who lived as a hermit in the middle of the woods.

First, she paired them off. Falcon and Cheri, Bass and Faye, and Behnam and Ebony. As they tried to learn the complex steps, there were immediate problems. Ebony resisted, trying to take the lead from Behnam. Faye kept stumbling over her own or her partner's feet. Falcon couldn't seem to find the rhythm.

After watching them for a few painful minutes, Tasmin waved to the musicians to stop. "Wait, wait! This isn't working. Why don't we switch things about a bit?"

"Fine with me," muttered Ebony as they stopped.

"Faye, you dance with Behnam. Perhaps he can keep you from tripping. Bass, take Cheri and Falcon, dance with Ebony. Let's see if that combination works. You look mismatched but...we'll deal with that later," she said, stepping back with a sigh. "Let's try it again. Music! That's it, listen to the music. Faye, relax, and let Behnam lead. Ebony, you've danced before. I want you to lead for a moment. Falcon, relax, close your eyes. Concentrate on the music. Cheri, do the same. Close your eyes. Let the music run through you and pay attention to Bass. Ah, that's it. I think we have a working combination. Now, keep dancing. Cheri, that's it, let Bass's movements guide yours. Falcon, take over the lead. Ebony, relax and let him take charge. That's better. Keep dancing. We need to practice."

Another half hour of practicing the first dance and Tasmin moved on to a second. This one was a faster tempo on top of requiring them to change partners as they danced as a group. Again, Faye stumbled when they changed partners, but they were all getting the hang of how the dancing was supposed to go. When they had gained some proficiency in the second dance, Tasmin moved on to a third, line dance. This one proved easiest for all of them. They weren't quite sure if it was the dance itself or their improving proficiency.

Then Tasmin had them change partners again and sent them back to the first dance. "Come, come. You'll have to change partners with every dance, ladies. You'll be expected to dance with most of the nobles. If you relax and listen to the music, it shouldn't be a problem."

"What? Strangers? That's easy for you to say. Will you be dancing?" grumbled Faye.

"I expect to, yes."

"You'll have had more than a couple of hours' practice. You already know how to do these dances," retorted Faye.

"Come on, Faye. Loosen up. This is fun. I mean, it's a bit old- fashioned...okay, a lot old-fashioned, but haven't you ever watched movies about the eighteenth century? *'Amadeus'*?" called Cheri. Now that she had learned the basics, she was doing just that, having fun.

"She's right. It is fun. Just relax," called Ebony from across the room where she was dancing with Bass.

Faye smiled brightly, maybe a little bit too brightly, and rolled her eyes as she danced with Falcon, who had finally learned to lead.

"Well, dears. I do think you all have the basics. You'll do

just fine tonight. Why don't you take the rest of the morning off and relax? I'll come find you when it's time to get ready," said Tasmin, abandoning them to their own devices.

"Can we practice just a little longer, Tasmin? We don't want to look terribly foolish tonight," asked Cheri hastily.

Tasmin turned at the door and regarded her thoughtfully. "If you really want to, I have no objections, but I have other things to do."

Once the door closed behind Tasmin, Cheri walked over to Ebony while motioning Faye to join them. "Don't you think it might be fair that if we have to learn their dances, they should have to learn a dance of ours?"

"What? You said you couldn't dance. Now you want us to learn another one and teach it to them?" asked Faye in disbelief, looking over her shoulder at their dance partners.

"Well, I'd never danced with a partner before. That doesn't mean I haven't moved to the music. Ebony, you choose, something simple. I'll go see if our musicians can scare up a drummer," said Cheri as if the decision was made.

"Ebony, surely you're not going to go along with this?" begged Faye.

"Actually, I think she has a point. We need to make it clear we come from somewhere else, with very different customs. I can't think of a better way than to show them, even teaching them, one of our dances. They're certainly a far cry from what we've just learned," responded Ebony thoughtfully.

As Cheri returned, one of the musicians left to find his nephew who was good on the drums. When they came back they began teaching the musicians the melody. Luckily, the drummer picked up on the rhythm quickly, helping keep the tempo. Finally, they pulled their partners onto the dance floor where Ebony began teaching them how to move to this different kind of music.

After learning the local dances, with their intricate rules, learning the more energetic dances of their world was almost freeing. Even the men found following the beat of the drums made moving easier, and within an hour, they had it down.

Finally, they let the musicians go, swearing them to secrecy, and headed for the dining room and lunch. There they found Gaban and Ochwatt at the table with Jakar and Gabriene.

"Gaban! You're here!" cried Cheri excitedly, rushing to give the old man a hug. Faye and Ebony were right behind.

After introductions were made and they had settled to eat, Gaban turned to them. "When we have time, we'll have to exchange stories of our adventures. Behnam, I went looking for you in Mojar. Now I see why I couldn't find you. Well, I did what I could.

"My old friend, Gabriene, was just telling me of the Imaldi that showed up on his doorstep. Apparently, magic is coming back into our world."

Faye smiled. "What's Imaldi?"

"Well, well. Those with magical ability without training have always been the Imaldi. In the past, all who were found were males, and they were known individually as Imaldo. Now, we'll have to come up with another name for the individuals when they're girls. Imalda, maybe?" explained Gabriene with a thoughtful look.

Faye scowled at the two old men. "Master Gabriene, in the past, did you look for magic ability in girls?" she asked suspiciously.

"What? What? Well, well. Now, come to think of it, I don't think we did," answered the old man, scratching his head in thought as he looked over at Gaban.

The blue wizard thought for a moment. "Wasn't there one girl who wanted to try out? A very long time ago?"

"Surely not. I'd remember if there had been." Mused Gabriene. "Then how do you know there weren't girls with magic out there all along? Typical male chauvinists!" growled Faye as Cheri and Ebony both glared at the wizards.

"Uh, well. Back to housing. There aren't enough of them to open the towers. If we keep them here in the castle, we'll have to make sure we aren't tripping over each other. Perhaps they could be fed in the smaller dining parlor or something? One of my greatdaughters is among them, and I don't want her to know I'm aware of where she is," suggested Jakar with a hearty chuckle, diffusing the rising tension.

"Well, well. The Imaldi are all yours now, Gaban. I'll leave the arrangements up to you and Madlene. The rest of us will be leaving in a week or two, at most," announced the white wizard, laughing at the shocked look on his old friend's face.

"What! I haven't trained an apprentice since Falarin, and that was..."

"When was the last time I had an apprentice? No, don't answer that. These Imaldi are difficult to train. They don't respond as they should, and I haven't even figured out what their talents are, for most of them. I'll need you to work with Beloria after lunch. I think it's probable she can become an animal. I think she's done it when asleep, but we're trying to teach her to do it voluntarily, while awake. If she can, I think she can control which animal as well. Yesterday we had an intruder, and we could use her skills to track this...thing. As for the rest of them, keep an eye on Briar Rose and Ciral. There's something about those two, but I can't put my finger on it," rambled Gabriene.

"In that case, I have a surprise of my own! Ochwatt will be continuing with you. I've found he can be quite useful. If the occasion arises, just ask him to smile," returned Gaban with an oh so innocent, smile of his own.

"Smile? I don't understand?" said Gabriene in some confusion. Eyeing the hairy giant suspiciously.

"Ochwatt, dear friend, please smile for Master Gabriene," asked Gaban, turning to the taciturn sasquatch.

Looking up from his meal, Ochwatt took a minute to swallow and then smiled broadly, his impressive teeth shining in the candlelight.

Gabriene, Bass, Behnam, and even Jakar drew back in momentary alarm. "Oh, now that is impressive!" applauded Gabriene. Laughter broke out around the table as they returned to their meal.

As they finished lunch, Ebony leaned closer to Gabriene. "Have we made any progress in getting ready for our...what... quest?" she asked.

"Well, well. Do you mean retaking the Taking? Actually, yes. We've received word one of the Black Ships ran aground at the small village of Lark's Meadow just east of Dhwittle. We all know Barakus's sailors aren't comfortable with being out of sight of land, and it looks like the storm played havoc with them. There's a reef enclosing a lagoon there, and they got hung up. From what we've heard, except for some broken bones, everyone made it safely off the ship. Unfortunately for us, it didn't get pounded to splinters by the storm. They've used their manpower to pull it onto shore and are attempting to make repairs. That's going to give us time. We've already sent the *Blue Pelican* out with a shipload of marines to take the ship, children, and whatever men we can. We'll bring the children here and transfer them to the *Unicorn's Magic* as soon as repairs are done. When we can, we'll send them to Jessamine. The rest of the Black Ships will be waiting in Yves when we get there.

"In the meantime, we haven't told anyone why we're doing what we are, but we're stocking every ship in the bay under the guise of taking on cargo. The troops are being called in from across the country..."

Gabriene's voice faded as a tall, thin footman ran into the

room and skidded to a halt just inside. After a hurried bow, he gasped out,

"There's a...situation...in the...stable."

Immediately, Behnam, Falcon, and Bass were on their feet and out the door. Faye passed them a moment later until she realized she didn't know where the stables were and dropped just behind Behnam who was in the lead.

Once outside and past the kitchen gardens, she spotted the stables where several men and boys were standing at the open doors, focusing on the interior while a cacophony of neighs, screams, shouts and...was that crying? echoed across the bailey. Also milling about the yard were several hounds. Faye sped up to push past the men, the last of which tried to stop her when he saw a woman.

Two grizzled stable hands were trying to calm Believer before he could kill the man lying curled up in the dirty straw beneath his hooves. This is where the crying was coming from.

Faye strode up to the one who appeared to be in charge. "Are you the stablemaster?" she asked, drawing her five feet two inches up straight as she imagined Ebony would.

With a grunt, the man turned to her before dismissing her and turning back to his helper. "It's useless, use the pitchfork!" he yelled. The second man ran for the instrument while the stablemaster turned back to Faye. "This is no place for a woman, leave!" he yelled, holding out his hand as if to take her arm.

Without thinking twice, she stepped into his grasp, clutched his arm, and turned to her right, throwing him over her back and onto the stable floor. Just as Ebony had taught her in the Haunted Forest.

As he landed, Bass walked over and put a foot on his chest. "Best stay where the savior has put you, don't you think?" he asked with a smile.

Behnam had already stopped the stable hand from reaching the pitchfork.

Meanwhile, Faye opened the stall door and walked up to Believer. "I'm here, Believer. I'm here. We'll get this sorted out. Calm down," she crooned.

Hearing her voice, the unicorn settled down to a quiver shuddering over his body. At least until the man groveling on the ground tried to move. Believer lowered his head and snapped with his large teeth.

Looking down, Faye got a thoughtful look on her face. "What have you, and your friends, caught for us?" she asked in a calm voice. Looking over at Behnam who was now holding Desert Wind's halter and Tiny who was still leaning on his captive, no matter how much Falcon tugged on his halter. Apparently the Chardell was waiting for Jakar.

Once things were under control, Bass leaned over and helped the stable master to his feet. "Why don't you tell us what happened?" he asked.

"Savior? That little slip of a gel is one of the saviors?" he asked scornfully.

"Yes, we've already established that! I think we've also established that touching them is a very bad idea. Now, from the beginning, tell us what happened."

"I dinna be too sure, 'xactly. When they comed," he began, giving Faye a head nod as Cheri, Ebony, and Jakar arrived. "Several of us was sent o'er 'ere to take care of the mounts. I brung me best men and we settled 'em in nicely. Although, dese three seemed a bit high spirited, if'n ye get me drift? Then, fer some reason, dese three men, who on'y been wit me fer aboot three weeks, comed over ter help. Said they been sent. Next thin' we ken, they be in de stalls and de horses be gone crazy, fer no reason at all."

"Not without reason, Master...?" said Faye, pausing for him to supply his name.

"Demal, my lady. I be Master of the horse, Demal," he answered, bowing deeply. "I be beggin' yer pardon, my lady. A thousand times, I be beggin' yer pardon."

"No, Master Demal. If you are truly a master of horse, you should know when to trust the animal. Especially over men you do not know well. In the future, if someone approaches these horses without your express command, do not hesitate to stop them. You have my apologies for earlier. I was concerned for you and your stable hand as well as Believer. But back to these men. Believer never does anything 'for no reason.' Neither do his friends. Guards, I think these three men should be taken into custody and questioned. There's more to this than meets the eye," said Faye, beginning to put the pieces together as she spoke.

Several of the castle guard were standing outside the stable by now, and their sergeant stepped forward, motioning for six of his men to take the three into custody. As they approached the two strangers being held by Behnam and Bass. The strangers quickly raised their left hands to their mouths and slumped to the ground a moment later, unconscious or dead. The man still being held by Tiny was trying to raise his left hand as well but couldn't move.

Behnam stooped to check the man on the ground next to him. "Dead," he said quietly, looking up at those around him.

Jakar stepped up to Tiny and spoke to him softly as two of the guards reached behind the huge horse, grabbing both arms of the man trapped there. Finally, Tiny consented to walk away to the far side of his stall with Jakar.

"Amner, run! Get the doc. We ain' takin' no kip this man die on us too," called the captain to one of his men.

"That's where I want to go," said Ebony to his retreating back. With a shrug, she turned to her own guard. "I wish to check on Sir Lakhvir. Please take me to him."

"I think we have things in hand here. I'll go with Gaban.

I'm interested in Beloria," volunteered Cheri, running to catch up to the old wizard, already on his way back to the castle.

*****

Once in the kitchen where Beloria was waiting, she introduced herself to the young girl before finding a seat against the wall. She had every intention of staying out of the way.

"Beloria, tell me about the animals. Tell me how they make you feel. How do you feel when you become one of them?" asked Gaban after introducing himself.

"'Ow do I be feeling? Afore I be changing? I be scairt or angered in me dreams. After? I be free. Sometimes I be powerful, lak a deer, fast, quiet lak. What dey h'animal feel, I ken. It be hard ter 'splain." confessed Beloria in a small voice while twisting a lock of her strawberry-blond hair around her finger.

"All right. Magic is taken and held by force. You must be stronger than the magic if you're going to control it. You said you feel yourself start to change when you get angry. Can you get angry now?"

"What if I can't control it? You said I have to be stronger, but I'm not strong. I'm fast and I can be sneaky, but I'm not strong."

"Would you try it anyway? I'll be here to help."

Cheri squirmed in her seat. This didn't sound like the way to go about taming magic at all. This sounded like the barbaric way they used to tame horses. Brute force and cruel spurs. Everything in her said this was the wrong way to go about it but surely Gaban had done this before?

Trying to follow Gaban's instructions, Beloria screwed up her face and tried to look angry, but...nothing. Taking a deep breath, she tried again, and...nothing. Then Beloria started crying. "I canna do this. Not apurpose."

"But...," began Gaban.

"Ahem...Gaban? Perhaps I can help?" interrupted Cheri respectfully as she rose from her seat. "You're trying to do this the way a man would, not the way a woman would. May I try?"

"Lady Cheri, what do you know of magic?" he asked with an almost condescending smile.

"Remind me to tell you about the whirlpool in the White River, when there's time. For now, Beloria, let's try something a little different. Close your eyes and think about how you feel just before you think you're going to turn into an animal. Only this time, you get to pick the animal, and you're going to allow it to happen," suggested Cheri.

Beloria looked at the girl in front of her for a long moment of doubt. This girl wasn't much older than she was, but they said she was a savior.

"Beloria, I believe you can do it, and I'll be right here with you," she assured the nervous little girl.

Nodding, Beloria closed her eyes and let her mind drift to the last time she'd been angry. As her skin began to crawl, she thought of a bright-red fox with a pert face and a bushy tail. As the feeling of strangeness increased, she did her best to welcome it as Cheri had suggested. Maybe it would be fun to be a fox. Would she be able to talk as an animal? Their mouths weren't shaped like a person's. Then she heard a gasp from Cheri and opened her eyes.

Cheri was staring at her from a great height. Wait! How had the lady gotten so tall? Wait! Snapping her head down, she looked at her paws. Paws! With more quick movements of her head, she soon found herself chasing her tail as she tried to get a better look. She was yapping in excitement as she reveled in her victory. Could she talk?

"Chark!" she barked in a high voice. '*No, that wasn't right.*' "Cheri, rowrr, kin ye unnerstan' me?" she finally got out.

"Oh! Wonderful! You can talk. Come with me, we need to check something out. Come on, Gaban," said Cheri, jumping up to lead the way out of the room. Now they could try to get to the bottom of yesterday's mystery.

*****

Ebony made her way to the infirmary, getting an impromptu tour of the castle grounds, beginning with the stables and moving on to a large grassy area for the horses. Almost as large as a pasture. Beyond the far rail, grass continued right up to the towering rose-covered wall, rising to protect the castle grounds. Set in the wall was a large set of iron-bound gates, closed and barred.

On the other side of the castle, separated by a large, formal, garden, was a strange building. A large domed building three stories high decorated with elaborate carvings she couldn't make out. At each cardinal direction stood a tower that appeared to spiral into the sky. Each one topped with a unique onion dome. Startled, she stopped to look it over. "What's that?"

"That be the Imaldi towers as was built a few 'undred year'n after de castle. Summat aboot another prophecy and a needs ter come, or summat," explained her escort with a smile. "I thin' it be a mighty pretty sight but ain' never been used."

"Well, from what I've heard, I think it's about to have residents soon. Let's go see Sir Lakhvir."

Obediently, the guard led the way to the small postern gate set into the larger door on the right. He had a great key for the door and locked it carefully behind them. Beyond the door was the knights academy: their barracks, stables, training grounds, and near the training arena, the infirmary.

Inside, Ebony found Sir Gurmail, sitting dejectedly on a narrow bed next to the one where Sir Lakhvir tossed and turned, sweating profusely. Absently, he rubbed an old scar on his face.

Ebony rushed over as a little bald man with a bit of a belly waddled across the room to try to intercept her. "Stop! Get away from that man. He's very sick," he called, turning from another patient where he'd just changed a bandage.

"Sick? What's wrong? He was injured, not sick," said Ebony, turning to the man and standing tall. Tall enough to tower over the doctor trying to stop her.

"Doc! Doc, stop. This be Lady Ebony. One of the saviors," yelled Sir Gurmail, standing quickly to get between them.

"Apologies, my lady," said the doc with a sketchy bow. "I must see to my patient." And he stepped forward to begin removing the unconscious knight's dressings.

"Wait! Stop! Aren't you at least going to wash your hands first?" yelled Ebony, grabbing his arms and holding him back. "Doctor... what's your name?"

"Well, I don't be a healer. I be more of a bonesetter. The healer done gone ter the castle. I be called Doc Afnar. Now let me through. Sir Lakhvir needs me."

"Doc Afnar? You know who I am, yes? You know I come from a far world, yes? Now I'm telling you, in our world we know things about keeping men well that you do not. Do you believe me?" asked Ebony in a series of quick-fire questions, getting a nod on the first two and a confused look on the last.

"Do you be a doctor or healer in your world?" he asked skeptically.

"I guess you'd call me a healer. I was a medic in a war zone for a time, but it doesn't matter. In our world, there are things about sickness known by almost everyone. I am going to teach you what I know, and then you will change how you do things accordingly, right?"

"Medic? What be a medic? You been to war? Huh! I doubt

that. Don't matter none, I don't take no orders from a woman." scoffed the bonesetter.

"Doc Afnar! Lady Ebony is one of the saviors. You...will... listen... and do...exactly...what she says! Or you will be removed from your position," insisted Sir Gurmail, towering over the other man.

The doc stared defiantly at the huge giant of a knight for a minute before capitulating.

When he bowed his head, Ebony approached and put one hand on his arm. "We are going to make you the best doctor in Persal, Doc. You're going to change the face of medicine as practiced in this world stuck in the middle ages," she said with a smile.

The doc frowned at her and Sir Gurmail defiantly before reluctantly nodding.

"Sir Gurmail, it's very important that his hands, all the way to the elbow, be scrubbed clean. With hot water and soap. I'll explain to him later about germs. He won't believe it, but it will be a beginning. Are there any helpers here? I need some things done while the doctor gets ready. Ah! You, there behind the door. What's your name?"

"Phredee, my lady," said the young boy with a bow.

"Well, Phredee, I want you to run as fast as you can to the kitchens and get some old bread. The kind with green stuff growing on it. Do you have needles and thread here? Do we need to send for some?" asked Ebony, pushing up her sleeves as she set to work.

"Uh, we have needles and thread but the green bread, Lady? Why...?"

"Don't worry about why, boy. Just do what the lady says," interrupted Sir Gurmail.

With a quick nod to the knight, Phredee headed for the door. "Make sure the bread doesn't have any seeds in it!" called Ebony to his retreating back.

"One of her guards looked at her with one eyebrow raised. "Mold on rye bread is poisonous," she elaborated.

Turning back to Doc where Sir Gurmail was helping him scrub, Ebony spotted another helper trying to stay out of sight in the next room. "You! What's your name?"

"G...Gart, my lady," he stammered.

"Great. Gart, go get us two buckets of clean water. Scrub out the buckets first with hot water and soap, if you can. The water must be as clean as you can get it. Go... Now!"

"Yes, lady," he answered with a quick bow before darting out the door.

"Sir Gurmail, what kind of alcohol can you get your hands on? The stronger the better," asked Ebony.

"Well, there's no whiskey allowed at the academy, but at the canteen they've got beer, ale, and even mead for the Mojar. Too sweet for my taste but some like it. Of course, at the castle...," he began, trying to remember what they could get quickly.

"Mead? *Ding, ding, ding!* We have a winner. Go get me two casks of mead, now!" she ordered her other guard, who took off running.

"Now, Doc, this is the part you aren't going to believe, and you'll just have to take it on faith. In dirt, on our hands, everywhere, there are these small little things like bugs called germs. They're so small they can't be seen. Not even with a magnifying glass. You do have those, don't you? Anyway, bad germs can make people sick and sometimes kill. Germs are responsible for all the diseases you have ever seen or heard of. From now on, whenever you tend to a patient, you'll need to wash your hands. Well, actually scrub them and scrub them again and again. When all the visible dirt is gone, scrub them again. All the way to the elbow. Any questions?"

"Ye wan' me ter believe there be little bitty bugs crawlin'

all over me? Why cain't I feel 'em?" asked the Doc as he scrubbed his hands harder.

"They've been there since you were born and they're so small... Look, I told you, you're going to have to take this on faith. Oh, good, here's Gart. In there, on the table. Now, put some on the stove to heat. Then go find more buckets. Get more water and lots of soap. This whole infirmary, top to bottom, needs to be scrubbed, and you and Phredee are going to do it. With hot water. I want is so hot it's hard to put you hands in it." She instructed as she readied a ceramic basin for the doctor to finish cleaning up.

Phredee returned with the moldy bread just after Gart came back and the two set to work, cleaning the rooms.

While Gurmail was helping Doc scrub, Ebony joined them and scrubbed up as well. "We're going to do this together. I caught a whiff of what's out there, but we're going to save his arm," she said with pursed lips.

"That is not possible. If you smelled it, you know."

"It is possible. It's the other lesson I'll teach you today. Cleanliness is the most important thing. Always remember that, but there is a way to kill the bad germs and cure such things. All I ask of you is to keep an open mind. If you can't, find the door," answered Ebony, the last comment dropping to almost subaudible.

"Gurmail, when he's done, rinse his hands with mead but don't touch him. Mead is made from honey, and honey is a natural antibiotic. Since we don't have rubber gloves, we'll just do the best we can. Then rinse the knives, needles, and thread in mead."

Doc Afnar shook his head at all this nonsense, clearly not understanding as Gurmail took it all on faith and vigorously continued to scrub under Doc's fingernails. Several minutes later, his hands and forearms scrubbed red, they returned to Sir Lakhvir's bedside.

When Doc started to reach for the blankets, Ebony stopped him, "Don't get your hands dirty. Let Sir Gurmail do that."

When the blanket was pulled back, the full force of the smell hit them, "Awghh!" That smells awful. What is causing it?" asked Gurmail, trying not to gag.

"It's gangrene, Gurmail. Don't worry, we're going to do our best to cure it. Get rid of that blanket, we'll need a clean one when we're through." Answered Ebony. "Doc, I know a great deal about wounds, but I'm not the doctor. You are. I'll assist you. "Sir Gurmail, can you remove the bandages, please?"

"I've done worse," he answered, gritting his teeth.

Working together, Gurmail carefully removed the old, putrid bandages. Ebony instructed Doc how to cut away the decayed flesh and then Ebony poured mead on it, carefully cleaning the wound. Finally, she had Gurmail scrape the mold off the bread and grind it up in a mortar and pestle.

"On our world, we call this penicillin. It will kill all those pesky germs that are in the wound causing the rot, allowing Lakhvir to live, with all his limbs. Sprinkle it into the wound and sew it up," she instructed, passing the stone mortar to the bonesetter.

Shaking his head, Doc Afnar complied. All this nonsense about invisible bugs and now this. Bad bread was going to cure gangrene? What nonsense, but there was no doubt when looking at Sir Gurmail or the other knights waiting outside, they believed in these saviors.

"Sir Gurmail, send word to the castle, if his condition changes. For better or worse," Ebony requested as she left.

*****

As soon as Ebony entered the castle through the kitchen, she could hear an excited bustle down the servant's hall off the grand hallway. Curious, she ran to see what all the excitement was about. When she rounded the corner, the strangest sight met her eyes.

In the hall was an excited Cheri, kneeling next to a bright-red fox. Standing over them was Gaban. Their other friends were coming from the direction of the library. When Ebony looked around, she realized she was about where the prophecy thief had disappeared.

"Hey, everyone! Beloria has answers for us, listen," called Cheri as the others joined them.

"Listen? Listen to who? To what?" asked Ebony in confusion, looking around for a little girl.

"Just hush and listen," insisted Cheri, scowling at her friend. "Go ahead, Beloria. Tell them what you told us."

"Yip, yip. I smelt 'im on'y 'tis not an 'im, if'n ye get me grif. What I smelled be ta wet an' ta stickly clay and ta sommat else. I b'leeve it be magic," came a high-pitched voice from the fox.

"What!" yelped Faye, jumping away from the animal in surprise.

"Calm down. It's just Beloria. Gabriene suspected she had been changing into animals in her dreams for years. We just needed the trigger that would allow her to change when she wanted to. Anyway! No one thought she'd be able to talk while she was an animal. Isn't it great?"

"Cheri, enough of that. The important thing is what she found when we brought her down here," interrupted Gaban. "We were right in our assumption the thief got in through the sewer. It apparently didn't use or know about any of the secret passages."

"And I was right! Yesterday I said he didn't look human? I was right!" exclaimed Cheri, taking over again. "From what Beloria can tell us, he wasn't really alive."

"Yip! Na, nor alive as we ken. Jus' mud and magic but

more. Smart, sort o'. I cain' 'splain it. 'E wen' down in dere," Beloria finished, pointing her nose at the adjacent room.

When Bass opened the door, it proved to be a water closet with a small hole for elimination.

"Eew. He fit down there?" asked Faye, curling her lip in disgust. "Not only did he leave by this route, he came in here as well," explained Gaban, shaking his head.

"You're describing a golem. It's from Hebrew mythology in our world. A clay statue brought to sentient life by magic," input Faye thoughtfully.

"That sounds like Barakus. Always breaking the rules," responded Gabriene.

As they were talking, Beloria ran off down the hall to a small sitting room where she had left her clothes behind a screen.

"Well, well. It appears our intruder has also revealed a chink in our armor. Falcon, would you alert the guards and have them see to the grates on the outermost sewer drains. They must be secured immediately," ordered Gabriene, making his way back down the hallway to the library door.

*****

Madlene hustled up to Tasmin and whispered into her ear as the others were following Gabriene. Nodding once, Tasmin turned to the ladies. "Goodness, it's time to get ready for the ball. This morning's activities had left you filthy and that smell. Let's get you into a hot bath, now!"

Upstairs, Faye was quickly ensconced in her room with three maids to help her bathe, whether she wanted it or not. They were there to help her get dressed and do her hair.

Emerging from her bath, she found a lace ball gown of azure blue with silver embroidery around the overskirt of satin. Under that skirt were many layers of chiffon in a lighter cornflower blue. Faye stopped to stare at the confection for a moment. "Oh, dear. Here we go again." She sighed as she allowed her maids to begin dressing her.

Two hours later, she was finally ready, with her hair pulled up into a pile of blond curls and a few stray ringlets brushing her neck. Looking at herself in the pier glass mirror, she tried to be objective and dismiss her shyness. Huh, she really was quite pretty. When had that happened?

There was a knock on her door followed almost immediately by Tasmin who entered with the sounds of music coming from below. "Oh, don't you look lovely! Faye, you're a vision. Well, come on. It's time for your entrance."

In the hall outside, Cheri was waiting in a seafoam green chiffon dress with dark-green embroidery similar to Faye's dress but with a drop waist. Ebony wore a mermaid style dress in burgundy satin with golden embroidery to emphasize her height and generous curves. Cheri's hair was done in a similar style to Faye's, but Ebony's hair had been combed out and oiled into curls. The curls had been pulled back so they could cascade down her back. The entire effect was striking.

Falcon, Bass, and Behnam in outfits designed to compliment the women were also waiting in the hall.

Quickly, Tasmin paired Falcon in his azure satin trousers and doublet with Faye. Behnam was wearing dark-green doublet and trousers to escort Cheri and Bass was wearing burgundy. With Faye and Falcon in the lead, the others followed half a flight of stairs later by Cheri and Behnam and at an equal distance by Ebony and Bass. Together they made a grand procession down the staircase to the waiting crowd of nobles and knights with their ladies waiting in the grand hall below.

Faye's stomach was churning by the time they were halfway down the staircase, and her shoe found the hem of her dress, causing her to stumble. Frantically, she grabbed tighter to Falcon's arm. With one foot firmly on the next step and the other leaving the one behind, Falcon's balance was compromised as he grabbed Faye with both hands and pushed back to keep from tumbling headfirst to the marble floor below.

There was a collective gasp of horror as they fell back from the crowd waiting in the foyer. Behind them, Bass and Behnam kept Ebony and Cheri from running to their friend. "Let Falcon handle it," they both whispered before exchanging a look.

When Falcon pulled Faye to her feet, she was blushing a bright red. "Perhaps you should hold up your skirt. It's obviously too long," suggested Falcon quietly as he helped her straighten her dress. "Are you hurt? Do you need to go back to your room?"

"Thank you, Falcon. I'm all right. I can do this. Let's get this over with," she said, smiling brightly for the waiting dignitaries.

When they reached the bottom of the staircase, the crowd parted, making a path to the ballroom where an elaborate buffet was set up along the walls, and the small orchestra was playing by the open doors to the garden.

Tasmin had directed them to a receiving line in the ballroom, and Gabriene took them through a seemingly endless set of introductions. Beginning with the regent and his wife. "Lady Faye, the regent, Lord Udan, and his esteemed wife, Lady Zillar. Lady Cheri..." Faye led the way by honoring the regent and his wife with a deep curtsy. Faye and Cheri did their best to follow suit. And so, the interminable introductions continued.

Some stood out. Such as Sir Suvaat, the Mojar knight from the tournament, Sir Gurmail and, of course, Sir Galad, the knight champion. Then there was Lady Shallan, a respected dowager and the regent's revered mother. As she met the saviors, she smiled as had everyone else, but when she smiled, her eyes sparkled in amusement. This was a lady with a genuine smile, unlike so many who appeared to already be calculating how to advance themselves. Most of the faces had blurred, and the names had run one into another by the time it was over. Faye found herself envying Cheri her eidetic memory.

Faye sought out Gaban once released, "Where's Ochwatt? He should be here."

"No, child. There are too many people. He also dislikes the piles of stone we choose to live in. He prefers caves as carved out by the Golden Queen, who guides his people. No, he's in the lower garden. I asked him to try to stay out of sight. It will be a disaster if he's seen, I'm afraid."

Before they could even think of approaching the food, the dancing began, and it was their duty to dance first. Their designated partners approached with a bow and led them onto the dancefloor. Then the evening began in a whirl of color and sound and changing partners. After the first three dances, they followed the music and the lead of their partners and survived the next two.

As they danced, Cheri glanced around the room, wondering how they were being received by these strangers. Most of the men, who weren't dancing and several who were, watched one or the other of them in open admiration. Most, including Sir Suvaat and Sir Galad, watched Ebony as she whirled about the dance floor.

Many of the women, especially the younger women, watched them with something akin to admiration, mixed with a noticeable tinge of envy. Lady Shallan sat in a large wingback chair, watching the dancing and tapping her foot, although Cheri had the impression, she missed nothing. When she caught Cheri's eye, she waved and smiled. On the other side of the room was the regent's wife, watching them dance and the men clustered around them with a sour look on her face. Sitting with her were three other ladies who Cheri remembered as being introduced as wives of some of the council. Two of them, in their late forties, and of an age with Zillar, mirrored her displeasure. What were their names? Ah, the Ladies Wandira and Bestia. The fourth, Lady Cantori, in her midthirties, was trying not to smile but her feet were tapping, anyway.

Then there was that strange little man, uhm, His Grace the Duc Pellatel, over by the punch bowl whose gaze flickered between Faye, where he glared, and Behnam where his eyes softened, into what? Ah, adoration. The man had a crush and thought Faye was his competition. He was in for a rude awakening.

During the sixth dance, Faye was changing partners when she tripped on her hem again and stepped on another woman's trailing gown, causing them both to drag their partners with them as they fell. At this point in the dance, everyone was holding onto two potential partners, so more dancers were toppled in a domino effect until half the nobility of Lohi were lying on the floor, instead of dancing.

Ebony ended up in the pileup, and Cheri barely managed to stay standing. They both immediately started laughing, joined quickly by Falcon, Bass, Behnam, Tasmin, Gaban, Jakar, and Gabriene. Faye's face turned a bright red as she gained her feet and tried to apologize to everyone around her. Then she lost all self-control and ran off into the garden.

When Bass started to follow, Ebony stopped him. "Not you. Not now. She's not going to want you to see her like this. She's gone to Believer. Just give her time." Neither noticed Behnam slip out the open doors.

Behnam caught up to her at the stable. "Faye, it's all right. We weren't laughing at you. We were laughing because you broke the tension. Couldn't you feel it? Everyone was uncomfortable, and your little slip broke that. You should have stayed to hear Lady Shallan laugh. It would have gladdened your heart."

"But, Behnam, why is it always me? Why am I such a klutz?" "Faye, I don't think you are a...what's that word? Well, I don't think you're clumsy so much as uneasy. Especially around strangers. From everything I know of you, you've never been clumsy when it really mattered. You're a very capable woman and those who count know this. Are you ready to return?"

Faye let go of Believer and nodded.

*****

When they returned, they found the orchestra had taken a break, and the others had finally found time to get some food. When Faye joined them, she found getting the food wasn't the problem. It was getting a moment to themselves to actually eat it that was the real challenge.

Most of the knights were gathered around Ebony, inquiring about her experiences as a warrior.

During the introductions, Gabriene had made a point of introducing Bass as the Woodsman, and many of the ladies approached to ask him what it was like, living in the Singing Forest. When he mentioned Cheri's singing to the forest, the young men trying to engage her in conversation overheard and the young women looked at her in awe. "Oh my, Lady Cheri, you must sing for us," several of them insisted.

Ebony stepped forward and added her voice to theirs. "Yes, Cheri, you must sing. It's either that or I give a demonstration of my...skills, and none of us are dressed for that! I've already agreed to demonstrate some of my forms tomorrow in the knights' practice arena."

"I'll sing, if you'll join me."

"All right, do you know 'Girls Just Wanna Have Fun'?"

"Let's go!" agreed Cheri, striding across to the musicians to give them the melody.

I come home in the morning light

My mother says, "When you gonna live your life right?" Oh, momma dear, we're not the fortunate ones

And girls, they wanna have fun Oh, girls, just wanna have fun...[****]

When they finished, the nobles and knights in the room rose and gave them a resounding round of applause. Many had not understood all the words, but they had enjoyed the singing.

Then Ebony looked out over the crowd and tried to speak. When the room didn't calm down, the drummer took over and did a quick drumroll.

As a hush fell on the room, Ebony nodded almost regally. "Ladies and gentlemen, with only a small mishap, we have been enjoying dancing with you all," she began, and there was a slight titter in the room until she continued.

"These dances are new to us, so we thought it only fair to teach you a dance from our world. If my friends would join me?" she asked, motioning to Faye and Cheri while Behnam, Bass, and Falcon followed them. "Please, join us. Line up, and we will show you how to do the Macarena," she concluded as the music started.

Then Ebony and Bass stepped forward, and on the third eighth beat, she extended her right arm, palm down. Quickly followed by her left arm. Then she crossed her right arm to her left shoulder. As she continued, and the others joined in, several of the younger nobles and their ladies tried to follow the moves, and the older ones were watching carefully. When she put her hands on her hips and rotated them, there was another burst of embarrassed laughter, and most were smiling. By the time she started repeating the moves, almost

---

[****] "Girl's Just Wanna Have Fun," Cyndi Lauper

everyone in the room had joined in. The exceptions were a few of the older women, who shook their heads but kept smiling. Lady Shallan left her chair to join them. When the music finally stopped, everyone was laughing and none harder than the dowager who was being helped back to her chair. None of them had ever had such fun at a court ball.

Abruptly, the night air was rent by a bloodcurdling scream, followed by a deep roar coming from the garden.

As the crowd rushed toward the open glass doors leading to the garden, a young couple in slight disarray ran into the room. The young woman was sobbing hysterically, and the young man gasped out. "A monster! There's a monster in the garden. Barakus must have sent it!"

Ebony, just a step or two off the dais, motioned to the drummer who beat out another drumroll, getting everyone's attention. "Please, please calm down. What you saw isn't a monster. He's a friend of ours. His kind is from our world. He won't hurt anyone. Please, just leave him alone. Please!" she asked with a worried look out the door.

While everyone's attention was diverted, Gaban slipped out to find his friend. "The wizard Gaban will take care of him. Please, return to the party," said Ebony brightly, enticing everyone back into the ballroom.

CHAPTER 26

Imaldi Well Met

Plans for the Retaking, as they were calling it, were gathering momentum. Knights were coming and going from the academy, but only Galad and Suvaat actually visited the castle regularly to plan with Gabriene, Bass, Falcon, Behnam, Jakar, and Ebony. All the visible activity took place from the knights' school, and even that was kept to a few key knights. Sir Suvaat, who needed a new squire, had taken on Matew, who's arm was out of its sling, and he was kept busy carrying messages hither and yon. Since he arrived with the saviors, his presence in the castle did not raise any untoward notice.

Ebony and the men spent a lot of time pouring over the maps of Yves. Cheri and Faye had glanced at the map a time or two, but neither one were versed in strategy.

The city of Yves was perched on a rough cliff with broad steps carved up its side. The homes and stores were carved from the rock of the cliff itself. At the bottom was the port and a fishing village. The piers and even the warehouses were built out into the bay on rock estuaries since the beach was sparse, disappearing at high tide. Perched atop the cliff was the castle of the governors who had been walking the edge of a knife for two thousand years. The one thing they needed to do was maintain their neutrality with Barakus. The stronghold of the great wizard was just beyond the Strait of the Claw, less than fifty leagues away.

Everyone knew this was where the Black Ships gathered before making their final run for Doome and many in Persal blamed the city for letting them pass. Most realized the people of Zabir had no more choice than the rest of Persal, but as always, blame must be put somewhere.

To the north of the city, the cliff climbed higher and its sides became vertical with fewer breaks. This barrier formed the western edge of the strait. On the other side was an island. A volcanic cone with the sides almost as sheer as the mainland. The rocky reefs surrounding the island made approach by sea nearly impossible. Next to this island, a symbol on the map was of a chimera. Once it was said they lived there, but now it was merely the name of the island itself.

This would be the terrain of the final assault. From the sea, if they could arrive in time, would be the fleet carrying the marines. From land, would come the knights already making their way northeast to Zabir and Yves. The saviors and those who traveled with them hoped to catch up before they were forced to mount their assault. They were still discussing how their attack would progress. Ebony wanted to have an aerial assault, but when she tried to explain hang gliders and how they worked, she ran into a wall. Worse, she didn't know how to build one.

*****

For the most part, on the day after the ball, Faye and Cheri were left to their own devices. When Ebony wasn't pouring over maps, she spent a great deal of time in the infirmary as Sir Lakhvir began to heal. All signs and smell of the gangrene were gone. She also spent a lot of time talking to Doc Afnar about anything she could remember concerning medicine.

At least anything they could put to use in these primitive circumstances.

Faye and Cheri decided to explore the castle, and it wasn't long before they found themselves in the west wing. "Isn't this where those girls—the Imaldi?—are staying?" asked Cheri. "It seems awfully quiet for where seven little girls live."

"It does, doesn't it? Let's see if we can find them. I'm a little curious about them anyway," answered Faye.

"Only a little curious? It's seven little girls coming into their magic abilities and going through puberty at the same time. They've got to be driving Gaban crazy." Cheri laughed.

"Then maybe we can help. After all, it's what I've been trained for," suggested Faye.

"You were trained to deal with children with magical abilities? I'm beginning to think you might be overqualified to be my guardian," sneered the redhead.

"No, I've been trained to deal with children as they adjust to strange surroundings. Ugh! You know this. Stop baiting me. Oh, and I chose to be your guardian, it wasn't a random decision, Cheri."

Cheri giggled to cover for being uncomfortable with that admission. They could hear voices behind the next door. Faye knocked lightly, and a young black girl with straight reddish-brown hair and golden eyes answered the door. Her long white tunic nearly covered the brown, baggy pants beneath.

"Is Gaban here?" asked Cheri, trying to peek inside curiously. "Yes, my lady," answered the girl, bowing nearly in half, reminiscent of those Behnam did so well. Opening the door to let them in as she straightened.

Inside, Ochwatt was sitting on one side of the room, and they crossed to him first. "Ah, Ochwatt, there you are. I heard you had a nasty scare last night?" said Faye.

"Not scared. Didn't like scarin' that gel tho. Just wanted ter be out'n de stone place."

"Oh, Ochwatt, she'll be fine and I don't blame you a bit for wanting to be outside. Especially on such a fine night," soothed Cheri, crossing the room to where Ochwatt was talking to three of the girls, Ciral, whose unique, dark and light coloring and short stature made her stand out, Meland and Beloria. They were peppering poor Ochwatt with so many questions he could barely get a word in to answer, as they stroked his recently washed fur.

In a corner of the room, Debora and Briar Rose sat on a settee, talking, while Carlise stood alone, looking out the window.

"No, no, Aliand. You must grab the magic and wrestle it to do your bidding," Gaban remonstrated to another young girl with green eyes and blond hair arranged in elaborate braids.

"But, sir, that doesn't feel right. If I try to force it, it just slips away," she answered, obviously frustrated.

"Gaban, can we help?" asked Faye, crossing the room.

"Help, Lady Faye? How could you help? We've already established you know very little about magic."

"That may be true for Faye but let me share with you a story. When Falcon and I were traveling down the White River, the Vortex changed direction. It was a very sudden change, not the normal drift so carefully tracked by the river pilots. As it veered, it tried to pull us in. The captain sent many strong men ashore with sturdy ropes to keep us close to shore. Still, they were struggling, even losing the battle. I wanted to help, but I didn't know how. Then I was moved to clutch the ropes. When I grabbed those ropes, a strange energy beyond anything I had ever felt coursed up the lines to the men. I still don't know how but it happened. It seems I might be an Imaldi myself. You saw how I was with Beloria.

"Besides, I know a lot about girls and how they think. The first thing you should consider is, the fair sex approaches the world differently than males. It's just a fact," Cheri finished with a shrug.

"Well, what have I got to lose?" muttered Gaban as he collapsed into the empty armchair behind him.

Cheri moved across the room to introduce herself to Debora and Briar Rose. "Hello. I'm Cheri, and I don't know a lot about your world yet. Please, tell me about yourselves."

"You're a savior, aren't you? Why are you interested in us?" asked Briar Rose curiously.

"I need to know about your world if I'm to help. Let's make a trade—you teach me something about where you come from, and I'll tell you something about my world."

Briar Rose's ever-present curiosity was instantly piqued. A chance to learn of the world the saviors had come from. "Well, I'm from the island of Jessamine. We are protected by the great Oracle Tree. We raise Chardell draft horses for export, although most of them are purchased by the knights. Our other export is Jessamine wine, the best wine in Persal."

When she turned to Debora, the girl's golden eyes were staring at her hands. "I...I don't know what you want to know. I am from the deserts of Mojar. We too have horses. The greatest and fastest in all the known kingdoms. My favorite food is tada. It's a fruit that grows in the desert. We send silk and salt to the rest of Persal," she said shyly, warming up to Cheri as she spoke.

Over by the windows, Faye and Aliand had joined the girls around Ochwatt. "Please, tell me where you're from and how you came to be here?"

Aliand drew herself up as her mother had taught her. After all, she had been raised as a noble daughter of Camir. Weren't they the most important people in Persal? "I'm from Rim, the capital city of Camir, in the east. I was having dreams, dreams of building wonderful things. My maid, Leha, and I came by horseback to the Dragon Inn, in the city. Late that night, I left my sleeping maid behind and stole a boat. Somehow, I managed to row to the tower. My hands are still rough from the work. When I left my father's house, I had to sneak away. My father, the Baron of Phym, is important and he would never have allowed a valuable daughter to leave, if I had asked."

"Where's your maid now?"

"I presume she's still at the Dragon. I left her all the money we had remaining and the horses. I knew I wouldn't need any of it."

"She wouldn't have gone home?"

"Home? No! My father would have made her life miserable if she returned without me. He might even have her killed. She has no other place to go," replied Aliand, surprised at the question.

"Cheri, everyone, come over here," called Faye, waving at her friend.

Cheri, Debora, and Briar Rose moved across the room. Briar Rose seemed most reluctant. As she joined the group, her gaze flicked to Ciral, who was watching her warily with those strange, pale eyes. She stopped just outside the group, as far from the diminutive girl with black skin and golden hair as could be without offending.

"Did anyone besides Aliand arrive with others?" asked Faye.

Ciral, Carlise, and Debora nodded. The other three merely exchanged looks.

"Gaban!" she called, rousing the old man from his nap. "These girls have friends in the city. We need to find them and bring them here. As soon as possible."

"Humph, they never said as much to me. Did you tell Gabriene?" he asked as he crossed the room to pull the bell.

"All right, we'll need to know the names and where to find your friends," said Faye. "Cheri, scrounge up some paper and pen to write this down. The first one is Leha, staying at the Dragon Inn."

Quickly, Faye got them organized. Learning what she could about the girl's companions.

Faye looked questioningly to Debora. "My uncle Ranjua and my brother Jondor came with me. When we last spoke, they were coming here. I don't know where they went after that."

"Ciral?"

"There were four young men. Cirroc, the man I was to marry in five years. Huge, very large for our kind, about eight inches taller than I. And the twins, Saith and Saird. When we arrived, I sent them to Lohi. I do not know where they may be now. Even in this city, they shouldn't be hard to find. If the outrigger is still in port, they will be here, somewhere."

"Well, if they're, what...four feet tall, or less, they shouldn't be that hard to find," commented Cheri.

"Carlise, who came with you?"

"When I told my grandfather of my dreams, he insisted I must come to the tower and fulfill my calling. I wasn't happy, my friend, Merind, and I were getting ready to join the resistance in Jamben. We were set to go in a couple of days when everything changed. When I set out, my uncle, Joban, traveled with me. On the road, Merind was waiting for us. I don't know if they're still here. Joban may have gone home, and Merind may be training in the woods outside Dink," she explained.

"Where should we start looking, to see if they're still in town?"

"One of the inns, I suppose. We didn't talk about it," admitted the girl with a frown.

"Ah, Madlene. It appears our new friends here didn't arrive in Lohi alone, at least some of them. Some may have come here first. Did two Mojar warriors arrive in the last two months?" asked Faye as Madlene joined them.

"Actually, yes. When they told me, their friend had gone to the White Tower, we decided they'd find more to do at the knights' academy. They should still be there."

"If you would send for them, please. Also, Aliand's maid, Leha, should be at the Dragon Inn. Then, Ciral had four companions. Cirroc, Huge, Saith, and Saird. Huge will be the tallest at about four feet and with their dark complexions and pale hair, probably not too hard to find. Start at the port where their outrigger should still be. Make sure it's there and see what the port authority knows. Ciral can tell you what an outrigger looks like. Carlise may have an uncle and a friend staying in one of the inns, but that's as close as we can get. The uncle's name is Joban, and the friend is Merind.

"Beloria, Briar Rose, Meland, are you sure there's no on we can contact for you?"

Beloria and Briar Rose shook their heads as they exchanged looks and shrugged. "No one came with me, and no one you know can get word to Jessamine, so no," elaborated the dark-haired halfling.

"I don' have nobody, here nor anywhere else," mumbled Beloria.

"That's not true, anymore, Beloria. You've got us," said Briar Rose, putting her arm awkwardly around the taller girl.

"I be from Lohi but me da an' me brother may be a frettin' after me. I left a note wi' the scribbler so's 'e could read it fer 'em. Kin I send word ter 'em? Tell 'em I be all right?" asked Meland shyly.

"Of course. We'll even arrange for them to come visit, if you'd like that?" said Faye. Just tell Madlene their names and where to find them.

"Yes, Lady Faye. Madam Madlene, do ye ken Smith's street? Me da be Happen, the farrier. Me brother be Gerard, apprenticed to Cantini the smith. Wanted ter be more than jus' a farrier and da said yea."

"We'll send a runner to them and a coach to the Dragon. I'll also see if I can find Debora's kin. What are their names?" asked Madlene, getting things organized.

"Ranjua and Jondor," supplied Cheri from her list.

"Madam Madlene, there are two horses with my maid. At least, there were when I left her. I'm hoping she didn't sell them," injected Aliand.

"I'll keep that in mind. Now, Ciral, finding your friends may take a little longer but let's hope not much. I have someone in mind who's very good at finding people. I'll ask him to find out what happened to your uncle and friend, as well, Carlise. If they're still in the city, he'll find them. If they've left, he'll find out when," finished the housekeeper before leaving the room.

Cheri had been watching the girls carefully as they talked, and something caught her attention. There was...a familiarity, when she looked at Ciral and Briar Rose. Yes, Ciral had mahogany-colored skin with pale hair and gray eyes while Briar Rose had a lightly tanned complexion, dark-brown eyes, and black hair. It wasn't just that the two wore their hair the same or that they were of the same small stature; it was more than that.

"Faye, can I talk to you for a minute?" she asked, stepping away from the girls. As Faye joined her, she turned her back to the group and lowered her voice, "Look at Ciral and Briar Rose for a moment and tell me what you see," she requested.

The petite woman looked first at Briar Rose with her pug nose and broad forehead. There, when she smiled, dimples appeared. She was so pretty. Then she did the same with Ciral. Pug nose, broad forehead, and as she broke into a grin, there were the dimples. They were negative images of each other!

"Briar Rose, would you and Ciral join us, please?" she asked as she pulled Cheri over to Gaban.

"Uh?" grunted Briar Rose as she exchanged an uneasy

look with Ciral. Hesitantly, they crossed the room to the three adults. Briar Rose stopped two feet to Faye's left while Ciral stopped two feet to Cheri's right, keeping them a good five feet apart.

Gaban rose to stand behind the two ladies, and all three could plainly see the resemblance, in reverse. "Oh my. I don't believe Gabriene caught this."

Cheri was looking at them speculatively. "Move a little closer, slowly."

The two girls glanced at each other, dark-brown eyes meeting pale-gray eyes before they each slid sideways, bringing them one step closer. Then, they did it again. As the gap between them closed, they were the first to notice an attraction. Drawing them closer, like a magnet. When they were less than a foot apart, a spark arced between them causing the watchers to gasp. Behind them, the other Imaldi were watching, and Aliand let out a squeal.

"Stop!" called Cheri.

Ciral found herself trying to stop, but the attraction between the two was too great. Briar Rose was fighting but found herself unable to stop and the gap closed. As their hands came up, and before they even touched, a breeze could be felt.

"Close that window," called Gaban, never taking his eyes from the girls.

After a quick look around, Aliand called, "There aren't any open windows, Master."

In that short time, those watching Briar Rose and Ciral could see the wind as it whipped at the girls' hair, teasing it out of their braids. A moment later, mist started gathering near the ceiling, quickly forming into a cloud. Small surges of electricity were jumping back and forth between them. A thunderstorm was brewing.

Cheri had been watching this in fascination, but it was time to take action. Without warning, she lunged for Ciral, taking her to the floor while Briar Rose stumbled back, falling away from Ciral. Rising to a sitting position, Cheri commented, "Well! Perhaps that bit of magic should be practiced outside. Maybe even outside the city. At least until they can control it. Don't you think?"

Ochwatt started making a deep grunting sound, his terrifying smile spreading across his face. As he continued, Gaban realized he was laughing and joined in. Then so did everyone else.

As things settled down, Faye returned to investigating the talent of the next girl, "Debora, could we talk for a minute?"

Debora rose gracefully from a pillow on the floor and gave her a traditional bow. "What do you wish, my lady?"

"I have one question. Carlise mentioned your dream of the tower was…different from the others. What did she mean?"

"Some of the other girls, as strange as their dreams were, I don't think they believe me."

"Tell me anyway. With all that's happened to us since we got here, there's not much I wouldn't believe, anymore."

"The first time I dreamed of the tower, it wasn't really about the tower. I dreamed I was standing in the rain. Rain like I'd never seen in a land greener than I'd ever heard of. Then the rain started to clear, and I was standing on wet sand. I'd never seen sand that wet. When I turned, I saw water, so much water, it was terrifying. It was rolling toward me and away, getting closer and closer when suddenly a…wave?… broke over me. I woke screaming, and when my mother came, she tasted the water, and it was salty. I had never been so terrified. The next day, I was taken before the women, and I left the oasis with my uncle and my brother, then, on the way here, I dreamed of the tower itself," Debora explained shyly.

"Well, let me think for a minute," said Faye as she went through what she was learning about the girls.

"Debora, I think it makes sense. What better way to get the attention of someone who lives in the desert than to get them soaking wet, in saltwater? I'm sure it got you moving faster than just the dreams would have."

"Yes! Of course. Thank you, my lady. At least now it makes as much sense as any of this does."

"Gaban, I think I have some answers for you!" she called as she crossed to the wizard who had fallen asleep, again.

"What? Oh, yes, Lady Faye. What insights do you have for me?"

"I'm thinking, you're a man who has, in the past, only taught magic to men. Therefore, you're using the same approach you always have, right?" clarified Faye.

"Well, yes, my lady. What other approaches could I possibly use? This is how it's always been done," admitted Gaban.

"It's the approach that's always been used with men and boys. Now, you are working with young women. Do you deny men and women think differently? That they approach the world differently?"

"Well, no. Women are less logical, for the most part, and less aggressive," he conceded with a confused look.

"Uhm, for the most part. I'm going to ignore that for now, Gaban. What I'm proposing is, women are more subtle about their approach to life. Men look at the big picture and push and shove to get that picture to come into focus. Women are about the details, and they will nudge a bit here and another bit there to accomplish the same thing. Try showing them how to recognize their magic and tap it here or there to make it respond the way they want it to," she suggested. "I think you'll get better results."

"Faye, when you have a moment, could you come here?" called Cheri from over by the tall windows where she'd been watching Aliand drawing at one of the tables.

"Gaban, do you understand what I'm trying to say?" pressed Faye.

"Yes and no, Lady Faye. What you say makes a great deal of sense, but I'll have to figure out how to do that."

"Ask Madlene or one of the maids for help. They will understand what I'm talking about. You might also ask the girls themselves how it feels when they try to touch their magic," she suggested as she went to join Cheri.

Across the room, Aliand was drawing, and Cheri was watching her art closely. Gaban had followed Faye and stopped as he was passing. Then he bent forward to take a closer look. "Uh...Faye, have you looked at this?"

Faye looked down and there, on the page Aliand was just finishing, was a detailed picture of Yves and the Strait of the Claw. Between the impossibly sheer cliffs of the mainland and the almost equally sheer section of the volcano, where it had fallen into the sea, was the raging waters in graphic detail. Just beyond the edge of the island could be seen an impossibly large and menacing crab claw, rising from the depths to grab at an unsuspecting ship above. On the top of the cliff, a small group of people were launching themselves into the air with a set of static wings. The wings weren't on their backs, like a bird, but above their heads in a frame that could glide on the incredible updraft ever-present between the cliffs. Below them were several of Barakus's Black Ships and the first of the fliers was diving toward the ship. As they looked closer, the incredible detail revealed a lion, watching from the lip of the volcanic cone of the island. An even closer look revealed wings and another indistinct, head. A chimera? An animal rumored to have once lived on the island that is inaccessible by sea. Just south of the Claw, where the bluff curved around the protected bay was a lighthouse, atop the headland.

"Aliand, what are these wings?" asked Faye, a glimmer of hope in her voice.

"Those? Oh, I call them my fliers. Here, this is how they would be made. My father calls such fancies foolish, and he tried to forbid me from creating them. To think of more important things like an advantageous marriage. According to my mother, no man would want to marry a woman who showed such signs of being unstable," she said with a sour face.

"Excuse me for saying this, but your father's an idiot and you're a genius. Gaban, what you are seeing here isn't magic, it's science. This young lady is an engineer. I don't know how she knows all these details of Yves but the wings? Those are hang gliders. Aliand, come on, we have to show this to the others and start building your fliers," said Faye excitedly.

"Lady Faye? Build one? Really? Lady Cheri, can I really build one?" asked Aliand with a surprised note of excitement.

"No, we're not going to make one, we're going to make a fleet. On our world, Lady Ebony has already flown on a machine very much like your fliers. Gaban, send a maid to Madlene. We're going to need silk. Lots and lots of silk."

*****

While Faye, Cheri, and Gaban were studying Aliand's drawing, several of the other girls wandered over to see what the excitement was about. One of those was Briar Rose. Looking at the drawing of the ocean approaching Yves and listening to the conversation got her to thinking. Once Faye left them alone with Gaban and Cheri, she approached Ciral, careful not to get too close, and got her attention. "Did you see that drawing? It's where they expect the Black Ships to be, soon. I think they're going to try to get the children back," she whispered from two feet away.

"The children? What children?" asked Ciral in some confusion.

"The children who were taken from the mainland. I guess Barakus doesn't even know Hawart exists. Every hundred years or so, Barakus sends his armies to take the children between five and twelve from their families and put them in the Black Ships, sending them off to Doome. In the past, trying to recover the children caused much more devastation. Jessamine was immune, of course, but we heard about it, and we never forgot. Imagine, all your brothers, sisters, cousins, everyone you know, just taken away. Gone. Nothing you do can stop it. It can only make things worse, if you fight back. Then you lose your other children. You lose your husband. You lose your wife. Whole villages were wiped out when this began. If they get them back, Barakus's men come back, kill everyone and still take the children who survive. It becomes a choice. Let Barakus have the children and hope for the best for them or kill the children themselves. Most of the people of Persal have learned to let their children go. It's called the Taking," explained Briar Rose, trying not to cry at the telling.

"Oh! By the face of my god! How can this be happening? Does anyone know why Barakus steals the children?" asked Ciral, in sorrow and outrage.

"Some of them become his soldiers and priests. The youngest ones, who don't remember, I think. No one is sure what happens to the others."

"You said the saviors are going to get them back? How will this be different?"

"I'm not sure. But the saviors are here! They've finally come, and anything is possible. I think they have somewhere to hide the children where Barakus can't find them again."

"Where could that be? I thought Barakus's men could go anywhere. That's what I've heard since I've been here, anyway."

"Yes, that's true. Except Jessamine, of course. Oh! Now I know... Well, that doesn't matter. I know a way we can help," confided Briar Rose, looking around to be sure no one was paying attention to them.

"Who? The Imaldi?"

"No. You and I and the weather," she said, lowering her voice and leaning closer until there was a spark between the two. Backing off quickly, she looked around to see if anyone had noticed. "Uh, maybe we should go to my room where we can talk in private without getting too...close."

*****

The strategizers were still in the library when Faye and Aliand found them. "Gabriene, Ebony, everyone! We have a solution to some of your problems!" exclaimed Faye excitedly.

"Faye, we have a multitude of problems. Which ones are you going to solve for us?" asked Behnam, turning to face them.

"I think the problem was originally Ebony's," suggested Faye with a teasing smile.

"You haven't narrowed it down, much, Faye. Who is your young friend here?"

"May I introduce Aliand de Phym of Camir. She's our new engineer," supplied Faye. "Aliand, may I introduce Lady Ebony, Lady Tasmin, Behnam, Falcon, Bass, and Jakar."

"Pleased to meet you, young lady, but what do you have for us?" asked Tasmin with a raised eyebrow.

"Here, look," suggested Faye, as she walked up to the conference table and set Aliand's first drawing down for them to examine.

Everyone stepped up, leaning closer to get a better look at her sketch.

"Isn't that...?" asked Bass.

"Yves. It's a completely accurate depiction of Yves and the

area around it," said Falcon, picking it up to examine it even closer. "I've been there before. The detail, it's amazing."

"Aliand, why did you sketch this? Have you ever been to Yves?" asked Jakar with a thoughtful look.

"No. I never left Camir before coming here. Mostly, all I've ever seen is the Duchy of Phym and Rim itself. I sketch what I see in my head. I always have."

"And these?" asked Ebony, taking the sketch from Falcon and pointing to the fixed wings above the people who were flying.

Faye produced the other sketch as Aliand continued, "These? Again, I sketch what I see. Sometimes, with...unusual things... mechanical things, I sketch how they work."

"You can build a hang glider?" asked Ebony, a note of excitement creeping into her voice.

"No. My father always scoffed at my 'little doodles,' as he called them, but if you know how to wheedle... Let's just say he allowed me to 'supervise' building some of my sketches. I can work with the carpenters and blacksmiths to get this built."

"I've already ordered silk for the wings. We just need to find the lightweight materials for the frame," added Faye.

"Aliand, come with me. Let's go talk to those carpenters and blacksmiths and see what we can do," suggested Ebony, taking Aliand's hand and heading out. "Tell me, what other marvels have you had built that your father didn't understand?" she asked as they left the room.

"Gabriene, I think we should tell all the Imaldi what we're doing. Who knows who else might prove helpful?" suggested Faye as they left.

"Well, well. No, I don't think so. They're too young, and they're untrained. We don't even know what they can do yet," prevaricated the wizard.

"We know more, now. When you bring Briar Rose and

Ciral together, they create stormy weather," commented Faye as she sipped a fruit drink.

"Weather? Really? Can they control it?" he asked, suddenly intrigued.

"Not yet, but I don't think it's a coincidence they have emerged from the woodwork right now. I think they are all supposed to help. Maybe they aren't all ready, but their help will be needed before this is over. I'm sure of it," insisted Faye.

"Woodwork? What...?"

"Uh...hinterlands? Do you mean you don't find it odd they have emerged from almost every corner of Persal right now?"

"She's right," agreed Behnam. "No one with magical ability has been found in almost two thousand years until now. Now, when the saviors have finally appeared. These three women may be our guides, but they are not going to do this alone. The Imaldi may be young and untrained, but they are in this as deeply as the rest of us." "They have a right to know what we're up to. They have a right to make a choice," added Faye. "After I fell through that waterfall in Seattle, I made a choice. No matter how young these girls are, they deserve the same respect you've given me. From what I heard when we talked to them, coming here wasn't a choice. Where they go from here should be."

"She's right, Gabriene. We're going to tell them what we're facing. Now and in the months to come. Then were going to find out more about what 'talents' they have. I have a feeling, we're going to find clues to their magical abilities when we do," agreed Tasmin, leaving no room for argument in her tone.

*****

Back in the Imaldi sitting room, Gaban was working with Debora, trying to discover what her abilities were. Madlene was helping keep the girl calm as they talked about her talents.

"Excuse me," called Faye softly as she entered the room. "Please, ladies, we need to tell you something before we go any further."

Expectantly, all eyes in the room turned toward her and Tasmin standing next to her. "Where are Briar Rose and Ciral? They aren't practicing their weather alone, are they?" she asked with a smile, hoping it really was a joke.

"I do be thinnin' they be in Briar Rose's room. Summat aboot talkin' anon gettin' too sparkly," answered Meland, with a shrug.

"Thank you, Meland. Would you go get them, please? They need to hear this as well."

Once everyone was together, Faye succinctly outlined what they were planning to do now and what kinds of challenges faced them in the next few months, maybe years, as they faced Barakus and his power. "There is no doubt in my mind you young ladies are going to be an important part of winning the battles in the upcoming war. It's going to be dangerous, and there are no guarantees you will survive. If you choose to go home, there will be no assurances you will be safe there either. You didn't have a choice when you came to the tower. Now, the choice is yours. You can join us and try to save all of Persal, or you can go home and wait for Barakus to come for you."

As she looked around the room, Cheri watched their faces carefully. Personally, she had her own doubts they could do it without the Imaldi.

Briar Rose and Ciral were the first to stand, saying, "We're staying," strangely speaking as one.

Debora was on her feet before they finished speaking, "And me."

Meland stood with a shrug. "I dinna come 'ere just ter go home agin."

Beloria looked up at Gaban before taking a deep breath and rising. "Lady Cheri, how old are you?" she asked.

"I'm fifteen. Not much older than you. Actually, I'll be sixteen on Carnival Day. If I can do this, so can you."

"I be in," agreed Beloria, nodding.

"Really Cheri? Are you sure?" asked Faye, turning to look at her red-haired friend. "I didn't think we'd been here that long."

"Eidetic memory, remember?" she whispered to Faye as she turned back to the girls. "Since we arrived, we have been attacked in Gaban's tower. Chased and attacked by Barakus's temple soldiers. When we went down the White River, Barakus did something to make the Vortex shift. When our crew was trying desperately to pull us away from disaster, I was able to send energy through the ropes, giving them the strength, they needed. Those are just some of the things I've faced. Lady Faye and Lady Ebony faced their own challenges. There will be nothing easy about what we're getting ready to do."

"I was getting ready to fight Barakus in the resistance. I may as well fight from here. I'll do whatever I can to help. Whatever that may be," Carlise said, bracing herself with determination. "Gaban, let's see if we can figure out what I can do."

"Debora, do you have a talent? A mundane talent that seems... more? Something you're really good at? Even too good?" asked Faye, turning to look up at the dark girl who was taller than she was.

"Music. I'm good at music. If you give me an instrument, even something I've never seen before, I can play it. I can play any song after hearing the first few notes. Not just some of it. Not just something close. The whole thing as it was meant to be played. My music has been described as hypnotic and mesmerizing. Some people have even been known to go into a trance while listening to it," she admitted, almost reluctantly.

"What about singing? Can you sing for us?" asked Cheri.

"No! No, I can't. I've been told my voice is sublime, glorious, and even entrancing. The problem is, it's literally entrancing. If I sing, I can make people do almost anything. I haven't been allowed to sing in public since I was three."

"Really?" asked Gaban, a thoughtful frown on his face. "Could you use this to get someone to say...confess to something?"

"Well, possibly but I don't know how to direct it at just one person. My singing has always effected everyone within hearing distance," admitted Debora doubtfully.

"We have a prisoner in the cells in the dungeon, why don't you practice on him? I'll be the only other one in there so we should be all right. Don't worry, the dungeons have never been used before. For being underground and a bit dank, they're not bad at all," he assured her. "We'll go down after dinner."

"Well, there's your power. Who's this?" asked Faye as a footman entered the room and bowed.

"My ladies, Master Gaban, Mistress Madlene, Lady Aliand's maid has been brought to the castle, and Lady Debora's uncle and brother are here as well."

"Bring them up, Philian. I'm sure Lady Debora would like to see her kin. Send someone to the smithy to find Lady Aliand. My ladies, where do you want us to put them?" asked Madlene, taking charge "Leha should have a room here, close to Aliand and the other girls," answered Faye thoughtfully.

"But, Lady Faye, she's a maid. I'm sure I could find a place for her in the servant's quarters with the other maids," objected the housekeeper.

"Here, she's a guest. I have another job in mind for her,

if she's willing. The men have been in the knights' academy. They might prefer to remain there. We'll leave it up to them," continued the petite woman, her mind churning with possibilities.

"Leha, welcome. Lady Aliand is with the smiths and carpenters, but we've sent for her. We'll get you settled into a room next to hers," said Faye in greeting as a woman in her midthirties entered the room. She was slight of build with pale hair done up neatly in a braided bun. Her gray dress was simple but elegant.

"Now that you're here in Lohi, you have a choice to make. I would like to hire you to be the house mother to the Imalda. There are seven of them, all about twelve going on thirty. They'll need someone like you to help keep them in line. Do you want the job?" asked Faye as she crossed to take the woman's hand and raise her from her curtsy.

"But...I'm Lady Aliand's maid. It's not for me to say," objected the woman in confusion.

"Not here, not now. Do you intend to return to Camir?" Mutely, the woman shook her head vehemently.

"Here, you have choices. You can choose to be someone different," said Faye gently as she drew the woman to a settee.

"What are my other choices?" she asked, trying to take in the concept of choice.

"Well, you can remain Aliand's chief maid, of course. Or if you have skills, like sewing or maybe, something else, we can set you up to apprentice in a shop in the city. What would you prefer to do?"

"It's my choice? Really? Would I be bossing Lady Aliand around?" she asked, warming to the idea.

"Yes and no. Within reason, you would make sure the girls behave themselves, but I don't want you to go on a vendetta against Aliand. You have to promise to treat her fairly. Treat her as you wish she had treated you. I'll make sure she understands how things have changed between you. This is going to be hard, so certainly you will be given a fair wage on top of your room. You will eat with the girls, and you will be provided with an appropriate wardrobe. So...will you take the job?" proposed Faye with a mischievous smile.

"You'll pay me? Along with everything else? Yes, I'll take the job!" replied Leha, finally getting excited by the possibilities of living in Lohi.

"Thank you, now excuse me for a moment," said Faye, rising to greet their next visitors.

"Ah, Lady Debora, would you introduce your kin, please?"

"Lady Faye, Lady Cheri, Lady Tasmin and Master Gaban, this is my uncle Ranjua and my brother Jondor of the Green Lizard Tribe of Mojar," she began as the men bent over in the ritual deep bow of Mojar.

"Uncle Ranjua, Jondor, these are two of the saviors of Persal. Lady Faye and Lady Cheri, uh...now of Lohi. Master Gaban is the wizard who will train me and Lady Tasmin is with the Saviors."

"We bid you welcome. We would be honored to have you stay as our guests unless you prefer to remain at the knights' college. I'm sure there's more for you to do there than we have to offer. Regardless, please remain for dinner with the Imaldi and for now visit with your niece. After dinner she will have an assignment," said Faye graciously.

"I will?" asked Debora, startled. "What?"

"It won't be hard, Debora. Nothing hard, I promise," said Faye with an enigmatic smile.

"Lady Faye, you're getting really good at this," said Cheri to her once shy guardian as they turned to speak to Meland.

Before they could begin talking to her, another page entered with a note for the young girl. "Here, Lady Cheri, would ye be tellin' me what it do say?" she asked, suddenly shy.

Cheri glanced at the girl as she took the note. "Of course,

Meland. It says, 'I am glad you're doing well. We can come visit at Carnival, if that is good for you. Da.'"

"Oh, that do be excitin'. He don' sound mad, do he? I do be glad," said the girl with a wide grin.

Cheri laughed with her. "No, he doesn't sound angry. You must invite him for dinner, and your brother too. Your family will always be welcome here."

"Will ye 'elp me write 'im?" she asked, eyes wide. "Yes, of course. Give me a moment. I'll be right back."

While Faye started talking to Meland about the depths of her talent, Cheri crossed to Madlene who was talking to Gaban. "Madlene, Gaban, Meland can't read or write. I think it's important we set up a school for any of them who need it. Madlene, what would it take to set up free schools for everyone in the city?"

"Lady Cheri? Everybody?" asked Gaban with an incredulous look on his face.

"Okay. I see the look on your face, and I know it won't happen immediately but let's start with all the children from the age of six through eighteen. They need to learn to read, write, and basic math. Oh, and history, for starters. And I mean all the children, no matter how poor. Especially the poor," she insisted, amazed at herself for being such a proponent of education all of a sudden. She had always taken her own education opportunities for granted. With her memory, she was reading by the age of two, so she had dismissed formal education entirely. Instead she had pursued her own interests in libraries.

When she returned to help Meland, Faye was trying to get the girl to open up.

"I be sorry, Lady Faye. I don' 'ave no talent. I be just an ordinaire!" she was objecting.

"Faye, may I?" asked Cheri as she joined them. "Meland, why don't you tell me about your ordinary day?"

"Surely ye don' wan' ter 'ere aboot dat. Me day be borin',"
she objected.?

"Tell us anyway. We don't know much about Persal or
Lohi so we might find it interesting," prodded Cheri gently.

"Oh! Awright. Well, after I do get up in the morn, I goes to
me da's shop below our place and start de fayer. Da says no
one kin start a fayer or get it 'otter quicker'n I kin. Tha's why
it be me job of a morn. Then I go in and eat the morn meal
wi' da and Gerad. Gerad usually be poutin' 'cause he has ter
make the morn meal. 'E thin's it should be me job, seein' as I
be a gel. Huh! Da sayed if'n he kin start a fayer like I kin, we'll
change," she said, grinning as she remembered her brother's
discomfort. "I thin' it be why Gerad went ter the smith's ter
'prentice."

"Well, Faye, that's it then," said Cheri, leaning back.

"What? What's it? She hasn't told us anything yet,"
objected the older woman.

"Meland, what else can you do with fire?" asked Cheri
with a look at Faye.

"Well, I ain' supposed ter talk aboot tha'. Da don' e'en
wan' me doin' them thin's agin," she objected.

"Don't worry, you won't get in trouble. I think this is why
you're here. Tell us, what else you've done with fire."

"Well...when I be little, aboot three, I used ter get flames
ter come out'n the fayer and dance 'em on the hearth. Scairt
me da somethin' fierce. Used ter yell at me a lot until I stopped
doin' it when he be there. 'E telled me oncet. I be getting' ready
ter set fayer ter de whole street. He don' ken I kin stopped me
fayer as quick as start it," she admitted.

Faye was smiling as she nodded to Cheri. "Of course,
the fire. Not only that, it looks like she's already learned to
control it. I'll go tell Gaban."

"Ye be thinkin' fayer be me talent? Fayer ain' no talent. It
jus' be me friend," objected Meland.

"That's exactly why it's your talent, Meland. Just think, you've already learned so much and now you'll get to learn even more. I'll bet we'll send you to the smith to work. Seems I saw an unused forge there yesterday," encouraged Cheri with a smile. "Now, let's get to work on that note to your father."

"Awright. Let's jus' not telled me da aboot the fayer. 'E be worryin'," suggested the little girl as Cheri pulled out paper and pen.

They were finishing when another page entered to announce. "Master Gaban, ladies, if it please you, dinner is served. The Imaldi are set up to eat in the petite dining room."

As Faye and Cheri were leaving to go to their own dining room on the main floor, Faye turned to Gaban. "You know, I really doubt only seven young girls in all of Persal have suddenly developed magical abilities. Just because these girls were called doesn't mean there aren't others out there. Both boys and girls, I'd be willing to wager. You might want to start by interviewing more of the children here in Lohi, for now."

As the two women walked away, Gaban shook his head. *What is it with these saviors and children, anyway?* he thought, shaking his head.

CHAPTER 27

Carnival!

Every year, at the full moon of the dragon, Lohi celebrated their unique independence from Barakus with Carnival. From early in the morning when they donned costumes and masks until dawn the next day when they stumbled into bed, their own or someone else's. They threw off all social shackles and partied. There was singing and dancing in the streets. There were parades both planned and impromptu. There were people on the streets selling food, drinks, masks, and anything else they could imagine someone would pay money for. In homes, great and small, were gatherings, ever-fluctuating, ever-changing. With the masks and costumes, the ordinary people mingled with the nobles. Social classes were ignored. No one asked. No one told who they really were. Everyone guessed.

Madlene and an army of seamstresses were busy making colorful costumes for each of the saviors and their companions. They also made copies, a dozen copies of each costume.

Ebony chose a costume common to this time, lots of material but so sheer as to barely cover the basics. On her legs, she wore a pair of harem style pantaloons with a very short feather skirt. The other basics were covered by feathers as well. Covering her bare skin were draped scarves of sheer blue-green floating everywhere. Her feathered mask, with a green scarf draped across her face, made her look like a bird. Her hair was tucked into a headdress also covered by feathers, trailing down her back. Cheri thought all those feathers on the top, which effectively hinted at everything while revealing nothing, would drive her crazy.

Cheri wanted something similar, but both Faye, her technical guardian, and Tasmin refused to consider it. Instead, they compromised on a costume common in Rio de Janeiro. Multicolored ruffles for the skirt, revealing her legs in the front with a train trailing in the back. The top had ruffled sleeves and bare shoulders. The bodice was bright yellow, cut low in front and with a bare midriff. Her headdress looked like a crown made of yellow feathers, and the mask was of red feathers sweeping to the sides, conveying a dramatic look.

Faye chose a costume commonly used at the carnivals in Venice. Swaths of teal silk covered with gray lace formed a wide, hooped skirt with a high neck coming up to her chin and long sleeves that came to point on the back of her hand. The headdress was also elaborate, but it was a silver framework filled in with more of the teal and gray cloth. The mask was a solid silver material. Once she was in costume, nothing of herself was visible. When Madlene's women finished it, Faye was quite pleased. She was fully covered.

*****

It was hours before dawn when the knock came on Cheri's door. Even so, she woke on the morning of Carnival humming to herself, "Happy Birthday to me. Happy birthday to me. Happy birthday, dear Cheri. Happy birthday to me." This was going to be the best birthday ever! She was finally sixteen, and the whole city would be celebrating. Okay, they'd be celebrating Carnival, but they'd still be celebrating.

After a hurried breakfast, Tasmin and Madlene hustled them all back upstairs to get into their fabulous costumes.

This carnival was the biggest event of Lohi's year, and they had to start off the first official parade, just after dawn. Of course, they had been drafted to start the celebration. They were the saviors, after all. There wasn't much time to get ready.

*****

Gabriene had sent Kitar, a short, stocky, auburn-haired man with a Samali mother and a Swaloh father, to the docks to look for Ciral's friends. Kitar thought it would be easy. Four men with dark skin, four feet tall, or less and a boat with a double hull. How hard could it be?

Instead he'd found no trace nor heard a word about any of them. If they'd come into Lohi, where could they be hiding. Well, the best course would be to look first for their distinctive boat, and that meant the docks. When he found not so much as a rumor, he started walking the shoreline.

It was early morning when Kitar headed east from the shipping docks. He was making his way to the good-sized fishing village of Sandy Spit, whose fishing fleet kept the city supplied with fresh fish. If he were a stranger in a strange land, he had no reason to trust, especially if he'd stand out the way these men would, he wouldn't go into the city, either. Better to hide in a smaller town where he might be able to find friends. After all, these men came from an island. Surely at least one of them was a fisherman too.

No one knew where the people of the village came from. They had appeared in the bay one month over a year after Barakus had taken over Kimball, now called Doome. Gabriene said they were refugees, but many believed they might be spies for Barakus. After nearly two thousand years, most of the people in Lohi had forgotten them. Those who remembered were either those who still didn't trust them or the fishmongers. The later just knew where to buy the best fish in the sea.

They were different from those in the city and the rest of Swaloh. Most of Swaloh was populated with people with a lightly tanned complexion, except the women of the nobility, of course, who powdered their faces to keep them pale. These people were deeply tanned like the sun off the water had cooked them to that toasty brown of a good roast chicken, fresh out of the oven. The people had a thick dark hair with a tight curl and they tended to be a bit shorter that what Kitar would consider normal. At six foot two, he was a head taller than the tallest of the fishermen. The women tended to keep to their stone cottages when strangers appeared, so he'd never seen much of them except their backs as they hurried away. It was the children who came running, laughing and smiling much like children anywhere when something new appeared. Only the littlest hid behind the older ones, peeking around shyly.

Kitar looked at the oldest boy. "Good morning, son. I'm from the castle, lookin' fer some strangers. The saviors up there wants ter see 'em. No one wants ter harm 'em. Kin ye help me?"

Eyes wide, he shook his head slowly. "Kin ye telled me who can?"

Slowly, the boy looked to the porch of a cottage farther down the strand before all the children took off running. In a matter of seconds, the only ones who could be seen were Kitar and the old man, looking older than Gabriene, sitting on the porch.

"Hello, Grandfather. Have you seen some short, black people around here? There's a friend of theirs livin' up at the castle who wants to see 'em. If'n they got the time. Leader's name be Cirroc," he said as he stepped up on the veranda.

"Whal, fishermens be out ter sea," he answered tersely.

"That's good. These men happen to be fishermen, I believe. Do it be awlright if'n I wait here wit' ye?" asked Kitar, pulling out a bottle of good mead.

"Umph," nodded the man, putting out his hand to accept the bottle.

Kitar settled back in another chair to wait. The fishing fleet would be returning by noon. As he sat there, the women nervously started emerging from their homes. They had work to do, and a stranger couldn't keep them from it for long. Shortly, a young woman came out of the stone cottage with more mead and fish, baked with slices of the citrus fruits from their orchards, farther up the slope from the sandy beach. Apparently, sitting on this man's porch qualified as being a guest. When she served them, she smiled shyly at the stranger.

With a nod, he smiled back but didn't deign to speak to her. It might offend his host, who was gently snoring beside him. Then he heard yelling from the children on the beach. The fishing fleet's red, triangular sails were racing across the waves, staying out of the shipping lanes where several merchant and warships were heading out. Well out in front of the fishing fleet was a low, strange boat without a sail. As it got closer, he could see the flashing oars, powering through the swells in defiance of the crosswind and a young boy, whose coloring said he was from the village, riding on a platform between the hulls. His gaze was focused on the fishing fleet behind them, and he was yelling loudly.

They were going so fast, when their boat hit the sand, it created two deep furrows in the beach. The boy jumped out of the boat and pranced about in jubilation. "Oohwee! Don be na una ken bate dem! I ain' e'er flan so. An I prom me dad'l ter sta far a water!"

Kitar didn't understand the boy's patios as he respectfully

approached the strange little men and bowed formally. "Sir Cirroc? Lady Ciral has moved to the castle and bids you and your companions to join her for dinner."

*****

Carnival was set to begin in the city's largest plaza, just to the west of the castle compound. It was the only area large enough to hold most of the people of the city and those who'd come in from the countryside as well. Every one of them was dressed in the best, most flamboyant costumes, they could afford. The crowd looked like a sea of flowers or the multicolored scarves magicians were so fond of pulling out of their sleeves. Ebony, Faye, and Cheri, escorted by Behnam, Bass, and Falcon dressed in equally colorful costumes made a procession to the central fountain and a temporary platform waiting for them. It was all very grand and stately which Cheri found somewhat absurd, considering how everyone was dressed. She also wondered why they called it a square when it was round. So very round, in fact, the fronts of the buildings lining it had concave facades, very subtle but there. The effect was to carefully preserve the circle of the paving and the grand fountain of stacked circles topped by a statue of a giant of a man symbolically sheltering Persal in the center. It was a representative of the savior. It was very effective, but it was also wrong.

There were musicians scattered throughout the crowd, and many were already dancing, singing and...well, drinking. She'd heard the maids talking, and there would be other activities as Carnival got rowdier. She was just a little nervous since, after they officially started Carnival, the six of them would be joining the party in the square. They were to lead the first dancing chain around the perimeter. After that, things would get really interesting.

Once again, Ebony took the lead as they joined Gabriene

and Tasmin on the dais. Tasmin's dress was very colorful and slightly risqué, but Gabriene had only changed into a pure white robe with gold trim.

"People of Lohi," her voice boomed as Gabriene gave it a magical boost. "Every year, you celebrate Carnival! A celebration to honor your faithful wait for the savior's arrival. This year, there is more to celebrate since your long-awaited saviors have arrived. Now, we celebrate once more before we begin the hard and dangerous work of freeing all of Persal from oppression, together. Today, it is time to sing, dance and party, one last time!" said the black woman, smiling brightly.

With her final words, Behnam, Bass, and Falcon jumped from the dais and turned as one to catch the women as they followed. Falcon led the way, lining them up. Several knights, also in costume, joined the line behind Faye before any of the crowd could get too close. As they danced away, the women were reminded of a conga line. They were to make a complete circuit of the plaza before breaking away to dance deeper into the city where the true deceptions would begin.

When they broke away to head down a side street, they also broke apart. Dancing together but no longer staying in a chain. Two of the knights stayed with them while the others led the conga line on another circuit of the square before they too left to dance down the main boulevard. Most of those who began by merely wanting to be close to the saviors would have lost them by then. Those who might be following them with other aims in mind had other distractions put in their paths.

Three blocks from their first turn, they were joined by six other dancers dressed exactly the way the saviors and their companions were. When the two groups broke apart a block later, Faye and Bass were with the new group while their doubles stayed with Ebony and Cheri. Two more turns and they met another group in identical costumes, and soon Falcon and Cheri went one direction while Ebony and Behnam went another. At times, their dancing took them through homes thrown open for Carnival, and as they passed through, each of the couples broke away to change while impostors took their places yet again.

Now, dressed in equally colorful, if less flamboyant, costumes, the six would make their individual ways to the northern gates where more knights, and their horses, awaited. The impostors continued to enjoy the citywide party well into the night.

Any watchers Barakus might have had should have been lost in the constant shuffle of people that had taken much of the day. Now, as Cheri and Falcon neared the northern gate, it got quieter. The heavy partying would be taking place in the multitude of squares in the large city or in the taverns, restaurants, and homes. The outer walls were no place to party. Before they reached the gate, Falcon pulled out plain brown cloaks from his pack, disguised as part of his costume. A block from the gate was a stable where six knights were waiting with another change of clothes. Everything they would need for the trip to Yves and Zabir was already packed in their saddlebags.

Cheri used an empty and thankfully clean stall to change one final time. The dancing, changing, and partying in general were already wearing her out, and they had a long way yet to go today. "Falcon, is Baby out there? They haven't tried to change horses on me, have they?"

"Baby's right here, Cheri. We finally convinced Gabriene your little mountain pony is sturdier, in his way than those warhorses the knights ride. He's also faster than the packhorses who're carrying all that armor. So, no, the disbelieving knights haven't switched horses on you at the last minute," he assured her with a chuckle, remembering how reluctant she'd been to ride at all.

The knights, with their large warhorses and the pages with their leaner mounts, had argued stubbornly that Cheri's pony would slow them down. It was only Falcon, coming to her aid, who convinced Gabriene differently. No one could deny Falcon's expertise with horses, and Behnam and Bass had both backed him up.

Cheri, for her part, was refusing to learn anew how to ride a bigger horse. She was comfortable on Baby, now. There was no way she was ready to change yet.

Emerging from the stall, in a dark-green riding outfit, she strode up to Baby. "We've a long way to go this evening. Are you ready?" When the horse nodded and pawed the stone floor, she took that for a yes and mounted in a smooth, practiced motion. Who would ever have thought a few months ago, she'd ever be able to do that?

Wrapped in their cloaks with the hoods raised, Cheri and Falcon followed two of the knights from the stable and out the nearby gate. They rode quietly while still in sight of the city wall, but once they rounded a curve in the hills and were out of sight, the pace got faster, they were riding hard for the Kindle Forest where Gabriene, Tasmin, Jakar, Suvaat, and Gurmail awaited with their squires and packhorses. Behnam, Bass, and Faye would follow in small groups with more knights. For this trip, the knights would make do with only three squires. Aliand and Ebony, with Galad and Jakar, were already on their way to Yves with her ingenious inventions, too many to carry on packhorses. She was aboard the *Mal de Verde*. The fastest ship left in port, when the rest of the marines were shipped out. She should reach Yves two days before they did. Hopefully, they would arrive several days before the last Black Ship who had been running into an inordinate number of obstacles in repairing their craft. The plan was to capture the stranded Black Ship before it relaunched. At least, that was the plan.

For now, they had twenty miles to cover before they could rest and another 250 miles in the next two weeks. From what Cheri had seen on the maps, some of that territory was going to be tough going.

*****

After dinner at the castle, Cirroc took Ciral aside. "We appreciate being invited to stay here, in all this grandeur, but what would we do? We are fishermen and hunters. We'll be back to visit, and you know where to find us, but we'll stay in the village and go out fishing with the fleet. They're due to leave soon. We had better be going as well," he said. "Good night, Master Gaban. Thank you for your hospitality. Ladies, so nice to meet you." And the four black halflings returned to Sandy Spit.

Madlene had provided strange costumes for them to wear while returning to the beach. The better to blend in with the celebrating city. Even children were allowed to stay out late on this one night. Capitalizing on this, Cirroc and his friends chased each other through the streets, pretending to be some of those children. As they ran, several local children ran with them, for a while, laughing and screaming before breaking off. A few minutes later, they were joined by more children.

They weren't running to go fishing; they were running to ready their boat for the secret mission Ciral had tasked them with. She and her new friend, Briar Rose, would be joining them outside the breakwater in Briar Rose's sloop. They didn't know exactly where they were going or what the mission was, but Ciral and Briar Rose had been quite emphatic, it was urgently important. But like the sea, there was always more beneath the surface when it came to Ciral.

Their mission was to stock the boat with as much food and water as possible and meet her and Briar Rose outside the breakwater. Briar Rose's sailing boat was small enough for one to pilot but large enough for all of them. They needed to hurry if they were going to be ready to leave with the fleet. They would also need to find a suitable place to stash the catamaran while they were gone.

*****

While the Imaldi hadn't been allowed to go out in the streets to join Carnival, Madlene had provided them with colorful costumes, so their dinner party was a mini carnival of their own. By the time the party was over and the guests not staying at the castle left, Ciral and Briar Rose had convinced Ciral's friends to meet them outside the harbor, later that night.

The costumes were perfect for their own escape since there would be partying in the streets to the wee hours of the morning. The trick was going to be sneaking out of the castle grounds without being seen since the castle was being guarded from would-be intruders. Ciral thought the key was in where the guards were looking. They'd been instructed to watch for intruders trying to get in from outside the walls. Not two girls sneaking out under cover of darkness and well shrouded in dark cloaks.

In the confusion of Carnival, getting out of the castle had been fairly easy, using the servants' corridors. From there they crept through the low hedges in the east garden, Briar Rose leading the way to the east gate. Beyond this gate was where the nobles lived, and she felt two well-dressed children during Carnival would be able to blend into the neighborhood and should be safer, at least until they had to make their way to the east end of the docks where Briar Rose's sloop had been taken.

There were pathways interrupting the hedges, here and there, but the most likely place to be caught was when they crossed the road paved in cobblestones next to the wall. On the far side was only a narrow strip of ground with tall, thin trees of a deep yellow. Hardly the cover they needed, but it was all that was available. Once they safely reached those trees, they slipped off their cloaks and put them in their packs. Among the yellow trees, they would blend in better in their bright yellow and light green costumes.

"Now, it gets tricky, so follow me and do what I do," instructed Briar Rose, once again.

"You know this is crazy?"

"So you keep saying. Now, keep quiet."

Ciral rolled her eyes. They had only gone over this about a dozen times once the plan had been made. Without another word, the two of them slid along the wall behind the trees, getting ever closer to the east gate and the waiting guards. When they reached them, the plan got really fuzzy. Briar Rose had said they would figure it out when they got there. Ciral found she was getting jittery as they got closer. The guards were being vigilant. Apparently, they believed the saviors were still in residence. Briar Rose had been sure they had already left, and she knew where they were going and why. Ciral had been unable to confirm any more than they were at Carnival. The only reason she had agreed to Briar Rose's scheme was because she knew Briar Rose was right. The same way Ciral had known she needed to come here. Doome! She didn't like feeling as if she had no choices.

Briar Rose turned, putting her finger to her lips and pointing ahead of her. There were two alert guards at the gate, standing at attention, their hands on the staffs of tall halberds, with thin, curved, blades coming to a sharp point. Then one of them whistled, making her start. Shouldering their weapons, they turned toward each other and paced the width of the gate, stopping and turning toward the grounds when they reached the other side. As they performed their maneuver, Ciral found she'd already flattened herself against the wall behind a tree. *Great! How were they going to get past them?*

The two girls stayed where they were while the men stood still for a few minutes, and then there was another whistle and a change of position. Briar Rose turned toward Ciral and mouthed, *Follow me,* before starting to slip behind the knights. Ciral followed while inside she panicked! What in Doome was Briar Rose up to? Then, something else occurred to her. Her father would be appalled if he knew how many times she'd cursed in her head tonight. She was going to have to watch that.

Briar Rose opened the postern gate as Ciral caught up and started to slip out. What she hadn't counted on was the loud squeal of the gate hinges in the quiet garden. Immediately, the two knights turned. "Who goes there? What? What are you two children doing here?" asked the whistler.

"We just wanted to get a look at the saviors, sir. We didn't mean any harm," stammered Briar Rose, turning to go and gesturing for the costumed and masked Ciral to go in front of her, out the portal.

"Well, it is Carnival, after all, but this is no place for children. Aren't you a bit young to be on your own? You'd best be getting back to your nanny."

"Yes, sir!" and they were away, off the castle grounds and running toward the docks, and Briar Rose's sailboat.

*****

When the last of them finally arrived at the campsite, bedraggled and exhausted, Tasmin was ready with the inevitable cups of tea. As she sat on a moss-covered log, Cheri sighed. "You know, someday, I would actually like to celebrate Carnival. It looked like a lot of fun."

"Well, well. There won't be another Carnival, will there? Carnival is there to celebrate Lohi's unique independence from Barakus. Once Barakus discovers our intentions, the war will begin. When it's over, we'll no longer be unique. All of Persal will have shaken off Barakus's yoke," said Gabriene pragmatically. "You're aware, once we rescue the children, we will be declaring war, aren't you?"

"I've been thinking about this, a lot, since we got here and that's not true, Gabriene. You have been at war for over two thousand years. Between Barakus's troops raiding for children and the oppression of the priests and their soldiers, you've had a very long series of cease-fires, but you've still been at war," corrected Faye.

"She's right," agreed Bass with a tight jaw as the others around the campfire nodded. "Look at Camir. Neigh on to two thousand years ago, Barakus wiped out the ruling family, unless you believe the rumors of a lost heir. Now the country has fallen into a constant state of political intrigue while the people have become nothing more than poorly, or unpaid, serfs. That's not what King Abnar of Rim was trying to build."

"There may not have been any open conflicts since Barakus retreated to Doome, but we've always been at war," agreed Falcon. "I've spent my life traveling throughout most of Persal, and except for Lohi, the people of this land have been held hostage for two thousand years. Even the rest of Swaloh is not untouched. They may not have any black towers but they know Gabriene can't really shield them. The rest of Persal may try to live their lives as if Barakus was but a distant threat until they go to town and see one of those black cathedrals, dominating the skyline. Or the priests and their soldiers come through town, taking what they want without payment. They hide their daughters and wives! Just as they find a new normal, there's another Taking, and they lose everything."

"Jamben has never stopped fighting, it's just not open warfare," objected Tasmin.

"You know, even if you discount what everyone has gone through for two millennia, I think Barakus declared war on Cheri, Ebony and I as soon as we came through that Doomed portal!" growled Faye.

"Then it's time long past for us to turn the tables," said Tasmin. "As for me, I'm tired and I'm going to try to sleep. We've a long way to go before we fire our opening salvo."

While everyone except the sentries wrapped up in their blankets and readied themselves for the night, Faye bent over the blank journal she'd found in the castle library. She was working on writing a chronical of their exploits up to this point. Wearily, she wrote of the jaunt through Carnival, trying to do the spectacle justice before wrapping herself in her own blanket for the night.

*****

Ciral and Briar Rose made it through the cavorting crowds still on the streets with barely any notice, but when they got closer to the docks, there was a noticeable difference in mood and costume. The sailors and dock workers were dressed flamboyantly and in colors just as bright but in a markedly different style. It was a style with knee-length, wide pants of a bright yellow or red and green or blue silk shirts open in the front, showing their bare chests hung with gold or brass chains. Their masks were painted in black, gray, silver or gold which appeared to be a mark of rank. Two young girls dressed as nobility would stand out, here. It was time again for stealth. Finding a quiet alley, they slipped in and pulled on their cloaks to cover their bright costumes. Then they donned small but deadly knives strapped to their waists. Once again, they kept in the shadows. Luckily, most of the mariners and stevedores were holed up in taverns and inns where the barmaids and harlots were. Carnival was in full swing, and the men staggering on the streets held bottles of rum or beer, making their way to the next tavern, looking for a better party.

They were nearing the dock where Briar Rose's sloop was tied. Unfortunately, it was tied at the end, and now the going was going to be much more dangerous. As they scuttled down the street, darting from doorway, to doorway, to alley, they were doing their best to stay away from the bars, but the closer they got to the docks, the more bars there were. Shortly after they passed one of the ubiquitous taverns, the door swung open and two boisterous stevedores in their bright blue pants and signature purple shirts, left open like the sailors but without the gold-colored chains emerged. They were almost past the two girls when Ciral stifled a sneeze, drawing the men's attention.

"Run!" snapped Briar Rose as she grabbed Ciral's hand, setting off sparks and drawing mist from the sea. Quickly, she dropped the hand and kept on running with Ciral close behind.

"Hey! Git back hare! Even on Carnival, ye should be abed," called one of them stumbling in their direction as they were lost in the dark.

"In here," whispered Briar Rose, tugging on Ciral's cloak, to pull her into an alley before starting to run, again.

"What are you doing? Aah!" yelped Ciral as she tripped over a large pile of...something squishy, going down hard.

"Come on, get up! At best they'll take us 'home.' I don't want to thin' about what at worst might be," hissed Briar Rose, pulling on Ciral's cloak, trying to get her up.

"Aah! My knee! I can't stand on it," cried Ciral in a low voice.

"Well, we can't stay here. Come on, lean on me, and keep our cloaks between us. We aren't that far from the *Bonnie Jean*."

Behind them, Ciral could hear the swearing and stumbling

as the big men came into the alley. Gritting her teeth, she managed to get up where Briar Rose could get under her arm and help her hop to the other end. There was some loud swearing, and a splat as one of their pursuers found the same pile of old clothes Ciral had tripped over. Then there was another bout of cursing as the other stevedore tripped over the first.

"What is it?"

"A drunk."

"Hey! Wake up!"

"Omigod, he's dead!"

The jumble of words followed Ciral as Briar Rose pulled her out of the alley. They were at the eastern edge of the docks. The pier at the end is where the sloop was moored, under guard, per Gabriene's instructions.

What? What were they saying? A dead man? She had stumbled over a dear man? Abruptly Ciral's mahogany complexion turned ashen, and she felt sick, as she pulled loose from Briar Rose so she could bend over and vomit.

Briar Rose turned back to her friend. "I heard, Ciral. It'll be all right. It's not like you killed him. Go ahead, get it out. We're almost there," she rambled, saying whatever came to mind as she watched for Gabriene's guard, their pursuers, or anyone else who might be around. Compared to the rest of the city, the docks were quiet. Since even the stevedores had the night off, it was almost peaceful. Certainly, quieter than any other time, night or day. She was trying to assess whether it was going to make it easier or harder to sneak onto her boat.

There, at the entrance to her dock, a guard, and approaching from the far end, another. When the two met, the first left the other there and started walking, his boots sounding hollow on the wooden walkway. Just before reaching the next pier, he stopped and turned smartly to walk past the other guard, away from the docks altogether. When he reached the end of the walkway, he turned smartly and strode back, continuing down the pier toward the waiting sloop and anything else that may be moored there. That was it! What else was moored on that dock? That could prove most useful.

"Ciral? Are you through being sick, now? I have a plan," she whispered to her collaborator.

"Yes, I'm fine, or I will be. My knee is still wonky."

"We can make that work for us. Cover up good in your cloak and hobble up next to the guard. You need to make him believe you're an old woman, heading for, let me see…I've got it! There's a smack down just past the sloop. Tell them you need to get aboard to get a good night's sleep. If they balk, just be real grouchy, like any little old lady who needs her sleep," instructed Briar Rose with a grin.

"How am I supposed to pass as an old woman of Persal with my dark skin? Oh, and what will you be doing while I'm pretending to be a grouchy old woman?"

"Don't be silly, they'd have to pull back your hood. These are Lohi knights. They wouldn't dream of being disrespectful of a grandmother. I'll be sneaking behind you and onto my boat where I can start getting it ready. Once they have both left you at the smack, they should go back to the end of the pier. Then, you'll be able to slip onto the *Bonnie Jean*."

"All right! All right! I'll do it!" grumbled Ciral as she pulled her hood lower and wrapped her cloak tighter, hunching her shoulders in the process. As she hobbled across the quay, she more than resembled a 'little old woman,' she was the essence of her grandmother.

Crossing toward the guards, she mumbled to herself, much too low to be heard clearly. "Where do she be getting' off givin' me orders! I ain' her dogsbody! She do 'ave a plan, do she? She ne'er asked if'n I might be 'avin' an idea. Humph!"

"Halt! Who be goin' there? No one is allowed without a pass!" called the guard.

"Pass? What pass! Do ye be thinnin' that oaf of a greatson o' mine be smart enou' ter give me a pass? Not afore he don lef' me in dat noisome inn, 'e dinnit. Whal, I cain get no sleep inna raxket 'neath my window at me inn so I needs ter be sleepin' on de smack, where I do belong. Now, do be getting' outta me way!" grumbled Ciral convincingly as she tried to push past the guard and hoped they didn't pull back her hood, regardless of what Briar Rose said.

"All right, greatmother. Me ma dinna rised me up ter be disrespect like. Let me take ye ter yer boat," offered the guard solicitously as the boots of his companion neared on the wooden pier.

"Umph! As if askin' fer me pass weren't disrespectin' me. We's gots differen' ideas on dat, boy!" muttered the dark halfling, keeping up her hobble as her knee started throbbing again. The limp got worse as they made their way down the pier.

"Greatmother, do there be anythin' I ken do ter help with the leg?"

"Jus' gets me ter me smack so's I kin get off'n it."

As they continued down the jetty, Ciral keeping up a running list of grumbled complaints and the guard getting more and more solicitous, Briar Rose slipped behind them, staying behind the guard in case the other one returned before she could reach her boat.

Finally, the guard and Ciral were passing her sloop, so she took a quick peek around the guard and ducked into the shadows by her low gangplank to port. As Ciral made her way to the low boat ten feet further down the quay and tied up on the starboard side, her hobbling was getting more and more pronounced. Briar Rose hoped at least some of the limp was being faked. The guard was steadying Ciral as she climbed the gangplank, so Briar Rose took her opportunity to scampered aboard the *Bonnie Jean* and lay flat on the deck, against the bulwark.

A few minutes later, she could hear the second guard approaching. "Hey! Watcha doin' here?" Ain' ye supposed ter be waitin' on de otter end?"

"I jus' be 'elpin' dis poor greatmother ter 'er boat. Don' worry none, de sloop be rijt dere, safe 'n' sound. Let's get back, anon."

"Aye! All right," the second guard agreed, and the two stomped off to the landward end of the dock.

After a few minutes, Briar Rose slowly raised her head to look after them, but they were gone and a fog was coming in. When she looked across the way, she could barely make out a small shape moving away from the smack. Ciral was coming.

Jumping to her feet quietly, she started getting the sloop ready to sail. She was almost ready when she heard a hoarse whisper, "Briar Rose! Please, I need help!"

Glancing over the bulwark, she saw Ciral leaning against one of the cleats securing the boat to the dock. Oh dear, the limp and been getting worse because the knee was worse. Quickly she scampered down the gangplank and braced Ciral so they could board the boat.

"I need to help," gasped Ciral as she sank to the deck.

"Help? I got here on my own from Jessamine. I think I can get out of the harbor by myself. After that, your friends will be here to help both of us. Sit here until we're away from the dock and then I'll get you into the cabin," sneered Briar Rose.

As she untied the mooring lines from the bollard, she took her first look at the bay. What? What was that? The bay was dotted with lights. Lights on small boats. Sloops, smacks, schooners, dinghies, and dories were floating out in the middle of the bay in close formation. Each one was loaded with partygoers. Carnival on the water! Perfect!

Once she had pushed off, Briar Rose allowed the boat to

drift away from the dock with the tide, for a few moments. Thinking furiously, the girl scampered down the gangway to the cabin and gathered all her lanterns and a strike kit. "Here, light these!" she instructed the other girl as she sat with her back against the bulwark.

While Ciral lit lanterns, Briar Rose hoisted sail and set out into the bay. Picking up speed quickly in the freshening wind.

"Halt! Bring back that sloop! It's under protection! Halt!" called the dock guard as he was returning to the seaward end of the dock. When Briar Rose didn't respond, he raised his bow and proceeded to begin firing arrows at them. A moment after that, he was joined by the other guard, but by the time the second bow was raised, they were out of range.

Laughing, Briar Rose moved Ciral to the rudder before she mounted the lanterns at bow and stern, saving the climb to the top of the mast for last. Then she took a moment to stash her cloak, revealing her Carnival costume.

"Here, give me your cloak. If we're in Carnival dress, we'll become just one of the many boats out here to party. They won't be able to find us, even if they manage to follow. Wooee! What fun!"

"Fumph? You call this fun? Having arrows shot at us is fun? Mangling my knee by tripping over a dead man, is fun? Briar Rose, your definition of fun and mine are quite different," grumbled Ciral as she tugged off her cloak.

"Haven't you ever done anything you weren't supposed to do? It's more fun if you get away with it. Your knee will heal, and as I said, you didn't kill that man, you merely tripped over him. No harm was done." Briar Rose laughed in return.

"Break the rules? No! I have never gone against the wishes of the elders. Until the dreams started, I was to be the new wise woman. My destiny was to marry Cirroc and care for my people. Defying the elders? Never!" answered Ciral, aghast at the very idea.

"Well, it's about time you started having some fun, isn't it? As your people's wise woman, shouldn't you learn to think for yourself instead of just following orders? In my experience, those who only follow orders aren't necessarily wise. It's time you learned that."

"What? In your vast experience of the last twelve years? No, make that nine years, the first three don't count. Now, you make me laugh, Briar Rose."

"No wonder you were so good at being a grouchy old woman, you're already halfway there. Just keep the rudder pointed to the right of the tower and don't hit any of the other boats, and I'll get you a wrap for that knee. I've got a salve in the cabin as well," said the dark-haired girl, scampering down into the cabin for a linen bandage. The sloop picked up speed, making it harder for Ciral to slip between the boats, many of which were anchored closely. As she maneuvered the sleek craft, her mind returned to what had happened when she took on the guise of an old woman. Something had come over her, aging her voice, making her bend as if with age. It had been more than acting as an old woman, she had become an old woman, as long as it was needed. Was this another 'talent'? Oops! She was sailing a little too close to a dinghy to avoid a brigantine when the boat dipped a little to port, and a tall young man bounded aboard. "Would ye be so kind as ter let me off near that smack over there?" he called cheerfully as she hurriedly pulled down her mask.

With a glance to where he pointed, she pushed the tiller to starboard and found a lane between the massed party boats. Apparently, this was part of the Carnival tradition.

"Oh, what fun! Just a tad closer and I'll swing right on over. Ta!" he called as he grabbed a halyard hanging down from the mast and swung onto the boat he was heading for. Or maybe, it was just another step on the way to his ultimate destination? Ciral found herself wondering what it would be like to be so carefree. Maybe fun wasn't really a bad thing. At least not all the time.

Briar Rose emerged from the cabin just in time to see their temporary passenger leave, and she immediately turned to Ciral. "What? What was he doing onboard?"

"Apparently getting a ride. He jumped on without asking just back there and, as you saw, dismounted here. I think we need to steer farther out from these party boats."

"There...there appears to be a clear lane there. It's even heading toward the Gate. Here, use this salve then bind your knee while I change course."

Finally bandaged, Ciral could feel a slight easing of the throbbing pain in her knee. As a healer of her people, she should find out what was in Briar Rose's salve. Right now, she was just too tired.

In due time, as they pulled away from the lively party boats in the bay, Briar Rose dimmed all but the light in the bow. That light she shuttered on three sides. It wouldn't do to be seen leaving the bay on a night such as this.

Once clear of the Gate, they sailed east, along the coast but far enough out to avoid the unknown dangers near the shore, Ciral kept a careful watch for the light Cirroc would shine to mark their position. It should shine any time now. "There! See that small inlet? They're there. Steer for the shore."

Quickly Briar Rose lowered the mainsail and used just the jib as Ciral turned the tiller. Sailing nearly blind, she dropped anchor a good half league from the beach. It wouldn't do to run aground. The catamaran had a shallow draft and could find its way all the way to the beach, but the keel on the *Bonnie Jean* was as deep as the mast above. Splashing could be heard as the twin-hulled boat was launched, bringing the supplies and men out to meet them. When they arrived, Saird and Saith jumped over the rail and started hauling supplies aboard, stacking them on deck. Being Saird and Saith, they didn't waste any time with small talk. When they were almost done, Cirroc joined them, starting to move things into the hold while Huge finished lifting things from the catamaran. "Okay, Huge. All done?" he called down the ladder.

"Aye. Be right up."

"What? Who's taking the boat back to shore? Cirroc, what?" asked a confused Ciral.

"Friend of ours, stowed away, now he's in it with us," explained Cirroc briefly as Huge clambered over the gunwale. "Don't worry, he's quite good with boats, and he'll be right back."

They had just finished stowing the last of the food and supplies when a singular wave came from the shore causing the boat to rock gently and a young boy with dark, very curly hair and deeply tanned skin came over the side. As he stepped down from the wave, he towered over the other occupants of the sloop, but he only looked to be about thirteen. One of the tall people, then.

Briar Rose turned to glare at the newcomer, while Ciral sat up straight to give him a good look. Seeing the reaction of the girls, Cirroc called his friend over. "Aenas, come over here. Let me introduce you to my friend Ciral. She came from Hawart, as we do. This is the owner of the boat, Briar Rose, and she's from Jessamine. Ladies, this is Aenas. He's the son of the fisherman we've been staying with. He stowed away 'cause he's sure he was meant to. He has a way with water and even more with denizens of the deep. I can't explain it."

"Let's get going. We've a long way to go in the next few days. We'll have time to talk, later. I do hope his being here doesn't cause us a problem, though," said Briar Rose, brushing off any more explanations. Even though she was sure, she knew why Aenas could do what he did.

"How can his being with us be any more of a problem than we're already in, Briar Rose?" asked Ciral acerbically.

CHAPTER 28

Off and Running

Patrice and Missy huddled together by the fire under a shared, thin, blanket. They had just been roused by the guards for breakfast, such as it was. Hender and the other boys were on the other end of the small beach with their own guards. The boys had been separated from the girls ever since they had been herded off the damaged ship. Patrice had come up with a plan to escape, but there were two problems with it. First was, Hender was at the other end of the beach.

Secondly, the plan hinged on the daily scavenging trips. Trips when the guards took the older girls out to look for food. Roots, berries, fruits, and anything else that might be edible. The boys were taken on hunting trips, but the guards did the hunting, boys just carried back whatever was killed. Patrice had been watching the guards and knew she could make a break for it with some of the other girls, but only the older children were allowed away from camp. Missy had to stay behind.

This was the dilemma she'd been wrestling with for the past several days, but now she had to make a decision. The ship was repaired, and they were reloading the supplies they'd scavenged after the wreck. Today would be their last chance. They could make a break for it, and Patrice could help as many of the girls who were willing to take the chance.

She was also hoping the soldiers would delay their departure while they tried to recover those who escaped. That might give her time to go back for Missy and Hender. She hated the plan, but it was the only one she had.

After she'd been taken to the jakes, she and the other scavengers were rounded up and herded into the woods to the west of the beach. She could see Hender with the other boys in the hunting party, going the other way. Hender caught her eye for just a moment. Did he just wink?

"All righ', ladies. This be yer las' chance ter get freshin' eats afore getting' back on de ship. Ye've already 'ad some o' de ships store, so I ken ye dinna wan' ter eat that any time soon," growled the sergeant in charge of the detail.

Obediently, the girls broke up into five groups of five, one for each of the five guards. Patrice thought all twenty-five of them were ready to run but knew it was possible some would give in to the fear.

As the girls searched for edible plants and roots, they moved farther and farther apart. First one girl would call out, "Here, look, another patch of wild turnips!"

Then another would exclaim, "Here! I've found some leeks."

"Leeks? We'll all smell like onions! Ew!"

"Especially the boys!" this comment was followed by giggling.

"Ere now! Shut it, if'n it ain' aboot food, I don' wanna 'ear it," snapped the guard.

Once the other groups of girls were well out of sight, Patrice gave a shrill whistle, and the girls dropped their vegetables from their skirts and ran. Each one set out in a different direction, away from where they'd started.

As Patrice ran, she thought she recognized another, faint whistle, coming from the east, where the boys had gone. Running as fast as she could, she hoped that whistle had come from Hender. The more of them who ran, the better the chances of getting away. Deftly, Patrice ran through the trees and ferns, frequently darting from tree to tree, putting as many between herself and the guards as possible. As she ran, she looked for a good place to hide until she could sneak back to camp. Then she saw Cantra flagging as the guard gained ground. Without thinking, Patrice cut over and called out, "Run, Cantra, run! You know that old man can't catch you!"

Immediately, the guard looked at Patrice with an expression of hatred as he changed tack and took off after her instead. Apparently, calling him an "old man" had hit a nerve.

Patrice had taken off before the guard did, knowing she would either get him to chase her or pause to decide which girl he wanted more. Patrice was heading back to a tall tree with wide leathery leaves and a hollow space among the roots. If she could duck in there without being seen, it was an ideal place to hide until it was safe. After that, she had another plan.

While the guards were looking for the runaways, she intended to go back for Missy and the other young ones. As she glanced from her path toward an outcrop she was passing, she felt a strong pair of arms encircle her, and looking down, she saw the sleeve of a familiar uniform. In terror, she started to squirm and kick, landing a good one on her captor's knee. As her captor bent down, dragging her with him, another arm came from nowhere, knocking out the man holding her.

Whirling, she swung a fist at the newcomer, landing a solid punch to his gut.

"Umph! I'm a friend!" said a quiet voice in her ear.

Now that she could see the newcomer, tall and blond with deep- blue eyes, he was dressed in shades of green. Not a guard then, reluctantly she nodded. "Who are you? Where did you come from?" she whispered.

"I'm Jesphar, part of the Sender Company out of Lohi.

We're here to rescue you and stop that ship," he answered in a low voice as the sounds of fighting came to them from the direction of the camp.

"Missy! I have to save Missy!" screamed Patrice, all thoughts of pursuit forgotten as she took off, back toward the camp.

"Wait! You can't go back. You'll only be putting yourself in danger," objected Jesphar, catching up to her in a few strides. "You don't run into a battle. Trust me, none of them are going to hurt the children. That's the one thing they agree on."

"Accidents happen, and Missy's so little. What if she gets in the way?"

"It's my job to protect her and you and all the other children on that beach. Now, do you want to help me? Start by tying that man up while I keep watch. Then we'll see how many of your friends we can round up. Barakus's men will be dealt with, trust me."

"But...but, Missy!" objected Patrice, worry etched on her face.

"I'm telling you, she'll be all right. Now let me help you," he insisted gently, taking the lead as they heard another girl screaming.

Off to the west of the campsite, the older boys had broken off running at Hender's whistle. Hender was running flat out when he noticed some young men he didn't recognize from the ship. These men were mostly tall and thin with light brown or blond hair, slipping through the trees silently, toward Barakus's soldiers. Curious, Hender circled around a thicket of tall bushes with wide green leaves to follow the strangers. He tried to remember what his da had tried to teach him when they'd gone hunting. Quiet, it was the most important thing.

Without warning, he heard a shout as Killen ran past, followed closely by one of their guards. Hender quickly ducked behind a clump of huge ferns and grabbed at the other boy, snatching him to the ground to hide them both. Meanwhile, one of the strangers took off running, soon overtaking the guard and bringing him down with a clout on the head from the hilt of his knife. As he flipped him over to tie him up, Hender pulled Killen with him to the stranger's side. "We be ter tie 'im up. Ye go getch 'nother," he said, recognizing an ally when he saw one.

"Thanks, I'm Villien. We're here to free all of you. Now, stay here while I round up the other boys. There are more of us out there, bringing down these brutes!" responded the stranger before he took off and disappeared into the woods. Searching out the other boys so he could bring them to safety.

"Patrice!" exclaimed Hender. "Stay here, I've got to find my sister!" he said to Killen before heading west toward where the girls had gone.

Getting to the other side of the camp was easier said than done. First, he had to skirt around the camp itself where there was the sound of battle. He only hoped Missy would be safe. Then, there was avoiding the guards who had gone out with the older children to gather food. Secondly, he had to avoid the newcomers. They were there to help, but they would probably try to stop him. Once on the western edge of the camp, he still had to find his sister, and there were girls running about everywhere. At last, while trying to avoid being seen by one of the strangers, he ducked into a thicket, only to find Patrice and several of the girls hiding there already.

"Hender! You're here! Now we just need to get to Missy. I'm so worried. They won't hurt her, will they? No, of course not. I know that. Don't I?" babbled Patrice as she hugged the breath out of her brother.

Gasping for air, Hender pushed her away. "I can't breathe, you're holding me too tight. Wait! Shh...do you hear that?"

Gennie cocked her head, listening, before answering, "Hear what? I don't hear anything."

"Exactly, they've stopped fighting. We need to go back to camp. It's time to get Missy."

"Are you crazy?" asked Cantra, pulling away as Patrice tried to get her to stand.

"What if the guards won? We'd be walking right back into their hands," added Gennie, with a shake of her head, shrinking back into the bushes.

"You're right. You three stay here until one of us comes back for you. If the guards lost, we'll send someone. We have to go get our sister," insisted Patrice as she and Hender made their way out of the bushes and cautiously headed back toward the camp.

As they left, Patrice could hear the youngest, Bella, crying. She was the third girl Patrice had rounded up, and she'd been crying most of the time since she'd been taken from her mother. Patrice couldn't fathom where all that water came from.

They made their way slowly, using all the stealth their father had taught them. Finally, they reached the edges of the makeshift camp without encountering any of the men, friend or foe. Maybe they had all killed each other? Not likely, but... where were the survivors?

Taking a closer look, they saw several of the younger children being released from the enclosures made of bound branches where they'd been kept. They also noticed several prone figures on the ground. Many of these were bound, and the rest were unnaturally still. It was the newcomers who were releasing the little ones. Several of the men must have been fathers; they were checking the children for injuries and holding those who were crying. With a loud cry of relief, Patrice jumped up and ran to Missy where a large bear of a man was holding her and swaying back and forth. Just as their own father did when Missy was upset.

As Patrice approached, Missy raised her head and asked the man, "Kin we go 'ome, anon?"

"No, I'm...not yet. We 'ave some'ere safe we be takin' ye to soon. Fer now, we be takin' ye ter a big, roomy ship. A ship ye kin explore. One where ye kin spend yer days on deck wit de wind in yer face."

"Sips? I don' be likin' no sips," lisped Missy with and emphatic shake of her head.

"Oh, I thin' ye'll be likin' this ship. She be named *Blue Pelican*. Do ye be knowin' aboot pelicans?"

Slowly, silently, Missy shook her head.

"Weel, I be tellin' ye wha' then. After we be settled onna ship, I be tellin' ye all aboot pelicans," promised the man as he handed the little girl over to her sister.

*****

As dawn broke, Cheri stumbled over to Faye and shook her shoulder. "Come on, breakfast is ready, and we'll be leaving soon, sleepyhead."

Groggily, Faye sat up and shook her head, trying to focus on a new day. Maybe staying up to write last night hadn't been a good idea, after all. Standing, she stumbled to the creek and splashed cold water on her face to wash away the sleep. Settling down on a rock by the fire, a plate of food was handed to her. "Thank you," she said, looking up to her benefactor. "Matew! You're here? I thought you were going to the knights' academy," she exclaimed, putting down her food before jumping up to give her friend a hug.

Matew blushed, "Lady Faye, I am pleased to see you as well. I did go to the college, but Sir Suvaat needed a new squire and he chose me. I'm squire to the second knight of Lohi!" he finished with thinly veiled pride.

"Matew! Are the packhorses ready to go? You can eat while on the road," came a strident call from Suvaat on the other side of the camp.

Faye and Cheri were as practiced in getting ready to ride in a hurry as any of the others by now. They'd spent over three months crossing most of the continent and when the others were ready, so were they. The knights around them appeared to be impressed. These were the same knights who had to be convinced Ebony was a warrior but who hadn't seen anything special about the other two saviors. They had yet to see Faye with her bow or Cheri with her knives. Well, they would. Before this was over, they would.

As they set out, Cheri and Faye began to discover how different it was to travel with a military contingent. Suvaat rode in the lead, with Gabriene and Gurmail. Ochwatt strode stoically to one side. No one told the sasquatch where to go. He was left to make his own choices. The squires brought up the rear with the packhorses. Scouts were sent ahead and behind. Falcon and Amalee became their roaming scouts. The man on his mount, the hawk in the air. Wolf, rode off to one side, disappearing in the trees, while the hawk circled overhead. Falcon showed his stamina and training with how quietly he would reappear next to Suvaat to report, before disappearing again, on the other side of the country lane. They made a point of avoiding the main roads.

Tasmin, Beloria, Cheri, and Faye rode in the second and third rank, but knights flanked them, keeping them secure. Bass kept close to Faye. Occasionally, he engaged the women in conversation when their pace would slow.

Behnam spent his time talking to the knights. Getting their measure. He's seen them playing at being warriors, but how were they going to be when battle finally found them?

Suvaat and Gabriene set a fast pace. Faye was surprised at the stamina exhibited by the short round wizard who had spent years studying in his tower with only rare excursions to the other realms or Gaban's valley. Did he have access to the fountain of youth?

Suvaat drove them onward, riding hard for a span then slowing to a sedate walk for half a span, and repeat. At noon, he stopped long enough to water the horses at a nearby stream and give the riders time to take a quick break.

Coming back from the jakes, Faye went over to talk to Beloria and grab some cheese and bread. "You ride very well. Where did you learn?" she asked.

"Neber been aside a horse afore," mumbled Beloria around a mouthful of food.

"Really, then, how...?"

Cheri looked up to watch the girl as she took a mouthful of water to wash down her bread. "I gets along wi' hanimal't. It jus' comes a' me."

Cheri shook her head as she remembered her first three weeks riding Baby.

"What's your horse's name? Did they tell you?" asked Faye, trying to keep up the conversation.

"Whal, 'is name be Dancer, now. Oncet it were Ginger, 'cause 'e bin a roan, 'e dinna lik dat one. Afore dat, it be Sir Meserscmidt. That be particular strange one an' 'e dinna lik dat owner, neither. 'E toldt me, if'n 'e 'ad 'is druthers, Dancer be jus' fine."

"Well, that's quite a conversation the two of you had. Did he happen to say what name he'd like if he could pick?" asked Faye, somewhat bemused by the matter of fact way Beloria related her story.

"He jus' say Dancer be fine. "Ow aboot yer unicor'? What be 'is name? Did ye asked 'im?"

"Uh, I don't have your talent with animals. I've been calling him Believer. It comes from a bumper sticker...saying on our world. 'Now I believe in unicorns.'"

"'Taint bad. Der ye wan' me ter ask 'im?" she asked with a quirked brow.

"Maybe tonight," deflected Faye, getting uncomfortable.

"Awright. Ain' it aboot time ter go?" asked the girl as the knights started to remount.

Once they were on the move again, it was the same punishing pace, and Faye leaned forward to whisper in Believer's ear. "Give us a little extra, boy. This is going to be a long haul. Uh...do you like the name, 'Believer'?"

The unicorn nodded energetically, and Faye could have sworn he was laughing at her. She should have known better than to ask.

When they slowed for a few minutes, Cheri pulled over next to her. "Maybe, instead of peppering her with a lot of questions, we should talk to her of our world," she suggested, with a nod in Beloria's direction.

*****

"Cirroc! Plea do tell'd dem. I kin makes it go faser. I kin e'en git de fishen ter keep us fra de rookers," begged Aenas, again. Just as he had been most of the night, when Briar Rose had been too busy keeping the sloop on the move and away from shore. The wind was in their face, so they'd spent the night tacking, back and forth. All the while, she was trying to teach Ciral and her friends how to pilot a ship with a sail. Now the sun was coming up, she had time to take a moment and find out what the boy was yammering about.

With a sigh, Cirroc nodded. "All right, Aenas. I'll tell them, but I don' know if they'll be believing. Ciral, Lady Briar Rose, Aenas has talents. He can get the water to do as he wishes. Then, there's the fish. They practically jump into his boat when he's fishing. You've never seen the like."

"So what has he been saying?" asked Ciral tiredly. Her knee was better, but she still didn't trust it.

"He's been asking me to tell you he can make the boat go faster. He can use the water to push the boat where you want it to go. Put that with your sail, and this boat will almost fly. He also says he can get the fish to help keep us away from the rocks near the shore. I know it sounds insane, but we've seen what he can do," admitted Cirroc, looking over at his young friend.

Briar Rose looked the tall young man over before exchanging looks with Ciral. "Imaldi," they said together.

"Wha'? Wha' be…Imald? Wha' ta' do mean?" asked Aenas in the village dialect.

"Untrained people with magical abilities are called Imaldi. Or more accurately, if you're a boy, an Imaldo. Briar Rose and I are Imalda. From what you're telling us, you're one of us," elaborated Ciral.

"Ah? T'er actual be a named fer it den? Do dere be other'n boyo's alike me? Kin ye do wha' I do?"

"You're the first boy to show up, as far as we know. Other than that, we each seem to have our own 'talents', Aenas. Well, let's see what you can do, then," urged Briar Rose.

With a shrug, Aenas walked to the stern, just to starboard of Saith, where he was manning the tiller and leaned over the side. The girls ran to the rail and either side of him to watch.

Aenas stretched out his hand to the water. A wave separated from the rest and rose to greet him, as an old friend. His fingers ran through the wave, encouraging more waves to join the first, and together they pushed against the stern of the boat. Gradually, at first, then faster, they could feel the boat surge as it sped up, pushing them due east. The sail started flapping as they lost the wind and Briar Rose, and Cirroc hurried to drop the canvas before it tore. Saird rushed to help Saith wrestle with the tiller.

"Not too fast, now," cautioned Briar Rose, worried about

the stress on her boat. "I think that's as fast as the *Bonnie Jean* can go."

"Nor ter worrit. If'n asket, I kin jus' pick 'er up ter carrin," said Aenas with a grin.

"What? Cirroc, what did he say?" she asked, alarmed.

"He said, 'Don't worry.' He can pick the whole boat up with the water and carry it, if you'd like?" he offered, hiding a smile.

"No! No, I think this will do nicely. Thank you, Aenas."

Aenas turned from the water and walked to the hatch to sit while Ciral watched him thoughtfully. "You know, at the castle, each of us had a story. I wonder, would you tell us your story, Aenas?"

"Me marm did go fisher'n wi da whe' I were aboot ter birthin'. Da try't ter stop 'er. She warn't 'avin' none of it. Said it 'ad ter be. E'er since I be born't, I be akin ter water," explained the tall boy with a shy smile.

"Do you know, I think I actually understood all of that," said Briar Rose with a smile of her own.

"Let us know if you start getting tired," instructed Ciral shyly. This tall boy was quite cute, even if he did talk oddly.

"Ah only's get it startled. Oncet it gets ter goin', It'll go till I be sayin' stop."

"Well, isn't that handy? I wonder if I could do the same with wind?" wondered Ciral.

"Wouldn't that be more dangerous? Aenas's water is only here, around the boat. If you start a wind, how would you control it once it was through blowing on the sails? I don't think it would be the same at all," objected Briar Rose doubtfully.

"Well, if we go according to your plan, we're going to have to learn to control my wind, and your lightning before we reach Yves. The sooner we start, the better. We'll need to control that and the weather as comes with it if we're to be any help," insisted Ciral.

"We'll start this afternoon, then. Right now, we're making good time, and there's no way anyone from Lohi can catch us. There's still a lot I need to teach everyone about sailing a ship. Well, perhaps all of you except Aenas. If he's spent his whole life at sea, he may be able to teach me a thing or two. I built the *Bonnie Jean* with my greatfather, and no one knows her better. Now, if the rest of you come here, we'll go over raising and lowering the sails. Then I'll teach you how to tack..." Briar Rose's instructions continued through the morning.

It wasn't until two spans after high sun, after lunch and a short nap for most, Ciral dared attempt to harness the power of the wind. In order to propel the ship, she stationed herself behind Huge, manning the helm, while Briar Rose cautiously took up a position on the bow. They weren't ready to join their powers yet.

First, Aenas bent over to the wave propelling them, and their speed slacked as the ocean dropped. Then Cirroc and the twins raised the mainsail. Once they were ready, they all turned to watch Ciral expectantly.

Taking a deep breath, she closed her eyes for a moment and gathered the air around her close, like a warm blanket. At least, that was how it felt to her. Opening her pale eyes, she stared past the waiting sail to the east, where they were headed and beyond. With a deep breath, she started to blow. Slowly at first, then harder.

The wind picked up, heading toward gale strength quickly, causing the mast to lean toward the bow.

"Slowly, Ciral, slowly!" called Briar Rose, taking a step toward the stern before stopping herself. The original gust was almost enough to rip the sails.

Mutely, Ciral nodded and dialed back on the wind, letting it build gradually as she directed the rising breeze toward the mainsail, but unavoidably, it spilled out and broadened, the longer she continued. Once she had it well started, she let it go. Time to see how long it would continue on its own.

For a half a span, it continued to increase in volume. Then it evened out, but like many things in nature, once it was started, it was inclined to continue, and the wind in the sail lifted the sloop as it skimmed over the waves. Briar Rose turned to look down at the water and saw most of the hull had risen above the crest of the ocean below.

"Weel now, we be skippin' aloonga, ain' we?" said Aenas in delight.

"Yes, we are. The question is, how long will it last? I mean, it's fast and doesn't seem to be putting a strain on my ship, but is it indefinite like Aenas's wave?" asked Briar Rose, getting to the heart of the matter.

"Yes, yes, indeed," agreed Ciral, unable to quit grinning as she watched the full sail drive the boat due east.

After a full span, Briar Rose called across the deck to Ciral. "All right, how much can you control it? Can you pull it back? I'd like to check the mast for stress."

Ciral looked up from where she'd been talking to Aenas and nodded. Again, she closed her eyes for a moment, feeling out the texture of the wind. Then she smiled as her eyes opened. Turning to the stern, she started to inhale slowly. Almost immediately, they could feel the wind slacken off. It was working, but how long could she keep it up? Briar Rose could feel Ciral's energy as it waned, even at the other end of the sloop. "That's enough, Ciral. It's back to 'normal'! you can stop," she called.

Aenas, who was standing next to her, shook Ciral's shoulder when she didn't stop. "Cira! Cira!" he called when she still didn't respond. In desperation, he brought his hand up to cover her mouth. Ciral slumped to the floor as she stopped inhaling, then her eyes fluttered before she lost consciousness.

Racing across the deck, Briar Rose stopped short as she felt the energy rising inside her. Ciral was close as a sister to her already, but they didn't dare come in contact. Fretfully, she paced and watched as Cirroc and Huge tried to revive her.

"Is she all right?" she called.

"She's breathing. I think she's just sleeping. Harnessing that gale took the wind out of her. Huge, take her below, we'll let her sleep it off."

Briar Rose let out a wry laugh as she backed away from the door to the cabin, "Well then. Saird, can you help me check the mast? We need to look for stress from top to bottom. I wish we could check the keel as well. That wind put a lot of stress on both of them, and we can't be sure the wave didn't do any damage either."

Saird grinned and nodded, rushing to follow her.

"Coo! Ain' she summat? Ah kin chock de keel inna morn. Jus' needs more'n ligh'," volunteered Aenas as he turned from watching Huge disappear.

Briar Rose noticed his look and smiled as she chose to ignore it. "How? Never mind, we'll see in the morning. Saird, help me rig a couple of bosun's chairs to haul us up," she said, instead.

A few minutes later, the strangest sound came from on high as Cirroc, Huge, and Saith looked up in amazement. Saird and Briar Rose were laughing. Most amazing was Saird's laugh. It sounded strange coming from the quieter of the two brothers who seldom spoke.

*****

Aliand stood in the prow of the Mer de Verde as it skimmed across the waves, sails billowing in the wind. Wildly, the breeze whipped her hair about her face, and she laughed.

Why couldn't her father have been in shipping? Maybe then she'd have been allowed to travel on the ocean before. For the first time in her life, she felt free! Well, and truly free! The rising sun behind her was shooting sparkles to rival diamonds across the water. It was grander than all the balls with all the nobles in their finery, it was simply the most delightful thing she'd ever seen.

Lady Ebony was on deck in a loose, white shirt and pants with a black tie at the waist. Hardly stylish but it appeared to be very practical, as she went through a series of exercises. She had started slow, with simple movements but soon she was moving quickly, and the movements got more and more complex.

Jakar was perched on a hatch, puffing on his pipe and watching her with appreciation. She was certainly graceful.

The knight Galad stood on the quarter deck, watching from the helm with a slight sneer on his face. He was obviously not impressed with Ebony's agility as she jumped and tumbled across the deck, cleared of sailors. Those who were not needed aloft were lining the rails and watching with much more appreciation, as were the squad of twelve soldiers who were assigned to the knight and Lady Ebony.

When the lady was finished and paused for breath, the crowd of sailors and soldiers along with Aliand and Jakar applauded and cheered, but Galad merely clapped slowly as he descended from the bridge to the main deck. "All very energetic and graceful, I'm sure. Not very useful in a real fight, of course," he drawled.

"Really? Would you care to test that theory?" asked Ebony with a wicked gleam in her eyes.

"Against me? You do know I have never lost in battle, don't you?"

"Well, I can't wield a battle-ax, broadsword, or mace

as you can, but I think I can hold my own in hand to hand combat. I'm game if you are."

"I know you're tall, but I've got both height and weight on you, but if you insist," capitulated Galad, removing his short coat and chain mail while looking at the gathered men. Although he was sure he would soundly beat Lady Ebony, he could hardly refuse in front of this audience. It hardly seemed fair. He was four inches taller and about seven stones heavier.

With a condescending smile, he returned her bow with one of his own.

Jakar jumped out of the way and moved to join Aliand. "This should be good."

Aliand turned from the sea to look down on the little man. "What do you mean?"

"The big man do be a bit arrogant, and I do believe Lady Ebony be about to bring him down a peg or two. That is always fun to watch," he said with a grin.

"I fail to see how this is proper behavior for a lady. Even one from another world," she said as she turned from the sea to lean against the rail as the battle began.

"Being a lady has little to do with what is proper, Aliand. It has a great deal to do with how you serve your people. If Ebony cannot convince the men of our world she can fight, and beat them, how can she ever lead them? If you watch the saviors, I believe you'll learn what a lady really is. Now, watch."

Ebony had started to circle Galad when he thought he saw his chance and grabbed it, rushing her. Before he could reach her, she stepped aside and turned to watch him run past before beginning to circle again.

"Are you going to fight, or are you just going to dodge me?"

"Don't worry, we'll fight. Care to try again?" Ebony taunted, making a "come hither" motion with her hands.

Goaded, Galad charged again, this time looking for her move and moving with her as she dodged. Instead of continuing to retreat, she moving closer, grabbing his right arm, she spun away to her left, leveraging him over her hip and onto the deck.

The clapping and cheering from the onlookers was deafening as she backed away, waiting for Galad to jump to his feet and turn again to face her. Jakar was cackling in glee, and Aliand couldn't help but smile. Ebony, on the other hand, was watching for just this reaction as she crouched a few feet away.

Galad didn't rush her right away, this time. Instead, he adopted her strategy of circling his opponent to get her measure. This time, Ebony rushed him, going low at the last minute and sweeping her leg in an attempt to knock his legs out from under him. Galad backpedaled and barely managed to avoid the maneuver.

"Your moves are tricky, I'll give you that," acknowledged the knight with another bow. "While that's all well and good for close combat, what if you face an opponent with a sword? Or for that matter, a mace or battle-ax?"

"As I said, I can't wield most of those heavy weapons, but I can handle a longsword or a scimitar or a knife. I can not only use a knife for defense, but I also have a set of throwing knives. I may not have Cheri's proficiency yet, but I'm getting better. Against the heavier weapons, I can move in close, where they can't reach me. Then my style of fighting is effective enough. If it comes down to a contest between brute force and agility, the advantage is mine. Don't tell me, once you have your armor on, you don't slow down," replied Ebony, standing straight now the fight was over.

Then, without warning, Galad, who had moved closer, went to grab her once more and, once more, found himself flying through the air and hitting the deck, hard. This time, he lay there laughing. "Oh, ho! Well, at least you don't let your guard down. Bravo! Lady Ebony." Once the battle was over, Jakar scampered over to congratulate Ebony, giving her another of his cakes for sea-sickness while he was at it.

Aliand returned to watching the sea, a thoughtful look on her face. A few minutes later, the cabin boy came up. "Lady Aliand, you're wanted in the carpenter's hold."

"Well, if she couldn't be on deck, at least she could be doing something constructive. Creating these hang gliders and making them light enough to work was a challenge greater than anything she'd ever been allowed to tackle back at her father's holding. The plan was to get the first one finished and ready for Ebony to test before they reached Yves. Then, once they had one working, they would finish the other nine frames they'd brought with them. There was a lot of work to do in the next two weeks.

CHAPTER 29

Falling in the River

Their small troop had been on the road for just over a week, traveling hard and avoiding cities and towns whenever possible. Twice they had crossed lethargic rivers rather than going through the townships built around the bridges. Cheri was feeling gritty and worn, but she highly doubted they would be staying at an inn tonight. As they made their way down the steep slope from the cover of the forest toward the riverbank, Baby's step was surefooted. The weight of the warhorses caused their hooves to slip on the muddy incline at times. When they did, Cheri would look over at Falcon and they would grin.

The city below was Berentii. It sprawled on either side of a deep gorge over the Cabriloh River where the Swaloh River came from the west; the south fork of the Zabir River dropped from the north; and the Camir River came tumbling from the Kintal Mountains in the east to meet just north of the city. From there it raged through the gorge as if in a hurry to get to the ocean. Where the three rivers met formed the boundaries between Camir, Zabir and Swaloh. The Cabriloh River itself was the boundary between Swaloh and Camir, twisting and turning as it made its way south.

Here the boundary between Swaloh and Camir was the gorge. On the western side, was Swaloh. To the east, was

Camir. Zabir was to the north of the Camir River. As they rode down the road from above, the differences of the city showed in the rooftops. On the west were mostly slate roofs with only an occasional cedar roof, near the bridge. On the east, there were a few slate roofs on larger buildings but most of the eastern roofs were of cedar shingles or thatch.

What really caught Cheri's attention was the tall black spire on the Camir side. It loomed in imposing menace over the city, casting its sinister shadow far past the city wall in the afternoon sun.

When they finally hit the road and turned toward the city gates, Baby trembled for a moment, reflecting her own nervousness. This was the first time since Dhwittle they might have to face the priests again. When she bent down to calm her horse, she was startled to find she was on a pale palomino gelding. Looking around, she saw that Faye's hair was a dark-brown as were her eyes. Believer was black and looked a lot like Desert Wind. She imagined her own looks had also been changed. Then she glanced down at the green charm she wore around her neck. Gaban had given it to her before leaving Lohi. It was designed to mask her "aura" from magical detection. Well, this would be its first test. Looking at Faye, she caught her looking at a similar pendant in blue. At least, she wasn't being paranoid, exactly.

Glancing back up, she realized they were almost to the city wall and she caught Suvaat looking back at them with a slightly puzzled look on his face. When their eyes met, he shrugged and turned back to the guards waiting at the gate, his glance briefly taking in the raised portcullis.

Apparently, the priest loitering at the portal wasn't there officially as the guard were careful to ignore him completely. He only bothered to look at their troop twice when he noticed Ochwatt, striding next to Gabriene, as they made their way into the crowded city. Cheri let out a sigh as she watched the crowd. Farmers were on their way out, heading home with their empty carts from the market. Merchants were closing up their shops for the night. There was a lot of talking and laughing as people passed acquaintances. These people weren't much different from the ones she had seen while in Lohi. The poor, the middle class, and she was sure, the affluent had been under Gabriene's protection, even though they didn't recognize the wizard as he passed.

Cheri was entirely expecting to ride straight through both cities and put as much distance between them and civilization as possible once on the other side. She was mildly surprised as knights and squires started breaking off in small groups, heading down side streets from the main thoroughfare they'd been traveling. At first, she thought this might be a way to minimize their profile while riding through the city of Berentii in Camir, at least until Suvaat turned into the Knight's Shield, a good size inn next to the Swaloh side of the bridge.

"Ladies, we'll have bathwater sent up as soon as possible," offered Suvaat once they were inside and their rooms had been secured.

"Ahh...what a wonderful concept. A hot bath!" exclaimed Cheri dramatically, as she followed Tasmin, Beloria, and the innkeeper up the stairs. Faye was right behind her.

When Faye and Cheri entered their room, Cheri looked around at the narrow single bed before turning to her friend, "I thought we'd be crossing the bridge and leaving the city before making camp tonight."

"So did I, but I'm grateful we'll be getting hot baths instead," answered Faye as she sank into the only chair.

An hour later, fresh from their baths and in clean clothes, they met with Gabriene, Suvaat, Behnam, Bass, Falcon, Tasmin, Beloria and Ochwatt, of course, in a private dining room with smooth tables from a striped wood. Matew stood against the wall behind Suvaat, in case he was needed. In the corner were grooved boards for some sort of game and on the walls were dartboards. Dartboards? Some things didn't change. Sitting at the table, just outside the door, were two of the knights with another of the squires, but no one acknowledged them. Bodyguards? Ridiculous! There were already four grown men and a rather large boy in his late teens in the room. Not to mention Ochwatt. Actually, from the look on Beloria's face, as she looked shyly at Matew, there might be an even bigger problem looming on the horizon.

"Is it safe to stay here tonight? I thought we were avoiding civilization," asked Cheri with a look at Suvaat with his mocha skin, close-cut reddish-brown hair, and hazel-green eyes. That seemed so weird to her, but it was also in keeping with Behnam's coloring. The biggest difference was the short hair. Behnam's was in long loose curls, just past his shoulders. Not as long as Ebony's, of course, but still, long and carefully combed.

"This side of the gorge is still in Swaloh and under Gabriene's protection. That priest you saw at the gate? Tolerated as long as they're alone, no Komas soldiers. There's also a regiment of soldiers from Lohi, led by some of our best knights, stationed here. Once we cross that bridge, we can expect things to get more...unpredictable," he responded with a smile.

Cheri's heart skipped a beat. Wow! That smile had star power.

"If we're still in Swaloh, and under Gabriene's protection, why have we been roughing it?" asked Faye as she buttered another chunk of warm bread.

"Well, well. Misdirection, my dear. We were attempting to confuse the trail. Making it harder to be followed for as long as we can. My magic does not hinder mundane observation.

Barakus has spies, everywhere," elaborated Gabriene with a raised brow.

"So what happens tomorrow? Once we cross the bridge?" asked Cheri.

"Well, well. Hopefully, not much. We'll cross in smaller groups to be less visible and meet up outside the city. If those talismans Gaban has given you work, you won't set off any alarms with the priests and once we regroup, we can continue without incident," said Gabriene with a shrug.

"Do you mind telling me when everything's gone according to plan? Okay, maybe the deception at Carnival, as far as we can tell. Since we arrived, that would be the first time. Personally, I doubt our luck will hold out once we're in territory under Barakus's influence," commented Faye acerbically. "Who will I be partnered with this time?"

"We'll only split up until we're well clear of the city. Faye, you will be with Myself, Behnam and Gabriene. I presume Ochwatt will remain with the master. Lady Cheri, here, will be with Bass, Gurmail and Denahar. Lady Tasmin and Beloria will be with Falcon and Matew. Matew will be masquerading as Beloria's brother. I believe he did that with you, at one time, and is quite good at it?" explained Suvaat.

Faye smiled at the memory, looking at Matew where he was talking quietly to Falcon. "He is still my brother. Family isn't only a matter of birth, you know?"

"That reminds me. How did you pull off that trick when we came into the city?" asked Suvaat, looking at Faye, and then Cheri, curiously.

"Well, well. What trick would that be?" asked Gabriene, suddenly interested in something besides his ale.

"It appears these ladies can change their appearances, when expedient. Not only that, they can change the appearance of their horses as well. It's a neat trick, and I can see the usefulness, but I would still like to know more. If you please?"

Faye glanced at Tasmin, who gave a slight nod and a shrug.

Behnam, Falcon, Bass, and Matew watched her but refrained from saying anything. This was for Faye to share.

"It wasn't me...us. My horse...he isn't a horse. He's a unicorn. He...masks us, sometimes. When he feels a potential for danger and if we're close enough together. He has other abilities as well. How much faster did we get here than you expected, Sir Suvaat?" she asked.

"Actually, we've made very good time. We didn't expect to get this far for another four days. Why?"

"Believer can revive us and the horses. He gives us more energy and stamina. The trick is to help, but not too much. Too much and he gets wearied, which could be dangerous for us all," explained Faye, revealing more of what she knew. The parts she thought Suvaat and the others should know.

"Hah! A unicorn? You expect me to believe your stallion is a unicorn? I don't want to disillusion you, Lady Faye, but unicorns are myths at best, or extinct if they ever existed."

Faye glanced at those who knew the truth. "No, Sir Suvaat. No, they're not."

Suvaat followed her gaze. "Do the rest of you believe this nonsense? Just because it's a white stallion doesn't make it a unicorn. This is ridiculous. Master Gabriene, do you believe them?"

"Well, well. Yes, yes, I do. I've heard the stories of their travels, and I believe the old things are returning to this world. The things we call myths, the ones Barakus threatened, went into hiding. Now they're coming back to us."

"Well, all right, but a unicorn? Where did you get a unicorn?" asked a very confused Suvaat.

"Actually, the unicorn came to me when I was called to Gaban's valley to fetch the saviors. I was buying horses, and when I left the town I was in, this white stallion showed up. I was concerned he and Wolf wouldn't get along, so I tried to shoo him away. Well, that, and I was sure he must belong to someone. Such a fine stallion doesn't usually run around free. Then I put him in the remuda with the others. Funny thing though, he and Wolf got along fine. No problems at all," explained Falcon.

"When they arrived at the village, I knew immediately what he was. It wasn't until later I realized I was the only one who was still a virgin. No one else could see his glowing horn," elaborated Faye. "When we left the village, the children could see him, but they didn't say anything. When we met Matew, he knew. Of course, Believer can hide his nature when he wants to. Even from virgins."

Suvaat's pale eyes slid to Cheri for a moment, when Faye mentioned being the only virgin but it was so fast, Faye wasn't sure it really happened. Cheri noticed though and ducked her head.

"I can see where all of this is going to come in handy and you've answered a lot of questions. Thank you," he finally said as he considered their revelations. Rising from the table, he suggested, "We should get to bed. Tomorrow's likely to be a demanding day."

*****

The Mer de Verde lowered her sails as the sun rose over the horizon. Menaril was already in the crow's nest with Ebony, waiting to haul the hang glider prototype up to the top of the mainmast for its maiden run. Sailors were hanging from the ratlines to keep the glider from fouling in the lines. Aliand stood on the deck below, watching her creation being hauled up and holding her breath every time a sailor missed and it bumped against the mast or tangled in the lines. She knew it was sturdy enough, but each bump made her second guess all the work they had put into it.

As the ship slowed, Aliand's hair was pulled from the elaborate braid she wore and whipped around her face by the sea breeze, and she wished Lisha had come with her. When she'd been told of the maid's new position, she had been furious. Until Faye informed her in no uncertain terms people were not possessions and she wouldn't be getting any preferential treatment as an Imaldi. After that, she had tried to adapt with all the grace she could muster.

Currently the plan was for Ebony to take off from the mast, soar over the water and return to the deck. Aliand just hoped the machine worked as it was supposed to and Ebony really did know what she was doing. There were just too many ifs about the whole thing.

Menaril had been training with Ebony on how to properly open and secure the framework once it reached them. Ebony's biggest concern was the weight. They'd gotten it down as much as possible, using leather for the hinges and lightweight wood for the frame. Well, no time like the present to try this out. Once the glider was ready, Menaril held it tightly while Ebony climbed up on the rail of the crow's nest. She was wearing a pair of trousers borrowed from one of the thinner crew. They were short on her but covered enough. This wasn't something she could do with culottes flapping about. It only took five minutes for her to settle into the cradle and get strapped in. As the morning wind freshened, she motioned for Menaril to back off and took flight.

Ah, she was soaring. It had been far too long since she'd been aloft. Oh, the exhilarating freedom! Well, this was a test run on new equipment, best she settle down and fly straight, as it were.

First, she let the updrafts carry her aloft. Then she tilted down and slightly to landward as she started circling back toward the ship's deck, far below. It was about forty-five minutes after her liftoff when she touched down successfully on the center hatch. She was laughing in triumph when she looked over at Aliand who seemed to be gasping for air. "We did it! Aliand, you're brilliant! That's one of the best flights I've ever had. Oh, my dear child, you need to let me teach you how to fly. You deserve it," exuded Ebony.

Aliand was grinning uncontrollably as she shook her head. "Creating it was my reward, Lady Ebony. I'll forgo the actual flying, thank you anyway."

Around them, Jakar, Galad, and the entire crew were cheering in admiration.

As Menaril folded the glider up, returning it to the hold, Galad stepped up to Ebony. "That was truly amazing. You are indeed a surprising woman, aren't you? Now, you'll just have to train the solders we brought with us to fly as well."

Ebony looked up at him saucily. "Just the soldiers? Not you? I thought you would be up for any challenge, but maybe I was mistaken."

Galad's jaw twitched as he returned her smile with curved lips that didn't meet his blue eyes. "Are you implying I ask my men to do anything I wouldn't do myself?"

"No. Not at all. I'm implying you might have a problem with... heights. Of course, I could be mistaken."

Galad glared at her for a moment. "All right. Tell me when you're teaching the men what to do, once they take off, and I'll be right there. Then I'll be the first off that Doomed crow's nest," Galad conceded, as he took off his jacket. "Then, after we've learned to fly, you can teach me some of your fighting moves. We're going to be dropping on those ships with nothing more than a knife, so we need to be able to counter their swords."

"Done!" agreed Ebony, ducking her head. She didn't want the tall blond to see the look of triumph in her eyes.

*****

Suvaat and Faye led the first group out of the Knight's Shield. Gabriene, on his Tobiano mare, Jessi, was close behind and next to Behnam who was watching their back. Ochwatt, as usual, was striding next to the wizard. The bridge gate on the Swaloh side of the gorge was manned by a complete squad of soldiers overseen by a knight. Those leaving weren't stopped, but many coming from Camir were briefly questioned. As they passed below the wide arch, Faye looked up and saw murder holes where arrows could be fired down on invaders. Then, at the far edge was a raised portcullis. This city might have one name, but it was definitely two cities.

The bridge itself was wide enough for two wagons to pass and still have room for pedestrians and horses on either side. On the Camir side, Faye could see another gateway, but this one was squared, instead of the graceful arch behind them. As they passed beneath, toward the checkpoint, Faye noted the defenses seemed to be the same as the Swaloh side. Okay, guarding against each other. There would certainly be no one coming up from the deep gorge below. That drop was definitely unsettling. She only hoped Cheri would handle the crossing well.

When they passed through the gate, the priests took a good, long look at their party, especially Ochwatt who was too tall to be inconspicuous, but they weren't stopped. Gaban's charms seemed to be working.

Berentii in Camir was nothing like the city in Swaloh. The houses were mostly wooden, and the cobblestones of the boulevard needed repair. The people in the streets appeared to be much like those in Swaloh, but the shops had fewer wares in their windows. This explained the cedar and thatch roofs when slate was available and would have been so much better.

"This side of the city doesn't seem to be as prosperous as over in Swaloh. Why do these people live here, on this side of the canyon?" she asked as she looked at the people around them.

"They are Camirians. For centuries, before Barakus changed everything, Camir and Swaloh would engage in wars. They were born here. Their parents, grandparents, and greatparents, going back thousands of years, were born here, on this side of gorge. Many of them have never crossed that gorge and seen what life could be on the other side. Those that have are not believed. If they're allowed to return at all. Life in Camir is not easy for any but the nobility, Lady Faye. Berentii is governed by the priests, so it's even worse here than in the country," explained Gabriene, moving closer so he could speak quietly.

Faye could only shake her head, but she knew there were places like this in her world as well. Sometimes, ancestry can mean everything. Lowering her head and closing her eyes, for just a moment, she said a silent prayer for these people.

Going through the northeast gate was much the same as crossing the bridge. The priests only gave them a cursory once over before moving on to the travelers behind them.

On the far side of the northeast gate, the road soon turned east as it found the southern bank of the Zabir River, winding its way from the mountains to the north. Then, they climbed past a series of stunning waterfalls. The first one had a drop of only a few feet from a rock-bound pool. The next one was higher and once they reached the top they were greeted by a stretch of rapids. A quarter mile on was a curve in the river and beyond that the third waterfall. It was ten feet wide with at least a twenty-five-foot drop. The sound of the water was resounding off the rocks on either side and the droplets of water in the air were sparkling. Faye's breath was taken away for a moment. Finally, as the road continued to climb and rounded another bend, they had reached the piece de resistance. The final waterfall was at least fifty feet high and thirty feet wide as it thundered in echoes down the valley behind them. Here, the road left the river and came back in switchbacks, climbing the steep slope. Once they reached the top, the road leveled out on a mesa. To the south, a forested hillside defined the other side of the road.

*****

Meanwhile, a half hour after Faye left, Tasmin and Beloria set out with Matew and Falcon. When they passed beyond the gateway, into Camir's Berentii, Beloria began to squirm. She didn't much like cities anyway, but this one felt particularly foul. The poverty and looming church tower made her feel like she was being watched by a predator.

She found herself urging Dancer to go faster, but Falcon grabbed her reins to pull them back. "I know this is no place for someone of the wild, but we'll be out of here soon enough. We don't want to draw attention, do we?"

Her eyes slewed toward him for a moment before she shook her head. Drawing attention could mean being detained, and she didn't want to remain any longer than necessary. Instead, she closed her eyes and trusted Dancer to keep her safe until they reached the eastern gate. Then she opened her eyes, trying to see the land beyond the city wall.

As they emerged into true sunlight, she realized how dark and oppressive the city had been. Here were crofts and farmland that fed the city. The homes of the farmers were low and made of stones cleared from the fields with thatched roofs. They seemed mean to Beloria as she compared them to the spacious farmhouses she'd seen dotting the Samali countryside where she'd grown up. Well, at least they were out in the clean air, or at least clean when the farmer didn't keep pigs. She'd never cared for pigs.

As they left the eastern end of the valley, she turned to look back and realized they had been climbing since they left the city, but now the real climb would begin. They were headed toward Rim, and the road had begun to meander up the path of least resistance to climb into the heights of the Kintal Mountains before breaching the Hero's Pass and traveling on to Rim itself. Of course, they weren't going to Rim. Falcon led the way as they came to a fork and turned north, toward Zabir.

Just as they reached the sixth switchback, Falcon headed into the woods, following what appeared to be a game trail. Beloria smelled as much of man as animal on this trail. It was evident to her; this trail was frequently used by men, but it wouldn't be so obvious to the casual observer.

Once they were out of sight of the road, Beloria started shifting uneasily in the saddle.

"Is there something wrong, Beloria?" asked Tasmin from behind her.

"No. Yes. I 'ave de urge ter change, yer see? I ain' never fel' this afore."

As she spoke, Falcon, who was in the lead, stopped to look at the young girl. "What do you want to change into, Miss Beloria?" he asked curiously.

"Well, a wolf an' tha' sure be strange. I ain' never seent a wolf afore."

"No! You're just a child. I won't have you wandering in strange woods alone!" objected Tasmin, shaking her head.

"This is why Gabriene brought her along, isn't it?" asked Falcon, turning to the older woman.

"But she's no older than my oldest granddaughter. She's too young to be wandering these woods alone," Tasmin insisted.

"If she were going to be wandering as a girl, I would agree. Remember, Tasmin, she'll be a wolf. These woods, this section of the woods, aren't hunted. She'll be safer than we are," insisted Falcon.

"Okay, girl, give me Dancer's reins and find a place to disrobe.

Just don't go too far," said Falcon.

Tasmin pursed her lips but kept them closed as Beloria dismounted and handed over the reins. "Lady Tasmin, would you collect my clothes after I change?"

Tasmin nodded, disapproval still on her face as she dismounted, so Beloria could go behind a large tree. When the huge red wolf emerged, Tasmin couldn't help but jump, and Falcon and Matew had trouble keeping the horses calm. Then, the wolf was off, racing down the trail ahead of them as if freed from all constraints.

Tasmin collected the clothes and put them in Beloria's saddlebags before mounting Anabelle.

Without another word, Falcon turned his horse Wolf about and continued down the trail, following the red wolf.

Tasmin found herself trying to look past him, waiting for Beloria to return although she knew it was much too soon. Well, she was still a grandmother. She was going to worry until the girl returned and there was no help for it.

Being a game trail, it didn't cut straight across to the river road taken by Faye and Suvaat. Instead, it wandered about, going up and down. At first it was more up than down, but then the decline became more noticeable. Beloria ran, following the trail, but even more relishing the freedom. Why had she ever resisted changing? Then her nose drew her aside. There was the distinctive stench of men ahead. Men with evil intent and unwashed bodies that was particularly offensive. Quietly, the red wolf padded around where they lay waiting to find out more. Suddenly she stopped and crouched to crawl closer, settling into a bush. There, seven thugs with bright and shiny swords. The swords looked familiar, but for now it wasn't important. Quickly backing out of her hideaway the way she had come, Beloria turned to run back through the forest to Falcon and the others.

As she loped back into sight down the trail, the horses started to dance and paw. Falcon's mount, Wolf, reared. Abruptly, she skidded to a stop and waited, with head cocked, for them to calm down.

"S...Sir Falcon," came her distorted voice from the wolf's muzzle. Talking like this was so...odd. "Der be mens waitin' aheed."

"How many? Can you count when you're a wolf? How far?" he asked quickly.

"Course I kin count. Dere be sev...seven mens. A short run, mebbe longer if'n yer not a wolf. What do be done? Me wolf thoughts told me ter fight, buts I ken I shouldna do it alone."

"Quite right. We'll do this together. Matew, off your horse," he said, dismounting from Wolf and giving Tasmin his reins along with the other two horses. "We're going to follow Beloria, quietly, and set up an ambush of our own. Tasmin, lead the horses down the trail and make no effort to be discrete. We'll want them to think we're all still together."

Beloria took off through the woods with Falcon and Matew quietly following. Amalee had swooped down to flit through the trees since she couldn't see from above. It wasn't long before Beloria lost the men and had to go back. It was so frustrating, trying to slow her pace to match theirs, even though they were moving quickly, for men. After a while, Falcon waved her closer. "All right, go around behind them and start to howl. Let them know you're there. Make them uneasy. Keep howling as you get closer and try to sound like a pack. Hopefully, they'll start to move away from you and toward us. With any luck, you won't have to show yourself. I don't want to give them an opportunity to attack you. Do you understand, Beloria? No matter what your wolf instincts are telling you, don't attack."

With a disdainful look, Beloria nodded once and took off as the men continued toward where the thugs had made camp, waiting for a traveler to rob. In a remarkably short time, the bloodcurdling howl of a wolf pierced the air. A moment later, there was another howl, closer and east of the first. The next one was closer yet but to the west. The waiting men were looking around, toward the north, wondering if an entire pack had picked up their scent. This is what Falcon had been hoping for.

"I be tired 'o waitin' fer 'ems ter get 'ere. I kin 'ear they's 'orses. Let's go. We kin give dem beasties summat else fer dinner asides us," said one. The way there was no discussion, he was evidently the leader. Mounting their horses, they headed for the trail, right between Matew and Falcon with their knives out. Quietly, the scout and squire waited for them to pass before quickly grabbing the two at the rear and cutting their throats. Falcon was dispatching the third when Matew's second catch squirmed loose and turned with a yell, ready to fight as he pulled his shiny new sword.

Now, Matew's knife seemed hardly enough against the longer reach of the sword. Soon Falcon, with his own drawn sword, joined them but so did the other three bandits, attracted by the sound of steel on steel and the curses coming from their living companion.

By the time the others reached them, Matew was finally able to draw his longsword, but they were still outnumbered, four to two. Matew rolled his massive shoulders and flexed his recently healed arm. They could do this.

It quickly became apparent to Falcon that these men were not the poorly trained soldiers attached to the priests and churches throughout Persal. These men knew how to fight and how to use their longswords. Not only that, they were outnumbered, two to one. He hoped Matew had learned enough while training at the knights' academy in Lohi, brief as that had been.

Falcon didn't have time to worry about his young friend as two of the well-trained bandits attacked. They kept trying to spread out so he'd have to reveal himself to one while fighting the other, but he'd fought two on one before, and he danced back, using the trees to force the two together, again.

The sound of clashing steel nearby brought his attention back to Matew, momentarily, but he didn't dare look away from his own attackers. Out of the corner of his eye, he saw Matew take a nasty hit on his left thigh while the other man moved closer for the kill.

Then he heard a low growl followed by a surprised yell as a streak of red fur and muscle surged into the fray, knocking the sword out of one of the assailant's hands, propelling the man to the ground. When he landed the knife in his belt was pinned beneath him. Desperately, the man raised his left arm to guard his face and neck, but the wolf was enraged, tearing his arm ruthlessly until the wolf ripped out a large chunk, taking muscle and tendons with it. Once his arm was useless, the wolf went for the throat, and the man ceased fighting, the life draining from him in a pool of blood.

While Beloria was taking down her man, Matew managed to kill his last attacker from one knee with a vicious up-thrust. Falcon had stepped closer to one of the men he was fighting, getting under his guard with a savage slice across his stomach. Leaving him bleeding out on the ground.

Looking around, Beloria saw Tasmin was tending a deep cut on Matew's thigh, and Falcon was disarming his last opponent. It was over. Embarrassed by the blood all over her muzzle, Beloria turned and ran toward the smell of fresh water. There was a creek skipping its way down the hillside not far from the battle. When she returned, she was relieved to see; her kill and the other dead were gone. The wolf in her wanted to eat the prey it had killed.

"That was nice fighting, Matew, considering how little time you had to train in Lohi," said Tasmin as she sewed the skin back together.

"Uh...me da...ahh...were a knight oncet...," the boy ground out through a clenched jaw, trying not to cry out in pain.

"Well, that explains a lot," said Falcon as Beloria shook water from her dripping but clean muzzle.

*****

The final ones to leave were Cheri, Bass, and Gurmail. Suvaat's lieutenant Denahar was coming with them as well. When she mounted Baby, Cheri noted he still looked as he had on entering the city. Evidently, Believer could make the changes last, at least for a while. She guessed that was a good thing, as long as it wasn't permanent.

As they set out for the bridge, she concentrated on looking up. Up at the buildings. Up at the rooftops and occasional spires and domes. Up at the first, graceful, gate as they passed under it, right behind a huge wagon stacked with heavy looking boxes. The wagon that was blocking her view to "up" now they were actually on the bridge.

"Take care of me, Baby," she whispered in his ear, leaning forward before closing her eyes as she intended. Oh, dear! Mistake! Big mistake! She was much too close to the edge, and her eyes looked down, down, into the deep, very deep, gorge, full of mist. There wasn't even a bottom. She couldn't see the bottom! Reflexively, she grabbed Baby's neck tightly and closed her eyes. *Oh dear, oh dear, oh dear.*

Looking over at her briefly, Bass caught on immediately and moved closer. "Cheri, my dear, why don't you move over here, closer to the middle of the bridge? I'd really like to see more of the view, and this wagon seems to be blocking everything," he said as he pulled his horse back, and let Baby pull ahead so he could maneuver to the outside. Luckily, Baby moved without any aid from Cheri who was frozen in her saddle.

"Lady Cheri! Cheri! You need to sit up now, we're approaching the Camir gate, and it's not a good idea to draw attention," he hissed as she refused to let go of Baby's neck or open her eyes. "Cheri, you don't have to open your eyes, but at least sit up. You know how sure- footed Baby is." Finally, she sat up unsteadily, but Bass continued to talk as the wagon ahead of them was stopped. "Well, they've stopped this wagon. I wonder what could possibly be on it? I certainly hope they don't open every single crate..." And on, and on, until they had gone around the wagon and through the gate.

"Cheri, you can open your eyes now. We're back on solid ground. Lady Cheri?"

Hesitantly, Cheri opened her eyes to look around the Camir city of Berentii. As they cut off toward the northeast gate, she wasn't impressed. "It hardly seems worth crossing that chasm to get here, does it?" she asked Bass.

Looking around, Bass's eyes turned cold. "You could be right, but you were very brave, none the less," he answered, smiling when he looked down on her.

"Are you crazy? In case you didn't notice, I was petrified with fear. That's not courage."

"Did you know you were afraid of heights before we left the inn?"

"Well, yes. The plan was to keep looking up, if worse came to worse, to close my eyes I just didn't close them soon enough," she said, shaking her head in humiliation.

"But you crossed the bridge anyway. Being afraid doesn't make you a coward. Doing something even when you are afraid, that makes you brave, Lady Cheri."

"Thank you, Bass. I appreciate it," she said with a weak smile.

Three-quarters of a span later, they passed the last of the priests and headed out onto the River Road Faye had traveled earlier that morning. Cheri found the waterfalls soothing after her harrowing experience on the bridge but she didn't appreciate the climb to get past them. Faye and her group, along with Tasmin and Falcon were supposed to be waiting for them by the shallow ford they were going to use to cross the north fork of the Zabir River. A ford, she liked the sound of that. Much better than walking a tightrope called a bridge over thin air.

*****

After Beloria told Matew and Falcon where to find their assailant's horses, even Tasmin agreed, having Beloria continue to scout ahead as a wolf would be prudent.

Pushing thoughts of what she had just done out of her mind, Beloria ran free through the woods. She was reveling in the feeling coursing through her as she ran around bushes and trees adjacent to the game trail. Her nose twitched constantly as the smell of habities, whirrers, and other game would flash by. After a few leagues, she didn't tire so much as lose momentum, and she took to trotting, keeping a sharp eye on her surroundings but nothing new appeared, and she couldn't smell any unfamiliar humans either.

Finally, she did hear the jingling of harness and smell of human and horse, but these humans smelled familiar. It was the rest of their party. Unwilling to spook their horses, Beloria turned before she got too close and headed back to Tasmin. There weren't any more bad men out here, and it was time to return to being a twelve-year-old girl.

Falcon had taken note when the infiltrators at the castle had killed themselves and pulled their captive's left hand with the poison capsule the moment he'd disarmed him. Now, he was tied over one of the spare horses they'd acquired. The other six horses were strung out in a line behind Matew, who was bringing up the rear, his thigh securely bandaged.

When Beloria appeared, Falcon leaned down to ask, "Did you find something?"

"Ye...yeah. Ta ends an' ourt frien's. Tasmin, I be readik ter be me," she answered, moving over to a nearby tree trunk.

Quickly, Tasmin dismounted and pulled Beloria's clothes from the saddlebags. After leaving them behind the tree, she returned to Anabelle and remounted. From behind the tree, she heard the sound of retching as Beloria became human again. At least she now knew, the girl was aware of what she had done. Knowing Beloria was safe, she was anxious to check on Faye and Cheri. Ah, the joys of being a duenna.

A league after they started moving again, they descended a final drop of four feet to the River Road where Faye, Gabriene, Behnam, and Suvaat were waiting. Then jingling harness and stamping hooves drew her attention down the road and here came Bass, Gurmail, Cheri, and Denahar. When she looked across the ford, she thought she saw movement in the trees. The rest of their escort were waiting. In front of them was the Zabir River, wider and shallower than farther west. It was easy to see the ripples of the small rocks and mud beneath the few inches of water.

Suvaat led the way with Falcon, his captive, Tasmin and Beloria. Matew, with his string of horses, was right behind. Ochwatt and Gabriene were next to cross. Then came Bass, Faye, Behnam, and Cheri.

Partway across, Faye saw a bright-red bird fly overhead, and she turned suddenly in the saddle to watch it pass, throwing Believer's step off, just a bit, but with Faye not sitting straight, she lost her balance. Riding close to Cheri as they crossed, she grabbed at the other girl and down they went. The water Faye landed in was just downstream from the ford and a little deeper as well. She floundered as she tried to rise. Behnam and Bass both jumped in after her, and Bass reached her first. "Faye, let me help you," he said as he reached her.

"Oh, I'm all right," she responded automatically, pushing him away in embarrassment.

While Faye was splashing about, Cheri was still in the ford. Dripping, she managed to pull herself up with Baby's reins, and the two of them started to wade toward shore.

Bass was standing on a slippery rock, and Faye's push was just enough to topple him over and down he went. Behnam came to Bass first and offered a hand to help him stand, but Bass slipped again, pulling Behnam down with him. As the two of them were sorting themselves out, Faye was still floundering on the slick bottom, stumbling into deeper and deeper water.

Three feet doesn't sound so deep, but when the river bed is covered in algae coated rocks and the river current is getting stronger, pushing harder, staying upright becomes a real challenge.

Faye was being propelled downstream by the current, pushed toward the boulders as the water got deeper and the rapids started. If she survived that, there was a waterfall a quarter of a league away. Alarmed, Believer charged around those still making the crossing and clambered up the rising bank. His horn started to glow as he raced downstream, running past Faye as the glow of his horn continued to grow, making his horn visible to all. Once well downstream of the thrashing woman, he stopped and directed his power to her, bolstering her strength.

Behnam and Bass regained their footing independently, fighting against the current as Bass headed for Faye. Hesitantly, Behnam turned toward shallow water and Cheri when she stepped on a loose stone, twisting her right ankle and fell in the water again, losing Baby's reins as she started to drift away. Before she literally got swept up by the river, the tall black man stood with legs spread for stability between Cheri and the waterfall. Nobody noticed when the glamours the unicorn had put on Faye, Cheri, Baby, and himself were washed away. Apparently, Believer had something else to worry about now.

Cheri managed to gain her feet, favoring her right side and fighting against the river, trying to hobble to shore when she stumbled on another slick rock and lost her balance, again. Helplessly, she was tumbling through the water as it got faster and deeper. She was a good swimmer, but this was going to require much more than that as she fought her heavy clothes as much as the current. She was angling toward the shore as she neared Behnam who was still on his feet and fighting to catch her before she got swept away entirely.

Downstream, Faye's battle was more desperate as she struggled to keep her head up, and her clothes tried to drag her down. Believer's added strength was helping, but the rocks were slick with water and algae. Determinedly, she kept trying to get closer to the northern shore. Bass was actually swimming downstream, using the current to get closer as he cut across to intercept.

On the far shore, Falcon turned his prisoner over to Denahar while Gurmail joined Suvaat who was bringing in his waiting men. Gabriene was already standing on the shore, mumbling under his breath as he gathered his power to try slowing the river but holding back that much water wasn't easy. As always, nature had a mind of its own.

Ochwatt loped downstream, looking for an anchor to help him reach her. Uneasy with the rushing water.

A moment later, Gurmail and Suvaat's squad were riding down the bank of the river, a good distance past where Faye was trying to swim to shore. Once far enough, the men dismounted in a hurry and six of them tied themselves together with rope before making a human chain to cross the rapids only a hundred yards in front of the waterfall. Ochwatt caught up and took the anchor position in the rapids, standing fast. If Bass or Behnam failed, they were going to catch the women and get them to shore. At least, that was the plan.

Faye reached out to grab at a boulder sticking out of the water. The first one was rounded and too slick with spray to get a firm hold. As her grip slid off, she reached deep, drawing more of Believer's energy as she swept her arms, swimming to the next boulder, this one more rugged with handholds. In order to remain there until help could reach her, her best option was to latch onto the upstream side. Desperate, her fingers grabbed and clung to this strange lifesaver. Praying Bass would reach her soon.

Meanwhile, Cheri was swimming just as determinedly, but she'd been closer to the riverbank when she lost her footing the last time. This gave her a head start, of sorts. Behnam, still on his feet, caught up to her as her strength was fading, just a few feet from shore and the two reached land together. They climbed the steep bank on hands and knees, coughing up water all the way. A few moments later, there were hands to help them and Denahar bent to lift the injured Cheri into his arms.

In front of the waterfall, Suvaat's chain of men was waiting with him at the leading edge, but their chain was precarious at best. Faye was clinging to her rock frantically, but Bass was finally getting close. It only took moments, but it felt like hours before he reached her.

"Climb on my back but don't choke me!" he yelled.

Faye nodded as she forced herself to loosen one hand and grab his sturdy shoulders. Then she loosed her other hand, swinging it around him so she could grab the wrist with the first hand. She kicked hard as he took off swimming toward shore, coming to the riverbank barely three feet from Suvaat's line of men.

Seeing Faye and Bass were safe, Suvaat started making his way to shore and behind him, one by one, his men began to follow. Suvaat was nearing the bank and Ochwatt when one of the men still out in the water slipped, pulling the men on either side down, in a blink, the man farthest out in the river started over the waterfall.

Slowly, one by one, Ochwatt started hauling men back to shore while the river furiously tried to wash the men away, Ochwatt's muscles strained as the men onshore, along with the man between him and Suvaat dug in their heels and refused to budge. Two, then three men were washing away toward the waterfall. The first one's feet were flailing as he tried to hold on to a rock. Then, Ochwatt pulled Suvaat and one by one, the rest of the men back to the bank. The men still onshore helped them climb out, pulling the rope and the men tied to it behind them. A few minutes later, the last of the troop were climbing ashore followed by Ochwatt, his water-resistant fur gleaming with droplets of water.

Once everyone was on dry ground again, they lay there for a moment, catching their breath. After five minutes, Cheri pulled her blanket close as she rose and limped over to Faye, where she sat dripping next to an equally wet Bass.

Faye looked up at her as she shook her head. "What?" Faye asked defensively.

"Well, don't we all look like a bunch of drowned rats?" responded Cheri with a mischievous grin.

Faye looked down at herself as she accepted a blanket from Tasmin, then around at Bass and Behnam who were coming up behind Cheri. Slowly she took in Suvaat and his men who were making mud puddles in the dirt with their boots as they came back to camp and started to laugh. "Yes. Yes, we do," she agreed, laughing even harder.

CHAPTER 30

Secret of the Marsh

After their impromptu dip in the river, Suvaat and his men made camp in a clearing in the woods. Out of sight of the ford and the road. Two of the men were sent to hide their tracks on either side of the river. They left the water to cover their trail through the ford itself. Faye, Cheri, Behnam, and Bass were able to change into clean clothes, and Cheri's right ankle was bound while their wet garments were hung out to dry. Suvaat's men weren't as lucky. Their only change of clothes were their padded shirts and pants to be worn under their chain mail and armor. Instead, they stripped to their small clothes and wrapped up in blankets for modesty while their plain, nondescript traveling clothes were hung on bushes to dry.

Faye sat next to the fire with her head lowered over her lunch, trying to hide her blush. She wasn't even sure why she was blushing. Because she'd caused them all to end up in the river or because the men were half-naked? Somehow, being in their small clothes seemed worse than a swimsuit.

Cheri, on the other hand, was busy sipping her tea while looking at Denahar out of the corner of her eyes. While all the knights were incredibly fit, Denahar's muscle definition was exceptionally impressive. Then, the knight draped a blanket around his shoulders, covering up the view. Sitting next to

Faye, she jabbed her with an elbow. "Did you see his body? Just when I thought he couldn't get any hotter! Whew!" this last followed by a long sigh.

"Hush, Cheri! He'll hear you! You really need to stop crushing on Denahar. He's too old for you," whispered Faye, looking around to see if anyone else had heard.

"We'll stay here this afternoon and tonight. We need to let our clothes get dry," said Suvaat, joining them at the fire and interrupting their conversation. He was holding a plate of roasted habity and some bread they'd purchased in the city. In his other hand was one for Faye. The men who had ridden out ahead of them had found game while waiting.

Faye looked at his plate and made a face. With a heavy sigh, she rose and walked further out into the meadow where she found leeks and root vegetables and something wild that almost looked like broccoli. Bringing them back, she showed her haul to Falcon. "Are these edible?"

Falcon stood and carefully looked over her selection. "None of these will kill you, but this one." He paused as he picked up a purple tuber. "This one tastes just awful," he finished, smiling.

"Good to know," she responded, bending over the fire and pulling out a pan before washing, peeling and slicing her finds after putting aside the purple ones. She'd rather eat cold habity with fresh vegetables. She was getting tired of meat, bread, and cheese.

"Oh...vegetables! Do you have enough for me?" asked Cheri as she looked over her shoulder.

"Sure. First come, first served. There should be enough for anyone who wants some."

"I'll try some," said Tasmin, holding out her plate as Faye began dishing them up.

Behnam and Bass joined the ladies.

"This is really good, Lady Faye. You're quite the cook," complimented Behnam.

"Mmph...," agreed Bass with a nod as he chewed on a mouthful of the vegetables.

Gurmail looked at the two relishing their food and put out his plate, "I'll take a little of that. It'll make my mother happy."

Suvaat looked at his well muscled friend with his scarred face for a moment and then burst out laughing. Gurmail looked around the campfire in confusion, "What? What?"

Everyone else who heard the conversation joined in the laughter.

After their hearty lunch, several of the men dressed and went out in two hunting parties. One back into the hills of Camir, the other deeper in the Zabir woods. Faye took Cheri, Falcon and Ochwatt with her, returning to the meadow and nearby forest to forage for more vegetables to round out their dinner. It was so rare to have down time and the cook in her wanted to know more about the edible vegetables in this strange place.

Gabriene was sitting at a small fire off by itself when Suvaat and Gurmail joined him. The old man was whittling a small piece of wood as the two knights sat where they could watch the women in the meadow. It was a few minutes before the wizard raised his eyes, waiting for Suvaat to speak. "Gurmail and I were appointed as savior knights, Gabriene. We can't do those jobs well and still lead the expedition. I think we need to step down and put Denahar in charge of the men while we concentrate on remaining close to Faye and Cheri."

Gabriene looked at the dark knight. "Well, well. The command of the soldiers and knights has always been up to you, Sir Suvaat, but I agree with you. Your primary concern should be the saviors. Ultimately, it is your decision."

Having decided on this new division of authority, Suvaat

and Gurmail wandered out to the meadow where Faye and Cheri were harvesting leeks.

While the women were hunting fresh vegetables, Bass and Behnam decided this would be a good time to talk to Falcon's captive and walked him over to Gabriene's fire.

"Well, well. You're here. But the question is, why are you here, isn't it?" said the wizard genially. "Oh, please, where are my manners. Sit down, and we'll have a chat," he invited, shifting his staff before resuming his whittling.

Looking about himself at Bass with his wide shoulders and strong arms from years of chopping wood and Behnam, head, shoulders, and then some taller than himself, the man's defiance faltered.

As the man sat, Gabriene looked over at him again. "My name is Gabriene, you may have heard of me? What? No? Well, well. How very disappointing. I was so sure Barakus hadn't forgotten me any more than I've forgotten him. Oh well, it's neither here nor there, is it? Just so you know, I'm a wizard. Now, tell, me, what's your name, young man?"

Now he was seated, the man had decided to ignore the impressive men standing behind and to either side of him and look only at the ancient little man with the bald head in front of him. When he heard Gabriene was a wizard, he blanched for just a moment but quickly recovered. Only tight lines around his eyes betrayed how tense he was. Clenching his jaw, his decision to keep silent soon became apparent.

"Well, well. I understand. You don't want to talk to me. After all, I'm the 'enemy,' aren't I? What could be the harm in exchanging names? I've told you mine, surely you can tell me yours?"

Briefly, the man's eyes flicked to the other men standing so near. "Well, well. Let me introduce my friends. Behnam is from Mojar and Bass here is a woodsman from Samal. All I'm asking from you is your name. You already know more than that about us," pressed Gabriene, looking down at his carving as he spoke.

Again, the man's eyes darted around as if looking for a way out before giving in, "Mi neim be Orander."

"Ah, now that's a good solid name, if I've ever heard one. Wouldn't you agree, boys?"

The two men watching nodded without taking their eyes off the prisoner. There would be no opportunity for the man to jump Gabriene, if they could help it.

"Well, well. Why were you and your friends camping in the woods, Orander? Can you tell us that? Bass has hazarded a guess that you were waiting to ambush or even kill us. Then again, I think you might just have been hunting until you were surrounded by wolves. Perhaps you could tell us which one is right. I've got a kine riding on this," continued Gabriene, allowing his eyes to glance up from under his bushy white brows for a moment.

Orander was staring at Gabriene with that stubborn set to his jaw again.

"Well, well. Did you see that? It appears you were right, Bass," said the wizard, looking up at the woodsman.

"I ain' say nothin'," growled the captive, looking even more nervous than before.

"Let me share a secret, Orander. What you don't say is also telling. Weren't you told that before they sent you out?" Orander's stare of disbelief bore into Gabriene, but he continued to refuse to speak.

"Well, well. Shall we continue? Who sent you? Would you be willing to tell us? No? Ah well, that's all right, Behnam here has a theory about that as well. Would you like to hear it?" asked Gabriene, still apparently absorbed in his whittling.

Orander's eyes betrayed his increasing panic. How much did these people know? Could this wizard read his mind?

"Ah, well. I can see you might be getting concerned about

what we have deduced so let me tell you what we think happened. Bass thinks you must have been sent by the priests back in Berentii. Behnam is sure that can't be true because you would have had to leave the city yesterday and how could you know which direction we would go when we left the city today? Falcon, that young man as caught you, he's sure you might have known if the priest at the Swaloh gate is especially sensitive to magic and could detect Gaban's amulets. Now, that would be a very sensitive priest indeed. Once he reported to the temple, the priests could have sent you out to wait for us. The only thing is, how could you know some of us would take that trail? After all, it's just a hunter's trail, not well known to most travelers."

Behnam stepped forward, "I have a theory. Maybe you can tell me if I'm on the right track," he said. "I don't think you knew any of us would take that trail. I mean, actually, the chances are pretty slim. I also think you're more than Komas soldiers. Your swords are too well made for that. So this is what I think. You and your friends were just one of several teams sent out and you just happened to be the first we came across. There will be more men waiting down all roads we can travel. Well, that's all right, we have a secret weapon, don't we?" As a look of confusion crossed Orander's face, Behnam continued, "You saw our secret out there in the woods, didn't you? You don't know how or why, but you know now, we have a wolf working with us. A wolf who can sniff out the other teams without them even knowing it's there."

"Well, well. Thank you, Orander. You've been most cooperative," said Gabriene, rising and handing the man a small chain that he had whittled from a long stick the width of his thumb.

Orander took the chain, a look of utter confusion on his face. "I dinna telled ye anythin'."

"Exactly. By not saying a word, you confirmed what we already knew," said Bass, pulling their prisoner to his feet.

"Gabriene, what do we do with him now? We don't need him anymore, right?"

"Well, well. Since the others chose to take their lives, we should leave the choice to him. If he still wants to die, I see no reason we can't grant his request. When the hunters return, ask Denahar to assign two men to escort him back to Berentii, Swaloh. Let them take care of him."

With a shrug, Bass and Behnam tied the man back on the tree. When they returned to Gabriene, the old man lowered his voice. "As long as he has that chain on him, he won't be able to run away, and no matter what he does, he won't be able to get rid of it either. Send him back to Gaban and Debora. They'll be able to get details about Barakus's forces from him."

*****

Aliand watched in awe as five of her hang gliders swooped in the sky, high above the Mer de Verde. As always, it was easy to pick out Ebony's graceful moves, but three of the others were now nearly as proficient. Aliand loved watching her inventions soaring like birds. *Look, Father. Look what I did!* she thought, grinning at Jakar.

The fifth flier was gaining in proficiency but still had problems gaining height and he wobbled as they descended. With Ebony in the lead, one by one, they landed. With practiced ease, they lowered their wings and ran to a designated safe zone, clearing the deck for the next pilot to follow. Finally, it was Galad's turn, and he wobbled as he lifted his legs. He was coming in too low, again.

As he stumbled to a stop, Ebony walked up to him, shaking her head. "Okay, Galad. You've proved you can do this, but I think you'll have to face facts. With your musculature, especially those shoulders of yours, you're too top-heavy to get the height you need, and you come down too fast. There's no control. It's not that you don't have the skills, you're just built to wield that two-handed broadsword of yours, not to fly."

By the time she'd finished, he'd regained his feet and slipped out of the harness. "You're right. I need to let those built for the job do it. For me to continue would be a waste of resources and might endanger the mission."

"Luckily, your aptitude in martial arts is better than your flying. Your men are getting really good, really fast. We'll be ready for our assault."

"If we're on time to make the assault, anyway. Let's get this ship underway. We've a long way to go if we're going to make it to Yves in time."

"Then I suggest you go tell Captain Sevalian we're ready to get underway." Ebony laughed, heading for where Aliand's carpenters and the soldiers were collecting the hang gliders, getting ready to stow them in the hold.

A few minutes later, with all sails unfurled, the mighty ship was cutting a wide swath through the swells. They were nearing the Malianna Peninsula in Camir, and the captain was heading out to sea. This was the last headland they would round before reaching the Raseri Ocean and heading north, past Rim and the Zabir River Delta on their way to the capital city.

Aliand stifled a giggle as she turned away from watching Ebony with Galad. The girl could see the attraction between them, even if neither was ready to admit it.

*****

It wasn't long after they got on the road the next morning, that they started to descend, and Cheri realized they were on a stone causeway. On their right was the turbulent north fork of the Zabir River racing through the narrow, stone canyons down the mountain. Beyond that, was a cliff face growing higher in giant steps as they descended. It looked to the redhead as if there had been a series of earthquakes, dropping Zabir while pushing up Camir over what was probably thousands of years or more. On their right was a heavily wooded slope with scattered boulders throughout. From the looks of the battered trees, it was apparent landslides from the bluff above were frequent. This also explained the number of boulders fighting with the water for dominance in the river.

As they rode, she noticed Gurmail had taken to shadowing her, never letting her get far away. Looking around, she saw Suvaat was no longer leading their band but seemed to be sticking close to Faye instead. Ahead Denahar appeared to be giving the orders. Scouts, including Falcon, had been sent ahead and behind as well as in the woods. Everyone seemed to be tense, keeping careful watch. They were all on alert for another ambush. Falcon came and went through the woods like a ghost while Amalee soared high above the road from west to east. Denahar's best scouts remained hidden as Ochwatt and Beloria, the red wolf, ranged farther than others could, looking for threats.

The men remained on high alert for the next few days, and as they traveled down the gradual slope of the mountain, their nerves stretched to the breaking point. No sign had yet been seen of an ambush. It didn't seem possible for the teams of assassins to stake out the only road branching out to the northeast from the ford and ignore the eastern route that headed into Zabir.

On the afternoon of the fifth day, they finally reached the end of the mountains as the road abruptly flattened out. The water in the river calmed and spread out. The causeway turned into one long, low, arched bridge, spanning a series of wide pillars rising from the marsh expanding out around them. Here, the marsh took over in earnest, and Banalar trees rose from the water on their sturdy roots, forming spaces underneath big enough to hide a house. Cheri craned her neck, looking up at the towering trees with their red- brown trunks and long, thin leaves hanging down and thin tendrils looking like long hooks as they curved back up toward the sun. Looking across the marsh, she could see these trees dominated the landscape. Interspersed between the taller trees, here and there, ancient trees looking very much like weeping willows were dwarfed by the Banalar.

Beloria soon returned from scouting, shaking out her paws. "Th- the wolf tha be me is na likin' they wets. I don' ken wha' hanimal't as lives here. Lady Tasmin, ken ye gets me clothes?" and reluctantly, Beloria changed and remounted Dancer.

Ochwatt returned to the road a short time later, wet from the knees down and looking miserable. He wasn't going to be able to range through the marsh as he had through the forest.

A half span later, Falcon came riding down the road from behind, also calling off his scouting. The footing in the marsh was too treacherous for his horse Wolf to continue. Only Amalee still had the freedom to keep scouting the wetlands as she swooped beneath the Banalar trees.

Denahar's scouts, out front and behind, were still out there, but their proactive ranging to the sides had ground to a halt, and the added benefit of Ochwatt's nose was blunted by being with so many people and horses.

They had almost reached a point on the bridge built wide for spending the night when the scout covering the rear came racing down the road. "Troops! Trained troops are heading this way! Fast!"

With a few terse commands from Denahar, interrupting what Suvaat was about say, the cohort surrounded the women while Suvaat and Gurmail reluctantly remained by their charges. Gabriene. Behnam and Falcon joined most of the troops now facing west while Bass and Ochwatt helped cover them on the east, expecting a trap set up to force them into the marsh.

It wasn't long before they heard the sound of hooves thundering down the causeway and a well-armed troop of men rode on them from the west. As Denahar's men prepared for battle, Behnam let out a yell. "Watch the east! More attackers!"

Amalee soared in from the northeast, screeching in alarm before she began circling, getting ready for combat.

Surrounded, Gabriene crossed to the two and a half stone coping wall bordering the road in the north, looking for an escape route through the marsh. They were outnumbered, and he knew something their assailants didn't. He dismissed the fact his friends weren't aware of his secret either as he spotted a string of hummocks venturing into the marsh.

"Ochwatt! I need you," he called to the giant.

Deserting his post, the sasquatch responded silently, joining the old man and looking to him for instruction.

"Do you see those hummocks leading out into the marsh? I want you to lead the ladies out to those. Just follow them until I can catch up with you.

Ochwatt regarded the hummocks of varying size before nodding to the wizard.

Meanwhile, Gabriene was speaking quietly to Tasmin. "Ochwatt's going to lead the way into the marsh, following those hummocks. Follow him. I'll be along with the others as we can break free."

"Do you know what they say about this marsh, Gabriene? No one who goes in there ever comes out," objected the older woman.

"Well, well. Of course, I know. I'm the one who keeps

those rumors going. As long as you're with me, we'll be safe. Now, go."

Without another word, Tasmin followed the giant with Beloria, Faye, and Cheri close behind. The sound of metal on metal echoed through the marsh, signaling the beginning of the battle. Suvaat and Gurmail hesitated before deciding to face the known threat.

Behnam's scimitar struck out from atop Desert Wind, cutting down the first two attackers but quickly he found he was facing three well- trained fighters while those around him were contending with their own challenges. Amalee began diving at the assailants behind the lines, going for their eyes. Denahar and two of the soldiers from their troop were fighting next to Falcon, but twelve men were attacking from the east, and behind them another seven men had fought their way through to Suvaat and Gurmail as they tried to cover for the escaping women. They'd managed to take down three of the attackers on the first pass bur Gurmail's arm sustained a wicked slash at the same time, and one of their own men went down, bleeding heavily.

Behnam took out another of the men he was facing, and out of the corner of his eye, he noted many of their assailants were down, injured or dead. So was one of the soldiers he was fighting beside. Two of the men he'd been fighting against pressed him while he was momentarily distracted and it wasn't until a couple of moments later, when the fight circled around again that he saw Denahar take a vicious hit to the neck and he was splattered with blood as the artery was severed. Angry now, Behnam's offensive became frenzied, quickly cutting down one of the men he was facing before exchanging blows with the remaining, highly skilled warrior and delivering a telling blow, severing his left arm below the elbow and knocking him off the bridge and into the marsh. When he looked up, the attackers from the east were either dead or disabled, but he could hear thundering hooves on the road, as another twenty men appeared from around a rock protruding from the bluff. Turning to assess the mayhem behind him, he saw two of the soldiers Suvaat had been fighting with were down, but the attackers on that flank had been defeated. Unfortunately the sound of hooves from the west confirmed more men were on the way.

Ochwatt was loping in long strides from hummock to hummock while the horses followed in shorter hops, finding their footing on the grassy mounds as best they could.

Next, Gabriene sent the squires with the packhorses out into the marsh while the battle on two fronts closed in and the fighting men backed toward the edge of the bridge where Gabriene was waiting.

"Follow me," called the old man, urging Jessi over the rail and onto the first hummock while Suvaat tied Gurmail's arm before helping him back onto his horse. Then the two of them and another surviving soldier were over the rail, following the wizard.

Behnam was checking on one of their downed soldiers who was only wounded, but he wouldn't be able to stay on a horse alone. "Easy boy," he said to Desert Wind as he put the soldier onto the front of the horse and climb up into the saddle behind the wounded man. He was holding the reins of the soldier's horse as well.

Then the arrows started zipping past his head, and he urged Desert Wind to go faster, "Archers! They have archers! Speed it up!" he called as he bent protectively over the man in front of him.

The arrows kept coming, but several of the attackers broke off from the main body of the contingent and started to find their own grass stepping stones into the marsh.

"Don't lose sight of the bridge!" called their leader. "If you do, you'll never make it out."

The hardened soldier leading the pursuit strung his men out as they tracked the saviors through the wetlands, trying to give them maximum penetration into the marsh but still able to find the bridge. Finally, he reached the actual island where the group had converged before continuing farther into the dangerous environs of the quagmire. Looking back, he could barely make out the last man waiting on a hummock where the causeway could still be seen through the towering Banalar trees. He shivered, these trees seemed aware and watching. Looking deeper into the marsh, he saw at least a dozen different escape routes they could have taken from here. There was no way for him to even investigate. All he could do now was hope the marsh lived up to its harsh reputation and would take out their prey.

Turning to leave, he couldn't see the man who should be waiting. Alarmed, he spurred his horse to return to the hillock where he should be. When he arrived, there was no trace of his companion. Looking toward where the next lookout should be waiting, he thought he saw something moving. What was that? Again, he spurred his horse back along the hummock trail. Again, his man was missing with no trace. Now, he found he wasn't sure which way to go, and he couldn't see anyone. Had he ventured too far? As he traveled in the direction of the bridge, he heard rustling in the giant trees dominating this marsh. He may not be able to find any of his men, but he wasn't alone. A few moments later, just after jumping to another hummock close to one of the ubiquitous trees, a net fell from above and snatched him out of his saddle while a small strange-looking creature jumped onto the horse and, taking the reins, guided it away. Another of the small creatures approached and rubbed something on his hand. A short time later, he lost consciousness, terrified he would never wake.

*****

Deeper in the marsh, Ochwatt had reached another, larger, island.

One large enough for them to stop and tend to their wounded. "Gabriene, why are we here? This is one of the most notoriously dangerous places in Persal. Many fear it more than Doome itself," asked Bass as he looked around nervously.

"Well, well. Yes, there is good reason for that, but you see, if you remain with me, we'll be perfectly safe."

Tasmin was tending to Gurmail's arm, and Faye had gone over to check on the damage done to the soldier's leg. "Matew, put on the pot to boil and then grab some of that moss over there," instructed Tasmin with a general wave of her hand.

"Suvaat, has any of our bread started to mold?" called Faye as she watched Tasmin clean Gurmail's wound before starting to clean the soldier's as well.

As she was working on him, the soldier started to rouse. "Hello there. How are you doing? I know it hurts, but I'm here to help," she said, talking mostly to keep his attention on her and not his injury.

"Lady Faye, I found some moldy bread. What do you want me to do with it?" called Suvaat from the other side of the island.

"Scrape off the mold into a cup, as much as you can," she called back before returning to her patient. "I'm sorry I haven't had the opportunity to learn your name. Would you tell me what it is now?"

"Argh! Tha's awright, my lady. I been out on scout most times. No need fer ye ter know me," he gasped out as she poured some mead Behnam had found on the wound.

"That's no excuse. You're very important to our mission. Where would we be if you weren't watching out for us? Now, what's your name?"

"Me name be Rogelo...me lady."

"Ah, is that the mold? Good, hand it here," interrupted Faye, grabbing the cup Suvaat brought to her so she could sprinkle some into the cuts on Rogelo's leg. "Tasmin, here, sprinkle some of this in Gurmail's wound, it'll kill the germs."

"What? Faye, what are you talking about? What are... germs?" asked Tasmin, looking doubtfully at the green powder in the bottom of the cup.

"It's medicine from my world, and I'll explain germs later. Just trust me."

"Argh! Do as she says. It saved Lakhvir's arm," ground out Gurmail through gritted teeth.

While they worked, Cheri took a good look around at the remnant of their party. "Sir Denahar? Where's Sir Denahar?" she asked Behnam since she'd last seen the knight fighting near the Mojar.

"He didn't make it, Cheri. I'm sorry."

"What? No, that can't be right. Maybe he was just injured. We need to go back for him," she protested, looking back toward the causeway.

Behnam took a step closer, putting his hands on Cheri's shoulders. "No, Cheri, there's no error. Sir Denahar is dead. The wound he received was fatal. Trust me, he died immediately."

"No! No, no, no," wailed Cheri as she leaned into her friend and began to cry. As her sobs eased, she looked up, "Are you sure? I mean really, really sure?"

"Cheri, I didn't want to have to tell you this, but his head was taken off by a battle-ax. He's dead," revealed Behnam reluctantly.

"What? Oh, no, no, no!" she wailed, pulling Behnam with her as she slid to the ground, her crying gaining new strength.

At a loss Behnam looked around to see if Tasmin or Faye were available for help. Consoling a brokenhearted teenager wasn't something he had trained for. Seeing both of the ladies working on the wounded, he just sat there, holding Cheri and let her weep.

Amalee was circling overhead, keeping watch when suddenly she began to screech a warning. Looking up, Falcon could see her circling tighter, but when he looked through the trees to the hummocks around them, he couldn't see a thing. Then he heard a faint swishing, rustling noise.

The sounds of movement high in the boughs of the Banalar trees drew the attention of Falcon and Behnam, followed shortly by the rest of their party who weren't otherwise occupied. Gabriene was smiling as several small mammals with long tails started descending on vines from the canopy above. Then, there were even more of the animals following the first and one by one they dropped onto the island and gathered around Gabriene until there were at least sixty of the beasts, filling every available space, all chattering away. Above, still in the trees or hanging from the vines were at least a hundred more.

Amalee was growing frantic, and Falcon let out a shrill whistle, calling the hawk down to his side.

"Well, well. My friends have arrived!" declared Gabriene with a big smile on his face. Excited as a boy, he sat on a protruding root of a tree and began conversing with one of the animals who appeared to be the leader. This impression was reinforced as the chattering in the trees ceased.

The arrival of the animals had another, welcome, effect as far as Behnam was concerned. Cheri ceased crying. She was as startled and curious as everyone else. Slowly, she started to rise, and Behnam stood quickly to help her to her feet.

Everyone on the little island, except Tasmin and Faye had stopped what they were doing to watch Gabriene and the little monkey person, with caramel-colored fur and a thick prehensile tail, talk. As she listened, Cheri began to feel she understood what they were saying.

"Wharpu Gabpu benju? Wepu misaju yop," said the simian female of indeterminate age

"Well, well. I know it's been awhile, but there's good tidings and I'm here now. I've brought new friends."

"Friendju whopu followi yop, be gonju. Werpu thapu wronju?"

"No, no. Those weren't friends, those were enemies, not friends. Here, let me introduce you. Everyone, this is Buchu, the matriarch of the Chugura. Before Barakus experimented on them, they were animals native to this marsh. Similar to an oppen."

Gabriene motioned for Cheri and Behnam to join him. "This is Lady Cheri, one of the saviors we've been waiting for. This strapping man is Behnam of the Mojar people, far to the west."

As Cheri approached through the throngs of Chugura crowding the island, she had no idea what an oppen was, but the Chugura seemed to resemble a mix between an otter and a monkey with long fingers and opposable thumbs on their webbed hands.

The small simian stood spryly and put out a tentative hand to Cheri, while she bowed formally. "I ampu pleaji teru meetsui, miladu. Anu yop alpu, siri Benamu." As she stood back up, Cheri noted there was a glint of purple crystal under the fur just above Buchu's heart. A sign of her status, perhaps?

Wearily, Gabriene rose to his feet and waded through the sea of Chugura, leading Buchu to Faye and Tasmin who were applying fresh bandages to the wounded. From there, he continued his introductions with Suvaat and the surviving soldiers, Falcon and Bass. Amalee screeched as the small animal approached. Normally, the hawk might see Buchu as prey until Falcon made a point of introducing them. His final introduction was to Ochwatt, who appeared to be enchanted with the small creatures. Buchu was equally fascinated with the furry giant.

Gabriene made sure to introduce everyone so Buchu would know they were all friends. When he got to Beloria, Buchu took the girl's hand in her own small paw. "Wees beju semi," she said with a smile.

"Wha? Wha be she did telled?" asked Beloria, confused.

"She said the two of you are the same. I think she can tell you can change into an animal," explained Gabriene thoughtfully.

Once the introductions were over, Buchu nodded as if satisfied. "Nasy wees gonju teru humua groovip." At these words, her entire troop scampered back into the trees and disappeared. Leaving Buchu alone to lead the way.

It took several minutes before everyone was remounted and ready to ride. Rogelo rode with one of the other soldiers since his leg wasn't strong enough to ride. Gurmail was having trouble remaining on his horse with his own injury, but Ochwatt volunteered to walk beside his horse and keep him steady.

As Gabriene settled into his saddle, Buchu bounded up a standing root and leapt on the horse in front of him. "Wepu gosi dis wayu.

Followi um landasu," she instructed, pointing through the Banalar trees to the northeast, expecting to be obeyed.

*****

They traveled for over an hour before reaching what might have been the center of the marsh and a huge, tightly packed grove of Banalar trees, surrounding a large raised island. As they neared the area, the rustling in the tops of the trees intensified. The Chugura people were gathering, and now that they were home, they were clad in primitive tunics made from animal skins. Many were also wearing necklaces and bracelets made of stones and shells tied in a rough twine. The excitement among the Chugura was palatable. They hadn't had welcome company since the last time Gabriene was here and never so many at once.

Cheri was fascinated by the trees and the clearing. There were three firepits evenly spaced in the center of the island where foods were being prepared. One of the fires had a large animal roasting while the other two were being tended by cooks with hardened wooden bowls for cooking vegetables. Root vegetables were being fished out of the ashes and set aside to peel for final preparation. In the center of the cookfires was a large pit where steam escaped carrying savory aromas through the...village.

Off to one side of the island were frames with animal hides stretched for drying. What she didn't see were huts of any kind. She couldn't help wondering where the Chugura called home.

Then she noticed the little simians, scurrying in and out of the raised portions of the trees. Ah, their homes were there, in the Banalar trees. Where else would they live?

Everywhere there were Chugura, and more were arriving. Some clothed, some not. Here, where they behaved as a community, she started seeing them as people and wondered. The humans dismounted as they gained the island and the squires took the reins, looking around, at the scampering animals nervously until one motioned to a nearby island large enough for the horses to graze.

Cheri approached Gabriene. "I have a million questions. Why weren't they wearing clothes earlier? Why are they wearing them now?"

Gabriene chuckled. "Well, well. Why would they? They don't see many humans, even fewer humans see them, so they don't need to be covered for modesty. With their fur, they don't need clothes for warmth. When they're traveling through the trees, clothes could actually be a hindrance. Here, where they are home, they can dress up. Especially for company."

"Oh...well, where did they come from? Why do they live in hiding?

Why...?"

"Cheri, stop. No more questions, now. I will tell their tale later. When everyone can hear. The Chugura love to hear it as well."

Temporarily defeated, Cheri walked away to see if she could be of help elsewhere.

That night, after eating the roasted fish and a pork-like animal from the pit along with dozens of other delicious dishes, Gabriene told the tale of the Chugura.

"Well, well. Where shall I start? It all began many, many years ago. Barakus was my apprentice. He was talented and hungry for knowledge. He absorbed his lessons like a dry sponge and read everything he could get his hands on. He always wanted to know more. One day, when I had been called away from the tower for some minor matter, he broke into my library and found the ancient scrolls. I thought they were hidden but not well enough. When I found him, I punished him and told him, some knowledge was forbidden. Our power was only to be used to help people. He refused to believe me. He said we had been given the power, so we had the right to use it as we pleased. According to him, in that final argument, we were superior to the rest of the people. Our powers, being able to use magic, was proof of that, according to him, anyway. This is not what we wizards teach the Imaldi.

"It was some time after that quarrel when he disappeared. One day he was helping me with potions, the next he was gone. It wasn't until much later I learned he had stolen some of my scrolls on dark, forbidden magic. At the time I thought he might have abandoned his magic and I was disappointed. He had so much potential.

"It was two years before I heard of a dark power rising in the northeast. This marsh had always been dangerous. It's the nature of marshes, after all. What with snakes and cougars. But suddenly, there were rumors. No one who went in came out again. Even men who had been hunting here for years went missing. There were other rumors as well. Rumors of strange things being seen. Rumors of stranger things happening. Hammil was called to investigate. When he didn't return, I came here. That's when I found out what Barakus had been up to. He hadn't abandoned magic. He'd simply been gaining power using blood magic, and he'd been experimenting. Unready to face my power, which was legendary at that time, Barakus fled the marshes but he left behind the Chugura. To him they were a failed experiment.

"When he had first reached the marsh, he found the oppen as they were known then and started experimenting. He wanted to create a race of intelligent beings who would worship him, give him his due, as he saw it. Only he didn't count on one thing, when you grant intelligence to a nearly harmless animal, you create a nearly harmless people. The Chugura refused to do his bidding. Changing a gentle, peace-loving animal into a tool for evil isn't as easy as it would seem. That takes generations, and my arrival disrupted his plans. The Chugura refused to follow him, and even with their newfound intelligence, they didn't understand the concept of worship. They still don't. When I tried to explain it, they thought it was the most absurd thing they'd ever heard.

"Later, when I found them, I realized if humans found them, they would be captured and either turned into slaves or exhibited as oddities. Neither option was acceptable. So, I taught them how to deal with humans who came unbidden to their realm and started spreading rumors of the dangers in the marsh. No one with innocent intentions comes in here, anymore. As men started disappearing, it only reinforced my rumors," he finished as he whittled another stick he'd picked up.

Cheri quickly piped up, "What happened next? We don't know the history."

Looking at the girl from under his bushy eyebrows, Gabriene paused to think. "Well, well. When I returned to Lohi and my tower, I discovered Jakar's uncle, the seer, had turned up in Jankaraa, in the far northern reaches of Samal, tucked in among the mountains. Gaban had gone to investigate. The next time I heard from Gaban was when he had found his valley and asked for help creating the portal and securing the valley. I took the remaining nine wizards and their apprentices with me.

"When Gaban's sanctuary and the portal were secure, we left, in small groups of two or three. When we were far enough from the valley, we found Barakus had been hunting us. Unfortunately, he started finding us and through deception separated us so one by one he confronted the other wizards and killed them and their apprentices. He only left me and Gaban alive. I don' believe he could find Gaban, hidden in his valley. As for me? Well, the last time we met, he still didn't have as much power as I. Since then, I have been doing what I can to make myself stronger in magic over the centuries, but Barakus has tapped into a type of magic...I...will... not...use. That alone makes him very dangerous, even if I can match his power and we're not at all certain of that, anymore."

"Now, it's time for us to get some rest. We'll have a long day of riding ahead of us tomorrow. If we move quickly, we've still got almost six days before we reach Yves," injected Tasmin, gathering Beloria, Cheri, and Faye together to follow one of their hosts over to a nearby tree. Even as short as Faye and Beloria were, they had to duck their heads under the roots.

Inside the tree, Faye's mouth dropped open in amazement. There were lanterns lining a circular ramp, winding its way up the interior of the hollow tree trunk. As they climbed, they passed a series of protruding sleeping platforms until they came to the one set aside for the four of them. There, they found their saddlebags waiting. The beds were made of the thin leaves and tendrils of the Banalar trees, woven into cushions, soft and springy. Fay sank into one and let out a sigh. This was the most comfortable bed she'd had since arriving in Persal. "This is better than a sleep number bed."

Seeing her reaction, Cheri sank into her own cushion of fresh leaves that let off a heavenly smell almost like vanilla and sighed. "Oh, this is wonderful! Don't you dare wake me at dawn tomorrow. Can we take these with us?"

Tasmin shook her head, "So sorry, but we will be rising at dawn. We're running out of time. I'll ask about the leaves in the morning. For now, get to sleep," she admonished, pulling across a curtain of woven leaves to block the light.

Cheri so wanted to argue but found herself yawning instead as she lay down and was asleep almost instantly.

*****

Late into the night, after the others were asleep, Buchu had several of her people raised the sleeping Gurmail, Matew, and Rogelo, and with Gabriene in tow, they wound their way deeper into the eastern marsh until they came upon a strange sight indeed. A half of a riant rock, glowing purple in the dark, rose like a bowl above the marsh, an island unto itself.

As they got closer, Gabriene could see the inside was filled with purple crystals and water, letting off an eerie light. While Buchu stopped Gabriene at the top of a nearby hillock, taller than the others, the rest of the Chugura carried their patients gently around to the other side where crude steps had been carved into the outer stone. As they mounted, they began to chant and Buchu, next to Gabriene, jointed their song. Once on the edge of the geode, strips of a woven cloth were wrapped carefully under the arms of the three men before they were lowered into the still, clear water within.

Gabriene watched in amazement as the water turned red from the blood on the bandages, clothes, and wounds themselves. After a quarter turn, the red was...just gone, and the water was mysteriously, almost spectrally, clear again, as if nothing could contaminate it for long.

When the Chugura returned with the three men, they were sleeping peacefully. Gabriene bent to unwind their bandages to find their wounds were gone, as if they'd never been.

Rising, he bowed deeply to Buchu and then to her people. "Thank you," he said simply.

CHAPTER 31

Are We There Yet?

The next morning, as promised, they were in the saddle and on the way north just as the sun was finding its way through the eastern canopy. Luckily, the rest they had gained, sleeping on the woven leaves, had been strangely invigorating. Cheri and Faye were more rested than they had been since leaving Lohi. The others of their party seemed equally refreshed.

Everyone had been astonished when they went to breakfast to find Gurmail, Matew, and Rogelo fully recovered from all their battle wounds and ready to travel. All Gabriene would say was the Chugura had taken care of them the evening before. During breakfast, Gurmail kept rubbing his face where his scar had been washed away with his injuries.

Beloria, on Dancer, was carrying a small bundle on her lap. "What's that?" asked Cheri curiously, as she pulled up next to the girl.

Startled, Beloria looked over at the older girl. "Uh, it's a present, from the Chugura. I'll show you when next we stop," she promised, spurring Dancer to leap to the next hummock and leaving Cheri behind.

"Now, that was odd," muttered Cheri as Baby bunched his front leg muscles for his leap.

By the time they stopped briefly for lunch, the Banalar trees had been left behind them, and the willows had taken over. The grass covered hummocks had grown larger, and the water between was flowing faster with clear water revealing the stone covered beds.

"While we're here, fill up the skins," instructed Suvaat who hadn't appointed a replacement for Denahar yet. The horses were watered downstream while meat from the feast and a pungent cheese was passed around.

After handing Baby over to Matew, Cheri scuttled over to sit by Gabriene. Whatever Beloria was going to show the wizard, she was going to be there to see it.

Beloria hesitantly handed her bundle to Jessufer, another of the squires, while she dismounted and almost snatched it back as soon as she reached the ground. The way she held it was almost like one would hold a baby or something precious.

Straightening her back in determination, she walked across to where Gabriene was sitting on a log, nibbling his cheese.

"Master Gabriene, sir. Afore we lef's Buchu say ter telled ye. It be import ta ha' Liliannia comes wi'. She be no troubles. I be takin' care," she stumbled as she explained, opening the bundle as she did.

Within, a tiny, female Chugura stood up and bowed. "I ampu teru heeps," she said, ruffling the fur over her heart with one tiny hand to reveal a small purple crystal implanted there.

"Well, well. So, you're Buchu's heir. Why is she sending you with us? Where we're going is dangerous."

"I keni. I ampu mora. I ampu lak Be...Beloria. I keni fas. I heeps," said the small Chugura.

"Ahh. Well, well. I suppose you will Liliannia."

"Lili, Master Gabriene. Lili."

"Welcome, Lili. Cheri, I'll expect you to help Beloria take care of our young friend when Beloria is occupied."

"That's so cool. Uhm, I mean, I'd be delighted," answered

Cheri as she reached over to shake the little hand...paw? "Pleased to meet you, Lili."

"Mount up! Time to get back on the road," called Suvaat as the squires returned with the horses. They were making their way north when he dropped back to hand packets of food to the young men. "Here, you can eat in the saddle."

*****

Tai chi training was over for the day, and Ebony and Galad were leaning companionably on the railing, watching a pod of dolfin-like animals racing alongside the ship. Leaping ahead and chattering. As they talked and laughed, Aliand found she could no longer hold her giggles.

Ebony turned to the girl standing nearby. "Okay, what?" she asked, putting one hand on her hip.

"You two are sweet on one another. It is sooo cute!" said the girl with more giggles.

"Don't be ridiculous. We've just become friends," denied Ebony while Galad watched the black woman he'd come to admire.

"Huh! A few days ago, when he was still flying, maybe, but I could see it. You forget, I grew up in the court of Rim. I also have three older sisters. I learned early how to tell when two people begin courting. I can also tell when they are getting close because there's something there and when it's purely political. In Rim, the political alliances have primary importance. If the two involved also like each other, it is so much more rare and easier to spot. That's what's going on here, trust me."

"You, young lady, have lost your mind. We're friends, nothing more," insisted Ebony dismissively.

"Well, like I said, that was true. At the beginning you would stand at the rail, looking at the bow cutting through the sea or turning to talk to each other. Then, there were about three kendars between you. Just now, your arms were touching. No, even if you don't want to admit it yet, there's more than friendship happening here now," finished Aliand, turning to skip to the stern where she could still see the dolfins, her giggle trailing behind her.

Slowly, Ebony turned to stare up into Galad's deep-blue eyes. "She's just a girl, she doesn't know what she's talking about. Does she?"

Galad turned to look at the young girl leaning over the aft rail before turning back to the striking black woman before him. "I don't know, yet. I like you, I agree we've become friends. I have no idea if it will go any further. Until our battles with Barakus have been won, or lost, I think it is too soon to consider either way. Perhaps we should cross that bridge when we get to it. If we get to it."

"Oh, I agree. Right now, we have far too much on our plates. This is a discussion for another time. Besides, I will be going home when the portal opens again."

Galad turned his too, too charming smile on her and she started to melt. "Agreed. After all, the fate of Persal rests in our hands."

As he walked away to confer with his men, Ebony couldn't help watching his broad shoulders. Unbidden, another image of a taller man with an equally impressive back, the color of milk chocolate came to mind. A back rising from a pool and glistening with water. Along with that image came the flash of a scimitar and a snake's head flying away to land on the edge of the pool. Unfortunately, she couldn't deny, she was attracted to Behnam as well.

Well, there's no use even thinking about it. When this is all over, and I go home, I'm not leaving any broken hearts behind me. Casual relationships may be normal on my world, but I have a feeling these things are taken much more seriously here, she thought. She couldn't help shivering in trepidation when she thought about telling Behnam she wasn't chaste. The man was so...rigid. Now, Galad, he might, or might not, take it better.

*****

For the next three days, as the trail led them out of the marsh, they began climbing into the foothills and away from the river. As they climbed, they left the damp heat of the marsh behind, and the weather cooled a little more every day.

While they rode, Lili refused to speak. When Beloria or Cheri would try to ask her a question, she would merely shake her head and point to her ears. She was listening.

Whenever they stopped, she took off running through the trees, touching and investigating strange plants and the droppings of strange animals. Occasionally, like with the willow bark, collecting samples and putting them in her satchel slung across her body. In order to keep up with her, Beloria turned into a bright-red squirrel and scampered off with her. The first time she had transformed, Lili had stopped to investigate this new development, walking around the squirrel curiously. Then she had chattered something quickly, and Beloria had responded just as quickly. After that, it was a given, any time Lili wanted to explore, Beloria would change into an animal she had seen locally and accompany her.

On their first day out, Beloria had seen a sloth-like animal moving incredibly slow. Curious about being one of these strange creatures, she changed. She quickly learned there was no advantage to moving so slowly and was eventually able to return to the ground and change back.

"Lady Cheri. It do be so strange. A'most as if'n me heart warn't beatin' much atoll. The beats was so far apart lak," she said breathlessly as she got dressed again and emerged from behind a tree.

"Well, well. Miss Beloria, that's all very interesting, I'm

sure, but we've a long way to go, and we're in something of a hurry, so, if you don't mind, please refrain from emulating the slower animals," suggested Gabriene as he mounted his horse in preparation for leaving again.

On the fourth day, they awoke to a heavy, overcast sky and they weren't on the road long when it started to rain. Slowly, at first, then harder and colder.

Swathed in ponchos of oiled cloth, Cheri hunkered down on Baby, leaving the slow climb to the mountain pony as they followed Believer up the narrow trail they were navigating. Then there was a loud neighing and shouts at the front of the column, and she looked up, trying to see what was happening. The column came to a halt as some of those in the lead tried to back their horses.

"Faye! Can you see? What's happened?" yelled Cheri, leaning toward the rock in her attempt to look farther up the trail.

"I'm not sure. There appears to be a problem with the trail, and that worries me. I really hate traveling in the rain!" came the answer. The last comment sounded really irked, but Cheri could understand her attitude.

"Even if we were on the paved roads of home, they wash out and remember all the sinkholes? You're just upset about the last time," teased Cheri.

"Really? I hadn't thought of that," rejoined Faye sarcastically.

A short time later, Falcon came riding back along the queue before stopping next to Cheri. "We need your help. About half a span of trail has washed away and Suvaat's warhorse is too big to continue. We need Baby to blaze a new trail which we'll reinforce with the smaller horses before allowing the Chardells to continue.

"Me? You want me to ride Baby across first? You do

remember I've only been riding since we arrived in Persal, right?" squeaked Cheri in surprise.

"Well, actually, it's Baby we need, and he would do better with you on his back. In case you haven't noticed, the two of you have formed a bond. If you insist, I can ride him, but he's not used to me," explained Falcon.

"Oh, all right."

"Faye, I'll want you and Believer to follow the lighter horses, once the trail has been blazed. I believe the unicorn might be able to shore it up for the weight of the heavier horses and their heavier riders."

"Oh, dear, here we go again," muttered Faye as they pulled out of line to follow Falcon. As they rode, they passed Bass who was lining up the horses by size. Faye stopped next to Gabriene while Behnam led the heavier horses to the back of the line, one horse at a time.

When Falcon and Cheri reached the head of the line, she gasped, then turned in disbelief to Falcon. "You expect Baby, us, to do what? Exactly? There's nothing here but the slope, running water and that gray mist hiding we know not what."

"Cheri, trust me and trust Baby and if he starts slipping, remember what happened on the *Gray Gull*. I believe, if you need to, you can give that strength to Baby, just as you did to those men on the shore."

Cheri stared at Falcon in disbelief before looking again at the distance to where the trail started again and noticed the far side was still being washed away. Oh dear, they were going to have to keep going until they found truly stable ground. Before proceeding, she bent forward on Baby's neck. "Baby, it's time to strut your stuff. I believe in you, and we can do this, together," she promised, trying not to think of the drop the gray mist was surely hiding from them.

Then, before urging Baby forward, she closed her eyes for a moment. As her eyes snapped open, there was a determined look on her face, and with a light slap of her reins, Baby started forward. For this crossing, she was giving the pony his head. He knew what he was doing; she was just along for the ride.

Taking steady, sure steps, the little pony walked uphill for a few steps before finding firmer ground and heading across the torrent of rainwater running down the hill. Cheri held on tight to the saddle horn with one hand while the other stroked his neck reassuringly. As they connected, they both began to glow, and his step became more solid. Placing one hoof after the other with care, each step seemed to land on solid stone. Carefully, Baby blazed a new trail across the side of the hill.

Halfway across, Baby stepped sideways for a moment but quickly regained his footing and steadily continued another half span, past the washed-out trail, where they found a wider, almost-level section of ground. Exhausted, Cheri turned to look back, and her mouth dropped open in shock. The trail they had produced looked like fused stone while the width was three times the width it should have been. "Oh, Baby, we did it! I mean, really, look what we did!" she whooped in excitement, before slumping in the saddle.

Baby let out a soft neigh and nodded drooping in his own tiredness. The strength for this had come from both of them.

Falcon, Tasmin, and Beloria, with Lili were the first to follow them across, and Falcon found himself catching Cheri as the exhaustion caught up with her. When Faye and Believer arrived, Tasmin was on the ground next to the girl, trying to revive her.

"Tasmin, here. Move over. Let's see if Believer can help," said Faye as she dismounted and brought the unicorn closer.

Moving aside, they gave Believer room as his horn started to glow, the light growing as he got nearer. Speedily, the light spread, first to envelope Cheri, unconscious on the ground, then Baby, barely able to stand. Silently, the light continued to grow, spreading through them all as it rose above them.

When it came back down, it formed a dome, stopping the rain. A slight tingle spread through the waiting men, women, and horses with varying reactions. Most grinned as they felt better than they had in days, but a few shivered at the thought of being touched by magic. This time, what Believer did was very different from what he'd done on the trip from Gaban's valley. Then he had been subtle, this time, those who knew him best were exchanging looks of awe. Fay leaned into Believer's neck with a grin. "I wonder what other surprises you have in store for us, my friend?" she whispered so only he could hear.

While everyone was watching the rain sheet off Believer's umbrella, they had forgotten Cheri, lying at their feet, until she gave out a soft moan and rolled onto her side. "Ugh! Did I pass out, again? How long have I been out this time?"

"Not long, dear. Thanks to Believer, not long at all," said Tasmin as Falcon helped her to her feet.

Believer dropped the dome just as Gabriene arrived. "Well, well. You can tap into the magic of Persal, very impressive. You were quite amazing, my dear. That new stretch of trail will be there for a very long time. I haven't seen such potential in anyone since... uhm..." Well, let's just say it's been a long time indeed."

On unsteady legs, Cheri walked over to Baby to lean against his neck and give him a hug. "You did good, Baby. You did good," she said softly.

Meanwhile, Lili crawled out from under Beloria's oiled poncho and jumped to the wet ground. Wet was something she knew well. In a couple of bounds, she reached the giant cedar-like tree just uphill from where they were congregating and put her small hands on its trunk. While Beloria watched curiously, the branches of the tree started to rustle and move, weaving itself together like fingers on a hand. Then the ground moved as the roots rose out of the ground, forming an area protected from the storm and the water running down the hillside. Although the rain seemed to be diminishing on its own, it wasn't fast enough. When Beloria looked around, she noticed Bass watching the small Chugura as well.

Dismounting, Bass walked over to their newest friend and bent to ask her a question. "You can talk to the trees, can't you?"

Lily cocked her head as she looked up at the tall woodsman. "Trees, flowers, any plant that grows. First, I listen to them, then they listen to me," she responded with a cute little shrug.

In amazement, Bass dropped down to his heels. "How is it your speech has improved so much?"

"First, I listen. It's what I do," she said as if it were obvious.

"You've been listening to us talk, haven't you? You're a tricky little minx, aren't you?"

"No, I'm a tricky little Chugura," she responded with a smile.

Bass's laugh rang out across the mountains. "Someday, I'll introduce you to the trees of the Singing Forest," he promised.

"A forest that sings? Really? Oh, I would like to know more of this Singing Forest," she begged, eyes shining in excitement.

"For now, why don't you ask Cheri? She actually got the trees to sing along with her. I grew up there, and it's more than I could ever accomplish."

While they talked, everyone else had crossed the new trail, and Suvaat was supervising as they set up camp. Here the mountain curved away from the edge leaving what amounted to a clearing in the road. Tents were going up while a large fire was laid in the sheltered spot Lili and her tree had created.

Cheri was ushered into the first and largest tent that went up. The same tent she'd been sharing with Faye, Tasmin and Beloria since they left Lohi. Lili was welcomed but so far had preferred sleeping in the trees. Today, in the rain and among alien trees, she came into the tent with the others, although her little nose wrinkled in distaste at the smell of wet canvas.

Once inside, Faye and Beloria helped the still weak Cheri disrobe and wrapped her in a soft blanket while Tasmin put extra water on a brazier to heat, brewing one of her ubiquitous teas with her teapot.

Matew soon called from outside. "Permission to enter, my ladies?" "Permission granted," called Tasmin with a smile.

Matew pushed open the tent flap with one shoulder. A large, round tub was slung over the other one. He was followed by another squire carrying two cauldrons of water, one of which was steaming.

"Behnam thinks you could use a hot wash," said Matew as he put down the tub behind a sheet that was strung in a corner of the tent.

"Thank you," replied Cheri, rubbing her temples. Believer had brought her around, but she still had a killer headache.

Matew left while the other boy began pouring in the hot water. Then he started adding the cold while Faye monitored the temperature. "Do I know you from somewhere?" asked Cheri, looking curiously at his face.

"My name is Timnon, my lady. I was Sir Denahar's squire. Today, they assigned me to help you ladies, but I've been traveling with you since Lohi," he answered shyly.

"No. That isn't it. I'm sorry about Denahar, by the way. I really liked him. I've seen a face like yours before, somewhere. Somewhere before Lohi. Where are you from, Timnon?"

"Uh, you probably wouldn't know it. No one ever goes there. It's a small village high in the mountains. We don't usually talk about it," responded the youth, refusing to look at her.

"Breymin! That's it, isn't it? I met your sister there," exclaimed Cheri, triumphantly.

"You know, Breymin, my lady? How? No one's supposed to know about Breymin."

"Timnon, I'm one of the saviors. How do you think we got here? We came from our world through Gaban's valley."

"Uh. Of course. Sorry, my lady. You met my sister?" he asked, looking up in sudden interest.

"Well, sort of. She yelled at me as I was leaving town, but I remembered her face. You look a lot alike, you know?"

"Yes, my lady. If you don't mind my asking, what did she yell at you? I mean she doesn't usually do that. Yell at people, I mean."

Cheri's eyes drifted away as she recalled, *Don't be too hard on him, he's my brother!* "I, uh, don't really remember what she said. I just remember her face," she prevaricated. "You know, I'd like to get in that bath while it's still hot."

"Oh, yes, excuse me, my lady," he stammered while turning to leave the tent and almost knocking over the center pole.

Cheri couldn't help giggling as he left, but then she winced as her headache attacked, again.

Cheri was slipping into the tub as Beloria climbed off the bedclothes in another corner to gather the blanket she'd dropped. A moment later, Tasmin and Lili returned with a cup of tea while discussing the benefits of different herbs. "I really think, for the type of headache Cheri has, you'll find willow bark works fastest," Lili was insisting.

"You've certainly learned to speak common quite well, and quickly, Lili. Is this a common trait for your people, or is it just you?" asked Faye, following them back into the tent.

"I have been trained since birth to listen and learn, Lady Faye, but yes, my people are very...adaptive, I believe the word is. Since Barakus interfered with our...what's the word?...ah, evolution? Yes, that's it. Anyway, since Barakus' interference, we've had to become very...flexible and learn a great many things, quickly, for survival. To be honest, Buchu doesn't believe Barakus intended us to survive. It's mostly because of Master Gabriene's protection we've had time to grow into our new state," explained Lili succinctly.

Cheri tried to refrain from giggling and aggravating her headache while Faye and Beloria burst out laughing.

"You know, Beloria, she could give you lessons," said Tasmin with a smile.

"Now, wha' be wrong wit' me talkin'?" asked Beloria before she snapped her mouth shut. "Awri' I heared it. Lili, ye wan' ter 'elp me speaks best?

Lili ducked her head shyly, "I'd be honored, Miss Beloria."

*****

"Here's the map I...borrowed. The way I figure it, the ships that left from Lohi will be staging here, this large bay south of Yves on the Raseri Ocean," began Briar Rose.

"Where'd you...find that map?" asked Ciral suspiciously.

"From the library, at the palace. They told us we could 'borrow' whatever we wanted."

"I believe they meant books, Briar Rose, not maps. I also don't think they intended us to remove anything from the palace," argued the small black girl.

"At this point it's irrelevant. Now, here, between Yves and Shairk Tooth Bay, is where I expect the soldiers and ships are staging for their attack, is a small inlet. Much too small for them but perfect for us. If we lay low here, we'll be able to keep an eye out for when they start their assault as well as keeping an eye on the Black Ships on the other side of this ridge. When either one of them move, we can mobilize and time our 'storm' perfectly," continued Briar Rose, ignoring Ciral's stormy scowl.

"How are we supposed to slip past the larger bay without

being seen? Don't you think they'll have lookouts?" asked Cirroc skeptically.

"With Aenas's help, we can head out to sea. Surely you have friends who can bring us safely back where we want to be, don't you?" she asked blithely, turning to the tall boy.

"I akin axed de whaltes," began Aenas. "See, no problem."

"Really? What was your plan before we brought Aenas along?" asked Saird, scratching his head.

"Uhm...," began Briar Rose hesitantly.

"We still can't control our weather. We're getting better, but how do we let loose a storm to attack the Black Ships without damaging our own fleet? How do we keep from sinking the Black Ships with the children aboard? Have you figured any of this out?" pressed Ciral, regretting letting herself get talked into this.

"Wai' I be try ter say, whaltes hees a mend o' theirn owns. Tha' won' hep less'n tha a mend ter," injected Aenas into the conversation.

"What? What was that?" asked Ciral in confusion. She still had some trouble understanding Aenas when he talked.

"He said, 'Whaltes have a mind of their own.' Basically, he can ask, but they'll make up their own mind if they want to help," explained Saith.

"What about dolfins?" asked Briar Rose hopefully.

"Dof's mi' tak' us'n outa then 'cide ter be off'n."

"They're not dependable. Once they get us out of sight of land, they might not bring us back," translated Cirroc.

"What about the fish? Can they help us? I thought you could control the fish," suggested Briar Rose.

"Fishes be stupe," he shrugged. "Cai' fin' way home, not else," he shrugged.

"All fish can do is find their way home, to spawn," said Cirroc, understanding only too well. "Other than that, they're rather stupid."

"Well, we'll just have to ask the whaltes, then, won't we? Unless you'd like to share your original plan, Briar?" suggested Ciral with a smirk.

"Well...I was going to figure it out when we got there. Now that Aenas is here...well, it's been figured out, hasn't it? Assuming the whaltes cooperate, of course," she said defensively.

"And the weather? Have you figured out how we're going to use it without killing everyone yet? It's not like stopping a water pump. For good's sake, it's the weather, Briar," pressed Ciral.

"We can do a couple of small test runs, while we wait. If the whaltes help us, we'll be in the cove tomorrow." Briar Rose shrugged as if it were a small detail.

"This 'plan' of yours appears to have a great many holes in it, Briar," commented Cirroc, disparagingly, while Huge and Saird nodded agreement. The entire crew had shortened Briar Rose's name to just Briar about the third day out, and Briar Rose found she rather liked it.

"No. That's not good enough. So far, this has all been your plan, Briar and, if you don't mind my saying so, it's only a half-baked plan at that. On this, I don't want to wait. We need to generate at least one storm, and see if we have any control, here, out in the ocean. Not in an inlet where we could find ourselves smashed against the rocks or stranded on the beach or even sink the boat. The men can handle the boat. It's time we created our first storm."

Scurrying to get out of the way, Saith and Saird took up positions on the rudder while Aenas stopped the wave carrying them across the sea. Huge stood in the bow with Cirroc, ready to take down the jib sail.

"Huge! Huge, come over here. We'll need you to stay close in case we have to be separated. If the storm starts getting out of hand and we can't control it, just knock us apart," instructed Ciral, remembering Cheri tackling them the only other time they'd dared touch each other.

When everyone was in position, Ciral and Briar Rose slowly approached each other in middeck. Ciral's wind started kicking up just before Briar Rose's lightning jumped between them and back again. Cirroc and Huge dove to the deck, covering their ears, as the thunder boomed, echoing right overhead. In the stern, Saith and Saird huddled over the rudder, trying to stay the course. They found themselves in the midst of the storm.

With the wind whirling around them and Briar Rose's lightning creating fireworks overhead, the thunder was nonstop. It was remarkable how quickly the clouds gathered, piling themselves one atop the other and the rain started. This was no gentle rain on a summer's afternoon. It wasn't even a little squall known to rise unexpectedly from the sea at this time of year. Nor was it slow in gaining momentum. It was a full-blown gale raging suddenly across the ocean, the wind whipping the waves, causing them to grow higher and higher.

"Bring it under control, before we're swamped!" yelled Cirroc as he wrestled with the jib sail.

Aenas ran to the rail, putting his hands in the rising waves, trying to counteract the effect of the storm.

Straining against the power running through her, trying to find a way to control it instead of letting it use her, Briar Rose struggled to find a way to make it...less, less violent, less all-consuming, less wonderful. She swelled with power as the electricity ran through her veins and part of her didn't want to let it go. "Ci...Ci...Ciral! Can you slow...slow down the wind? Maybe then...then I can gain control," she yelled, trying to be heard.

Ciral nodded as she sucked in the wind and it started to lessen. Seeing that, Briar tried again to pull the electricity back into herself as well and she screamed, dropping to her knees but not letting go of Ciral.

Gritting her teeth, she tried again. She had to learn how to do this, even if it hurt like Doome. This time, she pulled on the lightning slowly, very, very slowly. It hurt, oh it hurt, but the storm lessened. Finally they broke apart to crumple on deck and roll against opposite rails. Huge ran to Briar Rose, to see if she was still breathing. Saith started to rise from the rudder, but Saird pulled him back, it was going to take two to fight the remnants of the storm.

Cirroc ran to Ciral, who was slumped against the mainmast but still conscious.

"Huge! Is she breathing?" called Saith from the tiller, a frantic look on his face as he stared at Briar.

Gently, Huge lowered his head so he could listen to Briar's breath and heartbeat. Sitting up, he nodded. Then, still being as gentle as he was with small animals and children, he picked her up and with solid steps, took her down to the cabin.

"Ciral, how are you?" asked Cirroc.

Ciral sat up and shook the rain out of her golden braids. "Oh, I'm just fine. Thank you, Cirroc. Thankfully, the lightning Briar generates doesn't pass through me. How's Briar? Where's Briar?"

"She's unconscious. Huge says she's breathing, but he took her to the cabin. Maybe you should go down as well?" suggested the little dark-chocolate man with the close-cropped blond hair as he helped her to her feet.

Ciral looked at the closed door to the cabin thoughtfully. "Let me lessen the wind a bit first. Then I'll go rest."

Slowly, Ciral started inhaling, and the winds slowed, and the rain stopped, and the skies began to clear.

"Well, that might be something," she said thoughtfully. "It's time I talk to Briar."

In the cabin, Huge was taking up most of the room as he rubbed a near-naked Briar with towels, trying to get her dry and warm. "Huge! What are you doing? Here, I think you'd better let me take care of that," cried Ciral, pulling up a blanket to cover the other girl as she pushed the big man up the ladder and out the door.

When she returned to the berth, Briar was waking up. Ciral sat at the table as the pale girl with her black braids came fully awake. "Ciral, get me a basin!"

Quickly, Ciral reached into the nearby galley and pulled out a basin, sliding it in front of the other girl just in time. Briar Rose vomited until there was nothing left and then she retched for a while longer.

Finally, Ciral handed her a bota of water and took away the basin. "Are you all right, now?" she asked.

Numbly, Briar nodded. "Good. I have good tidings and bad. Evidently, creating wind, what I do, is fairly easy. Creating lightning, what you do, is fairly hard. I can control the wind; can you control your lightning? It didn't look like it to me. To me it looked like the lightning was trying to kill you. Now for the good tidings, once we're separated, your lightning ceases, and I can calm the wind. The storm stops, and we're left with only the waves."

Briar Rose was holding her head. "Shh... Don't talk so loud. Just so you know, it leaves my head pounding like the drums of Doome," she whispered, lying back down.

Shaking her head, Ciral rose gracefully and turned to open cupboards, looking for the honey. She was dribbling some on bread when she returned. "Here, eat this. You've sapped your strength, and this will help," she said, making honey bread for herself as well.

"I'm thinking we might need Aenas's help as well. More of a team effort, next time," she continued thoughtfully.

As Briar Rose nodded off to sleep, Ciral shook her head. *Huh!*

Next time. What a comforting thought that was.

*****

When they were still two days out from the lumber village of Hemlock Hollow, Suvaat sent Falcon and Amalee ahead to check on the barges he hoped were waiting there. When Falcon rode out, Ochwatt ran beside him, easily keeping pace with the scout's horse, Wolf.

"So you're coming with me? I hope you can keep up," challenged Falcon with a smile.

Ochwatt grinned back, and Falcon flinched involuntarily. "I run fast," he said succinctly.

Nodding, Falcon urged Wolf to go faster as the terrain allowed.

The time when everything was supposed to come together was getting close, and it was a two-day trip downriver with the lumber barges. Amalee's brilliant blue pinfeathers glinted in the sun as she soared through the hills and up the mountains toward Lake Annoura in the timberlands of Zabir. Oh, to fly free and not be contained by the movements of the troop, slowed by the uncertain footing and the climb as the trails continued to get steeper.

Halfway up the mountain, Ochwatt stopped. "Falcon, I needs ter go deeper inter de mounts. We be at Yves in a hand of days," he said, waving his arm to encompass the mountains behind him. With that, the sasquatch waved to his new friend and took off running through the woods. He had his own errand to run.

With a friendly grin, Falcon bowed to the retreating giant. "Until we meet again, friend," he called after him.

What Falcon found when he reached Hemlock Hollow was unacceptable. Three of the four men who'd been sent ahead to arrange everything were sitting despondently on the empty pier, looking anxiously across Lake Annoura and the lumber outpost on the far shore, Cedar Hall.

"What's going on here? Where are the barges?" asked Falcon as he dismounted from Wolf.

"Sir Falcon! Uh...they're over at Cedar Hall, loading up," said the red-haired sergeant, as he and his men stood quickly. Then he looked up at Amalee as she screeched from above.

"They are scheduled to be back tomorrow, aren't they? Gabriene, Suvaat and the saviors will be here by tomorrow night and ready to leave the morning after. We need those barges here or we'll miss the party in Yves. Our part in the coming battle is very important. Without us bottling up the way up the cliff, they might get some of the children out, maybe more than a few. What are they doing out there, anyway?" demanded a frustrated Falcon.

"They be finishin' gettin' dere logs lashed on dem barges, Sir Falcon. Didna 'ave enough logs on dis side so dey sent de barges ter Cedar Hall fer more. We tried ter stop 'em, we really did but, well, dese loggers ain' no weak Annies, now are they? We were more than a bit outnumbered an' dey carries axes."

With a rueful shake of his head, Falcon let out a shrill whistle, and Amalee swooped down to land on his leather patched shoulder. Opening the satchel on his hip, he fished out a small slip of paper and a piece of slate to quickly scratch a note. "Your friend, the one who went to Cedar Hall, he can read, can't he?"

"Aye, Sir Falcon. Gabriene's always insisted all the soldiers be taught ter read, write, and do sums. Right alongside the knights, if need be. Said he dinna want any of us ter be, uh, ig'nant, ye see?"

"*Ignorant*, the word is *ignorant*, Sergeant," said Falcon absently as he tied his note on Amalee's leg and sent her across the lake. With any luck, the barges would be back in time to leave, morning after next.

Curious, Falcon looked up at the mountains where Ochwatt had gone. "What's up there? Anything interesting?" he asked.

"Naw. From what I've heard, ain' even any trails and there be rumors of...strange things been seen, now an' agin. I wouldna take much stock in dat. I been talkin' ter de locals, ye see," answered the sergeant.

"You know, Sergeant, there is more in the sky and here below than you would believe," murmured the scout, looking back across the lake to see if Amalee was returning.

*****

Shairk Bay was defined by tall spires surrounded by jagged rocks lining the southern promontory, several of which ended in sharp spines. It was these jagged "teeth" that gave the bay its name. luckily, the one farthest east had broken off, sometime in the distant past, leaving a nearly flat platform. It made a fairly good lookout point, although the climb was treacherous. To the north, the promontory was wide and solid, until the eastern tip where two more of the "teeth" rose from the sea and broken rocks below. These spires, like most of those to the south were sharp and craggy. Among the marines, six men had been found who were willing to climb the flat-topped spire and act as lookouts. The lookouts assigned to the north had a much easier climb. Ropes had been rigged after the original ascent by a man used to climbing sea cliffs at his home, looking for birds' nests and the eggs within. These ropes were intended to speed up the changing of the guard and allow the scouts to bring news quickly.

Aboard the flagship, *Winter Storm*, anchored in the bay with several dozen other vessels of varying sizes. Admiral

Utheran of Gabriene's fleet had gathered the captains, both military and civilian to go over their plan of attack. Also present were the captains of the marine forces aboard each ship and the scout who had just come down from the shairk's tooth to report. He'd been on morning watch for three hours.

"Staivad, repeat your report. We're all going to need to know this," he ordered, once everyone had congregated on deck. There wasn't enough room in the spacious admiral's cabin, with this many ships gathered.

"Sir, yes, sir!" came the prompt response. "We don't know if it means anything, but there's been a series of violent but short-lived storms showing up to the south. They're headed this way, and if the pattern continues, we could be hit by tomorrow morning, sir," reported Staivad succinctly.

"This ain't nothin' ter be worriet aboot. We've all been through storms, we'll weather this too," said Captain Ta'Jar of the *Flying Seahawk* dismissively.

"Beg pardon, sir. You can't count on that with all of these storms. One moment the skies are clear and the sea is calm, then the winds and lightning begin, together. The waves, within moments they're towering and beating against the cliffs to the south. The clouds and the rain come after the lightning and thunder, as if they've been called. I ain't never seen that before. These storms are very violent and so far have been strangely localized but do not doubt, any ship, any ship at all, could easily be smashed against these cliffs you've been hiding behind," insisted Staivad. "I've been a sailor since I was a lad, sir. If these storms grow, or don't stop as quickly as they come up, like they have been, this entire fleet could be destroyed and so could the Black Ships, sir. I thought our mission was to rescue the children, sir."

"What you're telling us is impossible, storms don't act that way," insisted Captain Vandert of the brigantine *Summer Storm* of the naval fleet.

"Sirs, don't you think I know how this sounds? If I hadn't watched these storms come and go for myself... If I hadn't seen it happen five times, today...I wouldn't believe it either. But, sir," he said, turning back to Admiral Utheran, "this is what you placed us up on that spire to watch for. I was told to watch for any unusual movement. This, sir, is unusual movement."

The admiral stared at his scout thoughtfully for a moment. "What would you suggest, Staivad? It's two days before we're to move out to sea and head for Yves. If we move prematurely, we could lose the children."

"These storms were only sighted clearly today. Yesterday, we saw intermittent flashes of lightning on the far southern horizon. They stopped as suddenly as they began and each time, the skies cleared as if there had been no storm at all. There's more happening here than merely a series of storms, sir."

"You're thinking it might be Barakus? He's used storms before, but once he starts a storm, he whips it into a frenzy and lets it loose. Storms that start and stop without warning. That sounds like something entirely different. These storms do sound worrisome, so we'll continue to keep an eye out, even at night."

"Night, sir?"

"Lightning can be seen at night. We'll need the watches set both night and day until we're ready to set sail. Got that, Staivad?"

"Aye, sir. I'll set up the rotation, sir," Staivad responded with a sharp salute, before heading over the side of the ship to his waiting dory set to ferry him back to the base of the scout's pillar.

*****

Faye was wet, tired, and miserable. Believer had finally

reached his limit on being able to help. The rain had started when they were barely a half turn on the trail this morning, and while it was a soft rain, it didn't make her any less wet. The rain had slowed them to a walk, and it was nearly midnight. There was nothing she wanted, right now, more than to be clean, dry, warm, and well-fed so she could fall into a deep sleep. Even better would be if she could sleep in past sunrise. This is not the life she'd been raised to, and she felt it was wearing her thin.

She barely noticed they had entered a town until Believer pulled to a stop in front of the Potlach, the local inn. Bass was there before she could raise her head, pulling her into his arms and carrying her into the warm common room where he found a chair close to the fire. A moment later, as Behnam carried in a sleeping Cheri, Falcon brought dry blankets for the two of them as well as Beloria, Tasmin, and Gabriene, who had developed a wracking cough.

Lili jumped from Beloria's arms as she sat down and moved closer to the fire, shaking excess water from her fur in the process. She gave the wizard a worried look as she turned to Falcon. "I need hot water so's I can make tea for the master. If I can get two kettles, I'll brew another pot for everyone else."

"That'll be good, lady Lili. We could all use something about now," he responded, turning to the short, chubby innkeeper who was bringing out large bowls of hot stew and mugs of beer.

"We've got hot meals, hot baths and warm beds waiting for everyone," he beamed. "Sir Falcon has made sure we have everything ready and waiting."

As the food was set on the table, Suvaat and Gurmail came in from getting the horses, and Believer settled out of the drizzle. "Falcon, are the barges ready to depart in the morning?" called the black knight as he doffed his wet cloak.

"About that... They've been loading wood from the other side of the lake, and they'll be here by three spans after sunrise," admitted Falcon. "The good tidings are. Gabriene and the ladies will be able to sleep in a bit tomorrow, and from the looks of them, it's overdue."

Suvaat took a long look at the women and Gabriene, especially Cheri who was roused from her sleep by the smell of stew and Faye who barely had the energy to pick up a spoon. Gabriene's dry, heaving cough started up again as Lili put a strong-smelling cup of tea in front of him. "Here, master, drink this. Drink it all down. You should be better by morning, but I'll make you more for breakfast. Ladies, this tea should help you as well. Keep you from coming down with... whatever the master has."

"Well, today has been very hard on us all, especially them, I will admit. Maybe leaving a little later won't go amiss after all," he acknowledged.

"Where is our friend Ochwatt?" asked Gabriene, looking around as the tea took effect, giving him some respite from his cough.

"Just before we reached the town, he took off for the mountains. I'm not sure where he was headed. Said we'd meet in Yves in a hand of days," said Falcon with a shrug.

"You didn't try to stop him?" asked Suvaat.

"Would you?" responded Falcon with a questioning look to the knight.

"Good point. We can only hope he knows what he's doing," admitted Suvaat reluctantly.

"I'd say we can only hope he doesn't mess things up but do any of us really know anything about him?" asked Tasmin, looking around at the others.

Faye lay her head down on the table while Cheri leaned on Behnam. Exchanging glances, Bass and Behnam rose to take the two women up to their rooms and waiting hot baths.

Once in the room, the innkeeper's wife and two daughters took over, and in short order, they were clean, warm and tucked into warmed beds. They were both asleep before the bathtubs could be removed.

At two hours past sunrise, Tasmin came into the room and opened the closed shutters, letting the sunshine rouse the two women who finally felt rested.

"Time to wake up, ladies. The barges are due in about a span, and Suvaat wants to leave as soon as we're loaded. It will take two days to get down the river to Yves, and that's when the ships and Ebony's fliers are supposed to be poised to launch the attack. We're quickly running out of time," she said brightly.

Faye, feeling restored didn't even mind Tasmin's chipper attitude. "Come on, Cheri. We can't keep Persal waiting. After all, it's why we came."

Actually, they weren't all loaded and ready to leave until a span and a half after the two barges arrived, pushing their log rafts ahead of them. Just when Suvaat was instructing the captains to cast off, several burly lumberjacks, with axes in hand, jumped aboard each of the flatboats.

"What's this? We need to be going," objected Suvaat.

"Then, let's go. Sounds like fun," agreed a particularly tall and brawny man with blue eyes and a heavy blond beard, leaning casually on his ax handle.

Suvaat stared at the man and his companions hard for a moment before nodding. "Let's go, captains!" he called.

CHAPTER 32

Attack, Attack, Attack

Ebony, Aliand, Galad, and the men who had been training for the past two weeks with Ebony were climbing the cliffs north of Yves, leaving the *Mal de Verde* and Jakar far below. They had to reach the top by the end of the day to be in position when the attack on the Bay of Yves began the following morning. Most of the slope was at least fifty degrees, but at this point, it was a gentler slope than in the city itself and much better than farther north where the waves of the strait crashed between the mainland and Chimera Island.

When tomorrow's dawn broke, the *Mal de Verde* was to move out into the turbulent seas and watch for Black Ships making a run for home. Their goal was to give such longships pause while Ebony's troops soared down from above to take whatever ships they could.

There was a blanket of low clouds cloaking the offshore isle as Ebony came to a ledge and glanced across the raging sea to see the clouds disperse in tatters and reveal the broken peak of the island. Pausing, she noted what was obviously the cone of an old volcano covered in lush greenery. Just before the clouds closed ranks, she took a closer look at a promontory jutting out from the near side. Wait, was that an actual Chimera? Hadn't Gabriene said they were extinct?

Ebony blinked, and the clouds were back, hiding whatever she had seen in the mist.

Taking a deep breath, she turned back to the cliff and continued her climb. Behind her, Aliand was having some problems, and Galad was there, to steady her, but when she slipped a bit and he caught her, she laughed. "Oh, this is so much fun!" she exclaimed.

Galad shook his head, hoisting Ebony's hang glider up higher on his shoulder while Ebony joined the laughter.

"I bet you've never done anything like this before," she called back to the girl.

"Are you jesting? I was never even allowed to get dirty when I was a bairn. Being an Imaldi is so much better than being a nobleman's daughter with fancy dresses and endless dances where you're nothing but a political pawn. If my sisters could only see me now," she cried in excitement, wiping her muddy hands on her trousers, borrowed from the cabin boy, before continuing the climb.

*****

It was nearly dusk and two days out from Lake Annoura when the first water gate in the outer walls of Yves loomed into view. The coxswain of the first barge blew his horn and the guard, recognizing the barges, signaled to the gatekeeper to raise the portcullis. While the horses and Believer remained on deck with the lumbermen and boat crew, the women and knights huddled in the cramped cabin until they were through the first wall. Once inside, while the second barge was passing through, the first barge pulled over to the docks on the northern side of the river, deftly navigating their load of logs into a shallow bay next to the log yard.

When the men and women emerged from the cabin to lead their mounts from the barge, they were surrounded by the lumbermen who had come down from the mountains. The men onshore wrangling the logs barely gave them a second glance. The watch had let them in, and they had their own jobs to do.

They left the riverside warehouses in small groups of five or six, while Gabriene and Behnam made their way to the citadel dominating the upper city. The wizard's mission was to alert Imaland Hambertick, the governor of Zabir. Once Gabriene told the guards at a side gate who he was, they sent a runner to find the steward and Governor and announce their arrival.

"Master Gabriene. What a surprise. What are you doing here? You haven't left Lohi in…, well, years," stammered Governor Hambertick when they were shown in. The fat, florid governor was staring at them, amazed at the unexpected visitation. With an overly genial smile, he waddled across the floor of the great hall to greet his guests.

"Well, well. Ahem, sorry to come unannounced, Governor. We didn't dare send advanced notice. I need to speak to you in private," said Gabriene with a warm smile.

A short time later, they were alone in the governor's study. Gabriene sank into a cushioned chair with a sigh. "The saviors have arrived, Governor Hambertick. We've come for the children of the Taking. We're going to take them back tomorrow. We could use your help."

"Master Gabriene, my job is to protect the people who live on Barakus's doorstep. If you do this…if we get involved, we'll be annihilated."

"Well, well. I admit it's a possibility, governor, but think of all those children in the bay. It's time we put a stop to it. It's time we stood up to Barakus."

"I don't disagree with you, master, but what about my people?"

"Governor, how about this," interrupted Behnam, "You keep this quiet and recall your men. Pull them back into the citadel as soon as possible and keep them here until we've gone?"

"There'll be fighting at the docks and in the city, and you want me to do nothing? Send no one to protect the people?" asked the governor with feigned distress while a calculating gleam lit his eyes.

"Yes, not only that, we need to make sure no one leaves the citadel once they return. We can't have a spy warning the Black Ships," insisted Behnam, sharing a look with Gabriene.

When the governor hesitated, Gabriene cleared his throat. "Ahem. Well, we're going to proceed regardless but if we can't get your cooperation, we'd at least rather not have to fight your men as well. Will you pull back the guard?"

Warily, the governor's eyes shifted back and forth between the two men before he stood and went to the door. "I need to see Captain Alzo, now!" he snapped before closing the door again. "We'll call in the guard and set only our most trusted men on the gates. We won't interfere," he agreed, drying his sweaty hand on his robe before putting it out to shake.

Gabriene rose to take the hand while Behnam settled for an abbreviated version of his bow. Anyone else would have known it was an insult, but the governor had never met a Mojar before.

Once outside the citadel, the two men headed for the bay and one of the inns on the wandering track of Bay Road, where the others were waiting.

Meanwhile, Falcon and the lumberjacks who had joined their quest made their way to a tavern not far from where the river became a waterfall, plunging into the sea. This was where they usually spent their time at the end of the season.

*****

Late that night, as the city sank into the sleep of innocence and the lights blinked out one by one, dark shapes started to flow over the northern walls and into the shadows. Silently, they glided in flickers across lamp-lit streets to disappear again in dark alleys. The movements were so swift and graceful as to be barely noticeable.

Emeali, in her small apartment next to Bay Road, finished putting away the last of the clean dishes and turned to clean the sink when she noticed movement outside her upper window. *What was that? Was someone out there?* Looking closer, she shook her head. *No, no one was that tall. What was moving out there?* Then the shadows quit moving, whatever she might have seen was gone, headed down the switchback of Bay Road toward the port below. With a frown, she shook her head. Whatever it had been, it wasn't her concern. She had to rise early in the morning to return to Mistress Gandival's dress shop where she worked as a seamstress.

On the road to the bay, Ochwatt and his kin from the eastern mountains, male and female, were still flitting from shadow to shadow but finding them farther apart. Doorways, too short for the sasquatch, and spaces, too narrow for their frames, between the buildings had to suffice. Occasionally, they encountered a street corner where a narrow side street, carved into the cliff, curved to the north or south of Bay Road and was well lit. This was when they were most vulnerable.

Luckily, there were very few people about, and they were very good at passing unnoticed. Ochwatt had studied the map in Lohi carefully while the others were making their plans and his goal was the warehouses on the southern docks. They needed to be down there in time for the assault scheduled just after dawn.

Then, at one such intersection, the pounding of marching feet could be heard, coming up the road from the bay and headed toward the citadel.

Ochwatt's head snapped up, and so did his left fist. As the sound grew louder, he opened his hand wide and waggled it.

Immediately the bigfoot faded into any shadows they could find. When the troops marched around the curve of the switchback, the road was empty, and without a backward glance, the lieutenant continued leading his men to the citadel. He wasn't going to look too closely at having an unexpected night off duty.

When the troops disappeared around another corner, Ochwatt emerged, and he and his people continued flitting through the shadows.

*****

It was two hours before dawn. Admiral Utheran stood on the bridge of the *Winter Storm* as it sallied forth, leading the mismatched fleet of naval and merchant ships out of Shairk's Tooth Bay and headed north, toward Yves. The smaller coastal ships that had also been impressed for use were to follow an hour after sunrise, to help with the children. These ships were loaded with supplies for the children, blankets, and food, once they'd been rescued.

By the light of the full moon, without running lights, they sailed silently up the coast to blockade the bay and keep the Black Ships hemmed in place. They expected as much as a hundred and fifty vessels.

Before the captains had returned to their ships, he had emphasized again, "Our job is to keep the Black Ships in the bay. We are not to engage if it can be helped. We're here to save those children, all of them. Whatever else has to be done, do...not...use... your...cannon."

"What do we do if they fire on us?" asked Captain Vandert.

"They're carrying as many as a hundred and fifty children on each and every one of those ships. They have no room for cannon. Don't forget, they've never been challenged before. They aren't going to be expecting us. If they try to run the blockade, close in and board. We'll fight hand to hand.

Also, keep a lookout for the command ship. There will be something about it, making it stand out. A larger poop deck or perhaps a unique flag of some sort. Have your lookouts keep that in mind. Don't forget, stealth is paramount while we get in place. We don't want those ships to know we're there until the sun comes up. All right, gentlemen, it's time to go."

*****

It was during the dark before dawn when Suvaat sent his troops down toward the bay. In groups of two, or three, they made their way down Bay Road, as if on their way to work on the docks. The last two groups included Tasmin, Bass, Suvaat, Faye, Gurmail, Cheri, Beloria, and Lili. Keeping the saviors safe was still a priority.

Falcon and the entire group of lumberjacks made their way downhill first. Laughing and joking as they went. Looking for all the world as if they were still drunk from the night before. Occasionally, as they caroused, there were shutters slammed open, and heads popped out of doors.

"Shut it! I be tryin' ter sleep 'ere!"

"Keep it doon, some o' us be needing ter rest!"

Each time they were admonished, they would briefly lower their voices, with a low laugh before gradually raising them again after another turn on the curving road. Their job was to scout the warehouses and pick the best spots for the coming attack.

Gabriene, Behnam, and five remaining soldiers were in the next group, anxious to meet up with the others. They would also be rendezvousing with some of the marines coming ashore from the fleet. They had come around the headland during low tide and were waiting in the hills just above the warehouses on the southern side of the docks. Behnam was tasked with positioning them along the wharf, ready to board the twenty-six ships they expected to still be tied to the piers. Unfortunately, the bulk of the fleet was anchored throughout the bay, ready to head home.

The plan depended so much on timing. They must be ready to block all exits. Once the fleet blockaded the bay and the men aboard the Black Ships realized they couldn't get out without endangering their "precious" cargo, they well might try to take the children out through Yves and over the perilous mountains. At the very least, they expected some of the soldiers to try to desert rather than be taken prisoner.

*****

A half hour after Saith watched the last of the large fleet, made up of naval vessels and merchant ships sail past their hidden bay, Aenas called his friends the whaltes to help guide the *Bonnie Jean* to a good place where they could watch the upcoming battle. They had decided to watch for escaping ships. They were going to take that as their cue to start the storm.

When the whaltes arrived, a young bull stationed himself at the stern, his head towering over the small craft. He started to nudge the sloop while a cow lined up on either side, bumping the small boat to keep it in line and escort it out to sea.

Ciral, still highly dubious, wondered if this was a good idea. "What's going to happen to the Lohi fleet when our storm hits them? We can't control our powers well enough, to attack only the Black Ships and not have the waves crash against the fleet, Briar," she objected, voicing once more her argument.

"We'll send the storm to the north, away from the Bay of Yves. I have agreed we'd hold off until we're needed. Don't worry, I won't forget there are children aboard those longships," said Briar Rose, dismissively. She was sure her plan would work. It had to, or why had they come?

Ciral sighed. Wondering, not for the first time, why she had agreed to this crazy expedition.

*****

The sky turned as red as blood when the first rays of the rising sun crested the horizon. Admiral Utheran watched the water turn from black to blood red, to pink, to a deep green and sent a silent plea to the unnamed powers above that the water wouldn't turn red again this day. As the light spread across the large Bay of Yves, he raised his glass and began looking closely at the multitude of longships moored there. He was searching for the command ship. Taking that ship could make all the difference in the coming battle, and he expected to find it close to where the two estuaries curved toward each other, forming a constricted entry. The captain should be ready to lead the way home.

Raising his glass, he looked out at the fleet of black galleys spread across the estuary and he saw the activity begin at the docks. A few minutes later, movement increased throughout the other ships as they noticed his fleet barring the way out. Then the yelling could be heard cresting across the open waves, reaching his ears as more and more sailors and soldiers ran to the rails of their ships. Well, they'd accomplished one thing, they had surprised their prey. The next move was up to them.

Without lowering his glass, he said to his first mate, standing next to him, "Do we have a count?"

Immediately, the mate turned to the mast. "Ahoy the nest! Do we have a count?" he hollered, cupping his mouth as he did so.

The second mate, stationed at the base of the mast, relayed the inquiry.

From the lookout in the crow's nest, came another yell,

and again the second mate relayed the answer. "One hundred eleven in the bay. Unknown at the dock."

The admiral turned his glass to the fifty-seven ships in his blockade and thought of the fifty-eight still on the way. If the ground troops stopped all of those ships tied up to the docks, it was still one hundred and eleven to one hundred and five, once the rest of his fleet arrived. If they made a break for it, the estuaries formed a bottleneck, turning the odds to their favor, of course, but how were they going to keep them all in once they engaged?

Without worrying further on a future he couldn't control, he returned to his scan of Barakus's fleet. If they managed to stop them today, they'd not only save all those children; they'd cripple Barakus as well.

*****

When the morning sun turned the bay red, the marines and other fighters, waiting near the docks, moved out in a wave from warehouses, brothels, and taverns to board the few galleys moored there. The men on these ships would be the last to see the Lohi fleet but the first to be taken. The sailors, and most of the soldiers, were asleep when the attackers climbed aboard, overpowering the two guards per ship without a sound before making their way down the gangway to the captain's cabin. At the same time, other men started overpowering the soldiers on deck.

It wasn't long before Falcon tried to wake one of the larger soldiers and the man woke with his arms swinging, catching his attacker on the chin. Instantly, Amalee let out a shriek and swooped down from atop the fire-dragon figurehead, attacking the man's face and disorienting him. When Falcon regained his feet, he was quick to dispatch the man, but they were no longer operating in stealth. Several sailors and soldiers were roused by the ruckus and joined the fray, their noise waking those still sleeping on the neighboring galleys and the fighting began in earnest.

Gurmail and Suvaat stood restlessly at the doorway to one of the warehouses, guarding the women inside. As the men aboard the galleys began fighting back, Suvaat, started to take a step toward the closest ship but Gurmail snatched him back. "We are sworn to protect the saviors, Sir Suvaat. We cannot leave them."

Suvaat growled as he returned to the doorway, glancing back into the dim interior lit only by Gabriene's gleaming staff.

Out on a ship, Behnam was pressed against a gunwale and had just taken out two of the soldiers who had risen with swords ready when he turned to meet the next and noticed other galleys heading their way, presumably to help. Looking around, he assessed his position, was it time to move on? That's when he noticed about eight very large and hairy sasquatch he didn't recognize stepping in wide strides across the deck before bounding onto one of the ships coming to the aid of the docked galleys. Well, there was one problem taken care of.

Taking another look at the ship he was on Behnam saw only one or two soldiers hadn't died or been taken prisoner. The ship was theirs. It was time to free the children. Crossing to the hatch, Behnam struck the lock, snapping the hasp, and the lock while Tasmin and Beloria boarded the ship to help. He would stay to help watch over them while Suvaat and Faye boarded another ship and Gurmail helped Cheri on a third.

The men raised the hatches, finding the holds full of hundreds of scared and dirty children huddled in the corners.

"We've come to rescue you," said Tasmin gently, putting her hand out to the young boy standing with a girl about the same age to his left. Behind them were several more of the older children, ranged as if to protect the youngest who were hidden deep in the hold. Uneasy, the boy looked behind him, to the children he was trying to shelter. They hadn't seen a woman aboard before. "What was that noise?" he asked hesitantly.

"Well, taking the ship from those other men wasn't easy. There was just a bit of a battle, but now you're safe. Would you like to come out? We'll see you're fed and you can get clean. Seems to me it's a bit smelly down there," said the old resistance fighter, pushing stray strands of gray hair back in her bun as she gestured to Beloria standing behind her.

Nodding, Beloria stepped forward, and the boy looked again at the girl next to him who had stepped closer. "First, we must help the little ones," she insisted, moving aside. Behind her, slowly, the other children made an aisle to those in the rear, pulling the little ones to the front so they could go to safety first

In groups of two and three, and then in a flood, the little ones came. Then the next older children moved topside where the marines had already cleared away the dead. Finally, the oldest, who had so stalwartly tried to protect the others emerged. As they came on deck it was nearing high sun, and without a word, they found their kin, the oldest putting protective arms around their siblings in great hugs, be it one, two, or more. The few children who were alone stood slightly apart or moved together to create their own family. Silently, Beloria went to each of those who stood apart, giving her hugs freely to those most in need.

Similar scenes were playing out up and down the wharf as other ships were unloaded. On some ships, the children came out into the fresh air in a rush when invited. On others, they came out in small groups, families or children who had bonded over the last few weeks. In several of the ships, after most of the children emerged, there were a few children still hiding in the hold. Too afraid to come out into the sun. It wasn't long before almost twenty-five hundred children were milling on the decks, waiting to reach the wharves and the warehouses beyond. Looking about, Behnam's gaze went to the fleet still in the bay. Could Jessamine possibly take in all of these children?

*****

In the interim, the longships in the bay found all access to the open sea blocked and had to make a decision. Surrender or chance the blockade. The hastily assembled navy and merchant ships from Lohi numbered fifty-seven. They still had nearly one hundred ships that hadn't been taken by either the Swaloh marines or the huge and terrifying animals swarming the galleys who'd gone to the aid of the ships at the docks.

On the command ship, the *Hydra*, with its five dragon heads on the prow, General Zandert assessed the frenzied action in port briefly before returning his attention to the blockade. Carefully, he assessed the strengths and weaknesses of each ship. Where was their weak point? Ah, there, at the tip of the southern estuary, that ketch seemed a bit older and definitely smaller than the others. He turned to Captain Hindersen. "Look to the south. See that ketch? That's our way out."

"It do look ter be a bit shaky, mebbe. How yer thinnin' we be breachin' it? If'n we lead der way, dey kin still open fire."

"They won't open fire, fool! They've come for the children. They'll try to board, but we outnumber them. We'll send several ships toward the fleet as a whole, divert three to go for the ketch. They'll form the vanguard and we'll be right behind. We must get through to warn Lord Barakus. The people of south Persal are declaring war."

"War, Zandert? I woulda thought it was just they's a wantin' ter be reclaimin' dere chillins," objected the captain.

"They haven't tried to reclaim their children in over fifteen hundred years, Hindersen. Did you hear the rumors while you were in Persal?"

"Yer mean the ones as the savior 'as finally come? Yes, I heard. Them rumors 'ave circulated afore and always been not but dat, rumor. 'Taint no reason ter take stock now."

"Do yer really believe there's no connection to the rumors and this rather bold assault to save their children?"

"Well, ah…"

"Personally, I think it may be a bit too much of a coincidence. No, Hindersen, Gabriene, and the mysterious savior, or even saviors, are declaring war. On us, here and now and, by extension, on Lord Barakus. Signal the ships and keep the enemy troops from coming up on our rear. It appears we've already lost the ships on the docks," commanded the General. When it came to battle, he was in charge.

*****

When the signal flags rose on the lines of the *Hydra*, Admiral Utheran caught sight of them, and he lowered the glass to the ship itself. It was nearly identical to the other Black Ships, except…there, the figurehead. It was a hydra. Ah, he should have known. All the other ships had variations of dragons or snakes on their prow, only the command ship would dare sport a five-headed dragon. With a nod, he pointed her out to his first mate, but the Black Ships across the harbor had started to move. Raising his glass again, he noted the *Hydra* was holding back. They weren't going to make it easy to get to them after all.

Across the first line of Barakus's navy, anchors were raised and oars were being run out as several ships began to move across the bay. Many were headed directly toward the bulk of the blockade, but the admiral noted three ships heading a little to the south, which made no sense. Checking his own line of defense, he noted the ketch, Merrimar, was stationed there, making that end their weakest point. Apparently, someone on the command ship had noted their weakness as well. Perhaps he had made a mistake in leaving the other small ships behind. Well, too late now. With any luck, the rest of his fleet would arrive before they could break through. Ah, here they come. "Blow the whistle, Mister Adjun."

As the shrill tin whistle blew, the sound carried across the waves, and the blockade made ready to intercept any and all the enemy ships. They couldn't let any of them through or they would lose. They would lose children and they would lose the advantage of delay with Barakus. Their third goal today was to keep Barakus in the dark as long as possible.

Slowly at first, and then faster as their rhythm came together, the oars dug deeper into the waves and the longships sped up. Utheran spread his legs, bracing himself as the rudder of the *Winter Storm*, sails trimmed for battle, turned to port, bringing it closer to the oncoming ships. Once they picked their opponent, another slight turn back to starboard and they'd be in range to throw the grappling hooks and board.

Finally, the ship drew close enough and the helmsman turned the rudder just enough to intercept. A glance at his fleet confirmed the same maneuver was being repeated up and down the line. The battle was about to begin.

As the marines aboard started swinging across to the Black Ship, there was no more time to worry about the fleet. Now the battle was joined, he could only concern himself with the maneuvers of this one ship and trust his captains to do their best. What he really wanted to do now was join the marines with swords drawn, mounting their attack. He wanted to be fighting to take the ship in front of them, but it wasn't that kind of battle, and...he was the admiral.

Aboard the Black Ship with a vile looking green serpent on the bow, the marines were quickly overwhelming the few soldiers aboard. After all, how many soldiers did it take to keep terrified children locked up? The sailors aboard the *Winter Storm* lined the gunwales on both sides of the ship. Poised to fend off any attempts to be boarded by the enemy. While unlikely, there was no point in being sloppy.

Looking down the fighting line upon the sea, the admiral was gratified to see the blockade hold. Even as his fleet engaged the longships, they did well in holding the line; there were too many ships engaged for those still hemmed into the bay to find a way out. Admiral Utheran let his eyes shift to survey the battle to the south and the Merrimar, but there were too many sails in the way to get a good look. Once again, he sent a plea to the unseen powers to aid the small ship. The only saving grace he could see was if the command ship got past the ketch, it still had to sail out and around the eastern edge of the battle before reaching the Strait of the Claw. Then there was the dubious final defense, Lady Ebony's troop of fliers set to take passing ships from the air. No, that was a fool's errand. Those crazy machines would never work. It was his job to keep all the Black Ships from reaching the strait.

Once the bulk of his marines returned to the flagship, leaving behind a decicam to secure the prisoners and take care of the children, Utheran decided there was no hope for it but to pull his ship out of the line which was breaking apart anyway. It was time to position the *Winter Storm* out to sea, ready to waylay any ships breaking free from the south. Especially Barakus's command ship, the *Hydra*.

*****

Farther out to sea, Briar Rose held her glass to her eye and watched the activity at the mouth of the bay anxiously. This inactivity was frustrating her. So far, Gabriene's fleet was keeping the Black Ships hemmed into the harbor, but it was obvious it couldn't last. There were just too many of the longships. Especially since the navy wasn't prepared to open fire. What she was watching bore little resemblance to the navy battles from the stories her greatfather, Jakar, had told her as a child.

"Look! Look there, to the south, three ships are coming up. They're at full speed. Maybe they'll be able to overtake any ships that manage to slip through!" called Cirroc excitedly from the yardarm.

Startled, Briar swept her glass slowly to the south until the ragtag remains of the naval fleet came into view. Yes, they were at full speed, but she wasn't sure they could catch the longships. Then, they were so much smaller and had fewer men for boarding. It wasn't like Barakus's fleet would be caught unaware again. There wasn't a man on the water who didn't know what was happening now. Briar's mind worked furiously, how could they delay any ships trying to break out without causing problems for the Lohi fleet?

Beside her stood Aenas and Ciral, behind them was Huge and Saird. Saith was manning the tiller. The men appeared to be sharing Briar's frustration at not being able to contribute to the battle while Ciral seemed relieved the use of their storm would be a hindrance for all, so far.

Watching closely with his exceptional eyesight, Aenas was the first to notice when several Black Ships broke through and won free, heading out to sea, still several leagues ahead of the approaching fleet from the south. Only one of the allied ships, it appeared to be the largest, had moved out to head off any escapees but five ships had broken free. That was when the idea came to him. Bending over the rail, he made a strange call, a call to his friends the whaltes and the dolfins.

Slowly, a gigantic head rose from the sea, nearly brushing the side of the sloop. It was the matriarch of the whaltes pod who had helped them before, but as he continued to call, other whaltes came as did their smaller cousins, the dolfins.

Startled, Briar Rose looked over the side rail where the animals were gathering. "What are you doing, Aenas? We don't need to move again, and...uh...we certainly don't need... How many whaltes and dolfins are you calling?"

"I dinna ken. Cames ter me, the whales kin stop 'em. Ta dolfins comes ter see wha' up. Wants ter hep," he got out. Briar couldn't help but notice his speech had been improving over the last two weeks.

By now the others had joined them and looked out to a sea full of several different kinds of whaltes from the gigantic green ones to the flat-topped wide whaltes as well as the more common blues who had been helping them. Playfully, the dolfins were racing around their larger cousins, excited by the gathering but still avoiding the black striped killer whaltes who stayed on the fringes of the gathering under an uneasy truce. They were all curious about what this strange human who could talk to them wanted.

Aenas stood uncertainly at the railing, looking out at the gathering, amazed and overwhelmed by the response to this calling. Finally, he put his hand in the water and began humming. He wasn't sure of what he was humming, but he put into it the desires of his heart as simply as possible. *Stop the Black Ships. Don't damage them, just stop them,* he thought, picturing the black hulled galleys. Making the request as simple as he could.

The matriarch turned so one of her huge eyes could look directly at this human she'd bonded with and winked. Then she turned and led her strange pod into the fray. She had gotten one other image Aenas had not intended. There were calves to save. Calves being held in those black vessels the humans used on the water. They must be stopped so the calves could be saved. The *Bonnie Jean* rocked as the whaltes, big, bigger, and small, dove deep. They were going to come up under those black-hulled ships and stop them, but they couldn't hurt the calves. Human calves couldn't swim as hers could. They had to be protected.

Ciral's gaze never left where they'd disappeared as she said, "Oh, Aenas, what have you done?"

*****

Ashore, one of the warehouses was awash with children and the local women, awoken by the sounds of battle, had thrown on robes and come out from the taverns and brothels to help. Help that was sorely needed as they tried to settle children who had been cooped up in the ships, with too little to eat, for far too long. Many of the children still huddled together. The families and the shy ones, wanting nothing more than to go home, looking around the large warehouse in awe and unease. A few, mostly the older boys and girls, and some of those who were there alone, were running and screaming, enjoying their sudden freedom.

Tasmin was overwhelmed as she tried to organize things but knowing how many children there were on paper was entirely different than the reality of all those little people who needed..., well..., everything.

As best she could, Faye tried to follow her directions until it became apparent Tasmin was out of her depth. "Tasmin... Tasmin... please, let me help. No woman ever had this many grandchildren. This is what I was trained for in my world. Please," she begged, trying to get Tasmin's attention as she was dealing with five things at once.

"What? What did you say, dear?"

"I said, let...me...do...this. Taking care of children like this is what I did before," reiterated Faye. "Now, just let me get this organized. We need triage, of a sort, I think."

"Tri...what, dear?" asked Tasmin, pushing her straying hair back in its bun as she deferred to Faye.

"Triage, Tasmin. It's a way of prioritizing things. Okay,

first, do we have any children who are sick or injured? They should all be gathered together. How about the northwest quadrant of this warehouse? Tasmin, could you get someone to help you gather the sick and injured together and take care of them? Maybe Lili can help you? Now, let's put the families in sections throughout the rest of the warehouse. Cheri, find at least five women to take care of each quadrant. Now, let's round up these hellions who are running about and put them in the second warehouse. Put them to work getting it ready for the rest of the children. Behnam, could you and a few of these fine marines supervise? They'll probably respond better to a male influence. Now, for the ones who are alone, especially the small ones. Bass, could you and a couple of these ladies spread them in with the families? Ask the eldest sibling to help them. Once they're settled, see if any would like to volunteer to help out? We'll need the help and keeping them busy will make it easier when the other children are brought in.

"Well, that's a start. Next, Bromilide, can you find us some help feeding them all?" she asked one of the women of the night who had been acting as an intermediary with the other local women.

Bromilide looked around the warehouse, which was already full of children and thought of those still aboard the Black Ships, waiting to be liberated.

"Oh, dearie. That be a pizzle, ain' it? We nigh' need every kitch' in Yves ter gets dat done," she answered, shaking her head as she pondered the problem.

"Oh, Gabriene, how are we going to feed them until the supply ships arrive?" asked Faye as Gabriene arrived.

"Well, well. If your friend here, uh..."

"Bromilide."

"Thank you, Lady Faye. If the good lady Bromilide here could fetch, oh, about five kettles of stew, I think I might be able to manage it. There are some advantages to being a wizard, after all."

*****

Now that his initial bloody battle was over, Admiral Utheran returned his attention to the battle as a whole. He was gratified to see many of the ships they had conquered were now making the blockade stronger. Especially those who were lashed together. Unfortunately, a few of the Black Ships were still worming their way through while others were being taken. Here, in the open sea, his was the only ship not engaged, poised to stop them all. From the south, where the Merrimar had done its best before sinking, five were approaching, and with his glass he could make out the *Hydra* as one of them. Well, it couldn't be helped, he'd need to take them as they came. If only they could have gotten Barakus's command ship at the outset.

Seeing the intent of the other ship, General Zandert instructed the captain to head for the strait. They would engage the enemy when they met. The one thing both sides were sure of—they all wanted the children alive and unharmed. What his enemy wasn't aware of, was Zandert's own determination. He would not fail Barakus. He would rather die.

Farther south, the rest of the admiral's fleet were stringing out as they each raised full sail to get the most speed. They wouldn't make it in time to stop all the ships slipping through. Then the ocean itself started to boil and froth as...what? Whaltes? Slowly, the behemoths started to rise from the deep, surrounding the Black Ships who found their progress slowed before their oars snapped and they stopped dead. Their ships were surrounded.

"My lord! What's this, then?" exclaimed the admiral in astonishment.

"They seem to be leaving us alone, sir. Perhaps it's a sending from the old powers," exclaimed the first mate.

"Well, Mister Adjun, if it is a sending, it's best we take advantage of it, don't you think? Raise the topsail and head for the ship with the hydra on its prow, there," ordered the admiral.

In short order, the *Winter Storm* drew abreast of the *Hydra*, Utheran's green eyes met Zandert's icy gray ones as the general drew his sword. This man wasn't going down without a fight. Utheran sighed as he drew his sword with his left hand and grabbed a line in his gloved right hand swinging out to land on the galley. If the man insisted on a fight, he would give it to him. Being left-handed had often been an asset in a sword fight.

Eagerly, Zandert ran to meet the admiral, recognizing the importance of his opponent. Maybe he could help cripple Barakus's enemies before he died.

Utheran had a moment to set his feet on the rocking deck before the general reached him, parrying the initial thrust easily before slashing for the general's midsection. "You've already lost, why not surrender?"

"I swore to Barakus never to surrender without a fight. If this is the only fight you've left me, it's the fight I'll win," rejoined Zandert as he parried the slash and danced back before charging again toward his opponent, this time feinting low before raising his sword to a stab toward the heart.

This was where being left-handed had its greatest advantage. His sword was always where the opponent least expected it. Utheran easily parried the thrust and brought his own sword back around high, in a slicing movement, severing the general's head.

Panting, the admiral turned to scan the ship, only to find the rest of the men had surrendered and were being bound.

While the crew of the *Hydra* were surrendering with

minimal opposition, no one noticed another Black Ship slipping through the line to the north. Except the dolfins who found they were less intimidating when surrounding a ship than their cousins. Even when swimming close together. Frantically, their squeaks and squeals echoed through the water, calling for help but the ship was gaining speed, heading for the safety of the Strait of the Claw.

*****

High above, at the top of the cliff, Ebony and her team had been watching the strangely quiet battle below. With no cannon fire, the hand to hand fighting was muffled by the distance. Well, here came a ship; it was time to put on the wings and make ready to fly.

Galad had been pacing as the battle raged. He hadn't been trained to stand on the sidelines. Now, he busied himself with helping strap his men into these strange contraptions of Aliand's. They were so much higher than merely on a mast that even though he'd flown them himself, the prominence was daunting, and he found he was worrying about Lady Ebony. As he paused, he shook himself. It was a perfectly ordinary response. After all, not only was she in his charge, they had become friends over the last few weeks.

Well, now they had a runaway ship to catch.

One by one, the trained troopers made their way to the edge of the cliff and jumped without hesitation. Galad watched them soar and then dive toward the longship before it could reach the strait. As Ebony was getting into her own hang-glider, with Aliand's help, the first three men landed on the ship, one right after the other, just as they'd practiced. The men aboard the enemy ship were so startled by the incursion from above, they didn't have time to respond before the fliers were out of harness and attacking, using their new skills as taught by Ebony. While the soldiers and sailors on the Black

Ship finally raised their weapons, more of Galad's men were landing and joining the fray.

Finally, Ebony launched from the cliff, soaring out over the battle below. Catching an updraft, she allowed herself to climb for a moment, before beginning her dive. She had time to see the battle was over before another updraft picked up her wings and sent her higher, away from the cliff and directly for Chimera Island. Frantically, Ebony tried to regain control of her hang glider and just when she thought she had, a fierce downdraft slammed against the top of the wings, sending her down through the mist cloaking the top of the island. As she broke through, she could see a lush green valley, spreading across the caldera, the cone of the inactive volcano rising on all sides. She was spinning out of control as she caught sight of fluttering wings out of the corner of her deep-brown eyes.

Determinedly, she tried to regain control as the ground loomed closer. Unexpectedly, just before slamming into a meadow, something grabbed her, crushing her hang glider to slow her descent. When she hit the ground, she caught sight of a goat's head. *What?* she thought before passing out.

Galad watched Ebony's glider fly out of control into the mists of Chimera Island and felt as if a knife were twisting deep in his chest. Blinking sea spray and wind out of his eyes, he looked again at the ship below. His men had gained control of the Black Ship, and the *Mal de Verde* was overtaking it, ready to take it in tow. The dolfins appeared to be dancing around it. Well, it was time for him to get the rest of the team and Aliand to Yves. With the arrival of the whaltes, the remaining Black Ships had surrendered. The battle was over.

CHAPTER 33

What Next, Savior Mine?

The night of the battle, Ochwatt's friends flitted through the dark streets and over the wall, retracing their steps from the night before. Ochwatt and Falcon went with them as far as the wall before returning to the Long Ship Inn on the docks. Ochwatt went up to the room they were sharing while Falcon remained in the common room, listening to the joking chatter from the regulars. There was a great deal of humor as they called to the owner, "Hey, Kaldet! Do you think you need to change the inn's name, now the longships have been captured? I mean, they won't be coming back, will they now?"

*****

Late the next morning, Galad's troop finally wandered into one of the warehouses bustling with children. They had slept briefly on the trek from the high cliff face to town, and it had taken most of the morning to navigate through a postern gate, opening into Bay Road and the docks. The city itself was abuzz with excitement from the day before, and everyone was on the streets, talking to anyone who would listen. Most of the houses had a clear view of the bay, and the residents had been able to watch the entire battle. Now they wanted nothing more than to compare stories. The crowded streets slowed their progress.

Finally, they had reached the docks where Suvaat, and the knights were in charge. As Lohi's champion, his face, even in its filthy state, was well known among the knights and they passed into the warehouse without incident. Once there, he found Faye ordering people about, keeping everyone fed and wrapped in warm blankets. Tasmin, Cheri, and Gurmail were acting as lieutenants, passing on orders as they came.

When Galad arrived, everyone was getting ready to eat lunch, except Gabriene who was sneezing and wiping his nose between bouts of a terrible, hacking, cough.

Lili was hovering over the wizard with another cup of herbal tea and muttering, "I don't understand. I've tried everything. It's not paludal fever, I'm sure of it. Nothing is working."

Tasmin walked over to take a closer look at the miserable man. "A...achoo! I Haben't eber been sick before," mumbled the old man before his cough started up again.

"Maybe it's just a cold," suggested Cheri in passing as she took another bite of stew.

"No, he's not cold. If anything, he might be a bit too warm," argued Lili as she prompted the man to drink some more tea.

"No, I said he might have a cold. It's the name of a disease. It's common, on my world and hardly ever serious, but there's no cure. Keep him warm, give him plenty of fluids, and he'll be right as rain in about fourteen days. Actually, a little less since this started, what, three days ago?" explained Cheri, somewhat bewildered by Tasmin and Lili's confusion.

"How could he get a disease...is that the word, from your world?"

"Well, everyone gets colds sometimes, maybe we had the, uh, germs, on our skin, and he is susceptible?" suggested Faye with a worried frown. "He's been working hard the last couple of days, maybe he got overly tired. We should get him into a warm bed. Come on, Suvaat, let's get him to the inn. Behnam, could you help us?"

*****

As they left, everyone else was discussing how to get the children to Jessamine and Jakar was putting in his two decimars' worth, "Since Briar Rose is here, she can guide the ships to Jessamine and then return to Lohi," he was insisting.

Briar Rose, Ciral, Cirroc, and Aenas were sitting with the others, and Briar Rose objected, "Greatfather! I need to return to Lohi and continue my studies."

"You should never have left Lohi, Briar Rose. Now, you will make yourself useful and help these children find sanctuary."

"But..."

"I have other things to do, and there are only two of us here who can show the way to Jessamine. Therefore, the job is yours. Maybe next time, you'll stay where you're supposed to be."

"Uh...Sair, tha' ain' 'zactly truth. There be others kin show the way," interrupted Aenas hesitantly.

"Humph! Aenas, is it? Only those from Jessamine can find the way home, young man. It must be either myself or Briar Rose," insisted Jakar dismissively.

"No, sair. Dere be anoter opshun. The whaltes, ye see. Dey kin go everware. They would bring the chilluns ter safe haber, sair," he explained with a grin.

"See what? You mean those behemoths outside the bay? I've heard they helped but why would they take the children to Jessamine?" asked an amazed Jakar.

"Ye see, Sair Jakar, de mam be in charge. She be 'cerned aboot our young'uns. Wants ter protek our 'calves." He explained.

"Calves?"

"Tha' be wha' she be callin' 'em."

"Well, Briar Rose, it appears you've gotten a reprieve, but the *Bonnie Jean* is returning with the fleet, without you aboard."

Briar Rose opened her mouth to protest before she got a good look at her greatfather's face. Then she lowered her chin and nodded meekly. If she didn't, he might send her home after all.

That was when Faye, Suvaat, and Behnam rejoined them. "Aliand! You're here! Where's Ebony?" cried the redhead in excitement.

Aliand looked away as she teared up, again, and Galad stepped in, "A rogue wind came up and blew her into the mists of Chimera Island. We're not sure where she is," he admitted.

"What? We have to go after her! We have to look for her, she could be hurt," exclaimed Cheri frantically, her yell getting Faye's attention.

"Calm down, Cheri. There's no way to get to Chimera Island," began Bass as Faye joined them.

"Obviously there's a way to get there, or Ebony wouldn't be there, would she?" snapped a frustrated Cheri, putting her hands on her hips.

"Ebony? What's wrong with Ebony?" interrupted Faye with a worried frown.

"She's trapped on Chimera Island," growled Behnam, with a glare for Galad.

"All right, just listen to me. There is no way for us to get to the island and if someone could, they probably couldn't get back," amended Bass, trying to get Cheri to calm down.

"What's wrong with the other hang gliders? Surely there's at least one we can send after her," suggested Faye.

"Unfortunately, all of them were damaged. We've already

set the carpenters to making more, but it will be a couple of days before we can even try," supplied Aliand hesitantly.

"In the meantime, we'll need to come up with plans for returning. That's a dangerous island, ladies," said Galad with a worried frown. Cheri looked at Bass, Behnam, and the others as she slumped to an unoccupied pallet on the ground and started to cry. Furiously, she wiped at her face. She hadn't cried in years before coming to Persal. Now she seemed to be crying all the time.

Faye sank down next to Cheri and enveloped her in a hug. "I'm going to refuse to worry until I must. Ebony is very good at what she does. My faith is with her," she said levelly. "Do we have any volunteers?"

"Every man on Ebony's team has volunteered. I would go myself, but I'm too heavy, as she told me repeatedly," admitted Galad with a frown. "The main problem is how to get them off the island. They may be able to fly, but they can't flap their wings and take off like a bird once they've landed."

"Well, let's assume they're able to land without damaging any of their gliders and they find Ebony fit enough to be brought out. Then we'll assume they can climb to the lip of the volcano, with their gliders, and launch themselves away from the island. All we'll have to do is have a ship or two waiting to catch them or, if necessary, fish them out of the sea. Any ideas where we can get a ship?" asked Faye with a satisfied smile.

Cheri stared at her friend in amazement before she started laughing. "Oh, Faye, when you get going, you don't stop, do you?"

The battle hadn't been bloodless. Over three hundred of Barakus's men had died. Fifty-one marines and sailors from their side had died as well. Most of those had been aboard the Merrimar when it sank. They recovered as many bodies as possible from the bay before the sharks could swarm, and buried Barakus's men in a mass grave outside the city walls beyond the keep. For their own men, Galad presided over a memorial ceremony in one of the warehouses so the children who wanted to honor the men who had died for them could attend. Then there was a procession attended by every able-bodied marine and sailor up the winding Bay Road to the city's cemetery.

*****

A day later, the children were shepherded back onto ships, but not into the holds. Oh, they would have to sleep there, but they wouldn't be caged. As they were spread through both the Black Ships and the Lohi fleet, they wouldn't be as crowded, either. Faye's instructions were to leave off the hatches unless there was a storm, in order to give them more room, air and sunshine. She made sure there were enough supplies aboard each ship, and in small flotillas, the ships began heading out for Jessamine, in the company of the whaltes.

Amid the exodus, the *Bonnie Jean* also embarked under its temporary captain, Cirroc. Jakar had given him command of the small sloop while the task of returning Briar Rose, Ciral, and Aliand to Lohi and the care and teachings of Gaban fell to Captain Aberon of the Unicorn's Magic. Huge, Saith and Saird joined Cirroc as crew.

"I'm sorry you couldn't find a use for your storms, Briar Rose," said Jakar in parting.

"I'm just sorry we came all this way and couldn't help at all." The fair halfling pouted. "And you! You knew I was there all along! I was so careful to sneak off after you left."

"You did contribute, you know. You brought Aenas. Without him, it would have gone very differently. You also had the opportunity to practice your talent. As for the other, if you were determined, I knew you'd make it. If not, you needed to stay home," said the little man in his red suit, his long white hair blowing in the breeze coming from the sea. "Goodbye, greatdaughter, I'll see you in Lohi.

"Humph! Goodbye, greatfather, I love you," conceded Briar Rose, brushing away the unexpected tears in her eyes before kissing his scruffy cheek.

Six of the Black Ships had been commandeered to transport Barakus's men to Lohi. The hold of each one was packed uncomfortably tight. A hundred and fifty grown men had a lot less room than a hundred and fifty children but no one suggested it was unfair. Not after what the children had gone through. It was shortly before high sun when they set out, a full complement of marines on each ship.

A span after high sun, the last of the children boarded the last of the merchant ships, and they cast off. Faye had mixed the ratio of rambunctious children with families and small children. She was hoping to lessen the problems energetic children could pose for the sailors and marines aboard each ship.

Jakar said the trip would take nearly a month and Faye found herself worried more about the sanity of the men aboard than the children themselves.

*****

Throughout the day, troops of twenty and thirty had been leaving by land, heading back to Lohi. The knight, Sir Aberforth, led the last contingent. They were leaving with the lumberjacks, aboard the empty barges headed back upriver to Lake Annoura.

There was another complement of troops yet to be assigned, waiting on Gabriene to recover so he could speak to the governor of Zabir at the keep.

The knights, Galad, Suvaat and Gurmail took up their duties as personal guardians for Ebony, Faye, and Cheri, respectively. Cheri couldn't help thinking of Ebony. When she got back, she wouldn't be pleased to have a bodyguard.

When the day was done, only the *Mal de Verde* was left. Aenas had been dragooned as their new cabin boy, for the time being. Jakar seemed to think he might come in handy during the rescue operation. The ship itself was being readied to retrieve the glider troops when they returned from Chimera Island. Once that task was through, it would transport the carpenters, still hard at work on new hang gliders, and the men manning the gliders back to Lohi.

*****

Early the next morning, a message came down from the keep; on the outside of the folded and sealed paper it was addressed to *The Esteemed Master Gabriene.*

Since Gabriene was still in his sick bed and Faye was busy helping Lili in tending the wizard, Gurmail brought the missive to Cheri in the inn's private dining room where she was waiting with Bass, Falcon, Matew, Jakar and on an exceedingly sturdy bench in the corner, Ochwatt. The messenger was left cooling his heels in the common room.

Unwilling to open Gabriene's mail, Cheri went up to his room to see if he was awake. She stopped outside the room, looking Suvaat in the eye as he opened the door, but she couldn't read the man. What she found inside astonished her. To begin with, it was extremely hot and steamy. On the bed, the old man was gasping for breath while Faye placed hot towels on his chest. There went her plan of reading the message to Gabriene.

Tendrils of Faye's blond hair hung damply about her face as she turned at the sound. "It looks like it's turned to pneumonia," she said, turning back to her patient.

Nodding, Cheri left, returning to the dining room and the man she trusted most. "Behnam, Gabriene is very ill. It's worse than I thought, and Faye is busy taking care of him. I don't understand. It started as just a cold."

"I think it was a disease we have no defenses for, Cheri," he answered with a raised brow.

"Yeah, right. That went so well in the Philippines. So what do I do with the message?" she asked, raising the sealed missive.

"You'll have to read it and respond," he said, with a direct look in her eyes.

"Me? Why me?"

"You're a savior. The next highest in authority. Open it up. Let's see what the governor has to say."

"Just so you know, I hate this!" she said as she pried up the red seal and began to read.

Esteemed and honorable sir:

It has been several days since you successfully retrieved the children of Persal. Since that time, I have not had the honor of guesting you here, at the Keep of Yves.

Nor, unfortunately, have I even heard from you regarding the situation you have placed my fair city in. A subject I would dearly like to discuss with you at your earliest possible convenience.

With all due respect and consideration,
The Honorable Imaland Hambertick
Governor of the Sovereign Realm of Zabir

"He wants Gabriene to come to the keep and answer his questions? Gabriene can't go to the keep in his condition," said Cheri, holding the letter in dismay.

"Well, if he can't go, we'll have to come up with another plan, won't we?" said Behnam with a sly smile.

"What? Me? No, I can't go up to the keep!" she squeaked, looking around at Bass, Falcon, Gurmail, and Jakar.

"No, of course not. You're not someone to be 'summoned.'

You're going to make it clear the man must come to you. If he wants answers, anyway," stated Behnam calmly.

"What!"

"Sir Gurmail, you've had some training in diplomacy, as have I. Would you help me compose an answer for this, functionary?" said Behnam with a slight note of disdain in his voice on the last word.

Repressing a smile, Gurmail bowed, "I would be glad to help, Honorable Shik Behnam. Matew, find us a pen and some paper."

Behnam crossed to the table, passing close to Gurmail. "Honorable?" he said quietly as he passed the knight near the door.

"Sir Suvaat is a friend of mine. I know your position, sir."

"Not here, Sir Gurmail. Here, I am just Behnam."

After some discussion, the return message was ready.

Most Honorable Imaland Hambertick:

Unfortunately, Master Gabriene is unable to comply with your request at this time. The rest of the rescue contingent is occupied with other pressing concerns and cannot comply with your summons either.

As one of the esteemed saviors of Persal, Lady Cheri would be honored to take the time to receive you here, at the Longship Inn which has become our temporary headquarters.

Please send advance notice of your arrival so she can set aside time to address your concerns properly.

With all due respect and consideration,
Sir Gurmail Knight of Lohi and Savior's Guardian

Representative de facto: Lady Cheri Gaines
Long-Awaited Savior of Persal

"Really? Don't you think you're laying it on a bit thick? What's he going to say when he arrives and finds me? A sixteen-year-old girl who's drowning?"

"That's why we have to set the tone now before he meets you. We've told him you're a woman. For that alone, he's likely to be dismissive. The rest can be a surprise. Don't worry, we'll prepare you for the meeting. You're a brave young woman, Cheri. Just remember who you are and perception is based on attitude. Your attitude. From what I've seen, you have enough attitude to spare."

"You could be right. I've been told most of my life I have an attitude problem," she groused, slumping in her chair with her arms crossed.

"Maybe it's time you learned to make 'attitude' work in your favor." Leaning forward on the table, Cheri's green eyes met Behnam's golden ones for a moment before taking a deep breath, "Just tell me I won't have to wear one of those awful court dresses."

"You won't have to wear a court dress. You're too busy to visit the governor at the keep. Therefore, you're too busy to change clothes. We're going to make him wait while you give orders for the extraction of Ebony, but we'll make what he overhears generic, so he doesn't know it's Ebony we're talking about."

That afternoon, the same messenger arrived to see Lady Cheri Gaines. After a slightly impolite wait, he was brought into the dining room where Cheri was standing, looking intently at a map as several people hustled in and out of the room, squeezing past the poor man.

With a questioning look, Cheri looked up at the messenger and he began.

"If it please, Your Ladyship. Lord Imaland Hambertick, governor of the Sovereign Realm of Zabir, requests an audience in one span. He also respectfully requests immediate notice if this is not convenient for Lady Cheri Gaines, savior of Persal."

Cheri stared at the young man in amazement for a moment before nodding curtly and returning to her map. As the door closed behind him, she rolled her eyes and Behnam held up his hand for silence. When the front door could be heard closing, she giggled. "I was about ready to burst out laughing, you know?"

"I know, but your curt nod was perfect. You'll do well if you can just remember what I told you," he said with a smile.

It was just past a span when one of the maids brought a fresh pot of tea to the room where Cheri and her court of Behnam, Gurmail, Bass, Galad, Falcon, and Jakar were waiting. Ochwatt still sat on the bench in the corner with his arms crossed, while Matew and Timnon waited to serve. All were to follow her lead, and her heart was pounding frantically.

A sixth of a span later, a marine knocked on the door, and Cheri and the others at the table stood to lean over the table. Gurmail crossed to open the door, and Cheri didn't even turn to see who it was as the short, hefty man in red robes trimmed in silver fur and an upside-down pyramid on his head entered. With a haughty look, he took in the scene before him, trying to find this important woman he had come down to this dingy inn to see. A sudden movement at the far end of the room startled him as Ochwatt stood, his head brushing the high ceiling. The poor man took a step back for a moment.

As Cheri and the men around the table continued to discuss the upcoming rescue attempt and ignore the governor, he started shifting his feet, restlessly. It was apparent he wasn't used to waiting or being ignored. Just as he opened his mouth, Behnam, who had been watching him covertly, made a small movement with his hand and Cheri looked over to the sasquatch. "It's all right, Ochwatt, you can sit down."

Then, still dressed in her stained traveling clothes, she

turned to the leader of Zabir. "Ah, Governor, so good of you to come. As you can see, we have a rather urgent rescue operation to plan."

Again, the governor started to open his mouth at the audacity of this…this child, but this time he was cut off by Gurmail. "Governor Hambertick, may I present Lady Cheri Gaines, savior of Persal."

There was an audible snapping sound as the governor's jaw slammed shut. The whole room fell silent for a moment until a marine hustled in and whispered in Galad's ear, who then stepped closer to Cheri, and relay the message. "Are you sure? We might have to change the jumping-off point."

Finally, the governor found his voice. "Ye ain' nothin' but a wee bit of a gel. I do not kowtow to a wee bit of a gel!" he objected, drawing himself up but falling far short of the men around him.

Without warning, Ochwatt stood again, crossing his arms across his chest.

At the same time, Galad started to move until Cheri put up a hand.

She turned slowly and put both hands on her hips. "Lord Hambertick, you asked to talk to me. As you can see, I am a little busy here. I did not ask to be pulled, unceremoniously, into your wonderful world as one of your saviors. But! I…am… here. I have experiences from my world that may help yours. Do you want answers to your questions or not?"

"Well, uh, Lady Gaines. Yes, I want answers," he stammered with an uneasy look at Ochwatt, who grinned back at him, causing him to cringe, involuntarily

With a flick of her hand, Ochwatt resumed his seat. "Please, sit. Would you like some tea?" she asked graciously as she took her chair. The other men remained standing.

Having soundly been put in his place, the governor took the chair across from Cheri while men kept coming and going from the room. After he took his first sip of tea, Cheri began, "We would like to leave a full complement of soldiers here to help protect your city. While they're here, they will recruit volunteers and begin forming an army. Whether you understand it or not, we have just declared war on Barakus, and this is likely to be the first place he comes when he retaliates. Now, if you don't like this plan, you can refuse our troops and your new army. In which case, we will remove you from office and take our offer to your people. We will not let them die if you think you can make a deal with Barakus because you weren't involved. After all, Barakus has been known to be so forgiving in the past, hasn't he?"

The governor stared at Cheri for two full minutes in amazement. "That's it? You're leaving me troops and forming an army on Barakus's doorstep?"

"Yep, that's it. You're either with us, and we'll help you or you are removed from your position, and we make the deal with your people."

"Ah, well, yes. That sounds like a viable plan," muttered Lord Hambertick as he stood. "Thank you, Lady Gaines. I will let you return to your planning."

As he left the room, Governor Hambertick's back was straighter than when he entered as he wrapped his dignity around himself tighter than his cloak.

*****

In hopes of the mist clearing from Chimera Island, they waited until the next afternoon to launch the rescue team for Ebony. Gabriene and his diligent nurses, Tasmin, Faye, and Lili with Suvaat to watch over them, remained at the inn while the rest of them rode to the top of the bluff, where Ebony had leapt into the mists. Cheri moved as close to the edge as she could make herself and looked down. Below was the *Mal de Verde,* waiting for the fliers to come in.

Luckily, Bass was standing there when she began to sway

"I'm all right," she said as she took three hasty steps back and raised her gaze to the misty island instead.

Without a word, Bass nodded, but he didn't move far.

Galad helped his men into their harnesses, and one by one, they jumped off the bluff and caught the wind, soaring out and up to clear the edge of the volcano.

"I don't understand," murmured Cheri to herself.

"You don't understand what, Cheri? How they can jump off a perfectly good cliff? Heights don't bother me, but I agree. Only birds were meant to fly," said Bass quietly.

Cheri glanced up at the big man, "No. I mean, yes, there's that. What I really don't understand is why? Faye, Ebony, and I were brought here from Seattle, in our world, for a reason. Why would she go missing? It doesn't make sense."

"If it doesn't make sense, then we have to believe Lady Ebony is alive, don't we? There may be a reason she flew into that island, but we have to believe she's still alive. As you said, anything else just doesn't make sense," agreed Bass as the fourth man took flight and the fifth stepped to the edge of the bluff.

By the time the final marine took off, the first one disappeared into the mists surrounding the heights of the island cone, followed shortly by the second glider. Just before the third flier was to disappear into the mist, he suddenly lost altitude. When he disappeared, he was much too low to clear the top of the caldera. Behind him, the watchers on the bluff could see the final two fliers turn and dive toward the ship waiting on the sea far below.

Just before they landed, Cheri let out a scream and turned to bury her face in Bass's chest. Looking back to the island, everyone could see what had caught her attention as the third man's mangled body and wrecked glider tumbled into the rocks at the base of the island. Bass held Cheri tightly as she sobbed uncontrollably.

Once they saw the last two fliers were safe aboard the *Mal de Verde*, those atop the bluff turned to remount their horses. Now, all they could do was wait.

Suddenly, without warning, Jakar slumped to the ground. When they roused him a couple of minutes later, he started talking in rhyme, as he had when they first met:

> "The quest hangs by a thread
> Danger is on the threshold
> Delay is the beast of woe
> The guide is brought low
> Raised by faithfulness
> Hope to know
> With soaring success
> The time is near
> Reveal the heir
> There is safety in faith
> Enough to share
> Only with charity
> Can all find clarity."

When he was through, he lost consciousness again, and they were left staring at each other in bewilderment.

"Well, that was illuminating. All we know for sure is Faye, myself, and Ebony are all mentioned," commented Cheri sarcastically. "Do you think this means Ebony is alive?"

ABOUT THE AUTHOR

Margaret Lott began telling herself stories before she was six. When she learned to write, she started putting them on paper.

After her first husband became disabled, her formal education was refocused to accounting in order to support her family.

Informally, her insatiable appetite for the printed word continued to expand her knowledge, targeting fantasy novels but including a whole range of interests, from archeology to astronomy.

Margaret is currently living in Corsicana, Texas, with her husband and two dogs.